D1205804

TIME OF
DAUGHTERS I

BOOKS IN THIS TIMELINE

Inda

The Fox

King's Shield

Treason's Shore

Time of Daughters I & II

Banner of the Damned

TIME OF
DAUGHTERS I

SHERWOOD SMITH

Time of Daughters I
Sherwood Smith
First Edition October 8, 2019
ISBN: 978-1-61138-841-1
Copyright © 2019 Sherwood Smith
Cover illustration © 2019 Augusta Scarlett

Production Team:
Cover Design: Augusta Scarlett
Beta Readers: Deborah J. Ross and Jennifer Stevenson
Copy Editor: Debra Doyle
Proofreader: Sara Stamey
E-Formatter: Jennifer Stevenson

www.bookviewcafe.com

Book View Café Publishing Cooperative
P.O. Box 1624, Cedar Crest, NM 87008-1624

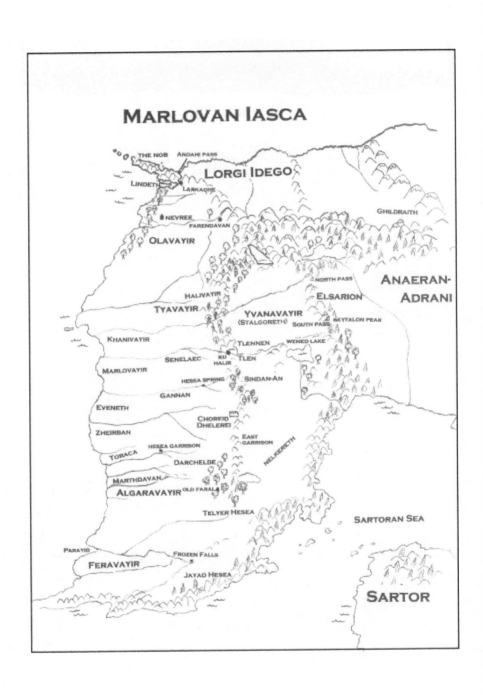

MARLOVAN IASCA

THE NOB · ANDAHI PASS

LORGI IDEGO

LINDETH · LARKADHE

NEVREE
FARENDAVAN

GHILDRAITH

OLAVAYIR

NORTH PASS

ANAERAN-ADRANI

HALIVAYIR · ELSARION

TYAVAYIR

YVANAVAYIR
(STALGORETH) · SOUTH PASS · SKYTALON PEAK

KHANIVAYIR

TLENNEN · WENED LAKE

SENELAEC · KU
HALIR · TLEN

MARLOVAYIR

HESEA SPRING · SINDAN-AN

GANNAN

EVENETH

CHOREID
DHELEREI

ZHEIRBAN

EAST
GARRISON

HESEA GARRISON

NELKERETH

TORACA

DARCHELDE

MARTHDAVAN

ALGARAVAYIR · OLD FARALA

TELYER HESEA

SARTORAN SEA

PARAYID

FROZEN FALLS

FERAVAYIR

JAYAD HESEA

SARTOR

PREFACE

The hundred years of Marlovan history after the defeat of the Venn at what became known as the Elgar Strait is a vexing one for archivists. As with any major war, the male population had dropped sharply, resulting in several generations of large families, in contrast to the traditional two or three, maybe four offspring.

That added to the shift of kingship from the Montrei-Vayir to the Ola-Vayir (now written Montreivayir and Olavayir) families, and the fractious nature of the latter, resulted in a shift of power from the throne to the jarlates.

This was the beginning of the period when jarls had private armies, called Riders. Riders are trained warriors, as opposed to riders, who are people on horseback. Some jarl clans were bolstered by Rider clans; others made up their Riders from local families. In the Who's Who list below, individuals are listed by clan or by city, and a few by vocation (such as brigands).

Because of the insularity of the jarlates, whose jarls were petty kings in all but name, there was a great deal of intermarriage among the huge, complicated clans, resulting in a proliferation of names.

For example, by the time Inda died in 3963, the academy was in the process of training thirty-seven Indas, forty-four Evreds, and twenty-five Haldrens. In self-defense most chose nicknames, which generally stuck for life.

Otherwise archivists despaired of telling them all apart. *Fellow Marlovans* despaired of telling them apart, especially the tangle of the great Eastern Alliance.

The Great Eastern Alliance

Tlen, Tlennen, Sindan-An, and Sindan, with the Senelaecs over to the west, were the principal horse breeders of Marlovan Iasca. The Sindan-Ans were the primary family among them, closely seconded by the Tlennens. The Tlens were by this time a much smaller jarlate, and the Sindans never held land at all — their many branches were spread among their cousins as Riders.

Not only were these clans constantly intermarrying, their family names were often given as first names, so new boys at the new academy could be

expected to meet similar-looking blonds named Tlen Sindan and Sindan Tlen
—until they got a nickname.

The Eastern Alliance jarls elected a chief among them who dealt with
outsiders, and commanded the alliance when the whole needed to be raised.

The Noth Family

There were three main branches of the family. The Algaravayir Noths
descended from Senrid (Whipstick) Noth of Choreid Elgaer, who features
prominently in the chronicles about Inda-Harskialdna. The Noths connected
with Parayid Harbor in Faravayir descended from Whipstick's second son.

Then there are the Faral Noths, plains Riders and horse masters connected
to Cassad, Darchelde, and southern points. They are descended from Flatfoot
Noth, Whipstick's cousin.

A list of who's who is at the back.

PART ONE

ONE

Marlovan Iasca, late summer 4058 AF

This chronicle in the history of the Marlovans begins nearly a century after the death of the man famed throughout the world as Inda Elgar, Elgar the Fox, Elgar the Pirate, and a few other less savory names. But to Marlovans, who cared nothing for the rest of the world's opinion, he was Indevan-Harskialdna, the king's war commander who never lost a battle.

It's always difficult to determine exactly when and where to start, because history is more like a river than a box: it bends and twists, flowing onward seemingly without beginning or end. But a chronicle has to have a beginning and end.

We will start in the northern part of the kingdom—an empire in all but name—once called Iasca Leror. Ever since Marlovan had become the language of government as well as war, the kingdom was more and more often referred to as Marlovan Iasca.

For reasons that I hope will become clear, at first I will avoid Choreid Dhelerei, the royal city, as well as the powerful jarlates, which in this time had nearly become small kingdoms on their own. Instead, we commence this record at a small freehold lying between the Olavayir and Halivayir jarlates, called Farendavan. Our primary concern here at the start is not with the holder (who was away more than he was home, serving as patrol captain in Idego) or his wife, who ran the holding, nor even with his son, but with the elder of his two daughters, Danet.

Though Danet Farendavan's mother's journal was scrupulously preserved by her progeny, anyone glancing at it could be forgiven for assuming the woman had no family feeling, as most of the journal is detailed accounts of linen weaves, dye lots, trade, and stable statistics.

For example, the day Danet's life changed, her mother's journal listed a complicated order for three different varieties of indigo, deep-water sponges and carmine fungi, saffron, and madder, then at the bottom is a brief note: *Spoke to girls about marriage agreement Olavayir eagle-clan.*

Danet was almost twenty. Her sister Hliss was sixteen. They had been out with their cousins and the stable hands doing ground work with the horses when their mother's runner appeared. "You're wanted. The both."

Surprise semaphored between the sisters, then Danet glanced at her closest cousin and grimaced, handing off supervision with a flick of an open palm. Mother never interrupted chores unless it was important. Danet's first thought was to wonder what she might have done wrong.

Hliss, as always, waited for her older sister to lead the way. They hurried back to the low, rambling stone house they called home, and into the big chamber where the looms were set up. The dusty smell of hay and horse gave way to the back-of-the-nose oily smell of wool; Danet sighed, recognizing the setup for weaving the sturdy cotton-wool twill from which their coats and riding trousers would be made. Winter work. Mother was starting the process of getting everything ready.

Hliss's face lifted. Danet couldn't understand how her sister could love being indoors working the looms and sigh over stable chores, when Danet felt exactly the opposite. The only indoor labor Danet loved was keeping tallies (what in other lands was called *counting, thus the origin of the title count*), because then you knew exactly what you had, and where you were. But once Danet had been trained, Mother kept the tallies and only let Danet observe. "I'm faster," Mother said with the hint of impatience that characterized her. "And whoever you marry will no doubt have their ways and rules. Enough that you now understand the method."

A flash of sun slanting in the narrow windows reflected off Mother's yellow-white hair as she looked their way. Then, instead of beckoning her daughters to help set up spindle or loom, she said, "In here, girls."

Hliss sent a round-eyed glance at Danet as Mother led the way into her private room, where shelves of carefully bound household tallies took up one wall, and the most precious of the dyes another, the narrow bed under the window almost an afterthought. This room, from which Mother ruled the house, flax fields, barns, and training grounds, was considered by the household to be as formidable as the seldom-used Family Chamber at the other end of the house, with the few and modest Farendavan trophies on the walls.

Mother dropped straight-backed onto her stool alongside the table and pointed at the bench. "Sit down."

As her daughters sat side by side, Mother compressed her lips and studied them—not as she saw them every day, but as strangers might see them. Both were lean and long-legged, Danet with dun-colored hair properly braided and looped, Hliss softer and rounder, with pretensions to prettiness (for those who looked for that sort of thing) in her fawn-dark eyes framed by pale cornsilk hair. Danet gazed at the world out of eyes too muddy to be either blue or brown, her thin, straight lips and set chin below round cheeks a match for Mother's own.

The truth was, Mother did not like what she had to say, but the good of the family had to come first.

Best to get it over with, then. She wiped a strand of damp hair off her forehead. "There's no time to waste, and you both know how little patience I have for questions I can't answer. I've just received a runner from the Jarlan of Olavayir. It seems the marriage arrangements concerning your cousin Hadand Arvandais up north have fallen through. Whatever the reason, that has nothing to do with us."

She paused, then said bluntly, "I'm certain that Han Fath suggested you to the jarlan. You know I used to ride with the Fath girls scouting for hill brigands, when I was your age."

From Mother this was a very long speech, and Danet had learned to evaluate what Mother didn't say as well as what she did. Danet already knew that the Faths—Riders for the Tyavayir jarlate—were one of the few clans Mother respected thoroughly. She thought less of the Tyavayirs, and less than that of the Olavayirs.

But Mother said nothing against them now. She went on, "You know I was trained by the Faths after I lost my own family, and I suspect they thought to honor me in putting forward your names. However it came about, the Olavayirs want you. Both."

Danet said in disbelief, "The *royal family? Us?*"

"Jarl branch. Eagle, not dolphin. You'll adopt in. The Olavayirs are all that way. Man or woman, if you marry into them, you take their name."

Hliss's eyes filled with tears. "I thought we could wait...until we were older."

Mother sighed shortly, and Hliss hastily thumbed her eyes.

Mother knew how tender-hearted Hliss was, and schooled her voice to patience. "I did say I believed we'd leave this question for the future, and Hliss, I understand that you and the draper's boy have been on fire since spring. But you know your romances have nothing to do with marriage alliances."

Danet had been hearing a lot about Forever and Love Till We Die from her sister, who had discovered boys half a year ago. To draw Mother's attention away from Hliss, Danet asked, "What do we get?"

Mother gave her a glance of approval. "We'll get trade favor for our linens and a pennon to send if we need protection. I hope just the word going out that you two marrying into the Olavayirs will cause those horsethieves up Cedar Mountain way to think again before trying any more raids."

She pursed her lips and made a spitting motion to one side; it was to one or another of these bands that she had lost her entire family, and herself left for dead. Those thieves had chosen a lair in the difficult country between Tyavayir and the great jarlate of Yvanavayir. Danet had grown up hearing the adults jaw on about how in the *olden* days, the King's Riders ranged the kingdom borders, seeing to that kind of trouble. But now the jarls had to protect their own borders because there were no King's Riders outside the royal city and its environs. And nobody ventured into those treacherous mountains unless they had to.

Hliss dropped her head at Mother's emphatic *Ptooie!* She hated the thought of violence.

Danet said quickly, "What do we have to give besides horses?"

Mother raised her hand, palm out, two fingers up. "Besides the two mares, a full bolt each of undyed linen and rider-gray linsey-woolsey — which I expect will result in plenty of orders for those trade favors, especially the first," she added, pride briefly showing in a tight smile.

The rest of the fingers went up. "And a riding if the jarl calls, same if the king calls, riding under Olavayir command. All equipment pertaining and a month's fodder."

"Nine riders and trained horses would be hard on us, if there's trouble anywhere near us, and the jarl is fighting somewhere else," Danet said. "You won't send our best, surely?"

"I will," Mother stated. "If we send them good horses, that helps our prestige, especially if our riding does well at their summer games next year. We'll make certain of that," Mother added. "Your father promised to send your brother next spring to pick the men and lead them himself."

It was just a wargame, but tender-hearted Hliss dipped her head again. Occasionally fellows came back from wargames with broken bones. And they all had heard about the second cousin who hadn't come back at all from a game up over the mountains, where they knew that their kin, the Arvandais clan, played very rough indeed.

Mother glanced out the window, squared her thin shoulders, and unlimbered another long speech to her silent, wondering girls. "Of course it's not the royal family. They only match with other jarl families. That's good, as far as I see it. I understand the royal city is quiet now under Kendred Olavayir as regent, but it wasn't when I was your age, or the generation before, and we don't know what young Evred is going to be like when he comes of age. I think it just as well to keep you in the north."

Danet had no argument with that. She had never experienced any desire to see the royal city.

"Danet, you're to go to the jarl's second son. I forget his name, and he likely doesn't use it anyway."

"Probably another Hasta," Hliss said with a soft laugh. "That will make six among us."

"Not among *us*. You are going to *them*," Mother reminded Hliss, who looked down again, her gentle smile vanishing.

"I?" Hliss asked, her soft brown eyes round with apprehension.

"Hliss, you're for the rider branch, but no sooner than two years' time. I stipulated for that. You're still training, and if they expect you to captain a border scout riding or manage the stables, then you'll need to know how to give orders. So no marriage until you're at least eighteen. Twenty if I can put them off, as the boy you're intended for is no older than you. Boys should never marry before twenty, they're too silly. I would put the marrying age for boys at thirty, but no one asked me. The Olavayirs want Danet right away. They seem to marry young."

Hliss heaved a quiet sigh of relief.

Mother turned her wide blue gaze on Danet. "We're all going to pitch in to get you ready. No Olavayir is going to scorn your things, even if we aren't jarl-family rank. About that. Your marrying among them will no doubt seem to their connections a jump up. Though we're kin to the Arvandais up north and through me to the Faths of Tyavayir, you'll no doubt arrive to resentment from secondary families who had ambitions for their daughters."

Mother turned her palm down flat. "This waiting until you're full-grown for betrothals is a bad custom for so many reasons. It was different in your great-grandmothers' day, when everyone knew from birth who was to go where, and you had a lifetime to settle to it."

And they'd heard about the difference so many times, Danet thought, hoping that the "Girls should grow up with the family they will manage" lecture wasn't hovering at Mother's lips.

But Mother felt she had jawed long enough, and there was work to be done. "So. We have what we have. Let's take a look at your gear."

"When is 'right away'?"

"I stipulated a month."

A month! Danet bit back an exclamation that would not be welcome. A month was at once too short and too long: too short for going away forever, and too long for curiosity.

But one thing about time, it passes, she thought as Mother charged out of her room, issuing a stream of orders. Especially when you're busy.

TWO

Danet had never expected to be living farther than half a day's riding from any of her family. Her first experience of Olavayir ways was the runner who came to fetch her.

Summoned by one of Mother's two runners, Danet reached the house in time to overhear the woman explaining that Danet's new robe mustn't be mistaken for runner blue-gray. "The Olavayir blue is *royal* blue," the woman said.

Danet held her breath, waiting to hear what Mother would say to that, and was surprised when Mother responded in a voice mild as six-comb flax that she had obtained the supplies for the right shade as soon as the betrothal treaty came.

Danet whistled soundlessly under her breath. She knew that Mother had for years, in anticipating hers and Hliss's marriages, set aside the best fabric from the best batches, to await dye once she knew the color of the House each girl would go to. Over the past couple of weeks she had insisted on supervising the dyeing herself, until the beautifully soft linen was the exact shade of the twilight summer sky. She had also inspected every stitch as Danet worked on her robe, adding a line of golden twisted-silk to the edging along the front and the sleeves.

Still in that same mild voice, Mother pointed out the guest quarters over the stable, and when the runner was safely out of earshot, Danet rounded the yarn rack.

Mother drew Danet inside her room and said with quiet ferocity, "You needn't say anything. Let facts speak for themselves on your wedding day, when you put on a robe better made than a queen's. They'll learn why Farendavan linens and dyes are famous. Runner blue-gray, tchah!" Mother flipped up the back of her hand.

From that, Danet discovered her mother's true feelings about this match. She said nothing, as done was done, but as the day for departure approached she was aware of more trepidation than pleasure.

The trepidation was sharpest the night before she was to leave, when she went to say farewell to her good-natured, gorgeous lover. Embas was as sweet and loving as ever, but when she left, he smiled benignly as he leaned in his doorway with his ruddy dark hair hanging over his shoulder and his shirt unlaced, and she knew that she felt her departure more than he did.

Mother had raised her girls to be practical in all things, including relationships. So Danet had always reminded herself that the fire between them wouldn't last, that the two friends she shared him with would no doubt be joined soon by another girl or two after Danet was gone. But it hurt all the same.

Next morning she rose, bathed, dressed, and stared at her breakfast until it was time to depart.

Mother took her by her bony shoulders. "I know you'll do well."

Danet, whose throat was too tight for speech, searched her mother's eyes, not sure if the glisten there was her imagination. Then Mother lifted her hands and turned away.

Hliss hugged Danet, whispering, "Write to me."

Danet promised, in a voice that sounded strange to her own ears, that if she could catch any runners going in the direction of Farendavan, she would.

They rode out.

Danet soon discovered that Gdan, the runner, was much like Mother: disciplined, straightforward, with no sense of humor. She appeared to be maybe ten years younger than Mother, in her middle to late thirties, light brown of skin, eyes, and hair, her only prominent feature a hawk nose.

As for Gdan, by the end of their first day's ride, when she saw that Danet dressed down her horse and cared for the bride gift mares before she did anything else, and did it well, she decided this girl would do, and unbent enough to answer the few questions Danet dared to put to her.

So on the rise westward over rolling countryside, where the sounds of harvest songs drifted on the air as people worked their fields, Danet learned that Gdan was runner to Sdar-Randviar—the woman Danet would one day replace—and though Gdan would not talk about her expected duties (that was the jarlan's prerogative) or about people, she did like talking about the horses and stables.

As Danet loved horses, riding, and anything to do with How Things Work, they found enough to discuss to keep the ride from becoming awkward.

They crossed the Tirbit tributary and turned their backs on the mountains Danet had grown up seeing—turned their backs on her home, and its familiar territory, and on Embas the Miller.

She kept her regret to herself, and tried to look ahead to her new life as they rode steadily west, until Gdan pointed out three hills surrounding Nevree, the trade town that the Olavayirs had made their capital.

Danet noted that Nevree's river, like its castle, was four times as broad as the Tirbit in full flow, cutting through the land to bend around one of the hills, the other two hills rising on the north side. Atop all three stood lookout and signal towers.

That, Gdan explained, was where the boys did their first watches away from the castle walls, and Gdan added in a dour tone that in his early days, with his first two sons, the jarl sometimes set Riders to make sneak attacks, and if the boys on tower watch didn't catch them, the boys wouldn't be able to lie on their backs for days.

Danet, after a lifetime of divining extra meaning from her mother's sparse words, got the sense that Gdan wished the same thing was happening these days, maybe to certain people.

The night before Danet's departure, her mother had warned her not to expect any special notice. That way, anything she got would be a pleasant surprise. So Danet firmly told herself she did not expect an outrider welcome, but she was gratified, and secretly relieved, to spot the dust of a full riding on approach.

The first thing she saw was the blue and yellow snapping heir's pennon; then individuals resolved out of the dust. The one drawing the eye was a big fellow—much too big to call a boy, and probably too old as well—he was enormous, with heavy shoulders whose slope the layered shoulder spaulders common to men's coats didn't hide. He reminded her of a war horse, with the straw-colored hair so common among Marlovans. His mount looked too small for him, until she noticed the huge chest and the long legs and the hooves like plates. The rider was so large he made his horse look small.

Gdan said, "That's Jarend-Laef."

The Jarl of Olavayir's eldest son! His horsetail made his long face look longer, a face dominated by the biggest pair of buck teeth she'd ever seen.

"Danet Farendavan?" he asked. His voice sounded like it came from the bottom of a well.

"I am. Well met, Jarend-Laef," she said, touching two fingers to her chest in salute.

He uttered a rumbling laugh, then said, "Came out to meet you, *hur hur.* Arrow said I should, *hur hur.*"

"Arrow?" Danet asked.

Another chuckle. "That's m'brother, Anred. But we don't say Anred, we say Arrow. On account of his mouth is shaped like an arrowhead. And because we got Uncle Anred and a cousin, too, but, *hur hur,* we all call *him* Bat, *hur hur.*" He chuckled again, then wiped his sweaty face on his arm, leaving a big smear. "Arrow has the hill watch today, so he said, come out and meet you, soon's the perimeter rider saw the pennon." He pointed to the limp blue and yellow flag Gdan carried on a pole, much smaller than the heir's pennon, of course.

And though Danet couldn't perceive anything whatever in that to laugh at, he chuckled some more as he fell in with them. He then asked a lot of easy, obvious questions that she suspected he didn't really hear the answers to, as his expression of good humor never changed; for his part, he found his brother's new wife to be easy to talk to, clear in her speech. Always glad to like anyone given a chance, Jarend did his best to welcome her by helpfully pointing out everything she could see for herself, and Gdan, riding silently behind, approved of Danet's manners as she thanked him, or commented appropriately.

It was nearing sunset when they approached the castle's outer wall. The whole, with its three rings, looked to Danet like the biggest hive in the world, with gray-clad bees buzzing in and out and crawling along the walls.

The old city lay along the river, most of it now warehouses and counting houses, with a guard outpost.

As they approached the outer gate, Danet kept her hand ready, watching to see what Gdan did about saluting: she knew from her one trip north over the Andahi Pass that some Jarl Houses expected saluting all the time. Her cousin Hadand Arvandais had warned Danet that they ordered floggings for those who forgot, for awareness of rank was a part of good order.

The Olavayirs, for all their reputation for trouble, did not seem to share that attitude. The gate sentries didn't move, except to brush a couple fingers over their hearts, to which Jarend made a lazy wave. Gdan didn't salute at all, so Danet shifted her reins back to her right hand.

Between the first wall and the second lay the city proper, shops closing up and others opening, eddies of cooking food aromas waking up her stomach. She stared at unfamiliar busy streets, so unlike their single street village in Farendavan. There were still round Iascan houses here and there, and the traffic as merchants ended their day and the riders' watch changed intimidated her. It was a relief to see familiar coats of Rider gray on the patrollers, horsetails bobbing down their backs.

Between the second and inner walls was the garrison and its stable. The inner wall surrounded the tallest part of the castle, what Jarend called the residence, where the family and most of the staff lived.

They rode under a third guarded gate, and here again exchanged the same casual salute. When they reached the stableyard—which was five times the size of Danet's—she felt as if a dull gray-blue whirlwind descended, runners beckoning her one way, the horses taken another way, Jarend and Gdan talking to people. Danet's Firefly was firmly led off, and another runner took her saddlebags.

A girl about Hliss's age said to Danet, "This way."

At first she was glad to stretch her legs. But the more stairs she climbed and halls she walked, the more she worried she'd get lost forever if left alone.

They entered a room that smelled of stale rye biscuits, and Ranor-Jarlan, a solid woman with flyaway gray hair, shot Danet an assessing glance as Danet laid hand to heart in salute.

"Danet? You don't have a personal runner?"

It was not a real question—more of a statement, as if a possible runner might be invisible. Danet said, "My sister and I shared our mother's at home."

"This is your home now," the jarlan said in a brisk voice very like Mother's. "As well you did not bring one. So much harder to retrain outside runners to our ways. When you settle on someone who suits you, speak up. Until then? Nand, get her situated. When Arrow rides in, see that they meet."

And Nand whisked Danet right out again.

The rest of that watch passed in a blur. Danet was shown to her room — her own room, with a bed big enough for two, a carved trunk for her clothes, a plain table and two sitting mats. Her attention stayed on the size of that bed as longing squeezed her heart. She missed Embas fiercely, but she knew he would never ride cross-country in order to see her. She wondered who would lie in that big bed with her, and what the customs were among the Olavayirs.

But Nand didn't linger long enough for questions. She swept Danet off to see where the baths were, and the stable where the women worked, and finally to the family mess hall, a smaller chamber up and to the right of the castle mess hall.

A single bell tanged: that had to be the evening watch change.

Danet discovered that everyone had their place. "The jarl's riding up around Andahi Pass," was the last thing Nand said to Danet before pointing out that she was to take the guest mat opposite the randviar, and then disappeared downstairs to the runners' own mess. An empty mat sat to the right of Danet.

She wondered who would sit there, and looked down the loaded table to the other end. Mother had told Danet that the jarl's randael — his brother — was dead, and there was his empty mat to the right of the jarl's empty mat. Danet wondered who commanded the Riders, but she kept quiet, having been trained to listen and speak only when spoken to when in new situations.

Sdar-Randviar sat down across from Danet, and they silently assessed one another. Sdar-Randviar appeared to be the jarlan's age, a generation older than Mother. The two women had to be in their sixties, the randviar a plain, straight-backed woman with graying hair streaked with rusty red.

Danet had just cut off a piece of fried fish from the big platter when in sauntered a skinny young man a few years older than Danet, splashed to the knees with mud, and smelling of horse. He folded up on the mat beside her. This had to be Arrow. They studied one another.

As his brother had said, Arrow had a mouth shaped like an arrowhead, an upside-down V. She thought he was frowning, but when he spoke she discovered behind his short upper lip a pair of sizable buck teeth. She wondered if he hated showing those two big teeth, so kept his mouth shut except to talk, unlike Jarend, always chuckling, *hur hur hur.*

She had been expecting another big fellow. But Arrow was spare in build, as if (she thought to herself, longing to write this observation to her sister Hliss) someone had taken half the makings of a boy out of him and stuffed the extra into his brother.

He was blond like his brother, skin the same brown as her own, eyes typical Marlovan bluish-gray, the shade of faded runner coats.

Arrow looked at her, wondering if she were smart, and if he'd be able to trust her with his father's plans. Only time would tell for that. As for her appearance, she wasn't any comparison to Fi, his current lover, as troublesome as she was tight. This Danet was plain and skinny. Like him.

He tightened his mouth to hide those damn teeth, hoping she wouldn't find him disgusting, because Father wanted children as soon as they could get them, and who knew if the Birth Spell would ever come again in the family. It hadn't for Aunt Sdar.

But anything could be managed as long as Danet didn't fall for Cousin Lanrid.

"Good ride?" he asked, then bit into a cabbage roll.

"Yes," she said, aware she was staring, so she glanced down the table again, wondering if those in the middle were cousins, and if one of them might be Hliss's future husband, the one Jarend had called Sinna during that long ride to the gate.

She was about to venture a query when the jarlan addressed them in her abrupt way. "I asked Tdor Fath to organize your wedding."

Tdor Fath—her birth-family name appended to distinguish her from several Tdors—was Jarend's wife, a tall, needle-nosed woman with thin braids like combed flax. Danet looked at her with interest, but didn't recognize her from the Faths she'd met at the horse fair a few years before.

Tdor Fath didn't say a word, just looked from the jarlan to Sdar with pale brown eyes as the two elder women in quick, practical tones fit the wedding into the castle schedule as they would a shoeing or an all-castle drill.

By then everyone was done eating. Arrow figured talk with Danet could wait until everybody else wasn't snouting in—and anyway, he had Fi to deal with, now that news of his wedding would be spreading. He'd told her at least twice that he had to marry for the family, but nobody ever said no to Fi, and she'd refused to believe him.

He took off, leaving Danet to head tiredly for bed—alone—where she lay staring at the two slit windows and the bare walls, and tried to compass the idea that this room would be hers for years and years, until she became randviar. She fiercely blinked back homesick tears, firmly told herself to look ahead, and wondered if she could at least get some hangings.

THREE

The unfamiliar sound of bells echoing off stone woke her at dawn. Nand had told her the women drilled before breakfast—no surprise there—so Danet did her best to remember how to get to the drill court she'd been shown. She could hear men's voices shouting in cadence over a stone wall.

The randviar led, and Danet discovered that her mother's drills, which she'd told the girls countless times came straight from her Vranid grandmother, who had served as second-generation defending commander at Ala Larkadhe during the Venn War, were much tougher than the Olavayir drills. She discovered that the Olavayir women didn't even do the *odni*, or double-knife fighting drills, except in the knife dance invented late in the last century, it was said by the great Hadand Deheldegarthe herself. Olavayir women didn't wear wrist knives except to ride the border.

Instead they did a basic hand-to-hand warmup, then went straight to riding and shooting in a circle in the corral. Danet could put a leg over any horse they gave her, but her shooting had never been great, and with so many watching eyes, she shot worse then ever. At least she hit somewhere on the target three times at canter, but she didn't come anywhere near the red.

Still, the jarlan, watching from the barn door, said nothing dire, just that Danet would ride out on her first border patrol after the wedding.

And so her new life began.

At first she was always going the wrong way, and always late. Even when she knew where she was going, everything was so far apart it took longer to get there. Then she had to get her own gear clean and ready, as she had no runner: she never saw Nand again, except at a distance, and she wondered if the girl was in one of those families who'd thought they'd marry someone to Arrow. There was some atmosphere here she couldn't define, except she felt she was being watched.

Her second night she found out where they kept the big barrels full of water enchanted to remove dirt, unsurprisingly located just off the baths, with lines stretched between posts in a court outside, for drying one's laundry. After the evening meal Danet ran down to start dealing with her pack of dirty travel clothes, when everyone else had liberty.

Arrow was gone all the time, and no one else spoke to her beyond immediate tasks. She saw him at meals, but now he sat next to his brother to the right of the empty jarl's mat, and he always arrived at a rush and was first one to leave.

A few days later, she spotted him and a startlingly beautiful girl with long, loose black hair worn over floating silks. They were coming down the hall from the opposite direction; this was how Danet discovered that Arrow lived on the same hall. The girl was clearly a lover, and not a Marlovan one.

Danet was carrying an armload of freshly sun-dried underclothes and stockings, but she thought, might as well begin on a friendly note, and started toward them.

The girl stopped, twined her arm around Arrow's neck, and said in accented Marlovan, "Is that *her*?"

The "her" was said with so much venom that Danet stopped short, appalled.

Arrow turned red to the ears. "Yes, that's Danet. Fi, you know how it works with us...." He opened his bedroom door and towed her in.

Fi sent Danet a nasty glare over her shoulder from those wide blue eyes, then liplocked Arrow, nearly causing the two of them to slam into the doorframe. Arrow got her inside and the door shut.

Ugh! How could someone so handsome have such terrible manners? Danet retreated to her room, determined to shrug off the feel of that venom. Just because that obnoxious Fi wanted to give it didn't mean Danet had to take it. Maybe this Fi wanted one of those outlander love matches you heard about. But Arrow hadn't said anything to Danet about how he was lifemates with this Fi, and he'd had plenty of chances.

Danet prowled around her room once or twice, then ran down to take another bath. Scrubbing her skin warm and breathing the scent of steaming water helped rid herself of the Fi feeling.

The wedding had been set two weeks on. The days passed quickly, everyone busy. Danet spent most of her time learning how to navigate the castle and its environs, and exercising Firefly once morning drill was over. Here and there she overheard bits and snatches of conversation, mostly as the delicious smell of almond cakes drifted along the hall near the bakehouse, which were only brought out for festival days, weddings, and Name Days.

Danet got the impression that Jarend's wedding had been planned for months. But he was the heir, and Tdor Fath was first daughter of the Fath Rider captain eastward in Tyavayir. They'd also made a festival of the Name Day of their little son, whom they called Rabbit (if you are guessing at big front teeth, you would be right) a not-quite-walking baby.

The day before the wedding, the jarlan sent out a party of teenage girls to gather boughs to hang up in the Hall of Ancestors. The jarlan also issued an order for beeswax candles instead of the usual leddas-oil torches. That was all the decoration, but for Danet it was enough. Boughs were customary at any wedding, no matter who, and the candles made it respectable. She hadn't hoped for anything beyond that.

The morning of her wedding, Danet encountered Jarend's wife Tdor Fath on the way to the baths, when she spoke to Danet for the first time.

Her expression was sober as she murmured, "Arrow's current lover Fini sa Vaka hasn't been asked to your wedding. But she's Iascan. She doesn't know our ways, and won't listen. She might turn up and make trouble."

Danet considered that. She certainly had no feelings yet for Arrow, whom she'd scarcely spoken ten words to. Marriage, Mother had taught her girls, was an alliance between households, with clearly defined work for each partner. Romance and love might come, or one might have to look for it elsewhere. She said cautiously, "*I* don't know all your ways yet. What ought I to do if that happens?"

"Our ways," Tdor repeated, flashing a rueful smile. "I'm a Fath, an outsider, same as you, adopted in. The Faths and the Olavayirs...let's say the families made a truce." Her hand swiped flat-handed, thrusting that subject aside. "At least we're both Marlovans. I thought I'd tell you, Fini's family is important in Lindeth. She was sent by her grandmother, Fini sa Buno, to run their counting house here at Nevree. So no one wants to risk her grandmother cutting off our trade with Lindeth-Hije Shipping. The jarlan says Fini-the-elder is fair, for an Iascan, so we don't say anything or interfere while Fi tries to court Arrow. But I think you should know."

"Is it a love match?" Danet asked.

Tdor actually laughed. "No chance. Before he took up with her, he, ah, he thought he was going to marry Hard Ride Arvandais, from over the mountains. While carrying on with half the girls in the castle, and another dozen in town."

Danet suppressed a whistle at the mention of her cousin, recollecting that a marriage treaty proposal had fallen through. Her brother had told her on his last visit that Hard Ride's family was negotiating with no fewer than four important Houses, including the regent on behalf of the king.

Tdor Fath's eyes narrowed. "You know something."

"Not really," Danet hedged. "I was only up in Idego once. When I was ten. To meet my cousins." Fourth-cousins, one generation before the kinship terms changed. The adults up in Idego had been looking her over as a possible match for Hal, Hard Ride's brother.

"Is it true that Hard Ride Hadand is that amazing?" Tdor Fath asked.

Danet wondered how much to say about that single visit. Hadand, the cousin closest to Danet's age, had been thirteen, Danet ten. Even then all the Idegans had called her Hard Ride. Danet's first glimpse of her cousin had been in the courtyard after their arrival, when Hard Ride leaped up onto the back of a restive horse and rode out at the gallop, not even holding on. Those long golden braids swaying across her back seemed shinier than everyone else's.

"She is...." Danet began, her gaze distant, and Tdor Fath waited.

Danet was trying to find the words for how her cousin had seemed somehow larger than life, except not in the sense of Jarend-Laef. She'd been the first to laugh, the first to shout "Good one!" if someone got in a good blow or shot in the constant competitions, even against her.

But she also had a temper like a flash of lightning, and then on some subjects she spoke in a fervent voice, her blue eyes wide and (Danet had thought privately) just a little bit crazy. Like when she'd blabbered away in Idegan to her first-cousins and friends, and instead of apologizing, she informed Danet that Marlovan was a barbaric tongue. *It doesn't even have its own alphabet! But Idegan is from Ancient Sartoran,* she'd said earnestly, as if that was tremendously important. Well, to her, it clearly had been.

Embas the Miller had told Danet just last year that everyone up north knew that by the time Hadand was seventeen "Hard Ride" had come to mean something very different. He'd said, *I'm told they all call her a flaxen-haired throwback to One-Eyed Cama during the days of Inda-Harskialdna because everyone wants her, same as they all wanted Cama.*

Tdor Fath said, "We heard she and her brother are the best in Arvandais with bow and sword."

"They were when I was there—that is, best among us, underage. The jarl was the best in everything, except for his sword master, who was even harsher." If Hard Ride Hadand glowed like a lantern, her father had been like the summer sun—everybody talked about him. Tried to please him. He shed a lot of light, but burned you if you displeased him.

"They have competitions up there every day. The loser gets a beating. Mostly from the jarl, though the men got it from that sword master and much worse. What was his name? Vana...Dana...not Sindan. Ah, never mind. My first day, I lost a scrap and Hard Ride beat me herself."

The jarl and the sword master had looked on in approval. Within a couple of days, Danet realized her cousin had gone easy on her—the Arvandais got a lot worse. Including Hard Ride Hadand herself. After that, Danet had made certain to be in the riding competitions whenever there was scrapping among the youngsters in the court, and Hard Ride let her get away with it. But there'd been no talk of a betrothal by the time they went home, Danet emotionally exhausted as well as physically.

Tdor Fath grunted, then tipped her head back toward the residence floor as they cleared the landing. "Some of the boys say that Fi is trouble at the gallop. She was after the new commander at the Lindeth garrison, and any of his captains related to jarls, before the grandmother sent her here to run their Nevree shop. Not that she does any actual work. She's always *here.* We all think the commander asked the grandmother to send her away."

Voices echoed up the stairway. Tdor Fath fell silent and hurried down the last few steps. Danet followed more slowly, watching the slow-rippling reflections of light from the air ducts high overhead as she wondered if the reason no one had talked to her this much was because they were waiting to see what she would do on rough trail as well as smooth.

Soon enough she stood alone in her room, putting on her wedding clothes, which had lain at the bottom of the carved trunk. She shook out the soft, almost silky double-heckled and bucked linen under-robe, wondering if putting on these clothes would make her feel different, but she just felt like herself inside clothes she didn't want wrinkled or snagged.

Her mother had insisted her daughters begin their braids behind their ears, which was practical and kept the loops out of their way as they worked. But some girls started their braids high on their heads, called the fox-ear look, making their loops stand out, and drawing attention to the shape of their heads and necks. Mother had given extra chores to any girl who wasted time on such frivolity, except on festival days, when at least half of the day was one's own time.

It was also impractical, for by the end of the day, inevitably strands were coming loose all over and the loops began to droop on girls with thick, heavy hair. Danet decided that for once, on her wedding day, she would braid fox ears. Even if no one else noticed, she would.

Then she pulled on her House robe for the first time, touched the thin gold-silk embroidered edging that she suspected would look downright plain to the wealthy Olavayirs, and walked down to the great Hall of Ancestors. She smoothed her hands over the beautifully woven fabric, loving the brilliant blue color that was a truer royal blue even than that on the sun-lightened tower banners and pennants.

Here she was in for a gratifying surprise. Every person who noticed the weave and color of her robe, the exquisite hang and sway of the fabric, had to stop and look, their eyes the size of horseshoes.

She cast covert glances at their House tunics, for they had all put on their best. Under the more elaborate gold embroidery, the royal blue was flat and dull, here too green, there too gray, and the coarse weave (in comparison to what she was used to) so kindled her family pride that she cared nothing for uninvited Fi in her embroidered Iascan silks of royal blue and gold, swinging her hip-length mane of waving blue-black hair as she clutched at Arrow's arm.

He had to shake her off before Danet reached the arch of boughs erected beneath the great Olavayir banner. When he stepped up, Danet noted his red nose, and whiffed stale bristic. Her bridegroom was drunk, but not so drunk that he couldn't see her reaction in her expression, and the way she took a half step back.

Annoyance and remorse washed through him, but at the fuzzy distance drinking always gave him. "Fi kept toasting us," he muttered to Danet.

He thought his voice was soft, but his ears, always alert for his hated dolphin-branch cousin Lanrid, caught the familiar loud snicker behind him on the men's side.

Arrow shut up and held out his hand peremptorily, with a sudden sea change in the current of his emotions, impatient to have this over.

Danet took his callused hand firmly: This was to be her life.

What were these two thinking about as they repeated the simple vows that adopted her into the clan and made them partners? He was wishing he hadn't drunk so much, and wondering how was he to get Fi out of there now that he'd actually gotten married — to someone else. He knew she'd expected him to dramatically reject Danet Farendavan at the last moment, right there under the boughs, in front of everyone, and thrillingly demand that his family accept Fini sa Vaka.

Danet was making a conscious effort to think of the Olavayir Hall of Ancestors as her hall. Much as she missed home, she knew that to return would make her a failure in her duty. So she exerted every nerve to feel like an Olavyair when the two of them took the wedding cup that the jarlan, as senior ranking person, handed to them to share.

He gulped. She touched her lip to the wine without drinking, then passed back the cup to the jarlan, who beckoned Danet away and passed the cup to Jarend.

He took a noisy gulp, then said in his deep voice, "Welcome to the family," with a smile so genuine that Danet smiled back. It struck her that she hadn't seen anything of Jarend since her arrival, except at meals, when he sat huge as a mountain, silent except for that occasional rumbling chuckle that was almost like a purr.

Jarend handed the cup to Tdor Fath, and the jarlan beckoned again, saying in an ordinary tone, "Danet, I've a question for you."

The everyday tone and behavior startled Danet, until the thought occurred to her that this was just another wedding for the jarlan and the randviar. They'd stood through many of them. This one was nothing special — Danet was nothing special. Danet stared down at the toes of her riding boots that she had polished so hard the night before, resolving to see this as another ordinary day.

The jarlan said briskly, "We and your family settled on the wedding trade, and I assure you we're well satisfied with the mares and especially the cloth your mother sent along."

"More than satisfied," Sdar said, her gaze running hungrily down the beautiful folds of Danet's robe.

"Would your mother be offended if we wrote to ask her to share your dye process?" the jarlan asked.

Danet said, "I can't speak for her, but I believe if you were to write and give an increase in orders, she'd be pleased, not offended."

The two women smiled with genuine approval. The jarlan liked this Danet Farendavan the more she saw of her. Sdar exchanged quick glances with Tdor Fath, both relieved that Danet was behaving toward that revolting Fini sa Vaka as if she didn't exist. Yes, she would do for Arrow.

The jarlan turned out her hand, and one of the younger girls, who had been watching for her signal, brought out a hand drum.

"Time for your bride dance," Tdor Fath said, coming up to take Danet's hand.

Danet followed, thinking of her mother's words about how marriage was like a castle, sturdy and enduring in shared work and family. Though she was now an Olavayir, Danet hugged to herself her pride as a Farendavan weaver, so she never once looked at Fi, after that first glance at her in her beautiful silks in the Olavayir blue and gold.

Instead, she danced with the women, beginning with the knife dance. She watched the men, even though Arrow only got up twice, and not even for the sword dance. He shuffled through the easier ones, swaying and braying with laughter as Fi pressed drink on him between dances, with vindictive intent.

When the night-watch bells rang, and everyone who had morning duty began breaking up, Danet started out after a departing clump of women.

Fi, who had hoped for at least a scene, despised Danet not only for her plain looks, but her dullness, and gave Arrow a push, nearly knocking him down. "Go give her her wedding night," she cooed. "She's not going to get it from anyone else."

Arrow blinked stupidly, and disgust surged in Fi. All this time she'd wasted on the bonehead. She bitterly regretted having crooked her finger at him during his summer stint at the Lindeth garrison. Of course he'd come to her like a trained dog. They all did. But her time had clearly been wasted.

"Waya...momun...." he slurred as he swayed after Danet.

The group of women heard the unsteadily rap of his boot heels, and the jarlan's second runner gathered the others with her eyes and drew them along as Danet turned a few paces in from the great doors, to face her bridegrooom.

"Ready for bed?" Arrow asked, with a drunken leer as he lurched toward her.

She put two fingers in the middle of the golden eagle wingspread on his chest and pushed him back. "You're sloshing to the back teeth."

"Fi sen' me," he mumbled. "Do it righ'."

"I'm sending you back. I can't stand drunks," stated Mother's daughter — not angrily, just a matter of fact.

Because they stood alone, Danet had thought them alone, until she heard a crack of laughter from somewhere behind, and saw the flush of anger on Arrow's face. She glanced up and caught a smirk on the face of the oldest of the Rider cousins, a very pretty one whose name she still didn't know.

She lowered her voice and said for Arrow's ear alone, "You're welcome in my bed when you're sober."

Then she walked out.

She hadn't gone ten steps beyond the door before she heard an unfamiliar voice say, soft and low, "Danet."

Danet turned to find that same big cousin addressing her for the first time.

He was almost as tall as Jarend, but far more slender, with splendid shoulders narrowing in to slim hips, what the slang of the day termed a tight body. His face was the definition of tight: square, cleft chin, bright blue eyes, and no hint of buck teeth.

He sauntered toward her, enjoying her slow up and down as he said, "I'm Lanrid Olavayir, dolphin-branch, here in Olavayir according to treaty." She heard the lilt of pride in the words *dolphin-branch*. "I'm Acting Rider Commander under the heir. Your sister will be marrying my little brother."

"Well met," Danet said politely.

He took a step closer. Now it was his turn to give her a slow rake from braids to boots that she felt as tingly heat, as if he'd touched her with his big, well-shaped hands. "You deserve a proper wedding night. *I'll* give you one."

His voice was low and coaxing and she gulped in air, heart thumping. A kind of giddiness serried through her, but she forced herself think past the feelings. If this invitation had come in her first few lonely days, she knew she would probably have responded, but why now? Mother had taught the girls early to heed any sense of contradiction, and to mentally cover the smile and look at the eyes for inconsistency.

His smile, bracketed by dimples, sharpened the tingles of expectation, but when she looked only at his eyes, and saw the complacent expectation there, and no reflection of the smile below, her budding attraction withered to ash.

At home, she would have been blunt, but she was still trying to fit herself into this family without making enemies, if she could. She said, "I saved this night for Arrow."

Lanrid did not accept that and retire, as custom — decency — required. He took a step nearer, as if he didn't believe her, and said, "I'm afraid it'll be a long, lonely night. You deserve better."

There. The words were kindly, and the smile, but the closeness — she could feel his breath on her forehead — and his unsmiling eyes warned her of trouble.

She didn't understand why, but she trusted instinct. "I can hope. And if not, there's always tomorrow."

He laughed. "Then we'll have this conversation again."

No we won't, she decided as she said out loud, "Good night." And walked away.

Her shoulder blades crawled and her heart continued to bang her ribs, not with anticipation, but a sense of having escaped something she still could not name. She looked back furtively a couple times as she retreated to her room, relieved each time that no one was there.

FOUR

She got up with the dawn bells and grimly made herself report for drill, for she knew that the rest of the household regarded it as another workday. Sure enough, she found, talking in a knot in the women's court, the jarlan, the randviar, their personal runners, and a couple of the cousins she still didn't know. Danet knew she was the subject when they broke up at the sight of her.

But the jarlan gave her a grunt of approval, and Sdar-Randviar thumped her on the shoulder with her fist. "Your place is now up front, when I'm busy elsewhere. Take the lead today. Make 'em sweat."

So there was Danet wearing her new working robe of royal blue over her old shirt and trousers, standing at the front. She hadn't brought out her knives, as Olavayirs didn't drill in the odni, but she decided to warm them up with the easy knife dance, and then put them through the odni hand drill without weapons, which she had been doing every day since she was six.

The others followed as she called cadences in Mother's voice.

It was the strangest feeling, as if she slept and was dreaming. But in a dream everyone's face is vague, or shows the same expression, and as she called the moves, she saw some trying hard, some watching for cues, a few resentful and sullen, and three or four girls at the back around Hliss's age or younger giggling when they thought she wasn't looking, until Sdar went back there and stood right behind them, making them repeat every move until they did it right.

After, when the older women broke up to head for the riding ring for shooting practice, leaving the younger girls behind for more drill, Gdan came up to her, leading another hawk-nosed girl about Danet's age, or maybe a year younger, wearing sun-faded runner gray-blue.

"This is Tes," Gdan said. "If you need a runner, Tesar'll do for you until you decide on someone."

Danet turned to Tesar. "If it's all right with you, it's all right with me."

Tesar ducked her head, brushed her fingers over her heart, and loped off without a word.

Gdan glanced off to the right, then also brushed her fingers over her heart and walked away. Danet had a few moments to consider how her status had changed. She began to wonder if a change of state was something that happened in how other people treated you, when someone approached, his step slow and uncertain.

Danet didn't recognize Arrow at first. His face was bruised and swollen, and instead of moving at his usual brisk bounce, he shuffled like an old man.

As Danet stared in bewilderment, from behind came the arms mistress's bawl, "No, Leap of the Deer from the *hips!* Turn from the *hips*—you've got 'em, *use* 'em! There's your strength!"

Arrow's bruised, swollen mouth got out the words with difficulty, "I hear Cousin Lanrid tried to spark you last night."

"Yes."

"But you turned him down."

Danet didn't see any reason not to speak the truth. "I don't know him, but I don't think he was sparking me so much as sparking trouble."

Arrow squinted at her as if he saw her for the first time. "He was," he said. "Can we start over?"

He sounded surly, but what little she could see of his expression past the distortion reminded her of her brother when he knew he'd done something stupid. And the last thing she wanted was the drag of resentment between them before they'd had so much as a single real conversation.

"Let's," she said.

"My head aches too much for talk," he said, gently touching his purple eye ridge. "Tonight. All right?"

"You know where I'll be."

He stumbled off, and Danet went in to eat breakfast.

Most of the table was empty. The jarlan, so congenial earlier, was now white-lipped and silent, which kept everyone else silent, so all Danet heard was the tap of knives or spoons on plates.

After breakfast she ran down to fetch the laundry that she'd left the night before her wedding, to discover that Tesar had been ahead of her.

Coming out of the hall, she spotted a cluster of the Rider cousins smirking and laughing as they swaggered in from the baths, but as soon as they saw her, Lanrid blew her a kiss, then they ran upstairs to the mess hall, guffawing.

When Danet reached her bedroom, there was Tesar smoothing the fresh linens on her bed. All the rest of the laundry had been shaken out, folded, and put away.

Danet said, partly to test the limits of their relationship, "Something happened. I mean, after I left, last night. Do you know what?"

Tesar tucked and smoothed down the blanket to military precision. Danet thought the girl was going to ignore her, and mentally resigned herself to losing a runner as fast as she'd gained one, until Tesar turned away and straightened up, and what had looked like a frown in profile was in full face the wrinkled brow of thought.

Tesar said slowly, as if choosing her words, "Lanrid Olavayir and his two cousins scragged Arrow last night. After Arrow had a shouting fight with Fini sa Vaka, and she went back to her Nevree counting house." Tesar made spitting lips to the side.

"They scragged him? Why?"

"And then threw him in the stable midden waiting to be wanded," Tesar said, softly, as if someone else stood in the room with them. Her gaze dropped, and Danet couldn't help notice that Tesar had the longest lashes she'd ever seen on a girl. "Said it was because he'd disgraced our connection with the Faths and the Arvandais, getting drunk at his own wedding and dishonoring you."

"They certainly didn't ask me, or I'd have told them I can speak for myself. But they didn't ask. They don't care what I think. What's the real truth?" Danet asked. "What's between them?"

Tesar's gaze shifted from object to object, her shoulders tightening. Clearly she thought she'd already said too much. "Ask him."

She was done, Danet could tell. So she said, "About wall hangings. Are there some in storage, or do I have to send for some from home?"

Sure enough, Tesar's tense shoulders eased, and she told Danet all they had were some old, moth-eaten tapestries. All the good ones apparently went south to the royal city with the first Olavayir king Aldren, and the secondary hangings when Jasid went south to take the kingship from Haldren-Harvaldar in '29. Clearly making more was not a priority for the Olavayirs.

Tesar left with the sheets and other laundry to be washed, and Danet, mindful of her first border patrol, changed into her sturdiest riding clothes. At the bottom of the stairs she encountered the jarlan, who said, "We postponed your first border ride a day." She took in Danet's clothes, then added, "You might want to take your Firefly out for a good long run, rather than just circling the training corral."

Danet slapped her hand over her heart, wondering what that was all about.

It felt great to get away from the castle. She galloped Firefly until they were both tired and refreshed, then brought her back, and though the Olavayir stable hands were excellently trained, Danet enjoyed the rhythms of a thorough curry. She didn't speak, Firefly couldn't, but they communicated through hands and muscles until the mare huffed and blew into somnolent contentment.

At dinner, Danet and Sdar-Randviar talked about morning drill, and where Mother had learned hers, and that led to stories about Danet's famous foremother holding Larkadhe—called Ala Larkadhe in those days—and the legends about how tough she was.

"If *she* had been with the Jarlan of Arveas and the women of Andahi Castle, they would surely have held out against the Venn an extra week," the jarlan said, and the randviar agreed.

Danet sensed that this praise of a long-dead relation was in a way praise for her. She said, "Mother told us once that our great-mother regretted not being there to her dying day."

At twilight she did not have laundry to deal with for the first time since her arrival, so she took a walk around on the walls, as it was a balmy evening. She heard singing on the air. One of the boys had a good voice, at least as good as any traveling bard she'd heard. But she didn't see where the singers were gathered.

When the night watch bell rang, she went up to her room, where she found Arrow leaning against the wall beside her shut door. He looked sullen and in pain.

She opened the door and gestured him inside.

She knew that the high ground here was hers, but she could see in his sideways glance and general hangdog atmosphere that he was aware of it. So she said in her lightest voice, "What does marriage mean in Olavayir? I want to know what to expect, so I start out right."

He dropped onto her trunk, and one hand fidgeted, his thumb running along the carved edge as if he checked the honing of a weapon. "What does it mean in your family?" he asked his knees.

She wasn't quite ready to sit on the bed, and the room had no other furniture besides the trunk and a tiny table with two floor mats, as she was seldom in there. So it was her turn to lean against the wall as she said, "My mother calls it a partnership. Each with their duties."

He glanced up, then said to his boot tops, "My father wants us having children right away."

No apology for his drunken beginning, but at least he was talking to her.

Danet didn't hide her surprise. "I know Olavayirs marry young, but I thought that was to get used to your ways. Isn't there plenty of time for children?" Then she remembered Jarend's little boy, though she had no idea how old Jarend was. He was so big he could have been forty as easily as twenty. She thought either would look the same on him.

Arrow lifted his one-eyed gaze at last. "You might not know that my father's first two sons, our older brothers, were both killed defending the last king."

"I heard a little about that, but not about your brothers being there."

"They were. Father wants the family strong," Arrow said.

It seemed strong enough to Danet, but it was clear that Arrow had orders from the jarl, and she didn't see any reason to start their marriage by arguing. Children were a part of the partnership. If you accepted that, then there didn't seem to be any reason why she couldn't get that part done now instead of in ten or even twenty years.

"All right," she said.

The side of his mouth not swollen into distortion lifted, and he said, "Give me a few days?"

She smiled back, thinking that it probably took all his strength just to walk.

"When you're ready," she said. "I'll tell the healer to give me gerda steep. I don't want to chew it."

The next morning, at breakfast, the servants brought in a small clay pot with gerda leaves floating in the boiled water. It was an odd smell, somewhere between ginger and anise, Danet thought. The jarlan looked on in approval as she poured it out and drank it.

The taste reminded her of summer grass, neither delicious nor repugnant, Danet was glad to find. Mother had told her that one early sign of pregnancy was that the taste would suddenly go off. As Danet conscientiously finished the contents of the pot, she thought that this was another potential change of state.

When she rose to leave, the jarlan broke off her conversation with two runners and gave Danet orders, sending her along with Gdan and a riding of experienced women for that postponed first border patrol. Tesar rode with Danet, to see to tent, gear, and weapons. They both would care for the horses.

They had not sunk the three hills beyond the horizon when they encountered a lone rider. No one stopped; Gdan raised a hand in salute to the tall silhouette who at first seemed to be wearing black. Proximity resolved into a midnight-blue coat cut like those of the Riders, tight to the waist and flaring out. The man did not bind his ruddy-blonde hair on the top of his head, but tied it behind, and the golden embroidery over the heart turned out to be a leaping dolphin.

Danet stared. This was a royal runner. Good-looking, too. Light brown eyes met hers then shifted away as he lifted a hand in polite salute, then he rode past them toward Nevree.

Danet slewed around in her saddle to watch his long tail of hair, golden against the midnight blue, bisecting straight shoulders.

"That kind," came Gdan's dry voice, "is all look but do not touch. Especially him."

One of the older women gave a rude crack of laughter.

"Him? What's wrong with him?" Danet asked.

"Nothing's *wrong*," Gdan said, as the older woman riding point laughed louder.

"Try sparking a Montredavan-An," she declared. "Just try. You'll get frostbite — either that or a knife in the back."

Gdan snorted. "Oh, button it, Vnar. You know that's ancient history. Probably not even true." And to Danet, "It's just that the royal runners keep themselves to themselves."

Vnar muttered in a relishing, broody voice as she gazed at the man vanishing beyond a copse of candlewood trees, "Only that one always seems to be riding to or from trouble."

Another of the cousins made a loud fart noise. "Of course they come and go when there's been trouble — they're *messengers*."

Vnar flipped up the back of her hand. "All I know is, after one of them comes, *especially* him, there's always rush messages going out, ride hard, sleep in the saddle, rush rush rush and never a word why. We're well out of it."

Nobody found fault with that, and they rode on, Danet doing her best to smother her wild interest. Obviously the royal runners dealt only with the likes of jarls and jarlans, and never the new brides of younger brothers. More important — and prospectively enjoyable — was this, her first border ride, and learning the landmarks for what she expected to be a lifetime of rides.

FIVE

Vnar was right, of course.

A webwork of messages did issue forth from Nevree, though few of them had anything to do with the slim packet of sealed letters that Camerend Montredavan-An delivered to the Jarlan of Olavayir. Always thrifty, and mindful of her resources, the jarlan combined as many messages as she could, sometimes saving less important ones for weeks or even months, until something urgent needed to be sent to family or ally.

This wave included the official invitation to the wargame that the jarl hosted every five years, to be held a month after Victory Day the next summer.

Not everybody enjoyed traveling all the way to Olavayir to do what they could just as well do closer to home.

Time to bring in the Senelaecs, whose importance will become apparent.

The Senelaecs—a relatively new jarlate roughly midway between Olavayir and the royal city—were among those who considered the Jarl of Olavayir arrogant for issuing invitations that nobody dared turn down.

The younger generation of Senelaecs usually liked nothing better than escaping such chores as they could be corralled into doing for camping and wargames, while everyone else labored to bring in the harvest and begin the arduous labor of readying for winter. But that was when they wanted to do it, and when they picked the ground. And when their usual opponents were either local youngsters equally happy to down tools and play attacking Venn or brigands or even pirates, or else their cousins among the Eastern Alliance.

Usually when Camerend Montredavan-An rode through the gate into the familiar court before the rambling Senelaec house, he was greeted with friendly comments and questions, or smiles and salutes if people were busy. Their grandfathers had trained together as Riders and runners respectively under the later years of Hasta, son of the great Evred, who had ruled all Halia, defended by Inda-Harskialdna.

This spring, though Camerend received the expected greetings, the smiles and glances ranged from sharp to questioning.

As he relinquished his tired and hungry horse to the expert care of the stable hands and circumvented the worst of the puddles and pools from the recent rain, he was fairly sure of the cause.

He was waved through by a bent, white-haired door steward who had probably been born around the time of the last Montreivayir king, and made his way through the series of large, low-ceilinged rooms that opened into each other, until he reached the vast kitchen, at one end of which the grizzled jarl sat, his bad leg stretched out on a small stool. Across from him sat his wife, a stolid woman whose ruddy-blond hair was as bright at forty-five as it had been in her girlhood.

They each had a chalk slate before them, but at Camerend's appearance, they looked up as one, then set the boards aside. They both smiled a welcome, but the jarlan's was a little livelier, for she always appreciated a comely young man.

"Camerend," the jarl said. "Wherefrom come you?"

"If you have any bad news," the jarlan said, "take it away again. Or else."

This was a joke, for everyone knew that no royal runner would ever breach the seal on a letter, or they would never have survived through all the governmental ructions of the past fifty years.

"Alas, the sniff test seems to be unreliable." Camerend pulled out a ribbon-tied sheaf of letters and ran it under his nose. "Bad or good news, they smell the same." He handed the thin sheaf to the jarl. "If I have to run, give me a count of ten, right?"

And while the jarl untied the ribbon and squinted down at the name scrawled on the top of each folded and sealed paper, the jarlan said, "Not sure if you know this, but Wolfie's wife Ndiran disappeared on us the first week the snows melted. Took little Marend up over the Andahi Pass. Left the boy."

"Did she say anything before she left?" Camerend asked, his expression so concerned neither jarl nor jarlan noticed his non-answer to the implied question.

The jarlan sighed heavily, as the jarl frowned down at a letter, turning it over and over in his hands. "Only a scrawl on the schoolroom slate to the effect that she wouldn't leave Marend to be married to some southern rat-shit."

Camerend only remembered Ndiran by her northern accent, she had been so quiet—unlike the rest of the noisy, boisterous, and happy Senelaecs. "Was it a bad match?"

"Wolf didn't think so," the jarl said, still turning the letter over and over.

"*The girls* didn't think so," the jarlan put in, her tone impatient. "Boys can't be trusted to know hay from horse-apple. As long as they're getting sex, they think everything is great."

The jarl looked up at that, his gray brows beetling. "Wolf told me she shut the door on him after she became pregnant with Marend. He *still* thought everything was fine, just that she was queasier with this one. You remember she was alone a lot, but when we saw her she was cheerful enough."

"What I remember," the jarlan said heavily, "is her flattery and compliments, and yes, I believed all that, too. I also remember her chatting up the Riders after a border run."

Camerend's interest sharpened at that.

Unaware, the jarlan went on, "Though that could have been because she was homesick, or hoping for stray rumors, or...what I don't understand is, she had *three years* on Wolf. You'd think she knew her own mind when the Jarlan of Arvandais wrote to us to negotiate the marriage treaty on her niece's behalf."

The jarl said mildly, "I still think she approached us to make the match because of you being the sister of a queen."

"But what could the Arvandaises think that would get them? Especially since my poor little sister was scarcely queen for a year?" The jarlan heaved a gusty sigh. She still missed her sister, slain by unknown assassins, though the pain had dulled over the intervening years.

The jarl's fierce brows knit as he turned the letter over and over and over, until the jarlan reached for it impatiently. "Oh, give me that. That's from that road-apple Ndiran, isn't it."

Camerend had his orders, but he preferred to not break the seal on the letters belonging to friends if he could help it. It wasn't that he couldn't replace the seal perfectly, for he'd been trained in that before his first ride. There were other ways to discover the contents that didn't push him over his own ethical boundary.

Sure enough, neither jarl nor jarlan chased him away as the gray and blonde heads bent over the neatly written letter.

"Scribe-write," the jarlan muttered. "She didn't even pen it herself. Yes, it's all formal language ending the marriage, and of course there will be no more island spices. Well, at least they won't get any more of our horses, though it breaks my heart that she took Moonbeam, whom I trained myself. Frisk was Calamity's. That's going to hurt. It seems *personal.*"

The jarl cast the letter onto the table. "I've half a mind to ride north with a wing at my back and demand my granddaughter's return. Along with the two horses."

"Don't talk like that in front of the young ones." The jarlan rubbed her eyes, her fingers trembling. "They might just go. We can send some of the girls north with you, Camerend, or one of other royal runners, in a few years, to scout out Marend when she's of an age to know her own mind. If she wants to come home, they can always bring her back. With or without her mother's permission," she added grimly. "Exactly as Ndiran asked Wolf's."

At the jarl's brightened expression, the jarlan smiled, then indicated the letter by his hand. "What's that one?"

"From Olavayir," the jarl said heavily, lips pursing as his head jerked to the side, more habit than intent this particular time.

"Ranor isn't so bad," the jarlan muttered as she slit the seal with her knife. "I wouldn't ride in her saddle for a crown. Two crowns. Oh, Norsunder take it, it's the jarl's orders. As usual, acting like a king. Those benighted boys of his are going to command the Olavayir wargame, and want two entire wings from us this time. A hundred sixty-two riders, and twice the horses, food and fodder — because you know they'll only feast them all on arrival and at the end. That is going to strap us badly, and right before harvest." She sighed. "It's always been two flights at most. What's going on up there?"

"The Olavayir boys are feeling their oats, of course," the jarl said. He was thinking of his heir, who had taken his wife's disappearance hard. At first Wolf'd been inseparable from his two-year-old son. He'd finally let the family near the cub again, but he'd been uncharacteristically silent ever since.

The jarl sat back. "This might actually be a good thing. Tell you what. Let's put Wolf in charge of picking them, and running their training over next spring. The Marlovayirs have to be sending two wings as well, and the prospect of beating them like a drum will surely put some frisk into Wolf's gait again."

"Excellent plan," the jarlan said, and shot to her feet. "No time like the present."

Camerend, who had faded back with trained expertise, stepped forward. "All right if I come with you? I'd like to say hello."

"Sure," the jarlan said. "As it happens, they're all up in their den. When the storm struck earlier, I put them to harness and bridle repair." She led the way through the door to the bake house into the storeroom, which smelled of rye and onion, and then to the old stable that had been converted into a barn, talking over her shoulder the while. "Overdue repair, like every other dull task around here! All year they toss broken bits up there where I can't see them, promising that they can work on repair over winter, when riding is impossible — and then all winter somehow riding is possible, usually scouting or running ruses on the Marlovayirs in the west." She cackled as she pounded up the dusty stairs to the long steep-roofed attic over the barn housing the family milk-animals.

Blonde and dark heads looked up guiltily at their entrance. The jarlan sighed, not surprised to see most of her wild brood of young people sitting in a circle playing a fast game of cards'n'shards. Only her daughter Fareas (called Fuss because of her tidy proclivities, which everyone else found alien) sat with a half-mended headstall in her lap, but her hands were idle as she watched the game.

Camerend, standing behind the jarlan, hid his amusement as the jarlan cleared her throat.

Startled faces turned her way, flaxen-haired Fuss blushing and returning to her work, skinny, freckled Carleas (known as Calamity) Senelaec laughing.

Camerend had brought Calamity himself—one of his first runs—when she was a shivering twig of ten.

He hadn't been much younger than that when she was orphaned at birth, both parents having fought to defend the young king and queen from the band of assassins that attacked one terrible night. Camerend's mother had coopted the young runners-in-training to help spirit the garrison children away to safety.

Camerend still vividly remembered that terrifying journey, no one knowing the truth of what had happened, and who might come after them, until the news came that Captain Mathren Olavayir had locked down the royal city, young as he was: his own little son had been saved along with the little prince, by his equally young wife.

Calamity had been handed off to one of the Noth families, who—typical for the Noths—had only boys, no girls. For the next few years, Calamity wore the boys' castoffs and more or less lived as a boy, until the jarlan and her elder sister as well as the Noths decided to bring Calamity to grow up with Fuss as Yipyip's future wife.

Calamity's vivid face changed from surprise to delight when she saw Camerend. He smiled back, glad as always to see her flourishing. But her expression altered to an unspoken question.

Wolf's grin had snuffed out like a pinched candle. "Camerend. Were you up north?"

"He was, and she wrote," the jarlan said roughly. "Not to any of you. Just a scribe letter to us. The marriage is over. But look at this. From the eagle-branch Olavayirs." She tossed the wargame letter toward the circle, and a cousin snatched it out of the air.

"They're holding another wargame. Two wings, they want, this time. Your father wants you to take charge," the jarlan said.

Camerend watched Wolf bend over the letter, squinting like his father. Wolf had received his nickname at birth, when he had come out with a full head of wild black fur as soft as a wolf cub's.

Now he was a tall, rangy young man in his early twenties, with a proud horsetail of thick dark hair that hung down to his hips. Like most of the Senelaecs, male and female, he rode like a centaur, as the saying was, horse and rider in perfect understanding—their Sindan-bred horses famed for being the best trained and fastest in a kingdom known for its horses.

Wolf's bony face turned to his younger brother and their cousins. The girls—most teens except for Fuss and Calamity, both twenty—also watched. Though of course they could not ride to a wargame, they would be participating in the training as enemies, along with as many of the local farm and artisanal boys as Wolf could commandeer.

"When should I start?" Wolf asked.

"Yesterday," the jarlan replied, to which the youngsters let out a war whoop. "But you get serious next spring, after planting."

Camerend retreated with the jarlan to clean up before the evening meal, reflecting on how the jarlan, daughter of Sindan-An Rider captains, still thought like a Rider. For that matter, so did the jarl, and Wolf clearly had been raised the same.

Back in the den, Calamity waited, and having lived with Wolf for half her life, knew what he was going to say moments before he spoke his decision: "If the Marlovayirs send Knuckles, we are going to *destroy* them."

Fuss paused in her four-strand hemp braid. "Why would they send Knuckles? Don't they usually send their best Riders?"

Wolf slapped the back of the letter with his fingers, mirroring his father's gesture. "Not with boys commanding, he won't. Da already thought of that, or Uncle Tana would be running our Riders, as usual."

The boys howled fox yips, Yipyip's shrill, hair-raising cry rising above all the others.

Fuss returned to work, and the rest all began throwing in ideas, no one listening to anyone else.

Wolf didn't listen to any of them. He had an idea.

He waited until the mess bell clanged, then cut Calamity out of the pack with a glance and a jerk of the chin.

"We can't win any individual contests except riding, if it's just us," he said to her, tapping his chest.

Calamity had to agree. They all knew that Wolf was somewhat short-sighted. Yipyip wasn't much better. So of course the boys tended to hone the skills they were good at. But good as they were with sword and double-stick and hand-to-hand, they would be competing against men. Not just any men, but some of the jarls would send their best to the Olavayirs, no matter who was commanding.

"Nobody outrides us Senelaecs outside of the Eastern Alliance," Calamity said, referring to the intermarried complexity of Tlennen, Tlen, Sindan-An, and Senelaec jarlates, with the Sindans serving them all.

His shoulder jerked up. "If they hold trick riding competitions, we'll win, yeah, but they probably won't. They haven't in the past."

Calamity turned her palm up in agreement. Trick riding wasn't war related, and though boys loved trick riding, it was the girls who really enjoyed it.

Wolf scowled. "That letter's full of grass gas about training everyone in the north and bark bark bark. My guess is, those Olavayir boys think they'll be army commanders some day, for Evred once he's crowned. All in the family."

"So?" she asked, aware of the two of them being alone in the den. She had been suppressing her feelings for Wolf for so long it was no longer a conscious thought.

He held his arms out wide. "So nothing. Just a thought, about *them*. About *us*, well, Knuckles Marlovayir is a good shot. He claims to be the best in the north—"

"But he's not," she said.

"Exactly," Wolf said, and as a way of getting nearer to his plan, he stated what they both knew, " *You* are."

She threw her arms out wide, mirror to his gesture. "So? I can't make a good shot of you by summer's end, if that's where you're going. I can't give you my eye for distances, though I wish I could, if only for the summer."

"But you could do exactly what we did when we rode to Marlovayir to scout Knuckles and his rats."

Her mouth curled with reminiscent pleasure as she thought back two summers, after the Marlovayirs had pulled a dastardly raid on the Senelaecs. Thirsting for revenge, Wolf, his two best rider cousins, and Calamity (wearing one of Wolf's old riding coats, and pulling her hair up, the way she had when she was living with the Noth boys) had sneaked into Marlovayir to scout.

She loved remembering the laughter and companionship, especially the night the four of them eased up onto the Marlovayir stable roof to watch the shooting drills to see how good Knuckles and his pack were.

Knuckles had been very good indeed.

Then it hit her. He was reminiscing because.... "You want *us* to go? In disguise?"

"Just you and your best eight. A riding. Dead secret. I don't care who wins the stupid wargame, and we haven't a hope in any of the individual competitions with steel and lance against more experienced men. But I want Knuckles Marlovayir to lose the ride and shoot, and to us."

Calamity dropped her gaze to her hands, trying to hide the extreme conflict. She had learned to make the Marlovayir-Senelaec feud her feud, especially after Knuckles started leading raids and making the feud personal and humiliating—though always careful not to kill anyone, which would commit the two clans to actual battle.

Also, she loved to win.

But could the girls in disguise fool anyone for more than half a watch? And then, if they rode north, who would do their work? She winced. The jarl and jarlan were unlikely to send her back south again, as punishment, but....

"We can make it work," Wolf coaxed. "I know Ma and Da'll be mad at us if you girls vanish, but if we come back with a banner, especially if Marlovayirs lose, then we'll only get a jawing, and stable wanding for a month or two."

He stepped closer. Calamity was as good as his sister. Better in a lot of ways he hadn't let himself examine since he turned twenty, as Ndiran had made it clear that their marriage would be exclusive. Then after she left him so suddenly, with nothing but insults scrawled on their chore board, he couldn't bear any relationship outside of run-and-comes with the girls at the pleasure house on the river, whose names he didn't have to know.

Calamity's heart knocked hard at Wolf's proximity. She'd grown into loving him in all the ways it was possible to love, but fought a heroic internal battle because it wasn't honorable when he'd made an exclusive vow—and now, after Ndiran betrayed him, he was clearly too hurt.

Neither was in the habit of talking out their feelings. What was the use of whining? That was life. But emotions are what they are, and their unspoken desires fluttered in the same direction, two moths toward the same flame.

"I'll talk to Fuss," she said, and her reward was his first real smile in what seemed like a hundred years.

SIX

I'll return you now to Olavayir, and Danet's own words as she wrote to her sister Hliss:

This far west, in late afternoon a breeze blows that they say is off the ocean, breaking up the heat. Imagine seeing the ocean! Anyhow, summer is on its way.

I will be so glad when you come here at last, and I don't have to pester Tesar to find out when the jarlan or randviar are sending runners in the direction of Farendavan.

Gdan brought me yours when she got back from the north, but it took me a while to write back, as I was so sick there for three very long months.

First, let me reassure you that I'm more used to life here. You know me. I always have to know where I am, what I have, what I don't, what to expect. I know you found it tedious to learn tally-keeping, and you never understood why I like it so much, especially when I'd rather be out riding. It's not mere liking, it's a craving, I finally understood when I came here and the jarlan assigned me to start learning the kitchen tallies, after I returned from my first border ride.

It was a relief, like a blindfold had been taken off.

The randviar does what Mother does, that is, oversee all supplies, from what they grow (food, of course, and sheep for wool) but what they bring in, like linens. I will like being randviar, especially with Tdor Fath as Jarlan. She reminds me of you in so many ways.

So from the first day I was always in the stables, barns, and kitchen, watching what comes in and what goes out, and then looking at the old tally books, the way Mother taught us. They were surprised, and the assistant steward was not pleased to have to dig the books up when I asked, but she couldn't say no because the jarlan gave me orders to learn the tallies right there where everyone could hear.

And Mother was right. There really are patterns in all these numbers. I saw what I thought was a small error, but it kept coming up, always the bristic barrels, and always in the fall.

To sum up, I caught a new kitchen runner stealing jugged bristic for sale at the harbor, and keeping the wherewithal. The jarlan was very pleased with me, and more with the savings.

I also learned that here, you don't go direct to people unless you want to lay on orders. Not like home, where everyone is in each other's pocket all day, sharing all the work. After I reported the thief I got some cold food and limp greens for two days, which I knew was no accident.

But then Aunt Hlar, who is chief potter, and you should see the deep blue on the dishes and especially the wine cups! Their fabrics are nothing, but their dishes so much better than ours. Anyway Aunt Hlar, who is nearly as tall as Jarend and every bit as big, and never once spoke to me, came to the kitchens to comment on how pilfering robs the entire family, not just in goods but also in honor.

Tesar told me that much. She is a real miser with words! I don't know what else happened, but apparently what Aunt Hlar says is important. Nobody crosses her, as she's sibling to the jarl. Next day my dish didn't have limp greens anymore, or cold oatmeal in the morning. Cold oatmeal is terrible, especially with grit that wasn't washed out, and most especially when your stomach is already unhappy.

But that didn't mean I was right with everyone. No indeed. After the jarlan demoted the thief to field work, I got more ice wall from the Rider branch—that is, the dolphin part of the Riders. I'm confused about that. All I know is, the Riders are made up of both clans, and cousins, and others. Acting Commander Lanrid, whose father is in the royal city as royal guard captain under the regent, favors the dolphin clan Riders, and is always taking them off for extra practice with lances, which Arrow says are useless for castle defense. I suspect that on my first day, this was what Gdan was hinting about.

I forgot to say that Lanrid, who sparked me on my wedding night as I know I told you, tried a couple more times before I got sick in the mornings, but always where Arrow could hear. When I said no he lost interest pretty fast, and rumor has it he took up with Fi....

Danet stopped before she got sidetracked into complaining about how Fi was still loitering around, but now, mostly at or near the garrison, where Lanrid lurked most.

Lanrid was elder brother to Sindan, known to everyone as Sinna, the teenage boy Hliss was betrothed to. Mindful of Hliss's request that Danet write everything she could about Sinna, Danet had done her best to learn something about him—while avoiding Lanrid and his pack of dolphin Riders. She thoroughly disliked Lanrid's knowing smirk as well as his compliments, always offered in too sweet a voice. Whatever she said brought the horrible laughter that owes less to amusement than to scorn. It was easy enough to see that Lanrid had taken a dislike to her, probably over her discovery of his thieving cousin.

From what she could see of Sinna, he was either the most practiced hypocrite she'd ever seen, or he was as unlike his brother as it was possible for a pair of siblings to be. She could accept difference—she was a plank of a person, and Hliss was like Brother, handsome. Hliss hated tallies and loved weaving, the opposite of Danet.

Danet had noticed at meals that Sinna was invariably quiet, which didn't mean much. It was manners for the young to say quiet while their elders spoke, and the jarlan invariably had plenty to say, especially at the evening meal, when orders for the following day were usually given out.

Danet had also noticed on her first Restday among the Olavayirs that someone in the family had a wonderful voice. At first she'd thought it as woman, for it was a high voice, clear and bright as struck metal.

One day, when a nasty bout of morning sickness made her late to the family gathering, she slid in among the servants behind the Riders and discovered that the singer was Sinna. He had his brother's pretty features, but when he sang he was beautiful.

Danet abandoned Lanrid and wrote about Sinna, adding:

I was up in the nearer stable attic, overseeing the airing and storing of the winter window-stuffing, when I overheard Sinna singing a Peddler Antivad song, and when I leaned out the hay window, there was Lanrid below, muttering something and I heard the word "jarl" and then he spat. His two favorite Rider captains spat as well. It was like habit, especially the way they looked around quick, after.

Why, you ask, would they slander the Jarl of Olavayir, who everybody else seems to like? There is this invisible stone wall between Lanrid and Arrow at meals. When I tried to ask Tesar, she was not only tight-lipped but she actually looked scared, the way her gaze shifted from door to window as if she expected someone to be hiding.

When we were growing up all the Olavayirs seemed to be one clump, but it's not that way here. There is an entire wall of silence around the royal family. It isn't a question of dolphin-branch family loyalty, as at the evening meal one night Lanrid was sneering about how his first-cousin Evred, who you'll remember will be king when he comes of age, never leaves the royal city, and he said it like Evred isn't allowed to. Nobody defended Evred.

About Regent Kendred, I've heard mumbles in the steward wing about how lazy he is, how much he likes his luxuries, but he can't be bothered to make certain that the northern garrisons get their share of the taxes, which is why the jarl holds the wargames, as a way of evaluating the training of the jarlates here in the north. But nobody has ever said anything about Commander and Defender Mathren Olavayir, Lanrid's father, except once.

I was going to the stable to ride Firefly, when I heard Lanrid's voice, and I stopped because I didn't want to go in there when he was there. While I waited for him to leave, he was ranting about how beautiful Hard Ride Arvandais is, and he deserves to marry her, hoola loo.

How you and I would have laughed if you'd been there! Too bad Cousin Hard Ride can't marry all those suitors. If anyone could rein them all, it would be she!

I was thinking that when an older Rider said, "You know what your father wants." And Lanrid actually went silent, for once!

So in short, this is what you will be marrying into, Hliss. I am sorry, but I do think it's better to be warned. At least Sinna himself seems nice, and I know you will love hearing him sing.

SEVEN

Festival days were somewhat perfunctorily observed in Farendavan, as Mother had always disliked anything that got in the way of work.

Andahi Day was different. It was considered a duty, being the anniversary of the fall of Andahi Castle in 3914 AF, when the Venn slaughtered every defending woman and began their march down the Pass, their intent to conquer all Halia. As the Farendavans had had relations at both ends of the Pass, Mother made time to sing the Lament, the household standing in a circle, holding drip-candles, and singing the Lament, after which the entire household got a halfday free.

So Danet had no idea what to expect from the Olavayirs when Andahi Day arrived, amid the castle's accelerating preparations for the wargame.

That evening she lowered her bulk onto her mat, so absorbed by her physical difficulties (like having to whisper the Waste Spell every single time she stood up or sat down) that at first she assumed the tense atmosphere was a result of unending labor in the summer heat.

But when she glanced down the table to see the jarl's usually empty mat filled with the nearly white-haired jarl, her gaze snagged on the randael's seat next to the jarl, and Lanrid sitting there proudly, attractive mouth curled in a smirk of pride.

And on the other side of the table, in his usual seat on the far side of big Jarend, Arrow, flushed to the ears with fury.

What did I miss? Danet's gaze swung toward Ranor-Jarlan, whose tired face wore a closed expression. No enlightenment was going to come from her. Danet then saw Tdor Fath looking her way, and she lifted her chin slightly toward the jarl, who had raised his cup.

Danet shifted to the other haunch as the baby inside her kicked her bottom rib. Danet pressed a hand against the baby, distracted from her discomfort when the jarl said, "Lanrid is now Riding Commander, in accordance with treaty. But it is understood that when Jarend replaces me as jarl, Arrow will be his Randael."

What? Danet thought, and understood Arrow's fury. As the jarl made a speech about courage and loyalty and protection of jarlate and kingdom, Danet worked out what it meant: that Lanrid was randael in all but name, and would effectively be running the military side of Olavayir when the jarl was away. Which was most of the time, as he was constantly visiting one or another of the garrisons, which were constantly short of both men and funds.

She let out her breath, wondering how much trouble that would translate out to be, as she thirstily drained her water and promptly had to whisper the Waste Spell again.

"Let us get to the walls now that the sun is down," the jarl said as servants began collecting the dishes in haste, so that they could join the Lighting.

Danet caught Lanrid shooting a toothy grin slantwise across the table at Arrow, who turned his back and vanished out the far door.

The rest followed in haste, as Danet struggled to her knees, then pushed her hands on the table to get to her feet. She understood why some people had chairs, though it felt good to lean there on her hands and let her stomach swing. She arched her back, then hoisted herself upright—to find the jarl standing there an arm's reach away.

"I came back to give you a hand," he said. "Since the boys have all run off. You're the Farendavan girl, are you not?"

"I am."

"I'm told Hasta Farendavan will be sending a riding of boys to fill out the East Company numbers, though he won't come himself, still being up north."

"That's my father," Danet said—then blushed. Obviously the jarl knew that. "He can never get back over the Pass, it seems. The Jarl of Arvandais always seems to need him guarding the coastline."

The Jarl said, pleasantly enough, "Apparently the inland castles up in Idego can't send anyone over the Pass to us due to some agricultural crisis. A young man they call Brother brought this riding. Do I have that right?"

"Yes. Brother is, um, my brother," she said, then blushed at how silly she sounded, stating the obvious. "He rode home, and brought Farendavan men."

"Brother? That's his nickname?"

"Yes. Everybody uses it," Danet said. "Even Mother and Father."

"Why is that?"

"Because there are four Hastas in the family. Five, when Brother was mates with Hasta Lassad. I don't know if they still are."

The Jarl laughed, a deep *hur hur hur* just like Jarend's, and took her elbow to guide her toward the door. "Four Hastas! Five! I should have known. All named no doubt for Hasta Arveas-Andahi, before the Idegans smashed two good Marlovan names into one impossible one. Arvandais! Pah."

He made a spitting motion, then said, "I'm the last of the Indas, except down south it's still a popular name, I'm told. When I was growing up, it seemed all the older men were Indas, if they weren't waving another banner, like Goatkick and Grass Ass. But that was back when they had the academy, and everyone trained together."

She stared at him, wondering at the leaps from subject to subject in his speech. Was there extra meaning? She was uncertain what to say.

But he didn't seem to expect anything. He went on, "Ranor and Sdar both say you've been trained well. Know your tallies and tasks. That's good."

He thumped her on the shoulder and added, "Ranor says the boy listens to you, too. All the better."

'The boy'? Could he possibly mean Arrow? Whom she scarcely saw anymore?

At that moment, Arrow himself reappeared. "There you are, Da. All the candles are ready, and the last of the stable hands are coming up the back stairs."

"They can wait a breath or two. It's not quite full dark," the jarl said, waving a hand that Danet could see was callus-thick and scarred.

Brown liver spots showed in his scalp under his thin horsetail. She had never considered how old he was. But he would be old, as he'd had two grown sons killed during the troubles in the royal city twenty-some years ago. The Jarlan had been well into her forties when Jarend and Arrow were born, four sons altogether and no daughters.

The Jarl said to Arrow, "Listen, boy, Ranor says this little girl here is banner-hand with tallies and tasks. You listen to her, understand?"

"Yes, Da," Arrow said, and gave Danet a look she could not interpret.

"Good. Now, help her up the stairs. Where are your manners?"

To Danet's considerable relief, the jarl let go her arm and Arrow took his place as the jarl sauntered off, his nearly white horsetail swinging. A spurt of amusement warmed her as she recognized Arrow's walk, only half a century older.

Arrow muttered, "What have you been saying to him?"

"Nothing! He came at me and said I'm good at tallies and tasks, and I don't even *do* that! I wouldn't dare! I only *check* the kitchen tallies after —"

"But you *could* do them, right? You could?"

She stared at him. "Of course I could! But last I saw, your mother is still alive and shooting. So I don't know what you're accusing me of, or why."

"No, no, you heard me wrong," he said as they turned toward the stairway leading up to the sentry walk. "I'm not accusing you of anything. Sorry it sounds as if I am. It's this mood I'm in. I could strangle anyone who looks at me wrong, thanks to Lanrid, so much worse now his da wants him commanding the Riders. Couldn't wait until he turns twenty-five, at least." Arrow scowled. "He's always been a strut, but now he's impossible, crowing all over, how as Olavayir Riding Commander he'll win the game, then marry Hard Ride Hadand. At least that'll probably send Fi flouncing back to Lindeth. I hope."

"Her again?" Danet groaned as she leaned forward to help heave herself up the stairs. "I thought we were rid of Fi for good till I saw her at the stable."

Arrow slid an arm around Danet, pulled her hip against his, and took some of her weight as he stepped with her. As they trod two or three steps, each trying to find the other's rhythm, he snickered in that typical male way that usually meant sex, as he said, "Oh, she's been running Lanrid ragged, and I don't mean in bed. Though that, too."

"What do you all see in her?" Danet asked. "There are handsomer girls who don't flounce and sulk."

"Handsome," he repeated, and flipped up the back of his free hand. "She's not just that. Tight. She's hot to trot." He laughed. "She isn't talking to me, so I'm not telling her she doesn't get a title if she marries Lanrid, and he doesn't know what I figured out too late, that what she wants from any of us is some kind of title added to her name." He added, "Otherwise she wouldn't have looked at me twice. And I don't care what Lanrid thinks. I'm sure it's the same with him."

Then he peered all around them, and stopped in the middle of the stairway, and turned her to face him. "Listen. You and me, we might have to go to the royal city," he whispered. "But keep that to yourself, mind. No one to know. Not even Tesar. *No* one. Until the jarl gives the order. Lanrid only got promoted early to keep Olavayir defended, that's what Da told me."

The sound of footsteps running up the stairs below them shut Arrow up. Danet suppressed the stream of questions that she knew would only irritate him. Arrow seldom bothered with details. She had also learned that if she was patient, she could satisfy her thirst for all the answers.

He helped her up the last few steps as the baker's boy and the barnyard and kitchen children raced past, each dipping hands into the basket to pick up a candle.

Arrow let Danet's arm go and bent to fetch two candles. He handed her one. She ran her fingers over the smooth contours, and sniffed the sweet clover scent. Though many families (like the Farendavans, as Mother hated waste) reused drippings for their Andahi candles, or used leddas wax, Danet had learned that the jarlan began setting aside beeswax for the next year as soon as one Andahi Night was over. "Proper is proper," she'd said to Danet on their first tour of the storeroom. "Besides, my grandmother said I had two kin on the walls at Andahi, both girls younger than you, sent up there for training. If their spirits are still around, I want them to see everything done right."

Danet rarely thought about spirits, or ghosts, or even Norsunder, the latter usually heard as a curse. Her mother had taught her to trust only what she could see herself, and although there were some who claimed to see ghosts—the rumor among the Olavayirs was that ancient Hesar-Gunvaer, the first Olavayir queen and apparently still alive down there in the royal city, could see them—Danet tended toward Mother's thinking, that she needed proof, just as she needed to see the tallies and count the barrels, baskets, bolts, sheaves, and jugs.

She watched as the jarl struck a spark from a stone battlement onto a twist of paper, then touched his taper from it. Light glowed ruddy-gold along the contours of his face, softening them into a semblance of his younger years as he bent his head toward Ranor-Jarlan and lit her taper from his. Both turned to pass the light, flame to flame igniting in a slow river down the sentrywalk battlement.

The pungency of clover candle perfumed the air, and a soft breeze caressed Danet's overheated cheeks as the tongues of flame sprang into light. Then the Olavayirs held up their candles, and the jarl and jarlan began singing the Andahi Lament, his voice a tuneless boom, hers a crow's screech, soon joined by younger voices, Sinna's pure tenor soaring over the rest, and pulling them into melody.

And as the camp below saw the lights spring to life on the castle rampart, swiftly tiny lights bloomed in the courtyards where the castle population had gathered, a reflection of the brilliant stars overhead, and the Lament echoed back in heart-achingly eerie melody, as if from the distance of history. For the first time Danet wondered if among those stars spirits dwelt, looking down at those still alive, or if they walked among the living, more intangible than a summer breeze.

The Lament had always been sad, but now Danet's entire being filled with wonder, and grief, too, for those women and girls long ago.

What Marlovans of the middle and northern part of the kingdom called Lightning Season had dried up the summer early this year, every day dawning hot and dry. The "lightning" was visible over the distant mountain-tops and closer; if you touched metal it sparked with a snapping sting. Hair crackled when brushed, even the thinnest, finest-weave wool clothing stuck to one, and felt like bees walking over you when you yanked it away. Above all, tempers flared like lightning.

Elsewhere it was harvest season, people working to get everything in before the autumn rains came sweeping over the plains.

For participants in the wargame, the jarl had reached no farther south than Marlovayir and Sindan-An, for there was no use inviting one Eastern Alliance clan unless you invited them all. Khanivayir, Halivayir, Yvanavayir, Tyavayir, the Eastern Alliance, and the garrisons at Lindeth, Larkadhe, and Andahi all began preparations for riding out, some the day after Victory Day, and those who had to ride the farthest had already left, and celebrated on the road.

In Senelaec, Calamity inspected everyone in the secret riding herself.

It was startling, how different the girls looked with their hair worn up in horsetails, and brothers and cousins' old coats pulled over their shoulders, some with padding carefully stitched in. She had never been more thankful that men and women wore more or less similar riding boots and trousers. Dressed as boys, the girls looked younger to her, which was good. No one would pay any attention to a bunch of young teenage riders, especially those rendered nearly indistinguishable by the dust of travel.

The girls had planned well. With Wolf and Yipyip's help, they kept their chosen mounts in a far field, with packed saddlebags heaped out of sight along a stream. The morning after Victory Day, the boys rode out.

As soon as they disappeared beyond the far hill, the girls raced beyond the training corrals to the hillock where their mounts waited, saddled up, and they crossed country, riding parallel to the boys for the rest of that first day.

As one day turned into a week, the girls kept the boys just over the horizon, camping when they did.

The boys rode more or less in column, until they fell in with the Sindan-An and Tlennen wings at a well-known crossroads. The girls followed their dust. When they camped, though the sky glowed warm among the campfires of the combined forces, and the somnolent summer air carried the sound of drums and songs for an appreciable distance, the girls' small fireless campsite was entirely overlooked, except by the indifferent stars overhead, and much closer by the equally indifferent night birds cruising the balmy summer currents.

In Nevree, by the end of the month, the dust of the first arrivals showed up on the border, reported by galloping outriders.

The number of participants stretched the jarlan's resources to the limit. They had planted as early as they dared, so that the first harvest could be gathered before all those wargamers were expected in. She was grateful that the gamble had paid off—this year.

Danet, at the waddling stage of pregnancy, had been put in charge of monitoring the flow of foodstuffs brought in from all over the jarlate and then sent to the big pavilions set up as storage. She relished exactly this kind of work, and those under her began to appreciate her previously maligned eye for detail. Though of necessity the perishables had to be gathered, cleaned, readied and stored in a fraction of the time allotted for game-related supplies, still her small army ran the smoothest, with the least number of crises, out of all the castle staff.

But there was a physical cost. Danet, very aware of the importance of her position—and of the jarlan's eye her way when she lumbered through on inspection—suppressed her growing physical discomforts.

No one wanted to hear about them, Danet knew. When she saw Arrow it was because he needed a safe place to pace back and forth, swearing at the slowness of his game captains, at Lanrid who was never to be found when there was grunt work to be done, at the sun, the heat, the signal flags when they were dust-caked and couldn't be seen unless swung mightily, and finally at the weather, which seemed to get hotter as the game days approached. Meanwhile Lanrid was off in a distant field drilling his handpicked lancers — what used to be called dragoon lancers — having left the Riders and castle guards he didn't want to Arrow.

The mass of Senelaec, Sindan-An, Tlen and Tlennen riders arrived at the great campground the day before the games were to begin.

Wolf rode off with representatives of the other two clans to report in at the row of big pavilions visible across stubbly fields still smelling of hay, and came back to report that they had been assigned a camp at the rump-end of the field, but at least near the river.

Calamity slipped away to establish her girls farther up the river, well hidden by clumps of willow and thickets of gorse.

They waited until Wolf showed up late, as in the distance the rolling, galloping rhythm of drums ran counterpoint to singing. "Here's some food from the banquet," Wolf said. "We had to wait until the end to grab it."

The girls sat along the river's edge to eat. When they were done, Calamity said, "Get some rest. Tomorrow is the ride and shoot."

EIGHT

When the sun rose to a sky filled with low, patchy clouds, the wargame competitors discovered that the Olavayir people had labored by torchlight before dawn to set up targets every twenty-five paces in a long line parallel to the great tents.

They'd placed the biggest tent—a pavilion that had been constructed with canvas walls within, creating little rooms that were hot and stuffy by afternoon—in the central position. The Olavayir family, including the women of rank, rotated in and out of this pavilion as duties permitted. At the side of the opening, under a shade canopy, the herald in charge of scorekeeping sat with his three scribes—two with slates and chalk, and one with paper and pen to record the final numbers.

Ranor-Jarlan, pleased with Danet's excellent work, had made certain that Arrow's wife would be among the first to get to watch the day's competitions. The jarlan's runners had reported that the welcoming meal had gone perfectly, and that everything else related to comestibles flowed equally smoothly. Danet had earned her ease.

The jarlan also remembered what it was like to be hauling a boulder around in one's belly that last month, especially at the height of summer, and so one of those little tent chambers had been filled with blankets for Danet to retreat to if she needed to lie down.

So Danet was at the pavilion, sitting on a mat under the extended flap that warded the sun, as the various teams each brought out ridings for the group and individual ride and shoot competition. She listened with mild interest to the gossip, hoping she'd get to see Brother among the nine chosen for his wing. He'd always been a decent shot, better than she and Hliss, who were competent, which was all Mother had required of them, their time being better spent on what she deemed more useful tasks.

Most of the gossip was about Knuckles, the Marlovayir heir, who was rumored to be the best—a rumor Danet gathered this selfsame Knuckles was doing his best to propagate.

The most intense interest was in the canter and shoot from fifty paces distance. It was difficult to see past the dust, as team after team rode hard down the dun-colored ground and shot, every arrow that hit the red causing a cheer to go up, always loudest from the wing the shooters belonged to.

Arrow and Lanrid, as rival commanders, had each picked teams of their best shooters. Danet was glad to see that Arrow's team got a respectable number of reds, though some shots barely touched the painted circle. They were edged out on the third run by Lanrid's team's better scores.

The Marlovayirs rode after, and Danet easily picked out Knuckles by the fact that he rode first, a big, square blond with a huge grin, easy and assured in the way he handled his mount, but with unnecessary swagger in the way he turned his horse fast, and kneed the animal straight into gallop. He was good, but on his second run, his horse was clearly overheated and faltered in rhythm, and Knuckles' aim suffered for it. Still good, but five out of eighteen reds.

His third run, he fell back to a canter, but his horse was blown from the heat, causing him to miss the last two shots. His team altogether was ahead, but he was tied for first with shooters from the Lindeth garrison and Yvanavayir.

Danet was nibbling at bread and cheese when the Senelaec team rode up. Wolf's most trusted cousins, ostensibly the shooters, had mixed into the back of the watching crowd as Calamity and her girls took their place—and at a perfect canter, horses nose to tail, Calamity led the way.

On the first run, she hit the red half the time, missing by a finger's breadth the rest, as the dust by then was choking, the sun at its worst glare, and she was painfully aware of all those watching eyes. Every nerve alive, she found her rhythm, the girls following her lead. Her second run was better, and on the last, she hit every single red. Two bordering the edge, but the judges allowed them, causing a shout to shiver the air.

Danet found herself on her knees, cheering as well. These riders were no more than teens! Even Mother admitted that the Senelaecs—closely related to the Sindans—bred and trained the fastest horses, and they were among the best scouts, but Arrow had claimed that their shooting was nothing special.

The jarl told his first runner to signal them in to be congratulated, but they didn't seem to see the limp flag in the stifling air. They rode off, and as the next group had already gathered at the far end, ready for their try, the jarl gave up. He'd compliment them when they came up for their banner—he had little doubt that their score would remain the best.

And so it was.

Danet found herself curious enough to wait until the competition was over to see the Senelaec winners up close.

But as the sun began dropping westward, and the captains of the winning teams came forward to receive their flags, the one who came for the Senelaecs was a tall, dashing fellow with curly dark hair—definitely not the skinny, blond young teen who had shot so well.

Danet looked at him doubtfully. Surely she would have noticed a fine-looking boy like this one among the shooters.

She found Arrow next to her. "That's Wolf Senelaec," he said, then lowered his voice. "His wife left him. The Idegan wing in my army say they don't know why, though they're all related in some wise to the Arvandais family. *We're* related, if you go back a hundred years. But she didn't even stop here on her way north."

Danet remembered something about the tangle of relationships, Cama One-Eye having had two families, one with the famous Ndara Arveas-Andahi, and the other through Starand Olavayir.

She watched Wolf Senelaec walk away as she said, "Was he that terrible a husband?"

"No one knows what happened or why. But Da says that's how feuds get started," Arrow replied. "I'll wager a horse that's why none of main branch of the Arvandais clan sent anyone down the Pass, and all that about farm problems is a load of horse apples."

Danet wondered if Wolf was another Lanrid, pretty on the outside, but trouble on the inside.

For the Senelaec girls, the high point of the entire experience was that first day. Calamity deeply relished the delight of the sun at her back, a perfect horse under her, and the bow she knew better than her own heartbeat in her hands.

She thrilled with incandescent pleasure at hitting the red every time on the third run. And as the girls rode away, she grinned to see Knuckles Marlovayir peering at them under his hand, looking fierce.

But when it was over, it was over. The girls were left to enjoy their win vicariously, for Wolf and the boys got the banner and the hails from other gamers.

And on the following day, the exhilaration began to ebb fast as first, a thunderstorm pounded through, and second, the individual competitions began.

These would go on for another three days, when the wargame would start. Wolf had warned her that it was likeliest nothing much but riding around would occur the first two days of *that*. It was always the last day that saw actual action.

At first Calamity and the girls enjoyed passing among the gamers as they listened to the way boys talked when among themselves. But this novelty wore off very fast—you can only listen to so much strut—leaving a long stretch of days to endure, eating their trail bread and either hiding along the river or passing among the crowd to watch the sword, double-stick, unarmed combat, and distance shooting competitions.

The only pleasure for Calamity was in sneaking over to watch Wolf doing the sword dance, relishing the tight fit of his coat that showed off his body, the swing of his hair and coat skirts whipping back and forth, the height of his leaps, and the sparks that he always raised when he clashed swords.

It was little enough compensation for the interminable drag of the sun across the sky, baking them mercilessly as they waited through the long, long wargame.

Wolf sent a scout to Calamity and Fuss when he had a chance, but they couldn't even find Knuckles and his followers the first day. The second day, the scouts found them, but apparently Lanrid kept them in reserve, preferring to use his favored lancers in various charges; the girls heard the thrilling trumpet calls on the air.

By the day the big wargame was finally nearing its end, the girls were more than ready for it to be over.

"Listen," Calamity said on the last morning, as they crawled out of their bedrolls. "Pack up. As soon as we're done with the Marlovayirs, or it ends, whichever comes first, we're heading out. We're not going to wait for the farewell banquet—we can't risk anyone seeing us up close. Wolf and the rest can catch up or not."

No one disagreed. They were all thoroughly tired of camp living by then, bathing in the low, muddy river, and drinking from their single magic-purified pail.

Calamity stood by, watching Fuss's neat, quick fingers as she rolled her clothes up for the saddlebag.

Mid-morning, Yipyip himself galloped to their camp and yelled, "They're using Knuckles to flank our side, and attack from behind while Lanrid runs a last charge." He pointed. "They're running along that ridge above the river bend, keeping behind those trees."

The girls mounted up, saddlebags already packed. They proceeded cautiously through the dust and noise, horse plops everywhere in the churned-up ground. As the horns blared in the distance, they occasionally saw someone or other galloping by with signal flags, but they paid no attention to those. They weren't the only ones; as she shadowed the Marlovayirs, Calamity was aware of parties slinking back to break camp, eyes turned toward the horizon, where thunderclouds built in slow tumble over the hills.

The closest the girls came to the main conflict was by accident, when they followed their quarry through a massive dun-colored cloud of dust to hear Landrid Olavayir screaming at ragged lines to follow his front line.

The girls trotted briskly away at what turned out to be a perfect oblique angle, flanking the confused Marlovayirs. Both parties cleared the last of Lanrid's army and approached the northern edge of Arrow's. When the boys began their run at Arrow's gamers, Calamity raised her hand, and the girls strung their bows, then pulled out the clumsy jelly-bag arrows used on these games, along with chalked wooden swords. The bags stung hard on impact, but more importantly they left sticky, bright-dyed evidence of kill shots—

which meant "dead" combatants were out of the game, no matter what they claimed to the contrary.

One by one the girls on their fresh horses streamed by the Marlovayirs, close enough to rile the boys' tired mounts. When the girls drew abreast of the Marlovayir line, they each shot their target, Fuss and Calamity both nailing the hapless Knuckles, one in the shoulder and one in the butt when he turned and half-rose in the saddle to protest.

The Marlovayirs' targets promptly started screaming that the sneak attackers were cheating, to come back and fight as they waved their wooden swords, but the girls faded back into the dust and rode away.

At last they could start for home! Then the two girls serving as outriders pulled up, looking troubled. "Where's south?" Pip, Calamity's teenage cousin, asked.

The dust hung motionless in the air the way it does when thunder is coming, and the sun was completely hidden. They couldn't see mountains or shadows to orient on. Fuss shouted, "Find the three Nevree hills, and use those as landmarks."

Pip, the youngest of Calamity's party, was partnered with Calamity's runner Ndara as scouts. They took off, the others following more slowly to allow their animals to cool.

Calamity finally spotted the Olavayir pavilions to the left. Much too close. Fuss and Calamity exchanged glances, and Calamity was going to ride ahead to get Pip and Ndara to skirt the tents as well as the castle when the two came bolting back, Ndara almost as pale as her hair. She pulled up before Fuss and Calamity, saying breathlessly, "We heard yelling for help so we went to look. Arrow's wife is alone except for a runner, who doesn't know anything, and I think she's about to give birth."

Fuss said soberly, "We can't leave her alone."

"But we can't ride for her castle — not in these coats and our hair up like this. If they see us close up, they'll know."

Fuss looked back and forth, then said slowly, as she shrugged out of her grimy coat, "Let's make braids as we ride for the pavilion. And we all have our robes in our saddlebags. We'll pull them over our shirts."

Danet was far too distraught to ask where these strange girls had come from. More uncomfortable than she had ever been, she had gone into one of the inner rooms in the pavilion to rest as her lower back and hips burned with intermittent pain. Without noticing her absence, the overheated, exhausted servants and runners had begun hauling things back to the castle, for they still had the last banquet to set up.

The building rhythm of aches abruptly shifted to the urgency of sharp pain wringing through her, and Danet sat up gasping. Tesar, left behind to fold ground covers and stack cushions, turned around, staring with stark eyes.

When water gushed from under Danet's robe, and Danet shrilled, "Get help!" Tesar panicked and ran for her horse to gallop to the castle.

Danet, alone, wailed with anguish—and then, miraculously, a pair of strange girls appeared out of nowhere and took over. Danet needed hands to hold her, and hands to catch the babe, and to knife the cord.

By the time Tesar got back with the jarlan and a stream of castle women, everything was done except cleaning up the mess, and Danet was curled up in the dusty tent with her little boy.

Calamity and Fuss met one another's gazes, and while the Olavayirs crowded around, everyone talking, they backed out and ran for their horses, kept at a prudent distance by the rest of the girls.

They turned their noses toward home as thunder broke overhead, drenching human and animal within three gasping breaths.

NINE

Rain hammered the dusty plain, now mostly empty except for a few stragglers struggling to fold wind-whipped tent canvas, and the Olavayir servants hauling goods and equipment back toward the castle. At the castle, dust ran off the stone and poured into the streets.

Lanrid Olavayir had left the servants and runners to deal with the detritus of the wargame, and to set up the formal banquet in the parade ground court.

In his view, the commander — especially the winning commander — was free to celebrate in his own way. He was not obliged to sit in that steaming courtyard eating hot food with Arrow sulking, and hundreds of fools too stupid to see a signal flag.

He, his younger brother Sinna, and their loyal cousins — all expecting promotion from captains of a riding of nine to captains of a flight or even a wing, now that Lanrid was officially a commander — rode back to the castle, splashing through new puddles. After the unrelenting heat, the sting of hard rain was exhilarating.

Sinna ululated the fox yip on a high, musical note until the rain and thunder drowned him out. When they galloped into the residence courtyard and scattered stable hands left and right, Lanrid held out an arm to his brother, who halted obediently. "I'm not going to say anything, but that win was not the smashing defeat I wanted," Lanrid said in an undertone.

Sinna, in his secret heart, was no fighter. But his brother had trained him to appear to be one, and he would do anything for Lanrid. "No?"

"The charges. The only ones who did well were ours. The rest may as well not have been there. I saw it, Sinna, that drill is *everything*. We're going to drill in charges and signals before we go on our raid."

Sinna's heart sank, for in his opinion they had already drilled in those things endlessly. But he loyally jerked his palm up in assent, and Lanrid rewarded him with a grin and a thump on the shoulder. "Spread the word. Dawn, tomorrow. Behind West Hill, in case that shit Arrow gets the same idea. I don't want him watching us."

Sinna assented with a flip of his palm, and they started after the others, Lanrid pausing when he spotted his spy among the castle staff lurking inside the stable tack room.

"Go on in," Lanrid said to Sinna. "Get something to eat after you tell the others, and order something for me, right?"

Sinna was going to point out that the banquet was at that moment being set up, but shrugged and splashed off, singing a victory song, his high, clear, joyous voice joined by others who sounded like crows by comparison.

Lanrid didn't like Wanreth for the very reason he paid him, because he was so willing to spy on anyone Lanrid asked, in hopes of becoming a Rider. As if Lanrid would ever trust a slimy worm like that!

But Wanreth was a useful slimy worm. "Wana?" Lanrid said, forcing a big grin, without any idea how false it looked.

Wanreth blinked blond eyelashes, glanced furtively at the stable door, then said, "The jarl is sending Arrow to the royal city."

"He is? When?"

"Don't know. Probably soon. But I saw the letter the runner brought, asking for them both."

Lanrid brightened, asking quickly, "From my father?"

"No. From the regent."

"Uncle Kendred," Lanrid muttered, flicking his hand away in disgust. Then, "Good man. I'll have a goldpiece for you come morning."

Wanreth licked his chapped lips, fingered the white-blond queue that he didn't dare wear in a horsetail except in his own room, and stepped nearer. "You said I could start riding with you."

"So I did," Lanrid said, thinking rapidly. If Arrow was going south...he'd better carry out his bride raid *now*, instead of next spring. He'd surprise everyone—his father, the jarl, Arrow—the kingdom! Especially that snively shit Evred, so-called crown prince.

Lanrid laughed again. Definitely time to act. If he waited, he might not get the time before his father summoned him. Drill, *hard* drill, until he saw Arrow's back, and then ride for the north, and Hard Ride Arvandais, the wife every man in Marlovan Iasca wanted.

"We'll talk about it...after Arrow leaves," he said, knowing he'd have time to figure out some other way to put Wanreth off during the ride north and back. "Get back inside. Looks like rain's lifting already. Don't want us seen."

Wanreth watched Lanrid stride off toward the command end of the Rider barracks, fury simmering inside him. He'd seen that quick, false grin, and heard the easy promise—the same promise he'd heard again and again.

Wanreth sloped off toward the gate, and to the hostelry where he ordered some newly-broached ale and waited for the brown-haired weaver who soon appeared. "Wanreth?" She sat down next to him. "You have news?"

Wanreth repeated what he'd learned about the jarl and his sons, then added, "That raid Lanrid keeps bragging about? I think he's going to run it now, not next spring."

Her light eyes narrowed. "Did he say so?"

"It was the way he lied to me, saying we'd talk after Arrow leaves. I think he'll leave as soon as Arrow and Jarend do."

She accepted that, brought out a pouch from inside her coat, and withdrew five six-sided Sartoran gold pieces, worth four and a half Marlovan golds in Lindeth Harbor. "You get the other half the day he rides north."

Wanreth smiled as he departed, running his fingers over his coins. Now he didn't care if Lanrid kept his promise or not. Wanreth would soon have enough to buy his own horse, and no more barrels for him!

While Wanreth was talking to the weaver, Lanrid was inside the castle guard command center, prompting the praise and compliments that were his due for winning the wargame. But there weren't as many as he'd thought. Everyone seemed to be more interested in watching the storm move overhead, and jabbering about how hungry they were as they watched the servants dodging rain gutters as they carried out loaded and covered trays.

Everybody always thinks about himself, Lanrid thought irritably and started up toward his new chamber — the Rider Commander's chambers. That never failed to cheer him, though Rider Commander was just a small step toward the true goal.

Lanrid stopped short before he reached the door when he saw the gorgeous figure waiting — Fini sa Vaka.

Before I relate this encounter, I need to disclose something that none of the Marlovans ever found out. Even Fi hadn't known. Though her mother, Vaka sa Fini, was a hard-working, sober trader, Fi's father had been nothing less than a pirate.

Lanrid stared in astonishment.

"Fi!" he exclaimed, forcing a smile. He'd been so busy drilling his lancers that he'd been avoiding her for weeks. "Who let you up here?"

She flung her hair back so that it rippled, her long-lashed blue eyes wide, dimpled arms crossed beneath her perfect breasts, which looked even fuller than usual, if that was possible. "I told your desk orderly I had personal information, and you and I could either talk in the middle of the court, or up here. He said I could wait here."

Lanrid let out a gust of air, more disbelief than laugh. Even when she annoyed him, showing up like this, he couldn't help the heat searing through him, especially with her silk plastered to her curves. And didn't she know it!

"I've waited *weeks* to see you," she said as she shifted a hip and lounged against the door, a slim hand up, two fingers folded down. "You said you had to get ready for that wargame. I understood," she finessed, not wanting to admit that she had felt, and looked less than perfect.

But she was perfect now. "You won. It's over. We have two things to celebrate."

"I can give you until first night watch," he said, mentally calculating. He had to be out beyond that hill by sunup, equipment ready...then he looked up. "Two things?"

Her soft lips curved up, smug, her deep dimples still entrancing. Perfect white teeth dug into her soft underlip, then she said, "Open the door."

She was standing with her back to the latch—but he sighed and reached past her, familiar with her demand that others open doors for her. Apparently important people in Iasca didn't open their own doors.

When they were shut inside, she put her hands on his shoulders and said, "I'm pregnant."

"What?" he exclaimed, backing away as if to escape.

"Preg. Nant," she enunciated, grabbing his hand and pulling it under her loose silks. Instead of the soft belly he knew so well, there was a distinct hard mound. "I came to discuss our marriage."

Fury burned through him. "I never said I'd marry you."

"Yes, you did."

"No I didn't."

"When you first slept with me," she stated. "Before I left Arrow. You said he wasn't free, but you were."

"All I meant was, he was getting married, and I wasn't." He scowled at her. "How do I even know it's mine? I'm not adopting any brat of Arrow's," he added in disgust. "Or some Iascan horse apple. Even worse."

"It's yours," she said. "I haven't been with Arrow since his stupid wedding, or anyone else while I drank gerda-steep. Which by the way is revolting. But I did it for *you*," she lied, and thoroughly enjoyed the lying. Boys were so very stupid. Fun, but stupid. "You promised to marry me. You Olavayirs get your children right away, so I got a head start. For *you*."

"You're trying to trap me," he said slowly, remembering when he'd caught an extra scent about her, but she was always changing her scents. One of those scents was probably the herb that they both should have discussed first. It was...it was...well, if it wasn't a law, it should be. But it was certainly *manners*.

He glared at her, angry at having been duped. Marlovan women didn't do that—they would scorn to.

She eyed him, seeing the rising temper in his tightened mouth and reddened cheeks. How *dare* he! She hissed in a furious breath. "I am an *excellent* match. My grandmother is one of the richest shipowners in Lindeth. I want to be Lady Olavayir."

"There is no 'Lady' Olavayir," he said, his tone corrosive as he repeated the Iascan title *lady*. "I'm not even officially randael—I just hold that position." He laughed. "Though Arrow is now under my command, and doesn't he hate it!"

"You are a lord in *my* language," she retorted, voice rising to shrillness. "You command an army, you live in a castle, and you have a title. I deserve a title, and a castle, and I mean to have both. And my daughter will be the child of Lord and Lady Olavayir, and take over our ships."

Lanrid remembered Arrow muttering something about how having Fi as a lover was like riding into a lightning storm. At the time, he'd thought Arrow was hinting at his great sexual prowess, like the bonehead he was, but now Lanrid was beginning to comprehend what Arrow really had meant.

Lanrid stared back at her, remembered his plans, and smiled. Once his bride raid was successful, the problem would be solved. As for the brat, if it was a boy, he could be a future Rider—a captain if he was good enough. She could raise a girl however she liked. But his future heir would be by Hard Ride Hadand, for surely between the two of them they'd raise a boy as great as Inda-Harskialdna.

Lord Olavayir. Ridiculous.

He was going to have a far better title than that.

Meanwhile, if he told her no, would she go slandering him all over, the way she had Arrow? He stepped close, tipped her face up, and gave her a bruising kiss that left her gasping, and him thoroughly roused. She attacked him right back, shoving him until his shoulders thumped the wall, and ripped his coat open so the shanks popped off.

Oh, yes, this was the way to celebrate his win. He'd give her until the night watch. And fend her off afterward until he departed north to fetch Hard Ride, his future queen.

TEN

The royal runner Camerend Montredavan-An sat in a small guest chamber on the servants' side of the castle late at night. He wrote in coded Old Sartora to his mother, Shendan Montredavan-An, who had recently relinquished command of the royal runners to her son, so that she might remain in Darchelde to teach magic.

Her descendants have written enough about her eventful life. For my purpose here, here are the salient facts: the Olavayir king known to history as Bloody Tanrid had clashed with her, reducing the royal runners to household servants and banishing her to Darchelde, which was still under interdict from the days of the first Marlovan king. It suited Tanrid to permit Shendan to rule as jarlan—he did not want any of the jarls taking Darchelde and in effect becoming as powerful as he was.

She was brought back by his son on his accession, but when he was killed, the new king from the other Olavayir branch, banished her again, while keeping her son Camerend as a hostage because the royal runners were so useful—they were the only ones who knew how to replenish the spells for water purity and bridge supports and the like.

Unknown to the new king, Shendan, who couldn't bear to sit home worrying about her boy, had gone out of the country in secret, learning as much magic as she could—including, for a short time, from the mage guild in Sartor, until she advanced fast enough for them to delve into her false background to discover she was one of those proscribed Marlovans. She was kicked out, but by then she had discovered other sources of magic learning. After Garid-Harvaldar's assassination, she returned to teach chosen among the royal runners what she had learned, directing the royal runners from Darchelde.

Camerend wrote:

The evidence could not be clearer that the Jarl of Olavayir, and his sons, however used to garrison life they are, have seldom emulated our ancestors in tent living.

The conversation I am about to repeat I overheard while waiting for the Jarl of Olavayir to finish dealing with the last of a string of servants and runners, shortly after the younger son's wife and her infant were carted back to the castle.

The Jarl arrived too late to see his newborn grandson, but he was clearly too intent on other matters. He told me to bide outside the grand pavilion that had been set up for his family from which to observe their Victory Day wargame. I was just as glad not to have to sit inside, as it was hot as an oven.

So I discovered that the jarl, like many who have never had to live in tents, assumes that what you cannot see cannot be heard.

I sat on an upturned bucket in what little shade there was and took the opportunity to repack my saddlebags.

The Jarl's second son, Anred ("Arrow"), arrived at the gallop, dismounted at a run, and splashed into the pavilion. "Where is she?"

Jarl: "In the cart with the last of the food. You rode right past them."

Anred: "I didn't come from the castle. I was talking to some of the Faths about the game, and what they saw."

Jarl: "You have a son."

Anred: "Good."

Jarl: "Better than good. We need boys. We can bring in girls to marry them. Far better than sending them out to other jarlates, taking our family secrets with them. You did well there."

Anred: "Seems to me Danet did well. My part wasn't exactly work." His voice rose. "I won the game, didn't I?" And when his father sighed, he added in a surly voice, "I would have, had my southern wing known the same signals as my lancers. And if those Senelaecs hadn't gone off on their own."

Jarl: "Arrow. It was the Senelaecs who apparently guessed Lanrid was going to try flanking you with those Marlovayirs while you were busy throwing everything you had at his damn charge."

Anred: "Which he lost. He won't admit it, but he lost."

Jarl: "No one really wins or loses a charge in a wargame, Arrow! Tigging lances just isn't the same as killing—all it does is train your arm to be able to tap your opponent's, and give you something to score in competitions. But in his turn, Lanrid was a bonehead to expect them to wheel and charge back on a signal no one could see or hear. Even in battle, no record has ever mentioned a charge doing anything but running wild after it breaks the line. And he broke the line only because this was a game, in which nobody wanted himself hurt."

Anred: "Then what's the use if nobody can win?"

Jarl: "It's experience—the sun, the noise, the confusion. The knowing that as soon as you contact the enemy, no matter how carefully you plan, things go wrong fast. You have to have a hundred possible plans ready, once you see the problem. If you see it. Command comes with experience for most of us. There's a reason we all sing about Inda-Harskialdna leading a mutiny against pirates at sixteen—because none of us before, or after, could do it and win. And that went for the Montreivayirs, too. People complain about us Olavayirs, and want the Montreivayirs back, but what they truly want is the Evred who had Inda Algarvayir as Harskialdna. Why d'you think we no longer even use the title anymore?"

Anred: "I still think I won."

Jarl: "Did you really send those Senelaecs to rout Lanrid's flank attack?"

Anred: "Well, I would have! If I'd seen—"

Jarl: "But you didn't see the flank attack, did you? I thought not. And did you even notice that the Idegans were gone?"

Anred: "Gone? Where?"

Jarl: "Someone said they were seen riding for the north at sunup."

Anred: "I <u>thought</u> I had fewer than Lanrid! How was I supposed to—"

Jarl: "Arrow, my point here is you didn't know your companies, any more than you knew where they were after you handed out your orders. You let Lanrid pick the best of them. And you didn't have a communication system that everyone was used to. Lanrid had you thoroughly beat there."

Anred: cursing.

The jarl cut through it loud enough that I saw some of the runners exchanging looks as they packed up the last wagon. "The boys Halivayir sent you scarcely knew one end of their swords from the other, which is entirely another matter. Even among those who sent good Riders instead of farmers or potters, surely you observed that training in one jarlate is not the same as that in their neighbors."

Then his voice lowered. *"We both know that Lanrid is an arrogant soul-sucker, but he's doing what he's supposed to do. And he's where he is because Mathren has kept his end of the Alliance treaty."*

Anred: *"Right, right."*

Jarl: *"This is what's important, that you learn to spot your own weaknesses. Those will never change if you always blame others. If you see a real problem, then fix the problem. That's command for those of us not born geniuses. Whining about your enemy's tricks is defeat talk."*

Anred: *"I get it, I get it."*

Jarl: *"Then forget the game. It's over. I sent for you because I got a runner this morning. Evred has been squabbling with Kendred, insisting that he be crowned king now, and he wants to marry that Arvandais girl and not the Senelaec one he's been betrothed to all his life. Kendred wants Jarend there to steady him, but I suspect it's to remind Evred that there is another heir—an eagle-clan heir—as agreed on by all the jarls, until Evred marries and has a son. I want you to go with your brother. Help Jarend steady Evred to the task, by all means, but there is no reason you cannot combine that with my original plan."*

Anred, in a flat recitation voice: *"'Discover the state of the Royal Riders, and why the northern garrisons have been cut off for three years running from their share of the royal treasury.'"*

Jarl: *"Yes. I want you on the road to the capital city by the end of the week."*

Anred: *"Just the two of us?"*

Jarl: *"No. Take the women. Especially with my orders to you, it's important to make it look like a family party, there for Evred's Name Day over New Year's Week."*

Anred: *"Right, right."*

Jarl: *"A last thing. Whatever happens, put Lanrid out of your mind. He's Rider Commander. It's done."*

Anred: *"I said I would."*

Jarl: "You can return directly after New Year's Week. If you discover something so important you think needs reporting sooner, then send one of the royal runners, and use our code words."

Anred: "The royal runners can't be trusted?"

Jarl: "Oh, you can trust them to get messages delivered. And the Montredavan-Ans among 'em are forbidden by that ten-generations law to interfere in crown affairs, so there's no reason for them to tamper with messages. It's just that I don't <u>know</u> them — they aren't runners I trained up from boyhood myself. They have their own training, nobody else allowed. It wasn't so long ago they trained them in Darchelde, which no one else can get into, until Bloody Tanrid, who ruled when I was your age, forced 'em to move to the royal city to keep 'em under his eye."

Anred: "So <u>he</u> didn't trust them?"

Jarl: "I don't know what he thought. All I know is, they survived the bad days under Bloody Tanrid. I like to use our people if I can, but there's the fact that the royal runners are faster. It's said they know old routes from the King's Runners days."

Anred: "I'll get ready."

The sound of the tent flap being thrust aside was my signal to pick up my saddlebag and walk around the steaming puddles to the front of the tent.

I wondered if I had been meant to hear all that. But when I met the jarl's gaze and saw the total indifference there, the slight pinch around the eyes as he tried for a heartbeat to place me in memory, I returned to my previous idea: no notion of tent voice. That art seems to be lost.

He said to me: "By request from the regent, I'm sending my sons to the royal city to celebrate New Year's Week with the royal branch of the family, so no messages. If you can wait to ride with them and show them the way, I'd appreciate it."

It was an order, of course. We both knew it. But his wording was far more polite than the Idegan runner had been when he handed off those letters to me at dawn, before they departed for the north.

I said I would, and so I am currently in the Nevree castle as another storm is breaking overhead, if you have any private orders for me.

ELEVEN

Let's leave the exhausted Olavayirs to recover, and shift southward to Senelaec to catch up with the tired, road-grimed Senelaec girls, who had long gotten over their triumph. By the time they neared Senelaec, they were worried sick.

So they rode slower.

Out loud, Calamity insisted that their sedate pace was intended as extra care not to run into any Marlovayirs while they were near the border between the two jarlates, but the truth was, they dreaded riding into the courtyard at home.

They dawdled so much that the boys beat them back, even though they had stayed for the last meal. Wolf said out loud that this was their last chance to talk to the friends they'd made, but he'd slipped away to search for the Idegan company, who'd always been somewhere else when he'd tried to find them all week. At that last banquet, as the storm pounded through, someone finally told him that the Idegans rode out at sunup, skipping the last day of the wargame entirely.

Wolf had never been in love with his wife, but he'd loved his little daughter, who he feared now he'd never get to see again. He rode in silence for half the journey, and by the time the boys reached home he'd made some new resolves.

When the girls rode into the courtyard several days later, the jarl was not there—he was out riding the border himself, as the Seneleaecs were so short-handed.

Oh, the moral superiority!

"We're dead," Calamity muttered to Fuss, who was in an agony of remorse by then, as she was a peaceful, orderly soul by nature. "Dead, dead, dead."

The stable hands didn't meet anyone's eyes. The only one who spoke was Ndara's little brother, who piped up with the righteous relish of one who'd been doing extra stable wanding for a solid month, "The jarlan's waiting for you. Phew, I wouldn't wear *your* boots for *anything*."

Fuss slunk toward the house, the image of guilt. Calamity stalked beside her, temper simmering. After all, the adults had been breaking rules for years, if it meant a good raid or sting. And she'd *won!*

"There you are," the jarlan said, arms crossed. "You seven go bathe and get to work. You'll find plenty waiting. And the stalls to wand afterward, in trade to the stable hands who had to do all your chores. You two." A jab of two fingers at Calamity and Fuss. "With me."

They reached the jarlan's private room, with its handsome desk that she had inherited from the daughter of a queen.

"Wolf gave me a full report. He took all the blame for your going off to skylark in Olavayir, leaving us wondering what had happened to you, as if none of you had the sense to tell him it was a stupid idea."

At the unhappy look on Calamity's face, and Fuss's genuine misery, the jarlan relented a little. It was clear that the girls, who could have been home days before the boys, had been punishing themselves a-plenty. "Though I suspect I know why you gave in," she said to Calamity, who flushed to the ears. "Yes," the jarlan said. "We're going to put it about you had to get back at Knuckles for what they did to our patrol last winter."

She cleared her throat, then glanced at the shut door to make certain it was indeed shut, and lowered her voice. "I have nothing to say about this feud. If it stays this kind of feud, raids back and forth. The stings. If it goes no worse, it keeps us sharp, and I know it's fun." She met the girls' gazes as she said, "But I do object to your adopting the boys' outlook on these big wargames, which makes it so easy to see war itself as the greatest game, with small raids that get bigger, and bigger, until they're battles, and then a war so terrible that for generations after we sing songs like Yvana Ride Thunder, and the Andahi Lament."

Fuss's eyes rimmed with tears at the mention of the Andahi Lament. She could never hear it without her throat closing up.

The jarlan pressed her thumbs against her eyelids, then dropped her hands, callused from years of bow practice and working with horses. "I will never understand why men go to war," she said low-voiced. "Think about what defense means. I know you're young. Everything to the young is a game. I know the family sees it that way. But war isn't a game. Especially for us women. My sister, your aunt, could tell you that—if she were still alive. And that wasn't even considered a war, because only a few died at the assassins' hands. But they are just as dead."

The jarlan hit her breastbone with a fist, right above her heart. "We fight when we have to defend our homes. What the men do...." She looked away, Fuss's tears falling when she saw the rare gleam in her mother's eyes. "We don't kill other mothers' sons unless they're attacking our own who cannot defend themselves. And yes, we can be, and are, vicious ourselves. But when men go looking for war as *fun*...." She sighed.

"I don't mean to say we weren't wrong," Calamity said earnestly, her vivid face as usual mirroring her emotions, "because I know we were. But, isn't making it a game a way *out* of war, for those who want it?"

"It can be. It can be, if both sides learn to let each other go home again. We aren't going to solve that now, but we can talk about it as you both move into adulthood's responsibilities. Which begin with not throwing over the important aspects of life in order to have fun. And yes, I know my husband, old as he is, thinks differently."

She sighed again, then turned to her daughter. "Fareas," she said as Fuss silently wiped her eyes. "You know that you are expected to marry Evred Olavayir when he comes of age. That means you will be thinking for the entire kingdom. And Carleas," she shifted her gaze to Calamity, "the jarl and I have decided that instead of waiting for Yipyip to reach twenty, you ought to marry Wolf, and now. It was Wolf's idea. He spoke to the jarl and me, and we agreed. How about you?"

Though Calamity had done her earnest best to keep her passion to herself, all three there knew her answer before she spoke.

The jarlan pointed at the door. "Go get yourselves a bath, and get to work. That extra stable wanding includes you. Since we have only ourselves to please, and not some outsider family, we can make the wedding come Restday." Then the jarlan said roughly, "Give him a girl."

About that same time, back in Olavayir, once again, Danet wrote to her sister Hliss:

I don't remember what I wrote last. I think it was before Noddy was born.

Well, having Noddy was the most frightening thing in my life because everyone thought I was asleep, and the wargame ended, so people began to return to the castle and there I was, alone with Tesar, who turned pale as death when I let out a yelp after my water broke, and I sent her to fetch the jarlan so her worried questions that I couldn't answer wouldn't make things worse.

It was still hot, but I kept getting cold waves, until a girl my age named Calamity Senelaec suddenly showed up with her foster-sister, I don't remember her name. All I remember is the relief because they knew what to do. Even if they talked to me like a mare in foal. I know that voice. I used it when Firefly dropped Biscuit.

Anyway, when it was over they left before anyone could thank them. Then Noddy and I got back to the castle and slept and slept.

I think we slept most of three days. I only woke when he wanted suckle, or when he cried, then someone would pick him up to change him into clean linens.

I never tire of looking at Noddy. They all insist he doesn't see anything, that babes are as blind as kittens or pups, but I think he looks at me. I know he tries to wriggle himself around to face me when I enter a room. I don't tell anyone that because I know they will laugh and say First Time Parent, as they did so often those first days. They said it to Arrow, too, when he came in to see us. That would send him right out again.

When I was feeling normal again, sometimes it surprised me he was there. I think I told you when I first put on my Olavayir House Tunic as a bride, I thought I would feel like a different person. I didn't. I felt like me wearing a new robe. It was the same when I looked at Noddy, wiggling there with his stream-colored eyes, neither brown nor blue, staring at the wall as the raindrops tapped against it. I don't feel like a mother—like a version of Mother. I feel like me who somehow squeezed out a baby.

I should also tell you I wrote to Mother before I wrote to you. I wrote a very long letter with a lot of questions. Then in the morning, before we left and I was going to see if some runner was going that way, I knew what Mother would write back. She'd say, You're among the Olavayirs now. You do things the way they like. Don't waste time and paper. So I threw it in the fire....

By the end of a month Danet was able to send off the long letter she'd written to her sister during her recovery, detailing every minute change in Noddy's expression. By now she was back to regular life, punctuated by Noddy's feeding times.

She was down at the stable grooming Firefly in preparation for a ride when Arrow turned up, eyes rimmed with tiredness as if he hadn't slept. He smelled of stale wine, but his voice was clear enough as he said, "We're off to the royal city. Not just you and me. All four of us. And the babes."

"What?" she exclaimed in dismay. "Why?"

"It's orders. We're to celebrate the New Year as a family with Evred, who seems to think he can declare himself of age and take the throne. Lanrid's Uncle Kendred, the regent, seems to think we might be able to talk him out of it, though I don't see how, if he's not listening to *them—*"

"Wait. I thought he was my age, or maybe a little older. Not twenty-five," Danet said.

Arrow's bow mouth flattened to a line, and she knew that once again, she'd managed to run into that invisible wall dividing the eagle clan from the dolphin clan. "We'll talk more later," he said, glancing over his shoulder at a clump of Lanrid's dolphin-branch Riders.

Danet took her ride, scarcely noticing her surroundings, her mind was so full of questions. On her return, Tesar was still going about with a harried, guilty demeanor, as she had all week. Danet suspected that Tesar felt badly for having left Danet when she was in labor.

The night before they were to ride out, Jarend was missing from all three meals. He seldom spoke, but he was a large presence Danet had gotten used to. She noticed him only when he was gone; in the stairwell, she overhead Tdor Fath telling the jarlan that he had another of his sick headaches, but he promised he would be able to ride in the morning.

The last meal was entirely taken up with Lanrid, now sitting where the randael ought to sit, loudly and forcefully arguing with the jarl that they ought to hold big wargames every year instead of every five—as if, Danet thought sourly, bellowing would convince anyone where a normal voice wouldn't.

"Even if it didn't seriously disrupt the work of the other jarlates, it's too costly for us," the jarl said in his even voice. "And so much of the castle work has to be set aside to prepare. Surely you can learn just as much wargaming Riders against Riders, or plan castle defenses, as usual, on Restdays."

It was not a question.

Lanrid sat back, his mouth tight. Sinna, his younger brother, whispered, "Won't a castle defense be fun?"

Danet didn't hear Lanrid's answer because Ranor-Jarlan turned to her and signed for her to follow.

When they reached the jarlan's room, Ranor indicated a mat, and they both sat down.

Ranor-Jarlan pushed a braid loop back, adjusted a cup on the table, then said, "Danet, you have brought a child into the family. You are now one of us. There are things you ought to know, and that I want you to do, for the sake of family. And for the kingdom." She reached behind her into the trunk where she kept household papers, and pulled out a flattened scroll, which she spread out. The hand was large and wavery, even sprawling, like a child's, except the letters were not the rounded ones you see from children. They were narrow.

The Jarlan said, "That was written by Gunvaer-Hesar."

When Danet stared in surprise, the jarlan said, "Yes, the first Olavayir queen, the eldest of the family. She is in her nineties, and she would very much like to come home. She will, once Evred is safely married—if she lives that long—but that's the future. This is now. Read it. I'll wait."

Danet bent over the text:

I believe the boy is going to throw off the regency soon. He refuses to have the Senelaec girl, who by all accounts would make an excellent gunvaer, and he keeps sending gifts and promises north, but there has been no definite answer from the Arvandais family. He will not listen to age. For once I agree with Kendred and Mathren, who I understand will ask your jarl to send the heir. Evred might heed youth, or at least he can be kept busy. He is always idle, and idle at that age is dangerous.

When Danet handed the letter back, the jarlan said, "I know you are kin to the Arvandais family. The girl is your age. Cousins, fourth degree cousins, can sometimes be as close as sisters. What can you tell me about them?"

"Not much firsthand," Danet said slowly. "I only met the Arvandaises once, when I was ten."

The jarlan turned up her hand, and it was clear to Danet then that the Arvandaises were not her chief subject here.

The jarlan said slowly, "My husband is forbidden by the Eastern Alliance treaty to ride into the capital city unless it's for Convocation, which has not been called for too many years to count. I would go, but Evred-Sierlaef would ignore an old woman only distantly related to him, and of course I have no authority whatsoever. You know Jarend by now, enough to understand that his strengths do not lie in remonstrating with an unruly cousin. I don't like sending both my sons to the royal city—you know what happened before—but it has been quiet these many years. Mathren Olavayir, who rescued Evred from the first assassination attempt, has kept the city well-guarded ever since his own wife was killed in the second assassination attempt. So I believe you will be safe enough."

Danet murmured assent.

"My sons will address their cousin, and Tdor Fath will look out for Jarend, who does not like travel, or things unaccustomed. But I have a very important task for you. I believe you are the best to accomplish it—far better than my sons. I need you to ask to see all the royal accounts, in order to be taught how they manage the tallies."

"The *kingdom* accounts?" Danet repeated, stunned.

"Yes," Ranor said. "Hesar is too old and too blind to act as gunvaer anymore. She is not permitted to know who is controlling the kingdom's treasure. Because there has been no Convocation for years, we have no idea what state the kingdom's affairs are in—we only know that the northern garrisons have been cut off from receiving their share of tax benefits, and it is our jarlate that has been making up the difference as best we can. It places enormous strain on us, and is not adequate. We need to know why this situation is as it is. I think you are capable of accomplishing that."

Danet stared. "But—the *royal* treasury...."

"Numbers are numbers. You have a knack for them. In truth I believe you're better at it than I am. If you can, find out who among the jarls is actually paying taxes, and who Kendred has bought off—and what he promised. It has to be Kendred, as Mathren only concerns himself with the Royal Riders—what used to be the King's Guard when there was a king—and castle defense. If Evred can't help you, go to Hesar. At least she ought to know whom you should speak with."

The jarlan's hand shook as she folded up the scroll again. "Will you do that?"

Danet placed her hand on her heart. "I'll do my best."

The jarlan smiled at last, and let her go.

Later that night, when Arrow came to her room to see Noddy, he picked the baby up, and over his small round head said to Danet, "Ma told me she talked to you about Evred."

"A little," Danet said cautiously.

Arrow said, "Here's what she probably didn't tell you." Then he fell silent, and looked around, though they were alone. Then he handed Noddy back and took a swig from his flask. "Look. The inside line is, the old people don't talk much about the last generation because they all knew each other. The way they talk, thirty years ago is like last season. But there's been bad blood in the family for a hundred years, ever since the the widow of the hero Hawkeye Yvanavayir married my great-father's second son. She worked it so her own boy took over as jarl, but it split the family into the two branches, and the feud got worse over the generations. Da remembers how bad it got when Jasid-Harvaldar killed Haldren-Harvaldar and took over as king in '29. There were duels and one ambush, though they always denied it. Other families got dragged in until the Eastern Alliance got the other jarls to impose a treaty on us. You know who they are, right?"

Danet opened her hand. "Everyone knows the Eastern Alliance is the horse stud families, the Sindan-Ans, Tlens, Tlennens, and Senelaecs."

"And the Sindans, who ride with them all. Amble Sindan is their chief—not a jarl. So, things were quiet until twenty years ago," Arrow went on. "How much do you know about *that?*"

"All I know is what my da told us. It was while we were riding up the Pass to visit our Arvandais kin. He said, while Kendred Olavayir was out with most of the royal guard on a training game in the plains, masked assassins killed Garid-Harvaldar, his gunvaer, and their first runners and honor guard while they were riding a shortcut through the woods to watch the training game. At the castle, the assassins tried to kill the little prince, but Mathren Olavayir, who was just a young riding captain at the time, managed to save Evred."

Arrow looked away. "Both my brothers were in that honor guard. They died defending the king and queen. We don't know who the assassins were, or where they came from. Everybody heard something different, that they were northerners, or southerners, or even Adranis from over the mountain passes in the east. The thing that bothers Da is that most of the witnesses had accidents, too. Except there's one thing no one talks about outside of the family. And I don't mean the cousins, or the Riders. Just us."

He held up five fingers. "Da, Ma, Jarend, me, and Tdor Fath. And now you make six."

Danet gripped her elbows with her hands as Arrow said, "A fourteen-year-old stable-girl, one of Ma's kin, had been watering the remounts at a stream a distance away, and I guess the murderers didn't know about remounts, because she had tied them up to crop at some clover while she came back for the saddles. She saw a blood splash on a tree and went doggo, crawled under some shrub, and looked out until she saw the queen lying dead, facing her way, her throat cut. She heard one of the assassins say, in Marlovan, *That's it. Leave the horses and come back here, for we have to find....* And then he—it was a man's voice—turned away and she didn't hear the rest. She lay hidden until nightfall, then rode those same horses away for home."

Danet said, "Why did you call that 'a thing?' It sounds like a witness to me."

He said, "Because the stable girl didn't *see* the assassins. Ma said there was no evidence other than the voice the stable girl heard. When the royal runners brought Great-Uncle Kendred's letter about the assassinations, declaring he, now as regent, would heed the Eastern Alliance Treaty, the older people decided nothing good would come of questions no one could prove, except maybe civil war."

Danet repeated, *"Civil war?"*

"Da says there are certain jarls, mostly in the south, who'd love any excuse to break up the kingdom. They could become kings on their own. Some already are, in all but name—he says Kendred has given way to them time and again. Everybody says Kendred hates trouble, and will do anything to avoid it. But now that Evred is older, rumor has it that he's getting harder to rein in. That's what we have to do, to keep Evred from doing anything senseless because he wants to be king now."

He bent over Noddy's sleep basket, and then said, "When's he going to look like me? He still looks like a little old man."

"He might look like me," Danet said, hiding her trepidation at this impending trip. Nobody wanted her opinion, they just wanted her to do her duty.

Mother would say the same.

TWELVE

The jarl left very early the next morning for Lindeth, to exchange the wargame recruits for experienced Riders to accompany him on his journey to deal with the latest problems at the Nob.

After breakfast, Jarend emerged from his room, and insisted in his quiet way that he could ride.

The entire castle gathered to see them off.

Fi watched from the inner city gate as Arrow and his brother and the rest of them rode by. She ducked back, but Arrow never looked her way. One they'd gone, the crowd began to disperse. She looked around for Lanrid, sure he'd be cracking jokes at Arrow's expense, but she didn't see him anywhere.

But of course, now that he was almost a lord, or whatever these Marlovens called their military leaders, he probably thought he was above joining the commoners. Well, she was, too — or she soon would be.

She returned to the family trade house to change into some flattering silks before going up into the residence to discuss her prospective wedding with Lanrid.

But when she arrived, it was to find the residence stable courtyard curiously empty, except for servants talking in clumps.

She walked around until she found a young runner-in-training whom she recognized, and confronted him. "Where's Lanrid?" she demanded in Marlovan, since these ignorant people knew no Iascan.

"He left on the north road," the boy said.

"What? When! *Why?*"

"He took handpicked riders for a field game," was the short answer. Fi was not popular with any of the servants.

"Where would he leave messages?" she asked. "He must have left me a message. Go fetch it at once."

"There was only one. For the jarlan," the boy said, with a little too much enjoyment.

She considered slapping some respect into him, but decided she could punish him properly once she was Lady Olavayir.

She stalked away to wait on his return.

Danet rode in the cart for the first few days, mostly for Noddy's and Rabbit's sake. The babies complained less with her there.

But then, as a vanguard of clouds slowly advanced overhead, the cavalcade pulled up. Danet peered irritably against the watery, glaring light at the three figures at the front, almost silhouetted against the diffuse sun: Jarend looming over the more slender royal runner, his hair touched to ruddy gold even in the weird light, and next to him Arrow, his shoulders and elbows points angling away from his scrawny backside.

Danet climbed out of the cart to stretch her legs and peered over the autumnal grasses, wondering what the problem was. Difficulties caused by the royal runner? She'd only seen him that once, on her first border ride, surrounded by an air of mystery.

Tdor Fath had ridden forward, and now trotted back, and slid out of the saddle to land beside the cart. She whistled to her mount, who shook her head and paused a few paces distant, nosing at the old summer grasses.

"Danet, we're going to part ways with the carts. We're going ahead with our personal runners and the babes only. Arrow insists," Tdor Fath said.

"What about Nunka?" Danet asked. Already she depended heavily on the old nursery minder.

"He stays with the carts. He's too old to ride as long and as fast as we need to," Tdor Fath said, and Danet's heart sank. But as Mother would say, duty was duty. If they didn't ask, then nobody wanted to hear what you thought.

"Bad weather coming, and the roads are terrible in the open plains of Hesea." Tdor Fath dug her fists into her lower back, then reached into the cart for one of the long baby cloths. "We'll have to pack a couple of changes of clothes for the babes, and dry things in the air as we ride. Here's how to make a baby sling."

Danet mastered it on one try, promised to teach Arrow, then they distributed Noddy's small needs between Danet's and Tesar's saddlebags, as Tdor and her first rider carried Rabbit's — all the other runners, including the nursery staff, had to ride with the carts.

Danet taught Arrow the baby sling. They traded Noddy back and forth, the runners and Riders carrying field tents and travel bread.

They reached Olavayir's border, a river dividing Olavayir from Khanivayir jarlate. The water was running low after summer, so the horses could ford.

Arrow insisted on carrying Noddy, saying he was taller in case his mount should stumble. She rode behind him, and kept her gaze fastened anxiously on his back every step his horse made, a journey of eternity while it lasted.

His horse stumbled once, and every muscle in her body flashed cold as if she'd been thrown into ice water. Arrow's arms tightened around Noddy, and she made herself breathe.

Arrow chose the eastern fork of the road because he'd been impressed by the Senelaecs' riding at the games, and their total lack of strut about it. He liked Wolf much more than he liked that strutting Knuckles Marlovayir to the west, so—in accordance with ancient custom—they headed toward Senelaec, expecting guest privilege, and knew that outriders would spot them long before they reached the valley above which the Senelaec fortress lay.

As each day of travel passed, swept by intermittent rains, everyone anticipated a dry bed and warmth the more. Danet also looked forward to thanking Calamity Senelaec, who had vanished before that could happen.

Senelaec riders greeted them half a day's ride out, and showed them a shortcut. The Olavayirs studied with interest the walled fortress built on a ridge above a valley, Arrow liked its commanding view—this position would be difficult to attack—and his brother the well-behaved horses the outriders rode. Though Olavayir horses were very well trained, there were still the occasional kicks and bites and whinnies of objection to one another, but these animals were mild as milk.

Tdor Fath also considered the defensive position of the fortress. Women could hold that, she thought, and because the Andahi Lament was recent enough to hear in memory, she shivered in the cold air. And when they had climbed the last of the switchback road leading to the gates of the single wall, and passed beneath, Danet gazed with interest at a dwelling different than any other she'd seen yet.

Shadowed by a single lookout tower, the house was low and rambling, an L shape with rooms that soon proved to open into each other—at one end a big barn, and the jarl and jarlan's living quarters at the other.

Calamity and Wolf ran out to greet them. At first Danet was not certain which of the two tall, light-haired women was Calamity and which Fuss. Within a few exchanges, Danet wondered how she could have thought them at all similar: Calamity's freckles and big, sunny grin were a dramatic contrast to Fuss's quiet sobriety. Even their Marlovan-blonde hair differed, Calamity's golden, and Fuss's a flaxen butter-cream color that brought Danet's sister Hliss to mind.

A cluster of Senelaec cousins crowded in. Danet handed Noddy down into reaching hands, and the babe was promptly swept away by a cooing sixteen-year-old, Rabbit right behind, swung gurgling with laughter between a pair of sisters.

Calamity said, "We can offer you guest quarters off the jarl's rooms, or else you can have our den. Here, I'll show you." She indicated the barn.

Danet looked at it doubtfully, but said nothing as they ran up a stairway to a big, airy attic loft with cushions and thick quilts everywhere, broken gear here, tools there. It was a mess. Danet suppressed the urge to straighten everything, yet even so, she found the atmosphere cheery.

Calamity rubbed her hands together. "I thought you might like this better. Half the time we just fall asleep up here! We always did when we were small. Let's go find out when we're going to eat, and you can get a hot bath. They've been cooking all day, and wouldn't let us in to pinch so much as an apple!"

She turned to go, but Danet caught her arm. "I wanted to thank you for helping me with Noddy. You disappeared so fast that I couldn't, and I did not want you to think me rude or ungrateful."

To her surprise Calamity blushed to the ears that stuck out between her braid loops. "Don't mention it. Really. We, ah, were not supposed to go north. To watch the boys. And we have a month to go of stable wanding!"

"Ranor-Jarlan figured that must be the case. I mean, that you rode with your boys just to watch them? She thought it odd, but then *we* were there watching, so why not?"

"Well, it's over now, for five years. Come, I'll show you the baths...."

The house was warm, redolent of food and hemp and horse and over it all the heady smell of malting, as they were brewing. The girls ducked under loose-woven sacks of drying yellow-blossom, which Danet suspected the Senelaecs used instead of hops to brew their ale. She found that intensely interesting, but she could see that for Calamity, it was merely part of everyday life. So she bit back her usual stream of questions.

After everyone was bathed and the babies fed and settled, the jarl and jarlan took Jarend and Tdor Fath off to entertain—Jarend, as heir to Olavayir, being regarded as stand-in in for his father, and Tdor Fath for the jarlan.

Arrow and Danet joined Wolf, Calamity, and Fuss in the den. Wolf's younger brother Yipyip was also there, a skinny weed with a prominent neck-knuckle and brown curls as luxuriant as his older brother's darker locks. A few younger cousins also drifted in, at first shy and tentative.

"Ma said we better get at it if we're gonna jaw." Yipyip spoke, hands on skinny hips as he surveyed the pile of harness repairs left over from the previous winter.

Arrow uttered a crack of laughter, and Danet said, "We can help."

"Right," Arrow said, interpreting correctly the hopeful faces around him. "I've seen plenty of repair duty, I can tell you."

"Let me guess." Wolf slanted a brief, wicked grin. "Penalty for scrapping."

Arrow shrugged as he dropped crosslegged on an old mat and reached for the nearest broken bit of gear. "Isn't it that way everywhere?"

Wolf laughed again. Though the Olavayirs didn't have that great a rep, and he'd found Arrow's cousin Lanrid irritating with his constant strut as if he were emperor of the world, he hadn't minded Arrow...he'd actually kind of liked him when he wasn't ranting and raving about how unfair his cousin was in a game no one else cared about once it was over.

Arrow and Danet proved to be deft, and the work party had made a significant dent before Wolf, feeling the prick of conscience, admitted that the jarl and jarlan got disgusted with them for putting off repair until the weather got bad. "It's not that we're lazy," he said. "But if you have good weather, and you're done with outside chores, wouldn't you rather have fun?"

Arrow's sudden grin made it plain he agreed, and before long, they were trading stories of various jokes, ruses, and stings, Wolf carefully keeping the talk well away from the game, and who had won the ride and shoot.

The last thing Arrow wanted to talk about was the game, and he loved stories about larks. But he began to notice that the Senelaecs' targets were always the same: the Marlovayirs to the west.

So he asked. "Why always the Marlovayirs? Wait, didn't someone once mention a feud?"

Calamity snorted. "It's *all* due to their greed, during our grandfathers' time, when they had the biggest jarlate in the north. Except for yours, of course, Yvanavayir, and the old Choreid Elgaer."

"The king was saved by my grandfather, who broke Marlovayir in half to create Senelaec," Wolf said. "It wasn't that we asked for it. Kings do what they're going to do, and everybody knows it's a very bad idea to turn them down when they want to give gifts. But the Marlovayirs have always acted as though our family robbed them, and they've been giving us trouble ever since."

"What kind of trouble? Is it a blood matter?" Arrow asked.

"No...not so much since the Eastern Alliance forced...ah, oversaw the treaty with your family. You know. The Marlovayirs don't want them coming down on them like thunder any more than we want our cousins giving us grief, so it's raids. And stings. Like, last winter, one of our border patrols got hit by a snowstorm and wandered into their territory without knowing. They camped to wait it out, dark overtook them, and when they crawled out of their tents, they found a wing or two of Marlovayir riders with swords drawn. There was only the single riding—they couldn't fight them all. The Marlovayirs robbed them."

"Why didn't I hear about that? Horse thieving is a serious—"

"They didn't take their horses. Nothing that could be presented before the regent in the royal city," Fuss said, looking at the corner of the room.

Yipyip piped up, his treble voice cracking suddenly as he said, "They took their pants."

Arrow had to bite his lip to smother his laughter. Danet took in the row of indignant Senelaecs and suppressed the urge to smile.

"And ever since, if they see any of us on patrol, they ask about the starkers patrol, or make some joke about moons," Yipyip said with honest outrage. "*I* think they lie in wait and save up their comments."

Wolf sighed, thinking that the younger ones did not need to provide quite so much detail.

Arrow exclaimed, "Well *of course* you'd want revenge for that. Have you tried....

He caused an avalanche of ruses, stings, tricks, and traps concocted by several generations of creative minds. When the discussion dwindled to the boys trying to outdo one another with outrageous dares, Danet decided it was time to go check on Noddy.

Calamity led the way to the nursery, where a couple of young girls were playing with Wolf's little Cut and Rabbit, who were roughly the same age and fascinated with one another. Noddy was sound asleep.

After a splendid banquet, full of singing and pounding the table until the hand drums were pulled out to spare the dishes, they adjourned for spiced wine and more talk, as below in the courtyard, the home riders entertained the visitors with roaring songs and dance, amid the rhythmic clash of swords.

Arrow had begun the dinner worried all over again about the wargame being brought up—that Lanrid had won—but it was soon clear that no one was interested in talking about it, and he enjoyed himself.

By the change of the night watch, Calamity, Fuss, and Danet were fast friends. Calamity liked everybody, if given half a chance, and in Fuss, Danet found another orderly soul, though even Fuss seemed to stutter and look overwhelmed at too long a string of *Why?* questions. They'd chatted happily about keeping household tallies (though Danet wondered how Fuss could bear to live in such chaos, cheerful as it was) until Calamity, bored with a conversation that seemed would never end, said, "Won't Fuss make a great gunvaer?"

Danet agreed, remembering what the jarlan had said, but there was also that gossip about Evred expecting to marry Hard Ride. Did the Senelaecs know about that? Oh yes, wasn't Wolf's first wife an Arvandais connection?

Could she ask? As a way of getting near the subject, she said, "That reminds me. At the game, I saw some of the Idegan people—"

The game! Horrified, Calamity reached for any subject to get away from that! "Did you know we used to have one of the Arvandaises here?" she asked, hoping that gossip about Ndiran would sidetrack Danet away from the disastrous subject. "Ndiran wasn't from the main branch."

"I heard something about that. What happened? I can't believe Wolf was a terrible husband."

"He wasn't," Calamity said firmly. "He did *everything* her way. Including being exclusive. Because *she* wanted it." Breathing hard, Calamity fought to keep her voice even. "I—we—thought we were so close. She was always telling me how great I am at shoo—at riding, and how beautifully Fuss organizes things, and chatting up the Riders, especially our Sindan cousins who'd come around after the spring roundup. It was all lies. She made it clear enough when she left without telling us how much she despised us. She not only took two of our horses — she took Wolf's daughter."

"She sounds like a snake."

"Oh, she was a real snake, all right, as slithery as they come. It wasn't till she was gone that it hit me that she never said a thing about herself. It was always the flowery talk, she admired us sooo much, she was everybody's *friend*. And all of it cold-blooded, *fake*. Wolf says she was that way in private, too."

"Ugh, good riddance," Danet said.

Calamity's mouth turned down. "Except that she hurt Wolf. He never said, but I could tell. Well. Gone is gone. And we are much better off now." She blushed to the ears, grinning in a way that caused Danet to grin back, though she wondered if she would ever feel about a man the way Calamity felt about Wolf.

The rest of the evening passed without any dangerous subjects being raised, and everyone parted with mutual good will. Calamity and Fuss went off to their old bedrooms, both sorry that Danet would be leaving on the morrow.

Danet made a nest next to Arrow under the slanting roof in the den, Noddy apart from her for the first time, warm and comfortable in the Senelaec nursery.

The next morning, she woke to aching breasts. By now she knew that when she felt that way, Noddy had to be hungry, so she got up and slipped down the back stairs that led to the kitchen. When she walked through the door she bumped into someone turning at that moment, having set down an empty mug of coffee.

A flash of midnight blue — hands steadied her shoulders — and she looked up into light brown eyes with a tilt at the corners: the royal runner. She blinked at his soberly queued hair of ruddy blonde, aware of heat all over.

She stepped aside, muttered an inarticulate apology, and passed on toward the nursery, but his image lingered so strongly that she had to blink it away.

As she picked up Noddy, who had just begun to stir and fret, she was glad to be alone with no more company than sleeping children. Not even Embas the Miller back in Farendavan had caused so strong a reaction in her. And a royal runner, too. Everybody said they kept themselves to themselves.

And so, as the Olavayir cavalcade departed (after being given a magnificent breakfast), she found herself looking for a reason to ride forward for the first time. I'm not seventeen again, she thought, and urged Firefly, who was frisky and impatient to move, back to ride sedately next to Tdor Fath.

"Good people, the Senelaecs," Tdor said. "I hope they invite us to make a real visit when we return north."

"When we go back, why don't we just stay longer?" Danet asked.

Tdor Fath flattened her hand, palm down, "Did you know that in the past, kings used near ruin jarls they didn't like by paying honor visits and staying until the last of the stores were eaten?"

"No," Danet breathed. She thought of all the extra food and fodder required, and regretted her thoughtless comment. Had she really forgotten the months of labor getting ready for the wargame? "I liked Calamity and Fuss so much," she said apologetically.

"Then write to them," Tdor Fath advised. "If they invite us, then it means they've planned for it. So much better manners."

Danet glanced at Tesar, her only runner, and Tdor Fath, easily guessing the direction of her thoughts, said, "One thing I've heard about the royal city is, there are always messengers going back and forth. We can talk to the scribes, and find out who's going where when."

Danet began mentally writing a letter to Calamity as she watched that blonde royal runner up there, riding near the banner bearers. Tdor Fath gazed out at the Senelaec field workers late in harvesting, and working at a frantic pace to beat the dark bluegray storm piling up over the eastern mountains. She wondered how such generous, friendly people could be such terrible managers.

THIRTEEN

Danet and Arrow got a better sense of the Olavayir family's standing among non-allied jarls from their welcome at Gannan.

Everything was scrupulously correct, and cold as winter. The two couples kept their little sons with them—there was no offer of a nursery, and they would not have used it had there been. The Riders were quartered in the courtyard in their tents; they were told most apologetically that all Gannan's Riders were in residence, plus family members, and there was no extra bunk space.

When Arrow found out from his personal runner, he was furious. "They wouldn't dare do that to my father," he said to Jarend, Tdor, and Danet.

"No, he wouldn't, *hurr hurr,*" Jarend agreed, chuckling softly. "Not to Da."

"We'll leave at first light," Arrow said to his elder brother. "Give the order. *Before* first light. That won't raise one of your headaches, will it, getting up before dawn?"

"I'll be fine," Jarend said, as he always did. Even when he felt wretched.

"Good." Arrow smacked his fist into his palm. "That'll let 'em know what we think of their hospitality. And I'm going to let Evred know about this soon's we reach the royal city. What happens to us reflects on him."

Jarend heaved himself to his feet and went out to summon the runner on duty outside the guest chamber door, his head ducking from long habit as he stepped under the lintel.

So it was; the runners had everything packed halfway through the cold, miserable night. They and the Olavayir Riders took grim pleasure in waking everyone housed in the barracks over the stable as they clattered back and forth, making plenty of noise.

At dawn the two couples and their fretting offspring walked out to the court to take their leave.

Danet, who had entertained herself during the ride south from Senelaec by watching Camerend Montredavan-An from a distance, discovered that he had departed even earlier. He had left a map behind, with all landmarks etched in on what was a straight road southeast to the royal city.

"Let's get there as fast as we can," Arrow said, eyeing the gray sky.

The big, burly Jarl of Gannan, distrusting what tales might be carried south, made an effort at apology and a friendly farewell, but it rang as false as Arrow's thanks, and the Olavayirs rode out.

The jarl trod upstairs again, and shed his coat to climb into bed. He shook his wife awake in order to curse the Olavayirs, both branches, until she said in the subdued voice she'd learned early on in a rough marriage, "I hope there won't be trouble."

She braced herself. But the jarl was too tired, and too pleased with himself, to lose his temper. "Soul-sucking Olavayirs. Don't fret. They'll be too busy squabbling with each other to bother about us. You watch."

The outer perimeter patrol spotted them three days outside Choraed Dhelerei, and sent the fastest among them to report to Commander Mathren Olavayir, brother to the regent, and father to Lanrid and Sinna.

Mathren listened to the brief report—Olavayir eagle banner, at least a flight of honor guards—and hid his surprise and annoyance as he dismissed the scout. As the eagle-branch could not approach the royal city without invitation, that meant Kendred had invited them without informing his brother. It was obvious why Kendred had invited Evred's putative heir: to scare Evred into behaving.

Mathren walked into his private quarters in the tower at the far end of the state rooms overlooking the city. He gazed up at the map of Halia, with its stylized representations of towns, villages, harbors, and red borders of the current jarlates, with the painted-out old borders glimpsed as palimpsests. Once or twice the rare scribes permitted in his inner citadel, with their eyes trained to niceties, had offered to paint out those faint lines with a light brown to match the aging paper of the enormous map left from Evred-Harvaldar Montreivayir's day.

Mathren always thanked them while refusing the offer. It was important to see those old lines—perhaps painted at the orders of Inda-Harskialdna. Those lines represented places and times in the Marlovan past. Painting over them would not paint over desires, or plans, to regain what was lost.

Mathren lifted his hand to touch the gold-inked Olavayir leaping dolphin, contemplating the importance of symbol. In youth, he'd seen the effect of displays of skill and strength in the riveted gazes of his comrades. It wasn't just being strongest or fastest, it was the seeming effortlessness that stirred men to follow a leader. This was the essence of the *elgar*, a word that hadn't even existed until a hundred years ago, and now was apparently in all foreigners' mouths whenever anyone talked about Marlovans.

Here in the Marlovan kingdom, "elgar" was less known, unused except by the coastal Iascans. Marlovans used that same tone of veneration when they uttered "harskialdna," which had once merely meant war chief. But it had been charged with such legend that only one man, a century dead, could wear it.

Mathren had read everything he could lay hands to about Indevan Algaravayir. There wasn't all that much direct written evidence, and nothing whatsoever left by the man himself. But the stories, ah, so many! Including those handed down in Mathren's own family tree, descended from two powerful jarlates, Olavayir and Tyavayir.

It was well-known in the family that Dannor Tyavayir, Mathren's great-great grandmother, had caught Inda-Harskialdna's eye right before he was married, but unfortunately, Inda's betrothed, a Marthdavan, jealously drove Dannor out before she and Inda could make a match. Dannor had left behind a tapestry she had designed and made with her famous artistic talent, which Inda had loved in her place, so family legend insisted.

Legends could blur, or even lie, but one thing Mathren Olavayir understood was the crucial importance of symbol. The Olavayir dolphin, joined with the Algaravayir owl, would be as strong a force in people's minds as the prowess of the never-defeated commander on land and sea who had made his name famous.

One thing was clear: whatever Kendred wanted would fail, but that didn't mean his gesture was useless. If it was true that both sons of Inda Olavayir of the eagle clan were about to walk into Mathren's citadel, then it was time to act.

But first he must alert his son.

Mathren left his private office for the outer room. The waiting runners leaped to their feet and snapped three fingers to heart. His gaze went straight to the most trusted of these runners.

"Thad. Ready yourself for a fast ride. You'll have my sigil for horse changes." He beckoned Thad inside, and said, "No one else to see you."

Thad's round face tightened. He saluted again, wheeled about, and vanished down the stairs four at a time.

Mathren sat down to write the order that he knew Lanrid had been waiting for. When Thad had reported back with his gear ready, he was dispatched with the letter. Then the commander sent a runner to warn the steward of the new arrivals in order to prepare suitable chambers, after which he pulled his remaining runners into his office to issue a stream of orders.

He retired late, satisfied with the shift in plans, until another runner appeared, drenched and shivering, as the midnight watch change clanged.

He said, "This had better be an attack."

"N-no." The runner could scarcely speak, his teeth chattered so hard. "Your son. R-rode out. The day the jarl's s-sons s-started south. Lanrid rode north. To Idego."

"He *what?*"

The runner swayed with exhaustion, and forced out the words, "S-said to t-tell you. Running a bride raid. Like the olden days. Return with a queen."

Mathren dismissed the man, hiding his annoyance. If only he'd showed up a day earlier! Now he'd have to send another runner north on Thad's heels.

He sat down to compose another letter, this one strongly worded. Bride raid! Lanrid had better work the last of the young buck's stupidity out of himself now; when he returned, it must be to his place in his father's careful plans.

It was time for Lanrid to act like a royal heir.

A few days later, Mathren met Jarend and his party along the bend in the river at the north end of the city, with a full wing in their honor. Even in the rain that turned the river and the sky to gray, and made the banners sag like washed laundry, he and the honor guard looked heroic and impressive, which only served to irritate Arrow.

To him, Mathren looked exactly like an older, harder Lanrid. More impressed with Mathren's striking profile and military bearing, Danet also saw the resemblance, and consciously reminded herself that family likeness didn't always mean like dispositions.

Arrow and Jarend saluted Mathren, three fingers to chest, hastily copied by the rest of their cavalcade.

Then Arrow glimpsed his royal cousin Evred slumped on his horse, half-hidden behind Mathren's commanding presence. Danet stared at the future king. He was blond also, round of face, his expression sulky.

"There you are," Evred said to Jarend as the newcomers slapped flat hands to their chests: only kings and commanders directly under royal orders in chief were saluted fist to heart. Even his voice sounded sulky. He didn't quite look at them as he said, "Uncle Kendred is off inspecting the mines, so you can tell your da *we* came and met you, everything proper, so he can't complain. Let's get in out of this rotten weather before it turns to sleet."

Mathren held up a fist, but correctly turned his chiseled profile toward Evred, who flopped a hand. Mathren opened his fist, turned his palm toward the gate, and the company galloped the last distance, trumpeters on the ramparts blaring.

The riders swept up the largely empty streets of early evening, those few still out pressing back against buildings, then ducking as they were splashed by the horses' hooves.

They rode into an enormous stable yard even bigger than that at Nevree. A squadron of runners sorted everyone in an organized chaos. Out of the torchlit swarm of men going in all directions, a short runner in dull gray-blue emerged, and faced Tdor Fath and Danet.

"I'm Tlen," the young runner said, and tipped his pointed chin over his shoulder. "I'll show you to your quarters."

Danet was surprised to see no women at all as they entered through a round tower, trudged upstairs, shedding clots of mud at every step, then trekked along an endless frigid hall of bare sandstone.

They encountered guards at every stairway they passed, and each time, Tlen stopped and introduced them as the guards gave the women a close scan. Danet found that odd until she figured out that these guards were trained to learn faces.

They were given suites next to each other three quarters of the way down the long hall. Each suite had three rooms, with smaller rooms off them. The walls were so thick that the single window could easily be sat in, if one didn't mind rough stone.

Danet found the windows odd. From the stonework, it seemed that the windows at least in this set of rooms had once been much wider, but had been narrowed. Instead of shutters and winter-stuffing to keep the cold out, there was wavery spun glass fitted into wooden frames that could be left open to hang against chains at the top. This was the same sort of glass, spun on a plate, that the Jarlan of Olavayir had been ordering servants to place in upper story windows against the coming winter, when Danet and Tdor Fath were leaving Nevree. She noted links for shutters that could be put up outside the windows. For defense, of course; she hoped she would not be in this castle long enough to find out if she was right.

She and Tdor Fath went exploring, finding doors in every wall, sometimes two. One of the small chambers gave access to both suites, a third narrower door opening into a dark, cobwebby space above a narrow stair.

"This has to be a servants passage," Tdor Fath said. "They mustn't use it anymore."

"I wonder what's at the other end." Danet peered into the inky gloom.

"I don't want to know." Tdor shuddered at the thought of pushing into all those spiderwebs. "We'll block this door with a trunk so Rabbit can't fall down those stairs, and make this room a nursery as we both can get to it. I hope Tesar comes soon with an ensorcelled bucket," she added, sniffing. "I think they both need diaper changes."

Danet nodded, and turned to inspect the outer chamber. The main rooms were furnished with a trunk, a mattress stuffed with old quilting, a table, and cushions that looked old and worn, though they were in good repair.

Their runners showed up carrying the saddlebags, and Tesar lugged in the freshly-filled wooden bucket. Its edges glimmered with the magic purifying spell.

The runners began to unpack as Tdor Fath and Danet changed the babes, plunking their sodden diapers into the bucket amid the greenish flash of magic as the waste vanished. They wrung out the now-clean cloths and spread them in the deep window embrasures beside the servants' stair, as there was no drying rack.

"There has to be a laundry chamber somewhere in this place," Tdor Fath said, her arms dropping.

"Where are all the women?" Danet looked around, as if a female might be stashed behind the low table, the floor mats, or the trunks. "I know the gunvaer died with the king. Doesn't the regent or Commander Mathren have a wife?"

"The regent never married. Commander Mathren's wife died, too," Tdor Fath said. "It wasn't too long after Sinna was born. She and her first runner gave their lives stopping the assassins coming back for Evred. None of us ever met her, of course—she came from the south—Marthdavan, I think. So. We're alone, except for the grand gunvaer in her tower. Whichever one that might be."

Since the men had been taken off somewhere, the two women readied for bed as soon as the unhappy children fell into exhausted sleep: young parents learned to sleep when the babes did. Danet was hungry, but she suspected that it would take half a watch for Tesar to find the kitchens, and then who knew if anything would even be available.

Danet woke early, hearing Noddy's hungry cry. Once he was fed and settled, she peered out the wavery glass in the slit window at the blue light of dawn, then looked back at the bed, where Arrow now lay sprawled over her half. She had not even heard him come in.

She decided to take some clothes, find the baths, and go exploring. But once she got outside the room, she gazed in either direction and thought, which way?

Pick one.

She remembered that the door to their suite had been on the right, which meant they'd come from *that* direction. She turned the other way and started off, counting doors as she went, so that she would be able to find her way back. She wondered who was behind all these other doors in both directions, if there was no royal family, and no Convocation, so presumably no royal guests besides them.

Now that it was morning after a good rest, she noticed details: suite doors between landings on either side of the hall, and various sounds and smells on the cold, still air. That stairway had to lead to the kitchens, and the farthest one smelled slightly dank, like water over stone. Baths? She ran down the stairs, whirled around at the landing toward the next set of stairs leading below ground level—and bounced chest to chest off a tall man.

Brown eyes. Ruddy light hair. It was the royal runner, the one who'd left them at Gannan Castle. The flare of attraction made her nerves tingle, and she stumbled back, aware of her entire face on fire. "You caught up with us—

you really are fast! Or did you ride ahead?" Realizing she was babbling, she blushed even more. "I, uh, was trying to find the baths."

"You're in the right place," Camerend said, opening a hand toward the stairs. "Bottom of these stairs."

"Kitchens that way?" She pointed.

"Correct," he said in a slow, pleasant voice. "To your left are the royal suites. Down that way, the garrison. Over the stable, from the tower south, is scribes and heralds. The third floor above us in the center here is the royal runner wing, off limits by royal decree." He pointed in the direction of each place he named.

"Which tower holds the grand gunvaer?"

He swung his arm in the opposite direction, and as she turned, her gaze slid over his sleeve straining against the curve of his upper arm, and she wondered if the royal runners learned weapons, too.

Of course they would. How else would they defend themselves while always traveling? She twitched her gaze from him to his pointing finger, then to the glint of gold on one of the curled fingers: a marriage ring. That usually meant an oath-binding and some type of exclusivity.

She croaked a word of thanks, and hustled past him down the stairs, toward the sound of female voices. It was a relief to discover that there were indeed women in the castle. They seemed to be scribe, stable, and weaver staff, judging by the bits of conversation she heard. Maybe the female runners bathed at a different time.

She soon sat in hot water, her fist pressed against her ribs as she considered the encounter with the royal runner. She had never even talked to the man before, and here she was feeling as unsettled as if she were sixteen again. *The head and the heart will take their own part*, so the old saying went. But he wore a ring, which put him on the far side of an oath.

She would use another stairway from now on, even if it took a little longer to reach the baths. In this gigantic castle, it ought to be easy to avoid him for the rest of the day, until that teenagerish heat died off.

Camerend Montredavan-An to Isa Eris, at Darchelde

My beloved: First, I hope you, Frin, and our little son are well.

In accordance with your desires, I only write with good news. On my way to the royal city, I passed through Gannan, and as one of my number was on her way from the west, I was able to turn the Olavayirs over to her and ride into Zheirban so that I could visit Frin's family, to see if they had any messages to carry. As you see, I folded this letter around their missive.

Another piece of good news, I hope: the Olavayirs. I know your ambivalence about that family, which I share, but I rode with the jarl's sons and their wives, and found them cheerful and determined upon maintaining the kingdom's peace.

Permit me to close by saying how much I miss you, give my respects to Frin, and I hope that we shall all soon be reunited.

FOURTEEN

Danet got back to the guest suite to find that Arrow's second runner had located the kitchens. After consultation with Tesar, he brought up coffee and rye biscuits with shirred eggs, and a pot of some purple compote, enough for two.

Arrow was awake, red-eyed and frowzy, tangled hair the color and texture of straw hanging down to his elbows. "There you are! Evred kept us up late drinking after Mathren left us. Damn, can he whine!"

"Mathren?"

"Evred. The best of it was, you know he and Lanrid grew up together...no." Arrow rubbed his eyes and winced. "You didn't know, did you? I keep forgetting you haven't lived with us forever. Ma said it would be like that. Anyway, Lanrid was born here. Lived here with the prince until he was ten or so. He was a horse apple about it for years after he came to us. *The prince and I, Me and the royal heir.* We dog-piled him once, and wouldn't let him up until he promised not to mention Evred in any form for a whole month. Then we scragged him again when he did it anyway."

"Did it stick?"

"Sort of, but he ambushed every one of us first. And the war was on. It would have been on anyway, because he can't breathe without strutting."

Danet had no objection to this judgment.

Arrow grinned sourly. "So anyhow, last night. Once we were alone, Evred told me right out that he loathes Lanrid. In spite of all Lanrid's fart noise how Evred followed him around, and tried to copy him, he said Lanrid was mean as a poison-snake and a good day was one he avoided him altogether."

He gave a crack of laughter, then slapped his hand over his mouth. Both parents held their breath as they glanced toward the nursery, but when no little wail issued forth, he went on in a lower voice, "When Lanrid got sent to us in Nevree, it was the happiest day of Evred's life to see his back, even though it was my worst day."

He yawned fiercely. "The rest was whine, whine, whine, he wants to be king now, he doesn't see why he has to wait a whole year and a half, he wants Hard Ride Arvandais—she's the best rider in all Idego and the most beautiful and who should marry her but a king, only he's not king yet, and *whyyyyyyy*...." Arrow sighed. "How's Noddy?"

"Sleeping," Danet said. "I think he'll be glad to be in one place. But Rabbit is miserable. He hates everything."

"There are some castle children," Arrow said, surprising her. "Evred said the guards' brats are always running wild garrison-side, and the rest out beyond the chicken yard and the kitchen garden. My brother is getting a tour of the garrison, so I'll see if I can scout some out before Evred wakes up, if you're starting on Ma's orders about figuring out the kingdom tallies. Maybe Rabbit will be happier with someone to play with, until old Nunka can catch up with us."

"Then I'll get to work," she said.

As the morning watch bell reverberated through the stone walls, Danet followed the royal runner's directions and found Grand Gunvaer Hesar's tower.

While she toiled her way up the stairs, the old gunvaer waited, nearly blind, hoping that one or another of the newcomers would arrive. She had survived this long by learning patience, and practicing defensive obliviousness.

When her servant announced Danet, she curbed her delight, and waited. It would not do to trust too soon. She had made that mistake twice, and both times people had died.

Danet cautiously entered the first fine room she had seen so far in the castle: a woven rug of blue and gold on the floor, two tapestries covering bare stone walls, carved wingback chairs made comfortable with thick cushions. By the fire sat one of these chairs, a tiny, withered old woman almost lost in it. Her milky gaze was diffuse, and Danet quickly looked away as the servant announced her.

"You arrived yesterday, child?"

"Last night, Hesar-Gunvaer."

"I commend your promptitude," the cracked, thin voice murmured.

Not knowing what else to say, Danet got right to business, quoting all that Ranor-Jarlan had ordered.

"Good girl," Hesar said slowly. "She is very right. Do not go to Mathren, or Kendred, or even Evred—he knows nothing whatsoever of the running of the castle or the country. What you must do is start at the kitchens. Tell them who you are, and that you wish to learn from the supply steward or his scribe. If they like you, they'll introduce you to the royal scribes. I cannot guarantee anything beyond that point, but it's always good to start low and work your way upward. No one pays much heed to the kitchens, as long as everyone gets fed."

The gunvaer shifted to inquiring about various Olavayir relatives, whom she invariably referred to as "little So-and-so" or "Young Such-and-such," even if they were ancient at fifty or even sixty. Danet replied with what she knew, until she saw the old woman's eyes close. She got up and walked noiselessly out.

By the time she had trod down the long spiral staircase, she had planned her approach. Remembering how the kitchen staff at Nevree had closed ranks against her when she'd exposed the thief, she expected a long siege. When she entered, she explained who she was, adding, "At Nevree it's my job to oversee kitchen and supply tallies. I'd like to learn how you do it here, and help if I may."

All heads swung toward a tall, grizzled, gaunt man who uncrossed his arms slowly. "I'm Amreth Tam, kitchen steward," he said. "One of my assistants will give you a tour, and explain how we do things."

Danet touched forefinger to heart in salute, and the steward unbent a degree more. By the end of the day, Danet was not only permitted into the kitchen archive, she had learned two important things: one, this establishment was exponentially larger than that at Nevree, and two, however it had been in the gunvaer's day, the royal castle staff was not at all united now.

"Here it all is," the steward said, a hand sweeping dismissively at the bound books in the stuffy little room. These books had been stored floor to ceiling in tightly packed rows against three walls, but the fourth wall was still half bare, books and papers stacked against the wall untidily. Her fingers itched to organize it.

"You saw the slate outside, right?"

She nodded, having passed by a huge slate fitted on one wall, with a basket of chalk bits beside it. Requisitions had been scrawled in many hands along this slate, some crossed off.

Tam said, "On top of everything else I have to oversee, it's I who has to make the time to transfer the finished requisitions to the paper, along with our own, and when the treasury scribe has marked it off, onto the list it goes, from which the treasury scribes take note, after which the list joins the others in that closet." Tam waved his hand in a circle, fingers wiggling as though shaking off something noisome from his hand.

"By rights a scribe ought to be copying the slate into our records, but oh no, the scribes are too busy with mighty affairs upstairs to trouble themselves with the lowly kitchens, which incidentally feed every mouth in the castle," he said heavily. "Including their flapping yaps. But I've kept my complaints in my own domain. That's the way to live longer."

Tam drew a deep breath, and, having enjoyed the satisfaction of unloading his very justified ire into fresh ears, he eased his tone. "At least I can say that, so far, anyway, there haven't been any but the usual complaints of slowness if each area deals with the requisitions they fulfill, and chalk them off. Of course, I'm the one stuck with jotting down the list at the end of each day, for the paymasters will not heed anything but a list. So if you want to take on organizing it, well, you'd be saving me extra trouble that never ought to have landed on my shoulders."

"I'd be happy to get it all into order," she said, sincerity ringing in her voice, and Tam smiled for the first time as he opened his hand toward the mess on the floor. He and his assistant left, both relieved to be rid of a duty that wasn't theirs in the first place. If this scrawny Olavayir wanted the drudgery, she was welcome to it.

At the end of a day's work, she ran up to the grand gunvaer's chamber to report her success, but the servant said that she was asleep, and not to be disturbed. Danet said she would return, and ran down to the guest suites in the middle of that long, lonely hallway to check on Noddy.

She found Arrow there, changing into his House robe, Rabbit howling in the background. Arrow tipped his head backward. "The castle brats are too old, and too wild." And when Danet sighed with disappointment, he went on, "Evred is waiting for us, and he likes us to dress for Restday. We're supposed to eat supper with him."

Danet finished feeding Noddy and turned him over to a sulky Tesar, who hated child care, then shook out her fine royal blue robe with its modest gold-silk trim. Her first glimpse of Evred had not impressed her, but then nobody liked riding in cold rain.

Her interest in the next king lasted no further than the eating of her first rye biscuit. "I notice *Uncle Kendred* isn't back yet," Evred began, his tone corrosive on "Uncle Kendred." "What do you wager he never went to the mines at all, but is holed up at Silver Shield?" His voice rose and his fingers flexed, flexed, flexed as Arrow gazed fixedly at Evred's gnawed nails.

Evred seemed to become aware of Arrow's gaze and whipped his hands behind his back as his voice dropped to an excruciatingly false, joking note. "Arrow, remind me not to take you there. It's his favorite. The Captain's Drum is better anyway, much more fun, and they don't mind a scrap now and then, you just pay for the damage. The girls are more fun, too. Unless you like boys?"

"Not for mattress-dancing," Arrow said. "Danet does."

Evred didn't even glance Danet's way. She caught Tdor Fath's gaze, and saw the faint line tightening her brow, then Danet noticed Jarend staring straight ahead, his jaw muscles twitching as his jaw locked. Another of his headaches? Who could blame him?

"...Uncle Kendred might have found a new one and he's tucked up tight with a couple of his favorites." There was that hand-flexing again. "And who would stop him? They all call me Evred-Sierlaef, but it means *nothing*, not until I'm crowned. *He's* really the king. He even lives in the king's chambers."

"Really?" Arrow asked. "Why don't you ask for those, at least?"

"Not until I'm really king! And I shouldn't have to *ask*. Everyone asks *him, he* gives the orders, and when we ride in and out, *he* gets the king's fanfare, short one chord. *Of course* he's in no hurry to let me be crowned, even though he pretends to be the humble regent...." And on and on he talked, so starved for congenial company — and so desperate for a validation that his auditors of course could not give.

Not that Evred was aware of that drive, except subliminally. His awareness extended only to a gnawing restlessness, and his growing desire for freedom.

That would come. Right now...he frowned at the newcomers. Danet was nothing to look at. Perfectly suitable for Arrow, but a king deserved a wife like Hard Ride Hadand, whose prowess everybody talked about. When Evred turned nineteen, he'd demanded that the royal runner going up the Pass to deliver messages carry a request for a drawing of Hard Ride Hadand. The Jarlan of Arvandais had sent him a sketch of her daughter galloping a horse. She rode like a centaur, and he'd been dreaming about her riding him ever since.

She'd be the perfect gunvaer, Evred thought, despising these plain-faced, boring wives of his beaver-toothed, boring cousins.

As the wearying evening drew on, Tdor Fath watched Jarend, whose throbbing head steadily worsened the more he clenched his jaw against it, and Danet fought yawn after yawn as she mentally worked out what to say in her letter to Calamity, knowing that Fuss would probably be reading it, too.

Once they were finally dismissed, Danet said to Arrow as they walked from Evred's tower suite down the long, empty hall to their rooms, "I'm not going again. He obviously doesn't think I exist when I'm right in front of him."

Arrow was annoyed because that loaded the burden of Evred's company onto him, but they both had their orders, and hers had nothing to do with Evred. "All right," he said.

The second day, Danet started on her letter over breakfast, fed Noddy, and watched him struggling to grasp things and work his mouth into shaping little sounds. She found him entrancing, but when he was ready for sleep, she was more than ready to run downstairs and tackle the kitchen records.

She could point to the exact time the scribes had abandoned those records and grudging kitchen staff had taken over. It wasn't just the change in hand from neat scribal print to a jagged, but readable, scrawl, it was the lack of organization.

At first the kitchen staff had gathered their daily sheets into the stiffened-canvas book covers without bothering to bind them. They'd stacked these on the floor rather than inscribing the range of dates on the spine and getting a stool to place them up on that fourth wall. After a time they'd apparently run out of book covers, the responsibility for making which was strictly confined to the scribe guild, and the closely written pages were stacked ever more sloppily on the floor in piles. She began organizing and tidying, occasionally stopping to read.

Presently she got up to shake her legs and swing her arms, and looked around in wonder. How could people consider tallies boring? Here was the record of daily life in the royal palace. She eyed the tightly packed books on the three walls, and held her lamp up to scan the beautiful scribal script along the spine: yes, right here in the upper part of the third wall were the records from when Inda Algaravayir and Tdor Marthdavan lived in this very castle, under the reign of the great Hadand-Deheldegarthe. In those books were the records of what they ate, and somewhere in another archive would be records of what they wore.

She thrilled to be so close to greatness, and longed to pull those books down. But no: first she must make certain that everything was in order in the contemporary tallies. Then she could read everything from the beginning.

"How are you doing?" Arrow asked at the end of their second week, on coming in so late that dawn was mere hours off.

Nobody could blame him, though the jarl and jarlan both had despised late habits, which to them were slovenly behavior. But Evred retired late and slept late, so Arrow and Jarend had to stay up late, then force themselves up at dawn. Jarend, as legal heir, was permitted to report to the Royal Rider courtyard for drill, while Arrow (denied access to the elite Royal Riders) had to hike clear to the opposite side of the castle complex to where their eagle-branch honor guard was housed, for their own morning drill.

Arrow minded the late nights less than he might have, since Rabbit screamed himself to sleep almost every night and was fractious any day he couldn't go outside and run himself tired. Rabbit hated this unfamiliar place, and hated unfamiliar people. He was much like his father that way, as Jarend had always hated any deviation from routine.

There was nothing Arrow could do about either.

Danet, in her turn, hated those late watches. She also hated hearing Rabbit's disconsolate sobbing as much as his shrill, breathless shrieks. She tried to help, but Rabbit only wanted his *Nunka, Nunka,* and—denied the nursery minder still traveling with the carts—he would only permit his mother and her first runner near him. That left the two to cope, as Tdor's second runner had departed with Tdor's and Danet's letters.

As usual Arrow smelled of stale drink, but at least he wasn't crapulous, as he'd been the mornings after the two nights he'd stayed away all night.

So when he asked *How are you doing*, she answered, "Everything is habits."

"Habits?" He yawned hugely. "What do you mean by that?"

"Even if they don't make sense to someone else. When you're new, you do what everyone else does, or you get them mad at you. I don't have to figure out how the mess down there got to be habit, though I'd like to know. I just have to sort the results, the records."

"Mmm?" he muttered, not really listening, but the assurance in her voice was soothing.

"What the royal family eats is a separate category from what the garrison eats, which is separate from the guilds who live in the castle, as opposed to the ones in the city. Each person has a line under their category. I've finished putting the last twenty years in order, and the way the royal family lines changed so abruptly...it does, when the person dies. But that's not what I meant to say. There's something odd, I think...." She glanced down, and saw his eyelids drifting shut.

He blinked rapidly, his voice husky as he struggled against sleep. "Something odd how? Military? Relating to the garrisons?"

"No. Maybe." Doubt assailed her—she might be imagining what wasn't there, just because she'd been successful in Nevree. "I need to start from the beginning, once I get the recent years in some kind of order. Then I need to compare supply lines with payment lines...."

He was already bored. His mind was entirely taken up with how thoroughly his own efforts at following his father's orders had been blocked. "At least you got something done." He sighed impatiently.

"Aren't you spending time with Evred?"

"Yes. Every day. For what that will get me." He sighed again. "Every time I try to ask the garrison guard captains a single question—and I can't get anywhere near Mathren's captains even to ask—they send me to Mathren, who tells me I'm so much more valuable influencing Evred. Only there's no influencing Evred," he finished with loathing.

"Why not?"

"Because he's a walking horse turd." Outrage burned through Arrow from the previous night, temporarily banishing exhaustion. He rose on an elbow. "He doesn't just drink, he does it with intent."

"What does that mean?"

"Evred keeps pushing bristic and whisky on Jarend, while telling him how well he holds it. Twice Jarend drank until he fell over."

Danet waited, knowing better than to ask why they didn't just quit. She sensed that same sort of male competition that had existed with Lanrid, which neither party seemed to be able to resist, no matter how much they disliked one another.

"Last night Jarend was late. You know his headaches. Maybe one or two a year at home, but he's having them a lot here. He was late, like I said, and Evred and I were alone, and he asks if I want to make a wager. I said what. *He* said, wager on how many drinks before Jarend topples. He thinks it's *funny*. He thinks Jarend is *stupid*. He went on and on about how Jarend sits there like a rock, or a big tree, drinks and drinks, then suddenly falls sideways. I wanted to rip his throat out."

"Does Tdor Fath know what's happening?"

"No—I don't know. What can she do?"

"See to it that Jarend is only waited on by his first runner, who can put water, or listerblossom, in those cups."

"Good idea. I should have thought of that! Though she's got her hands full with Rabbit." Arrow yawned. "I wish Kendred would hurry up and get back. It can't be as bad when he's here."

"I wish our carts would get here. Maybe Rabbit will be better with his own toys, and the nursery child-minder and his staff."

"Old Nunka is better than magic. You know what?" Arrow's voice drifted into a yawn, then he muttered, "Evred was rambling on about how the night before Kendred left, they had a big argument about his coronation. Worst one yet. Maybe Kendred is glad to just get away, and leave us stuck with Evred...." Two more yawns, as his voice softened in the huskiness of impending slumber. "I'd make Evred wait till he's thirty to be crowned. He sounds like a scrub of twelve. Why didn't they teach him anything...?"

Danet waited for Arrow to say more, but he was done. A deep breath made that clear. So she punched the pillow, which contained real down instead of old armor stuffing, turned on her side, and closed her eyes. At least, she thought drowsily, Evred considered her too boring to require her to be part of his daily audience.

The next morning, she pulled down the very first book of records in the kitchen cubby, which was thick with dust, only to discover that the earliest records were written in Iascan, which she couldn't read. So she checked the books one by one until she reached the years of Tlennen Montreivayir, father of the famous Evred who'd had Inda Algaravayir as Harskialdna. The change to Marlovan happened abruptly when Tlennen-Sieraec, which was what kings not at war called themselves in those days, became Tlennen-Harvaldar after the Battle of Ghael Hills. His brother Anderle, the first Harskialdna, had overseen all tallies, and had apparently issued an order that all records were henceforth to be kept in Marlovan.

No reason *why*, at least at this end of the castle. For that, of course, Danet would have to seek the royal archives. But she intended to breach that citadel armed with Tam's recommendation once she finished her task.

She smothered her curiosity and sat down to begin reading those first Marloven records, as rain beat intermittently against the windows over the following stretch of days.

FIFTEEN

The historical record, largely refashioned by non-Olavayir hands, has insisted that Indevan-Jarl Olavayir did too little too late, but the evidence is there, if one knows where to find it, that he spent his entire adult life tirelessly riding back and forth across the northern reaches of the kingdom below the mountains in a losing effort to maintain the three failing garrisons. Lindeth and Larkadhe, half a day's journey from one another, were only mildly arduous to reach from Nevree, but the worst was The Nob. That was a rough journey, invariably facing at least one attack from the mountain people, and at the Nob end he had to face stolid resentment and a long list of complaints and demands that cost money. His family's money, as somehow nothing from the royal city coffers ever made it that far.

Once every five years he dutifully traveled up through the Pass to the northern shore to inspect the three garrisons along the coast, where he was surrounded by the Jarl of Arvandais's honor guards, who accompanied him everywhere, providing every comfort he could possibly desire, feasted and flattered him at every resting place, and entertained him with exhibitions of trick riding and martial dances. His opinion was sought on everything from trade to tapestries, and everybody smiled until he was gone again.

Each time, the Jarl of Olavayir labored back down the long Pass convinced of the north shore's loyalty, and this recent visit was no different. Whatever problems they seemed to be having with the royal city were after all not his affair, as that arrogant turd Mathren was always the first to insinuate.

As for the hot-blooded boys who all sought to marry with the Arvandais family through the legendary Hard Ride Hadand, the jarl believed that no harm could come of Lanrid's hankering: Once the Arvandais clan chose someone (he believed that the jarl, if not the girl herself, had an eye on Evred and a crown), eventually Lanrid would grow out of his obsession.

A few days into the twelfth month of 4059, he had reached Larkadhe after an exceptionally grueling journey down the long path from the Nob, following a frustratingly evasive confrontation with the harbormaster up there, a local. He'd had difficulty catching his breath all day, blaming a series of hard rains on the road; he also blamed the shortsighted fools there, who acted like petty kings, and treated the people guarding them as nuisances. Except when the occasional pirate turned up.

In short, he thought as he wheezed his way into the courtyard, with a ball of ache deep in his chest that he assumed was a developing cold, everywhere he looked he found boneheads.

The garrison commander's head steward took one look at his face and had a runner take the jarl straight up to the best guest chamber, which had been readied as soon as his outriders reached Larkadhe's distinctive castle with its single tall, white-stone tower.

He wheezed his way up the stairs and sank gratefully onto his mat, then reached obediently for the small sheaf of dispatches waiting for him.

He opened the first, and read that Lanrid Olavayir, in full company, had passed two weeks before, going up the Pass.

The Jarl threw the scrap of paper down, cursing vehemently. He knew what was going on. Mathren's numbskull son was skylarking northwards, typically thinking with his prick, in order to impress that Arvandais girl.

In a fit of frustrated temper, he shoved the other dispatches onto the floor and reached for pen and paper. He'd send a blistering letter up the Pass after the young scoundrel, but as he reached, his left hand tingled, and sharp pain passed up his arm. As he looked for whatever had spiked the pain, his breath stuttered queerly before numbness folded him into its dark embrace.

When his runner appeared with a tray of food and hot coffee, he found the jarl lying lifeless, and the tray crashed to the floor.

Chief of the royal runners, Camerend Montredavan-An, wrote in coded Old Sartoran to his mother Shendan in Darchelde:

Mnar and I have both returned from touring the mines, using the pretext of delivering messages. Because of the risk of our effects being searched we left our notecases with the other instructors, as usual. The short report is, Kendred Olavayir has not been seen for days. I've sent our best scouts to track his movements.

But right now I believe we have another more pressing problem. On my return I retrieved my notecase from Fannor to find not only your letter, but also two from Vanda — arrived two days ago!

There is no mending the two day delay. I will give you an hour to read them, while I attend to things here to cover my absence.

He enclosed the following two letters from Vandareth Askan, boyhood friend and fellow royal runner, who had volunteered to serve the jarl family north of the Pass and to observe events there:

Yes, Cama, your faithful Vanda is alive. Or should it be, too bad, your faithful Vanda is alive? I'll leave you to decide.

That, I fear, will be the extent of my attempt at humor. I apologize for the lack of communication since you were here in spring. Hal Arvandais and I ended up on shipboard for most of the intervening time, and I didn't have this notecase on me, as part of our guise was being taken by privateers in order to investigate the harbors, and there is no privacy on shipboard—nowhere to hide it.

That report will have to wait. We sailed into Andahi Harbor today to discover that Hastrid-Jarl Arvandais is dead, assassinated at Middle Harbor at the end of summer. Two captains died defending him, Barend Veth and Hastrid Farendavan. You might very well have received a runner with that news by now.

Now to what you don't know. That Starand-Jarlan of Arvandais is gone, and what disturbs Hal is that no one knows where, or even if she's alive.

What we do know is that "Hard Ride" Hadand is claiming the jarlate over Hal. As soon as the memorial for her father was over, she began pulling all the Riders together for some big wargame. Or maybe two wargames. No one knew for certain, and Cama, we came back to a lot of talk in corners and courts, breaking up quick. But three times I caught the word "independence." And once a name, <u>Lorgi</u> Idego, Lorgi being, as I'm sure you're aware, Idegan for "old." You will see the irony here, as there is no resemblance anywhere here to old Idayago, except in the language, which is filled with Marlovan idiom.

This is the serious part: right before the watch change, Ndiran Arvandais sought out Hal, distressed and angry. She confessed to Hal that she had been sent by the jarl to the Senelaecs for a purpose, exactly as you had surmised. That purpose—she thought—was to obtain an exact count of the Eastern Alliance's horses, pending a demand for a number of same on behalf of Idego in return for taxes, but she's afraid that Hadand and her father had some other goal in mind.

"Hard Ride and her father were fighting all summer," she told me. "I can't say for sure what about, but now he's dead, and she is more crazed than ever to act now, so that his plans don't come to nothing. Hal, whatever <u>she</u> says, <u>you're</u> the jarl now," Ndiran declared, and insisted we accompany her to Hadand's room, where we saw a big map of Halia, with Ndiran's hand noting all the best horse studs, and their defenses. "If she really rides down the Pass to reclaim Cama

One-Eye's territory, as the jarl always intended, I'll be blamed," Ndiran declared, weeping.

Camerend looked up, startled, then read the passage again. The Arvandais family had made no secret of their desire — the entire region's desire — to separate from the south, but Camerend would stake his life on the fact that the jarlan, at least, had meant it to be accomplished over time, maybe even a couple of generations, beginning with her daughter marrying Evred, once he was crowned. After which Hard Ride Hadand could work on bringing northern concerns to the Convocation of Jarls, once that was reestablished.

He pulled the letter up to read the little bit remaining:

Hal asked me to discover if I can where this big wargame is that Hard Ride rode off to. Who she took and what type of strategy she wants to test should tell us a lot. I will leave as soon as I send this.

Send this on to Shendan after you read it, will you? I don't have time to write to her — Hal has been in here twice since I first put pen to paper.

The second letter, scrawled on a torn bit of paper:

Cama, Hadand Arvandais is on the march down the Pass not to a game, but to initiate her invasion of Olavayir by attacking one of the Olavayir boys, who is apparently coming up from the south side. Hal just came to me with a letter sent by runner from his sister. She claims that this is going to be the first strike for independence, and she says join her or exile. And she signed it Gunvaer-Hadand Arvandais of Lorgi Idego.

We're riding out to catch up as soon as I send this, Hal determined to talk her out of it, or die in the attempt.

Vanda

Camerend shut his eyes, trying to grasp how utterly they had failed to predict this, much less act to circumvent it. And he probably should have seen it. He remembered the first time he met Hadand — it was his very first ride north as a royal runner.

He'd arrived to witness her riding and shooting at targets, attaining shots that would have been respectable for an adult. Then she'd leaped off her horse and sparred with a gangling boy a hand taller than she — and put him down hard.

He'd complimented her on her win when they were introduced in the mess hall, as the jarl looked benignly on. She'd said, "I'm going to be a fighting queen, like the Hadand I was named for."

He remembered saying, "She certainly defended the throne from the Traitor Yvanavayir, but she never led an army to war."

Hadand had curled her upper lip, clearly despising him as the pedant he realized now he'd sounded like, and that was the last conversation they'd ever had. Though he'd often seen her at a distance on subsequent rides, a comet leading a long trail of followers, whatever she did.

He also remembered that Vanda had reported two or three years ago overhearing someone saying the Arvandaises were putting feelers out to one of the other dolphin-clan sons, but there had been no proof — and the rumor had died.

As he laid the letter down, he wondered if that had been a clue that everyone had not seen for what it was; he'd assumed Hadand herself was behind the rumor, querying about pretty Lanrid Olavayir, as no one was ever going to call Evred pretty, or even pleasant-looking.

Even with the aid of instant transfer of letters — and if they were desperate enough, magic transfer of themselves — there was no guarantee they could know everything going on across the kingdom. Vanda, sent to Arvandais to listen and to influence toward peace with his considerable wit and charm, had been completely blindsided as well.

No use in self-questioning now. They had blundered, and now he had better do what he could to repair the situation.

That meant going himself.

There was no one else to send; only three other royal runners had the magical knowledge to transfer. One had been sent south; his co-chief of the royal runner training, Mnar Milnari, was somewhere on the road; and the third was overseeing all the royal runner training, which could not be interrupted without notice....

Camerend walked out of the instructors' private room when he was certain he presented a calm front. He assigned his older students a research project, and took care of a few other pressing duties as he waited for the watch bell. At the last he drew on a heavy cloak against the bitter winds of the Pass.

When the bell rang, and he still had not received an answer from his mother, he closed his eyes, breathing deeply as he concentrated on Vanda. Using another person as a Destination was always dangerous, but they'd trained for such eventualities.

He transferred.

Magic transfer never was easy. The distance between the royal city and wherever Vanda was wrenched him badly, bone and muscle. He staggered, black spots swimming before his eyes, his teeth aching.

Breathe in, breathe out...the reaction vanished, never rapidly enough, and he became aware of Vanda's hands on his shoulders to steady him.

"I hoped you'd come." Vandareth wiped back sweaty pale hair. He'd cut it short, to his shoulders, Idegan style. Instead of the dark blue robe of the royal runners, he wore an Idegan short jacket and leggings. His dirty face was bruising down one side, and the clothes had the imprint of dirt, as if Vanda had recently fallen.

"Who did it? You know?" It took all Camerend's strength to cough out those few words.

"Assassinated the jarl, you mean?" Vanda asked. And on Camerend's lift of a palm, "No one knows. But he had enemies, that's for certain—though most everyone up here wants independence from the south, they do not agree about how to get it. The jarlan led the faction to gain it legally, over time."

Camerend knew that much. She'd spoken often about the hopes she'd placed in her bright, beautiful daughter. He'd assumed the entire family had agreed.

"Hal's been a lot more honest since we arrived to the news about his father. And we still don't know if his mother is alive," Vanda added. "You always knew the jarl was hardest on Hadand, right? We didn't know how much. Hal said one reason his mother traveled as much as she did was because she couldn't stand seeing him beat Hadand bloody—and then set her at the head of the table to practice being a queen. She loved presiding," Vanda added. "Even at the cost of the beatings. I saw it. Everyone saw it. She truly believed she had to be the best of the best. But nobody understood the real plan, how Hadand was going to be a queen down south, and the jarl would be king up here. But Hadand had begun to believe that to truly be as great as the Hadand she was named for, *she* must rule both north and south."

"That's what she and her father were fighting about?" Camerend asked.

"Yes—so says Ndiran. He wanted to attack now, while there is no king, she said that if anyone is to attack, it's to be her—but this is all hearsay," Vandareth added impatiently. "Irrelevant. We just caught up with her. She wouldn't even listen to Hal when he tried to get her to go back to the old plan. Or to me—as soon as I spoke she sicced three of her runners on me, holding me down while she held a knife at my neck. She threatened to kill me if Hal didn't acknowledge her as queen of the new kingdom of Lorgi Idego."

He yanked aside his hair, revealing an angry red line at his neck, blood crusted down into Vanda's collar. "The bloodlust is on them, Cama. Hal said yes, to save my life, but she didn't believe him, and had her personal runners tie Hal up and gag him. They know me as a runner, so they let me go. I offered to water the animals after our long ride, and brought them here to think out what to do."

Vandareth indicated the horses on a rope behind him, nibbling grass and and sniffing the wind above a chuckling stream. Great walls of sheer rock rose on either side of the deep canyon beyond the scree they stood alongside. Camerend knew those sheer walls had to be Andahi Pass: he recognized the distinctive slant of the layers of rock, and estimated their position was a few days above Andahi.

Camerend grabbed Vandareth by the shoulders. "Tell me exactly what's going on."

Vanda winced, and Cama freed him. "Sorry."

"No matter. I feel the same." With trembling fingers, Vanda lightly fingered the eye that had swollen shut in the moments they'd been standing there. "Lanrid Olavayir is coming up the pass with a couple of ridings. She rode to challenge them with Riders she recruited from Arvandais, and the harbor garrison. She's got a wing at least."

"Challenge?" Camerend protested. "Lanrid Olavayir has been bragging all over Olavayir about how he wants to marry her!"

"She thinks, or is telling them, that they're up here to...I don't even know what she said. She's got her followers, all the young ones, on fire to attack Olavayir, and not stop until she's retaken Cama One-Eye's lands."

"But Cama One-Eye never *lost* any lands! He was a second son, awarded the northern jarlate after the Venn War!"

"*You* know that. *I* know that. Camerend." Vandareth wiped dirty fingers at the trickle of blood on his neck, smearing it. "Hadand is throwing off Marlovan rule, and it's not just the northern shore she wants—"

Uniting all the kingdom. Camerend remembered those words, now sick with chill. This was exactly how wars began—

Trumpets blared.

Vandareth recoiled as if struck, then sent Camerend an anguished glance. "I've got to save Hal, at least. There's a trail up there—do something!" He gave Camerend a shove toward a goat trail winding around a spire to the left, then ran back down the trail to the plunging horses, who heard, or smelled, the tension of their herd on the other side of a jagged sheer of rock.

By the time Camerend had charged up the narrow goat trail to the spire Vandareth had pointed out, he could hear the echoes of many horse hooves, and above that rumble, human voices. Soaring over those, the urgent blare of trumpets.

Camerend reached the spire and paused long enough to mutter the emergency spell that would alert his mother far away in Darchelde: if there was any possibility that magic could save the situation, she knew far more than he did.

Then he stepped out onto a narrow ledge, to find himself at tower height, looking down into the Pass at two companies drawn within a hundred paces of one another, one with scarcely thirty including runners laden with baggage, and the other three times as large and fully armed.

Hard Ride's force blocked the top of the rise, their horses still, bare lances upright, shields on left arms.

Magic shimmered in the air next to Camerend, and Shendan appeared in a surge of air that brought the smells of home briefly, before dissipating on the wind. She leaned against a rock, looking old and gray.

Camerend backed up a step to let her recover, then knelt behind a rock so that he could see but not be seen from below.

Shendan blinked away the transfer nausea as her heart beat against her ribs: transfer hurt worse every year that passed, but when her son summoned her, she came. It was the least she could do, a parent's never-ending guilt for surrendering her only child as a hostage, leaving Camerend to grow up under the hard eye of the former king.

Below Lanrid's followers muttered questions to each other, here and there uttering short barks of laughter. Some in the front row made cracks about how they ought to have had some warning so they could put on their House tunics and look good. Few of Lanrid's riders had brought shields for what they had believed to be a romantic lark, and they carried only four lances, each with Olavayir leaping dolphin banners attached. They were in hilarious spirits, suiting a bride raid on the most beautiful Marlovan who surely, *surely*, would rather be married to their favorite Commander Lanrid in preference to that whining pup Evred in the royal city.

That had to be her, climbing onto a big boulder some twenty paces up a narrow path in the cliff above her lines of Riders. She was certainly beautiful in that coat somewhat like what men wore, except with elaborate shoulder spaulders in extra layers, the whole dyed a bright red. It was tight at the waist with chain mail over it, reaching down to her boot tops.

"I waited until you could see and hear me," Hard Ride Hadand called down as she tried to pick out which one was Lanrid.

Oh, that had to be him, the big one in the center, staring up at her with open mouth. She raised her voice, yelling the words she'd rehearsed while coming up the Pass.

"So I could have the pleasure of proclaiming the independence of Lorgi Idego," she shouted louder, watching as they stopped talking and turned their faces up to her. She paused to revel in her position above them, and grinned, burning with triumph. "This is the last time I will ever use your barbaric tongue—and *this* will be the last word you ever hear!"

She spoke so fast that most of those below turned to one another, muttering, "Did you catch that?" and "What is she saying?" as above, Camerend shouted, "Wait!"

But his voice blended with Hard Ride's shriek, "SHOOT!"

Archers rose from behind a tumbled scree on one side, and from behind a sheered granite wall on the other. A single hesitation from some, but when Hadand screeched, *"Shoot!"* again, a flurry of arrows spanged, then another wave.

Even if Lanrid had known how to gather his riders into a defensive line in that pass, he was outnumbered by a factor of three, facing an uphill ride, and they wore no armor or helms.

He was the fourth to fall from his plunging horse.

To enter the thoughts of another requires discipline and focus. It has been likened to being in the center of a crowd working themselves into a mob while one tries to discern the words of a single individual. Of course one is only dealing with a single person, but trying to make sense of that person's tumult of image, jumbled words, and physical as well as emotional reactions is comparable to the sensory chaos of the mob.

Before one gets to the pain of dying.

If the listener is not skilled, they will share that pain right into oblivion.

Necessity required I take the risk, and endure the sensory echo.

The arrow struck Lanrid in the chest, jolting him from shock to pain between one beat and the next, and while his ruined heart stuttered into quiescence his mind reeled from shock to disbelief to the urge to protect his brother. He tried to turn, to look for Sinna through the billowing dark clouds as he fell. The pain resolved into shocking cold except for the fire in the middle of his chest and he longed for home—Da angry—would he find out about Fi's and his son, because of course he'd have a son, the Olavayirs were like the Noths in that way, always boys....

That really was his last coherent thought as the cold numbed mercifully to a sense of floating outward into a starless sea.

He never heard the screams as horses and men panicked, struggling forward, backward, death hissing and thudding around them. A few brave souls ripped their swords free and rode to attack, only to be thrown back by Hadand's lancers.

Arrows dropped the four Olavayir lancers struggling to remove the banners, which threatened to get caught under the horses' hooves. Then Hard Ride's lancers charged among the Olavayirs, the ring and clash of metal reverberating off stone. Riders fell. Horses danced and sidled and reared, trying to avoid stepping on sprawled bodies.

It was a slaughter, not a battle, but Hard Ride Hadand grinned fiercely, because her plan—*her* plan—worked. It was happening! This was how you made yourself a queen!

Only there were so few of them. They were dying too fast, too easy.

She stared down at Lanrid, who looked so young, and even death did not diminish his beautiful features. She twitched her gaze away and up as her people grimly tried to catch the riderless horses, some of them wounded by arrows, increasing the chaos.

Up next to the spire, Camerend leaned against the rock, sick with horror and helpless rage. He was too high to be heard, he didn't even have a weapon as royal runners were forbidden to carry swords. He saw his grief mirrored in Shendan's profile: her lined face appeared to have aged twenty years.

Then, out of the mostly still figures below, and the muted noise of hoofbeats and terse commands from riding captains, rose an eerie sound. It was a young male, singing the Andahi Lament.

For a timeless moment everyone stilled except the animals, as Sindan Olavayir, briefly stunned by a glancing blow, crawled to his hands and knees to his older brother staring sightlessly at the sky, an arrow sticking up from his chest.

Sinna sat back on his heels, oblivious to the blood running down his face, threw back his head and poured all his grief through his voice, heart-rending and brilliant, as everyone turned his way as if yanked by invisible rope.

Hadand's victory exultation dissipated; excitement and victory withered into uncertainty, bewilderment, even sorrow in the faces of her own people as that soaring threnody echoed up the stones to the sky beyond. Some even wept, shocked cold by what they'd done.

Furious at how everyone seemed frozen by the anguished beauty of Sindan's voice rising and falling in the kingdom's most powerful lament, Hadand screamed to drown the sound, "Victory! We are *free* of the Marlovan yoke! *We are Lorgi Idego!*"

Her most loyal followers sent up a cheer, as below, Hard Ride's brother Haldren scrambled frantically up the path toward her, rope burns bleeding at both wrists, and Sindan's exquisite voice harrowed every heart.

In a red rage, Hard Ride whirled around, yanked the bow from her first runner, and loosed an arrow. Too late, a pair of dolphin-clan Riders struggled to defend Sindan, but both were wounded, one with a shattered knee.

They were too slow to block the arrow whiffling through the air to thud in the middle of Sinna's chest, right below his heart.

His head jerked up, eyes round and shocked. His fingers scrabbled at the arrow as he tried to gulp in breath to finish his song. His fingers came away bloody as he turned his fading gaze upward at those on the rock.

Then he toppled awkwardly atop his brother, twitching slowly. The two wounded men collapsed, one rising again to catch the reins of a plunging horse that threatened to trample the boys' bodies. Teeth gritted, Hard Ride sent three more arrows into Sinna, until he stilled. Then two more, until she got a grip on her rage.

"Here's how it's going to be," she shouted to her people. "You wanted independence. Now you have it. Don't let sentiment ruin that! It lasts as long as steam. *Victory* is real."

She pointed at the tumbled, blood-soaked Olavayir Riders. "*This* is victory! We did it once, and we can do it again! If any still live, slit their throats. Gather those loose horses, and form up in column to ride down the Pass. And we'll write our own songs—ballads of glory that will last a thousand years—"

A single arrow gleamed briefly in the air before it struck her in the throat.

She choked, dropping her bow as her fingers clawed at the shaft. Impossible! Impossible! Her lungs labored for breath to protest, then her legs gave out. She spun around and tumbled head first over the edge. She hit a jagged rock head first, a loud crack, then flopped lifeless onto her enemies below.

Her younger cousins cried out in rage and fear.

The more experienced among her warriors whirled to gaze in the direction from which the arrow had come. Camerend and Shendan whipped around; from their vantage only they could see the edge of Vanda's jacket as he vanished into the shadows of a crevasse, leaving those below gazing up at blank rock. On the other side of the Pass, Haldren leaped from rock to rock and scrambled up onto the ledge where Hadand had stood. He sidestepped the spatter of his sister's blood, then knelt and shouted into the noise, a hand extended.

Someone below tossed a metallic object up: a speaking trumpet.

Hal caught it, and blew a long, flat blast.

Everyone stilled, shocked by Hard Ride's sudden death. Her closest cousins reached for the weapons, fired into new rage, but most of the older ones' bloodlust had been snuffed out by the terrible effect of that mourning song still echoing in their minds.

Eyes turned Haldren's way, seeking answer, order. Absolution, justification. Sense. *Nothing* had gone the way Hard Ride had promised—the death was here, all around them, but where was the thrill of glory?

"What happened here cannot be undone," Hal cried, his voice breaking. "I am now the senior Arvandais in residence, and my orders are to retreat to Andahi Garrison. But first we shall Disappear the dead properly. *All* the dead." He opened his hand, palm up. "And grant mercy to the wounded. There is no hiding what was done today."

He turned his head to where Vandareth had reappeared among those below, reins in his hand from several Olavayir horses sidling restlessly. The bow was gone.

"Vanda, leave the Olavayir wounded some horses," Hal called in a lower voice.

First one, then two, and with many sideways looks, others began to follow Hal's orders as voices rose: *Who shot Hard Ride? Was it one of them?*

Was it one of us?

Camerend was sick with fury, at least half of it at himself for standing there uselessly.

Shendan eyed him. "If you'd tried anything, you would have been the first one shot." And when he lifted a hand as if to ward her words, she went on, "They might regret what just happened, but they wouldn't have followed her if they didn't agree in principle, if not with this approach. At the least, we'll lose the north coast entirely."

The "we" was an irony too well known to both to need definition. Montredavan-Ans were raised to take the long view, as their legendary forebear Fox had written privately: to never lose sight of their allegiance as Marlovans, in spite of the ten generations of unfair exile imposed on them seven generations ago.

Camerend remained silent, contemplating how clearly Hard Ride Hadand had taken pleasure in ordering the kill. That sort of craving was seldom sated this side of death.

Shendan turned to watch grim-faced Hal Arvandais as he climbed down to take horse behind the slowly forming rows of Riders, once the last of the dead had been properly laid out and Disappeared.

Shendan sighed, putting a hand to her aching lower back as she and Camerend retreated into the narrow passage between two towering rocks, out of sight of those below.

"It's done. We have about two months to try to figure out a way to mitigate the consequences," Shendan said.

It would take that long to dispatch a runner down the Pass to the royal city. There was no question of carrying the news by either magical notecase, or in person: the royal runners were already very strictly guarded by Mathren's tight security, with constant surprise inspections down to the bottom layers of their personal trunks. Every message they carried was triple sealed and coded—though they knew the most important ones were borne exclusively by Mathren's personal runners. Trust, over the past twenty years, was a scarce commodity in the royal city.

Camerend turned his gaze southward into the gathering shadows of the Pass, as below, the half-dozen or less badly wounded of Lanrid's once proud force painfully loaded their few surviving companions onto the horses and began the grueling journey south through the Pass.

"Mathren will surely pester Kendred into calling for king's service, if Kendred doesn't think of it first—once he returns. We can't stop that any more than we can stop the sun," Camerend said, stating the obvious as a basis for discussion: the king could, in a time of war, demand one of every ten men between twenty and sixty.

"We can't prevent Mathren from going to war even if we had six months to plan." Shendan sighed again, digging her knuckles into her lower back.

"We are powerless to act, but not to speak. We use our magic to stay aware of events for a purpose, never lose sight of that."

Camerend heard the tremble in her voice, and though he would not say he knew his mother well—he'd scarcely seen her while growing up—he understood that she was speaking to herself as well as to him.

Her voice firmed. "So let us consider how to communicate with those who *can* act. Go back. Use the time to get to know the second generation, who still do not know that the Jarl of Olavayir is dead. We need a better sense of how the jarl's heirs will define eagle-clan's place in these new events."

Her sorrowful profile turned toward the departing Idegans, Vanda riding at Hal's side. "I'll give Vandareth a chance to explain himself, for that is *our* rule. That was murder."

"Was it murder?" Camerend asked. "I don't question you because he's my brother in all ways except blood. But Hadand Arvandais enjoyed that massacre, and she made it clear that for her that was just the beginning. Vanda shot a killer who killed for the sake of killing."

"Is war ever lawful?" Shendan retorted. "I said I'll talk to him. But you must accept that we've lost him, for I cannot have him back among us now; that was in no way self-defense."

Camerend gazed at the back of that shorn head, suspecting that Vanda wouldn't mind exile as much as he would be missed. Camerend minded for him, but he had enough self-awareness to recognize that his ire on Vanda's behalf was not far from the resentment he thought he had buried over his own life as a hostage, ripped from his home at the age of six.

He laid his hand over his heart, his throat too tight for words.

The two used their transfer tokens to return by magic, he to the royal city, and she to Darchelde.

Below, the Idegans departed as the shadows filled the canyon, until all that was left was the drying blood.

SIXTEEN

"You reek," Danet said when Arrow showed up in her room after an absence of three days. He winced at the sound of Rabbit's howling, then scowled as Danet sniffed and made a face. "You smell like you bathed in bristic. You know I hate that."

"Can't do anything about it," he said shortly. "I keep getting the stone wall when I even try to talk to any of the Royal Riders. They're letting Jarend drill with them, but they don't talk to him, either, except about weapons and the like. Mathren told them my orders are to stick with Evred, and so I'm stuck sticking. Stuck sticking. Hah. Is that a joke? Sinna could tell us—if we could get him away from that shit Lanrid. Anyway, if Evred drinks, and he does, day and night, I have to. Keeps him from harassing Jarend, for one thing."

"Does he really have no responsibilities? No training of any kind?" Danet asked, skeptical.

"Not that I've seen." Arrow sighed. "He doesn't seem to do anything besides gamble with those boys at Captain's Drum, and pillow jig with the girls. He says Mathren won't let him wargame or even handle real weapons in drill, for his own safety. And he refuses to drill basics, no weapons, like he's five. Can't say I blame him, really."

Danet sighed. "I overheard someone in the kitchen saying that he can barely read." She felt Arrow's shrug. There were always runners and scribes for that. "I can understand keeping him safe," she said, dropping the subject of reading. "I wouldn't want to be the guard who knocks the next king off his horse and breaks his arm." Especially *that* king, she thought to herself. "What else does he do?"

"Not much. Says any time he has ideas, the uncles tell him he's too important to risk, or too young to understand. I thought my life was bad, dealing with Lanrid, but I'm coming to think we had the best of it, compared to life here in the royal city. No wonder Evred's hot to get crowned. Then he can order them to shut up when he wants to ride out the gates for a day!"

"It's that bad?" Danet asked, for she had been missing her own riding. But the urge to read and understand everything was a far stronger craving. Once she'd completed her orders, she'd be free to do some exploring with Firefly — when the weather wasn't sleet or snow.

Arrow sighed. "He makes it out to be. Kendred lets him gamble as much as he wants, and you know we spend half our time at the pleasure houses, which are all safely within the city, with guards always waiting to escort us there and back."

Arrow yawned, as in the far room, Rabbit finally whimpered himself to sleep. Arrow began to doze off.

When all was quiet at last, Danet lay awake, musing about pleasure houses. She could go if she wanted to. But she'd never been to one, so she didn't know the etiquette, or even how much it cost. When she first used the Waste Spell for her monthly, Mother had given her the lecture about sex, then considered the subject closed. Until now Danet had never thought about it, but she suspected Mother had no lovers, nor visited the pleasure houses — being one of those who was happy sleeping single, once her duty was done.

Danet hated going into any situation not knowing what to do, and anyway she was still trying to cure herself of watching for that attractive royal runner. That *ring-bound* royal runner. She kept catching herself looking for him, then being disgusted with herself.

Danet resolved to find out which house local women preferred, as that Captain's Drum sounded rowdy, loud, and she didn't want to be anywhere near Evred. Then she too, slid into sleep, to be woken, as usual, by Noddy in the middle of the night, wet and hungry.

Surely the carts ought to be arriving any day, she thought tiredly when at last she crawled back into bed.

At last, Danet caught up with the kitchen records to the events of twenty years ago.

As she ate a rye biscuit stuffed with shirred egg, she read the changes that signified the assassination of Evred's royal parents, and assimilated all the new patterns, and then pushed on, rereading the succeeding pages, which she'd already read once before when assembling the stacks of loose papers into stacks for each year. Only now she knew the patterns — and so she was able to recognize the anomaly she'd sensed on her first read: a single name, Parnid, whose requisitions were always made and signed off by the same person. A decade ago every two or three months, gradually increasing until more recently, every week or ten days, with gradually growing numbers of items.

The requisitions listed were all for everyday things spread across various branches of support and supply. They'd started in small quantities, but that had changed from year to year, nearly imperceptibly. No one would notice without looking at all the records: the requisitions were for food, fodder, and equipment of various types, but if you looked at the rising frequency as well as the numbers, it had gone from enough for a riding to a wing, then enough for a flight of wings, and in recent times enough clusters of small stuff spread over every branch to furnish a battalion. Every other requisition was made by various staff members—there was Tesar's name, for Danet's and Noddy's needs—and signed off by the person who supplied the requisition. All except Parnid.

So she set the book aside, and went back to the kitchens to hunt down Amreth Tam. She found him, morose as usual, inspecting the cabbages the kitchen boys and girls had just brought in. He looked her way in question.

"Who's Parnid?" she asked.

"Runner on the military side," Tam replied, waving a dismissive hand. "Night watch is my guess. But at least whoever he, or she, is, they do see to their own fulfillment. The requisitions are usually chalked and checked off during the night."

She accepted that, and got out of his way, sensing his impatience. She started toward the stairway, deciding it was time to brave the scribes after all, for the paymasters were located somewhere in the scribes' wing.

She entered the scribe annex to find a large room filled with apprentice-aged people in their undyed robes with blue edging signifying the scribe guild, lounging around a table with ink, pens, and paper. Two were reading. At first she thought they were working on something interesting, but before the circle of angry faces turned her way, she glimpsed a map and notes of some kind of complicated game.

None of them looked friendly. That included the girls among them.

Danet turned toward the eldest of these, but the girl spoke first. "Guilds are off limits," she said brusquely.

Danet tried politeness. "I'm Danet Olavayir, and it was on the jarlan's orders that I—"

"I fell asleep after jarlan," interrupted a tall boy lounging on a bench.

"For me, it was 'I am.'"

Amid much more laughter than the comment warranted, the boy nearest the door turned blank blue eyes Danet's way. "You Olavayirs stay on your side of the castle. You don't need to come nosing over here."

"I just wanted to ask a question, about requisitions, and when—"

"You're a scribe chief?" a girl of about thirteen interrupted, looking around at her fellows for approval. When she got it, she crossed her arms and shrilled, "Get out!"

Danet shut the door firmly behind her, and let out her breath in a huff. She refused to get angry, or feel humiliated. Either way, those snot-wads would win. She was obeying orders...and if she couldn't check her lists against the paymasters' lists, then there was another way to check: dispositions.

Every person who lived in the castle had two personal lines in the lists: one, itemized supplies for daily existence, or dispositions; the other, items they ordered for themselves, which would be deducted from wages.

She retreated to the kitchen cubby, thinking out her next step. All comestibles and raw materials were listed through the records she had just straightened out. By far the bulk of supplies was dispersed through the garrison, as the royal guard was the largest populace in the castle, seconded only by the castle staff.

She walked over to the east end of the garrison, bordering on the barns that housed the milk animals. Here, in an old much-segmented building, resided the quartermaster and his staff.

"I'm Danet Olavayir," she said to the bored young man stuck at the front desk, copying out orders. "I've just finished straightening out the kitchen requisition records."

"Kitchen?" The young man's face cleared. "Finally! We have enough to do having to run over there to chalk our requisitions on the board, since the scribes can no longer be bothered to bring the lists around to us, the way everyone knows it used to be done."

"I can believe that," Danet said with a sympathetic air. "One thing I can tell you, they left things in a real snarl. I just need to check a couple of your records to make sure I have everything square. I don't mean to make work for you—happy to do it myself, if you point me in the right direction." She brandished her closely-written pages.

As she'd hoped, the skinny young orderly (no older than Hliss's age, sixteen, she guessed) took one horrified glance at the stack and said, "Help yourself. Right through there. You'll see the year down the side of each shelf. Just put it back where you found it." And he went back to his copywork.

Danet slipped inside the stuffy building, and eyed shelves of stored books. At least everything was neatly labeled. She found the general lists, and checked, to discover that all those supplies Parnid had requisitioned were indeed noted, then leaned out to peek through the door. She spotted the boy at the desk, head bent, his bony shoulder blade working as he dipped his pen and wrote.

So she slipped down the narrow room and turned twice before she found what she was looking for: lists of garrison personnel.

She found Parnid listed sixteen years ago, and nearly put the book back. But she could almost feel Mother breathing down her neck, about to launch into her well-remembered lecture about unfinished work that makes more work for someone else.

Danet stood there, dithering. She loved doing a good job at any time, but she especially wanted to complete this task. It would be so satisfying to solve the mystery, and besides, the jarlan trusted her. She doubted very much that she would get anywhere near tax records for distant garrisons, but at least she could execute this one task.

And yet...she sensed that she wasn't supposed to be in this space. Not that anyone had said anything. It was the way everyone stayed in their own little island, for she hadn't missed that crack about the scribes, who certainly didn't appear to be overworked. It was possible—she supposed—that for some reason they weren't allowed over on this side, which made no sense that she could figure, but somehow it heightened this feeling, a tension, in the castle that made her want to watch her back.

She tiptoed out, peeked at the boy, saw him writing. She hustled back and began checking the runners' records, pulling book after book, only to discover that Parnid's dispositions were perfectly normal. Always the same.

Always the same?

Frustrated and anxious, she forced herself to move with calm deliberation as she backtracked to look more closely, and then it struck her: Parnid was listed as having the normal dispositions that all runners had, but there were no personal items. Not so much as an extra candle or a pair of socks.

She checked another year, and another. Same.

She only stopped when she heard a noise from the front area, and quickly put the book back, making certain it was neatly in place. Then she walked out, past the boy who had apparently just received a fresh batch of copywork.

"Thanks," she said as she passed.

He didn't even look up.

She hiked back to the kitchen cubby and sat on the floor, chin in hands, elbows on knees.

What did it mean—no, the real question was, whom ought she to ask? The quartermaster wasn't in charge of either garrison or royal runners. The grand gunvaer had said to avoid Commander Mathren, and the regent wasn't back yet. Maybe the grand gunvaer to start with, then. It was time to feed Noddy anyway.

She ran upstairs. When she got to their suite, she heard male voices: Arrow's familiar tones, and another quiet, slow voice that sent a warm shiver through her.

She opened the door, to discover Arrow sitting cross-legged opposite the royal runner at their little table.

Arrow hailed her with unmistakable relief. "Danet! You remember Camerend, right? Royal runner who took us south? Well, he's got some questions, and I was, uh, summoned by Evred-Sierlaef."

Gradually details accumulated: Camerend, sitting straight and tall, his hair glinting golden in the candle light, his expression masked, except for the marks of tiredness under his eyes; Arrow fresh from the baths this late in the day, his hair even combed out, his horsetail fresh, when most of the time he pulled it up into its clasp first thing in the morning and forgot about it until the next day.

Arrow and Evred were clearly heading to a pleasure house.

Arrow slipped past her and was gone in three quick steps, the rap of his boot heels diminishing down the hall. Camerend waited patiently as she became aware that she still stood in the doorway. Reddening to what felt like fiery heat, she entered the room and shut the door.

Tesar came out from the nursery with a kicking, wailing baby. "He's dry. But hungry."

"Shall I go?" Camerend asked as Tesar handed Noddy down.

With the swift movements that had become habit, Danet tucked the infant inside the loose robe that pregnant and nursing women customarily wore. The baby vanished within the warm fabric, uttered one shattered sigh of relief, and found what he sought.

"My question actually relates to the little ones," Camerend continued, making a conscious effort to settle to his task.

He had spent a terrible night fighting against the images of death, and the echo of that beautiful young voice so suddenly cut off. He'd finally given up any pretense of sleep, as tired as he had been, and lit a lamp to deal with correspondence, and after that to come up with various questions in order to provide an excuse to introduce himself to the Olavayirs.

He'd tackled Jarend first thing in the morning. The jarl's heir—actually, the new jarl, though he did not yet know it—was huge, pleasant in demeanor, slow in speech and movement. His squint made it difficult to see any expression in that massive face.

They worked at an awkward conversation until Jarend's wife appeared and quietly gave Jarend a hot cup that smelled like willow-bark steep.

Camerend understood then that the patient Jarend had a headache. He'd excused himself immediately, as the wife went to tend her child yelling in another room. Then he'd gone out to hunt down the second son, and found him emerging from the baths.

Now he was alone with the last of the four, a red-faced young woman who wouldn't meet his eyes as she said flatly, "Little ones?"

Camerend tried to see her expression, but she was bent over the nursing baby hidden in her robe. All he could see was the neat parting in her brown hair.

Grimly sticking to duty, he asked, "Do you know how long you're staying in the royal city? I ask because until Evred-Sierlaef was born, most education in the castle has involved us in some manner. Your little one there is too young for tutoring, but the other one, ah, Tanrid?"

"You can call him Rabbit," Danet said, glancing up warily at the husky note of strain in Camerend's voice.

As yet she hadn't the life experience to name what she saw in his demeanor. His mouth had fixed in a smile meant to be polite and friendly, but she looked past that at his eyes, as her mother had taught. She didn't recognize the lingering traces of horror, only that his forehead was taut with tension.

On Jarend, that meant headaches. "Are you all right?" she asked.

Startled, he met her gaze, saw only inquiry, and it was his turn to look down. Clearly his facade of calm was not as successful as he had thought. "I am," he said. "Thank you for asking. Nothing more than a slight headache," he lied.

"Oh." Her brow cleared. "Arrow's brother gets them. Tdor Fath thinks it's mostly when the weather changes. We have a good willow steep—but of course you have your own remedies," she corrected quickly, blushing and dropping her gaze again, aware that she was babbling.

He saw her remorse, but misinterpreted the cause, and got to his feet. "We can discuss the question of tutors later. If you like. Please be aware that we're always happy to help. Our younger runners must include teaching in their training before they're considered ready for the world. Traditionally they have offered tutoring to the castle children."

Once again, Danet found herself prodded beyond her tumbling emotions by curiosity—and the need to find out about Parnid, without revealing why she asked. "How is your training different from that of the garrison runners?" she asked. "Or is it secret?"

It was very secret, so secret that they all sidestepped that question with practiced ease. "Royal runners and scribes use similar lessons," Camerend said, sitting down again. "Most castle and jarlate runners aren't trained in Iascan anymore, much less Old Sartoran, which are useful for those of us assigned to work in the archives. Also, a few of us are also trained in what is called the minor magics. You know, the water purity spells on barrels and buckets and baths, heat for the latter when there is no hot spring, reinforcing walls and bridges, and so forth." The *and so forth* covered everything else.

"That's right," she said, remembering a gray-haired royal runner visiting years ago at Farendavan. "Is it fun, doing magic?"

"It's like anything else. You have to work and work to get it right. It's satisfying when you master it, as is anything else. But then it becomes routine. As I think is true for any repetitive skill. I remember our healer once remarking that after one has done the Beard Spell on the hundredth youth, it's become habit."

Danet's mind leaped to healers and their magics. And then, as always, questions proliferated like ivy vines. "A distant cousin of mine, they call her Hard Ride up north, where they see ships come in from all over, she once told me that in other kingdoms, they have healers who change the color of people's hair."

She saw the quick spasm in his face when she mentioned her fourth-cousin, almost a wince. She sensed that she'd said the wrong thing, somehow, and her next question—about the chain of command for runners —dried up unspoken.

She busied herself with shifting Noddy to the other side, which Camerend took as a signal to end this lumbering conversation and leave before he suffered any more nightmare flashes of memory.

SEVENTEEN

As soon as Camerend was gone, Danet let out a long breath of relief. Being around that royal runner was like drawing near a warm fire on a cold winter's day, except she knew very well if she got any closer, she would burn herself.

Once Noddy's round little belly was full, he sank bonelessly into sleep. Danet put him in his crib and tiptoed out, avoiding Tesar's brooding look. Danet knew Tesar hated child duty, but until the carts caught up, she had no one else.

Danet headed for the grand gunvaer's tower. The old woman sat up in her padded chair, eyes vague, but her wrinkled face lifted at an alert angle. "What have you found?"

Danet told her.

The old woman sank back with a long, hissing sigh.

"What does it mean?" Danet asked.

Hesar peered in her direction, seeing only a blur. But she could hear the genuine distress in the girl's voice. "It means danger, first of all. You must not go back to the scribes. They've been cut out of administration for years. All they do is copy general reports for the archives. Now. If there are no personal dispositions for this mystery runner, but everything that person requisitions is supplied and paid for, then...." The old woman breathed harshly. "The answers lie possibly with the quartermaster, but certainly in the treasury. Someone there knows the truth."

Danet stared in shock. "Truth about what?" she asked faintly, feeling that horrible cold tingle you get when you fall into icy water.

The grand gunvaer lifted trembling hands. "I'll send a letter to young Ranor," she finally. "Ah, if only it didn't take weeks and weeks to get answers! But needs must. You did well, child. Continue as you are, and say nothing."

"Even to Tdor Fath?"

"What can she do except worry? She has enough worry, from what they tell me. Say nothing to anyone—one thing I can assure you is, neither the regent nor especially the commander tolerate anyone questioning their orders, or venturing out of their own chain of command."

Danet left, hilarity streaming through her at the idea of the stolid, graying Jarlan of Olavayir being referred to as "young Ranor," a hilarity that lasted only heartbeats before being replaced by the gnawing anxiety of questions and a vague sense of dread.

As soon as Danet was out the door, the gunvaer dictated a letter to her runner, then sent her downstairs with instructions for the royal runners to get it as fast as possible to Ranor-Jarlan in Olavayir.

When the runner reached the third floor, she was passed directly to Camerend and Mnar Milnari, who served as his co-chief when he was on a run.

Mnar saluted, hand to heart — the salute for a gunvaer, acknowledging her orders — and said, "It will go out directly."

By the time the runner had returned to the tower, Camerend had drunk some willow-steep against a pounding headache. Grimly he removed the seal and read the letter out to Mnar, his tone flat. Mnar suspected that Camerend had slept little, if at all, since witnessing that slaughter in the Pass, which he had been unable to stop. Which even Shendan, with her years of magic studies, had been unable to stop.

Mnar copied the gunvaer's letter in scribe shorthand as Camerend read it. Then he resealed the letter and summoned one of their fastest runners to take it to Olavayir.

With the gunvaer's letter on its way, as promised, they locked the door to consider what they'd read.

Camerend dropped down cross-legged on the floor, his back to the fire, his hair a nimbus of loose golden strands against that beating light. Mnar took one look at his distraught profile and averted her gaze as she sat a few paces away. "It's clear from her letter that the grand gunvaer knows little more than we."

Camerend dug the heels of his hands into his eye sockets as he contemplated the lack of communication between garrison, staff, and government — all by strict orders, as a matter of security. Then he looked up tiredly, bloody images from the Pass still flickering in memory, sparked by sounds, sights, maybe smells too subtle to identify.

"Two questions," Mnar said. "First, did Danet Olavayir say anything to you when you went to interview her? She has to have gone straight from talking to you to the gunvaer."

"Nothing. Mnar, the gunvaer might not understand it, but I do: Someone in this castle is supplying, and no doubt paying, what amounts to a secret battalion."

"Who?" Mnar spread her hands. "Why?"

Camerend sighed, longing for sleep without nightmares. "Too many questions for anything but guessing. In any case, it can wait. Far more pressing is the fact that runners are on the way from Olavayir to the royal city with the news that the Jarl of Olavayir is dead. His heirs are here. And right behind that news will be runners to report on what happened at the Pass."

"We will have to be prepared to be sent in all directions," Mnar said, sighing. "Well, we can double up some classes, and the fledglings a year from promotion can make runs in teams. Good practice."

She got up to refill their cups of summer steep, noting that Camerend had not touched his. So she set that cup aside and fetched out the listerblossom as she said, "In the meantime, this Danet is a superlative ferret, at least as good as our own. Who trained her?"

Camerend spread his hands.

"I like the look of her, from what little I could see," Mnar commented as she dropped some treated willow into the cup and handed it to Camerend. "She looks like me—lanky and brown. Of course I'm predisposed to like her."

Camerend recognized an attempt to ease the tension, and forced a smile before he sipped the scalding, bitter drink. Almost immediately the pounding in his head began to lessen.

Mnar said, "Since Shendan asked you to get close to these Olavayirs anyway, maybe you ought to find out who trained her." She folded the copy of the gunvaer's letter, tucked it into her golden notecase, and tapped the sigil. The letter transferred to Darchelde. "Speaking of ferrets, you do remember I just sent our best two to find Kendred. Should we call them back to pursue this matter before the bad news begins arriving?" She bit her lip, then murmured, "Do you think we ought to ask Isa to come?"

Camerend longed to see his wife and his little son, but dared not until he could get a better grip on himself. "Better to leave her in peace," he said wearily.

He dropped his head, his eyelashes lowering. They were long and blonde, as they'd been when Mnar met him as a twelve-year-old fellow runner-in-training.

She thought back to Isa's first day in Choreid Dhelerei. In the flurry of magic transfer from Darchelde, Isa had forgotten her gloves, and she stood shivering, near panic, in one of the classrooms, having touched a handsome piece of furniture that had apparently belonged to Evred Montreivayir's murdered aunt.

That was how Mnar met Isa, who'd just witnessed through that touch of the chair the mystery of Ndara Cassad's murder by her own husband, more than a century previous. For her, it was as if it had happened yesterday, as spilled blood—even years old—always intensified what she experienced. Mnar had been so startled by the sight of this vague girl with the large, haunted eyes and the thin hands held out, fingers spread lest they touch anything more, that she'd stumbled right into a door.

Camerend said, "My understanding is that only very recent touches reveal clear details to Isa, except of course in situations of extreme emotion. When an object is layered with everyday touches she experiences a, oh, a merging of images. If there's anything violent in those images, she can't separate from the pain."

"Right, right," Mnar said hastily, remembering how quiet and tense and inward Isa had become over her years of study, her strange abilities sharpening by the year, until Shendan took her back to the peace and quiet of Darchelde, where the rare pain embedded in stone and wood was ancient and blurred, and she could live with calm, tender Frin, who as a faithful mate gave up her life as a runner to save Isa's sanity.

Where Camerend visited them when he could.

Camerend went on. "Finding the regent is our most important need now. This Parnid situation has been going on for years, so though it looms as an intriguing mystery, I don't see any need to rush to solve it. Whereas government affairs have to be piling up that only the regent can deal with before the bad news arrives."

While they were talking, down in the stable courtyard, a commotion announced the arrival of the Olavayir carts at last, the runners and escort Riders talking of an enormous snowstorm that had tied them down for a week, following which a frost set in, miring them for even longer. When that had melted enough to enable them to move safely, the roads had turned to mush, slowing them even more.

Arrow was on the other side of the castle, drilling with his Riders. Jarend was with the royal guard, as the Royal Riders had been out at lance drill. The brothers' personal runners were seeing to laundry and the next meal, as no castle runners had been assigned to assist them. So Danet and Tdor Fath had to do the unpacking, with only the help of the exhausted travelers.

Danet was hot and sweaty by the time all the baskets and barrels and bundles had been hauled upstairs, but she was glad to note the easing of Tdor Fath's expression at this long-awaited arrival of their nursery staff, and Rabbit's familiar toys.

"Did any runners catch up with you?" she asked at length.

Rider Nunkrad, the chief nurse, had been a lancer until a bad fall had removed him forever from riding horses. He'd taken over the nursery when Jarend was beginning to toddle, and had been in charge of Olavayir Rider captains' children as well as the jarl family ever since.

He smoothed back his silver hair, which had been dripping in his face, as he said, "No, but when the blizzard struck, they could have been a horse length away and we wouldn't have seen them. We ended up so far out of the way we missed Hesea Spring entirely."

"Blizzard?"

"You didn't get the blizzard here?"

"It must have gone straight west above us, along the river," someone else said. "Typical—when the winds change up north, we always get the worst storms before they see anything down here in the south."

Uttering the usual complaints about the weather which (as usual) nobody listened to, they dispersed to their various quarters to finish unpacking and settling in.

It was well past midnight when everything had been stowed, including the new staff, to Tdor Fath's satisfaction. Danet looked down at her empty bed wearily, having decided early the best way to catch Parnid was to go down to the kitchens and observe the traffic from the night watch.

But she was so tired she flopped down, shut her eyes....

Noddy wailed before dawn, as usual, jerking Danet out of deep sleep. Disgusted with herself, she pulled on a robe and went into the nursery, to discover Noddy dry and freshly washed, while Rabbit sat quietly, reacquainting himself with his wooden blocks under the benevolent eye of Nunka. Oh, what a relief to have a nursery again!

She took Noddy for a feeding. When he was content, she dressed and hustled down to the kitchen annex, where for the third time, she nearly collided with Camerend. She managed to sidestep, then stumbled to a halt.

"Do you always move at full charge?" he asked with a brief smile. His eyes were still marked with tiredness.

"I didn't know that I was." Danet looked at him with concern, feeling too awkward to ask if he was all right. "I guess I got in the habit at Nevree, because I was always lost, or late, till I got used to the castle. And this one is even larger."

She looked away from him to the slate—and there, six items from the top, was the familiar name.

And the requisition already crossed out.

Danet was too late. It might be another month before Parnid turned up again. She bit her lip, fighting sharp disappointment. "It's probably breakfast time," she said randomly, wanting to get away to deal with her clashing emotions.

But Camerend fell in step beside her. He asked a couple of questions about education, then about keeping records, listening with clear interest to her answers. Danet found it easy to talk about Mother and her methods, her frustration at missing Parnid dissolving—leaving her aware of the man by her side. If only unwanted attractions could be scrubbed away like a patch of dirt!

But she'd learned early how to take a tumble from a horse and keep going. This attraction to the wrong person was just another tumble.

That night, a letter arrived by magic transfer to Camerend's golden notecase. It was from his wife, Isa Eris:

My dearest Camerend, our little Senrid is well, and playing with Frin at this moment. I can see him laughing at the finger-people Frin is making as she tells a story.

Having sustained a waking dream that left me insensate for two nights and a day, I am taking up my pen at the urging of both Shendan and of course our beloved and steadfast Frin.

The exact recounting of dreams, as I have told you and Frin both, is never to be trusted, for the images seldom correspond with any precision to the objects of daily life—each with its burden—and so I will only mention that which I believe concerns you and the indwelling of inimical intent.

I understand that you, as well as the others, believe that my apprehension of evil, if even real (I understand that some are skeptical of easily brandished words such as "evil"), is merely an emotional reaction to my old life there before you and Shendan brought me to my refuge here in Darchelde. I understand that at least at times you, Frin, and Mother Shendan, the closest to my heart, believe my dreams are functions of what I suffered through inadvertent touch during my days as a student there.

This may be so. And yet, and yet.

I dreamed I was there in the royal city, by your side. My steadfast Frin, though she slept beside me here, was not present in this dream. You were very near the thickening strands in a webwork of sharpest crystal extruded by a spider made entirely of glass.

As yet you were not caught within this the web, or cut by these proliferating crystals, but they are passing close, carried on the air as light as whispers.

You are in danger.

There is little, or no, time, before you must be caught. I beg you to heed me when I say the web is strong, the edges of glass sharper than knives.

I called you thrice before my spirit winged upward toward the realm of the invisible, where eternal harmony sings eternal bliss. There, where spirits blend forever in exaltation, I strive for its cerulean intensity, where forever I shall fall and fall.

EIGHTEEN

As often happens when storms are severe enough to drive living things to shelter, the messengers ordinarily strung out by weeks in good weather arrived within a day or two of one another.

The first to arrive, late the next afternoon, was a runner bearing the East Garrison pennon. He was passed straight up to Commander Mathren's chamber, business as usual. But shortly thereafter everyone in the castle paused, looking upward as the slow tolling of the great bells announced an important death.

"What does that mean?" Danet asked Arrow.

He spread his hands. "Should hear something soon enough."

He was correct. Evred sent a runner summoning the eagle-clan Olavayirs to his suite. No sooner had that runner dashed out than Tdor Fath's first runner dashed in, eyes wide. "The news is all over. The regent is dead."

"We'd better get upstairs," Arrow said to Jarend and their wives.

They walked in silence, aware of the alert guards at the landings, and runners rushing to and fro. Whispers echoed along the stone walls, though no one spoke as their party drew nigh. Danet's heart beat near her throat. She had no idea what to expect from Evred—real grief? False grief?

The last thing she expected was nervous, badly suppressed triumph. But then she reminded herself that Evred had been impatient to take the throne at last. With his eldest uncle gone, it seemed likely to occur, maybe before she and Arrow and Jarend could leave for Olavayir.

She suppressed a sigh as her gaze shifted from Evred to Mathren Olavayir, standing behind and to Evred's left in shield position.

Evred said to Arrow and Jarend, "We've discovered that my uncle died in the service of Marlovan Iasca." His fingers flexed at the sides of his blue House tunic with the leaping dolphin embroidered across the chest in real gold.

He went on without any hint of grief, "Uncle Kendred and his runners were caught in the snowstorm. Their horses were found loose, and by the time the storm had passed enough to search, they were frozen, and somebody Disappeared them, we don't know who. But we'll have the memorial tomorrow at midnight just the same. So I summoned you all to tell you that I've decided to assume the crown on New Year's Firstday—two days from now."

He cast a wary glance over his shoulder at Mathren Olavayir's impassive face, then added in a stronger voice, "When I got the news, I sent out my own personal runners to tell the jarls. My first orders as king."

Mathren's expression remained blank, but jutting cheekbones so like Lanrid's showed a blotch of color. Arrow had been watching Mathren as Evred spoke. The commander's weight shifted, and the back of Arrow's neck gripped.

But Mathren didn't speak, so Arrow turned his attention to Evred, who hadn't stopped talking. "...and we'll have a *proper* coronation, with the jarls giving oaths, by Midsummer. By then I hope I'll have Hard Ride Hadand Arvandais here, and we can have a wedding, too. Then you can go home," he said to Jarend and Arrow, "because by then we should have an heir on the way."

He cast another look over his shoulder at Mathren, his fingers turning the shallow, beaten-gold wine cup in his hands as he said, "By New Year's Second-Day, I'll begin with how I want the castle to be run, and by the new year, the kingdom."

Everyone stared at him.

He said, "Aren't you going to salute the new king?" His voice was petulant, but Danet could see nerves, even fear, in the way Evred's eyes shifted between them all, as he kept flexing his fingers.

Mathren smiled, and struck his fist to his heart. Belatedly the others did as well. Evred broke into a grin that made him look almost appealing, and very much younger, and then they all had to drink, Danet forcing herself to sip as she loathed the smell of wine during the day. At last Evred seemed to remember that there had been a recent death, and tried to assume an aspect of sorrow.

Mathren set down his goblet and said, "I had better return to duty."

Three steps and he was gone, the door closing quietly behind him. Evred's brow furrowed. He forced out a strangled laugh. "Uncle Mathren forgot who is the new king!"

And so began a long, tedious evening of drinking, bragging, and speculation about how long it might take to get an answer from the north—and what kind of wedding would impress Hard Ride.

The next morning, while the Olavayirs slept in after their wearying, wine-sodden celebratory night with the new king, above them on the third floor, Camerend and Mnar sat across from each other on their mats pulled up by the fireplace, as far from the tall windows rattling with storm winds as they could get, as Mnar read Isa's letter.

Finally she handed it back, her expression pained. "A glass spider? What does Isa mean by that? Camerend, you know I've never understood her. She was the best of us at scribe training and magic, but sometimes I found her half-mad—and I say that with all respect and admiration."

"...Isa being Cassad twice over. I know." Camerend spoke in the tone of one who had heard that, and said that, many times. They'd all grown up excusing Isa's vagaries on this entirely justifiable ground. For though most of the Cassads were like anyone else, every so often that family was known to produce oddities, and Isa's particular family tree had two of these oddities in branches directly above her.

"Anyone who doesn't take Cassads seriously might not be half-mad, but they are generally all fool," Mnar commented. "We always take her seriously, but I can't make out what that spider of glass and the cutting crystal spiderweb...thing...means." She groped in the air. "I understand that symbols are different for different people. They're shaped by moods, and what we've done during the day, and even by time."

Camerend stroked his thumb along the line of his jaw, an absent, familiar gesture that had disturbed Mar's equanimity as a teen, until her intense passion for charming, easy Vandareth obliterated all her other crushes.

"You know Isa means only to help us," Camerend said.

"I know. I know! She was always so scrupulously truthful, and lies hurt her as much as touching things by accident did. And yet I don't see any utility in her warning at all, except that there's danger, which we know, and to be careful, which we always are, and to worry more, which isn't—"

A young runner gave a perfunctory knock and bounded in.

"—helpful," Mnar finished, and gestured the boy forward.

"Ivandred's back," the runner said. "He slipped in through the old bath tunnel, so no one saw him. He's on his way up."

Camerend and Mnar exchanged startled looks. With the news about Kendred's death all over the castle, nobody would think twice about royal runners dashing in and out, so Ivandred's needing to sneak struck them as sinister.

Ivandred entered almost on the runner's heels, the tips of his ears dark red from the cold, his queue a beaver-tail of frizz from the wet weather.

"Is Branid with you?" Mnar asked before Ivandred could open his mouth.

Ivandred ran his hands up over his high forehead and through his thick brown hair, sending water droplets hissing into fire as he said, "We were caught by the tail end of a snowstorm, passing north. Bad one. Raced back. Bran stayed behind for more evidence." Ivandred drew a breath, his scrawny chest expanding. "I wanted to make certain you heard my report first: Kendred Olavayir is dead," he whispered.

"We know," Camerend said. "East Garrison reported in yesterday. Foundered and froze in the snow below one of the mines. Memorial tonight."

Ivandred snapped away his words with a flat hand. "Murdered. He, his first runner, and Hlar Dei, who'd gone along to see to his meals as a favor."

"What?" Mnar exclaimed. "Hlar is a better fighter than Spindle!"

They all knew that; Spindle was a castle runner, but Hlar was a royal runner. She'd been temporarily helping at the bakehouse, which was close to the garrison housing for families, as she and Spindle had had a daughter just a few months ago.

Mnar's stomach churned.

"By?" Camerend prompted.

"The honor guard sent to meet them."

Mnar had started up, but she sank back again, as Camerend thought grimly that he was never going to be able to touch his wife again. Every horror he experienced was a fresh, invisible stain on his spirit that somehow she felt as strongly as he when she so much as laid a finger on his wrist. Only time muted the intensity of her mysterious ability to lift memories and emotions from physical contact, but it seemed of late there would never be enough time to render himself safe enough for the briefest touch of hands or lips.

Ivandred hunkered down by the fire, the other two moving back to give him space. His sodden clothes pulled over his thin ribs as he held his hands out, fingers spread as if to grip warmth. He mumbled over his shoulder through numb lips, "The second runner survived the attack, though he was left for dead. This was in up in the wooded slope of the mountains, outside Askan and Sindan Mines. We caught up with him four days ago."

"What happened to him?"

"He was found last week by some wood-scavengers. They Disappeared the dead. Had no idea who any of them were. Took Brana to their home. He didn't tell them who he was. Told them they were attacked by brigands. He was afraid that if Evred knew he'd survived, he would send more."

"*Evred?*" Mnar repeated in disbelief.

"Evred cannot assign an honor guard," Camerend said slowly.

"I know, but that's what the runner told us." Ivandred opened his hands. "Evred sent them to meet the regent and his runners to escort them to the capital. They took them to a dell in the wood and...." He gestured a sword slash.

Mnar sighed. "Someone's lying."

No one argued. They knew how tight a control Mathren Olavayir kept over his Royal Riders. No one gave them orders but him.

Camerend said slowly, "What if this supposed honor guard...weren't our guards at all?"

"Hirelings?" Mnar asked. "Who would dare to impersonate the royal guard? Who would dare to set up such a thing? It's a capital matter!"

"Let's assume that Evred really did send them. Neither royal guard nor Royal Riders take orders from him without approval from the regent or Mathren. But hirelings wouldn't necessarily know that."

"Hirelings?"

"If you have enough gold, anyone can be hired to do anything," Camerend said.

Ivandred turned up his hand. "True. Evred could easily hire some of those roisterers at the Captain's Drum he admires so much. I know at least two who were booted out of the guard, and there's rumor that that place is a safehouse for thieves."

Mnar scowled. "Thieves sound like just the sort that could be bribed to try anything. Especially if they know they have a prince in their pocket."

"Ripe for blackmail," Ivandred added sourly.

Mnar got up and walked in a slow, sightless circle. "All this is guesswork, but it makes so much sense." She stopped and faced the others. "But wouldn't someone report missing horses and gear to Mathren?"

Ivandred, the eldest of them, said dourly, "Unless he knew what was going on and chose not to see."

Camerend gazed into the fire. "One thing that never changed, all the years I lived as a hostage in this castle: Garid and Kendred played together, and Garid and Mathren drilled together, but Mathren and Kendred never got along."

They thought back to their fledgling days as student royal runners, observing the three princes from afar: laughing, dashing Garid, equally dashing Mathren who never laughed, and whose self-discipline ran counter to Kendred's lazy love of luxury. Since Garid's assassination by those still at-large brigands, Mathren and Kendred had lived separate lives, strictly dividing the kingdom's affairs. Clearly they hadn't liked one another, but in twenty years there had been no threats or signs of violence.

Ivandred said, "Of the two, I think Mathren the most capable, except why would he kill Kendred, especially now? It doesn't bring anything to him."

Mnar added in a dry voice, "Evred is the least capable of anything, but has the most to gain, as it's chiefly been Kendred standing in the way of him becoming king."

Camerend threw his hands wide. "If we investigate, what do we do with the result? Where is the right, here?"

"There is no right here."

They turned to where Shendan Montredavan-An stood in the inner doorway. No one could have entered unless by magic transfer. They waited as Shendan recovered from the wrench of transfer and walked slowly in, the firelight gilding her silver-white hair to gold.

Mnar leaped to lock the door; if Mathren sent a surprise inspection, at least they'd have a few moments in unlocking the door for Shendan to transfer away again.

She looked aged and worn, as she had on the cliff above the massacre. "You know that Mathren will never tolerate an investigation he did not order. We had better take the time to consider the consequences before we take action. Until then, do your regular duty as if you were oath-sworn to someone you could respect. Let your choices follow the right road, even if the road seems to be invisible to the world around you."

That sounded excellent, Camerend thought wearily, and he would always do his best to follow it, but the older he got, the more he wondered if anyone saw the same right road. "What about the baby?" He sighed, and answered his own question. "I'll go over to the garrison and talk to Captain Noth. Spindle was one of his Noth connections."

"Hlar was sister to Carleas Cassad," Mnar reminded him. "I expect he'll send the child to her."

Mushy snow was falling so heavily by the time the bell tolled midway between sunset and sunrise that Kendred Olavayir's memorial was perhaps more brief than it would have been. The singing of the Hymn to the Fallen was perfunctory at best.

As the former gunvaer had died not long after her favorite son's assassination, the only people who seemed to genuinely mourn the regent were his personal runners, who'd had easy lives, and perhaps those at his favorite pleasure houses—the sharpest regret perhaps felt by the owners, as the steady flow of silver from Kendred's carelessly generous hand had come to an abrupt end.

Half the leddas-oil torches hissed and spat, and some went out entirely. The singing was ragged, and only Evred made a testimony to the dead—the same words he'd spoken the day previous.

Then it was over, and everyone retired to warmth and dryness, the Royal Riders knowing that if the weather abated they'd have drill at sunup as always.

The storm passed on to the west with the darkness, and the Royal Riders roused themselves irritably. This was the day for weekly lance drill, which would be a real toil in the snow, but that never stopped Commander Mathren.

Sure enough, anyone who'd hoped the Commander had gotten uncharacteristically drunk after the memorial was disappointed, and they rode out as usual as soon as the gates opened for the day.

Mid-morning, shortly before the Royal Riders were due back, Ranor-Jarlan's personal runner, hawk-nosed Gdan—bedraggled after a long, wearying ride—rode alone into the stable that she remembered so well from her childhood.

She slid tiredly off her mud-caked horse, and approached the stable chief. "Gdan from the Jarlan of Olavayir, here to speak to Jarend-Laef or Anred-Dal."

She looked so exhausted that the chief motioned to one of the young stable hands, and tipped his head toward the castle. The boy took off, and Gdan was handed a scraper to get the worst of the spatters off her robe and boots before she could enter the castle.

Danet's runner Tesar happened to be right inside the guest suite, having just returned from taking a tray of dishes downstairs. She intercepted the stable boy, and when she heard who the arrival was, she debated internally for a heartbeat or two, then impulsively broke the rules and ran down to the stable herself.

Tesar found Gdan alone, beating the last of the mud off the back of her coat. "Auntie," Tesar cried, and halted, peering around the empty stable yard.

Gdan gave Tesar a speculative glance as she began on her boots a second time. "You look lost. They treating you bad?"

Tesar sighed. "I've been stuck with baby-minding, and I *hate* it. I don't buck meal fetching or laundry, but I was trained for the ride."

Gdan's heavy brows knit over her hawk nose. "Where's Nunka? He raised both Arrow and Jarend from the time they were weaned—"

"He and the carts just barely got here—"

Gdan cut her niece off. "Then stop whining and do what you're told," she said unsympathetically, for she hated being back in the royal city. But the randviar had said privately that it would be a mercy to offer to go, since she knew the way, and the jarlan's other runners were all over-burdened, the jarlan dealing with grief as well as the memorial for Indevan-Jarl. "Be glad you're alive," Gdan added shortly, her news boiling painfully inside her. But family-feeling prompted her to add, "Unless Danet treats you badly."

"She's not unfair." Tesar jerked a shoulder up. "Or mean. Just works on her papers a lot. We haven't touched halter or horse for weeks."

Gdan sighed. "We raised you better than that. If you're unhappy, you talk to Danet...." And she began to unlimber a lecture that Tesar had heard before.

The clatter of iron-shod horse hooves on stone caused them both to turn toward the gate as Mathren Olavayir, returning from the weekly lancers' drill, led the Royal Riders in at a gallop.

He drew both women's appreciative gazes as he reined in, tossed the lance he'd carried to one of his runners, and sprang down from the saddle pad. As he strode away, he called over his shoulder to his second runner, "Kend! Leave the horses to the stable hands, and come with me. I want you to run a message to Captain Gannan."

He vanished through the doors to the tower, yellow horsetail and gray coat skirts swinging.

Tesar turned to her adopted aunt and her mouth fell open. She had never before seen anyone actually turn ghost-pale until now.

Gdan stared after Mathren, her eyes stark as the words, the cadences, the timbre of that voice echoed back two decades, to when she was fourteen, and working in this very stable.

She knew that voice. She had heard it in nightmares for over twenty years.

She groped blindly, stumbling forward with no awareness of doing so, until Tesar caught her by the arm to steady her. Gdan flicked her gaze to Tesar's anxious face, which was paling as well. "Auntie?" she whispered.

What now? What now? Gdan ran shaking fingers over her face. "Where are they?" she muttered voicelessly, the lecture forgotten.

Tesar whispered, "Come."

She led the way into the stairwell, and, unaware that Gdan had lived here as a child, began explaining where things were. Gdan heard none of it as she fought to get her heart to slow down, and to conquer the tremble in knees and wrists. He hadn't looked at her. And even if he had, he didn't know who she was. It was twenty years ago!

But still, her shoulder blades crawled as she tried to work out what to say.

Danet and Tdor Fath were both in the guest suite, the former having visited the kitchen as she did every day, to write out the previous day's requisitions slate so that Kitchen Steward Tam wouldn't have to. Arrow had just returned from drilling his Riders out behind the barns, idling until Evred should waken and summon him. And Tdor Fath, with free time on her hands now that Rabbit's beloved Nunka was back, had been making up a fresh dose of listerblossom in case Jarend needed it.

All turned when Tesar brought Gdan in.

Gdan tapped fingers to chest in salute, saying, "Jarl-Indevan is dead."

Arrow let out a hoarse gasp as though someone had kicked him in the gut.

To his distraught face, Gdan gave the report on his death. "...a letter lying by his hand, saying that Lanrid had taken his favorite Riders up the Pass. Which we already knew — they left directly after you did."

"The castle must be a mess," Tdor Fath said, half-starting up from her mat, as if she could instantly run to Sdar and Ranor's sides.

"Sdar-Randviar sent me before the memorial," Gdan said in a weird, flat voice that at any other time would have caused question. "The message was, *Come home.*"

Danet and Tdor Fath looked at each other, each trying to read the thoughts behind the other's bewildered gaze: after weeks of tedium, suddenly life was changing much too fast.

Tdor Fath glanced toward the inner door, and lowered her voice. "Evred is declaring himself to be new king, and he seems to want Jarend and Arrow to stay until his coronation before the jarls at Midsummer."

Gdan didn't hear a word. She said, still in that strange, creaky voice, "Who was that? In the courtyard? Leading?"

"If it was the lance drill you saw going or coming, that would be Commander Mathren," Arrow said, his arms tightly crossed over his chest. "He always leads it."

Gdan recoiled at the name "Mathren." Then: "It was him. It was *his* voice."

"Him?" Tdor said.

"Who?" Danet said.

Arrow got it first, and took a step toward Gdan. "*You're* the stable hand, the witness, right?"

Gdan pressed back against the door, fingers spread wide and tense. "I am," she whispered, her face blanched. "I know that voice. He—said almost the same words. Same voice, same tone. I recognized it at once."

"Why didn't you say anything before?" Tdor Fath asked, instinctively backing to the side door, where she could see Rabbit peacefully asleep.

"Because I didn't *know* who he was. I'd never heard Mathren Olavayir speak. I was a stable hand, sent by Ranor-Jarlan to oversee the animals brought by Keth and Tana—that is, the Jarlan's first two sons...."

"My elder brothers. Assassinated along with Garid-Harvaldar," Arrow whispered.

"We'd only been there a month when it happened. I never met any of the royal family, only saw them from a distance. Never heard them speak. I saw them sometimes when they rode in and out, but never heard them talk. And after I heard the assass—*him*, and saw the dead queen's face, I caught the loose horses and galloped straight north."

"But Mathren's so duty-minded, so loyal to the kingdom, everyone says so." Tdor Fath spoke in the same urgent undervoice, as if invisible ears might overhear them though the door was firmly shut behind Gdan. "Could it be Mathren was searching for the assassins—that he merely found the dead?"

"The accounts all put him inside the castle, rescuing Evred and Lanrid in the nursery," Arrow muttered. "My father...." His voice hitched on the word *father*. Then he scowled, and continued in a higher, strained voice, "My father told me that much. And if Mathren did find the dead king and queen, and my brothers, why didn't Gdan hear him yelling for backup? I've heard the story over and over, ever since I was small: Mathren was in the garrison with the swordmaster. Someone reported seeing armed brigands. Mathren ordered the alarm bells rung and ordered out a company to search, then went to secure Evred, who was in the nursery with Lanrid, both guarded by his wife. The search company split into ridings, one of which found the king and queen. He wasn't anywhere near the site of the attack."

Everyone fell silent, staring at each other, then Arrow walked up to Gdan. "Think hard. Did the alarm bells ring before you found them, or after?"

"I don't have to think." Gdan's trembling hand turned palm down. "I was at the stream watering the remounts, because the king was going to join the game. I went back, heard that voice—*his* voice—and hid. Saw the queen lying dead. It was well after I ran away, I heard the bells in the distance, and I was terrified, thinking they were somehow after *me*." She flushed. "I was fourteen. The thing is, I know the bells came after I heard that voice."

Danet spoke now. "My question is, who exactly gave the alarm, and what did they see? I always thought 'assassins' meant an army storming the castle."

Gdan snapped her hand away. "There was no brigand attack. Everything was peaceful. King and queen talking about where they should eat supper, and the last I heard before they sent me to water the horses was her saying they never could keep grit out of the food after all the dust had been kicked up in the wargames. I never heard shouts or swords clashing. They were killed in silence, or I would have heard the fighting."

Everyone pictured Mathren—so very good with weapons—approaching the king, his elder brother, maybe even smiling and talking casually, then cutting his throat, and stabbing the queen on the backswing before she could draw in a breath to yell.

Tdor Fath said, "Then Mathren *lied.*"

A soft knock at the door, and Gdan jumped away as if she'd been stabbed.

Tesar moved to open it, as Tdor Fath drew Gdan into the inner room.

Camerend stood there, taking in the shocked faces. "I came with news, but perhaps you already know?"

"That the jarl is dead?" Danet asked, since his gaze fell on her face. She gulped in air. "Or that Mathren Olavayir was at the site of the assassination twenty years ago?"

Camerend's reaction was subtle, no more than a tightening of the muscles around eyes and mouth, and a shift in his stance to readiness. His voice was so low they could barely hear him. "Commander Mathren? No, that question must wait a moment. I came myself, as I have information relating to our earlier discussion." He faced Danet. "One of my fellow royal runners, who just returned from a message run, once saw Parnid writing on the kitchen requisition board. It was before dawn a month or two ago, and he thought nothing of it—"

Arrow jerked his hand up, cutting Camerend off. Then he wiped his hand over his face. "Who's Parnid?"

"It's that name I found in the tallies," Danet said, low-voiced. "Remember? I told you."

Arrow rubbed his eyes again, struggling to master far too many shocks, but his mind kept coming back to *Da is dead.*

Danet said, "Come in."

Camerend entered and shut the door behind him before he spoke. "I thought it best to deliver this report to you. Ivandred said he wondered why

Commander Mathren's second runner was writing a false name on the requisition board, but figured he was substituting for another runner. We don't know all Mathren's people—he has them spread between the three closest garrisons, and they are forbidden to interact with us, except to deliver orders."

"All right," Arrow snapped, overwhelmed by frustration, grief, and a sickening sense of helplessness. "Got that. What's it mean?"

Danet said, "If Parnid is Mathren's man, then Mathren is skimming increasing numbers of army supplies. But why would he do that? He already commands all the garrisons, including this one here."

To the rest, who stared, bewildered and angry, Camerend said with deceptive gentleness, "May I suggest a possibility?"

Arrow snapped his palm up, grief choking him. *Da, you should be here to solve this problem.*

Camerend said, "I believe it means that Mathren Olavayir is building a private army, possibly unknown to Kendred, certainly to everyone else. Judging by the increasing numbers in the requisitions, which one of us has been checking," he added, flicking a glance Danet's way. "He could very well be training them here, a few at a time, then equipping them and moving them somewhere else. Another riding went out this morning along with Commander Mathren's lance drill; according to the stable hands, these were new trainees being sent to another garrison."

"I still don't see why the commander of the Royal Riders, the chief of the kingdom's military, needs a private army," Danet stated.

Arrow said truculently, "Probably to attack *us*, up in Nevree. He and Da hated each other, that much I know, though Da always said he'd tell us why if Mathren ever broke the treaty."

"True." Tdor Fath flicked her palm up. "I heard him tell Jarend that at least twice."

Arrow began pacing, throwing words back over his shoulder. "What do you want to wager he plans to sic that army on us, and give Nevree to Lanrid? He could do it right now, with Jarend and me here, under his thumb. Damn! Damn! Damn!" He struck his fist against the stone wall.

Camerend's face tightened as he looked away, then he tried to recover a semblance of neutrality as he said, "Whether or not that is the case, who wouldn't like to have a covert army to carry out their personal will, without having to justify it to the jarls until it's done? Mathren cannot call up oath-stipulated warriors from the jarls unless we're under attack."

Arrow moved restlessly along the back wall. "While all around us is a castle full of guards who only answer to Mathren's orders. Camerend. Do you know the defense plan for the castle?" he asked abruptly.

Camerend said, "I do. It's something we're taught when young, as we generally live on the third floor. Why?"

Arrow shifted from foot to foot, longing for his father to make sense of everything, to take command. *But he's gone.* He said, "I've been checking. Nobody is in any of these other rooms around us. But here we are, a long way from the stable end. If someone wanted to attack us, not saying who, they'd have us boxed from either end."

Camerend said, "Not to deny your supposition, but you truly are in one of the royal guest suites. Those to the left are the royal suites, in the middle of the hall, deemed safest. You're right that the defense plan is indeed to close in from either side to protect the royal family. But I could see that as a threat as well."

He ran a thumb over his jawline, then turned his gaze to Arrow. "If I may request we return to the previous subject, what's your proof that the commander was at the assassination site?"

Arrow side-eyed Gdan, who stood against the wall. He recognized that sick expression on her face: she was terrified that Arrow would reveal who she was and what she'd heard all those years ago.

Arrow crossed his arms. "Let's just say that twenty years ago, there was a witness who saw the king and queen left dead. The witness heard Mathren's voice giving orders right after the murder, and ran away back to Olavayir. Didn't recognize his voice until today. So until we know more, I don't trust Uncle Mathren." As he said the words, previous annoyances altered to oblique threat. "*Or* the Royal Riders, who won't let any of us near them. Keeping my Riders out there beyond the barns."

Camerend studied them, reflecting that for the first time in years, he was hearing the truth without having to spy and dig for it. It did not seem to occur to this particular set of Olavayirs either to lie to him, or to order him to confine himself to running messages.

He made a step toward trust. "If," he added, "something dire were to occur, those old servants' stairs in the far wall have been unused so long that they aren't in the defense plans." He pointed toward the narrow door at the back, which Danet had ordered blocked by a sturdy trunk. He could see the gleam of tears along Arrow's eyelids—the numbness of the news about his father had to be wearing off.

"Good." Arrow's voice had gone husky.

Camerend slipped out. Arrow was about to yell for him to stop, to tell them what to do, but of course he couldn't. Camerend was a royal runner. They carried messages, they didn't give orders.

He turned to the wall and knocked his fist against it one, twice, and again. His breath hissed out, and he drew it in sharply, almost a sob.

Then he tensed all over, swung around, and said to Danet, "I'd better find Jarend myself."

The door banged shut behind him.

Danet turned to Tdor Fath, down whose face silent tears dripped. Danet was aware that she ought to feel grief, but she mostly felt sad for Tdor Fath and Arrow; she had only seen the Jarl of Olavayir so very briefly.

Danet said as gently as she could, "I think I'll check that nasty stairway, just in case. I'll get a lamp."

Tdor Fath longed to shut herself in her room to cry out her sorrow, but she couldn't. She knew Jarend was going to be hurt far more than she was feeling right now. And here was Gdan, looking as if someone was going to cut her throat.

Tdor looked wildly around, her eyes stinging, her throat aching. She hated this castle, its unanswered mysteries, and above all the inescapable lour of threat. But nobody was interested in her opinion. All that was left was duty.

NINETEEN

Evred woke late that morning, aware that it was the last day of the year. By tomorrow he would be king.

He sat up, fighting the usual back-of-the-eyes-banging headache, and found his morning dose of willow-bark waiting by his bedside. He drank it down and lay back with his eyes closed, waiting for the throb to lessen.

Why didn't mages invent something *useful*, like a spell for taking away all effects of drink? Or one that gave a king the strength of a full riding — a wing! Willow-bark was so bitter, and it only diminished the pangs. Listerblossom made him want to sleep. Kinthus — so hard to get, he had to steal it from the healers — blanketed his mind. Sometimes he liked the way it helped his mind just float, as if he drifted in a summer stream, but when it wore off, he wanted to puke, an effect that worsened with each dose he sneaked.

Stupid, grasping mages. They probably had all kinds of spells for themselves. Otherwise why would anyone want to study magic, just to fix bridges and water barrels?

He sat up, irritable and impatient at the need to get through another dreary day before he could start giving orders. At least Kendred's memorial was over and no one the wiser; his mind shied away from how it might have happened. He'd paid his picked men double to make it fast.

Better to think ahead. That's what Kendred always said when he was treating Evred like a baby, that time would pass fast enough, and Evred needed to...Evred ought to...Evred should...always orders, and scolding.

Well, he'd looked ahead. He'd sent all Kendred's worst runner-spies off to the jarls to report that he was now king, all without Mathren knowing, because the uncles never gave commands to each other's runners.

That was being smart, and looking ahead! He'd picked his men, gave orders, and they obeyed. The actions of a king, and now he *was* king!

He was almost king.... There was still Mathren. Evred had to be sure that everything would go right when he sat on the throne tomorrow. At *last*. But he had to see *everybody* obey. If the servants did what he wanted instead of running off to check with the damned uncles — now only one uncle, but the most powerful one — he would give orders to Mathren. And if Mathren saluted properly, then Evred would know he was king. If Mathren didn't...well, then he'd be forsworn, right? But who would the Royal Riders obey?

No, they were no longer the Royal Riders, they were now the King's Riders. But that was a name, just a name if they only obeyed Mathren....

Evred got up and fumbled for his winter robe, sucking in a breath to yell for a runner, then he saw his private staircase empty and dark. Oh yes. He'd sent all Kendred's spies away. All he had left was blind old Mard, and Tarvan, the pipsqueak runner in training.

Evred groped his way down the staircase, hating the way the lantern swung at each step, making the stones appear to move under his feet. He usually had four runners holding lanterns steady.

Maybe instead of keeping Arrow and Jarend around until the jarls came, he could send that bonehead Jarend north to escort Hard Ride Arvandais part-way south, then he could take his enormous, lumpish self back to Olavayir. He could put Arrow in charge of the King's Riders. Or something else he'd like, because Arrow was pretty decent, overall. And Evred knew at least *he'd* obey the king's orders.

But what to do about Mathren? Of course. Send him to the Nob. Everyone was always complaining about the Nob, what a miserable post it was, a waste of tax money, and how the people there gave Marlovan Iasca the back of the hand, except when they wanted defense against pirates. Mathren would scare them into behaving, oh yes he would—and he could stay there for the rest of his life, fighting pirates.

Evred sank into the hot water, staring broodily at the midday light slanting in from the north window slit, and striking green-blue lights in the water. What if Mathren didn't obey? What if Evred told the guards to put him in the dungeon, would they do it? His gut writhed with uncertainty. Everything depended on the oaths tomorrow. Now he wished he'd dared to have the coronation right after Kendred's memorial, instead of sticking to New Year's just because he'd already said he would do it then.

When he came upstairs after his bath, Mard was there, laying out his breakfast dishes on the table, the bed tidied and all the sour wine smell gone along with the cup and bottles.

Evred said, "Mard, send Tarvan to find out how far along in preparation they are for the feast tomorrow. I have some more orders."

Mard laid his gnarled fist on his chest. "Right away, Evred-Harvaldar." And he went out of the room, hand outstretched, fingers lightly touching the door frame.

That was one of his orders. The runners were to call him "Evred-Harvaldar" instead of "Evred-Sierlaef." He had to get used to it, he'd said, or he thought he'd said, but really he couldn't wait to hear himself addressed as king—for it to be real.

He toyed with his breakfast until Tarvan returned, his cheeks red from bounding up the stairs, his bony fist thumping his scrawny chest. He piped in his squeaky voice, "The bake-ovens are all full, and every prep table had people preparing food, Evred-Harvaldar."

Gratified, Evred sat back, dug into his oatcakes with better appetite, then said, "Where's the wine?" Yes, it was early, but he was king! He could do what he wanted!

Mard and Tarvan retreated to the side chamber to work on his new tunic —that was another order he recollected, more gold stitching around the dolphin and on the sleeve cuffs. He was a king, and kings wore lots of gold with their Olavayir royal blue.

Happiness flooded through him, expanding outward as he imagined the entire castle as *his*. But it wasn't pure happiness, because he still did not know if Mathren would really obey....

While he bolstered his mood with a second and then a third glass of wine, at the opposite end of the castle, over the garrison command center, Mathren had bathed, changed, and eaten a quick breakfast with his senior captains, during which they'd sketched out the general plan for the exhibition riding that Evred had demanded as entertainment on the morrow—assuming the weather didn't worsen.

When that was finished, he went into his office to check with the duty scribe on the night's and morning's reports. The efficient scribe was reciting the list in his nasal honk when someone gave the quick triple tap on his door that meant a new arrival with an urgent message.

Irritated, Mathren waved to halt the scribe, then yanked open his door. The waiting runners leaped obediently to their feet, as Mathren's gaze lit on the second messenger to arrive that day. The big man leaned on a crutch, with one leg missing from the knee down. His cold-mottled face had purpled with healing scar tissue across one sewn-shut eye, down to his jaw.

Mathren stared at that ruined eye, the blonde hair escaping from under a knit cap, then said cautiously, "Retren?"

Retren Hauth, a second-cousin five years younger than Mathren, had had strict orders to stick with Lanrid.

At the distraught expression lengthening Hauth's face, Mathren snapped his fingers and waved at the scribe. "Out."

The scribe clutched his slate against his chest and slipped out to sit with the runners, who waited for the door to shut before speculating in whispers.

Inside, at a gesture from Mathren, Hauth eased himself onto the bench, his clothes dripping, his hands a-tremble as he laid the crutch across his lap.

"Lanrid is dead. So is Sindan," he mumbled through cold-numb lips, his voice hoarse with grief and exhaustion, his right hand pressed to his left shoulder where an arrow had lodged. Like the wound that had cut his face open, it had healed very slowly on his long journey south.

His words struck Mathren with lightning-bright, searing pain. Mathern recoiled, gasping, as if real lightning had crackled in the room. It took him several harsh breaths to comprehend that the reaction was entirely internal, that the castle stood undisturbed, and he caught the tail end of words, "...both of them. Sinna fell beside his brother."

"What? *Who?*" Mathren shouted, and outside the door, conversation ended abruptly.

"Massacre. Led by Hadand Arvandais," Hauth said.

Mathren scowled in disbelief, refusing to credit it. "You could have smashed a rabble of brats all on your own, Ret."

Hauth's head bowed between powerful shoulders. "Lanrid had me riding rear guard. He wanted his cousins and the boys up front. They only had four lances, all with banners attached. No one expected an attack in the Pass...."

And, in broken words, he gave a brief but sufficiently vivid eyewitness report.

"I will kill them," Mathren whispered when Hauth finished. "I will *kill* them with my own hands."

Hauth stiffened, eyes stark. "She's dead. Someone shot her — maybe one of us. Before he died. Because it wasn't any of us who survived."

"I'll kill all of them." Mathren drew in a breath and held it, exerting himself to regain control, to think, but the sense had gone out of the world. His purpose had gone. Lanrid was to be king by next year — he was not even twenty-five! Sindan to take Olavayir, and preside over the northern shore...little Sinna *dead?*

Mathren held his breath again, then murmured, "Go. Report to the lazaretto. You look terrible."

"Commander, there's also news from eagle-clan. Indevan-Jarl is dead."

A faint pulse of pleasure soured to irony. What matter, with Lanrid and Sindan gone? "Just go. And say nothing to anyone."

Mathren held his breath a third time, eyes closed: when he opened them, the room was empty.

He let out his breath, and rage overwhelmed him. Nothing mattered anymore. *Nothing.* All his work, his careful planning, a fortune spent in building a private army to carry Lanrid to the throne...and it was all for nothing?

That drunken sot wallowing in his tower was *not* going to inherit it all. He should have died twenty years ago, but for Fnor's stupid sentimentality. *He's just a baby,* and four years later, *He's just a boy.*

Boys grow up, he'd said. Except little Sinna would never grow up. He lay somewhere beneath the soil in that damned desolate Andahi Pass, forever silenced.

Mathren pinched his fingers to his brow. He still missed gallant, laughing, singing Fnor, but she'd been too smart, too quick. And far too sentimental.

He whirled around and glared at his map: Algaravayir, dead center in the kingdom, the most famous name in the last century. He could still send Nighthawk Company to take it, but now, for himself. No jarl would lift a hand against an Olavayir matched with a descendant of Inda Algaravayir, once Fareas-Iofre was made to see the wisdom of a treaty marriage. And with that name he could raise the kingdom to go north and *obliterate* those conniving traitors, down to the last child and dog. Yes.

But first, the loose end swigging wine on the far side of the castle. There was no longer any use in letting Evred play at being king until next year. He would act now.

Mathren threw himself down on the bench and propped his forehead on his fists. He wished he could reach into the distance to pull back Thad and the new Nighthawk Company recruits, to send orders with them. But he needed to think out those orders first.... *Oh, Lanrid.*

Another spurt of fury that he forced down. It was time to act. Right now, everyone in the castle was busy, the guard rehearsing their riding and weapons exhibition, the staff cleaning and preparing, everyone else running about.

He opened his door. Six shocked faces met his eyes. He forced a smile, and controlled his voice. "I'm going to consult with Evred-Sierlaef—let us say, Evred-Harvaldar—about tomorrow's schedule. Tlen."

Tlen snapped palm to chest. That will be a fist by midnight.

"See if the Olavayir boys are at liberty, and can meet in the new king's tower. They ought to be consulted as well."

Tlen fled, instant obedience as always—kingship in all but name. The prospect of purpose, of action, tamped down the fire of rage. Mathren believed himself cool and calm, but anger revealed itself in his enormous pupils, rendering his light eyes black, in the taut skin around them, and in the hard line of his mouth. That barely controlled anger was palpable to his subordinates from ten paces away.

The runner named Tlen encountered Arrow just leaving the guest suite, having brought Jarend in. Arrow couldn't bear Jarend's sobbing—he had to leave, to do *something*, or he'd be in there crying with him. And things were too...weird, too tense. He wanted to jump on a horse and just ride, until he could get his head straight.

But here was one of Mathren's runners.

Tlen said urgently, "The commander requests both of you to meet him up at the king's tower."

"Did he say what it's about?" Arrow asked, the back of his neck prickling at the strain in the runner's demeanor.

"He said, consultation."

"I'll get my brother," Arrow said, turning back.

The runner tapped a finger to his chest, and ran off.

Arrow took two steps and stopped short, leaning one hand on the rough stone of the wall. Consultation about what? Mathren had never, in their entire stay, so much as asked them what they might like to eat. It *might* be real, but Gdan's revelation, and her horror, made everything about Mathren suspicious.

Something was wrong; every instinct jangled. Arrow faced the wall, leaning both palms against it until the grit dug into his skin. He longed for a drink, but all the good stuff was up in Evred's chamber. Where Arrow was supposed to be heading right now.

He drew in another breath, trying to identify that sense of threat. The news about his father made his head hurt—but there was Gdan and what she'd said about Mathren. Though that was over twenty years ago, somehow it loomed large, an immediate threat.

If it felt like a threat, then why not take some steps? Quietly, like it was a ruse. If he turned out to be wrong, then no outsider would have to know.

Arrow straightened up. The hall was empty. He ran downstairs and out to the guest barracks, where his Riders gazed in surprise to see him back so soon. He was about to tell them about his da, then decided it would have to wait. "Snag some runner coats, all of you. But I want every weapon you can carry under those coats. Go to every landing below Evred's tower. Every place there's one of them, there should be two of you. Two of them, three of you. Make up any story you want, be lost, or lurk if you can. Think of this as drill, and I hope it will be, but if you hear me yell for help, come running. Take out the guards if you have to."

Those words stilled everyone. Then the Riders, with shuffling feet and exchanged looks, selected Arrow's second-cousin Sneeze Ventdor, who said, "Arrow? There's only three ridings of us. And three battalions of *them*."

Arrow jerked palm up. "I know. If something bad happens, what I need you to do is cover our retreat to the stable."

He wiped his hands down his coat skirt. "We can't fight them all, but maybe we can buy enough time to make a run for it." He felt control slipping away with every word, and grimaced. "I know it's a stupid plan, and I might be jumping at shadows. But...." He remembered what Gdan had told them—and there was still that question about Mathren's secret army.

He jerked his chin up. "But this is as good as I can figure, and if they do come for us, it's not like a retreat is going to make anything worse than it already is. I'd rather die fighting."

At that, Sneeze and the others murmured agreement, some shifting from foot to foot, others looking around at the windows for attackers.

"So pack your saddlebags fast. You four, get the horses saddled, and be ready to ride like thunder."

They saluted him, thumb to chest. He ran out.

The Riders exchanged looks of tension, question, even disbelief, then Sneeze said, "Me and Keth can fetch the coats." And they broke into action.

Arrow found Jarend slumped on the edge of his bed, Tdor holding one hand and Nunka the other. Jarend wept silently, his face so unhappy that Arrow's throat ached and his eyes stung all over again.

Arrow turned his gaze away, to where Rabbit played on the floor nearby, a toy horse in hand, his little round face with its buck teeth puzzled as he regarded his father with tears dripping down his long cheeks. Arrow jerked his gaze desperately away to where Danet stood inside the door, swaying and jiggling Noddy, who fretted and drooled.

She caught Arrow's eye, and whispered, "Nunka said he's teething."

Arrow grimaced, feeling the pressure of those orders. The last thing he wanted was Mathren sending a riding of armed guards to see what was keeping them.

He knelt at his brother's feet. "Jarend. Right now we have to go to Evred's. Mathren wants us, and I think there might be some kind of trouble."

"Trouble?" Jarend said, wiping his sleeve across his eyes. "What kind?"

"I don't know, and I might be wrong. I might be seeing what isn't there, because of what we heard today. But we should be ready." Arrow turned to Danet. "That means all of you. If you hear anything out there—more than one person coming—get everybody down that old stairwell. Did you check it?"

"Yes." Danet jerked up her palm. "Left-hand turn leads to the old baths, and the straight-way to the barrel court between the kitchen and the bakehouse. There's another turn to the right that I didn't explore, but that's the direction of the stable."

"Makes sense," Arrow said. "So servants can haul out gear without getting in everyone's way. That's the route you'll take. Bring extra weapons so you can fight if you have to."

Danet clutched the hiccoughing baby against her, jiggling and swaying as she pressed her lips together in agreement. Guilt formed a rock in her gut. Now she wished she'd kept up with her drills. But this was not the time to bring that up.

Arrow turned to his brother. "Time to go."

As always, Jarend said, "All right."

TWENTY

Upstairs in the tower, Evred was on his second bottle, his mood expansive as he admired Mard's sewing. The man was so skilled even though he was mostly blind.

Scrawny Tarvan sat on the floor, carefully twisting the gold silk lengths for Mard, who sewed entirely by feel.

Mard worked in a rhythm, humming so softly only Tarvan could hear him. Evred kept talking about his plans for the kingdom. From long habit Mard listened to the tone, not the words, for he had had care of Evred since those terrible days after he was orphaned.

Tromp, tromp, tromp. Over Evred's continual mutter, the sound of approach. Though Mard's vision had worsened with the years, his hearing had always been sharp: the fast tread was Mathren's, the breathing harsh. Mard stiffened, tethered by the drumbeat of his heart.

In his experience, you didn't hear Mathren's step unless he was angry. If he went quiet, that's when he was most dangerous. Instinctively he turned toward where little Tarvan always sat. "Get out of sight." A quiet rustle was all he heard from Tarvan, as from the bedroom door, Evred muttered, "What was that?"

"Evred-Harvaldar," Mard said on a rising note, "I believe someone is coming."

Evred set the bottle down on the floor, and wandered to the outer chamber, where he heard footsteps coming up the stone stairs. "Hah, I thought Arrow-head and Beaver-teeth would sleep all day, after being up last night. Well, we can start celebrating now —" On Mathren's appearance, "Uncle Mathren? What are *you* doing here? I thought you were at lance practice."

"You would have to say my name." Mathren's haggard face contrasted with his red-rimmed, angry eyes as he advanced on Evred, his whisper guttural. "You've just condemned that old stick over there."

"What?"

"You useless, worthless sack of shit, I should have strangled you at birth."

Evred backed up a step, and tripped over the bottle. Mathren ripped his sword free. Evred flung his wine cup at him. It clanged off the wall, splashing the stone with dark red wine — and a heartbeat later, blood mixed with the wine in a spraying arc as Mathren struck so hard he half-beheaded the uncrowned king.

Mard tottered forward, hands outstretched. "Evred? Evred?"

From the open door, Arrow's voice merged with Mard's, *"Evred?"*

He and Jarend ran inside, then halted in shock.

Mathren faced them them, red-stained sword at the ready, his face haggard. "And there you two are, in time to see my tragic reaction in self-defense against you two assassins."

Mard turned his head from side to side, his voice querulous and high, "You murdered him—he has no weapon."

Mathren whirled the sword upward and slashed it across Mard's scrawny, defenseless neck, so fast the old runner's eyes and mouth had a heartbeat to round in surprise before he crumpled to the floor in his own blood.

Jarend stared in shock. Arrow took in Mathren's rictus grin, just like Lanrid's before he ambushed him. Arrow kept his gaze on Mathren's face as he flexed his hand once, in the old signal, hoping that Jarend saw, and remembered. Then he backed up a step toward the doorway, forcing himself not to glance at Jarend. Mathren turned to keep Arrow in view.

Arrow said, "You're a lying liar."

"The truth—" Mathren's teeth flashed "—is whatever I say it is. I believe I've established that, haven't I?" He uttered a soft, bone-chilling laugh, and hefted the slippery sword in his grip. "What a tragedy, jealousy among cousins strikes again." He turned his shoulder to Jarend, as the latter hunched just inside the doorway, empty-handed and hangdog, and faced Arrow, holding out the sword between him and the open door. "It'll go like this. I couldn't stop your bonehead brother from assassinating the next king, but I was able—at great cost to myself—to execute justice. Unfortunately, you died in the process."

Arrow threw his hands up, as if he was going to beg or plead. Lanrid had always liked that, and Arrow saw the corners of Mathren's mouth cinch upward in an angry grin.

"Why? Why are you gonna kill *us?*" Arrow said, letting his voice crack as he took another step. Mathren moved to face him, as Arrow said, his voice cracking, "We never did anything to you!"

Mathren's gaze followed his empty hands, for of course Arrow hadn't come armed. Livid with rage, he whispered, "My son was to sit on that throne. But he's dead. He's *dead!"*

"What?" Arrow yelped, and tightened his right hand: *Now.*

Jarend's huge fist smashed into the soft bone behind Mathren's left ear. Mathren spun in a circle, then dropped in a groaning heap, the sword clattering next to him.

Arrow lunged for the sword, blood-smeared as it was, and used both hands to drive it down into Mathren's ribs until the point caught against his spine. Mathren groaned, blood bubbling obscenely in his mouth as he tried to spit out threats. Arrow whacked the sword down two-handed to the man's neck. Mathren stilled.

Jarend choked. The sound halted Arrow's white rage. Arrow yanked the sword out and straightened up, sanity rushing back as he stared down at what he'd done. Bile clawed at the back of his throat, his entire body shivering.

Jarend massaged his bruising knuckles with his other hand, a slow, convulsive movement as he said in a pleading tone, "That's what you wanted, Arrow? Like we did when we got back at Lanrid? You gave me the sign. It was right, wasn't it?"

Arrow wrenched his gaze from the sprawl of death at his feet. Jarend stood near, distraught, his voice strained and high, veins stark in his forehead. Arrow swallowed again, then forced his voice to calm, though his heart jumped against his throat, and his stomach boiled. "You did right, Jarend. You did very right. Mathren killed that old runner there. He killed Evred. He was going to kill us."

A little noise from the inner room alerted them both.

"Who's there?" Arrow demanded, and snatched up the sword again.

Tarvan crept to the open door, his face stark with fear and disbelief. "Mard made me hide," he whispered. "Please don't kill me."

"We won't," Arrow said. And then, on a different note, "You're a witness. You saw Mathren kill Evred, right?"

"I heard it. I heard everything," the boy bleated.

"What do we do now?" Jarend asked, his voice as high and as strained as Tarvan's.

Arrow gritted his teeth, his breath short against the stink of fresh blood that roiled his stomach even worse. He gulped air, fighting the urge to puke, as black dots swam at the edges of his vision. Time counted out in heartbeats as he fought the black spots, and won.

He looked up. Jarend and the little runner both stared at him as Mathren's words echoed, *The truth is whatever I say it is.*

The truth? The entire day had erupted in truth—and truth had turned out to be deadly. Arrow cast a look down at Mathren. Lanrid, dead?

He couldn't think about that now. Arrow's gaze flicked to Tarvan, and he knew that whatever he said would be repeated by this boy.

He knew he had absolute right. Mathren had killed Evred. He'd killed that poor old runner. He'd said, right out, he was going to kill Arrow and Jarend, and then blame all the deaths on them. It was self-defense if anything ever was.

But would all those people Mathren commanded throughout this castle believe it? According to what they'd discovered that very day, Mathren had lied so much that no one knew what was truth and what wasn't. If Arrow called for the Royal Riders, they might take one look at their precious commander, and charge on a killing spree in revenge.

He blinked, as Tarvan gazed fearfully at him.

Arrow realized he still held Mathren's bloody sword, and threw it down next to Mathren's lifeless fingers. The weapon of murder ought to be seen at the murderer's hand. "Runner — what's your name?"

"Tarvan." It came out in a pitiful squeak.

Who in this place wasn't a madman or a murderer? Arrow recollected the conversation earlier, and let his breath out in relief. He took a step toward the door, then looked down at himself. That damned sword had sprayed blood across the front of his coat. No one would let him get by unquestioned.

Jarend whispered, "Don't leave me."

Arrow stepped over, reached — saw his bloody right hand, and patted his brother on the shoulder with the back of his left. "I'm right here," he said. "I'm not going anywhere without you." He paused, his throat raw with ache. He longed to escape, to ride for home. Sneeze and the rest were down there waiting —

And then what? Be hunted down by the Royal Riders as murderers? If they ran it would look terrible. And anyway, there was no running home any more. That is, no running home to Da, who always made sense, who had sensible plans. Da was gone.

Arrow looked up at Jarend's pleading eyes, and knew he had to act. Now. Before someone else did. Get someone he could trust, who would know how to lock down the castle, if it was possible.

He turned to the boy. "Tarvan? Your duty right now, as I see it, is to go fetch that royal runner. Camerend. He's the one. Don't talk to anybody else. He'll know who we can trust, to get control of the castle." *I hope.* "We'll wait right here. We don't want any more killing, right?"

"No," Tarvan said huskily, with absolute truth. His shaking hand brushed clumsily against his skinny chest, as his neck knuckle bobbed.

"Right," Arrow said, trying to sound calm and encouraging. But his own voice sounded weird, like someone else was using his throat to speak. "You've got the most important job here, so run your fastest. Get Camerend, tell him to send the right person to secure the castle. And don't step in the...."

Tarvan had already hopped past the pooled blood, slammed into the doorway, righted himself, and lurched out onto the landing.

There he stood, his knees so watery he was afraid he might fall. He gulped in a breath and started down the stairs, his mind reeling. Instinct drove him to avoid the careless brutality of bored landing guards, and he ducked into the moldy old servant corridor with its tattered webs, his usual route. Jink. Jink. Jink — he had to cross public halls twice, then slip into unused rooms as few of those old corridors led in a straight line.

But he finally reached the main stair that led upward to the royal runners, and he breathed a little easier. Commander Mathren had issued strict orders never to talk to the royal runners, but he was dead. And Tarvan had new orders. From an Olavayir.

His resolve stiffened, allowing him to face the woman at the top of the landing who held out her hand to stop him. "I'm to fetch Camerend and not talk to anyone else," he said, with no idea how terrified he looked.

"Wait." The woman pointed to the floor in front of his feet and rushed away, her robe billowing behind her. She returned with a familiar royal runner, the one who was always nice. "Tarvan, isn't it? Mard's assistant? Speak," Camerend invited.

Tarvan glanced cautiously behind him before it all came out in a rush.

The two adults stared at him with twin expressions of grimness, but no anger, and no hands raised to strike.

When he finished on a sob as his numb emotions began breaking loose, Camerend said low-voiced, "Tarvan. You're safe. Wait here." To the duty runner, "Could you get him something to drink?"

It was Camerend's turn to take to hidden routes now. He fought the instinct to race straight up to the tower to see for himself what Tarvan had described, but those words about securing the castle had been spoken twice.

Camerend's mind raced faster than his feet. Whom to go to? That was easy enough. Though all the captains were loyal, or they would not have survived this long, most were loyal to Mathren. Many, maybe even most, were also loyal to the kingdom. He needed one for whom the kingdom came first, no divided loyalties. Who was as honest as the summer sun.

Camerend stepped out of the empty harskialdna tower into the garrison side court, and forced himself to slow. Now was not the time to draw attention. With moderate speed he made his way to the city patrol duty station, and asked for Captain Noth.

Shortly after Camerend stepped into the noisy command center, he found Jarid Noth listening to a night patrol leader issuing his report as a scribe wrote it down.

Noth wasn't much older than Camerend, though he looked it at first glance, with gray streaking his hair at the temples, and lines at the corners of his eyes. He took in Camerend, who wondered what in his own demeanor gave him away, as Noth abruptly dismissed the patrol captain and the aide, and closed the distance between them.

Camerend made the palm-up gesture for open air, and Noth's eyes narrowed, but he didn't speak as he led the way up the narrow switchback stair to the sentry tower, leaping up the stone steps three at a time. Camerend ran after, and they proceeded down the wall until they were out of earshot of the sentries.

On his walk, Camerend had mentally ordered Tarvan's sprawling, nearly incoherent report into a succinct summary, which he gave quickly and bluntly.

Noth's eyes widened, and because he was scrupulously honest, he said, "Why did you come to me and not to my commander?"

Camerend, aware of the press of time, said, "Because you are loyal to Marlovan Iasca."

He watched Noth's eyes narrow, then color stained his weathered cheeks and his chin jerk up minutely.

"Where are they?" Noth asked.

"Still there, as far as I know. But I cannot vouch for how long that will be true."

Noth turned up his hand, then said, "That order to secure the castle is a good sign. What I would have said myself."

Camerend agreed, but his mind had raced down another path, that of the investigator. "May I suggest sending someone right now to secure Mathren's office, before anything else? The new king is sure to want that done."

The new king. As he'd hoped, the promise of orderly transfer of power seemed to bypass the suggestion coming from a runner.

Noth turned, and they ran back down the stairs four at a time, Noth stopping only long enough to issue some terse orders, and Camerend ran ahead to fetch Tarvan, the only witness.

In Evred's tower, Jarend stood rooted, one big hand massaging the other fist over and over as Arrow looked around for something to clean his hands. He spotted a water jug on a side table and plunged his hands into it, rubbing his fingers until the water had turned red, then he wiped them on Evred's new shirt, which lay on a trunk. Poor Evred wouldn't be using that again.

The way Jarend gritted his jaw, muscles bulging on either side—it had been that way ever since they were little. Jarend had to be regretting what he'd done, though it was defense, it was necessary. But all their lives, Jarend had never liked hurting anyone, even Lanrid at his worst. He'd always been surprised at his own strength, and the only times he'd been punished was when he'd inadvertently used too much of it.

"Jarend, you did right," Arrow said when his hands were more or less clean and dry. "Mathren was not only going for us, but I'm sure he'd finish off our wives and the babies as well. But now we have to make sure they are safe. Right?"

Jarend's painful expression eased as he raised both fists to touch his heart. "Right, Arrow. Right. What do we do next?"

Arrow thumbed his temples, as if the pressure would force clear thought into his head. What would his father say? *Lock down the castle.*

Noise from the stairwell caused Arrow to stiffen, and he bent, fingers outstretched toward that disgusting sword in case he had to defend them...but the first one through the door was Tarvan, who stuttered to a stop at the sight of the three dead men sprawled out on the floor. He slunk to the opposite wall.

Camerend entered behind Tarvan, his face utterly impassive as he took in the sight at a glance. He said, "City Guard Captain Noth is with me. He stopped to give some orders." He gestured toward the inner door.

The sounds of approach echoed up the stairs. Arrow ranged next to his brother, as two armed guards appeared, swords ready. At their shoulders, a broad-shouldered, trim captain with thick gray-streaked brown hair. This had to be Noth.

The guards stepped to either side. Captain Noth eyed Arrow and Jarend, brushed two fingers to his tunic, his other hand on his sword hilt, then took in the scene. The room was so silent that Arrow could hear Noth's breathing.

When he looked up, Arrow told him what happened.

"That's right," Jarend said several times. "That's right."

At the end, Noth glanced at Tarvan. "Tell me exactly what you heard."

Tarvan stammered his way through a fairly accurate account. Arrow suppressed the urge to correct details. He was afraid he'd sound like he was inventing a story. *Like Mathren.* So he forced himself to stay silent until it was done.

Noth looked around once more, and his hand dropped away from his sword. "Commander Mathren losing control like that—I would have said you made it up. He never loses, lost control. But if he just found out that his boys are dead...." He didn't finish his sentence, and shook his head. "I can check with that runner who arrived a while ago, just to make certain, but I believe you. I believe you. So what now?"

Camerend stood inside the door, unnoticed as he reflected on how decision—not quite the same as command—had passed from Arrow to Camerend himself to Noth. Though by now Noth's most trusted men were surely deploying through the castle, if it came to a fight, no one could predict what was going to happen.

The obvious course seemed to prevent that fight, and that meant following chain of command, all signs of order, no matter how ephemeral. He said, "I can send Mnar to escort the grand gunvaer to the throne room, if you like?" He addressed the center of the room. "Right now she's the senior authority."

Captain Noth studied Arrow and Jarend, eyes narrowed consideringly. "This probably isn't the time to get into it, but I don't know what's right, here. Camerend told me on the way over that you have a witness, after twenty years, who saw Commander Mathren kill Garid-Harvaldar, Evred's father."

As always, Jarend looked to his brother, and Arrow said, "She didn't see him. She heard him, and ran—she was a stable girl. Fourteen. It wasn't until today, when she came with messages, that she heard him speak and recognized his voice." And Arrow described what Gdan had told them.

The suspicion in Captain Noth's face eased to a frown. He propped his fists on his hips, his gaze now falling somewhere between the two brothers. "Fact is, every damn change of kings for the past three generations has been bloody, the worst finger-pointing always in your family."

Arrow bit the inside of his cheek to keep from shouting that he was telling the truth. In his mind the loudest voice yelling "I'm telling the truth!" was always Lanrid, always justifying himself. He wondered how to prove that what he'd said was true.

Noth glanced down at Evred, his expression bleak. "If what you say is all true, it seems clear enough now the commander never intended to let that boy sit on the throne. And some will justify it." He glanced over at Mathren's sightless eyes. "Then there are some of us who disliked how that boy was handled. Marlovan princes always trained in the academy, when there was an academy. Everyone in the previous generation says, that's what holds us together. Inda-Harskialdna was proof of that."

Arrow's temper flared. "Did *you* know about Mathren's private army?"

"His *what?*"

Camerend, standing behind Noth, grimaced as Noth's and Arrow's voices echoed down the stairwell. He heard the scrapes of footsteps and the mutter of male voices from below; word, or rumor, was already spreading.

"Camerend, you tell him," Arrow said. "You're the one who guessed about the army."

Camerend jerked his attention back to Noth, and he gave a succinct report.

Noth said dubiously, "Mathren's third runner Thad took off this morning with recruits for Hesea Garrison."

"How do you know they're really going to Hesea Garrison?" Arrow retorted.

Noth's lips parted, then he passed a hand over his face. "I don't."

"They've only been gone a short while," Arrow said. "Can you send search parties?"

Noth said reluctantly, "The Royal Riders won't take orders from me. Chain of command is strictly enforced, and—" He stopped, glancing down at Mathren's body, took a breath, then said with a glance of approval at Camerend, "I did give orders to my own men to seal off the commander's office, as well as secure the castle. If they were able to do so, then his papers will be untouched."

He swung back to face Arrow. "In any case, that's going to have to wait, if this private army is not actually storming the gates. Unless you want fighting to break out all over the castle, we need an orderly transfer of command. You can say the old gunvaer has authority, but she's been locked up for years. For her safety. That was Commander Mathren's doing, too, but again, he always had reasons for everything, and he was the hero who saved the prince."

The bitter irony of that struck them all at once, and Noth bit down on a curse. He had scarcely finished with sending off the baby belonging to one of his Cassad-territory Noth cousins, after Kendred's assassination, ordered by.... His gaze drifted to Evred, sprawled in death.

He breathed out, shifting his gaze to Mathren as he said heavily, "He was strong enough to keep order for twenty years. Now that he's gone, most will be looking for equal strength as well as order."

"Order is what I want, too," Arrow said, then added, "We." With a hand opened toward Jarend, whose well-deep voice rumbled, "That's right."

Arrow could hear his Da. "Lock down the castle, trusted men at every intersection. Say orders are coming."

"From?" Noth prompted.

Camerend interjected smoothly, "Perhaps all the Olavayirs should be seen united in the throne room, if the all-castle summons is rung."

Captain Noth grimaced as he glanced down at Evred, then up again. "I know who to talk to first. Who'll make sure there's order. Before the news gets to the Royal Riders." His gaze rested somewhere between Arrow and Jarend. "There are three times more of us than there are of them, right now; maybe it's a good thing that company rode out this morning."

Arrow nudged his brother, and Jarend said obediently, "That sounds right."

Noth turned, a flare of coat skirts. "Then I'd better get at it," he said, and ran down the stairs.

Camerend lifted his gaze to Arrow and Jarend. He spoke gently. "When the bells ring the all-castle summons, which I am very certain Noth will see to once he positions the garrison sentries and the city patrol. You must be prepared to speak. What you say, how you say it, will be carried through the doors into the kingdom." He glanced down. "As for them, leave the fallen to us. You can promise a proper memorial come midnight. We'll see to it they are properly prepared."

Arrow was glad for any excuse to leave. "Jarend, first thing, we need to tell Danet and Tdor Fath."

Jarend's jaw muscles had begun bulging again. But the mention of his wife caused a slight easing, and Jarend followed as Arrow led the way down the stairs, trying to figure out what to say first.

At the landing, he saw his own Riders standing in ill-fitting runner gray-blue, all eyes going to the blood splattered across his front.

"What's going on?" Sneeze asked, low-voiced. "People running around. Some with weapons out."

Arrow resisted the impulse to wipe his still-sticky hands down his ruined coat and said to the expectant faces, "Mathren is dead. He killed Evred. Don't say anything to anybody, just go and raise the rest of eagle-clan Riders. No dolphins. Be ready for anything. When the bell rings, if there's no trouble, report to the throne room. And you can put your own coats back on."

They tapped two fingers to their chests and ran downstairs. Two fingers. It was then that Arrow remembered how vague Captain Noth's salute had been, and that he hadn't saluted at all when he departed.

The truth slowly dawned on him, that as Evred's heir—by treaty between the two Olavayir families, made twenty-some years ago—Jarend was now not just the new Jarl of Olavayir, but the king.

Jarend was *the king*.

Well, unless someone else ran around the corner, sword in hand. Then there'd just be two more corpses for the memorial.

Arrow lengthened his steps, Jarend breathing hard as he stumped along beside. When they reached the suite, they found Danet and Tdor Fath each holding a sleeping boy in one arm and a knife in the other. Tesar had ranged herself beside Danet, also armed. Nunka stood behind them burdened with heavy bags, ready to go.

To the row of wide, questioning eyes, Arrow said, "Mathren is dead. So is Evred...." And he described everything in a backtracking, repeating ramble, until Jarend stirred, and swung his head Arrow's way, his eyes as puffy and red-rimmed as the knuckles on his right hand. He finished carefully, "And so by rights, Jarend here is king."

Jarend worked his jaw, then, "Arrow, I don't want to be king. I want to go home."

Tdor Fath's eyes closed. Tears glimmered in her lashes and slipped down her cheeks.

Danet flicked a puzzled glance from one to the other, and Arrow saw the exact moment she understood what they meant.

Tdor Fath turned to Jarend, and handed Rabbit's limp form to him. "Could you put him down in his bed, Jarend, since it seems we won't have to escape this very moment?"

Jarend bowed his head, carefully took his son, and shuffled into the next room.

Tdor Fath shut the door behind him and said, "Please, Arrow. Please send us back. Jarend knows what to do, at home. He gets these headaches when things change around him. He grew up expecting someday to be jarl, and his mother is there, and Sdar, and all the Riders Lanrid didn't like, which probably means the ones Jarend likes. Please, *please*."

"*I* don't want to be king either," Arrow snapped. "I don't know the first thing about being king. I've had enough bad dreams about not being able to figure out anything Da ordered me to discover. How am I supposed to command a kingdom?"

"Evred knew much less than you do," Tdor Fath stated, her voice unsteady. "And Jarend never trained for being king either. He was heir only in name, for a treaty that was a bandage over a wound in the family that Mathren's branch never would let heal, that's what the jarlan always said."

No one was going to argue with that.

Then she turned to Danet, swallowed a sob, and firmed her voice with an effort. "Right now, what Ranor-Jarlan always says is, the kingdom is really a lot of petty kings. The jarls can do anything they want. They need a king who can fix that, but also they need a gunvaer who can *organize*. And there is nobody I have ever met in my life who would be better at that than you."

"But..." Danet began, as she handed a sleeping Noddy carefully to Gdan.

Tdor pressed her hands against her eyes. "Don't say anything about tradition. What traditions are left? Assassinations? It's happened twice in one generation—and once when our parents were young. I think whatever you do is going to be better than Mathren or Evred."

"That's not what Mathren's Riders will think," Arrow said. "I'll wager you anything half the Royal Riders are *in* that damned private army."

"That can't be helped right now. It sounds like that royal runner went to the right captain, which means that the royal runners might be in favor of your taking the throne. Because he could just as easily have sent Mathren's people up to that tower to attack the both of you. Clearly not all the guards are Mathren's."

Arrow was going to point out that the royal runners were powerless—mere runners—but the women knew that. He knew they had no more answers than he did. He turned around in a circle, trying to comprehend as vast a world change as anything in his life. King? It seemed a joke, or a bad dream. Where were the great heroes of old, who always knew exactly what to do?

But this was now, and as his father had said many times, the days of heroes were over. There was just them, and what was that Mathren said about Lanrid being massacred by Idegans—a king would have to deal with that. But there was no king's army, not unless he raised the jarls....

"Norsunder take it, I don't even know where to start," Arrow said, his voice cracking. "Why does there even have to be a king? Aren't there places with no kings? Why can't *we* do that? Everybody goes home. Takes care of their own."

Danet could hear her mother's dry voice. "Because they *won't* just go home and take care of their own. Because even if you call the king a chief, or a guild chief over guild chiefs, or a...herald, or whatever other people call them, someone *always* wants to hand out orders. Better to choose them if you can. A riding of nine has a riding captain. The artisans have a guild chief. The holders and market towns have a jarl. The jarls have a king."

Tdor Fath added, "Better to have someone handing out good orders, rather than someone like Mathren, killing and lying and having private armies." She thumbed the tears from her eyes. "You know Jarend will do his duty if you tell him to. But he'll always look to you. Or if you go back to Nevree, he'll trust whoever is kind to his face. Whatever they said behind his back. You *know* that."

It was Arrow's turn to drop his gaze, remembering how, when they were boys, if Arrow wasn't on the watch, Lanrid had figured out how to sic his followers on Jarend, flattering and following him until they got him to do something they all thought was hilarious. They'd fooled him most of the time, because Jarend had a good heart. A clean heart. He always believed people were better than they really were.

But he would no longer be fooled at home if Lanrid was really dead. Jarend would have their mother and Tdor Fath to look out for him. The household, too, now that Lanrid's own followers were much diminished. Arrow knew they all loved Jarend, because he was steady, and kind, strong as a river, and always wanted to do the right thing.

Arrow turned to Danet.

They faced one another across that room, both feeling similar emotions: how sometimes it felt they had known one another since childhood, and other times they were strangers. How neither had ever foreseen anything like this situation.

Danet's gaze caught on Arrow's sleeve, as if noting small things would somehow make sense of this strange version of the world. It was Arrow's second best coat, with the left sleeve still slightly longer than than the right, and she had meant to fix it once the wargame was over. Better than looking at that horrible dark spray down the front. She didn't want to know whose blood that was.

She crossed her arms, feeling exactly as lost as he did, except for two things: first, the inner itch to wade into those archives, and second, the knowledge of what Mother would have to say about shirking duty.

"If you do it, I'll figure out the kingdom tallies," she vowed. "Whatever else is going on, a kingdom has to have a treasury, and a record of what comes in and what goes out."

Arrow turned away again, trying to hide the flare of fury. He knew that he'd let her decide, and she had decided. What's more, she'd chosen what was right—if anything could be called right in this mess—and not what he wanted, which was to go back home to the life he'd grown up to expect, and had been missing every day since their arrival.

He yanked off the blood-stippled coat and threw it down. In his shirt, riding trousers and boots he stalked to the nursery and plunged his hands into the ensorcelled diaper bucket to rid himself of the last of the blood. When he slouched back in, wiping his hands on his pants, he said heavily, "Everybody better put on their House tunics. We'll figure out what to say as we hike down to the throne room."

TWENTY-ONE

Later on, Danet remembered only shards of that hasty throne room assembly. First, stepping onto the dais in a vast chamber of stone with banners and shields on the walls below a high gallery under a vaulted ceiling. The throne room was so cold that even the entire castle population filling it, standing shoulder to shoulder, did no more than make the honey-colored stone of the walls darken with moisture.

Danet stood at one side of the throne on which the frail old grand gunvaer sat, and stared down at her scraped and dusty boots, holding her breath in expectation of being shot or stabbed.

Every shuffle and scrape, every whisper seemed imbued with threat, or derision. She sensed an equal tension in Arrow next to her, and eventually heard his voice, but the words he and the others spoke could have been in another language. She was too giddy, and too bewildered, to make sense of anything except her own two feet below her.

On stepping up onto that dais, Arrow had shared that same sick, grim sense that they were walking straight into ambush. The dais, to him, meant he presented a clear target.

But, though he knew he was no king, neither was he a coward.

So he stood braced for attack before the entire castle population, as the gunvaer stated in her thin voice that the former Commander of the Royal Riders had broken oath and struck down the unarmed Evred-Sierlaef as well as his blind first runner, which caused a murmur: most of the guards and all the castle staff had liked gentle old Mard.

As she spoke, Arrow forced himself to look back at all those staring eyes, and began to resolve the mass into individuals, and then to perceive patterns, specifically how Captain Noth stood at the front, flanked by those who had to be his allies among the captains, and Arrow suspected he'd salted his most trusted men among the mass gathered behind. He knew those subtle signs of eye and chin. They were all watching certain others, whose tight faces gave away leashed anger, or grief.

He began to perceive that Camerend Montredavan-An, in choosing Noth to report to, had been more aware of the inner workings of the castle garrison than maybe the guards knew themselves. But then, runners *would* know such things, passing in and out where others couldn't go, for years.

The grand gunvaer, who only saw a blur of faces except for a slender flame drifting toward her, ended by stating that there had been a witness, who would now testify to what he had seen and heard.

She gestured, and Tarvan, lurking behind Jarend on the other side of the throne, stepped out, his armpits prickling. He'd always been aware of being the smallest and ugliest of the runners in training, sent to serve with old Mard because the Commander Mathren despised him. Now he was suddenly the focus of the entire staff—it felt like the entire kingdom—and having all those eyes on him was acutely painful. Camerend had done what he could to bolster the boy's wavering courage, by rehearsing with him on the long walk to the throne room.

Tarvan spoke those words in a shrill rush. Only the front heard, but they whispered to those behind. The key words were Mathren's deliberate lies, and the fact that Jarend—unarmed—had felled him with one blow, though the commander still gripped his bloody sword, ready to kill again.

All eyes turned to Jarend, whom they knew was Evred's heir. Both Royal Riders and, when they went out to drill, the royal guard, had been drilling with the huge, silent young man for weeks, and had discussed his physical strength among themselves where their captains couldn't hear. Not everyone was loyal to Mathren, especially those passed over for the Royal Riders, or promotion to one of the garrisons. One blow? Hah. Those who had endured ferocious floggings for what they regarded as tiny infractions quietly reveled, wishing they'd seen it happen.

For Arrow, first came hope, then a gradual and amazed acceptance, as Jarend, racked with grief, looked as impressive as he ever would in his life: he uttered no laughter, or betrayed unease, for when he knew what to do, he did it. And the whispers were still ringing outward, *Took out Mathren with a single punch.*

With utter conviction, Jarend said, "As Evred's heir. Stipulated by treaty. I as king will give only one command. That is that my brother Ar, ah, Anred, here, remain as king. I will return to Olavayir as jarl. And only come if the king calls us to war."

Glances flashed between Noth and his allies and they sent up a shout, eagerly joined by Arrow's Riders. More joined, though some remained silent, angry, bewildered, and a few afraid. Arrow continued to pick out individual faces, and with an invisible gut-thump recognized Retren Hauth, a distant relation through Lanrid's branch of the Olavayirs, promoted to lance master when Lanrid got his promotion.

Hauth looked as pale as his hair, except for his one eye ringed with the dark skin of exhaustion, the other covered by a patch. Arrow remembered Noth saying something about Hauth having arrived that morning from the north. He had to be the one who'd brought Mathren the news of Lanrid's death.

Arrow looked up. Now everybody was staring at *him*. Time for his own speech.

He sucked in a breath.

All his life he'd lived in the shadow of bigger, stronger boys, Jarend at his side, and Lanrid against them. He had no notion that he'd grown into a straight-backed, taut figure in his own right. He would never be beautiful, but he looked as much like a young king as could be expected as he said, "We'll assemble here at midnight, then, for the memorial Disappearance, and I'll take oath as king. Captain Noth, dismiss the guard, and have them patrol the castle. You, Hauth, give me a report on what happened up north."

And so Anred-Harvaldar gave his first orders.

Retren Hauth limped painfully forward, and in front of half a dozen lingering ears, gave Arrow a vivid report on the massacre.

At the end, Arrow said, "What do you know about this private army Mathren has been raising?"

Everyone in earshot, already riveted stepped closer, shock ringing through them.

Hauth said quickly, stolidly, "There is no such thing."

"Yes there is," Arrow shot back.

Hauth's gaze shifted away. "I never heard of it. I was Lance Captain in Nevree. You know that."

Arrow did. But as he stared at the man, he realized that further questions were useless. How could he prove anything Hauth said was true? It was becoming more clear by the hour that Mathren had lived in a world of lies, which would be supported by everyone loyal to Mathren.

He waved Hauth off, unaware of how the news about the private army began burning through garrison guards, city guards, and perhaps most damaging of all, through the Royal Riders.

Arrow muttered under his breath to Camerend, "Isn't there some stuff like green kinthus, but stronger, that makes you tell the truth?"

Camerend said, "White kinthus. But I do not know that anyone in the castle, maybe even the city has any. It's extremely dangerous. Hauth is still recovering from severe wounds. He probably wouldn't survive a single dose. My suggestion is to avoid using it unless you are truly convinced that the individual in question isn't telling the truth."

Arrow wasn't sure. That was the whole point. But then he remembered Mathren's office, still guarded, and said, "Never mind."

By then Hauth was nearly at the door, having slowed his steps; he had made his report, but instead of swearing vengeance against the Idegans for their treachery, that idiot Arrow had brought up Nighthawk Company.

A day or two later, when Jarend's runner came down to the barracks to call for volunteers to return to Olavayir as the new jarl's honor guard, Hauth was first in line; it would be easy to vanish along the road, and make his way to Nighthawk Company's training ground, where they must decide what to do with their commander dead, and his plans in smoking ruin.

TWENTY-TWO

And so I have given you the truth behind the infamous Night of Four Kings. (The third being Mathren, for even less time than Jarend.)

Before the dawn of New Year's Firstday, Arrow and Danet had become king and queen.

Memorials for royal figures had always happened by torchlight midway between the end of one day and the dawning of another, with coronations directly after the old king was Disappeared, superficially guaranteeing that the Marlovans always woke to a king in place—but more often than not the intent was to establish an immediate legitimacy, which in turn would grant the new ruler the right to smite rivals. There had never been much in the way of ceremonial, when everyone knew that the most important element was who commanded the military.

That was not to say there was no ceremony.

The royal runners had done their best with Evred, clothing him in the fine tunic Mard had not quite finished. Poor, blind Mard was also there, victim of Mathren's ambition. And Mathren made the third, Camerend and Captain Noth having decided against relegating him to being Disappeared from before the prison, having cheated them of a traitor's death. The fallen no longer cared. Memorials were entirely for the living, and the inescapable truth was that a good part of the castle had been loyal to Mathren for years, and still was.

When the bodies were gone, Danet stood before the throne with a sword in either hand, her entire body stiff with self-consciousness as Sneeze Ventdor and his picked men began enthusiastically pounding a rolling beat on drums from up in the gallery.

Arrow walked up the aisle between those gathered to witness, and stepped up onto the dais.

Danet did not attempt any fancy maneuvers with the swords. Everyone there knew she was not a gunvaer trained in defense, and she wasn't going to pretend to be. She handed the two swords to Arrow, then stepped to one side of the throne as up in the gallery, Sneeze Ventdor and his hand-picked riding pounded with heartfelt enthusiasm on the big drums.

Arrow clashed the swords together, raising a respectable arc of sparks, threw down the swords east-west crossing north-south, and began the traditional sword dance, which of course he'd been doing every festival day his entire life, and often just for fun. He'd picked Captain—now Commander—Noth for one of his four guards representing the four borders of the kingdom, thus cementing his authority; Noth whirled through the dance as vigorously as Arrow. Jarend, of course, was North, lumbering grimly but powerfully through the dance, after a ringing clash raising a shower of sparks. The last two were Sneeze's younger brother and their father-cousin.

Danet stood there feeling awkward and self-conscious, her thoughts careening from memory to question to observation: the way Arrow danced, his bow-shaped mouth set hard with his effort not to fumble or stumble; Arrow as king; where was that army; what was it about the line of masculine backs and the curve of thighs that hit her so viscerally?

She blinked past the broad-shouldered Captain Noth to the side entrance, where Camerend Montredavan-An stood directly under the torches, his hair touched to gold in the firelight. Gratitude buoyed the purely physical reaction, for she knew how much he had helped: the thought occurred to her that his family had once been royal. They were in the old Hymn to the Beginnings. He even looked like a king.

She turned her gaze away, and grimly squelched her reaction.

Arrow ended the dance to a respectable cheer, and thought, *That's the easy part done.*

He raised his voice. "Evred sent runners to summon the jarls to Convocation at Midsummer. We'll keep to that. For everyone here except the wall sentries—they can rotate at half-watch—liberty today, and a feast."

They shouted with more enthusiasm, and were dismissed by their captains in military order. Arrow stood where he was, watching; Camerend had told him what to do to this point, but not what was expected next. Did he wait till they were gone, or march out the side door over there?

Then he remembered that he was now king. He was supposed to be deciding those things. He tried to look kingly as he watched Noth supervise the dismissal. Mnar and Camerend gently helped the grand gunvaer up from the side throne that had been dug out of storage.

Hesar paused to look around, then murmured, "Ah, that poor lost child."

"Child?" Mnar said.

Hesar raised a withered hand, pointing to a spot beside the now empty throne, as Arrow and Jarend closed in behind her. "Evred, right over there. Don't you see him?"

"I don't see anything," Arrow muttered, his skin crawling. He didn't *want* to see anything. He hated talk about ghosts, or weird things that couldn't be explained.

"Odd," Hesar quavered, unperturbed. "I see that poor lost boy much more clearly than I see any of you."

Jarend said to Arrow, "She sees Evred's ghost."

Arrow forced himself to respond normally, even carelessly. "Better than Mathren's."

Jarend uttered his old chuckle, which Arrow was relieved to hear. It was disturbing to have his brother so quiet. He sped up his steps, glad to leave the subject of ghosts behind.

Danet, too, glanced at that empty corner, but before she could follow, Hesar caught her by the sleeve. "Bide a moment," the old woman quavered. "Listen to me, Danet-Gunvaer."

Danet grimaced, finding the title attached to her name an absurdity, a fraud somehow perpetrated on her as well as on the world.

Hesar's rheumy gaze lifted in her direction as she said, "I never trusted Shendan Montredavan-An and her ambitions, after she sneaked away to Sartor for all those years. Perhaps I was wrong. Our troubles have never come from her, or from her runners. I advise you to begin with them."

Danet swallowed in a tight throat. "We have done that."

The grand gunvaer gazed off into the distance. "Good. Listen well. Whatever you decide, remember this: what you wish, what you want, what you will, it now matters. *Never* forget that for a moment."

She groped for her runner's arm, and shuffled away.

Danet sped out, relieved to escape that throne room, which she hoped not to have to set foot in again until Midsummer. Assuming they hadn't joined Evred as haunts.

Jarend was moving slowly. Danet caught up with the brothers in a few quick steps. The three stayed silent until they reached their suite, which was already being packed up by the runners, under Tdor Fath's orders. Danet skirted around trunks and sought out Tesar, saying, "If you want to go home with Jarend, I'll understand. I know you haven't been happy."

Tesar blushed dark red, her gaze fell, and she said, "I'll stay, If I can be a real runner."

Danet's face bloomed with a smile of relief, which gratified Tesar.

Danet said, "I've always wanted someone of my own to carry letters, instead of having to wait on others. And now I have so many people to write to. Like Fuss, for a start. She was supposed to be the next gunvaer."

Tesar was so pleased that she actually spoke without being asked a question, for the first time ever: "You won't have to wait now." And she smacked palm to chest in salute to a gunvaer.

Danet smiled, then it occurred to her that trained female runners were not going to sprout out of the ground. As Tesar set to packing with marked enthusiasm, Danet walked down the hall a few doors to where the royal suites traditionally lay, the king's overlooking the parade ground on the west side of the castle, and the queen's facing east and the inner courtyards.

These suites each had a number of spacious side-chambers, including those for attendants, and several exits. Danet promised herself to explore every single one of those exits, just in case.

She found Arrow standing in the middle of the king's outer chamber, hands on hips as he pointed at some fine old wingback chairs with legs carved into raptor claws. "Those can stay. Desk, table. Everything else goes."

A row of runners picked up baskets of silk-covered cushions, rolled hangings, and the remainder of Kendred's luxuries.

"I'll take those cushions," Danet spoke up, causing the line to veer through the doorway across the hall.

As the rest of the runners began toting unwanted furnishings out, Gdan pointed at a thin, wiry woman whose brown coloring was a lot like Danet's own. "This is Mnar Milnari," Gdan said. "Royal runner."

Mnar turned Danet's way and saluted. "Do you require runners?"

"Yes," Danet said simply, and with no pretension to an authority she was clearly unused to.

Arrow stood by unnoticed. Amusement sparked in him at how much Mnar and Danet looked alike. At least at first glance. Then the differences occurred: Mnar's triangular face (courtesy of her Noth ancestors through the Cassads, though he did not know that) so different from Danet's round one, how Danet talked with her hands, but the other woman didn't as she said, "Our original purpose was to serve the royal family. Of recent years we've mostly been confined to running messages and renewing bridge, firestick, and water spells. I can assure you, we have plenty of excellently-trained young people who need a place, and are well practiced in all runner duties, including scribe and archive as well as personal runners."

"Thank you," Danet said with real gratitude.

Mnar gazed with interest at Danet, whom she'd seen from a distance, but never met. As they crossed through the open doors into the queen's chambers, where Tesar was busy directing the distribution of bed linens, floor mats, and the embroidered pillows that Arrow had rejected, Mnar asked what types of runners Danet would need. Danet began slowly, and Mnar saw how frequently the new gunvaer hesitated, then asked precise questions that opened into new questions. Mnar began to appreciate a mind trained to hard work and orderly procedure.

The traditional nursery had once been on the third floor, where the royal runners were now housed. Danet chose the suite one door down from hers for the new nursery, and an army of servants got to work, so that by dawn, there would be an entirely new royal family in residence.

Arrow wandered back to his new suite, watched the runners busy at work, and reflected on how two days ago he couldn't get them to fetch him a cup of ale. But he didn't fault them. The atmosphere of constraint that had held the entire castle in its grip was beginning to ease. There was almost a festive sound to the voices, and a vigor to the work, now that people weren't looking over their shoulders.

He crossed back to the queen's suite, which looked just like his, only facing east. Fighting a gaping yawn, he gestured her out to the hall. "They know what to do. Let's go take a look in Mathren's office."

"Now?"

"We should have done it first thing," he said, hating this sense that there were a hundred things he should have done—and he had yet to go to bed.

He watched her mouth thin, and knew she was thinking exactly the same thing.

They approached the riding of armed guards at the ground floor entrance to the tower stairs.

"Any trouble?" Arrow asked.

Eight pairs of eyes shifted to one fellow dark of hair and skin, who said, "We just came on. Nothing reported from the day watch."

Arrow said, "Good," and passed by, Danet in his wake. They trod in silence up and around, each lost in weary, but nerve-driven, headlong thought.

The first landing opened into Mathren's command center, before which stood two more guards. "Anyone tried to get in?" Arrow asked the nearest.

The man shook his head. "Nobody made it this far."

The outer chamber giving onto the office had benches forming three sides of a square, below a huge dolphin banner.

"How many runners did Mathren have?" Danet asked, looking at the benches.

"I don't think anyone knows. Maybe Noth will find out something," he added, wondering how much trouble was going on in the garrison—if his promoting Noth over all Mathren's commanders would stick. I'm still looking back over my own shoulder, he was thinking as they entered the office.

It was a small room, with only the one entrance, and one window. Easily guarded, Arrow thought, looking at the two tidy desks, the storage shelves, the trunks, and dominating everything, an enormous map on one plastered wall.

"This is old," Arrow said, eyeing the map. "Real old."

Danet's gaze lifted to pins stuck in various places, each with a bit of paper appended, with cryptic marks. "A code," she breathed.

"Damn," Arrow said. "I hate that sort of horseshit." He turned his back on the map. "You're the one who figured out about the army. What exactly are we looking for?"

Danet thumbed her temples as she scanned the desks, the shelves, the trunks. "I don't know. Let's start with the easy and obvious: any mention of Nighthawk, or Parnid, or anything that you think points toward a secret army. You know military talk better than I do."

Arrow went to the large desk, and began rooting through the piles there.

Danet moved to the smaller desk opposite, clearly an orderly's workplace, shelves adjacent lined with bound books exactly like the one that lay open on the desk. Beside the open book lay a stack of paper, three quill pens, a pen knife, and ink.

Danet bent over the bound book. Here, too, was code, mixed with Marlovan.

"Nothing, nothing, nothing," Arrow exclaimed. "All rosters, reports from the garrisons, and monthly summaries from the quartermaster. Not a whiff of any Parnid." He turned away and surveyed the room, which was bitterly cold, the firesticks snuffed by someone; he noted with disgust that the fireplace floor was a bed of old ash. Since firesticks did not burn, but released captured sun warmth through magic, the ash had to be exactly the sort of evidence they sought.

He was distracted by the steam of his own breath as his gaze shifted from item to item: a sword (not the one that had killed Evred and Mard—that one Noth had taken away), a cloak folded neatly over a trunk. Several books above on a shelf. He reached for one: in faded ink, *Eyewitness Accounts of the Battle at Andahi Pass by Vedrid Basna, Branid Toraca, and Camerend Kened*. War reports. Of course. Arrow didn't bother with the other books—he suspected he'd already read them, sweating over his desk as a boy.

He kicked the cloak to the floor and opened the trunk, to discover tied sheaths of paper rolled up. "Damn," he said. "It'll take an army to paw through this stuff."

Danet said, "I'll do it. It's not only that army I want to find, it's treasury records, and everything else he hid."

Arrow heaved a sigh of relief, suddenly so tired he could scarcely stand. "You're better than the best. Ma was right."

Danet flushed. "Seems to me I have only the one talent, and I like numbers and breaking codes. It's satisfying. Besides, you have a lot more to do that I can't help with. Why don't you go get some rest while things are quiet? I'm going to sort through these and make some piles."

Arrow said, "First, I'm going to hunt up that quartermaster."

He ran down the stairs, already feeling lighter—and nearly knocked Camerend down. "Any new assassins or disasters to report?"

Camerend opened his hands. "Nothing new," he began.

"Good." Arrow grinned, not well enough acquainted with Camerend yet to hear that slight emphasis on the word *new*. "Who would I talk to if I wanted the academy to start again?"

"The academy?" Camerend repeated.

Arrow flushed as if he'd been caught breaking rules, but stiffened his stance. He was now a king, and his father had said repeatedly that the kingdom would only be united if the academy was running again. Even Noth had said it, standing there over the dead bodies.

He wasn't ready to admit to his worry that he would be terrible at commanding an army even if he had one. He knew he'd had as good a training as anyone in the north, at least. So there must have been something different, and better, in the days of Inda-Harskialdna. While boys got trained, he could get trained, too.

"We need it," he stated, rubbing gritty eyes.

Camerend heard the defensive almost-question, and said slowly, "Well, as for cleaning the academy buildings out and finding where all the furnishings have been stored, the castle steward for now, but the eventual Headmaster would need a staff for that as well."

Arrow's gaze shifted sideways, then back. "Where are the records about...how it was run?"

Camerend said, "There are of course records of competition-scores and dispositions and the like in the garrison archive. But if you mean, records about training...."

He hesitated, knowing that it would be a mistake to mention the extensive records written by his greats-grandfather Saverend Montredavan-An—known as Fox. And yet the last third of this memoir was comprised of direct quotations from the famous Inda Algaravayir, refinements Inda and the also-famous Headmaster Gand had worked up together—a training method aimed at defense, not offense.

So he finessed. "Well, as it happens, Headmaster Gand, I'm certain you've heard of him, left a training book, which we royal runners kept in our own archive after the academy was last shut down. I can send someone to fetch it, if you like."

Arrow smacked his hands together, his whole face alight with relief and delight. "Do it!"

Camerend said, "It'll take a few weeks for someone to travel to Darchelde and back in winter." That would give them all winter to extricate a suitable Gand record and leave out all the personal memories.

"That's fine," Arrow said, rubbing his hands. "I figure it'll take a year to get things ready. I'll tell the jarls about it at Midsummer, and they can send their sons the next spring."

"Very well," Camerend said, thinking, *It's time.* "There's something you should know, Anred-Harvaldar."

Arrow grimaced at hearing his given name, which he'd only heard when he was in trouble. The *harvaldar* just worsened it. Then the sense of Camerend's words sank in, and the grimace turned to a scowl. This couldn't be good. "What?"

Camerend watched the changes of expression that it never occurred to Arrow to hide, and out of hard-trained habit, began with carefully worded misdirection, "You can ask Commander Noth, who dispatched people to investigate—"

"Just tell me," Arrow said impatiently. "I can get details from Noth later."

"Very well. Kendred Olavayir was murdered, along with his first runner. His second runner survived, which is how one of us found him." Which was true enough — if he left out their own investigation.

Arrow said, "Mathren again?"

"It appears to have been at Evred's command," Camerend said. "That is, he hired the assassins. No one in either the royal guard or the Royal Riders was part of it. Commander Noth personally questioned those who had liberty that day."

"Evred hired assassins?" Arrow repeated. Hadn't he spent every day with Evred? But not in the mornings, when he'd thought Evred still asleep while he drilled with Sneeze and the rest of the eagle Riders, behind the cow barns. And there had been a few nights when he couldn't stand Evred's drunken drivel any longer, and came back to sleep in the guest suite. "Did Mathren find out?"

"We have no idea, as he communicated with us only to send us with messages, or to conduct inspections. But he has to have, as the assassins were disguised as an honor guard. Which means they possibly used guard horses, but definitely guard coats."

Arrow's bow-mouth flattened into a tight white line. "I bet I know where those assassins came from. I bet I even know who they are."

Arrow cast a fast glance toward the hall in the direction of the nursery, and Camerend understood: what he saw in the new king's face was the anger born of fear.

"Every stable hand and wood gatherer in the kingdom is supposed to be protected by the law. To be promised justice," Arrow stated, fists on his narrow hips. "But when it's kings getting their throats cut, and their families, suddenly it's just the way things are. But if I'm going to be a king, I'm going to change that." A quick step and a turn. "I don't want to worry every damn night about my boy getting stabbed in his cradle. So let's get Noth to yank every one of those shits out of the Captain's Drum and squeeze them until someone yaps."

"And then?" Camerend asked, aware that Noth was already ahead in this matter.

"For the ones who did it, the most public execution I can contrive," Arrow stated with fear-driven fury. "I hate that kind of shit. Floggings, executions. But I'll watch it and not even blink. I want the entire city to see that there will be consequences when they ambush us, whoever's behind the orders."

As a royal runner, Camerend was required to listen, not to argue. This new king had passed the first, easiest test — no. It was too easy to impose ordered hierarchies of trust over the fluidity of everyday human behavior, just because one desired. He would allow himself this much observation: Anred-Harvaldar was better trained than Evred, and far more transparent than Mathren.

Mindful of the communication net that the royal runners and Darchelde had exerted themselves to hide from the previous kings, as well as from the regent and his brother, Camerend felt the urge to tell Arrow about the golden notecases. But then he remembered the old story about Evred-Harvaldar becoming more and more obsessed with who had them, and whether or not they could be compromised. He had loathed magic and mages because he could not control them, and had finally got rid of them, forbidding his jarls to use them.

Arrow solved the question for the moment by taking off with rapid strides, determined to tackle the quartermaster, though it was still not yet dawn.

TWENTY-THREE

Camerend retreated to the third floor, where he found Mnar sitting by the fire with her knees under her chin, the way she'd sat since they were first-year runners-in-training, proud of their dark blue tunics too big for their skinny bodies. She sipped coffee, well dosed with with listerblossom from the smell.

A quiet step. Shendan entered and sank down in her chair. "Isa sent me," she said to Camerend's look of question. "She's keeping vigil, she and Frin, down in Darchelde."

"How does she even know?" Mnar asked. "It's not like she's touching anything here."

All three of them exclaimed, "Cassads!" and gave little smiles, humor an all-too brief relief, release.

Camerend then related his conversation with Arrow, and finished, "I like this young king so much that I was tempted to offer him a golden notecase. Not that Kendred was so terrible," he amended, uncomfortable at slandering three recently murdered people. "Just lazy."

Shendan, feeling no such compunction, stated, "Kendred was a selfish sot, and I believe the effects of his neglect are going to be a burden for these two new rulers to deal with, once they materialize. You were right not to mention the golden notecases."

"Agreed," Mnar said. "Arrow Olavayir might be grateful at present, but what if he starts brooding about how long we've had magic transfers, and why didn't we offer them to the other Olavayir kings? We don't *know* him, really."

"That occurred to me as well. Should I have kept silent about the other two matters? Fox's record, and the truth about Evred?"

"Probably," Mnar said, grinding her bony chin on her equally bony knees.

"No, on both," Shendan said, with a glance of mild reproach in Mnar's direction. "It was always possible that a king would start the academy again before our descendants could. That was an excellent notion, to mention Gand, rather than our ancestor Fox."

"That's why I did it," Camerend said. "If I leave out the Fox drills, the rest is all Indevan-Adaluin's ideas on humane handling, of shared command, of using the least possible force to attain the goal."

Mnar sighed. Just because you offered people the best didn't mean they would heed it. But she found this new young couple so profound an improvement on Kendred, Evred, or Mathren, that she kept silence.

"As for the golden notecases, why not wait? There's plenty of time to reveal their existence. We're sworn to the kingdom, not to any specific king, and our use of them is to that end."

"I'm too tired to argue," Camerend admitted. "And too much has happened too fast. We are no longer ahead of the news, as it's happened right under our noses."

Shendan opened her hand in agreement. "As for matter of Kendred's assassination, you could have left the report to Noth, but you want the new king to trust you. Bringing information to him will begin that trust." She shook her head slowly. "And so the last of Dannor Tyavayir's branch of the Olavayirs has come to a bloody end."

Mnar said, "The infamous Dannor's bad blood really was persistent, wasn't it? A remarkable number of them handsome and utterly without conscience."

Camerend raised a hand. "Not all. Not all." He still had nightmares about Sindan Olavayir and his singing.

Sleet rattled at the windows in wind-driven gusts. Then Camerend rose, and tapped the backs of his fingers to a piece of paper. "With so many runners now going into service for the new king and queen, we're going to have to shift ourselves about considerably." He turned Shendan's way. "Are the youngsters ready to come to training, say, by spring, assuming we deem it safe?"

Shendan said, "I wanted to discuss that very thing. Yes, by all means. And Senrid is another subject to be brought up. It's time to discuss the specifics of his training, early as it is."

Camerend heard this in silence.

Shendan went on, "You were forced to be raised here—that was my agreement with Tanrid Olavayir, to protect Darchelde. Though you were a hostage, and knew yourself to be, no harm came of it. I propose you not wait until he's older, but bring your son here right away, to be raised under your eye."

Camerend turned to gaze into the fire, hiding the extremity of his conflict. He knew that Shendan regretted their lack of mother-son relationship as much as he did: he had not been permitted to visit Darchelde until Garid became king.

He eyed his mother in silence, wondering if she had discussed this prospect with Isa, who he knew could not bear to come back to the royal city, which would mean effectively surrendering her son. Shendan had been forced to surrender him when he was small, but she had exerted all her influence through Tanrid-Harvaldar's gunvaer to make certain that the tutors the king hired were pre-selected by her.

Camerend said slowly, "Perhaps I'd better go talk to Isa face to face. I need to assure her that the danger is over. And it's always a delight to see my son." On Shendan's nod of permission, he transferred.

Up in the garrison wing, Arrow confronted Captain Noth, having come straight from his interview with the grizzled quartermaster. Arrow slammed the door to the central command office and said, "I thought that shit-sack was going to spit in my eye as he kept repeating he only followed orders. I can't have him shot for that, but I'd stake my life he's Mathren's man."

"Yes, he is," Captain Noth said. "Very loyal."

"Then he can go be loyal up at the Nob," Arrow snarled. "Along with that assistant, smirking around behind the door listening. In fact, that snake will be well-deserved by those turds up at the Nob, from everything my father said." His face spasmed in grief at the mention of his father, and he added truculently, "All Mathren's men can go with him. Starting with the supply annex."

Noth hesitated out of habit, then made a decision. Under Mathren, offering an opinion could get you flogged, demoted, even killed. He'd grown up with that system, thinking it eternal. The events—and the revelations—of the past few days, the last two watches, proved that wrong.

So maybe it was time to speak up. And if this new king was going to be like Mathren, best to find out now. "The fact is," he said, "we *all* took orders from Mathren. It was your life if you didn't. And we all considered ourselves loyal, as well. But with what we've recently found out—well, all around me I'm hearing there are many ready for a new life. Right now the Royal Riders are split over the private army business, for example."

"They don't believe us," Arrow said.

"Some don't, it's true. Many others do believe it, and feel betrayed. They had been told repeatedly that they were the elite, the most trusted. Clearly that's not true if there's this shadow army whose purpose is unknown. As for the rest, they may or may not know, but none of them are talking."

"At least they aren't fighting," Arrow muttered. "And so?"

"And so, my advice is not to gut entire service wings. Send off the captains and their own assistants, if you wish. But leave us a functioning castle. I believe we have enough trustworthy men deserving of promotion to ensure orderly changeover."

Arrow rocked from toe to heel, clearly turning these words over in his mind. Noth permitted himself a cautious hope.

"All right." Arrow smacked his hand on the desk. "You know 'em better than I do. I certainly can't replace the entire garrison with my three ridings, much less the quartermaster's staff. Whom do you suggest as a replacement?"

It was Noth's turn to think. Men were, in his experience, seldom all one thing or another. They had all professed loyalty. They had to. But some were more outspoken than others. He searched his mind for the quiet ones who did their work without talking hot. "As for the quartermaster's staff, Pereth oversees garrison repairs, and I know he gets along with the cobblers and the weavers. He's a family man, married local. Two small boys. Seeing as he's in repair, I doubt he was part of building a private army."

"Good," Arrow said. "He sounds good. Let's put him in charge, and everyone over him can get dispersed to other garrisons. None in command, either."

Heartened by this frank exchange—and the fact that this new king could take advice—Noth saluted, fist to heart. "It'll be done by day's end."

Back in the royal runner roost, displaced air stirred the fire, and Shendan turned her gaze toward Mnar. "I can see you still care for Camerend, though your heart is given to Vanda, who can never return from the north."

My heart among half a dozen others, at least. The words weren't spoken, but they both were thinking them.

Shendan said, "Why don't you offer Camerend the comfort he needs?"

Mnar sighed. "You're talking like a mother."

Shendan's mouth lifted on one side, into a crooked not-quite-smile. "Really? And yet I never had the raising of him."

"Then maybe you're not thinking like a mother. I don't know. I never was one, nor wanted to be. My fuzzies and fledglings are more than enough for me. As for Cama, first, I would never want back the terrible days of my teenage-passion. Second. He can get sex anywhere—if he wants to break his ring pledge—but what he can't get is a sister. Nor I a brother." Mnar crossed her arms.

"Ring pledge." Shendan sighed. "The ring is not a magical wall."

"That's right," Mnar retorted with the heavy sarcasm of hurt. "No stone or iron. Just a vow, so why not break it a little here and there?"

Shendan sighed again, more deeply. "Mnar. Ring pledges can be set aside, too, if people find themselves so changed that nothing keeps them together except the vow. As is happening here."

Mnar shook her head. "I don't believe it. I know Isa. I don't know Frin as well, but...."

"You haven't seen either of them except briefly in the past ten years. I live with them—I love them both—I'm training Isa to lead the family's magic learning when I'm gone, when Camerend must be here. But I see what I see, and that is, she's ever more bound to Frin. She lives with her with her gloves off, sleeps with her—and both Frin and I see her preparing for days, weeks even, to brace for Camerend's visits."

"I didn't know that," Mnar said.

"Of course not. He doesn't see it either. And Frin hasn't the heart to tell him."

Mnar looked down at her hands. "I thought if ever a three-ring pledge would last forever, it would be theirs."

"Three ring, two ring, ten ring, the number matters little." Shendan turned to the fire. "All permutations of human relationships can endure, can flourish — if the individuals want it, need it, make the day to day decisions and effort to strengthen it. Though I love Isa, the truth is, I was sorry from the beginning when she proposed to Camerend, because I could see, though he couldn't, she didn't want him in the same way he wanted her, she wanted what he represented."

"She loves him!"

"As a friend, as a duty." Shendan turned her palms up.

"But they have a child!"

"Duty. And now that little Senrid is weaned, I suspect she considers that duty done. Her passion is reserved for Frin. She gives herself to Camerend when she can bear to, not because she wants to."

Mnar squeezed her eyes shut. "I wish you hadn't told me that."

"Why ever not? You cared for him once, and Vandareth is in permanent exile. You will only see him if you go to the north coast," the older woman said.

"Cama's comfortable with me. I'm comfortable with him. There's no heat. I *prefer* it that way. We work together much better without the messiness of ardor. And even if he were free, and he did catch fire, it would be terrible because I know myself. I don't do love well," Mnar said with a wry, sidewise look. "I'm jealous and possessive. Every single relationship I've had was bliss for a short time, then torment for an eternity, until they had to get away from me."

She rubbed her temples, then dropped her hands. "The worst was Vanda. You joke about his half-dozen lovers, but there are more than that. Why do you think he really volunteered to go north? That was *my* fault, and all because I was 'in love.'" Her tone mocked the words. "Every boy or girl he was with was competition to me. Did he like them better? I had to fight against spying on him to know who he was with, to count who had him the most. Even though I knew from the start that he will never choose just one."

Shendan sighed. "Very well. I'm as sorry as I can be, especially that you never told me how serious your emotions were."

Mnar shrugged. "What could you have done? One thing adulthood taught me is, keep my messes to myself."

They fell silent, lost in tired reverie, the only sound the crackling of the fire, as far to the south in Darchelde, Isa clasped Camerend's hand between her gloved fingers and said, "The crystal web was me," she said, her beautiful eyes earnest. "I have kept you in a trap, bound by love. I have to set you free," she said. "And you must take our son, lest I ruin him, as I have our love."

Down a floor and farther along, Danet woke from a brief but deep sleep, at first bewildered by her strange surroundings. Then surged the tide of memory, and though she'd scarcely slept three hours, and not at all the night previous, she was now wide awake, her mind running stubbornly over things to be done. Duty had been the earliest prod in her life.

She had been raised to put duty first, which she had never quarreled with, as she reveled in order. Part of order was understanding everything in her immediate world, and her own place in that world.

She sat up in bed, looking down at her familiar palms as she tried out the word *gunvaer*.

It slid right into meaninglessness, impossible to grip. She looked around the enormous bedchamber—the very one that the great Hadand Deheldegarthe had lived in. Maybe she had slept in this very bed. Probably, considering how infrequently anyone ever changed furnishings, in her experience. Maybe even the same sheets, as excellent linen could last at least a century. Only the mattresses would have changed.

Hadand had never had the choice of becoming gunvaer either, in the sense that she'd come to the royal city as a two-year-old. But she'd done her duty. If a great woman could square herself to this duty, then Danet could only try to follow as best she could. Maybe that would help convince her that she was a gunvaer.

But first, she had to make sure that everyone else saw her as gunvaer.

What would Mother say? Make a list. Beginning with what you need to know.

She went down to the baths, then slipped back inside the gunvaer suite, trying not to disturb Tesar slumbering in one of the inner rooms. She dressed in her house tunic, rebraided her hair, and set out at a brisk walk back toward the state end of the castle.

When she bypassed the throne room and started up the stairs over the banquet hall opposite, she heard the clatter and chatter of preparations below. She marched through the door and sailed into the archive, where she found a dozen scribes of various ages sitting about idly, as New Year's Firstday was a liberty day in most of the world.

All looked startled at her entrance, then rose to their feet.

She studied each face, unaware of her own expression, which was pretty much a glare. Most of them recognized her, and remembered, vividly, the jokes they'd made at her expense the first time she came through that door.

Her eyes narrowed, and the oldest of the scribe students hastily recollected being taught the salute to a gunvaer, and snapped his palm to his chest.

Hands impacted chests. Danet waited another endless moment, studying the ruddy faces, all wary, many with the wariness, and awareness, of guilt.

"Today is a festival day," she said, arms still crossed. "But tomorrow morning, you are going to show me *everything*. I want someone here and ready for a thorough tour. Someone who can answer *every* question."

Her hot gaze met the eyes of that tall fellow who had been so sarcastic. Her breath hissed out. "And if you still find me boring, you can always go count ships up at the Nob."

His face blanched. Satisfaction surged in her. She bit back an impulse to lengthen the moment, but she could hear Mother's scorn for that. *Make your point, don't belabor it, or the point gets lost in resentment.*

She backed up, shut the door with a decisive click, and marched back to her new chambers, laughing under her breath in giddy exhilaration. She knew the exhilaration wouldn't last. The kingdom was a mess, the castle was worse. Those scribes were probably cursing her roundly, back in that room. She'd given herself the rest of New Year's Week to work through Mathren's papers. Along with learning how to do tallies for an *entire kingdom*.

She couldn't find the right way to describe her emotions, except terrifying, overwhelming, thrilling in a runaway-horse sense.

She found Arrow waiting outside her door, looking frowzy and red-eyed, smelling of drink. She couldn't find it in herself to blame him. He had to be worrying about Mathren's secret army, which might gallop up any day, swords waving. Then there was what to do about the massacre up north, and who knew what other problems she had no conception of, which never again could be passed along for someone else to deal with. She wouldn't let herself hate the responsibilities that had avalanched onto them, but she knew it would be easy to give in and blame the entire world.

"Noddy's awake," he said.

"I figured he would be," she replied. "I went to the scribes. Tomorrow, first thing, I'm getting a tour of the archives. All of them. Then I think we both better tackle the quartermaster, and find out what he knows."

"I've already done that," Arrow said. "Dead end — followed orders, did my job, is all he said. 'Don't know the runners, only the commander did, they just keep the records.' I've gotten rid of him." He stepped close, and peered down into her face. "Danet, I don't feel any Birth Spell mysteriously coming into my head, whatever anyone says about it, and I want Noddy to have a brother. We need to make sure there's going to be a future king, everything right and orderly."

He could have a sister, Danet thought, but she knew what he meant: he was afraid, as she was, that Noddy would become a target. And Marlovan kings had always been men. Maybe one day there could be queens only.

There certainly were elsewhere in the world, she'd heard, but she also knew that she, an accidental gunvaer, was not going to be able to change that.

"I don't feel any magic Birth Spell either," she said. "I think if it works at all, we both feel it. That's the way it did for my great-grandmother, anyway." Nobody knew how, or when, or if, the Birth Spell would come to someone who longed for children. Only that occasionally it did.

"Will you drink gerda?" Arrow asked, peering anxiously into her eyes.

"Yes," she promised, and in spite of the emotional inundation she caught at one tiny triumph: if she was about to be pregnant again, at least she'd nabbed those cushions.

"I will not be sorry to leave the ghosts here," the old gunvaer said, her voice quavering, as her runner helped her down the steps of her tower for the last time. "That poor boy is everywhere I look. He's so much brighter than the others...."

Danet waited with Tdor Fath at the bottom of the stairs, hands gripping in her sleeves. When Hesar-Gunvaer reached them, Tdor indicated for Gdan to take the old woman's other arm, and so they slowly, and safely, guided her out to the courtyard.

Danet cast a quick look upward, though the bright, almost brittle light indicated an iron-hard frost. She knew Jarend and company would travel as fast as they could while it lasted. She trailed them, trying to think of something to say, but everything was too strange, too strained.

However, the gunvaer was thinking of her. "Young Dannor," she said, as Danet grimaced, but didn't correct the old gunvaer. "You must reinstate the betrothal system before this kingdom tears itself apart. All of Hadand-Gunvaer Deheldegarthe's dynastic records are in the archive, which you now have the authority to unlock. Ranor and I will fill in the last generations. You must begin keeping records now."

Another task. Danet said, "Thank you for the advice. I'll see to it." She knew that Mother as well as Ranor-Jarlan would agree.

"Mount up," Jarend said. At the prospect of returning home, he looked as happy as he ever had, even though the knife of grief still cut his heart when people saluted him as jarl.

Arrow ranged himself alongside Danet as the Riders who had chosen to return to Olavayir formed columns ahead of and behind the tent-covered cart bearing Hesar-Gunvaer. Tarvan clambered up on the cart, smiling; Jarend's single blow to Mathren, who had terrified Tarvan since early childhood, had prompted the boy to beg to go with the new jarl. Jarend, kind of heart, had promised to find him a good place at Nevree.

Jarend's good mood was a startling contrast to Retren Hauth riding shield. He'd chosen—to Arrow's considerable relief—to return to Olavayir.

After Sneeze reported an altercation with eagle-clan's Riders, Arrow had forbidden them to harass Hauth further. Hauth'd been loyal to dolphin-clan, and an excellent lancer, though Arrow had always hated him for bullying Jarend. In contrast Lanrid could do no wrong in Hauth's eyes—Lanrid's bullying was "toughing up."

Glad that he'd soon see Hauth's back, Arrow smiled as Jarend stated the obvious, "Today's the first day of the new year. And I'm going home." Arrow knew that when Jarend told everybody what they already knew, he was making certain it was really true.

"That's right," Arrow said. "New Year's Week is over, a new year has begun. And you're the new Jarl of Olavayir, so ride out like a jarl, eh?"

Jarend raised his fist and turned it toward the gate. The cavalcade began to move, the trumpeters signaling *Jarl riding*, which would clear the streets to the city gate, where the trumpeters would peal again in final salute.

The brothers lifted their hands to one another, then Jarend rode through the gate, and Arrow cast a huge sigh. "I hope that's the last we hear about ghosts," he said as they turned back to the tower entrance. "I wish I could believe it's all old age and her blindness. The thought of Evred watching us makes my neck crawl."

"Me, too," Danet said. "Though I hope she's right about the dynastic archive. Hadand-Gunvaer's letters were located in one of the oldest archives, under some other old trunks. I've had them moved to my rooms. It's going to take time to go through them. She wrote a lot of letters, it seems."

She was going to say more, but saw the disinterest in Arrow's face, and shut her mouth. They both had too much to do—and Arrow was going to hold the execution of Kendred's murderers, who Noth's investigative team—all experienced city patrollers—had captured. Danet was relieved he hadn't insisted on her being there.

His thoughts paralleled hers. With a quick look her way, he muttered, "Let's go inside. It's damn cold out here." And when the stable hands had dispersed to their work, "I hate executions. But I told Noth to make it as nasty as possible, because I want every soul-sucking thief or would-be assassin to hear about it, and know that there's no more getting away with it."

"Did you get them all?" Danet asked.

"Three of them. Right there in the Captain's Drum. They seemed to think I'd reward them, because I was always there with Evred. Well, they thought wrong," Arrow said, brows twitching into an irritated line. "I told Noth to have the city patrol do surprise searches in that midden heap until they catch the last one of them. Someone's sure to turn him in if the patrols make life miserable enough."

He sent a quick look Danor's way. "You want to send those scribes down to watch? As a reminder?"

"No need," she said. "They've been working hard." Mother had always said it was a mistake to threaten people obviously doing their best, even if they made mistakes, or they didn't like you. *If you have to remind them of your rank, you've already lost their respect,* Mother had said when talking to Danet about becoming randviar, before her ride to Nevree.

"Some of them, I think they're happy to be given real work. Mathren didn't let them do anything but copy guild records, and general orders."

"Right. Noth's questions turned up nothing but more about how Mathren didn't permit anyone to question orders. So the sooner you figure out what he was hiding, the better," Arrow said, and Danet turned up her hand, smothering her annoyance.

Mother was right, she thought. Being reminded of your duty when you're already working your hardest doesn't make you work any harder.

But she kept that to herself, and they parted at the landing, he going on to the garrison and she to Mathren's lair, where she'd spent all New Year's Week sorting things into piles, and then listing abbreviations and symbols, and possible meanings.

All she needed was a single clue, even a date—

Then the obvious struck her. Wouldn't the royal runners have records of letters sent out, including dates? Obviously Mathren sent his own runners, especially with the coded ones, but maybe, maybe, maybe there was a week, a day, something, when he had to use the royal runners and there would be a record up there that she could use to triage the codes between Marlovan-written dates.

She whirled around and trotted in the opposite direction, then ran up the last flight of stairs two at a time, to the third floor, where the royal runners lived and worked.

She'd only been up there twice. There was usually a royal runner within call, but it was early. Mnar's fledglings were probably at their morning drill, and her usual assistants at breakfast.

She heard voices echoing from a room down the hall. Seeing the doors open, she headed down the unlit stone corridor toward the rooms that all faced east, and so were full of light.

Peering in, she saw Camerend Montredavan-An, who had been away all week. She hadn't seen him ride in—but obviously he had, probably during the commotion attending Jarend's departure. One glimpse of his distraught face as he held a tousle-haired child of two or three and she backed away, nerves stinging. Not certain why, for officially the royal runners now worked for her, and the entire castle was in principle under her rule, she did not want him or any of them to know she was there. It was the naked grief in his face, he who was always so very composed and aware.

Walking on her tiptoes so her boots wouldn't clatter, she stepped to the stairs, and fled down even faster than she'd come up.

TWENTY-FOUR

Shendan, Jarlan of Montredavan-An, paid a rare visit to the new king and queen.

She said, "I have sent Camerend to Sartor to refresh his language studies, so — with your permission — I'm temporarily resuming my old post as chief of the royal runners. When he returns, he will supervise your translation scribes who deal with foreign affairs."

Arrow looked at her askance, then to Danet. Both were too intimidated by the sharp-eyed old woman to ask why she'd taken it upon herself to send Camerend out of the country. But then the royal runners had their own chain of command, which it had not occurred to either Arrow or Danet to question.

Danet said firmly, "Very well. We'll carry on as we've begun."

The first days of the new reign turned into a week, and weeks into a month, then another; no army showed up at the gates. Danet finally cracked Mathren's record book code (based with cool arrogance on the words *Harvaldar Sigun*, or *war-king triumphant*), just to discover that there was no evidence in that office of the scrupulously noted orders and reports all enticingly labeled NHC, but those telltale ashes lying in the fireplace.

There were plenty of reports not labeled NHC. Such as pages and pages of spies' reports on secrets and weaknesses of every jarl and Rider Captain in the kingdom, including — especially — eagle-clan. After reading the malicious exaggerations written about Arrow and Jarend, and especially about their father, Danet burned those pages herself, joining their ash to the rest in that fireplace. She also decided to burn the reports labeled LH (Lanrid-Harvaldar), about Lanrid's improvement in various military skills. Lanrid was dead, as was his brother, whose reports were full of notes about how often Sindan bucked training in favor of going off to various taverns to sing, or hear singing, and the resultant punishments. She wasn't sure why those made her sad, but they did, and she chucked those papers hastily after the others.

She saved all the reports on the garrison and Royal Rider captains to hand off to Arrow. He could decide what to do with them.

Secret army details — there were none. Mathren must have kept all that off-site somewhere, or, given his penchant for secrecy and strict separation of chains of command, in his head. But she was not defeated. Oh, no. With access to the treasury and guild records, even given the lacunae in Mathren's records, there were ways to find out what she wanted.

And so she got to work, without noticing how the scribes' wary attitude metamorphosed to a grudging regard for how hard she labored, and then finally to genuine respect as their skills in turn gained her trust and confidence.

Meanwhile, Arrow, with Commander Noth's practical and circumspect advice, was slowly reorganizing the garrison and what remained of the Royal Riders. Most of them had been dispersed, under new orders that everyone in every garrison was to rotate every two years, to break up Mathren's coteries. It helped some when Arrow showed wavering captains the pages that Danet had uncovered about them, each bearing Mathren's distinctive handwriting.

And so life settled into what almost might be called normal, as winter roared on.

The first stretch of relatively benign weather brought another slew of messengers. One of these was a royal runner bearing a scribe-written treaty proposal, accompanied by a personal letter addressed to Evred, from Haldren Arvandais, new king of Lorgi Idego:

My sister's death after her massacre of the Olavayir Riders—who, I learned after the fact, had come to negotiate a marriage contract—put an end to any wishes by my family, kin, and people for war on either side of the Pass.

Our desire is for independence, and to be left in peace. If our treaty is accepted, as you'll see in the diplomatic language, we promise to preserve all trade south as it has been. All that would change would be the Marlovan titles imposed after the Ghael Hills War, for the truth is, Idego is not truly Marlovan—though Marlovan jarl families and riders married among them. The number of us who speak both languages is vanishingly small, for to communicate, the southern-born jarl families have always had to learn the local tongue. Though we have continued our military training in the Marlovan tradition, our tactics have evolved since the days of the Venn war, as our geography is not the same as that in the south. The sea is the heart of the north shore, not the plains. Our chief trade is by ship, as well as our main defense—though you know we can fight on land if we have to.

For us, belonging to Marlovan Iasca there on the far side of the mountains is a heavy cost that brings little benefit. The demand for army support if the king calls would only benefit us if the Venn—who we know are magic-bound to their own land—were to come again. Whereas it takes the better part of a year for our jarls to travel south for Convocation and back, leaving the north shore without effective command for defense during that time.

If you agree to my proposed treaty, we shall send back the horses my sister captured with those of us who would rather rejoin the Marlovan kingdom, and we will also give back the six ships the Evred-Harvaldar to whom we are both related sent north to defend us. They shall be laden with goods for you to use or disperse as you see fit, as there can be no true recompense for the lives lost in Andahi Pass at my sister's command.

Speaking now as one new king to another, I am as sorry as any human being can be over what occurred. What's more, I believe that many who struck those blows have come to regret their actions, for there was little complaint when I broke up my sister's force and scattered them across the north here, most to serve at harbor border garrisons, or on our own fleet, which will watch for pirates heading south as well as down the strait. I offer this promise: our fleet will regard the waters north of the Nob as our waters, and southward as yours.

The boy who sang—I am reliably told his name was Sindan Olavayir—has become a legend. Before my sister shot him he was singing the Lament of Andahi Pass, which celebrates the bravery of my foremothers, a Lament I understand is sung all over Halia on the anniversary. We share this much, and in that memory, and grief, I hope we can find our way toward peace.

Many of those who heard Sindan Olavayir say he still comes in dreams. He certainly comes in mine.

Arrow said to Danet in the privacy of her bedroom, "I've been having nightmares about Idego all winter. It's not as if I even have an army I could send against them. We're scattered more than I'd thought, with three entire companies, based at Hesea Garrison, wasted patrolling Darchelde."

"Why?" Danet asked.

"Because it's traditional!" He flung his arms out wide. "The answer to every question that makes no sense! The Montredavan-Ans have no army. Their jarlan is a woman who fixes magic on buckets and bridges. My first order was to stop patrolling the Darchelde border, as I think we can trust them not to come out. After seven generations of internal exile, she even told me it's traditional for them to keep themselves to themselves. But relieving us from Darchelde patrol duty is merely a start, a strip of bandage over a broken leg."

Under his tone of frustrated complaint, he seemed to be asking a question without asking. Danet understood that by now.

She said with as much conviction as she could muster, "I know nothing about army needs, but I do know we need those ships, and what they will bring. The treasury is a disaster. The northern garrisons got cheated because Mathren wanted the eagle-clan bearing the burden of supporting them. You grew up hearing your father complain that if he didn't pay for the most needed repairs and so forth, they seemed never to get done."

"Right," Arrow said. "That was one of his orders to me, once I got some of the Royal Riders to talk to me. To discover where that tax money was going. But—"

"Further, Kendred seems to have bought off, or overlooked, what was due to us from at least half the jarls, and what came in, Mathren used for the garrisons at which he rotated the Royal Riders."

Arrow cursed under his breath. Danet ignored it. "And. If we're forced to bring in cotton all the way from the east through Land's End below Parayid Harbor, it will double, maybe triple, in price. This is something *I* grew up knowing. So my advice is, if you can, protect that trade. So many in the north, not just the Farendavans, depend on it. Whereas a war up there, from what everyone says, would cost everything to win."

Arrow had endured enough nightmares concerning the truth of that. Idego, he had learned, had not liked being taken a century and a half ago. Now that Marlovans had mixed with them, there would never be a single battle like Ghael Hills deciding everything. It would be vicious, and protracted, facing their own training and terrain they didn't know. He muttered, "I guess that's that, then. Peace it is. *Lorgi* Idego. It sounds stupid."

"I'm told," she said wryly, "Lorgi means old."

Danet received two letters.

There was one from her sister, full of Farendavan gossip of no interest to anyone but Danet and Hliss, and one from Calamity Senelaec:

Danet: How is the royal city? By now you've been there more than a few days. Is it as horrible as everyone says? We've often talked about you—you must, must, must come to Senelaec when you return to Olavayir, and stay longer, even if the others return to Olavayir. The Jarlan and Fuss both agree!

There is little to report here. I am so bad with letters. That is, I love getting them but hate writing them. Everything I write seems so dull when I put it on paper, even though it isn't dull when I'm doing it, that I end up throwing good paper into the fire, and the steward glares when I go to get more. I am determined to finish this one.

I read yours three times, and shared it with Wolf, Yipyip, and Fuss, and they said to carry their greetings. But what is this rumor that came not a day before your letter—I hope it is not true about all Olavayir being slaughtered by Hard Ride leading an army of bloodthirsty Venn-damn Idegans!

Fuss wants to know if Evred is bearable since she is going to have to marry him. Her first order will be to send an order north with the army to bring Wolf's little girl back.

If you can, send by Camerend, who often rides this way, and tell us everything.

She did, in a letter carried by Tesar.

Winter closed in again, but the next melt brought Camerend back, after four months away.

It also brought another wave of messages, some carried by Danet's sister Hliss, who had bloomed into her eighteenth year.

The sisters threw themselves into each other's arms, a gesture that would have caused Mother's brows to rise, then Hliss sniffed, and let go. "I'm to tell you that Mother is pleased you stepped up to your duty, and that she's sending me to offer my services in clothing, linens, and household managing."

"Oh, that is exactly what I wanted most," Danet exclaimed fervently, as Hliss's bright blue gaze lifted past Danet to Camerend and Arrow, who had just entered, Camerend with a message from the chief scribe, and Arrow to see what was behind all the noise coming from the gunvaer suite's open door.

Inevitably her sister's gaze caught first on Camerend, who touched his finger to his chest politely, his expression mild and detached as he delivered the note.

Danet had only seen Camerend twice since his return. Though he looked exactly as he always had, except maybe thinner, she still remembered that grieved face and his bare finger where once he'd worn a ring. She had to suppress an instinct to treat him carefully, as if he were a spooked wild horse.

Danet said to both, "This is my sister Hliss, who was to marry Sindan Olavayir. Hliss, this is Arrow. And Camerend, chief of the royal runners."

Camerend said, "Welcome," and excused himself, leaving Arrow staring at Hliss with a look Danet knew well.

Danet smothered a laugh. It was inevitable that Arrow's roving eye would catch on Hliss. So very much preferable to him turning up with another Fi!

Danet grabbed her letters and went to her desk, leaving them to get to know one another.

Ranor-Jarlan to Danet-Gunvaer of Marlovan Iasca

Danet: Jarend and Hesar-Gunvaer have reached us safely. While the household is busy moving Jarend into the jarl rooms, I am instantly sitting down to write to you, as I try to comprehend all they have to tell.

After hearing the news we could scarcely believe, Hesar talked to me half the night.

I trust that by now you have found and catalogued Hadand-Gunvaer's papers tracing marriage alliances.

When Midsummer brings the jarls to the Royal City, I advise you to restore the betrothal system, and make it plain that it will be established within the year. Though I think the days of sending daughters to betrothal families at age two are past—the great Hadand Deheldegarthe broke that tradition herself—still, betrothals at birth will go a long way toward reknitting the kingdom. If a girl grows up knowing where she is to go, and that family knows she is coming, then everyone is prepared.

Enclosed you will find the marriage lines since Hadand Deheldegarthe's day. Hesar had sent my husband's mother a copy to keep in secret since the day Bloody Tanrid officially ended the system, allowing jarls to choose spouses for their own children. It is not surprising that clans have confined their marriages to their allies, further splintering the kingdom.

We have tried to keep the copy updated, but it's really only complete for the jarlates here in the north.

You will see treaty-designated heirs in black ink, younger brothers in green, children by consort or favorite not adopted directly into the family in blue, and daughters in red. Below, Hesar's and my suggestions for possible alliances, should the families bring forth suitable children, and my reasons....

[There followed ten pages of detailed genealogical notes]

Danet looked up from reading, to find herself alone. She turned to the chief scribe's note last, looked around for paper to write a note—then decided it would be faster to go talk to the scribes.

She returned as the bells rang the watch change.

She was about to call for a runner when Arrow charged into her study and dropped onto a mat, smelling of wine fumes—but she knew he was trying to limit himself to one or at most two cups of wine during the day watch. *It's the only way I can keep myself sane,* he'd told her.

He scowled as he threw a sheet of paper onto the neat archival piles on her desk.

"So what if I'm the ninth Olavayir king in sixty years? Does that somehow make us worse than the damned Montreivayirs, who had how many?"

"Actually—"

"Never mind the history lesson," he snapped, a vein beating in his forehead. "It's actually ten of us, if you count Evred—and there are jarls who still think he's king, as his runners ought to be reaching them right about now. Supposedly we don't know how to keep order—but that's just an excuse to set *themselves* up as kings. I gave in to Hal up north, because I didn't have anything to march up there with even if I'd...." *Been able to command a real battle.* "Even if I wanted to. So now Feravayir is saying *they're* independent, and there's rumors about the Jevayirs down there in Jayad Hesea. Apparently the Jevayirs think themselves separate from us, too!"

When he paused to draw breath, Danet said, "You're yelling at me. I didn't cause any of that."

"I know, I know, I know. I'm sorry."

"What do you want to do?"

He stalked to the window and back. "You're declaring your betrothal edict at Midsummer, when the jarls come for Convocation, right?"

"Yes. Only it'll take at least a year to send out the treaties and have both families accept—I discovered in Hadand Deheldegarthe's letters that it took that long back when she was sending them out, and it was expected then. Also, I just now returned from interviewing the scribes I sent to scour the archives. I've got some records, but I still have to fill in all the births, marriages, and deaths since Evred was born, take note of betrothal treaties already made, then work out the assignments. For instance, I'll wager you didn't know that Jarend's little Rabbit is already betrothed to the daughter of that new Commander Nermand up there in Lindeth. Treaty signed and sealed the month before you and I got married, right after your father put Nermand's name forward for promotion."

"That reminds me, I guess I'll have to confirm him," Arrow said. "He wasn't one of Mathren's men, which right now is my first requirement."

Danet eyed Arrow. "I don't mean to be defending Mathren Olavayir, but I thought he was very good at military training and planning. Why would you get rid of his people, if they didn't have anything to do with that secret army?"

"There's training for skill, and there's training for blood," Arrow said, a frown between his brows, which made him look unexpectedly like his father. "When Bloody Tanrid ran the academy, it was training for blood, under a savage named Vaskad, my da told us. Vaskad escaped the slaughter in the royal city when Tanrid died—that's who taught Mathren, who was thirteen when Tanrid was assassinated. Mathren and Hasta Arvandais were both taught by that soulsucker Vaskad—in fact, the next year, when Tanrid's son Haldren clashed with the Eastern Alliance, and Jasid came in as king, Vaskad ran up the pass to the north to run the training for the Arvandais."

Danet remembered the harsh drills her cousin Hard Ride had been so proud of, and suppressed a grimace.

"There I go, galloping down a side trail." Arrow smacked his thigh. "But it's related. In a manner of speaking. We'll have your betrothal edict—it's a good idea, and I know my mother has wanted it for years—but I'm adding another that'll start right away. It's the academy."

"You're starting that again? Even I heard horror stories."

"That was Vaskad, like I told you," Arrow said impatiently. "If we're to be a single kingdom again, and not a lot of squabbling little kingdoms, then we have to start the academy. Train our commanders to be loyal to Marlovan Iasca, not to this or that jarlate."

"I can see that," Danet said cautiously.

"We'll begin with second sons. Leave heirs at home, to keep the jarls from getting up on their hind legs and barking at me. This new academy, it'll be *second* sons and cousins, like Inda-Harskialdna was. I'll yap about the great days of old, and require the king's fifth—the royal tax—to include men as well as coin and kind, men who'll make up the King's Riders. They'll circulate between the garrisons. Keep 'em mixed. And their purpose will be to patrol the borders, like they used to. And of course they'll be there if we do need an army."

"You're starting it right away?"

"Well, I'll start small. I gave orders this morning to clean the buildings up. Fix what needs fixing. I'm going to pick the masters myself." He frowned again. "Da was right when he said half the troubles in the kingdom come from those private armies. I'm going to break those little kingdoms up." He smacked the dispatch on his desk. "'Perideth.' What kind of name *is* that? What's wrong with Feravayir? I don't even know what language it is *they* are claiming to speak down there."

Danet spread her hands.

"So once you get the royal tax straightened out, get the jarls and the guilds all paying their fifth again, no special—" He looked up at the runner standing in the open door. "Oh, what now?"

The runner saluted fist to heart and stepped aside as a soberly clad woman entered, still dusty from travel.

This courier hid her fear at the ferocious scowl the Marlovan king turned on her. She had expected no less. She regripped the handle of the basket she bore.

"What's this?" Arrow said, fists on hips.

The woman faced him, shoulders braced as she set the basket on the low table between king and queen. "This is Connar, the son of Lanrid Olavayir and Fini Daughter of Vaka. Fini Daughter of Buno, Chief of Lindeth-Hije Shipping, sent me to deliver this child, as the family has no use for boys. Those are her words," the woman added hastily in her heavily accented Marlovan, seeing the doubt in one face and the gathering wrath in the other.

"Where's Fi?" Arrow rapped out the question, not bothering to hide his annoyance.

"She left Lindeth," was the reply. "Fini Daughter of Buno dispatched me to bring the babe to you."

"Why did you come all the way here?" Danet asked with extreme skepticism. "Why not go to the jarlan, right there in Nevree?"

"We did," the courier stated stonily. "The jarlan told me to go away, and take the child to an orphanage in Lindeth," leaving out what the jarlan had said afterward: He will have a much better life growing up without knowing who either of his parents might have been—making it clear that she didn't believe Lanrid was the father. Even he wouldn't have been that stupid, she'd said in her blunt way, when everyone knew Lanrid was hot after that murdering Hard Ride Hadand Arvandais. Whereas we never trusted anything that snake Fi said.

Fini Senior had found that both insulting and incomprehensible. Whatever she thought of her granddaughter, if Fini said the father was Lanrid Olavayir, then the father was Lanrid Olavayir.

She'd said to the courier, Just because my household has no man to take him out to sea and train him to captainship of our vessels doesn't mean a child of our blood ought to be thrown away to be raised as a street wander. Those Marlovans do nothing but ride around swinging their swords. Surely they will need an extra chieftain.

The courier firmed her voice. "So Fini sa Buno sent me here, as you are blood-kin to the father."

Arrow said slowly, "There was no marriage that I was aware of. Lanrid died going north to fetch a wife."

The courier stated in that flat voice that hid her fear, "I am given to understand that Fini sa Vaka expected marriage on his return."

Danet grimaced. "There's something missing there. Is this really Lanrid's child? And what kind of name is 'Cnor'? It sounds like a girl's name."

"It is *Connar*, a name common among Sartoran kings," was the flat reply.

"Of course she'd name the brat after some outlander king," Arrow exclaimed in disgust. "But Lanrid wouldn't. I can't say much for him, but I will say this: he would not have agreed to have a child with one woman when he wanted another as wife." He stepped up and peered down into the sleeping infant's face. "Huh! Have to admit he does look like Lanrid, all right. Except for that black fuzz. That's Fi's."

He turned his head to address Danet. "I'll wager my right arm Fi tricked Lanrid somehow. It's something she'd do, and she was hot after a title—damn, *how* she squalled when I told her that nobody I married would ever have a title, outlander style. As if I'd done it on purpose." He flashed a grin at Danet. "Who knew I'd end up as king?" Then his face lengthened in comical horror. "Can you imagine her as gunvaer?"

Danet thought sourly to herself that half the men in the kingdom would love it, and for exactly the wrong reasons, but all she said was, "My guess is she's off chasing princes in some other land."

"Good riddance." Arrow peered into the little face, noting the feathery eyebrows with Fi's arch, the tiny, curved lips so like hers. But that was Lanrid's chin, and his broad brow: except for the hair color, this baby looked disturbingly like Sindan Olavayir had when he first arrived in Nevree, not long after his mother was assassinated.

No. Killed by Mathren, Arrow corrected himself. Another of those witnessed truths kept hidden out of fear.

Arrow's heart constricted. Much as he'd loathed Lanrid, he'd liked Sinna. Loved him, even. Everybody had. He would have made a little brother of Sinna had Lanrid not warded him off, making it plain that Sinna's loyalty solely belonged to him.

Maybe this baby, without Lanrid's poisonous influence, would be like Sinna. He looked up at Danet and said coaxingly, "We both feel the same way about Lanrid. And Fi. But Lanrid is dead, and this Cnor, *Con*nar, is a baby, as well as a blood connection. He's not to blame for having a couple of road apples as parents."

The courier pointed to the nearest window. "I can leave the nanny-goat here, if you haven't a wet-nurse. He's used to goat's milk now."

Danet, still feeding Noddy mornings and evenings while already struggling against the upset of early pregnancy, looked at that small face, her heart wrung at the flatness of the courier's words, hearing it as heartlessness. As the babe shifted, making small noises, she felt the internal squeeze of let-down. Women who had twins produced enough for two—why shouldn't she?

She picked up the basket and walked out, saying, "I'll take him to the nursery myself."

TWENTY-FIVE

As was traditional after a change of king, Convocation had been called for Midsummer Day. And all the jarls wanted to get a look at this new king.

The Jarl of Senelaec (who alone of the jarls had met Arrow) believed it a good idea for his son to accompany him, so that Wolf would get a sense of the royal city, the jarls, and how the traditional Convocation was going to be with this new king, before he had to begin attending as jarl. "This is the problem with waiting until you're well into your forties to marry," he said. "By the time your children are old enough to ride with, you're getting too old to ride."

Wolf disliked his father talking about his own death as much as he disliked being away at during the last weeks of Calamity's pregnancy, but he kept silent on both counts. It wasn't as if he could do anything whenever the babe decided to come.

"All right," he said. "I'll go with you."

"One thing," the jarl cautioned his hot-blooded son. "No trouble with the Marlovayirs, mind. Not in the royal city, the first Convocation in years. My guess is, they'll ignore us as if we weren't there. That's fine with me."

"All right," Wolf said, suppressing disappointment. He had been half hoping for a tangle with that strut Knuckles. At least the Senelaecs had won the most recent encounter, with Calamity's shooting at the wargame the previous summer.

Spring had ripened into summer heat. Once they were on the open road, Wolf felt less terrible about leaving home. He was interested in seeing the royal city, and meeting Arrow and Danet again. So long as the Marlovayirs kept their distance, he even looked forward to it.

The trip was hot, the city even hotter.

Wolf's best moment occurred the first day they rode into the royal city. He liked the rippling fanfare welcoming a jarl blaring from the towers as they trotted toward the gates, the Senelaecs' black hunting cat on the crimson banner flapping in the rising summer breeze, and then Arrow himself appeared in the stable yard to greet them. His flaring grin and his clear delight assured a fun stay.

Or seemed to assure. That assurance faded fast as the company dismounted and the runners fetched saddlebags—Arrow asked how everyone was, but scarcely listened before he started talking. "I'm going to...you'll see a lot of changes...you won't believe...."

Wolf could see that Arrow was excited, and full of plans, so he tried to adjust his expectations. Surely Arrow would find him again when he had time.

But Arrow—still new to the burden of kingship—had no free time. In his anxiety to establish himself, he felt obliged to heed every demand for a private interview by most of the jarls and garrison captains.

Wolf—struggling with a sense of betrayal over that treaty with the north that everyone else seemed to accept—refused to request an interview. He and his family knew that their sense of betrayal was entirely personal: Arrow had clearly forgotten all about little Marend when he dealt with the north. What was the use of bringing it up now?

Arrow had indeed forgotten, but more importantly, he had yet to make that vital alteration in perception expected of kings. In his own mind, he was still the Jarl of Olavayir's second son, scrambling to stay with the relentless current of events. So he labored from sunup until midnight through the week of Summer Convocation, but the only time he and Wolf glimpsed one another were when the jarls came forward to make their vows on Midsummer Day, and then again at the banquet, across the cavernous, stuffy chamber.

Wolf never saw Danet at all after her single appearance when the jarls made their vows, and she announced the betrothal system to be re-established within the year.

He didn't know that she was barely able to speak. This far into her pregnancy, she was still so ill that it took all her concentration to stand beside Arrow and not puke on her shoes.

As the jarls came forth one by one to mumble or bellow their vow to *heed the laws of Marlovan Iasca and to come to its defense at the king's call*, as Arrow in his turn promised to *protect and defend the lives and trade of the kingdom, and to respect their governance within their borders*, she gazed up at the proud new banner made by Hliss, the deepest and most brilliant royal blue from the Farendavan secret dyes. The soaring eagle was gorgeously embroidered in overlapping golden stitchery.

But Danet was too ill to take any pride or pleasure in the fine banner, hers and Arrow's splendid clothes, or the clean-swept and scoured throne room with its new torches bound with the usual leddas-imbued strips that had been stored in fragrant herbs. She kept swallowing, her body drenched with cold sweat as she fought against dry-retching from a long-empty stomach.

At the end of the vows, she slipped out the side door adjacent to the dais, leaving Arrow alone on his throne.

Whispering the Waste Spell over and over, she made it back to her bed and collapsed dizzily, muttering with her eyes shut, "Forget the interviews. You runners will have to track down the jarls and find out how many children they have, and who is betrothed to whom. If they even remember," she whispered acidly.

As that day blended into the next, Wolf tried to hide his impatience as he had to sit and listen to his father reminiscing with their Eastern Alliance connections, and on the third day, being hauled off to the pleasure houses with his Sindan-An cousin and his friends. Even the Marlovayirs were boring —Knuckles had obviously been given a similar lecture by his old da. Every time Wolf side-eyed him, Knuckles was looking away.

And he didn't see Arrow at all, except at the oaths.

Wolf's disappointment slowly turned to disbelief. Arrow certainly had changed from the fellow who sat in their den repairing horse stalls and talking about stings.

As it happened, at roughly the same moment Wolf was muttering to his father that Arrow seemed to be having too much fun strutting around being king to give any time to old friends, Arrow was sitting stiff and tense in a formal interview chamber, facing the Commander of the Parayid Garrison, and the new husband of the Jarlan of Feravayir—a tall, brown, hard-faced Noth in his late thirties.

This man had recently married the woman who called herself a queen, Arrow remembered, and who claimed to hold the title, as Ivandred Noth scrupulously launched into the speech he had promised his wife to deliver.

Noth's expertise, and interests, were in riding the border and protecting Parayid Harbor; he wasn't the least political, an observation that Arrow was as yet too inexperienced to recognize. The jarlan, who was extremely political, had sent Noth in her place, coached carefully with a speech that was supposed to intimidate this Olavayir barbarian.

Noth half-understood the palaver about differing languages and customs, and on seeing no encouragement from this stiff, unsmiling king he passed right on to the part he did understand. "But if it is your desire to return to the old ways, as you say, then we desire in our turn a promise that you will defend us if need be." *If this new king is forming an army,* (the jarlan had said) *make certain he's willing to use it for defense of the coast, unlike too many of his family, who were too busy taking our taxes in order to fight each other, leaving us to ourselves.*

"That I can promise." Arrow's expression lightened, and he leaned forward, rapping his knuckles on the massive table supported by legs carved with stylized raptor wings and claws. "I want us to go back to the way it was in the old days of Inda-Harskialdna. The best army in Halia. Every jarlate safe from outside and inside."

As soon as Noth heard that, his entire demeanor eased. That sounded excellent to him.

After that, the talk was much easier for both, as Arrow rambled on, enthusing about his new subject, and Noth offered stories handed down through the various Noth connections over the generations.

That interview was Arrow's first real success, so he ended up using the same words during the next, when he faced two jarls, the tall, thin, deceptively vague-looking Jarl of Telyer Hesea — which combined two older jarlates belonging to the Cassad and the Faralthad families — and the shorter, broad-chested, tough-looking Jarl of Jayad Hesea, chief of the biggest jarlate of the vast lands in the south.

Between these two sat a banner in the green of the Algaravayirs, with an owl stitched on it in silver. Arrow took in the owl, the silver, the green, recognizing this representation of a direct descendant of the legendary Inda-Harskialdna.

On the surface, they seemed benign, but Arrow had just enough experience to recognize the implied...not quite threat, but intimidation, most certainly, in this appearance of a threesome. That meant a strong alliance between the three.

"This banner represents Linden-Fareas-Iofre," Andas Cassad said in a calm, clear voice, his gaze steady. "Her brother Indevan has formally abdicated. He's remaining in Sartor to pursue the study of magic. Linden-Fareas is too close to giving birth to travel, and so she requested us, as first-cousin kin, to carry her banner and with it her vows."

Everything seemed fine so far, except he didn't miss the fact that this Linden-Fareas had not requested confirmation of her title. Like the Jarlan of Feravayir, she was claiming it.

Arrow had decided on the spot to go along with the Feravayir claim because he took a liking to Noth, who was the jarl, as far as Arrow was concerned. There was no representative of Algaravayir here, except that banner. But who was going to deny a direct descendant of Inda-Harskialdna?

"All right," Arrow said, suppressing the impulse to wipe his hands down his trousers. Then he stiffened his back and did his best to look kingly as he turned his gaze to the Jarl of Jayad Hesea, who had a son his age. "So it's just rumor, your wanting to turn your back on us and declare yourself a king?"

Arrow heard how truculent his voice came out, and fought against a grimace. He didn't want to strut as Lanrid always had, but how do you get back from that without sounding stupid?

The jarl placed fists on his knees, then said equably enough, "Rumor, as usual, gets it backward. What we like is what we have, free trade with you here in the north. Because of the mountains against our eastern border, it's also easier to get silk, spice, and even coffee from shipping down the west coast and inland from Parayid, with which we have trade agreements that don't have anything to do with you up here in the north. For generations, we've sent the required men, horses, and taxes to you up here. In my own family's Hall of Ancestors, there are monuments to those of us who died in the king's service — always up north, here or farther up. The Marlovan army has never come south. We've a tradition in recent generations of seeing to our own problems."

He paused, as if waiting for Arrow to disagree or deny. But from what Arrow had managed to learn in his six months of intermittent study of Marlovan history, he knew that everything the jarl said was true.

The jarl continued when Arrow didn't speak, "These past years, there was no academy, no Convocation, nothing in short that the crown used to provide. So our oath-promised levies bring us nothing."

Another pause—and Arrow said, in haste, "That's about to change."

"To whose benefit?" the jarl asked.

"To the benefit of Marlovan Iasca," Arrow said, looking surprised they would even ask—and sounding a little affronted. "I said yesterday, we're starting the academy again."

"Meanwhile," Cassad cut in smoothly, "there is the entire north shore beyond the Pass, apparently a separate kingdom again. Though both of us have ancestors who died up there. You say things will change, but does that mean another northern war?"

"No," Arrow said—not seeing the trap. "I concluded a treaty with them. Everything peaceful." And sensed it closing.

"And so," the Jarl of Hesea Jayad said, "there are those of us who want the same treaty."

Cassad added, "For all the good reasons it made sense to let them go."

"Except," Arrow said, fighting a rise of temper, "they have Andahi Pass." He heard the implied threat in his own voice—which was not what he'd meant—and he reddened, scowling in confusion. "That is, I don't want to lead an army up the Pass to a slaughter. They hold the Pass, and they have our own training, straight from the days of Bloody Tanrid. Also, I don't *have* the King's Riders in numbers and training that I can trust. But I will. You heard me yesterday, after the oaths."

At this, the two men shifted, narrowed eyes and stiff hands easing from wariness to question.

Arrow, subliminally aware, flashed his disarming grin. "The academy is not going to be run the way it was under Bloody Tanrid. First of all, I am not asking for heirs, as he did. You'll send me second sons, third welcome, too, and same with the sons of Rider captains. Ten years of training, they serve in our army ten years, then they can go home unless we have to muster the kingdom. If I have to put out the call to defend the kingdom, they come back as commanders. We're going back to the way things were in Inda-Harskialdna's day. Well, mostly. My point is, we'll have the best army in Halia. But it'll be for protecting our borders, north *and* south. I know Mathren neglected Parayid in favor of Hesea and East Garrisons, but I won't."

Neither the jarls nor Arrow wanted civil war, and they could see Arrow's resolve—and the enthusiasm of young manhood—and so the conversation ended with mutual assurances of good will, though in tones that didn't quite hide doubt.

Neither jarl said much over the next couple days. They explored the old academy buildings that the younger men had heard so much about and never seen, as the oldsters reminisced, not always fondly, for the duels and ambushes before it was closed had reflected the kingdom's fractures.

There was one last feast, at which Arrow promised that there would not be another Convocation at winter, but in five years' time, and whatever he had to communicate would come by royal runner before New Year's. This raised a heartfelt cheer.

The next morning early, under rain-scoured blue sky, fanfares resounded once again from the towers as the companies departed.

The jarls of Telyer Hesea and Jayad Hesea party rode together once again, in company with Commander Noth of Feravayir.

When they camped, Noth took the first watch guarding the camp.

The two jarls wandered down to a nearby stream, putting the horses between them and the tents before speaking.

"Well?" Handas Cassad asked.

The elder jarl grunted. "Young Anred is ignorant, but not irresponsible. He'll learn. Means well. I never thought I'd say this about an Olavayir, but I like him." He turned his face up toward the sky, lips pursed, then added, "For now."

"You'll send your grandson up to the academy, then?"

"Why not? Excellent way to compare our training to what he's putting together, though it might take him a year or three to find a good gait. I'll give him the time. I do like what I hear of who he's chosen for the masters. Stadas of Marlovayir, he's famous all down the coast for his archery. Seems to me Anred-Harvaldar listened to good advice, and bestirred himself to find the best. And ten years is fair enough, if he really does support the south, and reinforce our defense of Parayid, for instance."

Cassad accepted that with an open-handed gesture, and they walked back, talking over inconsequentials.

The journey proceeded quietly.

It wasn't until Handas Cassad rode into his own court and had closeted himself with his wife that he expressed his true thoughts. "The new king wants to rebuild Inda-Harskialdna's army," he said. "He said for defense."

Carleas Dei, his wife, said slowly, "But there are no Venn to threaten us."

"Exactly. I've been pondering this all the ride south. Jevayir of Jayad Hesea likes this young Anred, who's not only planning to build a standing army, he's beginning the academy again in order to fill it. He wants all our second sons, ours and our primary Rider families'. Third as well, though they're optional."

"No," Carleas said.

"No, what?" he asked gently. "Do we refuse, and become the first to defy him?"

"No," Carleas said, just as gently, for she was by nature a gentle person. "Here's my thinking," she said, her brown eyes narrowed. "Experience says those Olavayirs will be at each other's throats before you'd have to send little Barend anywhere."

"But what if they aren't?" Handas said.

Carleas continued to gaze down at her older son in the training yard below, and her infant second son rolling on his blanket as he babbled at Hlar's daughter, sent to them after Hlar and her husband were murdered defending the regent.

Handas flattened his palm. "Easy as Anred appeared, I expect he'd turn on us fast enough if we refuse."

Carleas said, "Don't refuse. We were all taught that the Cassad family deflects. We don't attack. Don't answer, or...just wait."

"But what if this king and his brother don't go at each other?"

Carleas turned away from the window at last. "Did you mention the children to anyone there?"

"No," he replied. "One of the gunvaer's runners chased after me, but I avoided her. I admit that this was pique on my part. I was not going to be summoned by a half-grown girl as if I were an erring stable hand." When his wife was about to speak, he raised a hand. "I know it was petty, especially when I learned just before we rode out that Danet Olavayir was flat on her back, ill with pregnancy, and not swanking about the way Mathren and Kendred Olavayir had, these past twenty years. My error. To the point, my talk with young Anred was all of sons in the plural, future tense, the context the academy. I never mentioned our children."

"So no one outside of us knows how many we have, or their gender."

"Us" meant their household, riders, servants included. The Cassad households were traditionally tightly bonded, with a protective layer of awareness between them and the rest of the Marlovan world that only they could see. That had only intensified over the past century.

Handas followed Carleas's gaze into the yard, and he exclaimed, "What are you thinking?"

Carleas smiled. "Officially, the Cassad family will report a son and a daughter instead of two sons. If Rider families are really included, the Noths can decide for themselves, of course. With two of them in the garrison guard, they might not mind their boys going north. But Barend stays here, and he can share a name with his cousin Chelis."

Handas Cassad turned his attention back to the training court, where the elder boy ran about with a pack of grubby castle children. Barend had turned about on his blanket to watch the shadows of leaves moving against the honey-gold wall, as Baby Carleas watched the older children at drill, waving her hands in the air, and calling, "Ba! Ba!"

He said, "So let me get this straight. Our Barend is now a girl named Chelis?"

"As far as the king is concerned," Carleas said serenely. "And when his brother or cousin replaces him in some bloody coup in five years, maybe ten, we can reevaluate. In the meantime, no one will know."

After he watched the last of the jarls ride out, Arrow ran straight upstairs to the queen's chamber, giddy with relief that his ordeal was over for another five years. By then, he reasoned, everything would be orderly and quiet, and he'd be used to being king.

Danet lay flat on her bed, staring straight up, as the early mornings were the worst, and by now even the smell of ginger steep set her stomach boiling.

"They're gone," Arrow said, twirling around and kicking in a couple of the sword dance steps, hands high. "I've got the academy. Second sons to start with. Though Noddy will go, of course. He'll need to know what they know, and his future commanders." He mimed swinging a sword.

Danet shut her eyes tight. Any movement—even seeing movement—caused burning nastiness to claw at the back of her throat. She had to swallow three times before she murmured through barely parted lips, "We still don't have all the current births and betrothals. My runners couldn't get some of the jarls to talk to them."

"Oh, Norsunder take it," Arrow exclaimed, hands dropping to his sides. "Well, send out runners to the ones you didn't get to, and I know it's gunvaer business, but after talking to them all, I have two things to ask."

She turned over her palm in invitation.

"First. If the Algaravayir Iofre has a daughter, I want Noddy to marry her. Inda-Harskialdna's greats-grandchild! Second, my father once told me that the Riders are really private armies. In the past, jarls had limited numbers of Riders, and the rest came here, but the jarls have been defending themselves for so long that...."

He saw her compressed lips and blue-veined closed eyes, then cut himself short. "Well, anyway, I was listening to a couple of them talking. The Jarl of Yvanavayir, a cheerful sort, admitted that he inherited an entire battalion, which is a lot of food and fodder."

Danet struggled up and fell back. "Was he issuing some kind of threat?"

"No." Arrow flattened his hand. "At least, it didn't seem so. He sounded pleased with everything, and offered to send his second son as soon as we got set up—said the boy has been army mad since he could toddle."

Danet let out a cautious sigh of relief as Arrow went on, "So I thought, the best way to break up private armies is to bring 'em in, instead of passing some new laws that'll get 'em rising up on their hind legs and howling. See, if the Riders' boys come to me, well, I'll have them in my own army for ten years, and if the Venn come, or we get more pirate fleets up the Narrows, or Hal gets murdered and the Idegans try to attack, I could get all the Riders under the same sort of command. Right? Right?"

Danet did not care. She longed for quiet, but she could see how important agreement was to him, so she wiggled her fingers.

Correctly interpreting that as agreement, he went on quickly, "So when you send out word, we can send along my plans for the academy. But. After," he corrected himself, "you find that army."

"Finished," she whispered.

"What? You know where they are?"

"Were."

"You didn't *tell me?* Why?"

"Don't. Yell." She closed her eyes. "I had to wait. For one last letter. Proof. Which I got yesterday." She had hoped to get into all this when she felt better, but he obviously wouldn't wait. She made a great effort to speak. "Arrow, it's not anything to worry about."

"How can a secret army not be anything to worry about?"

Danet had been considering for several days how to explain in the shortest possible words, knowing that Arrow would never read the records himself; the last time they'd discussed it she'd tried to explain that she was finding the evidence *around* the army through numbers, and he'd promptly lost interest.

He was paying attention now. Taking a cautious breath, she said, "We know Mathren destroyed direct reference to them. But. You can't hide large groups of people. They have to eat. They need horses. Those horses eat. Need stabling and shoes." She took another deep breath. "The scribes collected all jarlate tallies for the last ten years. Trade cities. Then all I had to do was look for bumps." She drew another shaky breath, and forced out a few more words. "All the evidence. Pointed to that old castle of your father's. The one they stopped using when your brothers were killed. Near the coast."

"I'll send—"

"Listen! Didn't you get a letter from Jarend?"

Arrow flushed. "I got a bunch of letters, but I've been too busy to read 'em."

"He probably explains more. Ranor-Jarlan's letter explains that Jarend sent all the Olavayir Riders to that old castle. Also all the Lindeth garrison. Found a few left. Bloody battle. Thad—the false Parnid—dead. Captains dead. Mathren's secret assassins—all killed."

Arrow grimaced. "So Jarend cleaned 'em out?"

"Faction fight before he got there. Because, no more pay. No supplies. Jarend offered to forgive those still standing and bring them into Nevree Riders. Or they could leave the country. Most went with him. Some went to sea."

Arrow scowled, thinking rapidly. That sounded just like kind-hearted Jarend. But if those soul-suckers were thinking of taking Nevree from within, in some kind of bloody revenge ruse—

Danet correctly interpreted his expression. "Arrow. Dolphin-clan is *gone*. Except for a few Rider-cousins. Like that Retren Hauth. The one-eyed one. Ranor-Jarlan says he's drinking himself to death. Though they offered to make him a lance captain again. Your mother knows who they are. There's only one clan now. Jarend the head." She waited for the obvious question—the one question she still couldn't answer, which was what Mathren had intended to do with that army—but it didn't come.

Arrow's mouth opened and closed. He kicked at the harmless cushions.

"I'd better read Jarend's letter," he said, looking at her fondly. She really was an excellent gunvaer, and if she had another son, he had nothing else to ask for. He bent down to put his arms around her—carefully—and held her against him.

She enjoyed his warmth, and the steady lump-lump of his heart against her ear. He might remind her now and then of a gangling yellow bird hopping around and then flitting off, but there were far worse sorts than birds, if you had to be married to one. And it probably didn't matter why Mathren Olavayir had spent years slowly building and training an army that no longer existed; she knew it was merely her wish for tidiness to find out.

She sighed. But even that much movement caused the nausea to well up. "Arrow. Have something to ask from you."

"What? If I can do it, you know I will."

Swallow. "If this is a girl." Another swallow. "We adopt Connar as ours. I think of him as ours. I nursed him with Noddy until I got too sick. He's an Olavayir."

"He's dolphin-branch," Arrow muttered. "I thought he could be Noddy's first runner. Or a Rider, if he has the skills."

"He's an *Olavayir*. If he's ours, then that wretched feud. Between dolphin and eagle. Ends."

Arrow sighed. "We don't really need three princes."

She struggled to rise, then fell back flat, moisture glimmering in her eyes. "He and Noddy are good together in the nursery. They don't cry nearly as much when they share that bed. And Connar's already making noises like he's going to talk early. I can't say, *don't call me Ma*, when Noddy just started saying Ma. I can't. He's just a baby. I want us to be his parents in all ways." She drew a careful breath, her face yellow-green and blotchy as she fought nausea. "And. I'm not going. Through this again."

Arrow looked down at her thin form shrouded by a single sheet, with the still-small mound between the bony protrusions of her hips. He glanced at the uneaten single biscuit on the bedside table that had sat there since the night before, and stirred uneasily: he knew she was still working with her scribes, sick as she was.

"Whatever you want," he promised.

TWENTY-SIX

Neither the Jarl of Senelaec nor Wolf spoke as they rode away from the royal castle into the breathless heat of summer.

"Now I know why Convocation was always winter," the jarl commented, once the trumpet fanfare had died away behind them, and they sneezed at the roiling dust of the Fath cavalcade a ways ahead.

"Father—"

"When we get home," the jarl murmured out of the side of his mouth. "Not before the Riders."

Wolf had to bite down on his temper.

At night, it was too hot for tents, so everyone slept in the open. It was so still you could hear the chirr of night insects a hundred paces away, and the shifting and snorts of the animals on the line. There was no private talk until they reached sight of home.

By then Wolf was anxious all over again, and so, when they rode into their courtyard at last, he left his father and the Riders and bounded inside, seeking Calamity....

Just to discover Calamity and Fuss shut up in the den, everyone else chased out.

"Wooooooolf!" Calamity shrieked on a long note—

And Fuss said, "Good girl! One last push...."

Wolf nearly killed himself vaulting up the stairs to the den. He'd made it in time! But barely. His eyes burned with tears as he stumbled forward and dropped on his knees. He promptly looked away again—what was going on seemed so painful. Worse than a sword wound to the gut.

"Girl?" Calamity breathed.

"Boy," Fuss murmured.

Calamity lay back, her trembling, sweaty fingers reaching for Wolf's. He took her hand, staring in wordless delight at his new, tiny son as Fuss rubbed the baby into rosy color, then laid him on Calamity's other side.

Calamity drank in the world-changing miracle of his little fingers opening up, the vague gaze that searched earnestly for her face, and the open happiness beaming from Wolf's countenance.

Both parents stared down ardently, until Calamity whispered, "How was the royal city?"

"Oh, *horseshit*," Wolf exclaimed.

Both Calamity and Fuss started, and turned twin gazes of affront his way.

He saw that, his face flooded with color, and he stumbled over his words in his haste to clarify. "No! It's not—faugh! You don't understand." When two pairs of female eyes narrowed, he yelped, "It's that turd Arrow!"

"Arrow?" Fuss looked around, as if Arrow had suddenly popped up in room.

"No, yes. That is...." Wolf scratched his head, then jerked his hair clasp straight. "No, we may as well call him Anred. Because he's just like all the Olavayirs," he added bitterly. "He decreed that all second sons have to go to the royal city to be trained for the King's Riders."

"At birth?" Calamity cried.

"Age ten, eleven, twelve. Train for ten years. And stay for another ten years, fighting his wars."

Calamity gazed down at those perfect fingers, each nail so miraculously defined, and the jarlan's broken voice echoed, *Killing other mothers' sons.* "No," she said. "No."

"No, what?" Fuss asked.

"No, he's not going."

"Then we'll be foresworn," Wolf snapped.

"I'll write to Danet."

"What can she do? If she even wants to?" Wolf hissed out a sharp breath, then added, "They didn't even *ask* those northerners about getting my daughter back. Da didn't say anything, but he hardly spoke a word on the ride back. Those Olavayirs just let the north separate off, and no one gave *us* a second thought."

Calamity stared at Wolf, not ready to admit that *she* hadn't given little Marend much more than a thought or two since she'd become pregnant. It wasn't as if Marend was dead. She was in another family—something that Calamity had experienced herself. Twice. Still, she knew how much Wolf grieved for the daughter the two-faced snake Ndiran had taken away from him. "Have Danet and Arrow changed really all that much?"

"Yes," he said bitterly. "They're *Olavayirs*. Who even knows how true all that is about Mathren being a secret assassin, the hero who held the city against the assassins twenty years ago—they could have made that little runner say anything." When he saw the twin stricken faces before him, he relented. "Oh, well, Da thinks it's true. And Camerend did say it was, even if he didn't see it."

"Then how does he know?" Calamity asked, as the baby marveled at the feel of air and light and sound, blinking slowly up at her face.

"He was the first one in after it happened. Calamity, the important thing here is that they want to take *this* baby, right *here*, *away* from us, for whatever wars Arrow—Anred-Harvaldar," he amended sarcastically, "decides he wants to fight. And he wasn't all that great as a leader last summer, as you remember. Lanrid, in spite of being a walking horse apple, was better."

Calamity pulled the baby tighter against her. Hadn't she heard some stories about the Cassads of old, when she was little? Or was it because she'd grown up as a boy until she reached ten, and was sent to Senelaec?

Whatever sparked the idea, she stared down at her new baby, and murmured, "Then he's a girl."

"What?" Wolf gasped, and frowned quickly down to check: nope, still a boy.

"What?" Fuss whispered, turning wide eyes to Calamity.

Passion's closest companion is anxiety when one feels any sense of threat to the object of that passion. Calamity said again, "He's a girl." And she drew a soft blanket around the evidence to the contrary. Now there were just waving arms and legs — with a diaper on, babies were just babies.

And once the words were out, she breathed deeply, *yes, yes*. It solved *everything*. "*She's* a girl," she stated, and turned her stark, determined gaze to Wolf, then to Fuss. "Everybody in the castle is busy around your Da, and making the welcome home banquet. Nobody knows this baby is here yet but us. We can keep the secret. We can!"

"Not forever," Wolf said wryly.

"But by the time he — *she* — gets old enough for it to matter, we can tell her what happened, and why. And she can keep the secret herself."

Wolf stared down at his little son. He hadn't even told them yet who the new masters were going to be in that damned academy of Arrow's, and shuddered at the vivid memory of Knuckles Marlovayir's smirking profile when the king had called up one of the Marlovayir Riders to join the academy staff on the dais in the throne room.

He absolutely loathed the thought of any strutting Marlovayir rooster having authority over his boy while he was not there to protect him. "Let's do it." And, once he'd said it, the sense of challenge — a prime ruse — sparked the old thrill. "But we can't tell anyone. Not even the parents. Da will insist we have to stick to the king's commands if they're reasonable, and he'll call this reasonable. I know he will — because he doesn't have to worry about me or Yipyip," he added unfairly. "So who do we get as minder?"

Calamity was way ahead of him. "Pip," she stated.

"Pip?" Fuss repeated. "But she wants to be a scout."

"She can be a scout sometimes, the way Ndara is when we ride out. Pip loves ruses more than anything. And she just turned seventeen, so she hasn't been assigned a permanent place yet."

"I'll go fetch her," Fuss said, and flitted out.

Wolf and Calamity spent the intervening time laying plans, until Fuss brought Pip in.

Pip—Ranet Noth—had been born when her cousin Calamity was five, a surprise after a string of brothers. She, too, had grown up treated as a brother, until she was sent to the Senelaecs at ten, to train with their runners.

She scowled at first, but when Calamity showed her the baby, and explained the plan, Pip's unremarkable face glowed with glee. "I'll do it," she said. "Oh, what fun! What's her name?"

"How about Ranet, for you. And Great-Aunt Ranet Sindan-An. Mother will like that." And, taking in Pip's glee, Calamity added, "Nobody can find out. Until later, some day, when we're safe from Ranet being sent off to that Olavayir academy."

Pip earnestly agreed, and ran downstairs to announce that Wolf had made it in time to see his daughter born, and Pip was to be her runner. Then, with an alacrity that surprised the jarlan, Pip bathed the horse hair and dust from her person and repaired straight to the nursery to get training—while insisting on all baby care for her new charge herself.

That was easy enough, as everyone was too busy trying to make certain that *this* year, they didn't get so behind on harvest and storage.

Pip was scrupulous about guarding the secret from anyone in Senelaec...but she could not possibly keep the delicious secret to herself.

The Jarlan's runner departed in the first stretch of good weather, carrying a sheaf of letters, including a short one from Calamity to Danet, reporting on the birth of a daughter (which committed her to her ruse), and one from Pip to her only female Noth cousin, with whom she'd been exchanging letters since she left Telyer Hesea at age ten.

Of course she swore her cousin to the strictest secrecy, but human nature being what it is, by the time a secret hits the third person away from the one most involved, any duty toward that original person has diminished.

This is especially true when, as was the case in the Marthdavan family—for whom this Noth cousin served as a runner—the family faced the same dilemma. And why not swap a he for a she? After all, the niece of the gunvaer assassinated by Mathren Olavayir reasoned, everybody in the world knows that Uncle Tanrid was born Aunt Tdan, but had grown up insisting she was really a boy, one of the fastest scouts in the Riders, with the best double-stick skills.

"But what about that order from the new gunvaer, about the old royal betrothals starting up?"

"So?" A shrug. "It's not the old two-year-old exchange, I'm glad to say. We'll have twenty, twenty-five years to figure something out, if the Olavayirs don't wipe themselves out first. As usual." A stern look. "But one thing for sure, no Marthdavan ever again is going to be murdered by any Olavayir in their soul-sucking fights, as has happened twice in four generations. Twice! That's what you get for loyalty to any Olavayir!"

And so, the Marthdavans decided as a family that their new son would be a daughter to the rest of the world, named Chelis, a well-respected and traditional female name.

Autumnal winds blew leaves skipping and dancing along the streets of the royal city when a lone rider approached the royal castle.

The wall sentries recognized the dusty, rumpled, sun-faded blue coat of the Olavayir Riders, and waved him through.

But when he got to the inner gate leading to the courtyard of the royal castle, one of the wall guards scowled at that eyepatch below blond hair, and spoke to the watch captain, who yelled down, "Retren Hauth?"

The tone was not particularly inviting.

"Sent by the Jarl of Olavayir, message for the king," Hauth called up.

It was not the job of the gate guards to sort people claiming to be messengers, and those who recognized him knew that he would have no easy time of it.

So it was.

But Retren Hauth was sober, and determined in the way of someone who had nearly drunk himself to death before discovering a new purpose in life. It had happened the night the nephew of a second cousin shook him out of his stupor to tell him that Lanrid had had a son. And that that son was now in the royal city.

He bore himself patiently, soberly, even apologetically as he was passed up the garrison chain of command until, at last, he faced an impatient king.

"Jarend really sent you?" Arrow asked skeptically.

"Yes."

Arrow knew his brother would not write a letter if he didn't absolutely have to. "What was the message?"

Hauth turned his one-eyed gaze skyward and repeated flatly, "'Brother, I am sending Lanrid's lance master back to you for your academy.'"

Arrow scowled. It was true that before Arrow left Nevree, Hauth had been good at teaching lance charge and mounted fighting, which had been Lanrid's obsession. And that did sound like Jarend. Arrow didn't know if this was Jarend's idea. But even if it wasn't, what harm could come of it? Mathren and Lanrid were gone.

"All right," he said with obvious reluctance. "We'll give it a try." Then added trenchantly, "But the first time you get soused and don't turn up for duty, out you go."

Hauth saluted, his expression serious and grateful, no sign of the old surliness.

Arrow sighed. "Report to Commander Noth."

Hauth saluted again, still grateful, until he was alone in the hallway. He'd become adept with a cane, moving almost as fast as before, except when he faced stairs. He permitted himself a glance upward as he wondered where the nursery was.

Well, he'd find out. There was plenty of time.

PART TWO

ONE

Spring 4072 AF

In the twelve years since Danet and Arrow found themselves thrust onto a throne neither had wanted, there had been gradual changes inside the royal city and through the kingdom.

The royal runners had been restored to their original purpose—a purpose shaped as well as guided by the Montredavan-An family.

To help furnish us insight into the twelve years since Anred-Harvaldar and Danet-Gunvaer were crowned, I shall introduce twelve-year-old Lineas, who happened to be born the first year of the new king and queen's rule. Lineas was one of the generation's most indefatigable journal writers, furnishing those with the wherewithal to find her to slip into her thoughts.

Let's join her the morning she first arrived at Choreid Dhelerei as a new runner-in-training.

When at last the towers of the royal city jutted up in the eastern haze, Lineas seethed with such excitement she shivered, though the spring day was quite warm. The pair of military runners passing through Darchelde from the south, who'd accompanied her at Shendan Montredavan-An's request, talked in low voices, paying her no attention.

It had been like that since they'd left Darchelde. That was all right. Lineas worked hard at being the sort of child people ignored. There was safety in being unnoticed, all the more remarkable an achievement for a child born with a wild shock of bright red hair and the freckles that usually went with it. Her head swiveled on her scrawny neck as she tried to take everything in at once. There were the much described three low hills, the divided river flowing on either side of the middle one, which meant that those towers over there on the north side must be the royal castle, her future home.

The muddy road was rutted from wagon wheels as carters drove through the mighty gates toward market. Her guides nudged their horses in line behind a wagon filled with barrels, talking as usual in voices too low for Lineas to hear everything. That was all right, too. Lineas found them as boring as they found her. She sniffed, trying to discover what might be in those barrels, until they neared enough for her to make out the sigil for brown ale on one.

The wagon was very slow. It was a relief when the runners turned off toward the left, toward another gate. That had to be the royal castle. Senrid Montredavan-An was inside! Her innards shivered at the thought of seeing him again.

He wasn't her first beloved, but he was the longest—three whole years. He must be almost *fifteen* now, getting tall. She was so excited her stomach churned, and she had to breathe slowly as they approached the royal castle gate.

The sentries waved them in, one calling down to grizzled, gray-haired Telna, who called something back up in some slang Lineas didn't know.

Then they were through, and riding into a busy courtyard. Stable hands took their mounts. Lineas slipped off, shaking her legs out of habit, though they'd camped not far from the royal city for the night, and had only been riding a few hours.

As her guides strode toward a tower with an archway at its base, Lineas noticed a young man lounging in the open door, blocking their way. He wore a fine House tunic of blue edged in gold, though it wasn't even Restday, much less a festival day. She was surprised to make out a dolphin on the front of his tunic, instead of an eagle.

His face didn't change as her escort chatted about whether to go straight to the garrison or to stop at the castle duty station to deliver Lineas. She watched in growing worry as they headed straight toward that blond young man who obviously had rank, but they didn't pause or salute.

Lineas held back, wondering if she ought to say something, when from inside the tower a young runner dashed right through the young man in the royal house tunic, and ran off toward the stable.

Oh. He was one of *them*. Well, that made sense, as he didn't match the description of the bucktoothed king at all, and he was too old to be either of the princes, who were supposed to be only a little older than she was. Glad that she'd said nothing, she held her bag tighter against herself and followed her guides into the tower.

Of course they'd noticed nothing. She'd learned before she could even read that most people didn't see *them*, any more than they saw ribbons of colored flame in the air, though some cats did.

They were halfway up the first flight of stairs when they heard the patter of footsteps from the landing above, and two young runners-in-training appeared, wearing midnight blue sashed smocks and riding trousers. One was tall and weedy, with swinging lemon-yellow braids, and the other....

Lineas stared at the familiar boy, his flyaway dark hair escaping from its queue. She shivered with delight in recognizing Savarend-Senrid Montredavan-An, Camerend's son and heir.

"Senrid?" she whispered.

"'Senrid,'" the tall girl mimicked, snickering. "Better corral your fuzz, *Senrid*. See you later, *Senrid*." Laughing, she ducked around the two riders, leaped down the stairs, and vanished out the door.

"Lineas?" At the sound of her name in his voice, the butterflies inside her turned into sparks whizzing around inside her like happy fireflies.

"Yes," she squeaked. Of course he wouldn't recognize her. Why should he? He was the heir of all Darchelde, and she wasn't anything, except a failure at magic, which was why she was here.

"I came to meet you," he said with a welcoming smile.

"Then she is given into your care," said the older runner, and the two of them promptly left, as if she were a burden dumped at last.

Lineas let a small sigh escape, then turned to Senrid, to find his eyes narrowed in laughter. "You might as well get used to calling me Quill. Everyone does."

"Why?"

"Got it when I was small. I don't even remember how. But I'm used to it, and anyway, nobody knows my first name here, and there are three Senrids that I know of, between us and the academy. The only one who gets his name is two years from the lancers. Those two runners sure galloped off fast. Are you that much trouble?"

Lineas's mouth rounded in surprise. She had spent her entire short life striving to be good, to be unnoticed. For a painful moment his humor didn't reach her. But his tone — laughing, warm — tipped her off, then she saw it, and laughed on an exhaled breath, blushing hotly.

He'd made a joke! Like she was a person you made jokes with! But he was waiting, so she guessed at what would be the best answer, and said, "Worse."

Her reward was a gust of laughter, then she said, "I think I was a duty they didn't want."

Senrid — *Quill*, she reminded herself — said, "You don't have to explain. It's happened to me, nearly much every time I went to Darchelde to visit my mothers. Since nobody can leave Darchelde except runners like us —"

She thrilled at that *us*.

" — perforce any runners carrying messages through got stuck with me, either going or coming."

Quill looked at his wispy distant cousin who stood there on the step, long, spider-thin fingers clutching her bag against her ribs, the mud of a morning ride dotting her trousers and robe, and said, "I'll take you upstairs to our lair. You can change, and I'll show you around."

She followed on his heels as he raced up to the third floor and along a torchlit hall that whiffed of old meals—unlike Darchelde, which was also large, but had been built by someone who understood how air moved.

When she sniffed, Quill said over his shoulder, "I know it stinks. Can't be helped. We'll get a bit more air when the warmer weather comes, and we can take out the window-glass and stuffing, and open up the doors to spring air."

"I wasn't going to complain," she whispered.

"No." Quill grinned. "But you noticed. Everyone does. You'll get used to it."

His lack of affront eased her dread of doing wrong, and she shook with silent laughter that was mainly relief as he led her through a door into a warren of interconnected rooms.

They moved too quickly for her to impress any of the spaces into memory, until he opened a door into a small chamber with a narrow bed, a trunk at the foot of it, and a desk on the opposite wall, and said, "This is yours. If you want hangings, talk to Mnar, but you won't be in here except to study and sleep. In the trunk you'll find clothes."

He whacked his chest. "The basket in the corner is for dirty clothes. If you want a bath, follow the stairs all the way to the left, and when you're ready, I'll be in our study. That's down to the right—the first open door."

He left her there, and she stood clutching her travel bag as she looked around uncertainly. She was actually here, in the royal city! And Quill himself had been sent to welcome her! Excited—apprehensive—curious, she wavered, then looked down at herself. Mud! And she probably stank of horse.

In dread of keeping Quill waiting, she dropped to her knees and opened the trunk to find two neatly folded sets of clothes—dark blue smocks, gray riding trousers—heavier winter wear beneath the lighter cotton-linen for spring.

She opened her travel bag, and hauled out her old, worn clothes, which were wrapped around her precious journal, two much-mended pens, and the ink she'd made herself. The journal, she stashed beneath everything else in the trunk.

Then she snatched up an undyed cotton-linen singlet from the neat, folded pile. It looked newly woven and sewn. She held it up, admiring a piece of clothing that nobody else had ever worn. She would begin its story, unlike everything she'd always worn, which had stories before they came to her hands: a mended tear here, from when and where? Worn elbows, from doing what? Sometimes she'd been able to guess at bits of the story, though not the entirety. Only Auntie Isa, Quill's mother, could touch a thing and tell you its stories.

Lineas pulled out a dark blue tunic, this one soft, with worn edges, so it had a history. She sniffed, but it just smelled like sunshine, as did anything that had dried outside. Trousers, new and sturdily stitched. She upended her bag to pull out her last, wrinkled pair of drawers, and flung the rest of her underthings and socks into the laundry basket in the corner.

Then she fled down the many stairs to the baths. No one was there, as everyone was busy with the day watch. She took the fastest bath of her life, then dressed, sashing her smock with more care than she customarily gave her clothes.

She raced back up, counting the doors. She opened the correct one, tossed her old clothes into the basket on top of the rest of her dirty laundry, shoved her feet into her boots—glanced in despair at their dirty state—then rubbed her old smock over them, wondering when and where she would deal with her laundry. She had no new underthings for tomorrow. She had to remember to ask.

She raced down the hall and stopped outside the open door, assessing the tone of the voices inside, then stepped in. All conversation ceased, and Lineas's gaze found Quill, who sat at a table on which were spread several books, a stack of chalk slates, chalks, and an open box containing paper, with inkwells and quills beside it.

"You must have flown," Quill said, hopping off his stool. "Come on!"

He charged toward the door where she still stood, halted, then whirled around. "Oh. Everyone, this is Lineas, the new fuzz. This is...no, better to meet 'em one at a time," he said, and shot out the door, pulling her after him by sheer speed.

"Middle stair, right over here, takes you to the royal chambers on the second floor," he said rapidly. "So don't use it unless you're serving them. That stair to the left goes down to the mess hall and the kitchen gardens. You'll learn the gardens well," he added, with a speculative glance.

"We do gardening at Darchelde, too," she said, lest he think her lacking in some way. "Weeds. I know all the kinds. *And* pulp and rag shredding and pounding for paper-making."

"Good. Far end stair goes to the stable, as you saw, and over that is the state wing...."

And so it went, Lineas running beside Quill down one stairway and up another, with quick glimpses into various rooms. She sniffed as well as looked, trying impress each space into her memory. It was both thrilling and unnerving to be with him, after those brief glimpses in the past, which had been followed by imagined conversations, and thoughts of what he would say when she showed him her favorite places in and around Darchelde, because of course he would have loved everything she loved.

Only why was he hurrying so fast? Perhaps he was in some way testing her, though she didn't see challenge in his face, or hear it in his voice, and she knew all the signs from her life in Darchelde.

When they hustled back from a fast glance at the garrison side, a bell clanged—not the tower bells, but one at the back end of one of the stone buildings, and Quill let out a whoop. "We did it! And we'll be first in line."

They shot through the door ahead of a stampede of runners in training, servants, and stable hands.

"This time of year, there's never enough fizz," he explained as he led her past the food to the far end, where a big wooden tureen sat, with a ladle next to it. They each filled a clay mug with purple liquid. Lineas smelled fermented citrus and tartberries. "When they get to the last tier of barrels, they only put out one bowl a day," Quill said. "To make it last until the berries ripen in early summer. We'll be helping with the picking."

So this was why he'd hurried her along!

He led her back around to the food tables, where she found offerings little different from what she was used to: rye biscuits, cheese to stuff into them, pickled cabbage, and apple-nut rolls that were more nut and raisin than apple, as usual in spring, with more honey than usual to hide how dried the nuts were.

When they sat down across from each other, he hunched forward, gaze earnest. "I don't know where to start first. What's your interest?"

"I like studying everything," she began, and when he rolled his eyes at the conventionality of the answer (though it happened to be true) she said, "Will I meet the princes and princess?" She cared little about meeting boys, especially older ones, though she was curious to see them. But she was really curious to meet the princess, who was exactly her age.

Quill turned his palm down. "The princes aren't around much since they were sent to the academy, except in winter, and then they have tutoring. You might see them on festival days, and once in a while at the stable. We see more of the princess, as she studies with the fledges, though she spends all the time she can at the stable, and the barns."

Lineas smiled at that. Then, "Fledges," she repeated. "And what did you call me, fuzz?"

"Hatchlings." Quill walked his fingers uncertainly over the table top, mimicking a chick learning to walk. "Fuzz, fuzzies, are first year chicks fresh out of the egg. Fledglings before you've been appointed a post, or declared your preference. You'll pick it up fast enough. Not much imagination. The inventive stuff," he lowered his voice, "we usually say in Sartoran, which no one outside us understands. But never around the seniors."

He flashed a conspiratorial grin, and Lineas consciously turned her gaze away so she wouldn't be caught staring at the light freckles on his nose, or the golden tips on his eyelashes.

She swept her gaze around the rest of the room, noting those wearing dark blue staying together, and those wearing gray in their own groups.

Quill watched her assess the familiar space and wondered what she saw. How it compared to Darchelde, which he remembered as brief, bright colors, and a blur of faces, except for his mother's cottage deep in the woods, where he spent most of his visits, when he wasn't in the castle studying. His father had told him that he'd met Lineas, but he hadn't been able to distinguish her from his memory of a cluster of more or less red-haired youngsters.

Trays slammed down next to them, and here were three girls and a boy, curious about the newcomer.

At first, they all looked alike to Lineas, whose nerves prickled at those unwavering gazes. "You're the new fuzz from Darchelde," one girl said. "Kind of young, aren't you, for a fuzz?"

Lineas was uncertain how to answer such obvious utterances. She didn't have to worry about it because Quill said impatiently, "Hasn't been tested. Just got here. Bunk off."

The boy, the most blond, and apparently the youngest, snorted as he pointed at Quill's mug of punch. "Of course you fingered some. As usual." He reached for the stone water jug on the table and poured water into his empty mug with a notable lack of enthusiasm.

"Got the last of it," the tallest, weediest of the girls said with satisfaction, her hands cupped protectively around her mug.

"Hog," the girl next to her said, but without heat.

"*Why'd* they send you?" the short, round girl asked, then her brows twitched together as she studied Lineas's small form. "Are you even ten?"

Lineas suppressed a sigh. "I'm twelve. I'm here because I was slow—" She remembered then that she was no longer in Darchelde. Her guides, in ignoring her, had not given her the chance to practice what she ought to say and what not to say.

She heard the word "slow" suspended in the air, and closed her lips. It didn't matter, did it, what sort of slow they thought her?

Maybe it did, for the others exchanged looks, then the tall one said, "Well, you're here. If you like the stable, I'll see you around. I'm asking for road training."

The round girl stated with flat conviction, "*I'm* for the scribes."

Quill said, "Dannor is the best of any of us at drawing."

Dannor, the round girl, smiled, her cheeks pinking.

Lineas was glad to get the attention off herself, and stayed quiet as the others began chattering about their day, using so much slang that Lineas had a difficult time understanding much.

They'd all nearly finished when an older runner-in-training—this one with an actual blue coat that was fitted and had shank buttons—approached to say, "Quill, you're wanted in the roost. Take the fuzz with you."

The little group had fallen silent. Quill finished off the berry drink that he'd been sipping slowly. Lineas gulped hers down, picked up her tray, and followed Quill to a table where a huge bucket of water waited. Lineas blinked away the faint ribbons of light weaving around the edges of the barrel. She hastily popped the last of her bread into her mouth and dunked the tray into the water. Magic scintillated in a million greenish silver dots of light. She blinked them away from long habit, stacked her wet tray on Quill's, and followed him out, insides roiling at the prospect of being tested.

The roost turned out to be the schoolroom area of the royal runners' lair.

Camerend and Mnar were there, both unwilling to leave Lineas's testing to the other instructors. It wasn't their competence in question, but their patience: Camerend and Mnar would have a thousand questions about the child's words, tone, and demeanor, far more important than the results, which assuredly would be satisfactory at the least, or Shendan would never have agreed to send her.

But after all, Lineas was here because she had failed at magic studies.

So they sat side by side, unaware of how stern and imposing they looked to Lineas, who tiptoed in, her fingers stiff at her side lest she forget herself and begin pleating the folds of her tunic.

She recognized Senrid's father, of course, who had occasionally appeared at Darchelde, but she had only heard about Mnar Milnari, chief of the runners-in-training, as Camerend Montredavan-An was chief of the royal runners.

Both chiefs, to test *her?*

Her throat constricted in fear.

Camerend and Mnar took in the tiny person before them, almost lost in her garb, her twig-thin wrists barely visible beneath the rolled sleeves, her long fingers stiff, her triangular face wan beneath the freckles. Tufts of ridiculously bright, wiry red frizz escaped from her stiff, thick braids. Mnar suppressed a flutter of laughter at the notion that there was far more hair than person in this unprepossessing little mite.

Camerend sent Mnar a look, which she correctly interpreted as invitation to speak first. "Welcome to the royal runners, Lineas. What can you tell us about your progress in your studies?"

Lineas was desperately honest, in the way of someone who has had to carefully check her perceptions against others' all her life. "I'm not very good at...." But here she had to stop, as she had been trained never to mention her magic studies outside Darchelde.

And then there were all the other things she couldn't do! She couldn't construe the ribbons of color in the air, or the patterns in the wind harps high above Larkadhe City in the north, though the beauty of both made her soul yearn with a hunger much sharper than an empty belly ever could.

Mnar's brows shot upwards at Lineas's vacant expression. Camerend gave Lineas a puzzled look that shaded into concern the longer Lineas gazed into space. Shendan had insisted that Lineas was not burdened in the way of Isa. Could that be wrong?

But then a far simpler reason presented itself, and gratefully he tried it. "It's all right, Lineas. With the two of us, you may talk about magic, though not to anyone else. I know you were not able to master elementary magic, but I also know it was not for lack of trying."

To his relief, Lineas's expressive little face altered, her relief echoing his. That was it, then—the child had merely made a verbal stumble. It was now clear that she had been coached not to mention magic, a subject forbidden outside of Darchelde's tower given over to magic studies. It was equally clear that she was scrupulous in observing that boundary of silence.

"I did try," she whispered. "I tried so *very* hard. I know all the elements by heart, but they won't go together. For me." Her lower lip trembled. "I can't even renew firesticks," naming the most elementary and useful of spells, which beginners do repetitively each summer. "The one time I tried, it caught on fire."

Mnar waved a hand. "We've enough help with the firesticks, and everything related to magic renewal, as I'm certain Shendan told you. You're here, where different skills are needed. What we want to find out is what you *are* good at, what you like to do, and what you don't like to do, plus any problems you feel we should know about—"

"I don't have any problems except magic," she said. "I love to study and I am very, very normal!" Her voice rose, reminding them of the piping of a bird, as she smiled brightly.

"Excellent," Camerend said, restraining the impulse to sneak a look Mnar's way, to see her expression. "Begin with a list of Marlovan kings, and the principal events of each reign...."

Lineas gulped in her breath and reeled them off.

Maths, Old Sartoran alphabet and vocabulary, modern Sartoran, Iascan, all went by in quick review.

"Now your report capability." Camerend and Mnar began a conversation, mentioning names and places and what had been said by whom, after which Lineas had to report it all back.

Just before the end, Mnar suddenly swung an open-handed slap at her, but Lineas knew that move from drills, and up came her forearms. She stepped in, turned against Mnar's arm, and stuck her bony little hip into Mnar's side as her foot trod inside Mnar's ankle and she pulled at Mnar's wrist.

Mnar let herself be pulled off-balance, as Lineas had executed the defensive move properly. Mnar then patted her on the head, as Camerend set down a slate and chalk, and said, "Now, last thing, a map of the kingdom."

Lineas's heart expanded with anticipation. "What do you want on it?"

Neither Camerend nor Mnar missed the pleasure lighting Lineas's face. "Whatever you think belongs on a map," Mnar said. "We'll be back presently, after which you will be finished with the testing."

Lineas scarcely heard the last few words. She sank onto the cushion before the low table, staring in delight at the large slate. She did not regard herself adept at drawing people or animals or anything that moved, unless they remained still enough for her to sketch from. She loved detail, and inevitably when she finished one bit, her model would have shifted and the whole thing always ended up distorted. But maps...she adored drawing maps. Any kind of map. With sure strokes she sketched the shape of the kingdom, and began happily putting in the jarlates, rivers, trade cities, and provincial capitals.

In the far room, Mnar and Camerend sat down together.

"I'm very normal?" Mnar repeated, uttering a soft laugh.

"Probably left over from her early days. Shendan told me that Lineas's mother is deaf, her father a blacksmith. Until she was four or five, Lineas never spoke, or considered words relevant. She played in silence with village children until some brat decided to mock her, and she learned fast to put sound and words together."

Mnar flicked open her fingers. "You'd think she would have forgotten that by now."

"Well, Shendan also said she has two Cassads in her family tree, one on each side." *Like Isa.* "Not just two Cassads, her grandfather was a Dei. From the branch that changed their name. But that doesn't keep Dei oddities from cropping up, the Cassads insist. However, her mother is a Noth, which seems to steady down those oddities. Noths might turn up deaf, like her mother, but they're steady."

Mnar accepted that with relief. She was related to the Noths herself, a family not known for flights of fancy. Unlike the family-tree-obsessed Cassads, who were careful not to match with any Deis. Too many offspring had been strange in ways that had made life difficult for them as well as for those around them. "She does seem *present,* as you'd expect from a practical Noth. Truthful as well as quite advanced in vocabulary."

Camerend held up a finger and opened the door. Through it they glimpsed Lineas's bony shoulders hunched up as she drew carefully with a bit of chalk, so absorbed she didn't notice Camerend coming up noiselessly, glancing down, and retreating.

He shut the door. "Her map is very nearly perfect," he said. "She's working in the woodlands and the eastern hills."

Mnar said, "But she's so small."

Camerend said, "And in some respects, Shendan says, young for her age. We have plenty of time to figure out if she'll do for Bun."

Both the king and queen were quite firm about it: none of the three royal heirs were to have a royal runner assigned as personal runner until they turned sixteen. They were to make do with the family runners until then.

"So we needn't say anything now," Mnar agreed, knowing who among the runners-in-training wanted such a prestigious appointment, and who might side-eye anyone obviously being trained for it. "I think it will be salutary for certain of our more ambitious slackers to see what appears to be a nine-year-old put among them. Lineas's appearance should shake up the lessons nicely."

Camerend opened his hands in assent, then went to his own duties, leaving Mnar to rejoin Lineas, who was detailing major springs in the hills between the capital and the Nelkereth Plains.

"You may take the rest of the afternoon to explore and acquaint yourself with your fellows," Mnar said. "Report to our mess at the watch change. After the meal, everyone will come up here for study, recreation, and what we call mend and make."

"Is that when I can do my laundry?" Lineas asked, and blushed. "Everything is dirty."

Mnar laughed. "To be expected if you've been traveling. The next door down from the baths is the staff laundry, which opens into our drying court. We recently shifted to the outside lines, now that the sun is getting stronger."

Relieved, Lineas slapped her hand to her skinny chest, and Mnar stepped into the next room, where a group of teens awaited their lesson. The door closed quietly, leaving Lineas alone.

She ventured onward, studying everything. Her attention snagged on the big slate on the opposite wall, with what looked like a map of the castle painted on the smooth stone, and between and adjacent to those lines, chalked initials and symbols.

Those had to be the day's watch assignments, Lineas thought, ignoring them in favor of the map itself.

The instruction to meet her fellows slid off a child raised as she had been. She had no idea how to "acquaint herself" with strangers, and besides, what better way to spend the rest of her free time than memorizing this enormous castle?

From her journal that night:

At first I got completely turned around. I think it was because I lost count of the landings bending back and forth, and because the door let me out between buildings from which I could only see bits of the cloudy sky, so I couldn't find the sun. So I swapped east and west, north and south.

I came out of a short but dark tunnel that I knew S. didn't show me [will I get used to Quill?]. It was cut through a wall even thicker than anything in Darchelde.

I knew I was lost, but then I made out a bright spot in the clouds atop some roofs, and it nearly made me dizzy as my sense of direction righted itself. That was west, not east, toward the kitchen gardens and the dairy animals.

So those roofs were the academy, and to the right lay an open space. I think it must be the parade ground. When I understood how lost I was, and where I almost got myself into, it felt like a slug right in the ribs. I right around fast, started to run back, and smacked hard into a boy—so hard I knocked him on his butt.

I tripped over his feet and fell on top of him. Hit my elbow. Others laughed as the boy and I shoved away from each other and got up. They stood behind me in a row while I stood at the mouth of the tunnel, blocking my way to what I knew now was east. They had obviously been running toward the parade ground.

What's this, a spy, one said in a snaily voice. I got that slimy feeling, he wanted trouble. All big boys. At least fourteen, maybe even fifteen.

I'm not a spy I said. I just got here and got lost.

A bell rang in the distance and the pale-haired one I knocked down yelled look what you did you made us late. Late for what I said. I got lost. I'm new.

Late to be picked for headmaster's runners said one. This is our last year. Shut up said the one I knocked down. She ruined our chances.

I could tell the pale haired one wanted an excuse. I was so afraid it would be like that horrible M at home or worse so when he swung a slap at me saying they'd teach me my directions I yanked his thumb and when he went off-balance I side-kicked out his forward leg at the knee.

He screeched as he fell over holding his knee and the biggest one came at me. It was that sick feeling all over, my heart banging my ribs and me shaking all over as I put my fists together and turned inside his arm and thumped his chin good.

He screeched as he fell. They were all screeching and I think I might have been too but then the yelling turned into deep voices. A royal runner, I'll call them RR, at the inner end and somebody in gray at the other, maybe even a master.

It had to be a master, because the boys wouldn't stop for a stable hand or servant I don't think.

The RR grabbed me and the master yelled something at the others. The RR pulled me all the way to an inner court that I found on the map just now, before asking what happened.

He listened all the way as I explained. Then said, you should have asked for a guide. The academy is off-limits, as are the state buildings. Those boys will rough-house at the slightest opportunity. Yes I understand that you got lost. With a guide you wouldn't have. Go to the mess hall and sit there until the bell. Now I have to report this idiocy, and I'm already late for what actually matters. Do you need directions to the—no, I'll walk you there myself.

He didn't say another word. I couldn't stop crying but as least I didn't make any noise.

When I got to the mess hall and told the kitchen staff I had to sit there they put me to work. I was glad. That made time go faster, though nothing made me feel any better.

When the bell rang, Chief Mnar came herself and sat with me to hear it all over. I felt so sick I couldn't eat until she said it was our mistake not to give you explicit orders to find one of your fellows who was free. I remembered that she did say find people, but that was only when I came upstairs to write this.

They are all in one of the rooms where they have free time. I did not get gated or punished, but a rebuke on my first day is worse.

I can hear the voices—

Someone is knocking. It has to be bad.

That was S, no I should write Q, with two others. I hid this before I opened the door.

He said why didn't you find us and I said I don't like to go up to people I don't know. What do you say to them? Especially when I can see they don't want me? At D you stayed with your group, and we magic students had to stay away from everyone else, even the scribes, though we were called archivist-scribes.

I could not say that I belonged to a group until I wasn't able to do magic and then nobody in archivist-scribes wanted to be near me because they thought I was kicked out for being bad, and how when I left no one came to say goodbye except Papa from the masonry as Mama was still traveling.

I couldn't even <u>write</u> that until now, I just saw when I went back two pages.

Q said I didn't know it but it's a very bad thing, fighting against Them. (The academy boys are Them. You can hear the capital in their voice.) Especially that one.

He told me that academy boys in the lower school can be headmaster's runners, which means they get wider bounds than the other boys. Everyone wants to be one, but they can't be after thirteen. Q said Senrid Gannan (who some call Big Mouth) and Frog Noth and Horseshoe Toraca would never get picked because they are always in trouble or too wild but now they can blame me, as they didn't get there by the watch bell.

The tall girl whose name I still don't know said, also fighting with the scrubs is bad because they think they have to win, don't I see. Us, we aren't army. We only defend ourselves or whoever we are assigned to.

Most of Them ignore us, the other boy said. (No name yet either.) Anyone interfering with runners, they get caned if they get caught.

Q said, maybe Noth and probably Gannan might come after me again, and if I want the academy boys to leave me alone I have to lose.

The other boy said, and if They do pick on someone, we can report it and They get Their coats dusted good, and gated with stable cleaning.

I said thank you, and I didn't know, and I'll do everything they say, and they left and went away to their rec room and I'm alone again and I'll always be alone for ever and ever and I. FEEL. SICK.

TWO

Lineas woke up remembering her undone laundry.

Convinced that she had become heinous to everyone, she stayed in her room until the stampede of feet toward the baths had come and gone before venturing downstairs with her laundry basket. She found several grown women at the bath. None of them gave her a second glance.

She washed her hair, put on her second set of clothes with no drawers, which felt odd, then found her way down the narrow hall to a huge, airy room with empty drying racks for winter. At the end of the room adjacent the baths there was an enormous tub into which water dripped in a stream, draining away in a channel that obviously led back to the baths. Lineas stared at the sparkle of magic around the tub's rim, which she usually found reassuring, but she was too upset to enjoy the flare and ribbons of color as she rapidly dunked her clothes. She put them through the wringer next to the barrel, then ventured through the door beyond, which opened into a court on the north side of the castle—which would get the most sun.

Hempen lines had been strung from wall to wall. She looked for dark blue, and found where her peers hung their things to dry. How could you tell yours apart from anyone else's? (She would soon discover that nobody did; if you hung out two items, you were entitled to fetch away two similar items. The clothing for the youngsters was interchangeable, except for underthings, which you embroidered with your initials.)

She neatly hung hers, knowing that if you put things to dry all wrinkled, they dried wrinkled. Everyone else had neatly hung theirs, too. She retreated to her room to tame her frizz into ferociously neat braids, so tight her scalp pulled and her eyes watered. The mess bell rang halfway through this process, but she ignored her growling stomach. She couldn't face anyone.

She waited until she heard the voices and feet again, then slipped out to join them, using the stealth she'd mastered early on. Staying close to walls, and keeping her head low, she didn't see Quill looking around worriedly for her. He hadn't seen her at breakfast.

When he spotted the telltale red braids on the other side of the room, he sat back in relief, and turned to his particular friends, who were staring at one of the school slates on the table.

Usually someone wiped the slates clean each evening and stacked them for morning. Sometimes the tutors kept someone's work out to serve as an example, or as a sign of excellence.

Quill elbowed his way in, then whistled under his breath when he saw a detailed map of the kingdom. It was not quite right, too long for the width, but in every other way it was really well done. Far better than the work of his particular class, which he would have recognized.

Mnar entered.

The runners in training fell silent.

Mnar said, "We teach you that among the ineffables binding together family, clan, guild, and country, are loyalty and honor, truth and law. We talk about them constantly, because these are ideals to strive for. The reality is...us, which includes individuals whose definitions of these four don't always quite match."

One of the seniors behind Quill whispered, "Is this the honor lecture again?"

Mnar sent a sharp glance their way, and silence fell. "So we sing stirring songs to bind us together, by emotion and by shared definitions. We all agree that the epitome of honor and loyalty was exemplified by the women at Andahi Castle at the start of the Venn War, who sacrificed their lives in delaying the entire Venn army. Though the king no longer permits us to sing the Andahi Lament on its anniversary, we all know the story."

Quill couldn't remember ever singing it as part of the summer Victory celebration, but the elders had said it used to be customary until Lorgi Idego's craven slaughter above Andahi besmirched the name, not the event. Now only the old women still sang it on Andahi Day, but everyone knew it. Once you heard it, it was impossible to forget.

As the eerie threnody echoed in every mind, Mnar said, "One of the ineffables—one of the strongest, so strong we don't make songs directly about it—is memory."

She paused, and lifted a hand toward the map chalked on the slate. All heads turned. Lineas strained to see what they were looking at. She was astonished to discover it was her map, and further—now that she could see it at a distance—it was horrendously distorted.

Her head dropped and her eyes stung as she braced herself for being made an example of for sloppy work.

Mnar said, "I would have made corrections for a senior, but it was not a senior who drew this entirely from memory. It was made by a first-year." She raised her voice as the runners all tried glancing furtively around, "Memory binds us together more effectively than our notions of honor and so forth. Memory comforts us and goads us. It is not only a skill, but a tool. Those among you who were born with excellent memory might start ahead, but it takes work to stay there—and it's those who put in the labor in this and other skills who are entrusted with the most important posts."

When she saw all attention on her, she drew aside the cloth covering the big slate with the day's study and work schedules on it.

Her voice altered to crisp warmth as she said, "Our newest student, Lineas daughter of Tdor Noth and Tanrid Stonemason of Darchelde, drew that map. Lineas, everyone is marked here by a sigil. Yours is this one, LN. Each day you'll find your morning's study chalked here, and your afternoon work."

Mnar paused to watch the students taking in the small figure hunched in on herself, then the board, which testified that Lineas was scheduled to study with the third and fourth years for every subject but Maths & Maps, where she'd be with the first-year seniors.

Mnar took in the faces, and, satisfied with what she saw, said, "Dismissed."

"Why the memory lecture?" one of the seniors muttered covertly, though everyone around was listening.

"Because she's got a new pet, of course," was the reply, though in a mild voice. The speaker was from a minor family on the western coast, where Iascans had slowly mixed with Marlovans. "From the looks of yon map, I'd say it's deserved."

"And better she pick one of us," added a sturdy boy of sixteen.

The seniors all opened their hands in agreement, and the listening juniors agreed.

All they knew of the newcomer was that she'd knocked that obnoxious academy scrub Gannan on his butt a heartbeat after her arrival. As for pets, if it was true, Dannor repeated to her particular cronies as she headed down the hall, "Good that it's one of *us*. I have nothing against Bun—I adore her— but proper is proper."

Lineas didn't hear any of it. Her head buzzed with relief. She wasn't in trouble? Her hands picked up chalk and slate as she followed the shuffling line, then she paused to glance at the diagram to orient herself on which room she was to go to.

Quill watched, hesitating until a fifth-year girl Quill's age turned dark, friendly eyes on Lineas and said, "Lost? Scribe class is with us, down the hall. I'll show you."

Lineas's buoyant mood carried her through her first day.

Scribe class helped Lineas steady herself, despite her being lightheaded from no breakfast and very little dinner the previous evening.

Her handwriting was excellent, but that was because she drew the letters rather than writing them. The tutor was calm and patient, showing her how best to grip her quill to speed up writing an alphabet that had been designed for right-handers. She much preferred Old Sartoran, which favored left-handers.

After that she had history and reports, both of which she loved. The latter was an exercise in memorization of words and tone, as taught by scribes.

Following that was the midday meal, and she found herself in a group of girls who all had questions about the mysterious Darchelde, which no one was allowed to enter or leave—except for runners.

"Quill comes from there," a girl said, her light blue eyes round and bright. "But he only goes back for his Name Day, and he says he doesn't see much, because his mothers live in the woods."

"I can't compare it to anywhere else," Lineas said with her usual scrupulous care. "Because I don't know anywhere else. But once, when I was learning to ride, my mother took me to deliver messages...."

From the other side of the mess hall, Quill observed Lineas looking a lot more cheerful as she chattered with a mix of second and third years. He relaxed inside. Though he'd done what he'd been told to do the morning before, guilt still poked at him for the mess that had happened in the afternoon. He should have looked out for her, a fellow runner in training from Darchelde, and a relative, however distant.

He turned back to his friends, breathing easier—and unaware of Camerend watching them both from the other side of the mess hall. Both youngsters were easy enough to read. Lineas was settling in at last, and his son was developing a sense of responsibility.

At the same time, up in the gunvaer chambers, Mnar said to Danet, "I will *not* make a pet of Lineas."

They often met to talk over runner and tutoring affairs. This particular evening, Danet triumphantly offered a taste of the latest delivery of coffee from the islands, brought in from Lindeth after the snows melted.

Mnar paused to sip appreciatively, then said, "I hadn't thought I'd made a pet of Bun in tutoring her myself."

"*They* make a pet of her." Danet turned up her hands. "Everybody makes a pet of my daughter. I think your seniors looked for what they expected to see, and since no one really minds, where's the problem? Bunny likes you, and I want you tutoring her. You're the only one with enough authority. Everyone else, she charms them into letting her skimp work to escape to her animals."

The door banged open, thrust by Arrow's impatient hand. He and Commander Noth walked in. Arrow plunked himself down on the nearest cushion, as Noth rounded to the other side, and sat next to Danet. Mnar watched the subtle signs between them—the way the gunvaer turned slightly, the touch of Noth's thigh against hers, and sighed inwardly. This bond showed every sign of permanence—which she didn't begrudge either of them—but she missed the days when she and Danet went together to the Rose on Restday evenings. Danet had stopped that ever since she'd taken up with Commander Noth.

"What now?" Arrow asked, looking from one face to another.

"A new fuzzy," Danet replied. "One they think might do for Bun someday."

Arrow shrugged. That was someone else's worry, and he had enough of his own. He leaned forward. "I was just telling Noth that this year, I want to try something new with the academy, now that we're finally a good size, and have sent two classes on to the garrisons. So far, the reports coming back are good. We're making *Marlovan* captains here, rather than individual jarlate ones. But we can always improve."

Danet opened her hand. She still was ambivalent about the academy's purpose, but that was Arrow's affair.

He saw enough assent to be satisfied, and went on. "Inda-Harskialdna insisted that youngsters learn faster with rewards rather than punishment, so I'm going to give out medals for the winning commander of the Great Game, as well as the Victory Day competitions. That means we have to figure out what they look like. I'm thinking little eagles, silver. Gold. Down the sleeve, which is where actual command chevrons are worn, but maybe the left instead of the right sleeve...."

Mnar got to her feet, knowing that the conversation would be entirely taken up with academy minutiae, now that the king was here. It had been this way ever since that first admittedly awkward year, when they had only twenty-seven boys: the king was always changing things. She might as well get back to work.

THREE

Spring had abruptly turned into summer when Lineas reported to the roost to find herself assigned to the garden. She and the others with that duty trooped downstairs that afternoon, grumpy at the prospect of not just weeding, but toiling down the rows with buckets of water from the canal, as the bright blue sky gave no hint of rain anytime soon.

She had gradually gone from dreading a second encounter with the academy boys to largely forgetting about that first terrible day. Like the other runners in training, at her first glimpse of the undyed sashed smocks and gray trousers of the academy boys she whisked herself out of sight, taking another route.

That was until midway through the afternoon, as Lineas labored with her friends in the far corner of the garden, and they spotted roaming academy boys — who spotted them at the same time.

"Heads down," spindly, second-year Cama muttered. "It's Big Mouth Gannan and the Poseid twins."

"They're not even supposed to be here," Lineas whispered back. There were rules!

"They're definitely out of bounds, unless they're on a tracking game." And even then, they weren't supposed to harass any of the castle staff, which included both garrison and royal runners in training. Fnor, who was finishing her first year, snorted a hard sigh through her nose. "Lineas, if they go after you, best to lose."

Lineas obediently lowered her gaze to the cabbages in front of her, but she knew from sad experience that her red hair was a beacon for bullies.

"If they want me to blub, I won't." Lineas scowled.

"Why not? Everybody does." Fnor sent her a quick, covert glance. "You fake it if you can't make it."

Cama whispered as he yanked up a handful of tangleweed, "Saddleback Fath and his gang went for me after a storm last spring, when I got stuck sweeping leaves on the west end of the parade ground. I howled so loud that all the scribes in the state wing heard through the windows, which they'd just opened, but Saddleback and his gang didn't notice. The gunvaer was with the scribes, and heard everything."

His mouth curved in reminiscence as he banged his trowel into the ground. "They all came a-running to the window. Saddleback had only smacked me once but I howled as if he'd ripped my arm off. The gunvaer ordered Fath and the rest dusted on the spot. By no less than Commander Noth."

Fnor glanced over her shoulder, then whispered, "They got gated an entire month in the stables, too. Sh! Here they come. If we ignore them, maybe they'll move on."

Senrid Gannan and his Rider-family third-cousins had been half-heartedly playing a long game of hide-and-find (scrapping when you got found) with others in their year when they spotted Lineas's red hair. The heat, their fruitless search, and boredom vanished like smoke. Gannan remembered that girl, and though he had not in any of his previous three years been picked as a headmaster runner, a privilege extended to few and easily lost through (for instance) the sort of trouble he was about to get into now, it was always easier to blame someone else rather than yourself.

As for Lineas, Cama had said exactly the right thing. In the time it took to yank two handfuls of sprouting sticklewort and tangleweed, Lineas's heartsick determination not to let herself be humiliated changed to teeth-gritted determination as the academy boys tramped straight toward them.

Gannan scowled, in a bad mood from the heat, the boring game, and especially from Connar's sarcasm in the barracks that morning, just because he'd called Noddy a rockbrain. Which he was! How Gannan hated that swanking, strutting Connar, prettier than a girl.

The twins perked up, hoping for entertainment. Gannan's irritation sharpened. The red-haired fuzz was even scrawnier than he remembered, scarcely half his size. That only made his defeat worse, at least in his eyes; he was certain that everyone in the academy was still laughing behind his head, though in truth most of them had forgotten between one meal and the next. But Gannan, grown up under a bully of an older brother and a brute of a father, nursed grudges like a fire in winter.

He waited for her to attack, but she just kept messing around.

"You think you're so tough," he prompted, kicking a clod of dirt onto her knee.

"I never said that," Lineas replied after another, larger, clump of dirt hit her in the stomach.

"Oooh, that's not what *I* hear," taunted one of the twins, side-eyeing his brother. They didn't care at all about what had happened eons ago. They were looking for fun, and Gannan going after someone else was a thousand times better than him taking his temper out on them.

"Then you heard wrong," Lineas said, as the other two runners-in-training kept weeding. She bent over to yank a stickleback. "I don't know any of you. I certainly haven't talked to you, so whatever you heard didn't come from me."

The second twin, who alternately sympathized with his Gannan cousin, and privately thought that he could use a dose more of what he'd apparently gotten in the tunnel (which he wished he'd seen) crooned, "I heard you scrapped with Gannan here."

"No. We bumped into each other."

Gannan shot her a puzzled frown. She didn't act like the whirlwind she'd been that day.

But then came, "What's happening here, Big Mouth? These feet giving you lip?"

Feet, Lineas had learned, was academy slang for runners in training.

All six looked up at the boy sauntering their way. Tall at nearly sixteen, Manther Yvanavayir looked old and tough to their eyes.

Gannan refused to answer, dead set against accepting Big Mouth as a nickname. None of the bigger boys had used it until now, so he had to squash it—and yet you ignored the bigger boys at your peril.

Lefty Poseid didn't mind teasing his cousin, but stopped at involving older boys. He said quickly, "Just some talk with Red here."

"That's Pimple," Gannan snarled, unable to let the earlier grudge go. "She's *Pimple*."

"That the fuzz that dumped you on your butt, Gannan?" Manther sneered. "What is she, six?"

"She caught me off-guard," Gannan retorted, relieved that Yvanavayir had used his name.

Lineas's lips shaped the first word of *That's a lie*, but she caught Fnor's warning glance as she and Cama kept working as if no one were there. Lineas forced herself to kneel again, and feel with shaking fingers around a cabbage for weed tufts.

"Nothing to say, *Pimple?*" Gannan goaded, this time kicking her directly in the side.

It was not a bruising kick, but strong enough to knock her into the dirt. She fought the instinct to roll to her feet, hands up and ready, and forced herself to tumble flat.

He came at her again, tromping two cabbages as he leaned down to swat at her, for he'd been raised to take out his anger on those below.

Lineas knew how to deflect blows, but Gannan was faster than her fellow runners-in-training, who were all so careful not to hurt each other in drills. She flung herself aside, as one of the twins hissed in protest at the cabbages Gannan kicked up.

Gannan didn't even see. Being a jarl's son, he had never gone anywhere near the kitchen garden at home—unlike the twins, who along with all the youngsters of Riders and castle staff had to help at harvest time, and when small, in the kitchen garden all spring and summer.

Lineas scrambled away, mindful of Cama's advice, but Gannan just kept coming, trying to provoke her. One of Gannan's slaps caught the side of her ear, and she rolled away, her ear stinging. "Ow!" she shrilled, then caught Cama's covert smirk of encouragement, and howled, "That hu-u-u-u-u-urts!"

"I barely touched you," Gannan retorted. "What a rabbit!"

"But *you're* so tough," Manther said goadingly, laughing at how easy it was to fetch Big Mouth.

Gannan caught himself up short, completely thrown by this unexpected attack, when he'd just proved that he *wasn't* a coward, and that he could beat the snot out of the brat.

"Go away." Lineas hated the way her voice quavered. It was not fear, but anger. She reminded herself of Cama's window, and shrilled, *"Go away!"*

"Go away," Fnor added, arms crossed, a short, stolid figure with ash-blonde braids.

The academy boys knew they were breaking rules, if not bounds, and there was nothing whatsoever warlike in Fnor or Lineas kneeling there, twelve years old, feet bare because summer weeding was so much easier barefoot.

But Gannan — who saw himself not as a bully but as a victim — couldn't let it go. He couldn't lose, he was *right.* He scowled at Lineas. "Stand up and fight, *Pimple,*" he snarled.

Lineas bit back her anger. She was a veteran of a pair of roaming bullies in Darchelde, who'd had a talent for catching their victims out of sight of anyone who might defend them. She knew from hard experience what escalation cost.

Where was the supervising kitchen staff, she wondered as she dodged another kick.

Not a hundred paces away and coming fast, running alongside the roaming patrol sentry, who had been flagged by a wall sentry.

The sudden adult voices caused all six children to recoil, startled into stillness.

"What's going on here?" demanded the sentry.

"Who ruined these cabbages?" demanded the kitchen runner.

"He did!" All three runners in training pointed at Gannan. The twins just stood by, stiff as posts, hoping to remain unnoticed. Yvanavayir laughed — then choked it off as the sentry crooked his finger at him.

"You're all going to the watch commander," the sentry said, annoyed at his utterly unnecessary hot run during summer. "On the double."

"And I'll be lodging a complaint about the damage," the kitchen runner added, pointing at the ruined cabbages.

The boys slunk away, arguing and protesting all the way.

The kitchen runner squinted against the sun at the rest of the unfinished weeding and the scattered cabbages, and said to the fledglings, "Let's see if we can rescue any of these."

Silent, the young runners bent to do what they could to replant the cabbages, then they were sent to fetch buckets of water from the canal.

Lineas's fingers ached as they lugged buckets of water from the canal to the vegetables.

They were all drenched with sweat and bursting to talk when at last the watch bell clanged, the kitchen runner dismissed them, and they were finally alone.

After thoroughly and repeatedly reviling against the academy boys, Fnor said with gloomy satisfaction, "What you want to bet they got dusted?"

"How many, do you think?" Cama asked.

"A hundred, I hope," Fnor retorted. "*Two* hundred."

Lineas's head pounded by the time she entered the cool, shadowy building and stood in the mess line.

But her headache was forgotten after she sat down, and Quill stopped to say, "Cama told me what happened. Good job!"

Lineas hadn't meant to say anything, but out came the words, "He kept calling me Pimple. They're all going to do it." Tears threatened. She had grown up hearing the horrible nicknames of famous Noth elders.

"They might try," Quill said. "If you don't like it, don't answer. And all of us will say 'who'? until they drop it. He hasn't the sway to make it stick."

You like Quill? Lineas thought miserably as he went away to join his own table. But it would never occur to her to question anything Senrid said.

The older girls at home had laughed at her when she admitted to her first crush, at age eight. She still remembered that black-haired shepherd's boy and his turned-up nose.

"Oh, you're *in love*," Haret had cooed, laughing. "Because all seven-year-olds are so-o-o-o-o-o experienced with heats."

And tall Chelis had said kindly, though patronizingly, "What you say, Lineas, is that you hope you will be friends. Heats aren't appropriate until you're out of smocks," she added with a squelching look at Haret, "and have at least a faint idea what that means. Same with 'in love.'"

Lineas had crept away from those tall, knowledgeable twelve-year-olds, no longer wanting to explain how much she liked looking at Keth the Shepherd, and how, when he looked at her, he made her feel outlined in light.

But one day he'd shoved a snowball down her neck after she brought him a tart made from the last apples, and he'd howled with laughter as she danced around trying to shake it loose.

After that she wondered how she had missed how mean his grin was, and her infatuation withered. At nine, she was in love with Lnand, the miller's second daughter. Lnand was eleven, and everybody said she was the prettiest girl in Darchelde, and had the best singing voice.

Whatever Lineas did to try to please her, Lnand accepted with the calm smile of one who knows what is due to her, and finally Lineas noticed how many other people also gave Lnand gifts, and tried to get her attention.

Lnand gave them all that smile that Lineas gradually sensed was smug, though as yet she didn't know the word.

After that, Senrid came to visit his mothers, and lightning struck again.

In her journal that night, Gannan and Yvanavayir got a paragraph of insult-laden description, and the rest of her scribbling was about Q and how pretty his flyaway hair was and how wonderfully he played the drums on Restday.

While she was busy writing, Commander Noth had been pulled away from the staff wardroom, and his all-too-rare rec time. He joined the headmaster in facing the boys, who sat there with a variety of expressions from sulky to grim endurance. They had been left to stew all day, and all knew what was coming.

Noth compressed his lips against a brief impulse to laughter. They reminded him so much of young animals. They *were* young animals, somewhere between lanky pups and colts, exhibiting the unconscious grace of strength and skill when enjoying themselves in the sun and wind, but seeing no further than their noses. They should have known the inevitable consequence of their actions, but boys typically looked little beyond some version of *We won't get caught.*

"The headmaster," he said without preliminary, "tells me that your rec periods from now until the Great Game will be in the stable. And you'll shortly be getting ten reminders of the price of stupidity from me, so brace your shoulders, boys. But before that. Yvanavayir. Next spring you'll be a senior, handling lances, and — ostensibly — commanding ridings in wargames. I can't believe someone who has been here six years could act like a scrub."

Stung into self-righteous defense, Yvanavayir protested, "I didn't *do* anything!"

"No, you stood there goading Gannan into recklessness, which he obediently complied with. Gannan, do you need to go back with the ten and eleven-year-olds to learn basic rules?"

Gannan flushed. "No, Commander."

"Meanwhile, none of you seemed to be aware that you were harassing the runners-in-training who were busy working on raising the food you *eat every day.*"

Sulky, resentful gazes dropped to the stone floor. They were on the verge of shutting Noth out as they nursed resentment and mentally spun out all kinds of retribution on one another and the hapless runners-in-training.

So he tried again.

He snapped his fingers, and they looked up, startled. "Imagine ten years from now. The king calls us to war, say, up north."

They looked puzzled and wary, but they were listening.

"We might even be meeting the Venn, or the Chwahir, or some other empire-seekers in the Pass, where too many of our ancestors bled out their lives. You fight all day, maybe take a couple of bad wounds. The weather turns foul, because it's always going to turn foul on you. The medics are spread too thin. Your personal runner is dead, defending you on the left—"

"But—" Gannan began to protest.

"Your personal runner," Noth sharpened his voice, "is dead. There's no one around but royal runners. 'Feet.'" His teeth showed when he repeated the word. That predatory flash of white was not pleasant to see.

He paused. Their mulish expressions had not changed, but the angles of heads, the tight shoulders, indicated they were still listening.

"The royal runners bandage who they can, and set up tents as fast as they can, and take away bloody clothes to mend, then, while you're lying nice and dry, they're over at the cook tent fetching water and food—maybe helping with the cooking. And while you're asleep, who's riding to the royal city with news of the battle?"

Yvanavayir's eyes shifted.

"These are not Iascans who not-so-secretly despise us, or foreigners who endure us. They are fellow Marlovans, with the same pride, who sing the same songs at Restday and Victory Day—but all during their training years, who treated them like enemies?"

He leaned over to pick up the ash switch. As he cracked it experimentally on the air, he added, "Gannan, every Restday until you go home, you will report to the kitchens, and do whatever they tell you. It seems that you are unaware of where the food comes from that appears before you each mess, and how much work went into putting it there. Now, Yvanavayir. You first, while my arm is fresh."

FOUR

For Gannan, the first Restday was the worst.

He was convinced that the entire academy, all enjoying themselves at their ease, were laughing at him trudging to the kitchen gardens behind a tall, grim-faced woman wearing the apron of kitchen staff.

As is often true, others are far less interested in our movements than their own, unless we've become notorious. Being stuck with kitchen duty was good for a laugh, but most of the academy had forgotten long before the marks on the boys' shoulder blades faded.

That first Restday, the adults in charge made certain that Gannan would be alone so that he would not be distracted from the lesson in garden protocols. Also, both kitchen and garrison chiefs agreed that making the boy work hard would get the point across.

He was acutely miserable, his ears red with vexation and shame, as he began work that was unfamiliar to his hands. But one thing about weeding: it's simple, and repetitive, and as time slid by under the hot sun, and no one came around to poke fun at him, he actually...didn't hate it as much as he'd expected to.

His back still ached—and that was before he had to lug pails of water to his assigned rows—but he, like the rest of the boys, lived in an atmosphere in which muscle ache equated with the gaining of strength.

When he returned to the academy for Restday drum, the others knew exactly how far to go with teasing lest they get themselves into trouble, and his worst enemy, Olavayir Tvei, wasn't even there. He and his royal Ain (for the academy had resurrected the ancient practice of number brothers in birth order: *ain, tvei*) were up in the castle, doing Restday with the king and queen. The princes always returned at lights out.

And so things settled down to routine for the next couple of weeks, until Connar decided enough time had passed.

It was Gannan's fourth weekend, and probably his last, since the entire academy would ride out for the Great Game the next week, following which would be the Victory Day competitions and then home till next spring.

Connar said to Noddy, "Let's go see Big Mouth grubbing in the garden."

Noddy accepted this suggestion, as Connar knew he would, and so they set out, Connar leading them the long way around past the back end of the stable yard, and behind the weavers' buildings, where linen stuff soaked and dried. As they skipped over a low wall intended to keep sheep from wandering in, they caught sight of Chief Weaver Hliss at the same time she saw them.

She stood by the dye shed, her hands pressing into her lower back, her huge stomach sticking out. "Hai, boys," she cried, smiling wearily, for it was the hottest day of summer so far, still and humid. "What are you doing?"

"Just walking around, Aunt Hliss," Connar called. "It's too hot for anything else."

"Don't wander beyond the back barns," she warned. "Sunset's not far off."

"We won't," Connar promised, and Noddy echoed, "We won't."

She smiled and turned away to speak to someone, as the acrid smells of dye wafted in the thick air.

"I think it's going to thunder," Noddy ventured.

Connar ignored that with a lifetime's habit—Noddy was always making obvious remarks about animals, the weather, and everything else that had nothing to do with their evolving plans *now*.

"Slow down," Connar breathed. "We're just wandering around."

Both boys knew that the wall sentries as well as the patrols always watched them, or rather, watched over them. They knew it was for their safety; as yet it had never occurred to think beyond that for other motivations, any more than they perceived how laughably predictable boys their age were.

Everyone in the lower academy knew about the feud between Gannan and Connar, which had originated when they were ten-year-olds when Gannan tried to gain the admiration of their fellow first year scrubs by calling Noddy Rockhead. Of course Connar would want to see Gannan grubbing among the vegetables.

So they moseyed along toward the kitchen gardens, as if it were a surprise to find themselves there.

Gannan, by now practiced enough for his hands to keep busy while his mind wandered, had been trying to count up the days since the Restday meal had included honey cakes. His count broke when he heard the crunch of footsteps. He looked up, scowling—then gloated when he saw who it was. When he'd cut through the garrison on his way to the garden, he'd been stopped by a garrison runner in training who shared a juicy rumor. Gannan had been saving it for the academy, but this would do.

"Big Mouth," Connar exclaimed with a fake start of surprise. "All alone? What happened, scare off all the six-year-old feet?"

Simmering with anticipation, Gannan snarled, "You're out of bounds."

"It's Restday." Connar flicked his hand down his House tunic with the eagle embroidered on the front, a reminder that the princes attended Restday with their parents. "And when we're in civ, the *whole castle* belongs to us. There *are* no bounds."

Noddy opened his mouth to point out that that was not true—they were not permitted in the state wing, or the third floor—but Connar, knowing his elder brother's proclivity for extraneous details, dug a warning elbow into his side, and gave Gannon a toothy grin.

And Gannon shot his hoarded bolt. "*Nothing* will belong to *you* if the weaver chief has a boy. And won't we laugh!"

"Huh?" Noddy looked puzzled and Connar wary.

Gannon dropped his handful of weeds and sat back on his heels, giving a hearty, scornful laugh. "Are you too stupid to know what *everybody* knows? That child inside the weaver chief is the king's, and *you* aren't. If it's a boy, he'll be a *real* prince, and you'll be nothing! Ha ha ha!"

Connar stared, too stunned to move, then fury ignited, but before he could launch himself onto Gannon, Noddy caught his arm in his much stronger grip, his other hand making the two-fingered sign for eyes. Connar remembered the sentries who of course were watching, and enough of the white heat subsided for him to take in Gannon's triumphant grin at having fetched him.

Connar curled his lip in scorn. "You're stupid, Big Mouth." Then, seeing no reaction to that nickname, he observed in light-toned sarcasm that cut like glass, "Look at you, enjoying yourself grubbing in those cabbages. Right where you belong. *Cabbage.* Let's go, Noddy." He turned, and as he started away, kicked up a spray of soil into Gannon's face.

He walked away, his righteous fury intensified by doubt.

When they were out of earshot, he said, "What did he mean by that?"

Noddy shrugged. "You *know* not to believe anything Big Mouth says."

"Cabbage. From now on, he's Cabbage."

Noddy said equably, "All right."

Connar brooded. He'd always known he was adopted. Well, he remembered finding out when he was around five, when the stable chief was about to have a baby and he'd asked his mother how long he'd had to stay inside her. She'd said he was inside someone else, but Ma and Da wanted him as a son, and so he came to them. She'd said, "Me and you, we're both adopted. People come into a family in two ways, birth and adoption. And there are two kinds of birth."

That was already more than he wanted to know, but Ma's voice reassured him, and so he'd run out to play again. But he remembered it now and then, like on Noddy's and Bun's Name Days, when some old person or other would bring up how Noddy was born at a Great Game, or how Bunny had come during a terrific thunderstorm. But nobody said anything about his birth on his Name Day, because nobody was there.

He didn't even know when his true Name Day was, but he liked having it on Spring Firstday. Ma had said, "We picked that day because everybody celebrates it. So everybody celebrates your Name Day."

He hadn't thought much about it since then. He had no interest in what the adults did, if it didn't impact what the boys were doing. But lately he'd noticed how Aunt Hliss sat beside Da for many meals, and sometimes she wasn't there, and Commander Noth was sometimes there, sitting next to Ma. It all had something to do with favorites and mates and sex, which were as remote as the idea of being grown up.

For the first time, as he and Noddy trudged through the garrison in the simmering heat, he began to put together favorites, sex, and birth. It was still confusing.

When they reached the top of the stairs, Connar said, "Go find Bun, and get our horses saddled. We can ride before the watch change."

Though Noddy was the physical defender, Connar had been the leader of their games since they were small. Noddy turned obediently and ran off.

Connar sped down the hall toward the royal suites. Ma could be anywhere on most days, but on Restday she almost always stayed in, writing letters.

She was deep in composition, a letter she'd put off since the Restday previous. She hated writing to the Jarlan of Feravayir, who packed her letters with Sartoran phrases, and who seemed incapable of stating a straightforward truth. When dealing with the woman, Danet never forgot Arrow telling her that the jarlan was reported as having said that she was Queen of Perideth.

Writing to her was a battle sentence by sentence, so Danet glanced up impatiently when her door burst open, and there was Connar, his startlingly blue eyes wide, the fine black hair escaped from his tied-back hair lying across his high forehead in damp strands.

His distraught expression, with the anger flattening his arched brows, turned a half-formed sentence to smoke. "What's wrong?"

"That baby inside Aunt Hliss. If it's a boy, will he be a prince, a *real* prince, instead of me? Because Da is his da?"

Danet laid aside her pen, her mind working rapidly. This was the second time she'd been caught off-guard, expecting this sort of question later. The first had been when Connar and Noddy were around five.

"You *are* a real prince," she said. "What bonehead put the idea into your head that you aren't?"

Connar's gaze dropped. "One of the boys." While he loved the idea of royal retribution on Gannan, he knew what everyone else would say about snitches, and anyway it would be extra horrible if the beaks landed on Gannan for it. Then Gannan would know he'd got to Connar. Which would be worse than a thousand tortures and death by fire.

"Well, you ought to know better than to listen to them. First of all, boy or girl, that baby is Aunt Hliss's. It won't be adopted into the Olavayirs. It will be a Farendavan, unless it adopts into some other family later. Aunt Hliss wants a child to inherit the Farendavan weaving secrets. And she tried hard for—that is, she hopes it will be a girl."

Connar skipped over the "tried hard," assuming it meant wishing hard. "Farendavan," he repeated.

"That's Aunt Hliss's family. My birth family, too."

A new question occurred. "What's my birth family?"

Mother's gaze shifted away, then she looked back at him. "I don't know. That is, your parents didn't marry, so there wasn't any adoption treaty. And your birth-mother's side don't name families the way we do. They're Iascan."

He'd learned at the academy that Iascans were mainly sea traders or fisher folk. "So she went away to sea?"

"Yes," Danet said, grateful to see the lessening interest in Connar's face. She had promised herself never to lie to her children, but she did not look forward to discussing Fi. Especially as Connar seemed to have inherited her temper. But he wasn't Fi, or Lanrid, she reminded herself. The one who calmed him the fastest was always Noddy. The boys were loyal to each other in a way that Arrow and Lanrid never had been.

"But my birth father was Olavayir."

"Yes. He died in the Pass, when Lorgi Idego split off from the kingdom."

Connar nodded, relieved. He *was* a real prince, then, and he had a hero as a birth-father. A last doubt assailed him. "He said everybody knew."

Danet let her exasperation show. "Who is this everybody? If 'everybody' knows something, wouldn't we all be hearing about it?"

That was certainly true. Connar let out a breath of relief. No one had said anything until Big Mou—*Cabbage* Gannan yapped those words. Hatred burned deep at how Gannan had gloated.

"You should know by now that when someone starts jawing about 'everybody knows', they're inventing rumor to convince you, instead of stating facts. Even if they didn't make it up outright, it's still just rumor." She laid the cover over her ink, then said, "If I were to tell you that everybody knows that Lorgi Idego is a staging base for a Norsunder invasion, would you believe it?"

"Yes," he began, then scowled.

"Right," she said. "Most of us can't forget that slaughter before you were born, and they hate the Idegans for it. So it's easy to believe that they invited Norsunder in. But the truth is, there's no evidence that Norsunder had anything to do with that attack."

He shifted impatiently, and she heard the echo of her own words beginning to sound like a lecture. No wonder Mother used to clip her words short.

Danet choked off what would have been useful instruction about always asking for sources, and waved her hand. "Go play. The bell will ring soon enough."

He flashed a grateful smile and fled, determined to get that new name for Gannan well spread before lights out. Much better vengeance than snitching.

She watched him run off, so unconsciously graceful, with that clear, musical voice, unlike her darling son. But she had only to see Noddy's bony, bucktoothed face, or Bun's round, equally bucktoothed countenance, and her heart brimmed with love.

Connar...though she didn't think of herself as a mothering type any more than her own mother had been, but in the course of nursing him she had come to love him fiercely. But it was a conscious love. She couldn't help but notice certain expressions, especially as he altered from round-faced babyhood into boyhood, that brought Lanrid to mind, and once in a while, Fi. Then love would surge up, smothering that inward catch as she reminded herself that he *wasn't* Fi. He *wasn't* Lanrid. He was *hers*.

She turned her gaze back to her letter and dipped the pen with a determined tap, but then held it suspended as she labored to retrieve the careful phrasing she had toiled over.

No use. Gone. Instead, questions bloomed until she gave an exasperated sigh and threw down the pen again. Glad that Restday afternoons were understood to be her own, she left without catching curious eyes, and took the back way via the baths to the ground floor, then roundabout to the airy, open barn where Hliss had caused the looms to be moved in spring.

There was Hliss, recognizable by the thick braids wrapped around her head to keep them off her neck. Her hair had darkened to the rich honey-brown of good ale, glinting with golden highlights in the slanting shafts of light.

Danet crossed the space, watching dust motes from her steps whirl upward like tiny fire-stars, and she breathed in air heavy with the scents of cloth, wood, dust, and the home-smell of wet flax laid out to dry before hackling.

Hliss spoke to a cluster of youngsters in training, then flicked her fingers and they dispersed to their various tasks. Some, catching sight of Danet, pulled up short and slapped their palms against their hearts in salute.

Danet brushed her fingers outward to indicate they should carry on with their tasks, and Hliss lumbered over in the swaying gait Danet remembered unfondly, when the joints of hips and legs seemed loose as baby teeth in childhood.

"Danet?"

"Not here," Danet said.

Hliss's face, rounder and fuller than twelve years ago when she was eighteen, glowed with the warmth. Danet thought that Hliss had been appealing in their young days, but she was beautiful now, her expression so mild it always reminded Danet of the first spring day, when you breathe in and know that winter is over.

Hliss led her down into the cellar, where baskets of lupin waited for the dye pots.

"Seeding done?" Danet asked.

Hliss nodded, rubbing her hand over her damp forehead. "They were quite happy over at the kitchen with this year's crop. We'll begin the salting tomorrow, or the next day if the storm everyone says they feel breaks tonight." She gave her sister a whimsical smile. "The bell hasn't rung yet. Why are you down here, when I'll be up there shortly?"

"Because I want to talk to you with no listening ears around," Danet said, and repeated her exchange with Connar. She ended, "Has Arrow been pestering you for adoption if you do have a boy? I want to know where this rumor came from."

Hliss shook her head. "No." She laid her hand on her stomach. "He knows she's a Farendavan." Her broad, smooth brow puckered, the closest Hliss ever came to bad temper. "He also knows how bitter Mother was about my having a king's child."

Danet remembered the long letter their mother had written, spelling out what horrors lay in the future if Hliss did have a boy, and the inescapable civil war that she would lay directly at her daughters' doors.

Hliss's smile faded and she stared down at a basket. "I suppose it might have been wiser to marry someone else. It's not as if I haven't had offers, even now. But...."

"No," Danet said, coming forward to take her sister's hands. "Arrow is better with you. You're the only one who can calm him down. He drinks less when he's with you," she added.

It wasn't in Arrow to stay with one person. Danet always knew when he took up with a new favorite, usually from the Shield. At least he tended to choose professionals who wouldn't make trouble; he'd learned that much from Fi. But when he ventured away from Hliss, he drank more, because professionals were expected to bring money into the house, and Danet could smell the result when they met in the mornings.

"I think so, too. Anyway, I'm as sure as one can be that I have a girl. And if I made a mistake," Hliss chuckled, "I could always make him a Ranet."

"A Ranet?"

Hliss pressed her knuckles into her lower back and said, "You know. Ranet Senelaec."

"What?" Danet exclaimed. "Ranet, daughter of Calamity and Wolf?"

Hliss stared, aghast. "You didn't know?"

"Are you telling me that Ranet...isn't a girl?"

Hliss sank down onto an upturned barrel, weary and horrified. "I thought you knew." She blinked with that lost face that Danet remembered from late in her pregnancy with Noddy, when the heat seemed to boil your brains. Hliss gave Danet a puzzled, unhappy look. "Calamity is your friend."

"I thought she was my friend," Danet said slowly.

Silence fell between them as Hliss pressed her hands over her face.

Aware of the growing silence, she looked up, to see Danet looking shockingly like Mother.

Her mind might not have been working before, but it was now, as the implications of her careless remark proliferated remorselessly.

Hliss sighed. "Danet, I want you to be Danet Farendavan for a moment, and not Danet-Gunvaer. You felt the same misgivings that I did when Arrow started his academy again. We talked about it, all that winter, especially after little Bunny was born, and you were so glad that she was a she, and so wouldn't be drawn into it."

Danet crossed her arms, her fists tight. "All that is true. But what has it to do with Calamity making a fool of me? Ranet, or what I thought was Ranet, is betrothed to Connar!"

Hliss grunted as she swung to her feet and reached for her sister's hands. "Think of what people have said about the Olavayirs for years, all the bloody changes of king. The fear of war up north. Remember the stories about the academy. Not the ones about how it was a miracle under Inda-Harskialdna, but how terrible it was when the Olavayirs took over from the Montrevayirs, and then, under Bloody Tanrid, all the duels and fights that led to it being shut down again. Would you—you're a mother now—want to send your little boy so far away, to be put under people you know hate your family?"

Danet could see it...just. Yes, she could see it. And, ruthlessly honest with herself as always, she sought for the source of the pain. She wasn't really upset about Arrow being denied one more future army captain. It was because she had been exchanging letters with Calamity for twelve years. Almost thirteen. But there had never been any mention of Ranet not being a girl, not even after Danet had sent the betrothal letter—a betrothal that Danet had intended to be an honor, pairing Wolf's and Calamity's daughter with the second prince. She had even wanted to make Ranet Noddy's wife, but Arrow had insisted on a descendant of Inda-Harskialdna as soon as the news arrived that the Iofre had had a pair of female twins.

"Why didn't she tell me?" she whispered, eyes closed. She hated to say the word *betrayal*. So dangerous and bloody a word. Her eyes opened. "What did she think was going to happen twenty years after they called a boy a girl, when it came time for all the pairs to meet and marry?"

"But that would be in *twenty years*. Even more. Anything could happen. Danet, remember, when that baby was born, it was right after all those dolphin-clan murders. Which everyone outside the Olavayirs sees as Olavayir murders. Everyone was afraid there would be more and more fighting, especially as neither you nor Arrow had been brought up to rule."

Danet let out her breath. She herself hadn't believed she and Arrow could hold the kingdom. There had been times, especially that first couple of years, when any sudden noise in the night sounded like assassins coming for her children. She had drilled hard every day that first year, until she got too sick with Bunny. For four years she slept with a knife under her pillow, and the inner door open to the nursery; she hadn't let the children be moved into their own rooms until Noddy was almost five, even though the traditional crown prince's suite was next down the hall from the king's.

Danet's thoughts shifted. She eyed her sister. "How did *you* find out?" Her voice sharpened. "I take it they're all laughing behind our heads? At *me*, and my betrothals, which I worked on for *two years*, as a way to keep the peace?"

Sick at heart, Hliss realized the least said the better. Which meant, for the first time, the unconscious freedom of their communication had ended.

No, stumbled. She had to save it if she could.

Her eyes filled with tears. "Danet, I truly thought you knew, and like me, kept silent for Arrow's sake, as well as for Calamity's. I don't believe one boy more or less will harm Arrow's academy, especially a boy whose family doesn't want him to be there. Arrow didn't give anyone any choice."

"There was *never* any choice," Danet said tiredly, her anger draining out, leaving her feeling sick. "Everyone always considered it an honor. All the records say that boys couldn't wait to go—and girls longed for their two years at the queen's training. I suppose there's no use in my even thinking of starting *that* again," she added bitterly. "Will everyone call their girls boys, to keep them away from me?"

"Danet," Hliss whispered, the tears dripping off her chin. She drew a breath, then attempted to shift a subject becoming more disastrous by the heartbeat. "Were you planning to begin the queen's training again? You know we've sort of annexed old queen's training barracks for dye storage, and so forth."

"Yes...no...sometimes." Danet's gaze wandered sightlessly over the stone walls. "Things have changed so in the last hundred years. The truth is, I think girls would be better training in the academy, because one thing I saw when I lived with the Olavayirs is that we are faster riders, and many of us better archers on the gallop. If it came to defending the country, why are the fastest riders and archers confined to the castle walls?"

Hliss's gaze shifted down. "I think...I think there are others who might agree." She glanced up again. "Danet...."

"I know what you're about to say, that when Calamity met me, I was the wife of the second son to a jarl, meant to be a randviar. She was originally supposed to be a randviar, too. Maybe my becoming gunvaer broke something between us that I wasn't aware of at my end. Maybe she thinks of me as a jumped-up gunvaer, maybe they even resent my falling into the place meant for Fuss. But she's had *twelve years* to tell me. Do all the Senelaecs know about this boy-Ranet?"

"I don't know." Hliss's gaze shifted again, and Danet strongly suspected that her sister knew a lot more than she was saying. "Listen, Danet, the important thing is, you're aware now. What are you going to do? Tell Arrow?"

Danet compressed her lips.

Hliss said coaxingly, "Please, Danet, write to Calamity before you do anything. Tell her I was irresponsible — blame me."

So many questions arose that Danet couldn't follow any of them. She walked out, and circled around the kitchen garden as the bell began to ring. She was so deep in thought she didn't even see Gannan, who had straightened up wearily as he finished his last weed. He startled in horror as none other than the gunvaer tramped toward him, scowling.

To him that scowl meant one thing: Connar had snitched! He stiffened, readying to be hauled off to a flogging in the parade ground. Maybe even executed! Excuses streamed through his mind, and he barely kept himself from gibbering until she marched on by without giving him a second glance, leaving him limp and sweaty with relief.

He waited until she was well ahead, then cautiously followed, not breathing easily until she turned to the left toward the residence. He kept going straight toward the north end of the academy, where its stables abutted on the garrison stable yard.

He checked when he spotted the runner-in-training, leaning against a hitching post. He straightened up. "Gannan."

"Fish," Gannan said warily.

Fish (born David Pereth, but renamed by his elder brother when he first glimpsed his goggle-eyed newborn brother), a scrawny urchin with a face dominated by those pale, protuberant eyes, was often seen around the castle grounds as well as the garrison. He was well-known as a snitch. His big brother Halrid led the garrison boys whose fathers weren't captains, the important distinction being that the general run of garrison boys were no longer invited to the academy, unless they showed some exceptional talent. Only captains' sons, now that the king had achieved the numbers from the jarl and Rider families that he wanted. The result was a complicated relationship between garrison and academy youngsters.

"I happened to be running a message on the wall," Fish said — too casually, offering an excuse Gannan hadn't asked for. "I saw the princes rousting you. Or did you roust them?"

Now that the gunvaer was safely out of sight, Gannan's triumph reignited. "I told them what you said about Snot not being a real prince. You should have seen his face!" Gannan crowed. "Red as fire."

Snot was Gannan's nickname for Connar. He used it as often as he could, but somehow neither it nor Rockhead for the older prince caught on.

Fish laughed along with Gannan, then, "What did he say?"

"Nothing," Gannan gloated. "Said I was stupid and ran off."

They parted, and Fish lingered until Gannan had vanished beyond the academy wall. He ducked through byways until he found his elder brother finishing the cleaning of horse tack. He sidled up. "You know that thing I told Gannan, about the pr —"

Halrid smacked his hand over his brother's face. "Shut up, blabbermouth," he muttered. "Do you want everybody hearing?"

Fish decided against retorting, "Why not?" His brother could be a little too quick with his fists when annoyed.

Halrid dragged him to a corner of the barn. "What did he say? *Him*, not Gannan."

"Nothing, Gannan says."

Disappointed of a juicy story, Halrid shrugged. "Keep it to yourself." He waved his hand, and his brother scampered off.

When the mess bell rang, and their father got off duty, Halrid reported what had happened. "Good," Pa said under his breath. "Maybe he'll take the bait."

Bait? Which he? Halrid wasn't certain what the point was — or the plan — but he knew from his father's tone that he'd best keep quiet.

Pa gave him a narrow look. "Say nothing more. To anyone."

"I know, I know," Halrid whispered, hoping to ward off a lecture. Every time Pa got together with Uncle Retren, he acted the same. It probably had something to do with that slaughter up north, where Uncle Ret lost his eye, and half of a leg.

Pa waved a hand in dismissal, and Halrid ran off, disgusted. It would have been a lot more fun if the academy boys, who (in the garrison boys' collective opinion) were all prigs about their rank, had gotten into a royal scrap on Restday, bringing down heavy retribution.

Oh well.

FIVE

By the time Danet reached her room again, she simmered with righteous anger.

She flung herself down on her cushion, glanced at the letter she had been struggling over, and swept it off her desk. Her fingers trembled as she pulled a fresh paper in its place. She flicked the lid off the ink, shook a couple drops of water into it, and impatiently mixed it with the ink stick. Then dipped the quill—and halted.

She had always addressed her letters to Calamity, which was a nickname, a friendship name. Now she wondered what sort of friendship it was when one party sneaked behind the other party's back, no doubt laughing with their entire clan.

Danet threw the quill away, infuriated afresh as ink splattered all over her desk. The urge to write formally seized her, but she wasn't certain she even remembered Calamity's given name outside of her connection with one of the three Noth clans.

Maybe she ought to send a royal runner with a formal spoken message.

To say...what?

She got up again and wandered to the window, hands gripping her elbows. The burning desire to get a letter written and dispatched before the family gathered for Restday wine and bread had begun to cool as she considered what exactly to say. To do.

The first setback was law. Angry as she was, she could not call to mind any actual law that had been broken.

She and Arrow had both sworn, not just before the jarls in the Convocations since their coronation, but to each other, to stick to the laws. They were not going to be like Mathren Olavayir, or worse, the long-dead Sierlaef, elder brother to the famous Evred, who in regarding himself above law and tradition had made himself so hated that several generations later, people still didn't refer to Noddy as "the Sierlaef." He was Olavayir Ain at the academy, Noddy in the family, or in formal situations outside the academy, people would use his full title, Nadran-Sierlaef, as if to distinguish him from that Montreivayir prince dead a century and a half ago.

There wasn't even an academy rule. She knew the history of the academy, and all its rules. Arrow had talked about little else (except guarding the borders) those first few years, prompting her to read everything in sheer self-defense. This situation, as far as she was aware, was new: no one had disguised a boy as a girl to keep him out of the academy.

The opposite—girls disguised as boys—had happened three times, according to official records. Two were sisters close to brothers, one a twin who refused to be separated from her brother, and both were summarily sent home. The third had been murkier in motivation, something having to do with a Rider family connected to the Jayad Heseas hiding a problematical son by sending his sister instead. This girl had even managed to survive till summer, the year after Inda-Harskialdna returned to his homeland to become Adaluin. She'd excelled in everything, but when she returned the next spring she hadn't been able to hide body changes, and back south she was sent, to re-emerge ten years later as the famed scourge of the brigands always infesting the mountains above the pass to the Sartoran Sea.

Danet remembered wondering why, if a girl wanted to be there and her skills were equivalent, she shouldn't be there. Just because she had a basket below the waist instead of a pickle-and-plums didn't seem relevant to much of anything. But in other moods, she thought the academy was a disaster waiting to happen and women were well out if it.

The point now: There was no law, or rule, to grant Danet the moral high ground. Which didn't lessen this sense of betrayal a whit.

As Danet glared through a shimmer of hot tears at the dusty slate rooftops below, it struck her how easy it would be to throw all her authority at the Senelaec family...who were not going to attack the capital. Or even their loathed neighbors, the Marlovayirs.

Their back of the hand was directly solely at *her*. Well, no, not exactly. If Hliss was right, the back of the hand was directed at Arrow....

A tap at the door, and a runner poked her head in. "Commander Noth is here, Danet-Gunvaer."

Not trusting her voice, Danet waved permission. Jarid Noth entered, broad of shoulder and chest, his shaggy salt-and-pepper horsetail swinging at his martial step, his craggy face breaking into a tender smile that she on their first meeting would have thought utterly foreign to him.

She still didn't know quite how it had happened, how over ten years interest had turned into friendship, and then one winter night into something warmer, until he rooted as strongly into her heart as her children.

His smile faded, and his eyes narrowed. "Danet?"

The sound of her name on his lips warmed her down to her toes. The urge to confide in him was so strong. Her throat worked as words shaped her lips, but she resolutely killed the impulse.

It was that last thought, about Arrow. The Senelaecs' back of the hand might have included her when she arranged the betrothals, but it had begun with Arrow and his academy and army. She knew Arrow. His temper was like tinder, especially about the academy, his chief pride. It would be so easy to point his finger and launch, say, Commander Noth, northward, to attack....

And Jarid would have to do it. Or be foresworn. All because Calamity had put her boy in braids.

What you wish, what you want, now matters, Hesar whispered in memory. Danet understood it now, what the old gunvaer had meant. As a someday-randviar, Danet could laugh and gossip and nothing would come of it. She had lost that luxury the night she handed Arrow those swords before the throne.

Chill crawled up the back of Danet's neck. She launched herself into Noth's arms, and hid her face on his shoulder so he wouldn't see anything of her thoughts.

"Danet, what happened?"

"Nothing," she muttered.

"That expression on your face isn't nothing," he murmured into her neck.

"I have a problem, but it's something I need to work out on my own," she said, locking her fingers together behind his broad back.

They kissed, and then both heard the pounding of footsteps that could only be youth running in the simmering heat.

"Your young are here," he said with his twisted grin. "Which means the bell is about to ring for Restday Drum. I'd best get back down to the garrison. See you later."

As commander, of course he had to preside over the guard-side Restday ritual. He smiled as the door burst open and her three children raced in, coltish in their lengthening limbs, Noddy's hands and feet seeming larger every day. Bun danced right past with only a smile over her shoulder, but the boys, used to academy protocol, touched three fingers to their chests in salute. Noth dipped his chin at them, then exited and vanished down the hall.

The bell rang a short time later. While the children clamored at Danet, talking over one another, Arrow finally entered, rubbing his hands, and the children fell silent. "Noth and I finished setting up the Great Game. Everyone thinks a big storm is coming, so we'll camp out at Gold Hill so we don't get flooded. But right after the bell rang, I thought of three questions." To Danet, "Is he coming back later?"

"Yes."

"Good. Tell him to bang on my door first, will you?" He turned to face the children. "What have you been doing all day?"

Bun said, "I was just telling Mother, or trying to, but Connar was yelling over me—"

"Bunny, you were just as loud," Danet chided.

"Go one at a time," Arrow said. "Youngest first. Bun?"

"I was down at the stable with some of the first-year feet, and we got to braid manes!"

"No wonder you smell of horse, Bun," Noddy said mildly.

Danet felt Arrow's gaze on her, and she wondered what her expression was like. She turned a mock frown on her daughter as she sniffed. "Phew! Stink is more like it. Bun, this is Restday."

"It's too hot for House tunics, and mine is too tight," she whimpered.

"At least go wash and put on a clean smock. Quick."

Danet turned to the boys, mostly to get her back to Arrow, then chill gripped her neck again when she saw Connar's expression. She was thrown back to the rumor that had sent her down to Hliss in the first place. Connar's eyes seemed bluer, somehow, when he was upset, the fine bones barely emerging in his face subtly enhanced.

On impulse, Danet said, "Noddy, will you go make certain Bun doesn't wave her fingers over her water pitcher and consider herself clean?"

"All right."

As soon as he was gone, Danet put her back to the door, and said to Connar, "If you're still worried about that foolish gossip, you can ask your father directly."

Arrow was heading toward the room where they usually gathered for Restday. At this, he swung around. "What's this about?"

Connar looked down, his long lashes hiding his eyes. "It's all right. I know it's nothing."

"What's nothing?" Arrow said.

Danet watched Arrow. "Someone told Connar that Hliss's child, if a boy, would replace him."

Arrow's face reddened. "What shit-brain said that?" he demanded, too loud for the room. And when Connar hesitated, Arrow waved a hand. "Never mind, never mind, I know the world will end if you snitch. Connar, your Aunt Hliss would have plenty to say about that. You can go ask her, if you're worried."

Yes. Too loud, too forceful. He's been thinking it, Danet realized, and wondered how many times she could be shocked on such a hot day.

But Connar's face cleared, the other two reappeared—Bun's sweet round face shining with vigorous scrubbing—and Noddy and Connar finished talking about some game they'd been playing. Danet didn't realize she hadn't heard a single word until the boys brought out their drums.

Danet forced her thoughts to focus, and she and Arrow picked up bread and wine to begin the ritual.

Ordinarily Danet cherished this time with her family. During the academy season, she never saw the boys except for this one time a week, and of late Bun, who used to be her little shadow, had taken up more and more with her agemates among the younger runners, the kitchen help, the weavers, and especially in the stable, when she wasn't in lessons.

It was quite warm, and she trusted the children to want to launch out the moment they were done. As happened.

As the door banged behind them, Arrow scowled her way, and said before she could open her mouth, "Is that why you've been glaring ever since I walked in, because some brat's been farting rumors?"

Danet drew a breath, making sure her voice was even. "Arrow. I heard your tone. Don't deny you haven't thought it."

"It's just thought. Who wouldn't?" He threw his arms wide. "*I* can't help it! *You* were there when Mathren attacked Evred, and tried to kill us. I mean, you weren't in the room, but, shit, you know what I mean. After which, we found out he'd done for not only the previous king and queen, but his own wife!"

"But Mathren is dead."

Arrow turned away, his hands stiff, then turned back. "Hliss's baby will be named Farendavan, which makes him not a target, see? That's my thinking. So if the worst happens, and someone gets to Noddy, well—"

"Noddy and Connar."

"—we'd be able to adopt him into Olavayir...and, what?"

"Them. We have two boys."

"That's what I said."

"You said Noddy."

"Him, them, you know what I mean." Arrow made an impatient gesture, but he didn't meet Danet's eyes.

She said, "We are Connar's family in all the ways that count. He calls us Ma and Da. He and Noddy are close, not at all like you and Lanrid."

"I know, I know," Arrow said, swinging around again. "They're both loyal to each other." He flashed a grin. "Noddy might not have Connar's looks, but he's got my brother's strength, and some of your brains. Connar will be his commander."

"And Hliss tried for a girl," Danet reminded him.

Noise outside brought their attention to the door. A runner tapped, then announced that Commander Noth was there.

Arrow rubbed his hands. "Let me have him for two words, then he's yours." And he shot out the door, leaving Danet to wrestle with her roiling emotions.

SIX

Whenever he could, Arrow rode out into the plains to watch the all-academy Great Game for at least part of the stay. They always left a day or so before Andahi Day, so he wouldn't have to hear the women singing.

He'd tried forbidding the Lament altogether, insisting that the Idegans of Andahi, in slaughtering Lanrid and his Riders in the Pass, had tainted it forever. Most had obeyed, sufficiently disturbed by the reports that had trickled outward after the slaughter.

However, the older women had reacted to his decree with stubborn indifference. Every one of them had vivid memories of their own elderly relatives who'd lost mothers, aunts, sisters, and cousins up at Andahi. What could he do against those obstinate old toughs?

He'd discovered that their thin, high voices haunted him worse than the entire castle singing. Somehow — he had no idea why — their voices always caused him to dream of Sinna's beautiful singing of the Lament. No, not dream. Those voices caused nightmares in which he found himself in the middle of a battle he was supposed to command, and he had no idea where anyone was, or even who the enemy might be. And when he tried to move, it was like running through water, with that haunting, heart-ripping voice echoing through.

So, even though everyone knew a storm was going to strike, they rode out as scheduled. Sure enough, the storm hit them before they could make camp, a miserable experience that at least the king shared with them. "This is what war is like," he kept saying — which no one could argue with.

In the royal city, as thunder crashed, reverberating through the thick stone, Danet wondered how her boys were doing, floundering around in mud with their wooden swords.

Two Days before Victory Day, on the eve of their expected return, Hliss sent a runner to Danet, who had gone to bed not long before. She dressed and made her way through the dripping world to Hliss's quarters above the looms, thinking she had plenty of time, but she had scarcely walked in when she heard one of Hliss's younger runners shout, "Here it comes!"

Within two heartbeats there was a slippery baby, all awkward limbs trying to work back into their familiar ball. The Birth Healer swathed the infant in soft cloth and began to rub gently as Hliss gasped, "Let me see her."

The Healer said, "Him."

"What?"

Hliss sounded so aghast that the tired Healer actually opened the swaddling cloth to double-check as Hliss's runners crowded around.

"He's a he," the youngest runner said, looking at her chief with a wide gaze.

Hliss dissolved into breathy laughter, tears leaking out the sides of her eyes as she held out her arms.

With practiced ease the Healer and her assistants supervised restoring mother and infant to clean comfort, then everyone but Danet left.

Candlelight struck Hliss's hair to gold, restoring her youth again as she smiled pensively down at the babe. He blinked around with the vague gaze of newborns, his fists bumping up against his face.

When he made a little noise, Hliss gave Danet a startled look. "What do I do now?"

"He'll let you know what he wants," Danet said, and then added, "Speaking of boys. When you change him, put a cloth over that little dangle, or you *will* get shot in the eye."

"Really? On purpose?" Hliss asked, her brow puckered, midway between tears and hilarity.

"With boys, who knows? I can only tell you that Noddy's first laugh was when he got me right in the neck. I suspect it was my startled expression that made him laugh, but then then, we don't know when boy humor starts." Danet thought back to that sweet, husky little sound, and the big infant grin, and chuckled.

Though the storm had washed most of the heat out of the air outside, the small chamber was still warm. Hliss laid the babe on her lap, letting the cloth fall open as she stared down. "Strange, isn't it, how the sight of that little dangle—or absence of one—somehow lays out an expected life path. Without that one bit, we all look the same."

"We don't grow the same," Danet said, somewhat tartly.

Hliss scarcely heard her. Still staring down at her little son, she said slowly, "Arrow will *not* make him a prince."

"What's your fear here?" Danet asked. "That his being a boy will make him ride to war, even if you raise him exactly as you planned to raise a girl?"

Hliss looked up, the candlelight reflecting in her eyes. "It sounds arrogant, a bit, doesn't it, when we consider that the most bloodthirsty person in our family connections was Hard Ride."

"But then there is Olavayir history." Danet spread her hands, palms up.

"Yes," Hliss admitted with a sigh, her voice softening to a whisper. "It didn't seem right, to ask another man to have a child with me, when I'm with

Arrow. I keep expecting him to move on to another favorite and stay, but he always comes back."

Danet looked curiously at her sister. Hliss had appeared to be content, and she was so very good for Arrow. Danet knew she herself was too much like Mother. At best she'd been able to get him to stop yelling, but that was not nearly as effective as Hliss's ability to actually calm him down.

Danet asked, "Do you love him?"

Hliss looked up, then out the window before saying softly, "How do I answer that? There are so many kinds of love. Do *you* love him?"

"I do," Danet said. "It's the love that comes of being a family. It was never a passion for either of us. Until you came, I didn't think he could be 'in love.' Actually, I didn't think I could, either."

"But then you met the commander." Hliss smiled tiredly.

"And that happened without my being aware. It took six years before I realized that we were mates. Maybe even lifemates. I don't know. No one is ever going to come to me for wisdom or insight about love."

Hliss chuckled under her breath, then thumbed her eyes with her free hand, holding the wriggling baby close with the other. "I do love Arrow, but like you, I'm not certain what being *in love* means," Hliss went on in that low, almost dreamy voice, "I don't know that Arrow does either. I did tell you, if I reached thirty, I wanted a daughter to hand on our secrets to. And Arrow loved the idea of my having a child...." She sighed. "What's the use of talk? I now have a son. He can be a weaver. But he's *not* going to be a prince."

Danet bent to look into her sister's face. "You've said that three times, now. Is that aimed at Arrow and me? Do you think we're raising the boys wrong?"

Hliss blinked at her, as if trying to bring her into focus. Then she said, "No. That is, I don't know how princes should be raised. But I do think that two princes are enough." Her voice broke. "I was going to name her Danet."

Danet bent down, hugged Hliss, kissed the baby, then stepped back, saying, "You're tired, and it's nearing dawn. Were you up the entire night?"

"I couldn't sleep. But I didn't think it was time. It was only mild discomfort, until suddenly it wasn't."

The baby began to fret, and Hliss looked panicked, but Danet talked her through the first awkward attempt at feeding, insisted it was all right for him to yell a little, and promised her she would easily learn to differentiate his cries. It seemed no sooner had he figured out feeding at his end than his eyes shuttered and his breathing deepened.

"He's dozed off. That's your time to get some rest."

Hliss lay back down again, the babe held in the circle of her arms, but she gave Danet a considering glance and asked, "Did you write to Calamity?"

"No," Danet said, and at her sister's strained expression, she added, "I was going to, but I was too angry. It can wait. It has for twelve years."

Hliss's gaze dropped. "I feel terrible."

"How did you find out? You may as well tell me. I'll find out one way or another."

Hliss sighed. "One of my weavers, Lnar. Her brother married into one of their Rider families. I sent her to get North Valley sky berries for your royal blue. Bad weather drove her into Senelaec, and she found out, and told me."

"When was that?"

"I don't remember. A few years ago. Ranet was a toddler. He—she—everyone called Ranet she, even though he ran out of the bath naked, and almost tripped Lnar. Pandet came running after and grabbed the child into a towel. Pandet swore her to secrecy. She told only me."

"Did she find out if there are any others?"

Hliss lifted a shoulder. "No notion. It wasn't as if we talked about it much after she got back. She said it was a secret, and I thought that that was why you hadn't told me. I don't really know the Senelaecs—we only stayed the night when I came down from Farendavan to the royal city—so I forgot about it, until we were talking. I don't even know why it popped into my mind."

Danet said, "Get some rest. No. First, do you want me to arrange the Name Day party?"

"It'll just be you, me, Bun, and both my runners if Arrow isn't back by tonight. I can send Liet to get some wine and any tarts left over. That's good enough."

"Tomorrow is Victory Day," Danet reminded Hliss. Arrow and the boys should be back by noon. Would you like it here or up in the Residence?"

"Here." Hliss's eyes drifted shut.

"I'll put it all together. Sleep."

Danet walked out, her mood a weird mixture of laughter and grim.

The worst of it was, this new knowledge about the boy-Ranet placed her squarely between these *bonehead* Senelaecs—what were they *thinking* would happen?—and Arrow. Unless she could figure a way around it.

She retreated to her suite and tried to return to sleep, but her mind would not quiet. So she bathed and got to work, intermittently mulling the problem until noon, when, as she had predicted, Arrow arrived with his usual great clatter.

She had stationed the youngest runner to report when he appeared. Danet left her desk, and walked out in time to meet Arrow coming down the long hall, three runners following, each taking turns to report.

At the sight of Danet everyone stopped, and the runners slapped hands to chests.

"You have a son," Danet said to Arrow. "Are the boys back?"

Arrow's eyelids flashed up. "At the academy." His voice was husky.

"Send someone to fetch them. I gave orders for a Name Day celebration tonight, at Hliss's rooms. Bun is down in the kitchen, making certain they have enough tarts."

Arrow chuckled, flushing with pleasure. "If he'd waited a day he could have had Victory Day as his Name Day." He started away, then halted mid-step. "Is she awake?"

"By now she must be."

Arrow rubbed his hands. "Shall we name him after my father? Another Inda?"

"I expect Hliss has names picked out," Danet said.

He raced off as fast as one of the boys, and Danet returned to her desk, wondering if he would have been that excited at the birth of another daughter. No. That was exactly the kind of question that got one angry, and confused the other party who had no idea what one was thinking. If she wanted to know, she should ask him—and there was no use in asking, because of course he would say he'd feel exactly the same, and then she'd have to determine whether or not she believed him.

She'd let him answer through his future actions.

She pulled forward a newly delivered report on early harvests, forcing herself to concentrate on the list of jarlates and their numbers. As always, the columns of numbers steadied her as they built a mental map, and she worked until the bell rang.

On the last reverberating *tang*, Arrow burst in, wearing his House tunic. "Come, Danet, get a leg over the saddle pad. I got the boys ready."

"Send them on down," Danet said as she neatly stacked her papers before handing the results to the waiting scribe to take and make copies.

"Down?" Arrow repeated, surprised.

"I know I told you. She wants the celebration in her quarters."

"I thought she'd want to come up here," he said. "More room. I'll tell Bun and the boys. Meet you there."

Danet bathed quickly and changed. As she crossed the castle to the east side, here and there she heard shouts of jollity. The import struck her: Arrow had given the entire castle Name Day liberty.

When she reached the looms, sure enough, Arrow presided proudly as the entire textiles staff gathered, tightly packed, against the wall. Hliss's ancillary chiefs stood like sentinels on either side of Hliss, all wearing formal garb.

This was a Name Day for a royal prince, in every way except the ringing of the bells and a royal fanfare salute from the towers.

Danet's attention went to Hliss, who smiled happily as she walked around, showing everyone the infant. She stopped in the center of the room and said gently, "I'll lead the toast."

Arrow looked surprised, but smiled and stepped back.

"Today is my son's Name Day. Andas Farendavan, welcome to the world," Hliss said, lifting the infant.

Everyone cheered, and drank.

Danet noticed a couple of covert looks as people repeated "Farendavan." Then newly-born Andas wailed, startled by the cheers. The circle dissolved into knots of conviviality as people helped themselves to food and drink, the youngsters going for the tarts, as usual.

When the food had been demolished and most of the wine drunk, Hliss's staff took their leave. As the boys and Bun foraged for crumbs on the tart trays, Arrow said low-voiced to Danet, "Why not any of the family names?"

"Andas *is* a family name," Danet said. "Our great-great grandfather, famous for making our linens what they are today."

Connar's boyish treble rose, "Is he going to the academy?"

Danet turned to see him standing next to Hliss.

Arrow opened his mouth, but Hliss said, "No, he is not. He's going to be the future Chief Weaver. He'll make all your banners just the way you like them."

Connar grinned. "I want my own banner!"

"You'll have one as Commander of the King's Riders," Arrow promised, grinning as he flipped Connar's glossy horsetail. "Actually, you'll have two: your own, and the kingdom's, whenever you ride out on royal orders."

Connar's dark-fringed blue eyes rounded with excitement, and Arrow laughed indulgently.

Danet said, "Andas is beginning to fret. Let's leave so he can be put down to sleep."

"You boys have to be up early," Arrow reminded them. "Victory Day competitions tomorrow!"

The boys shouted, Andas wailed, and Danet shot an apologetic look at her sister as she herded them all out.

They started back to the Residence, Danet watching the boys gambol ahead, Bun, as always, their shadow. Laughter rose suddenly, Noddy's voice, never lovely, beginning to drop into the nasal bark of an adolescent. Connar's voice was exactly as clear and pure as it always had been. High above them, Bun's bubbling laugh, and below Arrow's guffaw. Had to be a fart joke. She rolled her eyes. Arrow's sense of humor had never grown up, to the boys' delight.

Too soon that they would be braying teens, scorning apple tarts as a reward, and Da's old jokes....

A solution struck her then. It was so neat, perhaps too neat—too much a back of the hand gesture to the Senelaecs, so she had better think it out.

She kept silent until everyone had withdrawn to their chambers, then sent her youngest runner with a message to Mnar with their agreed-on code for discussion with kingdom-wide ramifications.

When the girl returned, it was to say, "If you can wait one hour, Danet-Gunvaer?"

Danet suppressed impatience. Mnar was as busy as Danet herself was. Danet almost sent the girl back to say never mind, but restrained herself. The royal runners had been too consistently good with their advice, when asked. Even Arrow agreed on that. So she turned over an hour glass, then saw to a stream of minor tasks, including inspecting Bun's House tunic to see if it was too small. It wasn't. The palace runners had not been neglecting the royal children, though those ungrateful scamps might wish differently.

When the glass was empty, she went upstairs, where to her surprise she not only found Mnar waiting, but Shendan, looking older and more frail than the previous time Danet had seen her.

"I did not know you were here on visit, Shendan-Jarlan," she exclaimed.

Shendan touched fingers to chest as she said, "It's much easier for everyone if I come and go with the runners. And you have all been so very busy."

Mnar watched Danet accept this evasion, aware that Shendan would not want the gunvaer finding out about magic transfer or its terrible cost. *I shall officially retire when I cannot transfer anymore,* Shendan had said.

Danet sat down on the waiting mat, and—having thought out what she would say and what she wouldn't—stated flatly, "I discovered that the Senelaecs lied about Ranet, rather than send her, that is, him, to the academy. There is no law preventing it."

The only one who betrayed relief at that secret being popped was Camerend, listening from the inner room. He'd dreaded what might happen when it was discovered.

"There is no law, but I know that Arrow will take it as a personal slight," Danet went on, and explained her idea—to invite jarls' and Rider captains' girls to compete in the Victory Day competition.

The two women before her listened all the way through in their usual manner, and then, without once looking at each other, said, "Excellent notion."

Mnar added, "That will give the Senelaecs plenty of time to provide a suitable wife for Connar-Laef."

Danet was pleased, relieved, and also tired, for she had been awake since that midnight call. She looked at old Shendan, who was so wise and sensible, and though she hadn't meant to, poured out a disjointed tale of Andas's birth and what she'd seen in Arrow. "No one is wrong here," she said hastily. "I'm not saying that. Not at all. It's just that my sister kept repeating that Andas will not be treated like a prince, and I feel in part that that's aimed at me."

Mnar kept her lips closed. She'd thought Hliss was walking blindly into danger to risk having a child by a king, in case it turned out to be a boy, but no one had asked her opinion. She wasn't about to deliver it now.

Shendan said slowly, "I understand the Chief Weaver's concern, and though I did not hear her say it, I don't believe she had you in mind at all. Her worry would be the same whoever the royal family was. The fact is, though our history offers enough examples of princes, or cousins of princes, or jarls related distantly to princes, leading a war party in order to make themselves kings, so far no woman, much less a princess, has led a war to become gunvaer."

"Well, one did. I'm related to her."

Shendan looked down at her hands. "True. She was raised to be a warrior. But I believe most of us are killers only when we are very angry, or very afraid."

Danet said, "That's true."

Shendan sighed, easing herself on her cushion. The ache from magic transfer still throbbed in her bones, but Camerend's instincts were far too good when he sensed trouble. She'd had to come, then pretend it was a regular visit.

She said, "In Colend and other places, apparently that instinct to violence has been mitigated by custom. The first king of Colend once said that their royal policy is like their winding canals along handsome countryside, which curve and meander pleasingly, and at the same time lessen the river's terrible strength. In Colend, though politeness is tied in with their notion of honor, they are still human. But their custom, like the canals, tends to force their conflicts into expression through words and manner. Their duels with fans and fashion, from what I hear, can be just as vicious as our duels with steel, but at least everyone walks away alive."

Danet could see how tired the elderly jarlan was, and rose, thanking her.

They had agreed to her idea. It was a good idea, but what would inviting girls for the competition lead to?

As she walked downstairs, she wondered if it was time to bring up the queen's training again, though a stab of guilt made her pause. She had fallen out of the habit of morning riding and shooting drill after she'd recovered from Bun's birth. The constant demand of work, the lack of time...she went out to ride, mostly to exercise Firefly, but the truth was, Mother would be disgusted with her. She wasn't even certain which trunk held her old bow.

But that didn't mean other women, who had the time, and the skill, and the desire, couldn't be part of kingdom defense.

She fell asleep during a mental redesign of the castle, and after she woke and bathed, she sent a runner across to Arrow.

He showed up shortly after, his hair still wet, like hers. "What is it? I've got to get over to—"

She forestalled him before he could launch into a long ramble about his day. "I want to send out an order, so the jarl families can start planning. Most of my betrothals are beginning to reach our boys' age. Within a very few years they're bound to be interested in who they are to marry. I think the girls ought to come to the royal city, say for the Victory Day competitions. Then the girls can either return home, or perhaps go for a visit with their betrothed's family to see their future home. Get to know each other."

"To stay?"

"That's up to them. Stay, or return home again. I want them all first meeting each other around fifteen or sixteen, which you know is generally when interest starts. Get used to each other."

Arrow propped his hands on his hips, which were still as skinny as when they first met. But as he stared down at the stone floor in thought, she saw that his hair had begun to thin around his temples. When had *that* happened? He wasn't even forty yet!

He looked up. "I don't know. Girls! I have enough randy teens to deal with."

"Girls used to be in the Games, during Inda-Harskialdna's day," she reminded him. "We don't have to hold the defense game, since many girls aren't trained in castle defense the way it was in our great-great-grandmothers' time. Let's invite the girls to compete in riding and shooting exhibitions. You know they're good. Maybe it'll make the boys try harder."

Arrow gave her a peculiar look.

"What?" she asked.

He wiped his hands over his face. "I take it you also knew that my father's summer game ride and shoot was won by Calamity Senelaec and her cousins, dressed as boys."

"What?"

They stared at one another, she in shock, and he surprised to see her surprise.

The sense of his words hit Danet, bringing up scattered memories of that week. Calamity again! "I didn't know," Danet said slowly. "They were there, I remember that! Calamity and Fuss helped me with Noddy. I always thought they came to watch the boys."

"Knuckles Marlovayir figured it out," Arrow said, laughing. "He told me at last Convocation. You know it was his first, his da having handed off the jarlate. I thought you knew! Kept mum for Calamity's sake."

"How did he figure it out?" Danet asked as she struggled inwardly with a fresh flare of those emotions she'd thought conquered.

"That feud they've got going, the Marlovayirs and Senelaecs. What with all the back and forth, they all knew each other by sight. He didn't see Wolf at that ride and shoot. But he recognized Wolf and the Senelaec riders in all the other competitions. Then on the last day, out came the strange riders again, and shot the Marlovayirs out of the wargame when everyone else was riding around in the dust yelling at each other, Wolf included. Knuckles saw them up close—thought at first they were a bunch of scrubs, then figured out they were girls. Now he's the jarl, it's more'n ten years later, and he admits it was funny, though he'd never tell Wolf that, of course." His eyes narrowed.

"You say you didn't know, yet you want girls in the games. Is this a covert plan to get girls in the academy?"

"Why not?" Danet retorted.

"I want them defending their own borders," he said. "Especially if I have to call for the men."

"Against?"

"*I* don't know! If the Venn come back. If those northern shits come back down the Pass for a second try." He wrinkled his forehead. "Would I have to start all over again, trying to figure out how run women riders?"

She snorted. "Not if you think of them all as warriors. And you would, if they trained here."

Arrow rubbed his hands over his face and up over his head, then dropped them. "Send out your order. Let's see how they all do with the Victory Day competitions. We'll go from there."

He left, and Danet stayed where she was, knowing it was unreasonable to be angry with Calamity all over again, this time for the girls' ruse at the wargame when they were all young. In no way had that been aimed at her — they hadn't even met yet.

Still, the feeling of betrayal would not go away. She decided not to write to her — or to any of the Senelaecs. She'd send a scribe-written decree to Calamity, as well as to all the other jarlans, inviting girls to the Victory Day competition. The question of reviving the queen's training could wait: first, take a look at what sort of training the various jarlans' daughters received. Or, supposed daughters.

"Over to you, Calamity," she whispered under her breath.

SEVEN

Summer at last gave way to autumn, and then winter, which closed in everyone except hardy runners crossing the kingdom back and forth.

Correspondence was fitful, arriving between storms and frosts. Danet didn't expect to hear any reactions to her new order until spring, excepting possibly the closer jarlates. There were both verbal messages and letters acknowledging the invitation, including from the Senelaecs, and that came from the jarlan's hand. Danet read that with conflicted feelings: she could not, of course, know why Calamity hadn't written back, and it was too easy to ascribe negative emotions to her because Danet felt wronged. She threw the letter into the fire and forced herself to turn to the ongoing river of work.

Early spring brought a larger spate of letters, everything as expected — except for one.

She took the letter into her chamber and sat down, contemplating the sealed paper. She knew almost nothing of Linden-Fareas Algaravayir. What she did know was that in the past several generations — since the Olavayirs had inherited the throne — the much-reduced lands that had produced the famous Inda-Harskialdna were now generally known as Algaravayir.

"Iofre" was the last of the Old Iascan titles, meaning female holder of a principality. Back in the Iascan days, Choreid Elgaer had been a principality, Mother had said when she taught Danet the map. It and the Cassadas lands were the only ones the Marlovans had acquired by marriage instead of war. Choreid Elgaer had kept its old name when a Marlovan captain, Algara, married its princess. He'd added *vayir* to his name along with the rest of the early jarls.

But now there was no Adaluin, or prince. The last male Algaravayir had gone to Sartor to live, that much Danet knew. Arrow had insisted that Danet arrange a betrothal for Noddy with one of the twin girls born to the Iofre.

Danet-Gunvaer:

I write to you to assure you in part of my acceptance of your decree about betrothed daughters coming to the royal city at sixteen to meet their future husbands.

I see the reasoning, and agree. I am heartened by your sensible compromise between sending full-grown strangers into a new land, expecting to fit in, and the cruelty of the old two-year-old tradition.

But this order, coming now, causes me to reflect on the fact that the next few years are unlikely to see material change in my daughters. I know that Hadand (firstborn by moments) has been honored as your choice for Nadran-Sierlaef, and that Noren is intended to go north to the Yvanavayirs.

But I believe it would be better for Noren to come to the royal city instead of her sister. And also, I would prefer to find one of Hadand's cousins for the Yvanavayir boy, as I believe she will be better remaining at home.

I apologize for this disruption of your plans, but hope that the change can be made while none of the young people involved have met, and have no expectations other than a name.

Linden-Fareas Algaravayir

Danet read the letter through twice, then summoned her First Runner, Loret, and handed her the letter. "What do you make of this? Don't you come from that area?"

Loret bent her head over the letter. She was stocky and brown, unremarkable to look at until she got outside at the shooting range. Those shoulders and arms enabled her to shoot as far as many men.

Loret looked up, pale eyes solemn. "The Iofre says what she means."

Danet sighed inwardly. "Isn't one of those twins deaf?"

"Noren," Loret said.

"Who knows Hand-speech among you?"

"Shen is the best," Loret said. "We all know some, but we're not expert, as we don't have any deaf runners at present. Though one of the fledglings has a deaf mother, and is equally fluent in Hand."

Shen, Danet's Second Runner, was Danet's liaison with the guilds and the few foreign contacts—she knew more languages than any of the other runners, and they all learned several.

"The boys—no, all of us—are going to have to begin learning Hand, if Noren comes to us instead of the other sister. But," Danet said, thinking sourly of Calamity and the false Ranet. "I want to know why the switch. What's wrong with the other twin? I wish I could go investigate myself. You really don't know more?"

Loret's gaze blanked, then she said, "I've been here in the royal city since I was ten. I've never seen those girls. And I can't answer a question like that, when all I've heard is hearsay."

"Hearsay like what?" Danet asked, exasperated. Everybody gossiped...except the royal runners, who would only repeat what they'd verified themselves.

Sure enough, Loret just turned her palm down without meeting Danet's eyes.

Danet scowled at the letter. Mnar had chosen both Loret and Shen. Danet found them honest, scrupulous, and good at their work. They carried out her orders exactly as she wished. Even young Sage, her new Third Runner, demonstrated a quiet maturity beyond her eighteen years.

But that quiet maturity — that refusal to indulge in anything that might whiff of gossip — did not serve Danet now.

She looked up. "Pass on the order to Shen, will you? It's too bad the boys just went over to the academy, but at least Bun can start lessons in Hand-speech."

Loret said, "The younger Mareca boy is deaf, and the academy fourth-years are all learning Hand from Master Denold."

Danet tapped the letter against her fingers. Her boys had just become fifth years. To send them to join the fourth year classes would be obeyed, but the boys would regard being sent to a lower year for lessons as the deadliest of insults, she knew. Everything was life and death at that age — except real life and death, the first taken for granted, the second as remote as the stars. And they all wanted to be grown up yesterday: it was only when youth was gone that it was valued. "Tutoring," she said finally.

Loret touched fingers to chest and walked silently out.

Danet dropped the letter on her desk, made herself read the last of her correspondence, then lifted her head, about to summon Sage to fetch Tesar, who by now should have had a meal and a bath.

No. That wouldn't do, either.

She mulled over the questions raised by the Iofre's letter for the rest of the day, until she came to the inescapable conclusion that she must take the royal runners' rule to heart, and investigate herself.

That evening, she went in search of Arrow, finding him coming back from a long day of wrangling the guilds.

His face looked flushed as he said abruptly, "We have four excellent harbors! Five, if you count The Nob —"

"Which I don't," Danet said, steadied as always by the unassailability of numbers. "It's merely a resupply and transfer point. We get almost nothing out of it."

"Except preventing an army marching down the peninsula," Arrow said. "But that has nothing to do with —" He interrupted himself mid-stride. "Why are you here? Something happened? Is it the boys?"

"No," she said. "Surely you'd know that before I," she couldn't help adding; she had scarcely seen the boys all winter, for they seemed to have reached that age when elders were anathema, preferring to stalk the garrison boys in interminable games that too often brought them back with bruises and roughened knuckles. But Arrow enjoyed hearing stories of their wins. As long as they moved together, he insisted it was good for them, leaving Danet little to say.

"So what is it?" he asked.

She summarized the letter and her consequent questions, then said, "I've decided to go to Algaravayir to see for myself what's amiss."

He stopped dead, his eyes wide and suspiciously pink. Yes, he smelled like double-distilled bristic. By now she was expert at assessing him: he'd obviously stopped to drink the edge off his irritation, but he wasn't soused. "You can't go," he said.

"Are we at war?"

"Of course not."

"Then I don't see why I can't go. Don't say gunvaers mustn't travel. Hadand Deheldegarthe went all the way over the mountains to the Adranis and survived just fine. There is no reason why I shouldn't ride down to Algaravayir. It's spring. I'll be back before the first strawberries ripen. I'll only take Sage, so Tesar will be here if you have to send for me. Loret and Shen know my routine as well as I do, and you're here for major decisions, and for the children."

Arrow scowled. "I don't like your going."

"Why not? Arrow, this is Noddy's future wife. The future gunvaer. When I asked Loret, she wouldn't talk. Wouldn't meet my eyes. Which means she knows *something* about them down there, but it's thirdhand. I need to see and hear for myself."

He rolled his eyes. "All right. But only if you take an honor guard."

"They'd better be fast," she warned. "I'm not going to dawdle for weeks, and come back to half a year's worth of reports to catch up on."

He grinned. "I'll pick the men. You'll have to keep up with *them*."

She snorted.

She and Arrow walked back together, and as Bun had not turned up by the time the watch bell rang and the runners brought up supper, they sat in Arrow's inner room, and gave each other detailed comments on the day's doings, Danet adding what she expected he might have to deal with during her absence.

Bun ran in halfway through the meal, covered with dust and dog hair, and plopped down. Arrow and Danet spoke at the same time, "Go wash up!"

Bun cast a dramatic sigh, dashed out, and returned to a covered dish, not that she ever noticed if her food was hot or cold. When she finished a running stream of commentary on how clever her animals were, Danet said, "I'm leaving in the morning for a trip south to meet Noddy's future wife."

Bun dropped a rye biscuit. "I want to go too!"

"No." This time mother and father said it one after the other.

Danet said, "You need to be more responsible with your studies, instead of running off to the stables whenever you think you can escape actual work."

"I do my work!"

"Then why is it you cannot name all the kings and queens of this kingdom, and yet you know the name of every single dog, cat, and cow in the entire castle—not to mention all the horses, including those only here for a short time?"

Silence fell.

At Bun's miserable face, she added, "In a couple of years, if she comes to visit, you might ride to meet her. If you show more responsibility...."

Bun interrupted as soon as she heard the familiar words about responsibility, and offered passionate promises. When she saw that her mother remained unmoved, she sighed, accepted what couldn't be changed, and the rest of the meal passed with Bun speculating on which horses would go—which ones got along best with one another, and so forth.

At the end of the meal she pelted out, leaving Danet to say wryly, "She'll miss the horses more than she'll miss me. As for the boys, they won't even notice I'm gone."

Arrow flashed a grin. "They'll notice on Restday. Though I might just let them stay over there with their friends. They keep begging me to let them stay in their barracks. Why not let 'em. I can spend Restday with Hliss, Bun, and Andas, or go over to the garrison with Noth."

"Then the boys'll hate me when I return and they have to wear House tunics again," Danet commented.

"Too bad," Arrow retorted. "If I have to dress fine, they have to dress fine."

Danet laughed, then crossed to her rooms. She called in her runners, told them what was going to happen, and was sorting things on her desk when a knock came at the door.

She expected Noth—and looked forward to a night with him—but when Shen opened the door, it was Mnar.

Danet exclaimed, "I was going to talk to you in the morning, before I left. Unless there's something I don't know about?"

Mnar skipped past that with the ease of old habit, and said, "I have a request."

"Yes?"

"That you take Lineas."

"Lineas?" Danet repeated, then remembered the fox-faced little runner-in-training with the red hair, glimpsed occasionally now and then. "Why? Does she have some connection in Algaravayir?"

"Her mother's twin brother is Aldren Noth, one of the Algaravayir Riders, but of course Lineas has never met him. More to the point, Lineas grew up using Hand-sign as well as speaking Marlovan, as her mother is deaf. So she'll be of help with you there. Also, if you remember, we're training her to be either Bunny's or the future gunvaer's First Runner."

Danet exhaled an "Ah-h-h-h. I assumed there would be translators aplenty in Algaravayir, but this would be far better. She can begin to teach me while we travel."

Mnar was aware that Camerend, who had always been close to the Iofre and her brother Indevan before he left for Sartor, had gotten a great deal closer to the Iofre after Isa had ended their marriage. But that had nothing to do with the security and welfare of the kingdom. "Lineas can also visit with the girls while you and the Iofre speak, and if you ask her for her impressions, she will give you as truthful a report as she is able."

"Can she ride?" Danet asked doubtfully, remembering that tiny weed of a child—then recollected the stringent training sessions she'd glimpsed in the far fields, when the academy was elsewhere. "Never mind. Of course she can. Excellent notion. Have her ready by daybreak."

At last she had the night to herself. She considered sending a runner ahead to warn the Algaravayirs she was coming, but hesitated. She recollected what Tdor Fath had said about beggaring jarlates, but that was with enormous parties. Arrow wouldn't send more than a riding, and Danet was taking only Sage and now Lineas.

No doubt they'd be spotted by border riders when they reached Algaravayir, which would give the Iofre a day or two of notice. Much more than that, and what couldn't be hidden?

Danet hated thinking like that, but her confidence in herself—in how others viewed her intentions—had been severely shaken by that discovery about Calamity and the boy who'd been called a girl.

EIGHT

Ghosts, Lineas had discovered at an early age, seemed to have a logic of their own.

Since her arrival in Choreid Dhelerei, the royal city, she'd regularly seen four ghosts in and about the royal castle. One, glimpsed the single time she was in the heir's outer chamber, was in the doorway. Lineas was glad that Nadran-Sierlaef was away when she was sent to put a corrected slate in his room, as she had not yet met either of the princes, and dreaded encountering both the heir and a ghost at the same time. At least it was a vague ghost, no more than a tall, pale-haired figure, probably male, though even in that she was not certain.

The brightest and most frequently glimpsed was the young man she was fairly certain was Evred, as someone had told her the ancient gunvaer who used to live in the south tower had said his ghost was in the throne room the day the king and queen were crowned. Lineas believed it, for it made sense that a prince who would have been king had he not been murdered might stay — except that ghosts seldom demonstrated any logic that she could figure.

Since no one but her seemed to see ghosts, she couldn't ask about them. Anyway, another was so faded it was no more than a blur, *more there than here*, Aunt Isa had said once.

When Lineas asked, There where? Aunt Isa had blinked and opened her hands. Where the music goes, my great-great aunt used to say. But then, she heard music that no one else did. And only at times.

Like the windharps above Larkadhe, Lineas had decided — another subject she couldn't discuss, because normal people didn't hear singing counterpoint to the soughing mountain windharps, any more than they saw ghosts. Most didn't believe ghosts existed.

Her single trip to Larkadhe, early when she first commenced magic studies, had furnished her only exposure to what she thought of as ghost music. The royal castle had no ghost music (at least, none that she could hear), but late that summer, when she was finally trusted enough to run errands to the royal residence on the second floor, she discovered her first and only ghostly scent: in Bun's room, she walked into the faint, heady scent of flowers.

By then she was used to Bun, who seemed to be at the stable every time Lineas was sent down for riding lessons. Bun didn't act like the princesses in some of the records brought from Sartor into Darchelde. She was a stick figure much like Lineas herself, only with a round face, and lank brown hair instead of bright red frizzle. She had a short upper lip exactly like a kitten, Lineas privately thought, but apparently when Bun was born, her head was covered with short, soft hair, and she'd been small and round: bunny.

She talked to everyone with the same cheerful demeanor, always ready to laugh, so when Lineas was sent to fetch Bun, she was not too intimidated at the prospect of meeting one of the royal family on their own turf.

She found Bun kneeling on her floor, waving around a feather tied to a stick as kittens scrambled and pounced.

Lineas loved kittens, but she was so surprised by a faint but heady scent as she walked in the door that she stopped short and exclaimed, "Oh, where are the flowers? And where did they *find* them during winter?"

Bun glanced up, her laugh like a bubbling stream. "Everybody else says it stinks of dog in here. Or cat. Or horse. Really, you really smell flowers?"

Lineas sniffed harder, and now all she could smell was dust, dog, and horse, probably from Bun's clothes, which were dusty, and her knees covered with horse hair. She'd obviously been currying. "Now I don't smell it," she admitted. "Maybe I imagined it."

"If you did, you aren't the first," Bun said as she scrambled to her feet.

"Really?" Lineas asked, cautious in case she had stumbled into another not-normal thing.

"A long time ago," Bun said with her usual cheer. "Everybody said this room was haunted, but by smells instead of ghosts. I should love to see a ghost," she added. "If it wasn't horrible, like carrying its own head if it was executed, or something nasty like that."

"I wouldn't want to see that either," Lineas said, mentally adding Bun to the enormous list of those who didn't see ghosts. "I was sent to fetch you for tutoring."

Bun groaned. "I always hope they'll forget me, but they never do." She dusted herself off, eyed her smock, decided it would do, and they ran out together, Bun asking Lineas who were her favorites among the horses.

After that, Lineas had occasion to go to Bun's rooms twice more, and each time, if she just breathed, not thinking of anything, there were the flowers again. But the moment she concentrated, or sniffed for location, it was gone.

By spring, the anniversary of her arrival, she was so thoroughly accustomed to her new life that she no longer reacted with alarm at unexpected summonses.

So when Mnar herself arrived in the runners' recreational area, where Lineas was busy setting a sleeve in her new smock, she only looked up, touching finger to chest.

"Pack for travel," Mnar said. "As soon as you're done, come upstairs for instruction. You'll be leaving at daybreak."

Before the sun rimmed the distant hills, Lineas shivered in a wind scouring over snowy mountains to the northeast. She waited in the stable yard next to the horse chosen for her, amid armsmen who seemed impervious to the cold checking saddle girths, weapons, and pack distribution. They talked quietly, their breath frosting in the air.

The gunvaer appeared, another person Lineas had only glimpsed from the safety of distance, as well as the king. Lineas was not afraid of the gunvaer—nothing she'd heard made her fearful, and Bun talked cheerfully about her mother—but intimidated, yes. Danet-Gunvaer strode toward them, straight-backed and narrow of eye as she took in every detail. At the gunvaer's shoulder walked Sage, who had been a senior runner-in-training the previous year, and who had helped Lineas with her handwriting.

Danet stepped aside as Sage reached up to load her travel pack onto her mount. Danet glimpsed knife hilts at both wrists, and remembered that royal runners traveled armed. She reflected as Sage went to load her own mount that she had never actually seen the royal runners drill.

Sage flashed a smile Lineas's way, then the two turned to face Danet, their expressions mirroring expectancy. As were the faces of the honor guard.

Danet cast her own expectant gaze around. They were all ready. What were they waiting for?

Ah.

As ranking person, it was for *her* to give the command that had always been Jarend's on their previous long journey.

"Mount up," she said, and they all got into the saddle. "Ride out."

The trumpeters, who had been rubbing and biting numb lips as they waited up on the wall, blew the king's fanfare in reverse: the queen was riding.

That cleared the streets, which were mostly empty except for the returning night patrol and early wagons heading to market. All pulled aside as the small cavalcade trotted out—Danet was not one for showy gallops.

She missed Firefly at once, mostly out of fondness, but also because when she rode Firefly she didn't have to think about her riding. On the other hand, it was interesting to get a feel for a new horse's signals. The stable chief had told her that Firefly was getting too old for sudden long journeys during the uncertain weather of early spring.

When they were through the gates, Danet saw the two scouts glancing expectantly back at her, and opened her hand. They rode off down the road, hooves kicking up clumps of mud.

The guards arranged themselves in column, and Danet looked around for Sage and the little runner girl. Sage rode behind and to her left, very properly, but the child had dropped way back. Danet beckoned her forward.

Surprised, Lineas urged her mount into a trot outside the column, and when she neared the gunvaer, she was motioned in beside Sage.

"What's your name? Lanet?"

"Lineas, Danet-Gunvaer."

"Lineas, I understand you know Hand-speech. I want you to teach me, so we'll know enough to get by when we reach Algaravayir. Sage? How much do you know?"

"Only what we're taught—the basic twenty signs. My extra languages are Sartoran and Iascan."

"Then teach us both, Lineas."

Lineas struck her hand flat to her scrawny chest, flushed with pride at the idea of teaching the gunvaer, but she was also a little afraid of doing badly. Sage recognized that fear, and started them off with the first of the basics: Come, Go, Stop, I/me, You.

By evening, Danet's thighs and hips reminded her she hadn't ridden long hours for years, but she grimly walked it out while the others set up camp, aware that everyone else had jumped off without any apparent discomfort.

They ate a cold meal then retired early. She'd forgotten how much tents stank and got stuffy.

They woke before dawn, and rode with first light.

She'd recovered her old muscle tone by the end of a week, and could form very simple sentences in Hand, but she had to ask for two or three repetitions before she could translate what others signed. It turned out that Hand-speech was not predicated on the Marloven alphabet, and had its own word order and verb tenses.

By the time they skirted Darchelde and turned the animals southwest (Danet staring with interest into the forest-covered hills of the forbidden jarlate, and Lineas wistfully) Danet was beginning to assemble a rudimentary vocabulary.

"It's Spring Day," Sage said one morning, surprising Danet.

She thought immediately of Connar. Though she suspected he'd been a winter baby, or even New Year's, she'd suggested they pick a festival day that everyone liked for his Name Day, one that wasn't close to Noddy's, so Connar's would never be overshadowed. And she'd made certain that he had exactly as much attention on this chosen Name Day as Noddy did on his Name Day.

She hoped Arrow hadn't forgotten. He always had to be reminded of anyone's Name Day, including his own. But would Connar understand that? She leaned her head against her horse's warm neck, struggling with guilt, but then reminded herself that the boys had reached the age when peers and not parents were all-important. Noddy would remember, if Arrow had left them in the academy.

Lighter of heart, she mounted and slowly, awkwardly formed a sign to Lineas. Or tried—what was the sign for spring again?

At week's end they crossed the eastern tip of Marthdavan, where people were busy planting, the rise and fall of old planting songs carried on the balmy air. They crossed a last great river, then headed into the hills that divided off Algaravayir. Here and there they glimpsed clusters of the distinctive Iascan houses with their round roofs.

"Find out all the stories about Inda you can," Arrow had told Danet. "We have almost nothing. Did he write anything? Either bring it back or copy it!"

The days had warmed considerably. By the time the towers of the Algaravayirs' Castle Tenthen jutted above the hills, they were sleeping out under the stars instead of closed in the tents.

At last they rode into view of Tenthen Castle.

Danet was surprised to discover that it was a lot smaller than the Olavayir castle at Nevree, which she had learned was considered awkward compared to the splendid Yvanavayir castle. Tenthen was more like an outpost.

Small as it was, it was well maintained, the fields around it orderly, crops growing, with two orchards glimpsed. The scouts, having gone ahead on this utterly uneventful trip, rode back to say that the Iofre was waiting for them, just as Danet had expected.

And so they found Tenthen's walls lined with guards both male and female, the brisk breeze fluttering the green-and-silver Algaravayir flags and royal blue-and-gold Olavayir, striking a festive note.

Danet had envisioned Inda's direct descendant somehow being larger than life. Instead, the woman who met her was short and round-bodied, her head made rounder by a halo of thick flaxen braids.

But her countenance was friendly as she welcomed Danet and introduced two sturdy blond girls, her hands fluttering so quickly that Danet sighed inwardly. She caught perhaps two Hand words in a hundred, if that. At least Lineas was able to keep up, judging by her own fluttering.

Lineas, of course, was thrilled to every nerve to meet these cousins her own age whom she had thought she would never see. They fell in step beside Lineas, one signing as fast as she could a series of questions, as the other smiled down at her feet, each foot placed just so.

Lineas answered as speedily as they were conducted upstairs to the heir's suite, which the twins shared. Lineas looked around the bright room, with its old furniture. Central, covering the stone floor, lay a now-threadbare rug in Algaravayir green, its silver owl almost obscured by the footsteps of generations of Algaravayir children.

Noren signed that Lineas would be right next door, in what used to be the second child's room, as there weren't any other Algaravayir children, and the guest chambers were at the other end of the castle.

In the courtyard, horses were led one way, and runners carried gear in another.

Danet was conducted by a runner to a guest chamber that didn't look much different from any other stone-walled chamber she'd ever been in.

She was invited to bathe and join the family for a meal. The Iofre asked about the journey, and made easy conversation, hands and mouth going at the same time in what was clearly thirteen years of habit. Afterward, the castle folk did their best to entertain their guest with ballads and drumming, then all retired early.

After a grateful night in a bed again, Danet—a light sleeper—woke to the sunrise bell calling everyone to drill. She rose and dressed, and when she got downstairs, she found women and girls lining up in the courtyard.

The Iofre saluted her formally. "Would you like to lead drill, Danet-Gunvaer?"

Danet said, "The truth is, I haven't been drilling seriously since my daughter was born. All I find time for is the basic warmup and the occasional ride, and little enough of that. I'm happy to follow from the rear."

The Iofre held out a pair of wooden practice knives as she said, "I expect if any of us woke up and found ourselves gunvaer, we'd have to give it up as well. I wouldn't face your workload for a barrel of gold."

Danet laughed, and took her place in the back, behind the girls.

The Iofre led them through the old odni drills that Danet's mother had been so proud of. Danet was soon sweaty, and muscles that she hadn't thought about in years trembled from the unaccustomed effort. It felt good to move like this again, though she knew she would be sore later.

The women put away their wooden practice knives and fetched the bows for archery drill. Danet took her turn, expecting to be terrible, and she was, but old habit at least sent her arrows close enough to the target.

After that, the Iofre dismissed them to ready for breakfast. They retired to bathe as the men gathered for their longer drills.

After breakfast, the Iofre and her daughters took Danet, Sage, and Lineas for a ride around Tenthen. As Danet peered westward at a cluster of round Iascan houses on the other side of a shallow river, Noren and Lineas were deep in conversation, hands moving in a constant flutter as the other twin looked on, her expression never changing.

And rather than force a visual language into unnecessarily awkward diction by attempting transliteration, I shall translate it the way I would any language.

"What is the heir like?" Noren wanted to know. "Does he like animals? What's the princess like?"

"I haven't met him," Lineas signed back, scrupulous as royal runners were trained to be to differentiate what they observed from what they heard. "But everyone likes him. He loves to ride, and likes the princess's pets. She loves animals. We all see her often at the stable, where she goes whenever she can."

"Is she a great rider?"

"I know not. All I've seen is how she loves to take care of animals. All of them, not just the horses."

They went on to talk about the royal castle and the city. For Noren, who had never left Tenthen or its immediate environs, the idea of a huge city was at least as exciting, maybe more. The idea of marriage was hazy at best.

As the girls rode in front, Danet finally said to the Iofre, introducing what she assumed would be an easy, pleasant subject, "It probably won't surprise you to know that my husband admires Inda-Harskialdna."

Linden-Fareas kept her face neutral, but her muscles tightened so that her horse sidestepped, ears flicking to catch whatever had startled her rider.

This gave the Iofre an excuse to bend forward, ostensibly to soothe the horse, but hiding her face as Danet, still looking at the light on those round roofs, went on, "He modeled the academy on what he and the famous Headmaster Gand put together. When I get back to the royal city, he'll ask if I saw any tributes to Inda. I know there is that tapestry —"

"Which he loathed," the Iofre put in, her wide-set dark eyes crinkled with laughter. "He refused to look at it, we're told."

"Really?" Danet asked. "I was told that he loved it, or that's what's been handed down in the family. And I thought it was beautiful. Why did he object to it?"

"He said everything about the pose of the central figures was completely wrong, and he used to laugh and ask when he'd ever been as tall as the ceiling. But mostly he hated the woman who designed it, Dannor Tyavayir, though she only supervised a part of its making. Everything else was done by the household. We've kept it because of that work, but it can be a bride gift to your son, if you like," the Iofre said with a shrug, causing Danet to slew around in the saddle and stare.

Linden-Fareas wished she could take the words back. Not so much because she was fond of the tapestry, though she was. It was because her careless gesture might have exactly the opposite effect from what she'd meant.

Then she saw the honest surprise in Danet's face, and let out her breath, trying to shed the old anger. Camerend had told her in person, and Mnar by letter, to trust Danet in the sense that what you saw was what you got.

Linden-Fareas was aware that Anred-Olavayir venerated the Algaravayir name for all the wrong reasons, but in this he was no different from all the other kings who had pestered the family for marriage alliances since the death of the great Hadand Deheldegarthe.

She took a deep breath and, watching Danet covertly, answered her question to get the subject of Inda's artifacts over with. "There's a shield in the Hall that Inda's runners brought back from the Venn invasion in the Pass, but we're told he never used it. His old practice blade is with it. Other than that, there isn't much. That is, the people have changed the names of some of the places along his old route. Like Indasbridge, where he used to stop and chat with the old men in a trade town on the river, and there's Indascamp, which eventually turned into an outpost. And everyone knows the field where he died, though there's nothing to mark it. Ho! It's coming on rain. Well, that's it, really, unless you want to see the peach orchard that we've tended ever since Joret Dei, who went over the mountains to be queen, sent rootlings to Tdor-Iofre."

"It looks like thunder's coming," Danet said, eyeing the dark clouds in the east, rather than admit she wasn't particularly interested in inspecting orchards. She knew Arrow wouldn't care, either.

The Iofre turned her horse, and as they rode back under big splats of rain, Danet watched the girls. She still couldn't tell the twins apart, except that one seemed to have a lot to say, and the other little, judging by the hand movement.

When they arrived back, the girls were dispatched to help pull in the bedding and mats, which had been washed and put out to dry. The Iofre excused herself to see to castle business, leaving Danet—stiff and sore from the morning's workout—standing at the upper window. Ow, every muscle hurt. She could so vividly hear Mother's disgust, and envisioned herself having to muck out all the stable stalls, and haul in fresh hay. The sure cure, Mother always said, for sloth.

From now on, every morning at least the knife dance, and if she had time the most basic odni drill, she promised herself as she watched the girls dashing about the courtyard below, gathering things to be brought inside. The twin named Hadand was immediately recognizable by her unchanging expression. She moved in a repeated pattern of straight lines, a hand touching the rim of the well, the hitching post, a stone jut of one of the towers. It was as if she were blind and guiding herself, except it was plain she could see.

She was also slower in gathering mats and blankets, as she meticulously lined up corners precisely. No one interfered with her, or chivvied her to hurry, even though the rain was coming faster. It wasn't until thunder rumbled that she started violently, and sped back along her route, touching each thing in reverse. So she wasn't deaf, though Danet had yet to hear her speak.

After the noon meal, Rider Captain Aldren Noth took the three girls into the stable to play with two newborn foals while he got to know his niece. The Iofre took Danet around the castle, introducing her to weavers and carpenters, stonemason and so forth. All very friendly and open, and yet Danet got the sense that she was seeing the outward components of their lives, as if this all was rehearsed.

She distrusted this impression, wondering how much she was reading into the situation, just because Calamity had lied to her.

A couple more days passed, beginning with odni drill with the women before breakfast. Danet observed the twins, noting how well Noren got along with everyone, and how athletic she was—everything her twin wasn't. She held back from formally interviewing the girls, suspecting that they'd be on their best behavior, perhaps saying what they had been coached to say. She was content to observe.

They all rode down to the harbor one day, and while Danet thoroughly enjoyed getting her first glimpse of the ocean, she still felt that the Iofre was keeping her at an affably polite distance. It felt as if she were being guided over the surface of a frozen lake, with all the underwater life hidden below.

She had always been a light sleeper, and that had only worsened after she and Arrow found themselves king and queen. The occasional nights she slept alone she still put a knife under her pillow, though she knew it was senseless —anyone who could get past the castle defenses would strike her down fast. The knife was a compromise, yet even deep in sleep, the softest unexpected noise brought her instantly awake.

So it was her fourth morning: She woke abruptly to the sound of rain below her open window. Her inner sense was of very early morning, at least an hour before dawn. She was about to turn over and go back to sleep when a slight cough, followed by a soft *Shh!,* shocked her nerves. The sound resolved into not rain but the soft thud of many footfalls.

Attack?

But the bell wasn't ringing. No one was shouting. Except for those soft, steady footfalls, those below were completely silent. Sneak attack? Except no one was running.

She got up, stepped to the side of her window, and peered down. There outlined in the dim, ruddy light of a wall torch, were the Iofre's twin daughters. They joined a cluster of castle people all moving in one direction. With them walked another twig of a girl—was that Lineas? Yes. As they turned in one direction, the light fell across that triangular face. Danet's alarm cooled to wariness and intense curiosity. She slipped barefooted out of the room and down the hall in the direction they were walking.

The castle was not that large; Danet came up against the tower stair, and peeked out of an arrow slit into the court off the kitchen yard, with the water well central. Here the group she'd seen met up with a bigger crowd already gathered. Yes, there was Sage! In close ranks, with the Iofre at the front, they launched into what looked like an odni drill, except it was far faster, with alterations that she could see drew on male strength, rather than always driving from the hip.

They were so fast, yet so close together, she could see why they didn't hold blades—except, as it finished, everyone precisely in place, she suspected that if they had been drilling with weapons, no knife edge would have come closer than a finger's breadth from the person at either side, in front, or behind.

When it was done, they began to disperse as silently as they had gathered, leaving the yard empty. Danet ran like a girl back to her guest chamber, her toes cold, for the stone had yet to warm up.

That was not the regular odni drill. That was something much more lethal. And her own runner was a part of it, as well as that little twig Lineas. Royal runners did get hard training, she knew. Among their many duties, they were expected to protect whoever they were assigned to. The strangest part was that these Algaravayirs apparently did two sets of drills, and further, the royal runners and the Algaravayirs shared that secret one.

Secrets again! She lay in bed wondering what, if anything, she should say. As if sanity dawned with the sun, she remembered that she was not Danet Farendavan, she was Danet-Gunvaer, who had every right to put any question she wanted.

She got up, bathed, and dressed with a little more care than she usually bothered with.

When the bell rang, sure enough, she found the women forming up for the customary odni drill, as though nothing had happened. To the Iofre's friendly greeting, she said as neutrally as she could—because they hadn't done anything wrong, precisely—"If this is for me, since you've already drilled, you don't have to put yourself to the trouble."

The Iofre sighed. "So we did wake you up? I apologize."

"I don't mind that," Danet said. "And I was impressed by what I saw. I was also impressed to see my own runners in there with you."

The Iofre checked slightly at that, her gaze dropping. Then she looked up soberly. "I'd already decided to discuss certain things with you, and that can be part of it, as you wish. The simplest answer is that we're trained much the same as the royal runners are. As for why, can it wait until a bit later? There's a feel of a storm coming, and I'd like to get our outside chores done beforehand."

Danet knew that a lack of anger and a steady gaze didn't necessarily mean truth, but instinct inclined her toward liking this older woman who seemed without pretense. "Certainly," she said. "If you can give me something to do, I'd be the happier for it."

The Iofre's bright smile flashed. "If you would help over at the stable."

"Gladly."

The stable chief was another Noth, tall, narrow-faced, with red-toned light hair, about as unlike her own dear Jarid as a man could be, but then Jarid's branch of the Noths came from elsewhere. This man was slow, mild, and had a patient hand with animals and young people alike.

The three girls showed up, two bouncing and giggling, Noren's giggles a breathy keen very much her own sound. Her twin never laughed, but she seemed more animated than Danet had ever seen her, and less wooden, as they all worked to exercise the restless colts.

The animals seemed to sense the coming storm, the young ones friskier than ever, which caused much running around, but finally all the stalls had been mucked out, and those who needed exercise had gotten it, and the midday bell clanged as the first heavy drops splatted around them.

Danet discovered her mood had lightened. As usual, work cleared her heart, if not her head. The air as they crossed the courtyard was greenish with impending thunder, and everyone scurried, the two girls holding Hadand's hands.

Then the Iofre, who had been wrestling all week with an increasing instinct to trust an Olavayir — something she had never expected to happen — said, "Will you come up to the library?"

The storm that crashed overhead darkened the library so that the Iofre went about lighting lamps as she said to Danet, "You've had time to observe my daughter Hadand, I'm certain."

Danet knew she was no good at subtlety, so she didn't try. "I believe I understand why you swapped the girls. Noren is outgoing and sociable. Hadand...isn't."

"Yes. She can hear — if you go downstairs, you will see her with her head buried under a cushion to muffle the thunder. The fact that she can hear is why I'd thought she'd be best to send away, when the girls were tiny, and we discovered that Noren was deaf. It runs through the Iascan side of the Noth family."

Danet opened her hand, accepting this, without perceiving how carefully Linden-Fareas watched her.

"Since you wrote to me about a betrothal treaty, we've come to discover that — as far as we can tell — sound is irrelevant to Hadand. You can speak to her, but she seems to hear our words the way we hear dogs bark, or cows moo. She doesn't speak. Never has. It's always been Hand. I think she learned it not from us so much as from her sister. She and Noren have their own language, though most of it is recognizable Hand. Your little redhead is catching up remarkably quickly," the Iofre added. "That was a thoughtful gesture, bringing the girls' cousin."

"It was the royal runners' training chief's idea," Danet said.

"Mnar Milnari? I know her," the Iofre said. "She used to visit here as a child, before she was sent up north. We still correspond when we can. She knows the situation, but I can understand her not wishing to say anything unless forced by circumstance, as she has never seen my girls, and I know the royal runners set great store by first-hand observation."

The Iofre waited for a blast of thunder to roll away. She sat head bent, her profile somber, almost unfamiliar. Danet hadn't recognized until then how much those lines of laughter around her dark eyes were characteristic. The Iofre was a head shorter than Danet, but somehow within a day, the force of her personality had made her seem larger, in the way a summer garden looks so much larger than itself after a good rain.

Danet said slowly, "This is in no way an accusation. I ask only to learn. But why didn't you write to me about Noren and Hadand before I sent out the order about the visits once the girls turn sixteen?"

Linden-Farias said bluntly, "Because I wasn't always certain we'd keep that treaty."

Danet hid her shock. "Why?"

"Every generation since the Olavayirs came to the throne, *everyone* wanted alliance with the Algaravayir name, while the Olavayir kings made it clear that they didn't want anyone but themselves allying with us."

"I didn't know that. The betrothal records I have didn't show...."

"Didn't show the broken ones," the Iofre said. "As for my own experience, the threats," her teeth showed, "began with Mathren Olavayir. Judging by his behavior, and the tone of his demands, he was obsessed with the Algaravayir name and past. *We* knew all along that he murdered Fnor Marthdavan, his wife. After which he made noises about coming after me. We did not know how much your husband would resemble Mathren Olavayir."

"*How* did you know that?" Danet leaned forward. "That rumor started going around when his secret army turned on itself. We heard there was a witness, but never who."

"The witness was a kitchen boy, who'd crawled under the hay to sneak a nap. Woke when he heard a shout, peeked down in time to see Fnor and her runner both murdered by Mathren and his first runner. The boy managed to escape with help from his grandfather in the stable. We kept that secret lest Mathren retaliate. I understand that Mathren's regicide also had a witness of sorts, who didn't come forward for twenty years, probably for the same reason." She lifted her hands. "The frightening thing was, the world believed Mathren to be a hero, and yet there were all these secrets. People kept them out of fear, without knowing that others kept the same, or similar, secrets."

"Just the way Mathren wanted it," Danet said. "Everyone living in fear. It's taken us years to overcome the shadow Mathren cast."

"Yes. It still exists in places." The Iofre sighed. "Anyway, Mathren made it very clear that any marriage alliance I made without royal permission would be considered, oh, call it a threat to the throne. And then after Fnor's death...well, to cut it all short, why do you think I waited until I was almost forty to have children?"

The Iofre spread her hands. "The very week I learned that Mathren was dead, I chewed gerda. Aldren Noth is the girls' father. He's my randael, though he also functions as our stable chief. You met him today. He and I were together at the time. He's an excellent father."

"And so you accepted my treaty offer to buy time, in case Arrow might be the sort of king who would send an army?" Sickened as Danet felt at this evidence of Mathren's long reach, she was glad she had come. She knew she would have learned none of this through writing letters.

"Pretty much," the Iofre said with a brief, sad smile. "But that was then. We've had twelve years of peace, nothing dire has happened, and meanwhile, Hadand is the way she is, but Noren loves the idea of living in the royal city. She loves history, she gets along with everyone, and she longs to travel."

"As a gunvaer, she won't get much of that," Danet commented wryly. "This is my first trip. Might very well be my last."

"I realize that. Which is one reason we're talking today." The Iofre recrossed her legs and leaned her elbows on her knees. "I think I need to talk about the Algaravayir name a little, and what that might mean to your future grandchildren. We understand how our name is perceived on the outside. You have to understand that Inda was beloved here, but it wasn't for foreign battles, or even for what happened way up north. That was his duty, and he was duly honored for it, for he carried the scars as proof of the cost. He was beloved in Choreid Elgaer for his heart. The old people insist that *their* old people said he was always loving, always trusting, when he was small, but the truth was, he was also...odd. And he was away for so many years, during which things here...well, that's another old subject useless to rake over."

The Iofre wiped back a strand of hair. "The one we all consider truly great was Tdor-Iofre, whose room I sleep in, and whose tapestries I look on each day, but whose greatness I could never measure up to. She, and the Fareas-Iofre I am named for, held Choreid Elgaer while Inda was away, and it was she who made life bearable for him on his return."

"Bearable," Danet prompted, mindful of Arrow's request.

Linden-Fareas gazed into the fire, waiting out another crash of thunder. When it had died away to an uneven rumble, "I'm told that everyone in the kingdom talks about Grandfather Inda's great battles, but *we* all grew up hearing about how his shouts during his nightmares echoed through the castle. How, before he turned forty, he needed help getting out of bed in winter. How his scars and badly healed bones ached ahead of blizzards, so they used him as a weather vane."

"I had no idea," Danet said.

"Few do. He hated disturbing others with his weaknesses, everyone knew that. He also hated writing. Really hated it." She waved a hand at the solid wall of books and scrolls behind her. "Though he did like to read. He bought books, the way his mother had, but you won't find a scrap of paper in his hand anywhere. Youngsters pestering him for stories of his days of piracy on the seas, and so forth, would cause him to go silent, rocking back and forth, until they learned not to ask."

Danet opened her hand in agreement, and Linden-Fareas sighed. "This is what you need to think about. You've already noticed Hadand's ways. Let me tell you, she's not so very different from how Inda behaved as a small boy, I'm told. Oh, she's got more of it, but the trait is inherited. It was that way with my brother, who's better off in Sartor, where he can be away from people altogether, and spend his days peacefully translating ancient magic texts that take others three times as long to parse."

Danet said, "What trait is that?"

"It's hard to describe, but it's a way of being here and not being here, then suddenly being here and seeing things that others don't. The family name for it is 'the waterfall'. Inda would go around seeming blind or drunk, definitely heedless, while seeing all the elements of battle, then suddenly he'd fit them together faster than actual events, which, I'm told, to everyone else is chaos. The cost to him was terrible, because he didn't have the nature to be a killer, but events made him one. A *good* one. And my brother has the trait. He sees the connections between words, no matter how ancient or obscure. It's something about patterns, and for my brother there's no terrible heart-cost outside of being tired from working without sleep sometimes."

Danet's stomach cramped. She had come to determine why one twin was swapped for the other, and that had been easily seen. She'd thought that would be an end to the matter. But this conversation was making it clear that the solid ground she'd assumed was not so solid — there was an entire cavern beneath.

The Iofre paused and glanced sideways. "My aunt saw, um, we'll call them ghosts. Again, things no one else saw. You can argue that such things aren't real, but then, what do we really know about real and not real?"

Danet shifted on her mat. The sudden veer to ghosts made her feel slightly queasy. To her, who spent most of her waking moments ordering what was real, "ghosts" were merely a metaphor for madness.

In a disturbing parallel, the Iofre went on. "We're told that Fareas-Greatmother feared for Inda's sanity, because her sister had showed the trait. She was sent to Sartor, but the Adaluin would not let his boys be sent outside the kingdom. We know that the great Tdor Marthdavan, who will never be written about by the scribes, but whose praise we all sing, kept Inda happy, and as sane as he ever could be, until he died."

She gestured toward the south. "The Cassads believe our two families crossed too many times. We think Hadand-Gunvaer and Greatmother Tdor might have had a letter exchange about that, but if they did, it must have vanished, unless it's in your royal archive. There's no sign of it in this castle, and everything of Tdor's was preserved as a treasure by Greatmother Rialden and her daughter-by-marriage. Anyway, I believe Noren will make a fine gunvaer, especially if you tell me what you would like her studying in the intervening years. But there is a chance her children might inherit some measure of the waterfall."

Danet's mind streamed in several directions, but one thought persisted: Arrow. The Iofre was being frank about the possibility of madness in the family, and seemed to be offering the chance to break the betrothal. Danet wavered, then mentally gave herself a shake. Arrow would call it all hearsay.

The only betrothal he cared about was this one. If Danet offered to break it, he was more than likely to ride down here and reinstate it.

To gain a little time for thought, she said, "That training,"

The Iofre didn't react to the shift in subject. "It's what Inda taught at the academy, refined again by Greatfather Savarend, known as Fox. But it seems to have been largely forgotten during the years when there was no academy."

Forgotten except by the royal runners, whose chief came from the Montredavan-Ans of Darchelde, and who had always had close connections with the Algaravayirs. The royal runners' mandate was to serve and protect the royal family. They were in no sense an army.

The one preoccupied with armies, and the Algaravayir name, was Arrow. He and the rest of the Olavayirs, according to....

A glimpse of vivid memory — that fast drilling in secret — and shock iced Danet's nerves: she was certain she had the last piece of the puzzle now.

Mathren had been even more obsessed with Inda-Harskialdna's fame and name. What other purpose could that secret army be stationed directly to the north be, but to swoop down to take and hold the legendary lands of Inda-Harskialdna?

And the Iofre had expected it. The Tenthen people drilled to resist attack, not from the Venn, or pirates sailing up the little harbor at Luwath, but from their fellow Marlovan. Over a name and its bloody fame.

No, that was too simple. Over what the Algaravayir name meant to those who wanted power.

Danet pinched the skin between her brows. "I truly appreciate your telling me this history," she said, her voice firming. "We would be glad to have Noren come to us. As for her sister, if you can find a cousin to send in her place to send to Manther Yvanavayir, that would be a great help. I know that the Jarl of Yvanavayir was also pleased to unite with your family."

Linden-Fareas Algaravayir suppressed a sigh. She had expected no less. "I will see to it," she promised. "There are several suitable girls in my maternal family."

Two more pleasant days passed.

Danet managed to exchange a couple of brief, child-simple conversations in Hand with Noren, who was patient and attentive, in contrast to Hadand, who didn't seem to see Danet even when she signed a greeting. Danet did little better trying to speak slowly and enunciate, as Noren watched her mouth.

Sage took her aside to tell her that over-enunciating was wrong, and that Noren had trouble seeing speech in people she didn't know. "But the Iofre is going to bring in tutors," Sage said cheerfully. "And Noren is going to work on maths, as you suggested."

The following day, a perfect spring morning, Danet called for their departure.

As soon as they were clear of the walls of Tenthen, the rolled Inda tapestry carefully packed as a gift from Noren to Noddy, Danet said to Lineas, "You spent the most time with Noren. What did you think of her?"

Lineas knew the gunvaer was not interested in what a wonderful time she had had, and how much she liked Uncle Aldren. Likewise, she was not going to tell anybody that she'd seen Hadand staring at the ribbons of color in the air that she thought nobody but she saw.

The gunvaer would want to know about Noren, who was expected to marry the next king and would someday give Lineas and the other royal runners orders.

Lineas said, "Noren is very good to her sister." And, conscientiously, as she'd been taught, she offered witnessed evidence. "Whenever Hadand interrupted us to tell us *again* the birth-lines of each horse, going back a hundred years, Noren acted as if it was the very first time. Noren also lets her put the mats right around the table before sitting down, and doesn't get upset if Hadand has to put them just so. I saw Hadand go back and fix them three times, yesterday morning, but Noren told us to wait...."

She went on with similar anecdotes, but that was enough for Danet. Noren seemed a promising prospective gunvaer—she couldn't have asked for better. Furthermore, Lineas, a serious, hard-working child without a mean bone in her body, might be the right First Runner for sweet, animal-mad Bun.

Yes, all in all, though Danet no longer enjoyed camping outside, and dreaded the prospect of the long, uninteresting journey home, she had learned a great deal.

She waited until Lineas was finished, thanked her, then said, "You and Sage and I will speak in Hand from now on, until we return to the royal city."

Sage saluted, hand to heart, thinking of the private conversation that she'd been invited to the previous night.

"You've met the gunvaer, and talked to Lineas," the Iofre had signed to Noren, as rain roared overhead. "Is this marriage still something you want to do?"

Noren looked from Sage to her mother. She signed slowly, "Can I change my mind?"

"Of course you can," the Iofre had assured her. "But the closer we get to a possible departure, the more difficult it becomes. However, if you find you cannot do it, we'll manage."

Sage waited, and when Noren turned her wide gaze her way, she signed, "I like what Lineas told me."

"Then we are going to have the first of some adult discussions. If you do decide to go to the royal city, they're going to be looking at you and expecting to see the glories—" On this word she snapped her fingers, face wry, indicating irony. "Of our past. So here's my thinking. We want to change that, yes?"

Of course Noren agreed, her eyes wide.

"But to change it, you have to gain their respect. With something that isn't war or battle related. But something you enjoy."

At that Noren's solemn little face transformed. "Riding?"

"Exactly. There is no one faster in the kingdom than the royal riders, but they don't compete with the academy. Never have during any of the academies. Grandpa Dignose says he'll train you. So if you do go, you'll be ready to earn their respect in a way that has nothing to do with Greats-Grandpa Inda or battle."

Noren flashed happy agreement and ran off.

Sage then said, "You still have misgivings? Why hold to the betrothal, if so?"

The Iofre said, "Because I like Danet, and the king doesn't sound like the worst of his Olavayir forebears. Danet's staff seems to be content with her." When Sage signed that it was true, the Iofre went on, "Plus this betrothal is a protection of a kind. If we broke it, then we would surely be pestered by others, most certainly that Lavais Nyidri in Feravayir, who calls herself Queen of Perideth."

Sage looked startled at that.

"Never mind," the Iofre said. "It's possibly a clash of personalities. The main thing is, Noren will be happy, and the gunvaer will leave Hadand be. We'll find a volunteer right away to gradually take Noren's place in Hadand's life."

Sage left, and the Iofre turned to her own women. "Let us make certain that when Noren goes to the royal city, she'll give them the Algaravayir they expect to see. That'll make it easier for her to hold to our plans."

NINE

"Olavayir Tvei, hold up."

Connar reined in his mount, looking at Master Hauth in surprise, as the other boys trotted back toward the stable. They'd just finished mounted hand-to-hand on a clear morning, as rain puddles lay on the green-tufted ground, reflecting the sky. The midday watch had begun, and his stomach was already gnawing with hunger.

But Connar waited obediently, hoping he hadn't been *that* bad. At least he hadn't fallen right out of the saddle, like Tevaca. But Master Hauth was legendary for strictness, and this was their first year with him. He mostly taught the big boys.

"Not bad," Master Hauth said, his one eye narrow, the other hidden behind a wicked-looking patch. A puckered white sword scar extended down from it to his jaw. "You don't have Olavayir Ain's reach, but then few do."

Connar touched two fingers to chest in acknowledgement. Noddy was big and strong, everybody knew that.

"You could, with some work, match him for skill," the master said.

Connar gazed in surprise. "Me?" Sometimes he dreamed about being as tough as Noddy, but he kept those imaginings strictly to himself.

"You." Hauth dipped his chin slightly. "But it would take work. Extra work."

"How?" Connar asked dubiously.

"Start lance practice early."

Glee thrilled through Connar, as he imagined surprising his entire class on their first day of lance practice — which was notorious — only he wouldn't fall out of the saddle, or catch the lance on the ground, or smack some other boy across the head while losing control of his horse. He'd gallop straight for the target, and *bam!*

Except nobody *bammed* the first month. Or the second.

The vision faded and he gave the master a wary, puzzled look. Everyone admired Hauth because he was the biggest master, bigger even than Stad the archery master, and looked the toughest because of the missing eye and the scar. The older boys had scared the first-year scrubs by insisting that there was a burning red eye under the patch that could see in the dark.

And this master had stopped to talk to him?

Master Hauth said, "You expect one day to be the kingdom's army commander. That means you must be the man everyone wants to follow. Your birth father was that type." He was careful not to say *real* father. "As was his father."

Connar scowled. "That traitor?"

Hauth's mouth tightened; too soon, far too soon. He made an effort to ease his voice. "Never mind what happened at the end. When Mathren Olavayir was not much older than you, he worked harder than anyone else, he rode faster, shot straighter, never lost a duel, and everyone wanted to follow him. Would you like to be that kind of commander?"

Connar wanted nothing more. He dismissed Mathren Olavayir from mind—easily done, as he was just a name—and there again was that delightful vision of him surprising everyone with his lance skill. "What do I have to do?"

"Meet me in the training corral behind the barns every day before sunup," Master Hauth said. "And don't tell anyone."

Connar stared. "Why not? My brother—"

"He doesn't need the extra practice."

"But he'll help me rise early. I know he'd love to see me get stronger."

"Maybe now," Master Hauth said. "But when you get older, and the competition is tougher?" He watched doubt furrow Connar's forehead, and then came the narrowing of his eyes in wariness. Hauth said easily, "Even if Olavayir Ain doesn't follow the trail of most older boys, wouldn't it be fun to surprise him? You know how much he'd like that."

Connar's brow cleared. "He would!"

"So. Another part of command is learning to keep your own counsel when necessary. Here's your challenge. I'll know how serious you are by your actions: if anyone finds out about these lessons, that will be the last. And I'll pick another candidate," he added, as he had seen by now that though the heir had no vestige of competitive spirit, Connar was driven by it.

Connar gazed up at the master, longing and doubt evident in the tightening of his jaw, the set of his shoulders. So very like the father he would never meet—it hurt Hauth to see.

Connar was debating mentally. He and Noddy always told each other everything. They shared everything. Their stalks were more fun together. Noddy had protected him from the older boys when they got too rough, and if someone had a nasty tongue, it was Connar who defended them. He didn't like the idea of keeping a secret from Noddy, even a fun one.

It even felt kind of wrong, somehow, coming from a master with nobody around, instead of orders from Da, or even from the headmaster. But then there was that image of surprising everyone one day....

What was right? The impulse to ask his mother seized him, but she was far away.

Hauth saw that debate so clearly in Connar's puckered brow and averted gaze. Twice now he'd used his nephew-by-marriage to cast doubt on Connar's birth and status in Connar's mind, but both times, it seemed, the gunvaer had blunted his arrow. This was why he'd chosen this moment to approach Lanrid's son on his own, while the gunvaer was safely gone.

If he got to Connar successfully, by the time the gunvaer returned from her journey, Connar should be established in a new habit. To boys that age, a couple of months was akin to a couple of years.

Time to dangle the bait. He said in a doubting tone, "It'll be tough. Maybe too tough."

And of course that did it.

Connar put two fingers to his chest, his chin lifting in decision.

Hauth said, "Tomorrow morning. No, don't worry about getting a horse. It'll be a long time before you try anything mounted. There's plenty of work on foot to be done first."

Connar discovered the truth of that the next morning, when, shivering and bouncing on his toes, he slipped out after a sleepless night, in the inky darkness with only the faintest smear of color above the eastern hills.

Master Hauth was already there. He put Connar through a series of exercises that very swiftly warmed him up, and then left him water-kneed and sweaty. How was he going to get through the rest of the day?

"Tomorrow morning," Master Hauth said grimly. "If you aren't here, then we're done."

Of course Connar was there, and the day after.

It had become a regular thing by the time early summer had dried up all the puddles.

One sunny morning the gunvaer and her party rode through the castle gates. Danet didn't like fuss and parade, but her guards knew what was proper, and the scouts riding a little ways ahead signaled to the wall, so that when Danet's dusty cavalcade rode through the gates, the queen's fanfare not only cleared the streets, but her three children, over at the castle as it was Restday, came running.

In the courtyard, Danet looked about in satisfaction, glad to be back. First order of the day, a bath.

Sage quietly went about unloading the animals, looking forward to catching up with Loret and Shen. Loret would want to hear any news of her homeland.

Lineas was probably the most excited. She could hardly wait to see her classmates again, and exchange news. Then there was always Quill; every conversation she had with him was faithfully recorded in her journal.

She pulled off her saddlebag, and waited to be dismissed, when three figures shot through the doorway, right through the Evred ghost hovering there, and shouted, "Ma!"

Bun was first, flashing a smile at Lineas before jabbering about a litter of new kittens born since her mother had left. Next was Connar, he of the sky blue eyes and curling black hair and the beautifully chiseled face. An instant in which his gaze met hers, and Lineas flashed hot then cold all over.

In that moment, as Connar dashed indifferently past, Lineas—so responsive to beauty—launched into the exhilaration of emotional freefall, her innocent passion arcing past Quill to Connar.

Connar trotted beside Noddy up the stairs behind their mother, waiting until Bun ran out of breath and surreptitiously feeling the reassuring shape of his arms. He thought about telling his mother *some* of the secret. Just to make sure everything was right.

But when they reached the residence floor, she turned around and faced them. "Noddy, your future wife will be Noren Algaravayir. She'll come to visit in a very few years. So, beginning now, we're going to have a new rule: Restdays will be talked in Hand only."

And, slowly, awkwardly, she asked how each of them was.

Noddy gave Connar a long face. Connar signed back covertly, *Stupid.*

They actually liked Hand, once they'd discovered that they could use it as private code (as long as no fourth-years were around). But the signs they liked best weren't the ones they could use around parents or masters.

So Connar sat tight on his secret as the family struggled through an entire meal without speaking, except when Da barked out a curse or two when he got frustrated. The boys and Bun did get some entertainment out of Da signing that the sun stank, and that his feet were hard. Arrow finally left early, leaving all the tarts to Connar, Noddy, and Bun.

The children vanished the moment the dessert tray was empty, whereupon Arrow slunk back in, slanting shifty glances right and left before he said, "I can't stand waiting any longer. What did you learn about Inda-Harskialdna?"

"There's a tapestry that the Iofre sent along as a gift to Noddy, made while Inda was alive. But there isn't anything else, really."

"He didn't write down his thoughts on strategy?" Arrow's eyes widened. "Every commander does that! *I* do that!"

"Not a word. According to her, he hated talking about his wars as much as he hated writing. I was in the library one afternoon while they were at work. The only signs of him are the books he bought, and they're all old histories and travel books, and one about ship building. All the family stories handed down are about his nightmares, and how he couldn't get out of bed in winter, because of all his scars and broken bones."

Arrow thumbed his jaw. "I've heard some of that passed down through the Noths, but I thought that was just what outsiders heard. Damn. Well, I'm glad you're back. But I hate this Restday rule of yours. Do we really have to do it?"

"If we do, Hand'll become habit as much as our speaking, just as on the coast they all speak Iascan as well as Marlovan."

Arrow sighed, then said, "Be sure to tell Noth when he turns up. If I can't get out of it, he can't, either." And he left.

It was too early for Jarid, who usually came after the night watch changed. Now that she was alone, Danet hurried over to the archive, and as it was Restday, no scribe was on duty. She unlocked all three doors, and when she reached the inner vault, she uncovered her lamp and crossed to the sturdy, iron-bound chests that contained all Hadand Deheldegarthe's papers.

She set the lamp down beside her on the floor, and methodically went through them until she found what she was looking for: Hadand's own family tree, written in the women's code in some places, and in a private code at other times, the ink varying in color denoting how many times she had come back to this project over the years.

Danet hadn't really looked at it once she'd seem the code, deeming it useless for the present. She'd assumed it had been a hobby for the gunvaer, something to do on long winter nights. But after what she'd heard from Linden-Fareas, she felt she had to break the code in order to corroborate its truth.

She set aside that sheaf of papers, carefully restored everything else, picked up the papers and the lamp, and locked the archive behind her.

TEN

Three new patterns began that season.

It was well known by any who cared that the gunvaer and Commander Noth were lifemates. When this sort of thing happened between people with responsibilities in different parts of a huge castle, a room was usually found in a central location. It was partly for that reason and partly because Arrow temporarily put his fledgling army under Noth—now that he had his first academy graduates beginning their ten years in the forming King's Riders—to assign him the old harskialdna tower, an awkward suite that had been empty for over fifty years. From here, Noth could more conveniently run the garrison as well as the King's Riders. It also halved his walk from garrison command.

Danet no longer felt she must sleep near the nursery. She and Noth discovered that her own chambers, with their many windows, were more comfortable in summer, and the nearly windowless harskialdna chamber was much cozier in winter, as it could be kept warmer. Both had access to a small court directly below so that she, her runners, and Bun could do odni each morning; Noth always did sword drills with the guard.

The second pattern that developed that season—everyone understood "season" to mean the half year of the academy season—was that Hliss no longer came to the royal suite. She said it was for practical reasons, as the king's chambers had no place for a babe. Arrow found it annoying at first, but he discovered that he liked her quiet rooms, where he could leave aside being king for a short time.

The third pattern was Hauth's training Connar in secret.

It temporarily ended with the academy season. When the boys went home after the Victory Day Games, Hauth was assigned to the new barracks to train the King's Riders over winter.

Before he dismissed Connar for the last time, he said flatly, "If you turn up next spring, I expect you to have kept up these exercises. I'll know in a heartbeat if you slacked off. And of course, you can always give it up."

He was ready for that, or considered himself to be: Connar's black hair was a constant reminder that half of the boy came from that obnoxious Iascan woman that both Lanrid and Arrow had been so hot after. Had her blood tainted Connar too much? He'd not been above slacking off when it was exceptionally warm, or when he'd had a rough day previously.

From Connar's boyish perspective, Hauth had told so many stories about Lanrid's brilliance that he had begun to believe that Lanrid had never whined, or slacked, and had always been first in everything, like his father — both natural commanders.

Connar craved being recognized as a *natural commander*. Hauth made it clear that his birth-father and grandfather had been faster than everybody, and stronger than most, so that everyone turned to them whenever ridings were chosen for a game.

Attaining that goal seemed impossibly distant, because nobody in his year at the academy was turning to him. It was always Noddy, or Ghost Fath of the nearly white hair that tended to stand out around his head when the dry winds of Lightning Season blew, or sometimes skinny, rusty-haired Stick Tyavayir. At least it wasn't Cabbage Gannan, though he tried hard enough to flatter or bully the others by turns.

Still, after a season of arduous training in secret, Connar had begun to notice a gratifying change in his standing in both class competitions and private squabbles. In the first, he was no longer somewhere in the middle of the scrum, but had begun to win his way behind the three leaders — Noddy of course always first in anything that had to do with strength. He just wasn't fast. In private scraps, there were times when Connar at least held his own.

With that in mind, as winter began to close in, Connar kept up his habit of rising at the single bell an hour before the clangor of the dawn watch change, when those who had to be ready and on duty for morning watch rose to get ready.

It was difficult to keep up the habit when there was no Hauth, just himself in his room. But then came Noddy's Name Day, when Da measured Noddy against the inner door, and there was a three-finger spurt, and how Da laughed in pride. Connar knew he hadn't grown much at all, because his togs from spring still fit. He couldn't do anything about his height, but he could about his strength.

And so the long slow harvest season passed, ending in the howling storms of winter.

The problem with secrets, Danet decided as she dug her knuckles into the sides of her neck and twisted her head from side to side, was that it was easy to justify keeping one's own, but one could still begrudge someone else for keeping theirs.

To test her theory about madness running through the Algaravayir family, she'd worked at Hadand Deheldegarthe's family tree off and on over the months since her return from her visit to Linden-Fareas Algaravayir.

First, she'd discovered that there were actually two handwritings, belonging to Hadand and someone else.

It took months of close, meticulous work, but Danet liked these types of puzzles. Over New Year's Week, with the castle blanketed under a four-day snowfall and with no duties to pull her away, she systematically tried every name associated with Hadand—down to grandchildren and pets—in every combination, and finally she cracked the code.

As often happened, the solution turned out to be simple, once she had all the information: the code was based on the name of the king of the time, Evred, plus his old academy nickname, which Danet discovered completely by accident one night when Arrow was telling the boys stories from the old academy days: Sponge.

Put the two names side by side, and the code unraveled itself.

But that only uncovered more puzzles, like the page that featured one Isa Cassadas, who had instead of a death date a note that she disappeared. And in the second handwriting, a small notation next to it: *Gold = R?*

And finally, at the root of the entire project—with significant holes, more frequent the farther back the research went—Adamas Dei. That would be the mysterious and legendary Adamas Dei of the Black Sword, who according to all the oldest legends and songs had traveled Halia righting wrongs while working as a blacksmith, teaching the Iascans how to make the swords that the Marlovans coveted when they came a-conquering.

Danet had seldom paid much attention to legends, as Mother had said that most of them were fireside pretense that people would then pass on as truth, usually through ballads.

But here was the name *Adamas Dei*, and next to it, *Siar Cassadas*.

Leading back down the timeline toward the present, it was apparent that Dei family had intermarried with themselves and the Cassadas family over generations, until small diamond shapes began popping up more frequently. Danet guessed that these diamonds represented relatives who had turned out to be...call it odd, instead of mad, as there was one next to Inda's name on the first page, and also next to his mother's sister.

As she tidied up the old papers and her notes, she reflected that the scale of this Algaravayir-Cassad-waterfall secret made Calamity's silly boy-to-girl ruse seem trivial by comparison.

So she hid the papers away under her records of tax lists, and bent her mind to her new list of Hand vocabulary words.

Winter slid slowly into spring, and at the first thaw that lasted longer than a week, the boys began clamoring for their move over to the academy for another season, Noddy's voice an unlovely adolescent bray, Connar's reminding Danet of the silverflute she'd heard once, on her visit in Idego.

It was always the same—they moved over the week after Spring Day, and Connar's Name Day—but they never tired of trying to wheedle an earlier date.

When the time came at last, and Bun was off on some pursuit of her own, Arrow and Danet sat down together for the evening meal. After they'd gone over the affairs of the day, Arrow said, "You'll remember that this year you wanted girls in the Games. You've got a season to think about how to organize it."

"Me?" she exclaimed. She'd never had anything to do with the academy.

Arrow's brows shot upward. "Kind of late to change your mind."

"I haven't," she said. "So far I've got the Marlovayirs sending a riding of girls, and the Faths as well, along with a Tyavayir cousin. That's in the first batch of letters to arrive. But I thought the Victory Day competitions were arranged by the Headmaster."

Arrow turned his palm up. "You've got to let him know what you want."

"I'll see to it."

She sent Loret to ask if Mnar was free. When Mnar sat down on the guest mat, Danet summarized her conversation with Arrow and her subsequent thoughts, adding. "Since making a change works best when someone can point to tradition, I looked through Hadand-Gunvaer's papers, but there's nothing like a schedule of events for the queen's training girls' competitions. Only glancing references to who won what in a given year."

Mnar reached for the Idegan-trade coffee that the queen always thoughtfully provided. "I expect they knew the traditions so well no one thought to write it down. Or if it was written down, it was all tossed out when the queen's training was abandoned." She lifted the cup in both hands. "You might go farther back in her letters, if there are any, to when she was a girl. Did she write to Tdor Marthdavan about the games, once she could be included in them? You might also see if there are any letters from Joret Dei, the one who went over the mountain to become a queen among the Adranis."

Danet gasped. "Of course. I should have thought of that."

Mnar opened her hand. "But there's still the matter of what was expected of girls in those days. Do you want to go back to women on the walls? What is it you want to accomplish with bringing girls here for Victory Day games?"

Danet hadn't expected that question from anyone but Arrow, and of course, herself. Maybe it was time to break that circle of questions chasing each other's tail through her mind. "I'm not sure, except that going back to the walls doesn't make much sense. If anything, we should be testing for field skills, considering how much border patrol women do. It isn't always possible for scouts to get away from a fight. My own mother, as a girl, scouted with the Faths, and twice got caught in skirmishes with horse thieves from over the mountains. I know that the Jarlan of Yvanavayir went home with her best runners to help her Tlen relations against that huge raid in the Nelkereth. She died there, along with a lot of other women."

Mnar said, "I remember that, though I was just a girl."

Danet recollected her mother complaining bitterly that people over the mountains were rumored to pay something like ten times over the normal price for Marlovan-trained war horses. *And if it's true it's the crown paying, then we're going to see more and better raids,* she'd warned the girls one hot summer day, when they were sloppy in drill.

Mnar opened her hand. "I wondered, because I've gotten the impression over the past decade that your feelings about the academy are ambivalent at best."

"They are," Danet said. "But then I think that having sensible girls in the academy might be a benefit overall."

"Shall I state the obvious?"

"I know all girls aren't sensible. But most of them, at least in my experience, don't think of war as the highest form of life. Yes, I remember my cousin Hard Ride Arvandais. The fact that it's her name that comes up every single time there's any sort of similar discussion proves that she was an outlier, not one of many, doesn't it?"

Mnar spread her hands. "I don't know. My job is not to make policy, but to teach those who serve and protect you policy makers." She smiled wryly. "Speaking as a teacher, one subject I know well is teenagers. I'll confine my advice to this: when those girls come, keep 'em busy. What they do during the competition is less important than what you have them doing all day before you let them have rec time. Give them specific boundaries, or you'll have them running wild all over the academy chasing the boys as soon as they get back from the Great Game, at which time discipline will go straight into the midden."

Danet's lips parted. "I never thought of that."

"I didn't think so. From what I can gather, your own upbringing was a model of order. That won't be true for all these girls. Secondly, if you do decide to bring girls into the academy, start 'em young, just like the boys, as there is no longer a similar standard for girls' training any more than there is for boys outside of the academy. By their teens, habits are already set in. Good and bad."

Danet had been thinking of integrating only the best-trained girls among the lancers—academy jargon for the senior boys—again to serve as examples. For the first time she considered how little she knew about how other girls were raised, and how they acted.

"I'll consider your words," she said, promising herself as she walked out that once she'd finished delving into those letters, she'd better talk it over with Hliss.

ELEVEN

"And so," Danet said the Morning of Spring Day, and Connar's sixteenth Name Day, "as we promised, you may choose one of the eligible royal runners to be your first runner."

Connar stared at her in surprise, trying to hide his dismay. How would he ever be able to hide his secret training from a royal runner always at his elbow?

The words *I don't want one* would not be spoken, because he knew they would ask *why not?*

Danet, seeing his hesitation and completely misinterpreting it, said, "You don't have to follow your brother in this."

Both parents looked at him in approval.

Connar knew they liked him and Noddy doing things together. Then he realized what had hitherto escaped him: Noddy's Name Day had come and gone and *he* didn't have a royal runner as personal runner.

Arrow said, "If you feel the same way, that's all right. It can wait."

"I do," Connar said quickly. "I'm fine with the house runners coming by to sweep and change out the linens. I don't need anything else. I could even do that. We have to over academy-side."

Arrow tapped the breakfast table. "I have to say, I like the self-discipline you two boys are beginning to show. So, Connar, today is your day. What do you want to do?"

"I've got some ideas," Noddy began, and grinned.

"Go on," Arrow said. "Have fun."

As soon as they hit the hallway, Connar said, "I guess you got the conversation about royal runners on your Name Day?"

"Heh, I remember." Noddy smiled, as he invariably did. "Told 'em, why? Even if they give us one, what would he do? Sit around on his thumbs all spring and summer? We can't have 'em in the barracks."

"Right," Connar said. "Right, right!"

"And in winter, I'm so used to seeing to my own tack, there's no real work for a royal runner anyway. It'll be different, I guess, when we finish out, and get orders."

"I feel the same," Connar stated, immensely relieved. By the time they were seniors, the secret training would be over and he would be the best of the lancers.

The next morning Arrow told them it was time to dig out their academy togs to see if they fit.

Connar ran to his room and shut the door. Then, shivering in the frigid air, he opened his summer trunk and pulled out last season's academy clothes. He pulled the tunic-shirt on, and sharp disappointment roiled in him when it fell to the same spot mid-thigh as it had during summer. He already knew that he still had no body hair. As he pulled his winter clothes back on, he reminded himself that most boys didn't get body hair until they'd reached their full height. Tall as Noddy was, he still hadn't a single pit or prick hair. Which meant he was still growing.

Connar heard voices and laughing from Noddy's inner chamber next door. He opened the joining door as Noddy held his tunic shirt up against himself. He'd grown half a palm over winter.

"As I thought," their mother said with a sigh. "If you boys still don't want a royal runner taking charge of your clothes, then get down to the stringer to be measured. I don't want the staff being harassed to make up new clothes in a day."

"They only need to make them for him. I guess I don't need new," Connar muttered bitterly.

Danet could see his deep chagrin, prompting an unwanted, vivid memory of Lanrid towering over her right after her wedding.

She smiled at Connar's flushed face, the bone structure so like Lanrid's, the pout forcing up a vivid memory of Fi.

But he was not them.

She smiled wider, consciously banishing the images. "We'll have new made up for you as well as Noddy, with plenty of growing room. When you do get your growth, it'll probably be suddenly. It certainly was for my brother. One New Year's Week he was exactly my height, then at Midsummer he was a full hand taller. As I recall we had to summon the boot-maker four times that year."

Connar flashed his own dimpled grin that was nothing like either Lanrid's well-remembered leer or Fi's smirk as he ran off with his brother to the tailor to be stringed. Danet reveled in this proof that he was indeed his own self.

The boys waited impatiently for the rest of the week to pass. Suddenly all their winter pursuits were stale. Their minds were already down in the academy as they repeated the same conversations: speculation about what their bunkmates had done over winter, which end of the barracks would be best, what the year would be like.

Finally one morning Arrow sat back after breakfast to say, "It's time to head over academy-side, boys."

Letting out joyful yips, they went to their rooms to get their gear bags full of new clothes, then raced each other downstairs and through the short, mossy-smelling tunnel through the castle wall into the academy, where the balmy weather had brought some early arrivals.

Noddy, as always, looked forward to the year with sunny good will. Connar's joy was mixed with apprehension: would he be the shortest boy in their class by now? And would Hauth have forgotten about him? Or worse, had Hauth been transferred to the army altogether?

Their new digs were on the north side, closer to the stable. One more year put them closer to lancers, but they could easily be given an extra year. It had happened to the previous sixth year class. At the thought of lance training, Connar grimaced. Over winter he'd worked, but now he doubted it was enough.

"Two windows left," Noddy said with quiet satisfaction, then his tone altered. "Hey, got a gut ache?"

Connar looked up to find Noddy regarding him with a puzzled air.

He forced a grin. "Nah. Just griping to myself about how window bunks will be runny shits until the weather warms up."

"It'll warm fast enough," Noddy said, with his usual easy confidence.

Someone had already claimed the prime bunks under the windows and closest to the storage shelves, so Connar and Noddy each took the next window over, across from each other.

As he tidied his clothes into the trunk, Connar wished again that being a prince meant something here. It seemed senseless for it not to, when everybody knew who they were. But if he said anything he'd get howled down for swank, and probably find mud in his bunk, if not worse. And if he said it over castle-side, he'd get lectured at, *the best way to get and keep their respect is to earn it, lally-lally-loo.* If only he could be certain that Hauth was here, and that they'd be meeting!

Finished, they went outside seeking others, everyone exchanging wisecracks and insults while either covertly or openly checking each other out. By nightfall about a third of the barracks had filled. Connar noted with disgust that Ghost Fath was not only half a hand taller, but bigger across the shoulders. He was already one of the best in class. He sure didn't need extra size. At least no one else looked much different.

When the mess bell clanged at last, Connar's eyes searched the place on entry. Among the masters lining the wall...there was Hauth! His one squinty eye, cold as ice, glared right *at* him. What did that mean?

A sharp jab in his side, and an impatient, "Going to stand there all night?" from Cabbage Gannan (of course he was one of the first to arrive, with a family probably glad to get rid of him) jolted Connar into awareness that a huge space had opened between him and the boys forward in line.

He grabbed one of the waiting trays and hustled to catch up, snatching randomly at whatever was in the serving dishes. His mind was on Hauth, full of anxious questions.

Which was what Hauth saw from across the room, and smiled inwardly. He had him, no doubt about it. That mutinous mouth so like Lanrid's. If Lanrid's boy hadn't inherited his grandfather's self-discipline any more than Lanrid had, it was Hauth's duty to train it into him.

He maintained the façade of ignoring Connar through the loud, noisy meal—as the season had not yet officially begun, certain rules were relaxed. He waited until the general scrum on the way out, and when Connar's eyes turned his way for the hundredth time, Hauth twitched his fingers of his free hand down by his side, flashed *Tomorrow, same place,* and watched the revealing flush of triumph in Connar's face.

Connar ran behind the others, almost blind with the joy that he could not reveal. He wouldn't; he recognized that some of this ferocious joy was the secrecy.

After a night of almost no sleep, because he was so afraid of missing the muffled single clang that served as signal for those who had to rise and report for duty before the dawn watch bell, he slid out of bed, the stone floor icy on his stockinged feet. He yanked on his clothes, fingered his hair up into its clasp, carried his boots outside before putting them on, and ran all the way to the appointed spot, relishing his strength.

When he arrived, words spilled out of him. "I worked all winter! Even when we couldn't go outside, I ran up and down the steps in the south tower. And look!"

He glanced about for a spot that wasn't muddy, then did a handstand there in the mud, steadying himself in the slippery mess, and then bent his elbows and lowered his head almost to the ground. His horsetail draggled in the slime as he straightened his arms, then repeated. His face was purple by the time he finished ten.

When he flipped upright again, Hauth caught his horsetail painfully. "Don't let that mud dirty your clothes. How will you explain that?"

Connar stilled, wincing against the yank on his scalp. As Hauth roughly combed the worst of the mud out with the fingers of his free hand, he scolded Connar. "I see you worked hard. That's good. But we've any number of muscle-bound rockheads in the army. Turning yourself into another will never make you into the commander Lanrid would have been proud of. You need to start using some mental discipline, beginning with being aware of your terrain, and then considering the consequences of every action."

Hauth had decided to substitute *Lanrid* for *Mathren*, until he could clean out the prejudice with which Anred, living example of mediocrity, had poisoned the boys.

Connar gulped and stood still for Hauth's ungentle ministrations. When at last Hauth stepped back, his fingers now muddy, he added, "Stop by the stable on your way back, and clean those hands in the horse trough."

Connar jerked his head up, and there was the tight-lipped mutiny again. "That's *all?*"

"It will be all for good if you start whining like a scrub," Hauth retorted.

Connar flushed and belatedly tapped his chest in salute.

"This is going to be a year for strength, yes, but before you get on a horse and pick up a lance, you're going to need the wits to command lancers. I keep telling you, a commander doesn't just give out orders, he lives a life that others want to follow—"

"I know, I know," Connar muttered.

Hauth sensed that he was losing Connar by repeating himself. Annoyed, he tried again. "Watch the leaders among the seniors. You'll never see them lazing around. They work hardest and longest. As for your wits, because the king doesn't see fit to educate your brain, we'll work on that, too." As soon as the words were out, he knew they were a mistake.

Sure enough, Connar's brows met in an angry line parallel to his mouth. "Da makes sure I get the same tutors my brother does."

"Oh, yes, the king always treats the two of you very strictly the same. The trouble is, most people are unaware that no one is exactly the same as anyone else, so though it might be considered *fair* by some, it's never *just.*"

"What do you mean by just?" Connar asked warily.

"Let's take your winter training, for example. It's too easy. That's because Olavayir-Ain is not nearly as smart as you are. Yes, he's brave, and honest, and strong as a horse. But who's the real commander in your private games? I'll wager anything it's you."

"Noddy isn't stupid," Connar said, eyes narrowing.

"I never said he was. I said that he's not as smart as you. If I were in charge of your tutoring, I'd have you working with the guild masters, and learning affairs of state, while he works on his reading. But no doubt that will come in time," Hauth amended, seeing the resentment tightening Connar's shoulders. "I know the king counts on you to help the Sierlaef when he inherits the crown."

And if that didn't provoke the boy to start thinking, *Why shouldn't I inherit it,* then Hauth would have to knock some sense into him. Connar was stubborn, clinging to those sentimental prejudices so convenient to the king and queen, but then Lanrid had been stubborn in his own way, too.

Hauth said, "So there will be other exercises. And as before, a missed day without real cause—any sign of whining or slacking—and we're done."

Connar jerked his fingers up in another salute.

"Then go." Hauth lifted his cane toward the path leading around the back barn. "I'll see you here tomorrow, ready to work."

Hauth watched him run off, and let the smile come as he headed over to the nearest rain barrel to wash his hand.

And that set the tone for the rest of spring.

Connar mastered the urge to tell Noddy; though he knew Noddy would be thrilled on his behalf, he also couldn't keep a secret.

Connar always took defeat hard, the more because Noddy won every single competition that tested strength or endurance, not only among their own class, but against many of the older boys. And they weren't letting him win.

Connar felt that a prince should always win, or how could he really lead? But as training matches came and went through days that steadily grew longer and warmer, the sharpness of defeat was undercut by his secret training, the kind of training a prince *should* have.

One gratifying thing happened when spring's mild afternoons began to promise the heat of summer. Connar leaped down from his horse, by habit ignoring the pinch of his toes in his boots, when Noddy signed, *You all right?*

"Of course I am," Connar exclaimed, surprised and impatient—then he looked down at his feet. Then up. "Oh."

"Outgrown your boots, have you?" Noddy asked with ready sympathy. He was very familiar with the sensation.

"I have," Connar said, and exulted inwardly. New boots had to mean he was finally growing, didn't it?

It's human nature to expand wherever space permits.

In anticipation of the girls coming, Hliss had to clear her people and supplies out of the old queen's training barracks that three, five, eight years ago they had slowly taken over as temporary solutions, now that the castle population had grown, and showed every sign of expanding with the king's plans. The new young captains in the fledgling King's Riders had already filled all the old barracks on guard-side, as Arrow wanted them serving with Noth's guard for a year before he posted them elsewhere.

Not that Hliss asked. Part of her quiet campaign to keep Andas—now toddling from puddle to puddle in the nearby kitchen gardens and helping the younger kitchen children chase seed-raiding spring birds—from the military world was to never ask Arrow about academy or army subjects.

If he talked about them, she listened, but never offered a comment. And so there was always a firm but gentle wall between her wishes and his desire to coax her into letting Andas attend the academy when he turned ten. Often when they parted, she believed that time would firm her wishes, while he was thinking, *There's still time to convince her.*

Mild as she was, Hliss was still Mother's daughter. When Connar, Noddy, and Bun brought toys for little Andas, the dolls and toy horses and dogs and cats all stayed, but the toy swords vanished as soon as the boys' footsteps diminished. That is, if Danet didn't spot and confiscate them first.

As spring ripened into summer, those old barracks were swept out, repaired, and furnishings brought out of storage. Right before Andahi Day, carefully selected older runners were installed at either end of that wing, and the soberest of younger runners, including Lineas, squeezed into the tiny chambers across from each other at midpoint.

As Hliss and one of her older weavers stood watching the runners cart their gear to the girls' barracks, the weaver said, "What is the gunvaer expecting out of these girls?"

Hliss said, "She wants to give the girls a chance to meet their future husbands, the way she never did."

The old weaver grunted, stealing a glance at Hliss's serene conviction. Much as she respected the stories she'd heard about Mother Farendavan, she thought that neither of her daughters had any conception of what might motivate girls not raised in that strict atmosphere.

Time would tell.

And so the day arrived when those stone walls rang for the first time in over a century with shrill, excited female voices: three parties had met on the road, and decided to ride in together.

Runners led the girls' escorts one way, and the girls themselves finally quieted long enough to be heard: "The gunvaer will address all your questions."

The word *gunvaer* diminished the noise to a susurrus of whispered words. The senior royal runner said, "I'll explain the layout of the castle as we go."

Pony Yvanavayir paid little attention, as she had grown up in an exact replica of this castle, built by one of her more ambitious and infamous ancestors, who was executed after leading an attack on this very castle.

Most of the girls had grown up hearing stories handed down through their families about great-mothers during the queen's training days; it was the beloved Hadand-Gunvaer Deheldegarthe who had, in fact, stopped Pony's ancestor in a duel before the throne. Not that Pony had much interest in history.

Her interest was entirely bound up in meeting the other jarls' daughters — and demonstrating her skills with the bow, which she was quite proud of. Of course she would be the best. Hadn't her father said she was the best, as good as her heroic mother?

She also wanted to meet the academy boys.

She wasn't the only one.

Soon gunvaer and girls faced one another, Danet seeing a crowd of young faces wearing a variety of expressions, and they a tall, brown, straight-backed woman, her unmemorable face dominated by a pair of very sharp eyes.

Is that something they taught gunvaers, Genis Fath, sister to Ghost Fath, was wondering, as Danet spoke her carefully planned short speech of welcome. Except that hadn't this one come to her rank by accident? Even so, she had a stare on her as pointed as a sword.

Short as her planned speech was, Danet saw within three sentences that their attention was already drifting. So she got right to it. "The academy is out of bounds for you," she said abruptly, and sure enough all those wandering gazes snapped right back to her. "Once the boys return from the Great Game, this area will be out of bounds for them, a caning offense," she went on.

Caning—that caught their attention. Side-eyes of consternation flickered between some of the girls. Pony, who was the spoiled darling of a household of men, asked with barely concealed impatience, "Then how are we supposed to meet the boys?" She ignored the flicked looks from others, with the confidence of one who had grown up the undisputed leader of the girls at home.

"Once they return, those who get rec time will meet you in the city," Danet said. "They'll show you all their recreation lairs, and you can whoop it up as much as you want. But that's when you have earned recreation time."

Silence.

"Earned?" Genis said cautiously, as Pony looked askance.

Thank you for the warning, Mnar, Danet was thinking, then she said, "I've been considering restoring the queen's training."

Gasps of surprise, and in a few, the burning gazes of delight, met this news.

"But I won't be able to convince the king that girls are anywhere near as disciplined, or as skilled, as boys, if you're chasing boys all over the castle from first to late bells," Danet finished.

Some looked down guiltily, and Pony flushed. At home, where she was the only female of rank, she was used to doing what she wanted.

"So we'll be busy with our own competition," Danet finished. "Any girl who hasn't got basic skills isn't going to be allowed to go out on the parade ground to serve as a laughingstock."

Chins came up, and mouths tightened, heartening Danet: whatever else these girls might be like, it was apparent they were certain of their skills.

And so it proved over the next few days, as the last of the girls arrived from the farther jarlates.

Danet watched from the queen's suite, which she'd discovered overlooked what had been the old queen's training grounds.

The day the girls were all there, she stood at the windows, her hands clutching her elbows, as she watched those young bodies moving with blithe assurance, and struggled within herself.

What did she really want here? In the old days of tents and plains wandering, women had had a purpose long since superseded by the move to castles. Did she want the girls learning that knife style that the royal runners learned? Who would they use it against—and how long before the men took it away again, and made it their own?

And why shouldn't they, she argued with herself. Were they not all on the same side? War between the sexes would be horrible....

Any kind of war was horrible.

Once again the weight of responsibility pressed on her: she, a single being, could make a decision that affected the kingdom. She hated how that awareness made her question herself into an anxious fret, usually late at night, but there was no use in whining. She could hear Mother's emphatic scold. Mother's solution to every dilemma was to *stop complaining and do your duty*.

That night she ventured into revealing some of her worries to Jarid Noth, and as always he listened sympathetically, but he invariably spoke like a military man. "If we don't have order—everyone understanding the same rules, and obeying commands—then we get trouble."

"We also get trouble if the commands are senseless," she retorted as she leaned against him.

She felt his sigh, then he said, "You won't give senseless commands. Is that what worries you?"

"I don't worry about giving foolish commands so much as I do about giving the wrong ones. One person in command...." She shook her head.

They had been lying in bed, but here he hoisted up on his elbow to gaze down at her, moonlight highlighting the surprise lift of his brows. "You're against kingship? But what else is there? We can't all be giving each other orders!" He snorted. "I know the argument, what about bad kings. My answer to that is, people have a way of getting rid of really terrible kings."

She knew she would get no answers from him, and because she couldn't even express what it was she sought, she let him sidetrack himself into enumerating the sanguinary ends of previous bad kings, which just goes to show (he rapped his knuckles on his forehead for emphasis) that people want order.

What kind of order was that? People mostly want to be left alone, she thought before she drifted into sleep. But Mother would say such an attitude was another word for selfishness, and avoidance of duty.

After restless dreams, she woke when Noth readied himself to depart for the garrison. She forced herself to get up and dress for drill, when Arrow's impatient rap presaged his abrupt appearance. "We've been back for two days. When're you letting those girls loose?"

"Tonight," she said. "Today is our last drill."

Arrow expelled his breath in obvious relief. "If you hadn't, Andaun swore he'd have a mutiny on his hands." He stuck his head out the door, yelled, "Tell the Headmaster to cut 'em loose," then popped back in again, grinning ruefully. "Pity the shopkeepers!"

"As long as the girls spend as freely as the boys do, no one will make a peep," Danet predicted. "And it isn't as if the taverns and shops didn't have plenty of warning."

The academy boys were used to either being ignored by the city girls, or regarded as flirt-worthy but little else. And while the pleasure houses held the obvious attractions, here were new girls besides sisters and female cousins who spoke the language of horses, territorial patrol, and the drill — their language. One of them might even be a boy's future wife. The rest wanted to be admired for their own sakes. Many looked for nothing more than a night of dancing, bragging, and maybe a quick trip somewhere private.

The shops and taverns whose trade was primarily with the academy had all been warned to close up by the end of Third Watch, as the Victory Day competitions would begin early the following day, and of course the academy students would be celebrating even more at the end of it.

The girls, who brushed and braided shining hair up into fox-ear loops or coronets, tied their sashes tighter, and sashayed through the castle gates into King's Street, high voices chattering, avid eyes seeking out the teenage boys in their neatly sashed gray coats, their horsetails brushed and their blackweave riding boots polished.

They converged in Market Square as the sun sank toward the west, braying laughter meeting high giggles. Boys and girls both prowled around in clumps, then in twos and threes as brothers, cousins, and friends wrangled sisters and girl-cousins into introductions, and vice versa.

Eventually they began to disperse in all directions, most to the boys' hangouts, where the drums came out for singing and dancing. For the first time, those male precincts featured women's dances, to enthusiastic approval — especially the knife dance, when some of the girls did whirling and spinning tricks with steel, causing roars of approval. As darkness closed in, some paired off and disappeared into the starry night.

At home in Yvanavayir, Pony, as a motherless moppet, had become the mascot to the entire family, but now only her father still fondly regarded her that way. What had been adorable at age six had become less so for her brothers by age ten, and downright annoying by the time she reached sixteen

—an irritation spiked as she began flirting her way through their friends among the Riders and other castle youth, dropping them without a second thought.

Consequently there was little habit of conversation between Pony and her brothers. She gave a perfunctory look for her brother Manther, now a senior, then shrugged him off; she could find someone else who could point out her betrothed, Ganred Noth.

It was Dannor Ndarga, regarded by the girls as the prettiest among their group, who spotted the problem, and in her typically friendly manner, left her own group and towed Pony toward several boys who stood in a knot. "Are you looking for Rat? Here he is! He's my third cousin, I think, or fourth?"

The pause turned into a silence as Ganred Noth, given this opportunity to speak, just stood there, staring at the tops of his boots.

Pony said, "Rat?"

"Everybody calls him Rat," Dannor said cheerfully. "His little brother is Mouse. Have fun!"

She ran off, leaving Pony staring at her future, who stood like a skinny post, his squinty eyes under his broad forehead shifting to either side of her and back, making him actually look like a rodent. At least he didn't have beaver teeth, Pony thought, like the crown prince.

For the first time in her life, she felt obliged make an effort, and started in with questions about where he liked to go for rec time, and what he liked to do.

Every question elicited ever shorter responses as he stared, stunned, at this self-possessed, golden-haired girl. His shoulders hitched tighter as he felt his childhood stutter threatening a return. And clamped his lips shut.

She found herself talking more and more to fill in the painful silence, until one of the girls called, "Let's do the knife dance!"

Pony had never worked so hard in her life, and for what? Much better-looking boys at home fell all over themselves if she glanced their way, but this rat of a Rat was *impossible.*

The future could take care of itself. Right now, she intended to find someone cute, and have some fun. She flipped her braids back and walked away, from sheer habit expecting him to at least catch up, or call, or *something.*

But a quick glance showed him standing there as if his boots had been nailed to the ground.

She turned away in disgust, and scanned the boys, lighting on the best dancer among them, a pretty boy with white-blonde hair. But everyone else seemed to be watching him, too. He was surrounded by girls.

Used to being the center of admirers at Yvanavayir, she had no idea how to break through the group to get him to notice her. So she danced harder and leaped higher, twirling twice and three times instead of once, until her robe whirled about her hips and her braids came loose and streamed out like shining ropes, but was he watching her? No.

Time sped by unnoticed until the bells rang, and everybody started moving toward the doors. Already? She swayed, suddenly tired, then spotted red-haired, freckled Lineas, their runner guide, and said, "What's going on?"

"The boys are under strict orders to report back within a glass after the bells," Lineas said. "The Victory Day competition will start early. The gunvaer ordered me to remind you all that you need your sleep."

Pony sighed. She'd been ready to ignore the bells, but not if there wasn't anyone interesting to ignore them with.

Lineas walked away, girls spotting her and joining up from all directions. Tired and irritated, Pony followed as two of the girls wove unsteadily, singing an old ballad and cackling inanely whenever they forgot words.

"Try putting 'kissed' in place of anything you forget," one suggested, poking her friend — or trying to.

"Jayad and Cassad galloping thunder,

forefront the enemy — uh, uh...."

"Kissed!"

"Forefront the enemy, Gannan kissed the.... Kissed who?"

"Horseshoe Toraca!"

"Then the rhythm's off-gait...."

They dissolved into drunken laughter.

Pony scowled at the crapulous pair, their braids half undone (she was unaware of her own state), their robes slopped with drink. At least they weren't Yvanavayirs. They'd be terrible at tomorrow's competition.

Too bad, she gloated.

She would ride them all down, in spite of pretty white-haired boys who didn't look at her once.

TWELVE

Excerpt from Lineas's journal:

...and so, mindful of the new orders to be more observant of what is, instead of seeing what I want to see, I was glad that I was finished with the visiting big girls. There was nothing more for me to do. The others had games duty, and the big girls' own runners were responsible for them.

It was at first very strange to be at the Victory Day competition, and to hear girls' voices. I tried not to think about myself as I walked about. I attempted to empty my mind and observe.

Things I observed: the gunvaer was there. She had stopped going four or five years ago—

Now she was there to see the girls, and everybody knew it. Liet insisted the gunvaer used to sit next to the king with papers in hand, and watch the sky as much as she watched the boys. Then she stopped going at all. I could see it in the way they looked up at the stands, and in their straightened posture, and manners.

She watched with that close attention that makes everyone want to please her. I saw her smile twice. One time was when Pandet Tlen shot three reds in a row at the gallop, and the other three were close—I think she might even have hit it six times, but by then the dust was so thick I'm surprised Pandet saw the targets at all.

The girls rode out hard. In that they were not so different from the boys. I wonder if it is something in our age, or if it's just the excitement of the game. While it goes on everyone is giddy, and to win is everything, and nothing else matters. It is the opposite of what we fledglings have been taught—that our strength is in our trust of one another and our vows.

But it is so exciting to <u>watch</u>. I wonder if this is what they talk about, feeling the effects of drink, which makes everything bright and intense in a way that withers to tawdry and cold when the drink wears off.

When I was sent to fetch water, I heard Old Sartoran at the side-stand, by the barrel. Those of us who had rec time, or were within call, watched from there.

Though they had their backs to me I recognized Quill and Vanadei. They look so much alike. Perhaps it is because they have shared a room ever since they were little. And yet I recognized instantly which was Quill and which Vanadei, though they both wear runner robes, and their hair is the same shade of dark brown. No, not the same. Quill's has more red, and more curl. But I hadn't noticed that difference at first, so how had I known which was which? Why is the eye and ear so much faster than the conscious mind? The angle of Quill's shoulders, the way he leaned his arm against the fence, even the sound of his voice, which has gone deep into his chest as they talked over the academy seniors' sword competition.

I won't write down everything they said, as I know I will never care about who they thought the best, and who the worst, or how they evaluated strength and skill in individuals. I don't know those academy boys.

My observation was this: the first time I was sent for water, the boys finished and the girls ran out by the time I got my turn. I passed by Quill and Vanadei again so that I could observe them from the front. Quill's expression was very intent. I know his face so very well, but I discovered that I don't know __that__ expression, except in that his eyes didn't blink but once despite the dust.

Though Vanadei also watched, he wasn't intent in the same way. But when I came back a third time, the boys were out again, doing their ride and shoot. This time it was Vanadei who was intent, but Quill was looking more at where the girls had gathered to sit on the corral fence than he was at the boys.

Because of Mnar's orders, I asked Liet of the seniors later if she noticed the same, and could name that expression. She is the most patient of the seniors, but she laughed at me. Ndand said with that twist to her eyebrows she gets when she's being mocking, Lineas, isn't it obvious? Quill was undressing the girls. (She tapped her head.) Here. Dei was undressing the boys.

Liet hissed at her.

What? Ndand exclaimed, her hands out wide, palms up. You know they do it.

So do we, Liet said, and pointed at me. The point is, Lineas isn't out of smocks. Not appropriate till she wears a robe.

Ndand gave me owl eyes. How old are you, Lineas, you have to be sixteen, or near, as I'm nineteen and I remember when you came, I was exactly — no, no, Liet, I'll stop, never mind.

She walked away and shook her head, and Liet said to me and her voice was kind, Never mind. You'll wake up one of these days. There is no hurry.

I went away, feeling very confused, because I __am__ awake, if they mean loving someone. I've been awake since I was very small. But all these pages, like Restday last, when C. brushed against me, and I thought he did it on purpose, and the day of the thunderstorm when I helped Bun with the pups, and the princes came in and he smiled at me —

There. Six pages! I ripped them out. It's stupid to imagine his interest and speculate on our conversation. I saw what I wanted to see, I know that now, because he didn't have __that__ look. Not even a little. Though I wanted him to. I'm furniture, just as I thought.

What IS love? I thought I knew....

With the girls and boys went a copy of Danet's carefully worded letter that made her request an order: for the first time in Marlovan history, jarlans were to accompany jarls when the latter arrived for the next Convocation.

And meantime, in the interim year, girls would be once again invited to the Games, an invitation endorsed with enthusiasm by most of the girls who had been to the first.

Even Pony, having arrived home to Yvanavayir, tossed her glossy braids back and announced that her relay team had won the fifty-pace gallop-and-shoot, and came in second in the saddle and racing relay. She didn't mention that she had placed second and third (at least to older girls) in the individual competitions for bow and riding, and as for that boring old odni knife fighting, she'd been terrible, but so had other girls, at least — few of them knew much more than the knife dance.

Next year she would do much better.

Her father, assuming that meant more discipline, clapped her on the back. "I knew you'd make me proud! Did you meet the Noth boy you're betrothed to?"

"Yes," she said, and he didn't recognize the danger in her jaw jut.

"Good," the jarl exclaimed. "A third son, brought in by the jarlan's second marriage, but Feravayir is larger than most jarlates. Most three jarlates. Some say a kingdom on its own, and the boy is one of the best. The king has his eye on him for future command, that's what everyone says."

Pony was going to snap that she didn't care, that she'd rather stay in Yvanavayir, but the visit to the royal city had caused her to think for the first time of the future. Specifically about when Eaglebeak, her older brother, would bring home his own betrothed, one of the famous Cassads. This Chelis Cassad (who had *not* been in the royal city) would be the jarlan, and Pony would have to take her orders. She already hated her.

Pony returned no answer, and threw herself even more violently back into her usual habits, flirting recklessly with every fellow who looked her way. But she still brooded about the boy whose name she'd discovered on her last day in the royal city: Anderle Fath, the pale-haired one the academy boys all called Ghost.

Danet's letter made its way to the rest of the jarlans.

When the Jarlan of Telyer Hesea received it, she took a day or two to think it over, then one morning summoned her children to her study, where she read out the letter.

Her second son, Barend, (the one Danet thought was a girl named Chelis) looked up at the last.

Little disturbed his tranquility. "That doesn't sound like we're being accused of deceit," he said. Unlike his distant cousin in Marthdavan, who had been making trouble about being denied what sounded like prime fun that every other second son in the kingdom got to have, Barend was glad he'd never been forced to go to the academy. He loathed morning drill, and skipped it as often as he dared. "If they want a girl to come along, and Colt doesn't want to go, you've only to offer Cousin Chelis in my place."

"I'm not that worried about your cousin standing in for you in the betrothal treaty. The fact that all these years have gone by without any of the trouble that has always beset the Olavayirs gives me to hope that the gunvaer will forgive our deceit, if she even finds out. As for this summons, it appears that *all* the jarlans, and not just me, are being summoned to the royal city. This is a first," the jarlan added, for despite her words, her tone betrayed uncertainty. "Since there is no real alternative short of leaving the country at the gallop, of course I must go."

She paused and regarded her niece, whom the Riders had nicknamed Colt when she was barely three. The girl stood straight before her, her fine dark hair pulled up high into a boy's horsetail, her coat the Rider's gray, her sash worn at her hips as the boys did, not round her waist. She stood with her booted feet planted solidly, hands behind her back, the way the Riders waited at attention when receiving orders.

In contrast, Barend lounged peacefully by the table, where he could watch the passing clouds out of the window, and try to define the exact shades in the light as it passed the edge, then hid behind the mass of gray, then emerged again into golden brightness. He contemplated measuring where the sun must be to thread gold through the subtleties of other colors.

Carleas was so used to her son's wandering attention that she gave him no heed now. Her concern at this moment was Colt. "I know you don't want to ride with the girls to the games come summer," she began slowly.

Colt flattened her hand and struck it away. "I don't ride with them the rest of the year. It would throw us all off our gait."

Carleas approached her idea tentatively. "Ever since I was a child, we've ignored the government as much as possible, as we could do little about it, short of uprisings. Mathren Olavayir made it fairly clear what would happen to those," she added.

Colt stood impassively, and Barend gazed out the window. Mathren was just a name to them both, Carleas could see that much.

So Carleas left that subject, and got right to her plan. "I thought about taking you with me, Colt. Because there's a rumor from at least three sources I trust that the gunvaer is summoning us to talk about starting the queen's training again." She tapped a letter on her desk. "I know you wanted to go to the academy...."

"But queen's training would be more of what the girls do, right?" Colt stated.

And here was the crux of the matter. Carleas said, "I know the Riders accept you as one of them—"

"Because I *am* one," Colt stated, her heavy brows like Carleas's own drawing down. She had the same domed forehead Carleas's sister had had, and Colt's expressions so often brought her sharply to mind, bringing up all the old grief. "I'm a Rider," Colt said. "I'm a boy to them. To me."

Carleas gazed at her, then shot a puzzled glance at her son, who just a week ago had been wearing that flowing gown from overseas, his hair hanging down his back, as he walked around in a circle up in the sun room.

She said in a bewildered tone, "Are we at fault here, for causing you two to trade places?"

Barend looked up at that, his usually vague gaze suddenly acute. "Fault?" he repeated.

Colt braced her shoulders back, her chin jerking up, a boy's gesture, and entirely unconscious. "Why's there 'fault' here? Who did anything wrong?"

The jarlan's glance toward Barend caused him to say, "Did it bother you, my wearing that Colendi silk? I told everyone, I wanted the feel of it, the move of it so I can get the folds right in my design."

Colt turned her palm up. "*You* know how he is, when he designs a new tapestry."

Carleas let out a slow breath. Yes, it was ill-advised to think that a single cause lay behind the paths her two had taken. In truth, Barend had never done anything but the basic lessons in self-defense training, and that with an attitude of weary endurance, even when he was seven years old. His life was entirely bound up in color and design, pattern and texture, and had been since he could hold a chalk in his chubby fist. No surprise. The Cassads tended toward artists. Colt had from the earliest age wanted to ride with the Riders, and the swap had been so easy that—Carleas saw now—she had never raised a question about its very ease. She and the jarl had just been vaguely grateful that the deception had been so simple. Unlike it had been for their connections in Marthdavan.

Carleas laid aside the question of the royal city. "Colt. Would you say that you are a boy inside your skin, but given the wrong form?"

Colt shrugged sharply. "Mostly, I don't think about it at all. Unless someone starts in with how I ought to start running with the girls, I should braid my hair, get a robe." She made a face. "Just because everyone else does. In truth, wearing a robe makes me feel naked. I don't even know why it's the way it is, that only boys wear coats—"

Barend's mild voice interjected here, "I can tell you that."

"I don't care," Colt said impatiently, but at the twin looks of quiet reproach the jarlan and Barend turned her way, her tone became less combative. "But I'll listen."

"The Marlovans have no drawings from the old days," Barend said with the assurance of one who had spent a great deal of time looking. "But the Iascans did. Especially our family. All in the old archives, the really old ones, at Telyer Tower. When the Marlovans left the Venn, everyone wore coats. It's always winter up there, or so the ballads say. The Marolo-Venn moved south to the warmer lands and they turned to robes in summer. When the Marlovans invaded the Iascans, everything changed fast, as near as I can tell, including trying armor, though it interfered with fast riding, and so, during summer campaigns, they stayed with robes, but for winter brought out their old Venn coats...."

Colt suppressed a sigh, already bored, but the jarlan listened to what she already knew with as much of an air of interest as she could project, as her son seldom spoke even this much. Most of the time his mind seemed to be somewhere else, which was another Cassad trait. At least, she thought gratefully as he described various types of clothing tried in the days when Marlovans first took to life in castles, he lost himself in tapestries and weaving instead of the world of ghosts.

"...and many later ballads say that the first Montreivayir king stabbed Savarend Montredavan-An in the back. But in fact, he cut his throat from behind, and the jarls knew it, though the king wouldn't let that be written in the archives. His jarls took to sitting in wingchairs, so they couldn't be attacked from the back, and many began putting that little band of steel in the high collar of their coats, the way we have it now. According to the drawings these were really high collars, almost to the ears. You couldn't get a knife past steel. And the king knew why, but he could say nothing. But everyone liked the coats with the high collar so the habit stayed, and since you can't put a collar on a cotton-linen robe, much less a collar with steel in it, the coats required heavier construction." He indicated the seams on himself.

Carleas thanked her son, and said, "I remember Great-Aunt Lissanre Dei always saying that there is a story behind every fashion." She turned to her daughter. "As for our previous subject. You probably don't remember Great-Aunt Ndara, on the Danold side."

When Colt shrugged again, Carleas said, "She was born a boy. Said from a child she was a girl. The Danolds offered to send her—when she was a him, you understand—to Sartor, where they have mages that can emulate what shapeshifters can apparently do without much effort. Only it takes time, it's apparently painful, as you are forcing change within your body, which takes time for healing even when there is no weapon involved. And it's expensive. Though the Deis in Sartor can well afford it. Anyway, the Danolds, I was told, wanted her, when still him, to wait until age twenty, because young people's minds so often change. As soon as that twentieth Name Day came off he went, and came back Ndara, but said that the transformation was the worse because they'd waited so long, for all the physical changes that had to be undone. They should have sent Ndara earlier."

Both were paying attention now.

Carleas said, "So, is this something you want, Colt? Because you have a much closer claim to the Sartoran branch of the Dei family than the Danolds, through me and your mother. We could find a way to share the cost."

Colt glanced down her male-clad body—*his* body when he rode in the sun and wind as a fellow Rider—as though seeing what wasn't there, or evaluating what was. "I don't know...I didn't know you could do that."

"Outlander mages do a lot more things than we Marlovans are aware of, apparently. I could write to my Dei cousins today, if this is something you want," Carleas said. "You still wouldn't be able to go to the academy, as you'd return at, or older, than the age of the seniors."

Colt's brow furrowed thoughtfully. "I'd be away a long time?"

"I believe at least a year. There's the healing and adjustment. We can find more out."

"I'll think about that," Colt said, but the aggrieved look returned. "I wish you'd asked when I was five or six. No, don't speak. I know you'll say I was too young. I didn't even think about those things then. I was glad because Cousin Inda let me do sword with the rest of the boys. But the academy, why *is* it a *man's* life? We shouldn't have to go to Sartor to grow a prick. I mean...what if somebody, like, oh, Cousin Chelis, who likes being a girl, wanted to go to the academy, and she was as good as any boy?"

The jarlan met Colt's gaze somewhat helplessly. She had grown up knowing that the Cassads could be odd, and her son becoming a tapestry artist—an art customarily belonging to the women, and in some places jealously guarded—didn't disturb her. Colt was half-Dei, a family for all its faults usually known for practicality as well as ambition, but she also was half-Noth, and nobody ever equated the Noths with anything but stolidity, strength, and steadiness.

Colt snorted, glanced Barend's way, and suddenly recollected a story he'd told her after one of his delvings in the family archives. "I wish I was Yxubarec. They just think whatever form they want to be."

Barend blinked, his usually serene brow puckering with mild disapprobation. "They mimic forms. Then they usually kill the person they mimicked."

"Exactly." Carleas brought up her palm in a ward. "Child, aside from their evil practices, they aren't truly *human*. They just take human form as a game. Male or female, it means nothing to them."

"I don't see that being human is much to brag on," Colt stated, then sighed. "Thanks, Ma. I know you mean well. Let me think on it."

"Do. And if you choose to ride into the royal city with me next Convocation, when women are called for the first time, then that would be fine, too."

THIRTEEN

Despite the alterations reported above, it was said by many later that this next two years saw everything begin to change.

Change is a constant; though one summer follows the next, each summer could not have occurred but for the events in the previous. Incidents that snag at memory take on importance, and later, when the surrounding days are forgotten, might seem isolated. More subtle variations in the daily routine sink into the deep waters of our minds, whence they might furnish the stuff of dreams, but otherwise remain unremembered.

One change that was remarkable only for how unremarkable it was considered at the time: when Lineas reached sixteen, the same age as the princess, she was officially made Bun's royal runner.

Because we can never see the importance of events except in hindsight, I think it's interesting to observe that no one in the royal castle outside of Lineas herself regarded her appointment as an event of note.

It was a dreary day in winter, everyone's breath clouding as Mnar and Lineas — the latter self-conscious in her new dark blue runner's robe — walked together down to the royal floor below, and then to the princess's rooms. There, the castle runners who usually dealt with the royal children's things stood in a row, waiting, aware that the gunvaer was expected at any moment. The princess was there as well, for once almost still, which she rarely was unless asleep. Her merry eyes in her round face, and her short upper lip, made her look more like a rabbit than ever as she regarded Mnar and Lineas solemnly.

Danet had been alerted by Sage, her third runner, that all were assembled, so she set aside her own work and walked past her sons' closed doors to her daughter's rooms.

Danet said, "Lineas, welcome." She turned to the runners lined against the wall. "Your chain of command now goes directly from Hadand-Edli...." At this rare mention of her given name, poor Bunny jumped, her eyes blinking rapidly. "...to Lineas, and to you."

The castle runners saluted, and at a wave of Danet's hand, filed out the door. Mnar followed; everything she had to say had been said already.

Danet turned to Lineas and her daughter, and said with such fondness that there was no sting whatever in her customarily acerb voice, "Bunny, you might be a thoughtless creature at times, but you show responsibility when it matters. So consider said the lecture about giving no orders that you wouldn't want Lineas to have to bring to me. She's trained to be loyal to you, but you must repay that loyalty by earning it. Lineas, I give the care of my daughter into your hands. Serve, defend, and protect her."

"I will," Lineas said, hand to heart.

Danet went out, utterly unaware of the tension in the room going with her, commensurate with the respect everyone held for her. In her mind, she was still Mother Farendavan's dutiful daughter, of no particular looks or smarts or talent, trained to her duty.

Alone, the two girls turned to one another. They scarcely drew breath before the clatter of boot heels approached, and the two princes appeared in the open door.

Lineas's gaze went straight to Connar, who was, if possible, even more beautiful seen up close than glimpsed down the hall, or across a courtyard.

"There you are, royal runner," Noddy said, his deepening voice still very much an adolescent honk. "Heyo, Bun, never thought it'd be you, first one of us to get a personal runner."

Connar was thinking just as well he didn't have to deal with an extra pair of eyes shadowing him, but he wasn't going to say that. "Good, someone we can send to get us a jug of bristic of our own," he joked.

Lineas suppressed the shiver ringing through her nerves at the sound of Connar's voice. It was so unlike any other voice, slightly husky, but it sounded somehow like music. Though she'd never heard him sing.

With her mother's admonition echoing in her ears, Bun said firmly, "No, you won't. She's mine-mine-*mine*. You get your own bristic. I hate that stuff anyway."

The boys laughed and clattered out again, Lineas fading from their minds within five steps out the door. Not so for poor Lineas, still enjoying the intensity of her secret love; that brief moment when eyes met eyes, forgotten in five heartbeats by him, from her earned a page and a half of description and speculation in her journal that night.

So Lineas's bright red hair was seen even more often on the royal floor, which no one remarked except Lineas herself. She poured out her feelings in pages and pages of minute, deeply coded journaling with the tireless ardency peculiar to the age of sixteen.

Connar's own passion was reserved for hard winters of exercise in his own room, and for readings of battles in records passed to him by Hauth. These records had been hoarded in the dolphin-clan of the Olavayirs, brought out by Mathren Olavayir for training Nighthawk Company. These papers had been rescued and preserved by Hauth when the company broke up in bloody violence after Thad tried to take command by having all naysayers flogged—and ended up dead himself, having never realized that his own authority had vanished the day Mathren dropped to the stone floor in Evred's tower, felled by Jarend Olavayir's fist.

This treasured sheaf of papers contained not only records of Olavayir dolphin-clan heroes, but—valued most of all—One-Eyed Cama Tyavayir's reminiscences of his academy days and the battles after, as recorded by one of his sons.

A small portion of the papers was about Inda-Harskialdna, who was only in the academy two seasons. Most of the academy stories were Cama One-Eye's memories of Evred-Harvaldar's academy wargame wins and losses, usually against the equally famous Whipstick Noth, father of all three present branches of the Noth family. Cama insisted that Inda's plans lay at the root of these academy battle games.

The latter half of the memoir described Cama One-Eye's governing of the lawless north in the days after the Venn invasion, interspersed with conversations with someone known only as Fox, who described Inda's battles at sea. Initially, Connar skimmed these sea battles with little interest, as they were mostly about ships, maritime customs, and foreign kings. His attention was reserved entirely for the wargame accounts, each with a name that began with "Inda." Inda's River Defense. Inda's Two Hill Flank Decoy. Inda's whirtler arrow signals.

Most of those academy sites still existed, and many even had the same names. What Connar picked up in poring over these accounts was that terrain was important, and so, on wintry days between snow storms, when he and Noddy went riding, he explored those sites as closely as he could, without ever telling Noddy why he chose this or that destination.

Noddy never asked. He just liked to be outside, under the broad sky, no noise except the crunch of hooves and the rush of wind through the trees.

The time arrived at last to be measured for their first coats, Connar intensely relieved to discover that he'd grown nearly a palm in height that winter.

The day their coats were ready, of course they had to stun the castle denizens with their manly appearance. They set out full of expectation, which was soon dashed. Though Connar noted the lingering glances of castle girls their own age, he wasn't quite sure what to do about those. Anyway, the people he wanted to impress—guards and castle staff—didn't seem to see anything new until Noddy dropped hints with the subtlety of horse farts.

"Ah, yes, seniors at last," the baker said with good humor. "Very fine! Would you like a tartlet? Just fresh out of the oven."

Connar was disappointed, but not enough to forego tarts. Noddy grinned. "I hear the pups back there in the churn court."

Connar shrugged, but followed willingly enough. He wanted to sit and eat, so as not to slop blueberry mixture on his fine new coat, and the barns weren't far, with their small courtyard annex.

They found the castle children there, playing some kind of tag game. "Heyo, there's Andas," Noddy exclaimed.

One of the grubby four-year-olds looked up, his face breaking into a grin. They smiled back. Noddy broke his tart in half and held it out. "Want some? It's blueberry."

"Yes," Andas yelled, and pattered toward them, half the other little ones on his heels.

Noddy handed down the pastry, which Andas turned to share out among his friends, but there wasn't nearly enough. While some stood around eating and then licking sticky, grimy fingers, the slow ones who got nothing began squalling.

The young kitchen helper in charge of them called, "Will you watch them if I go see if there are any more?"

Noddy shrugged. "Sure!"

Andas and the others turned speculative gazes up at Connar. "Share!" a pugnacious girl yelled.

"Maybe...." Connar blocked them with a boot. "Let's see you duel for it."

Noddy said, "They don't have practice swords. Or even toy ones."

But the girl, the oldest of the bunch at six, had swept her gaze around the court, and spotted the long poles of the dash churns, set out to dry in the sun after the morning's churning.

The children flocked to these promising weapons, and promptly began waving them at each other, their crimson-faced efforts excruciatingly funny to Noddy and Connar.

"Go at 'em," Noddy bellowed, his deep honk echoing through the stone canyons.

The garrison urchins were easy to pick out, as they had some rudimentary training, if little skill, unlike the kitchen, carpentry, stonemason, barn, pottery, and clothyard youngsters. Noddy was fond of little creatures of every kind, and to him those earnest faces, the squeaky voices, the astoundingly bad skill, were adorable.

"Look." Noddy elbowed Connar. "Andas whupped the stick out of that one's hand! Go, Andas!"

The child grinned proudly their way half a heartbeat before the boy's assailant landed on him from behind, and they went tumbling in the dirt, wrestling and shouting.

Connar was also entertained, but he was also aware of mixed feelings. He knew it was despicable to secretly wish Andas had lost, but it was clear to him that Andas was a natural. He and that sturdy girl were easily the best of the entire pack of brats, most of whom swung wildly and then yelled insults when they lost. She used that dash with an instinctive swing that both

Noddy and Connar, after years of training, recognized as correct, her yellow mouse-ear pigtails bouncing at every strike.

Noddy nudged Connar again. "What you want to wager the runners nab that girl in a year or so, and make her a long rider?"

"Wouldn't take that bet," Connar said, watching Andas. What if their da saw how good he was? He, unlike Noddy, had figured out that Aunt Hliss did not want Andas playing with toy swords. The urge to rat the brats out was so strong. But he couldn't. If it got out, everybody would despise him for being a snitch. *He* hated snitches.

As it happened, he didn't have to. Noddy's booming honk, aesthetically unlovely though infectious in its sheer good-nature, was recognizable all over the castle. Hliss, crossing in one of the far courts where the dyeing was going on, recognized it and wondered what Noddy was doing in the churn yard, when churning time was long over.

As she neared, she heard the shrill voices of the castle children, who generally played about, watched by either a prentice or an adult. Noddy's laugh rose again, and she entered the yard, taking in the brothers sitting side by side on the fence, looking older than their years in their new lancers' coats.

In the yard, the little ones were busy bashing each other with the churn dashes pulled out of the churns. And in the center, his flaxen curls drenched with sweat, Andas.

She strode into their midst, the utterly alien look of fury in her eyes terrifying the children. Sticks clattered and dropped all around, as the more savvy children scampered off. Others started yelling and wailing, as Andas cried, "Ma, look, I won! I want my tart!" before his mother yanked the dash out of his hands.

"Get inside," she said in a furious hiss.

Shocked and frightened, Andas began to howl. She grabbed his hand, then glared up at her nephews. Noddy looked as shocked as he was. Connar was harder to read, but she didn't care what he was thinking — if he'd been thinking at all. "Who left you two stone-skulls in charge?" she demanded.

"But nobody got hurt," Noddy said reasonably. "We told 'em, no hitting heads —"

"Get. Out," she said, still in that furious whisper they found more unsettling than the worst curses bawled by any sword master. "You are *never* to come here again."

Noddy and Connar looked at each other, then as one swung their feet over the other side of the fence. They retreated as fast as they could, Noddy saying, "What's wrong? Nobody got hurt!"

Connar was fairly sure he knew, but instinct kept him from saying that he was sick and tired of everybody in the world maundering on about how beautiful and clever Andas was getting to be. All he knew was, he didn't need, or want, a beautiful and clever king's real son following on his heels. Because every time Hauth reminded him how skillful a leader his *true* father and grandfather had been, no matter how much Connar resented that "true," he knew that he was being reminded of his own shortcomings. As if he couldn't see how much stronger Noddy was, and how much faster Ghost Fath and Stick Tyavayir were, no matter how hard he tried.

He jammed the tart in his mouth so he wouldn't have to speak.

"I really don't get it," Noddy said, panting along beside him.

"All I know is, we better play least in sight until she gets over it," Connar said thickly around the pastry. And, after he swallowed, seeing Noddy still upset, "We've strutted our new coats around, but now we better change. How about a ride. See what the terrain looks like now that the thaw is real?"

So the boys were nowhere in sight when Hliss confronted Arrow up in the royal residence. All the way over she'd mentally rehearsed bunking him out, but by the time she'd trod up the stairs to the third floor, passing all the sentries and runners, reality caught up with her: She was the royal weaver. She still had to live here. And though she could order Arrow out of her life, she couldn't order him away from Andas.

Her conflict sharpened when she saw the honest confusion in Arrow's face, after telling him what she'd seen. It was clear he'd had no idea where the boys had gone—he had not given them permission. But the little grin, quickly quenched, when she said, "And your boys were cheering him on," made it clear he truly didn't understand what the problem was.

"I'm sorry, Hliss," he said when she snapped her teeth shut on a tirade. "I'll tell the boys the kitchen and back end is all out of bounds," he said.

Too late, she wanted to say. Andas had been so proud of himself. And who wouldn't, cheered on by those boys who looked to the uncritical eyes of the small ones like the kings of the world in those dashing coats and high boots.

Hliss stared at Arrow, silent as exasperation and affection and uncertainty boiled inside her. Yes, and guilt. It wasn't as if Mother hadn't warned her....

Mother. That was the solution, she decided, though it came near to breaking her heart at the prospect. She couldn't forbid Arrow to see his boy, but she could make it very hard to do so. And incidentally, get Andas away from the garrison boys.

"Thank you," she said.

She went straight to Danet, and two days later, a party led by Danet's fastest and best armed royal runners departed for Farendavan, Andas riding in front of one of them as he chewed on some honeycomb.

It wasn't until nightfall that he was told he was not going back to Ma, but on to meet his grandmother and Uncle Brother. The young royal runner and Hliss's most trusted assistant sat up all night with Andas, who screamed until almost dawn, when he fell into exhausted, sweaty sleep.

He was not the only one who spent a sleepless, grief-stricken night. When her work was done, Hliss slipped out of her rooms and ran down the back way. To every person she encountered, she said she was going to a different place to check on this or that, and made her way by as circuitous a method as she could contrive up to the north tower, which afforded a clear view of the road.

She thought she remained unseen, but Noth's sentries were too vigilant to miss a lone woman—the king's well-liked favorite, no less—slipping along from little-used stairwell to servant hall to wall. One glimpse of a tear-streaked face revealed in torchlight caused a watch captain to send a runner to Noth, who happened to be sitting with Headmaster Andaun, Camerend, and Quartermaster Pereth as they went over the logistical needs for the coming academy season.

Noth said, "Tell Captain Toraca thanks. We'll take it from here."

The runner departed, and Noth turned to the other two. Silence extended as they all considered the obvious: Hliss Farendavan had not gone for comfort to the king, who they knew was up in his suite. Nor had she gone to the gunvaer, her sister.

"Do we tell them?"

Camerend said, "My suggestion is, leave it. She knows where they are. She might need to be alone."

So they left it, and got back to their lists.

Noth met up with the queen in the old harskialdna tower, which was warm and smelled of mulled wine, he said, "Your sister was reported on the north tower."

"I know." Danet's welcoming smile vanished. "One of her runners told me, and Loret checked with the watch captain. If she wants to be alone, she should be. She knows where we are if she wants us."

Noth accepted these words as he accepted his cup of warm wine, and they talked of other things, Hliss gradually sliding from the forefront of their attention.

But she stayed in Camerend's mind, and when he ventured up to the north tower as the first blue light of dawn began lifting the shadows, he found Hliss standing alone, shivering in a thick cloak as she watched the north road. He let her hear his footfalls, and when she turned, her expression eased minutely when she the cup of freshly boiled summer steep he carried.

He joined her and silently held it out.

When she had first arrived at the castle at eighteen, she had of course noticed the fine-looking royal runner and felt the same flare of attraction that her sister had: their tastes were much alike. Danet's had died away, but Hliss's never had.

He'd been too heart-sore for anything beyond appreciation for the queen's lovely sister. But now, all these years later, he was powerless against grief.

FOURTEEN

Arrow did not find out about Andas being gone for several days. He was furious, but he kept his reaction between the walls of the royal suite. "What did she want me to do, thrash Noddy and Connar bloody?" he said to Danet.

"I suspect she didn't think you took her wishes seriously."

Arrow was going to deny that, but he knew it was true. "Well, what of it?" he grouched. "He's my boy, too. And what if he doesn't want to be a weaver? What's wrong with him maybe serving his brothers?"

Danet heroically kept her opinion to herself. She knew he was saying these things to her so that he wouldn't say them to Hliss—or anyone else. And as long as she didn't tell him he was right, which she would not do, he wouldn't. At least he knew where Andas was, and that he was safe.

The princes were late in finding out. Noddy was genuinely sorry, and missed his little brother. Connar, as always, kept his mouth shut, and anyway, they were suddenly busy, as Arrow told them to get their gear ready for the academy.

The days dragged until the morning when they were released like bolts from a cross bow. They only slowed when they reached the tunnel between the castle and the academy, for it wouldn't do at their exalted age to look overeager.

They sauntered to their new barracks—where, as always, the early arrivals eyed one another, seeing who had grown and who hadn't, and bragged about how much drill they'd gotten over winter.

Connar was not the only one who had practiced with a lance over winter, though his had been in secret. Some had begged training from accommodating older brothers on the grounds that the family would be disgraced forever if they looked ignorant when the class finally started their lance drills. Though he hated it, Connar couldn't complain.

Two days later, they began classes, and in the afternoon, for the first time, the princes' barracks rode out to their first real lance drill. It galled Connar to see Ghost Fath pick up a lance, jam his heels down into the stirrups, and charge at the target, nicking the top of the straw man in a respectable first strike.

Noddy went next. As expected, he hefted the lance with no trouble at all, grinning as he urged his horse into a trot. The boys whooped and cheered, for he was well-liked (and would have been had he not been born a prince) but when he tried for the target, he forgot everything he'd been told, and his strength utterly betrayed him as the lance caught in the target support, he made the mistake of gripping it tight, and described a neat parabola over the horse's head.

When he rose up unhurt from the mud, he laughed right along with the boys, as the junior master sighed in quiet relief, and Hauth remained impassive.

Connar held himself strictly in check until the master called him forward. Then, controlled from wrists to heels, he couched the lance comfortably, and kept his horse at the ordered trot, though he longed to gallop. When the lance struck the straw man dead-center, the boys roared with approval, and he rode back, exhilarated, glorying in the admiration and surprise in all his bunkmates' eyes.

This was what he lived for. And it was everything he had hoped.

He didn't see the junior master's knit brows—the man experienced enough to recognize how easily Connar had handled that lance. It was familiarity, not miraculous instant skill. Clearly Olavayir Tvei had been coached by Hauth, who had said nothing. No one would have a second thought about a king's son getting coached, but for some reason Hauth had kept this training private.

The junior master shrugged it off. At least Connar's form was impeccable, which couldn't be said for some of the others who also betrayed familiarity with the lance—which is why they told the boys not to experiment on their own, and pick up bad habits that had to be unlearned.

Connar ended the class in the heady glory of triumph, and didn't stop grinning as the boys discussed everyone's performance, Connar and Ghost being voted the best.

But admiration doesn't last unless you keep earning it. Everyone else, he discovered over the following days, was too busy trying to earn it for themselves. And one day he arrived to an unpleasant discovery: Rat Noth and several boys from the class behind them had been ordered to join them for this class. At first Connar thought they were there to watch, but no, Hauth motioned them to practice, a whole year ahead of when *they* got to! The howling injustice!

Of course at first they were terrible, and Connar felt justified in bawling insults along with his class. But they were there the next class, and the next.

Some worked harder than others. Noddy never worked hard. He was too easy-going for that. Even so, within a month, Noddy whacked the target clean off the fence, right hand and left.

One morning, when Hauth put Noddy on a big war horse nearing retirement, the animal responded to the man-sized weight in the saddle, or maybe it was only something in the air, and broke from trot to gallop. Noddy rode easily with it, his big body locked down in the stirrups, and when he struck the target, it not only burst apart, but the practice lance—made of flimsy wood—cracked with the violence of lightning hitting a tree. The entire class shrilled *Yip-yip-yip!*, the truest praise.

Connar forced himself to cheer with the rest, for he'd seen the derision that jealousy raised. But for the first time, he was startled by a spurt of hatred for his brother. That caused an equal surge of self-hatred. Noddy was never jealous. Noddy cheered everyone equally, and he laughed at his own errors.

Connar and Hauth were still meeting for their secret training, a habit Connar didn't question, though there was strictly speaking no longer a necessity. The next morning, as soon as Connar saw Hauth, the pent-up words burst out: "Why is Rat Noth with us? *We* had to wait until this year to begin lance training."

Hauth saw Lanrid's jealousy staring out of Connar's eyes. Mindful that they hadn't done well to curb it with scorn and punishments while Lanrid was alive, he and Quartermaster Pereth had spent uncounted hours discussing a different approach.

He tried it now. "On the king's orders," he said impassively. "He's clearly marked for the army. But think of it this way: he will be one of your captains."

He watched Connar's expressive brows lift, and the tension in his face ease to a reflective expression.

Connar was thinking: a captain, right. Everyone could see Rat Noth was born for the crazy skirmishers in the cavalry, being lean and light in build, but strong, as the saying went, as if made entirely of snapvine and steel.

Rat Noth would never surpass Connar in the chain of command. He had to remember that. None of them would. Besides, there were still the class against class wargames to look forward to, and everyone knew that when Noddy commanded those, he invariably let the riding captains do what they wanted, which often ended up in a loss.

As the season wore on, Connar had to get new boots twice, but he was so preoccupied with the competition of academy life that he was scarcely aware of shooting up: all he knew was, he always looked up into Noddy's face, but at least he caught up with Ghost Fath and Stick Tyavayir, the class leaders.

He was chosen to command wargames three times, between their barracks house and another. Only the senior class got to command the all-school and overnight games.

After his first command, Connar left early for his meeting with Hauth, half-expecting the master not to be there anymore. After all, lance drill was now a part of classes, and Connar had lost the wargame he'd commanded the day before. Sick with certainty that Hauth would give up on him in disgust, he raced out into a cold morning, his breath steaming. But he found Hauth waiting.

Hauth saw him coming, and breathed with relief. Connar's loss the previous day both annoyed and reassured him—there was clearly much that Connar still needed to learn. The annoyance was a mix of disappointed expectations. By now Hauth had forgotten that Lanrid had only won when he ran at the front, using brute force to bowl over his opponents. Lanrid had never been a planner, but in Hauth's memory (in those early days, wine-soaked), Lanrid was forever the bright, shining son of the great Mathren, strong, skilled, and a natural commander. A natural future king, and it was Retren Hauth's purpose, his vow, to see that Connar became the king his father should have been.

Clearly he had to train that Iascan woman's bad blood out of him.

He greeted Connar with a terse, "You lost yesterday. Do you know why?"

Connar launched into a disjointed explanation, with plenty of self-exculpatory sidetracks, until Hauth cut in with, "I can see you're ready to blame everything and everyone else. Some of that even might be true. Let me ask instead, what did you learn?"

Connar stared at Hauth, loathing that sense that the mystery of successful command slipped away exactly like the mirages on the plains during the height of summer. "I...." Seeing Hauth's scowl deepen, he said quickly, "I couldn't *see*, from the middle of everything. Everything started all right, but then it all fell apart, and I couldn't see. I think I have to get where I can *see* everyone." He remembered a stray fact, and his tone changed. "In the very first story, the very first wargame. Inda got outside, somehow, and sent Mouse Marthdavan for the flags.... He *saw* things."

"All right," Hauth said. "Next time, make sure you do the same." Frustration sharpened his tone. He'd really expected Connar to come out a winner, after studying those hoarded papers that no one else even knew about; one of the prospects keeping him awake at night was that Connar would arrive at their meetings full of resentment for Hauth's bad teaching.

Hauth knew he wasn't a leader. Mathren had valued him as a lance captain. His proudest moment, which he'd had to keep secret all these years, was his promotion to Nighthawk Company Captain of First Lancers. On Connar's behalf he'd sought the key to command ever since, and had truly believed that the secret lay in those carefully hoarded old stories about Inda-Harskialdna, which, joined with dolphin-clan blood, would catapult Connar to leadership.

They parted, Connar with a plan, and Hauth with self-doubt, because surely the fault was his.

After Connar's second command, "I didn't *really* win," he said truculently. "We did get the flag, and we did the drum dance, but it was really all Ghost being fast, and doing what he wanted."

"Why did he do what he wanted? Did he ignore your orders?" Hauth asked, his pale brows a line over his deep-set single eye and the black patch.

Connar struggled against the burn of envy, so familiar. But learning command was too important, and envy wouldn't get him anywhere. "Yes. No...well, everyone told me my plan sounded great, but once we started, there was too much of it to remember. I did have a lot of contingencies. I thought they were all good. Cab—some ignored me, or got bored and didn't listen." The instinct not to snitch was still strong.

"Gannan," Hauth said, lip curling. "He wasn't the only one running wild."

Connar sighed. "It doesn't say in the papers how much Inda said to his company. I thought maybe he explained everything, all contingencies."

"He may or may not have, but that doesn't prevent you from doing it."

The third time, everything started out perfectly—as perfect as drill. Then all of a sudden, it fell apart and they lost.

Connar was in a vicious mood, all the worse for having to hide it. Everyone despised a commander who couldn't lose well.

"It started right," he said resentfully. "A perfect three wedge attack on both flanks and to break the middle."

Hauth opened his hand. From his vantage on the hill Connar's company was supposed to be defending, he'd seen it—and also seen Manther Yvanavayir's flag shoot a whirtler arrow signaling a wheel and oblique attack, after which the skirmishers cut up the flank attacks and converged on the mass in the middle, which promptly turned to chaos, everyone trying to take everyone else prisoner.

Hauth said, "Yvanavayir saw it coming. That's a common attack."

"I picked it because it was simple," Connar muttered. "Since nobody listened to me on the defense along the river. I couldn't see anything, because I led the point." *The way Rat Noth does.* He couldn't make himself say it, as Rat was in the class behind them. That made his skill somehow more insulting.

"You have next year," Hauth said quickly, seeing the mutiny tightening Connar's features.

"I should be winning *this* year," Connar retorted.

"You're up against your own future captains," Hauth reminded him. "And we kept Yvanavayir an extra season to get him better trained in captaining foot as well as mounted."

Manther Yvanavayir was a mere side issue to Connar. "Yes, and because I'll have to be the future commander in chief, I don't see why I shouldn't get to see the problem first," he burst out, knowing very well that he was suggesting in a roundabout way that the master brief him on the game details ahead of the others.

Hauth's eye widened, and Connar stepped back. "I didn't mean it like cheating," he started.

Hauth knew exactly what he meant, and a brief pulse of memory brought Lanrid's voice expressing a similar sentiment in the same roundabout way, his voice breaking on the word "cheating" with eerie precision in exactly the same way. He had actually forgotten that until now.

To smother the disloyal memory, he said all the more forcefully, "I'm relieved you're not asking me to cheat on your behalf." He let out his breath, aware that he had all Connar's attention now. "There's a reason the headmaster is careful not to bring out the chalk board until everyone's ready to ride. It's as close as we can come to what happens in the field, when the scouts report what they find of the enemy. A commander is not going to be able to send a runner to his enemy asking for him to wait a day or two so he can come up with a plan. Cheating might net a win, but it won't teach you anything...."

And Hauth relieved himself of a long lecture about how a natural commander didn't need to cheat, only followers cheated. Connar's focus shifted inward within the first words of the familiar hectoring tone.

So Hauth wouldn't let him scout ahead. It wasn't *really* cheating. After all, spies got extra information. That was the entire purpose of spies! For that matter, Cama One-Eye's Inda papers were really extra information. Of course, they were descriptions of past battles, and anyone who wanted to read about past battles could do it if he found them. Maybe Rat Noth and Ghost Fath had similar stuff at home!

Anyway. Scouts finding maps or plans or orders of a future battle was different, but really, a commander didn't send them back, saying, *Nope, unfair advantage here. Can't listen to you unless you share it with my enemies at the same time.* There were all kinds of ifs, if you thought about it.

War wasn't launched by two commanders seeing a setup and a goal chalked out on a board, and given exactly the same briefing.

When Hauth finally finished, Connar walked away, having not heard a word past *it won't teach you anything.*

Spring came late to Senelaec, but even so, once again planting was even later because Wolf had taken every rider over the age of eighteen to reinforce their family connections in Sindan-An, where, not long after the first warm spell of spring, five horse studs were attacked at the same time. It was entirely by chance that a patrol rounding up yearlings on the plain caught sight of the dust of a mighty party coming from the direction of the east, and raced belly flat to the ground for home to warn everyone.

Wolf—now the jarl—took his eldest son Cub for his first foray. Calamity remained behind in command of Senelaec, which was protected by teens and oldsters who alternately patrolled and helped with the planting. Near the end of summer the outriders spotted the dust on the horizon, galloped to a high point, spotted the Senelaec pennons, and raced home with the news that the jarl was back at last.

Wolf, Cub, and their Riders trotted into the homestead, tired and dusty, to general cheering, and general questions about the success of the foray (lots of chasing, a few scraps, nothing definitive—as usual). Calamity was glad to see Wolf, but they knew each other well. Nothing was said as they both went about the day, but as soon as they were alone, he turned his back to the door, crossed his arms, and said, "What?"

Calamity sighed. "The girls want to go to the royal city to compete in the Victory Day games."

His tone completely changed when he exclaimed again, "What!"

"It seems every letter that comes in goes on and on about how much fun it is, the most fun ever, hoola loo. And Vole Patrol encountered some Marlovayirs on the border—"

"Was anyone hurt?" Wolf reached for a sword that, for the first time in three months, wasn't at his side.

"No, no, it was all talk. Stand down, Wolf, you know the girls take care of themselves. And it was Marlovayir scouts, mostly girls. Young Tdor said they were bragging about their wins, and dropping hints as delicate as horse apples about how *some* people didn't dare ride to the royal city to compete because they knew they'd lose."

Wolf smacked his hands over his face, then sighed loudly. "So of course they want to go."

"And I don't know that we should stop them."

Wolf turned and kicked the toe of his boot against the door. "You and I have to ride to the royal city come this winter. Do you think it's a good idea to send them before we've scouted the terrain?"

They both recollected receiving that astonishing notice, inviting the jarlans to the royal city for the next Convocation. For the first time in history. Calamity glanced toward her desk, where the letter still sat in the wooden casket where she kept important mail. She didn't need to take it out to remember the fine scribal hand, and the fact that Danet hadn't signed it.

Even so....

Calamity said, "Nothing bad has happened since Arrow and Danet took the throne. All the gossip goes the other way, mostly, about the academy, and how everyone loves going."

Wolf said slowly, "So you think...?"

Calamity said, "I think we might pick out the best of the girls from the three patrols, and let them go."

"Not Ran," Wolf said quickly. "And Kit's too young."

"Kit's definitely too young. And, of course, not Ran," Calamity said, just as quickly, as with the same heartfelt conviction. "In fact, this might be a good idea to let Cousin Ranet go along. Since she's taking Ran's place, she ought to get a chance to meet Connar. Scout the territory."

Wolf grimaced. When that notice had come about jarlans to attend the next Convocation, his mother had said, "I told you years ago your Ran-ruse would throw you ass over horse's head. You deal with it," before riding off to support her sister in Sindan-An, who had taken a bad fall that had permanently disabled her.

So they'd had plenty of time to consider what to do. In family councils that had started secret and widened, as usual, to include everyone from old, toothless Cama Miller to the youngest barn brats, they had agreed that Fuss's daughter, also named Ranet, was the best choice to take the false Ranet's place when the time came. She was smart. She even had the right name.

The Keriams (long allied with the Sindan-Ans and the Senelaecs) had said she could decide, whereupon she nearly bounced through the roof at the very idea of marrying a prince. The only drawback was her age: she was almost three years younger than Ran.

"Do you think she can pass for older?" Wolf asked doubtfully. "She's a good filly, but on the small side."

"Both riding captains say she's held herself well on her first border patrols. In fact, she was there at that Marlovayir encounter, and Pandet says she comported herself well. And remember, the younger prince isn't going to be pushing for marriage. He's only a year or two, three at most older than our Ran. At that age, the last thing they're thinking about is marriage. By the time he's ready for marriage, she'll be as well."

Wolf said, "True. All right, let 'em go to the summer games. But bite their ears good about behavior."

"Oh, you know I will," Calamity said grimly. Those girls were going to get the benefit of all her sleepless nights about the consequences of flip decisions.

They did.

At length.

As soon as she was gone, Ran and the girls retreated to their own particular hangout, which was the south harvest barn, conveniently empty. There, they all faced one another.

"We're going," Young Pan shrilled. "We'regoingwe'regoingwe'regoing!"

"Clip the rat squeak," Ink, an older girl, ordered.

Ink had gotten her nickname at age six after a close encounter with a fresh bowl of ink, when she was taken with an urge to express her artistry on the side of a barn; after much scrubbing, they still had not managed to get it out of her flaxen hair, which had turned green, and stayed green, until she took the sheep shears to her hair at age ten. Despite an unpromising start, Ink was likely to become a patrol captain before she turned twenty.

Ran introduced the subject on all their minds by saying, "I'm going with you."

Silence. They all remembered Calamity beginning that long jawing with, "Of course Ran will stay here, but...."

Ran looked at the uncertain faces, and said, "It wasn't orders. She just said, *of course*. And I didn't say anything. Right? You all heard me."

"True," Ink said slowly.

They all respected the jarlan very much. But there was, right here before them, the prospect of the ruse of a lifetime.

"Why not have Ran come?" said a freckled fifteen-year-old they called Trot. She lived for risk and adventure.

They all scrutinized Ran. They had regarded him as one of the girls for all their short lives, but of late a couple of the older ones had become aware of little things that weren't girl, and further, that they rather liked...when it wasn't awkward.

Ink, three years older, narrowed her eyes as she studied Ran, who stood still under this inspection. It was easy enough to guess what they were thinking. "The Marlovayirs've never raised a question, not once," he said.

True. Ran was nearly sixteen, and until recently—this spring, really—had been a skinny reed, much the same size and shape as Trot, Young Pan, and Fnor there. But since winter he was starting to get shoulders on him, and his arms, when bare, weren't girl arms. However, nobody would be seeing his arms, covered by his robe.

"What about the baths?" Trot whispered.

This was a poser. Calamity had abruptly declared when Ran was twelve that he had to bathe with the boys from now on, which everyone had accepted, unaware of the fact that when the patrollers passed their favorite pools on hot summer days, they'd all stripped down without a second thought. No one had been interested in the single dangle among them— though Ran, just this summer, had found himself noticing in the others what he'd always taken for granted, and sometimes had to consciously make himself not stare, lest they catch him at it and all the easy sisterhood suddenly got weird.

Yeah, his old life was definitely ending, and the fact that Cousin Ran was now living with them, ready to take his place when the time came to marry the second prince, was the proof. So why not go out with the triumph of the world's primest ruse? "If we take along one of the buckets will the spell on it, I can make do with that," he said. "Or. It's only for, what, a week? I won't stink in a week—"

"Yes, you will," Fnor stated.

"Says the biggest farter in the kingdom," Ran retorted.

Ink snapped her fingers, cutting a promising insult fight short. "Definitely the bucket. Every day," she added with a frown, and Ran suppressed the urge to sniff his pits. Nobody had complained before; it had yet to occur to him that he was beginning to smell like boy, and that some of the girls had noticed.

"Here's what I think," Young Pan said. "Ran's the best rider alongside me, you all know it. And he's the best shot. Even when he doesn't do that trick with two arrows."

They had to acknowledge this: while Ran had trouble seeing details up close, like writing, he had inherited his mother's distance vision, and could name correctly the type of bird that others barely saw as a speck on the horizon. Coming from two naturally athletic parents, he brought this sharp eye to archery. In that he was as good as Ink, and this last year, especially since winter, he'd begun shooting much farther and faster while riding, the most coveted skills besides accuracy.

Ran sighed. "You know it's gonna end. Da told me before he rode east that next year I can ride with him'n Uncle Yipyip, as Cousin Ranet is old enough to take my spot in the patrols."

"Next year you'll probably have to do the Beard Spell." Trot's eyes rounded.

Ran didn't mention that sometimes, when he was alone, he looked at his reflection in his knife to check for hairs on his chin, as he didn't have any anywhere else. So far, they were few, and as blond as his braids.

Fnor said, "Oh, let's have Ran with us. Wouldn't it be a blister?"

"It's dangerous," one girl murmured, half-ashamed.

Sure enough, the others turned on her with Senelaec scorn. "That's what makes it fun," Young Pan stated. "All Ran has to do is act like usual. The Marlovayirs haven't figured it out. Why should anyone in the royal city?"

Ink jerked her head in a nod. "Let's do it. But it's going to take planning, or one day out, you know someone will come after us hot and yank us back by our braids."

She turned her eagle eye on Kit, Ran, and Cousin Ranet. "You'll have to help."

Kit had already been told she couldn't go, and she didn't insist. Nobody ever said anything, but she knew she wasn't ever going to be as good as Ran, as she seemed to have gotten her da's and Uncle Yipyip's lack of distance vision.

But she was a loyal sister, and clapped her hand to her skinny chest. "Sure!"

This decided, they broke up lest someone come around curious to see what the conclave was about, and anyway everyone had chores.

As they parted, Trot elbowed Ran. "You'll look *really weird* with your hair in a horsetail."

He snorted. "Who cares? I don't have to see it!"

FIFTEEN

As summer wore on, those who made it their business to notice such things were aware that the king was rarely seen at Hliss the weaver's, but the royal runner chief was often there.

Danet, who knew her sister better than anyone, suspected from subtle signs that Hliss, for the first time since their teen years, had found her heart's mate. She couldn't get a read on Camerend, but since no one was communicating with her, she kept her surmises to herself.

As summer ripened toward the end of season expectations, she had the girls' games to plan for—and that usually prompted all the old questions about purpose.

One fine summer evening she sat at her desk, hesitating over which games to arrange, when Arrow burst in, scowling and bringing a strong waft of hard bristic.

"If you're drunk," Danet said, laying aside her pen, "you can walk right out again."

Arrow flung his hand toward the door. "Hliss's with *him* again. Camerend."

"So?"

Arrow prowled the room. "I went to see her. He was there, eating with her. Sitting where I do when I eat with her. They were...." He screwed up his face, trying to express what he had seen in their faces, in the way they sat shoulder to shoulder, hip to hip, how their voices blended. "I hate it! She's— everybody in the castle has to know...."

"So? She can pick who she wants, just as you do, and I do, and everybody else who didn't make a ring vow." When she saw his scowl deepen, her voice sharpened. "Arrow, if you dare start in about how a king shouldn't have to, or what a king expects, I am going to puke up my dinner."

Arrow flushed to the ears.

Danet said in a softer tone, "I'm glad those two have one another. I think it's good for them both."

"But I—"

"Arrow, you aren't in love with Hliss."

"Yes, I am. Well, most of the time," he amended, and when she uttered a dry laugh, he glared at her. "It's not funny."

She sighed. "No, it's not. Feelings are, well, feelings. They splash everything. The truth is, she didn't go looking for this kind of love. It came. Seems to be the same with him. As for you, Anred-Harvaldar, you've got an entire kingdom full of women who'd love being a king's favorite. Let her go."

"But I miss her. It's not just the sex."

"So go sit with them. I don't think either of them would ever turn you away. I know she still has good feelings for you, and Camerend has always been our best help."

"All right, I do miss the sex," he muttered. "But she said she's exclusive now. And don't tell me it's easy to find someone like her. There isn't anyone like her." He also didn't like women who obviously wanted something besides him, the ones he thought of as just like Fi. Nor did he like them too young. The sex was great, but afterwards, and lately even before the sex, the way they looked and talked was different from when he first became king. They made him feel old. And it was harder to find professional women closer to his age, as a lot of them tended to retire to other lives.

He looked around Danet's empty room, then said, "Can I stay here tonight? With you?"

Danet gazed at him in surprise, for it had been years since he'd shown any interest in her that way. But they were married—in fact, another year or so, and she would have been married as long as she'd been alive. "Of course you can," she said immediately; Sage could intercept Noth. "If. You're done with the bristic for the night."

Arrow halted mid-step, for he'd been about to fetch his cup and jug.

"Never mind." He slammed out, and went off to one of his regulars in town, who wasn't any Hliss, but at least she never gave him any trouble about how much he drank.

Far to the north, a stronger current of cold air than usual bullied its way into the streams of warm air breathing across the continent, smashing into hundreds of smaller whirlpools that towered into angry clouds, hammering the land below with thunder and driving rain.

In Marlovan Iasca, these storms caught ridings of girls converging on the royal city, forcing them to find whatever shelter they could as the roads turned into brown streams, and rivers became torrents.

Between the storms the travelers raced for the royal city, and so arrived in waves, as the puddles steamed and shimmered in summer heat.

When the Senelaec girls left home the day after Andahi Day, amid shouts of farewell and exhortations to win, Ran was seen riding with his younger sister and her patrol, heading east for a border inspection that usually lasted about ten days. A day out, Kit covered for her brother when he claimed he had to return due to a bad knee, and the patrol continued with eight.

They returned ten days later. Kit had been practicing her story about Ran and his bad knee, but counted without Calamity and Wolf knowing immediately on their arrival that something was amiss: eight riders, no Ran. He had not been seen since the two ridings departed.

With twin expressions of grim dismay, they returned to the house, leaving poor Kit trembling with trepidation—and hidden excitement.

"You know as well as I do where he is," Wolf said heavily when they got inside.

The old jarlan, who had accompanied Cousin Ranet from Sindan-An and remained for a visit, snorted. "What did you expect? He's just like you two." She sighed, then said with trenchant relish, "Better prepare for the King's Riders to turn up demanding your heads."

"I'll ride to the royal city, and throw myself on Danet's mercy. There must be something of the Danet we met, somewhere inside that gunvaer," Calamity exclaimed.

"No." For once Wolf wasn't smiling. He looked like someone else to her. Older, harder; the Wolf she knew even grinned when he rode into battle. "At heart, this was about my avoiding sending my son to the academy. I'll go."

"Take all the Riders," she said. "Everybody who can lift a sword. You know every single one would volunteer."

Wolf flattened his hand. "First of all, I want to be fast. Catch the girls before they get there, if I can. But if I don't, whether I've got two or two thousand Riders at my back, if we start fighting our own people, then nobody wins. If Arrow wants me to stand against the wall, it should be only me, and I'll make him look straight into my eyes when he gives the command to shoot me."

He walked out, calling for his personal runner, while ten days to the south, Ran—secure in the belief he'd gotten away with it—grinned along with the others as they *finally* spotted the towers of the royal city on the horizon.

They'd vowed to reach the royal city in a record run, until the first of the storms caught them flat.

Now, ten days later, with what seemed to be every fiber of their gear gritty with mud, as well as both their skin and that of their mounts, they splashed across the river, their pennons as unrecognizable as those of the other two ridings of girls they met at the road on the other side, where it curved toward the distant city.

"I'm Pony Yvanavayir," the lead rider from one of the other groups spoke as soon as they were all in earshot. Pony swept all the rain-washed faces, and said, not without sympathy, "All new to the royal city, then?"

"Yes," Ink said, speaking for the Senelaecs, and introduced herself.

"Yes," said a girl who appeared to be Ink's age, from the third riding. She did not introduce herself, and Pony was too impatient to assume command of the combined parties to ask. Yvanavayir was the most prestigious House — and Pony had worked harder than she ever had on her skills. This was her year to be first in everything.

So why not begin leadership now?

"As it happens," Pony said, "we've been going since the first time. Just follow me, and we'll show you everything you need to know."

The Senelaec riding, completely oblivious to this establishment of hierarchy, gratefully accepted this offer.

Pony then turned to one of her runners. "Dip our pennon in the river and get rid of the mud. Then ride ahead, so the gate sentries will see Yvanavayir yellow to give us our salute."

She turned her head, and called, "If any of you are jarlans' daughters, of course you should get your pennons out. Fall in behind me."

The Senelaecs exchanged furtive glances. Ink's gaze fell on Cousin Ranet, and she jerked her chin at Fnor, who shifted her gaze back and forth between them all, then joined the Yvanavayir girl at the riverside. After all, waving their banner wasn't giving anything away — it seemed to be expected.

Pony wound her hand in the air, and her riders formed into column.

Ink turned toward the silent group of girls whose banner was still rolled. They waited in a line, their horses perfectly disciplined.

Impressed by these displays of order, the noisy Senelaecs fell in behind Pony Yvanavayir's group and for the first time ever, and with hisses and chin-jerks, jockeyed each other by riding in more-or-less spaced pairs.

"Who *are* they?" Ran whispered to Ink, as the third group fell in behind, two by two.

A shrug and a roll of her eyes was all she answered, as Cousin Ranet looked on with huge eyes. Tdor sidled her mount over and hissed. "Sit up. You're supposed to look sixteen."

Cousin Ranet, a thin, flaxen-haired girl who strongly resembled her mother, jerked upright.

The big party had rounded the first low hill when the outriders began to canter, and all three banners rolled out as the horses' hooves kicked up thick mud clots.

They could now make out all the towers of the city, which looked enormous to those who had never seen any city.

Pony reveled in the fact that she rode at the front of a long column — in fact, a flight, as three ridings made a flight — as they topped the last rise and there before them lay the royal city.

She grinned, and made the twice-pumped fist command for a charge, thinking that it would be grand for the city to see them galloping through the gates as the trumpeters blared the chord for Yvanavayir. The girls obediently urged their horses into the preliminary trot.

But as the outriders reached the city, the girls barely made out the splotches of color flapping: crimson, yellow....

And *green?* A silver owl on green!

Pony dropped her hand and her followers began to gallop the last distance, as the trumpeters blasted the fanfare for a prince.

Prince? There was only one family rating that fanfare: Algaravayir.

Pony realized her mistake as her riding splashed through the gates, and people stared round-eyed from them to the others approaching more sedately.

"We should have waited," Fnor breathed to Ink as the waiting outriders each fell in with their own party.

"They didn't say anything," Ink retorted.

All eyes turned to the head of their column, to Pony, who had told them to fall in behind without asking who anyone was.

The city people drew to either side of the street, staring as the Algaravayir girls rode through in twos. Everyone had to take a look at the first Algaravayirs to come through the gates since the days of the last Montreivayir king.

And the inevitable whispers ran along ahead, faster than the wind: the Yvanavayirs had taken precedence over them.

Pony caught what seemed like a thousand affronted gazes, and as their column proceeded more slowly toward the stables, she waved her girls ahead and lingered, addressing the first pair of Algaravayirs, "Why didn't you tell us?"

"You didn't ask," a younger girl signed and spoke.

Her sturdy blonde partner silenced her with a cool look, then gave a slight nod to an older girl, who said neutrally, "We don't mind following. As you said, this is our first time in the royal city. Lead the way."

Pony did, but all the pleasure had gone out of showing off her inside knowledge. She pointed out the main buildings until they reached the castle stable, where royal runners waited, Lineas and Bun having raced down three flights of stairs and along four halls after the gunvaer's first runner burst in on them at lessons, saying, "Noren Algaravayir is here!"

Bun had been somewhat lackadaisical in practicing Hand. She regretted it now when Noren, immediately recognizable from the crowd by her fast fingers, exchanged greetings with Lineas at lightning speed.

The Senelaec and Yvanavayir parties dismounted—Cousin Ranet thoroughly intimidated now—as Lineas turned at Noren's open gesture to say, "Noren Algaravayir gives everyone greetings."

Cousin Ranet stared at the older girl who was exactly her height, though much stronger in build. Here was the person she was going to be serving under for the rest of her life. Feeling entirely out of her depth, she said slowly and distinctly, "I'm Raw-net. Sen-eh-lay-eck," she added.

Pony rolled her eyes. "She's deaf. Not slow."

Cousin Ranet flushed scarlet, her gaze dropping. Fingers touched her wrist, and she looked up as Noren tapped her chest then made the forefinger-up, thumb out sign next to her chin.

"She's telling you her name is Noren," Lineas said.

Cousin Ranet turned to her gratefully. "How do I tell her my name is Ranet?"

Lineas showed her the common sign for the name Ranet, and Cousin Ranet copied the gesture, earning a brief smile from Noren. The others went on to exchange introductions, Ran hanging back with Ink.

Then Bun said, "Come with me! I'll show you where you stay."

Thus Pony lost the leadership again, perforce following the pack as hands fluttered here and there, and high voices chattered.

Cousin Ranet watched Lineas, Noren, and Bun carrying on a silent conversation, and mentally resolved to find someone to teach her this new language. She was good at languages. She'd already had to learn Marlovan when the decision was made to send her to Senelaec, as she had been born in the western hills of Sindan-An, where a dialect of Iascan was still the everyday tongue.

Ran trailed them all, walking between Ink and Fnor. No one had given him a second glance so far.

His first challenge occurred unexpectedly, when they reached the barracks and nearly ran into a pack of Marlovayir girls coming out. What might have been a bad moment almost anywhere else was averted by the fact that both ridings were self-consciously on their best behavior.

But as Ran followed the rest inside the barracks, he heard a couple of Marlovayirs muttering back and forth: "Did I get that right? That scrawny rat is Ranet Senelaec? She looks like she's twelve!"

"Probably rides like a twelve-year-old, too, hah!"

"All the better, ha ha ha...." They vanished around a corner.

Ran caught up, to discover the rest of his riding muttering among themselves.

"Just stay away from them," Ink reminded them in a scolding voice. "You remember we promised Calamity-Jarlan. *No* trouble." She rolled her eyes meaningfully Ran's way, in case any of them had missed the hint.

The barracks was filling fast, but the Senelaecs were ready for that. They chose the end farthest from the door, so fewer would pay attention to them, and tossed their gear onto the beds surrounding Ran's, so that he'd sleep in the middle.

Then Cousin Ranet, eyes bright with anticipation, said, "Let's see if the prince is around." Because of course he'd be as interested in seeing her as she was in seeing him — or so she thought.

Pony overheard, and because she couldn't stop herself from attempting to reclaim the position of experiential (if not moral) superiority, said airily to the entire room, "They won't be. They're still days away at their big wargame."

And so they would have been, had not the Great Game been declared a washout, after all the tents collapsed and half of them had vanished in the same storm that had forced the girls first to take cover, and then to ride covered in mud.

The senior royal runner in charge of the girls appeared in the doorway. "The gunvaer is going to address you now," she said, and everyone hastened out, falling into the pairs they customarily rode in.

A row of boys, including both princes, lay flat on a rooftop as the girls passed below them. It wasn't the Senelaecs who caught their interest, once Cousin Ranet passed below their hidden parapet. The notion of wives belonged to the hazy future for both Noddy and Connar. The boys were all there, for word had passed about the fanfare, to see the descendant of Inda-Harskialdna.

The boys' avid gazes locked onto the short, pear-shaped blonde girl in the silver-trimmed green robe: an actual Algaravayir! Her hands fluttered hummingbird-fast at Bunny (the latter struggling to keep up) as the two strolled at the front of the crowd.

Most of the girls remained blithely unaware of their hidden audience. They were too busy assessing one another as potential competition in the field. Noren, however, who relied on other senses besides hearing, had been aware of the uneven shadows bumping along the roof line as they passed the back end of the stable, and guessed who they might be and why.

"We're being spied on, aren't we?" she signed with considerate deliberation to Bun when she had her back firmly to the roof.

Bunny sighed. "My brothers," she signed back.

Noren accepted this. She'd been prepared to be stared at and evaluated. You can't change your ancestors.

As soon as the queen came out, the boys retreated fast, most of them believing the queen could see through stone with those steely eyes of hers.

Danet began with the same speech as always, conscientiously repeated in Hand, then ended, "Since there are so many of you this year, we'll drill in a larger courtyard, which the runners will show you at dawn bells. When you get back to your barracks, the runners will have a list of the games the boys compete in. You can sign up to compete in any of them. I look forward to watching you."

She paused, ignoring the rising murmur of comments and questions.

Lineas had stood nearby, translating the speech far more effectively than Danet's stiff, studied attempt. Bunny watched with concentration. Now that there was a real person who used this language exclusively, Hand was no longer a game to be played when she was in the mood, and she regretted her lack of real practice.

Danet dismissed the girls, except for her sons' future wives and her daughter. When the girls came before her, Danet studied them. Noren looked well grown and capable. The Senelaec girl whom Calamity and Wolf had sent regarded her through a pair of steady, serious eyes that reminded her of Fuss. Good. However (Danet thought to herself) if that girl was any older than thirteen, she would be very surprised. Just as well that neither of the boys had expressed any interest in their future wives.

When the girls lined up before her, hands flat to chests in salute, she said, "Since tomorrow is Restday, I'm inviting you to an early drum, to meet my sons. My daughter will bring you up and give you a tour. After the meal, you'll be released early to join all the others in the city," she added kindly.

After that they were released to get settled in, and the most conscientious wanted to check on their mounts in the stable.

The Iofre had warned Noren that she was likely to be treated as a curiosity, and so it was. At least the girls asked very little about her family and home, much less the past. Mostly they seemed to want to stand close to the future gunvaer—to be noticed themselves. They talked far more than they listened, even the ones who had to wait as their words were translated.

The rest of the day passed swiftly, ending early as everyone was tired from their grueling rides.

The next day, Ran watched in relief as Cousin Ranet went off with Noren Algaravayir, both dressed in their House tunics, their blonde hair brushed shining and done up in double loops high above their ears.

The Restday drum with the royal family was awkward, but not painful, due entirely to Bunny. Arrow had resigned himself to a boring interval, as Restdays inevitably were, ever since Danet insisted on communicating only in Hand. He'd managed to master a hundred phrases or so, but there was never time for more; it seemed to him that as soon as he got a new one, an old one fell out of his head. Anyway, Noren was women's business—and of course Noddy's, once they were wed.

So he sat there. As he had no idea how intimidating he appeared to the girls, his silence made all conversation an effort. The boys, much better at highly idiomatic Hand, had to concentrate on not using academy slang. Cousin Ranet, of course, knew nothing at all, but Bunny—bad as she was at the language—clearly didn't mind the boys laughing when she made mistakes, and so she cheerfully translated for Cousin Ranet, which incidentally brought Arrow in.

Noren had already decided not to use speech. She'd been proud of learning to say words until one of her Totha cousins told her frankly that she sounded like a goose honking. She also decided not to let on how much lip reading she was able to do. It was tough enough with new people, especially when they talked fast, or the worst of all, got up into her face, over-enunciating so much they looked like they were being tortured as she stared down the backs of their throats.

Most of all, she didn't want to deal with questions about her ancestors until she gained a sense of how they would take the answers.

Which of course was the first thing they asked. "Did Inda-Harskialdna leave any weapons that were his?" Noddy asked.

"Or written records?" Connar asked.

"All we had of him is the tapestry we sent before," she signed.

Noddy grinned. "Thank you for that. It hangs in the best interview chamber. Sometimes I go in to look at it."

His open curiosity, and his easy acceptance of her answer, caused her incipient resentment to ease. The other prince, the beautiful one, looked disappointed, and she suspected that he wasn't going to let it go—but she had prepared herself for that, too.

Danet asked after her mother and father, the boys played the drums, and the girls sang, Bunny trying hard to repeat the songs in Hand, which caused some laughter. The meal ended and the youngsters were free.

Arrow sat back, swallowed off his wine, and said, "I followed more of that than I expected."

Danet said dryly, "That's because Noren was polite, and matched her tone with ours."

"Tone?" Arrow asked.

"Speak. Ing. Like. This. Be. Cause. We. Are. That. Slow."

Arrow grimaced. "Well, looks like Bun's taken charge there. Good. That should keep her out of the stable."

"Maybe," Danet answered dryly, both parents unaware of the fact that Bun had scarcely been in the stable ever since the royal runners had been deployed to make ready.

Bun had told Lineas she was ready to help, without stating the true reason: Quill Montredavan-An.

SIXTEEN

Ink tried to talk Ran out of going with the rest of them to meet the boys in the city, but the prospect of testing the ruse was just too irresistible. He loved the notion of putting something over on everybody, especially those Marlovayirs swanking about.

As yet, no Marlovayir or Senelaec rider had addressed the other. The Marlovayir girls had endured a hard lecture by the jarlan before they left: *any* whisper of bad behavior and they would never go again.

"What if the Senelaecs show up and start something?"

"Then you defend yourselves. But you'd better be able to back your claim that it was self-defense," she'd said.

Ran expected to enjoy getting away with his disguise. What he didn't expect was his gut twinging with envy when they passed into the great square and got their first glimpse of the boys on the strut in their horsetails and academy coats as they shot academy slang back and forth. To him, their lives looked like so much fun.

He shook it off, his sense of humor steadying him. When someone started organizing singing and dancing, he volunteered to drum, which he was very good at.

Pony sorted through the boys impatiently, looking for Ghost. Of course he ended up surrounded by flirting girls, who had also sought the most prettiest of the boys, but didn't quite dare flirt with beautiful Connar unless he made some sign he wanted to be flirted with. But he was over with the dancers — with a big crowd watching.

Cousin Ranet stayed close to her particular friends in the riding, feeling intimidated by all these older, taller, strangers. But as soon as the dancing began, she joined the girls, and began to relax and enjoy herself.

Bun made her way to the biggest clump of boys standing about. She'd spent her entire life around boys, marking no distinction between castle boys, academy boys, and her brothers. She knew who every horse belonged to, and began putting faces to names.

Without any self-consciousness whatever, she introduced her way through the crowd until she came face to face with Rat Noth. "Oh, are you the one who belongs to Grasshopper?" she asked.

The boys around Noth watched with interest, a couple of them exchanging the age-old signals for wagers. Rat Noth, tall, lean, broad of forehead, turned his narrow gaze on Bun, and to everyone's surprise, he spoke. "You know Grasshopper?" Three actual words!

"Know her! She's one of my *favorites.*" Bunny went on to talk about a mare that everyone else considered cranky and notoriously skittish, taking instant exception to many humans, most other horses, and all cats, dogs, and tumbleweeds.

Rat already knew that the horses were excellently cared for when the boys weren't able to ride, much less get to the stable to curry their own animals. He looked right at Bunny, rather than at the ground, as she said, "Tell me, how did she get her name? I like it so much!"

The boys wagering whether Rat would talk (and the number of words) all held their breath.

"When she was first born. Two days old. She hopped." Rat held out his broad, strong hand, palm to the ground, about waist height. "Like a grasshopper."

"I can just see it," Bunny exclaimed, clapping her hands in delight. "Did you train her yourself? She's a dream on the longe line, once you figure out her ways."

Rat stared. This girl was so easy to talk to that even the horses knew it, if Grasshopper tolerated her. His gaze dropping, he muttered, "We learned together. Got her when I was ten. Last year was the first time I brought her."

Three complete sentences!

Bunny chattered on about Grasshopper's excellent qualities, then, noticing his bright red ears and his earnest gaze on his dusty boot toes, she said, "I'll be watching for Grasshopper in the games." And she turned sunnily to match another horse with its rider, leaving Rat's friends to pick up their jaws.

Rat Noth! Talking to a girl! His particular friends muscled him off to revive him with liquid courage after his ordeal. He went willingly, though he seemed more dazed than devastated.

Bunny breezed her way through the senior boys with sisterly friendliness, and Lineas shadowed her at an unobtrusive distance. Though Bunny was not at all what anyone would call handsome, with her round face, buck teeth, eyes set too close together so they sometimes looked crossed, framed by plank-straight brown hair that was more often messy than not, she seemed to make friends wherever she turned.

No one had the least idea how troubled she was over the fact that the one boy she liked as a boy treated her with friendly respect, exactly as a royal runner ought to treat a princess. And she had no idea how to change that.

Noren observed her—she observed everyone. Very aware of the stares and pointed fingers ringing outward wherever she walked, at first she regretted wearing her House tunic, except that all the girls had theirs on, having come straight from Restday drum at the barracks. But she knew that even if she wasn't wearing the Algaravayir green and silver, she would still be pointed out. Better to get it over with.

She didn't regret her decision not to tell them that she could sometimes read lips. Even in the flickering light of the lanterns that enterprising tavern owners had strung out, hoping to lure the youngsters in to spend their coins, she recognized the lip shapes of *Inda-Harskialdna* over and over again. She didn't want to know what question formed around that name. Returning a blank look, she told them in Hand that she didn't understand, and moved on.

She was ready to return to the barracks when she came up unexpectedly before a tall, broad-shouldered boy. She recognized Noddy the same moment he recognized her. He spoke, then wiped his hands down his pants and signed slowly, "Anywhere you want to see?"

Unsurprisingly, Bunny's Hand name was signed with bunny ears. "Bunny took me around. Thank you."

He wiped his hands again, and this time asked if she wanted to try the strawberry mountains up the down street. She could see in his face how hard he was working, and that he meant well. And he hadn't said a thing about the Algaravayir family. That might come, but right now she appreciated his kindness, awkward as it was.

They made slow, painstaking conversation until the drum beats changed. She hadn't been watching the boys in the center circle competing against each other by doing the sword dance with cups balanced on their heads. The familiar reverberations of the girls' falcon dance caused her to look up.

A few girls had taken drums from some of the boys. The rhythm pounded in her bones. She glanced up, but Noddy smiled and made little motions as he said, *Dance, dance!* Then he blushed and wrung his hands the way people did when they didn't have a word. He clearly didn't have the Hand for the girls' dances.

She demonstrated, he repeated it, and she turned away, flanked by her two runners. Pan Totha and Holly of the bright green eyes followed obediently. She invited them to join her, and though the girls were cousins, and looked a lot alike, their expressions were so typical of each—Pan Totha sober and dutiful, Holly flashing a grin of delight, then signed a cautious, "Are we allowed?" as she stood back.

"Just come," Noren signed back. If the royal city people were going to shut out runners, too bad for them.

So Holly took her hand and they broke into the circle, clasping outside hands with unknown girls as they found the circle's rhythm. Noren loved dancing, especially when the drums were strong enough to feel through her body. She stomped, clapped, leaped, and twirled, unaware of her own easy grace, borne of years of hard work, promise of what was to come.

Arrow looked up from the words chalked on the slate, and frowned at Danet. "Whose idea was this, letting the girls mix in with the boys? We've always run them separate."

"Mine."

Arrow's brows shot upward. " *You?* Why?"

"I gave the girls the opportunity to sign up for any of the boys' regular events," Danet said. "Instead of setting up a separate program. If they hadn't wanted to, they wouldn't have. Maybe I need to remind you that before us, there hasn't been an academy for several generations. A lot of these girls and boys train together at home, then divide off according to tradition, yes, but also according to need. When there're going to be battles requiring swords, the men go."

"Three girls signed up for the sword melee on horseback. Here's one signed up for the standing sword competition." Arrow frowned at the chalk markings. "It just says Vesea."

"She's a cousin to the Tualan—"

"Riders to the Toracas, I know, I know. Standing toe to toe, she'll be hammered."

Danet said, "I've watched her. I don't expect her to beat any of your biggest senior boys, but she'll hold her own among the rest. All these other events, let them match their skills. I think it'll be good for them all."

"All right." Arrow tipped his head. "Give it a try. And if those girls look good, then find money for your queen's training. There's a tradition for it."

Danet had been thinking about little else during her rare leisure time. The problem with it, she had discovered in poring over Hadand Deheldegarthe's old letters, was that the traditional queen's training was for a purpose that was no longer in use. But all she said was, "We'll talk about it afterward."

The day before Victory Day, all the puddles dried up and the sky cleared, leaving a beautiful day. But everyone over the age of twenty or so peered to the west, where there were no clouds, and muttered to one another that Lightning Season was striking early.

When the sun rose the following day, it was to a brilliant blue sky, sparks igniting from every bit of metal. After breakfast, Arrow and Danet went straight to the parade ground, knowing that Andaun and the masters had rearranged the schedule.

Usually the riding contests—the most popular events—were last, but this day they were moved up to early morning to spare the animals the afternoon heat.

They began with races the length of the parade ground, which the Sindan-An or Tlennen boys usually won. Interest perked up when the girls rode out with the boys, heads turning as they side-eyed one another, or stared outright.

Headmaster Andaun dropped the flag. The moment the fluttering cloth hit the dusty ground, the horses, sidling impatiently, leaped into the gallop and bolted down the length, boys shrilling the fox yip.

This year's race ended with a clump, led by a Sindan-An girl a nose ahead of a Fath girl and Rat Noth on his Grasshopper. Baldy Sindan-An was neck and neck with two Tlennen cousins, boy and girl, and a Jevayir boy, with Ran and Salt Marlovayir barely a nose behind, these last two eyeing one another narrowly. Salt knew if he was caught slanging any girl, even a Senelaec, he'd catch it hot, and maybe get tossed out altogether, if she whined to the beaks. And any Senelaec would of course whine up a storm.

As for Ran, under Ink's watchful eye he kept his mouth shut and his face averted. But the ferocious longing to win seethed inside him.

Boys and girls readied for the obstacle course, the most grueling of the riding events, which Rat Noth had won the past two years, and had come in second the year before that, beating out all the seniors.

The race started in a mass, circling out beyond the academy itself, into the fallow fields at the north end of the city and back behind the garrison to the other end of the parade ground.

By the time the dust was seen at that end, the mass had thinned. Ran was neck-and-neck with Ghost, another Fath girl, and a Sindan-An Riders' boy, all three desperate to catch up with Rat Noth thundering ahead of them....

And ahead of him, Noren, daughter of the Algaravayirs.

No one could touch her. She galloped across the finish line three horse lengths ahead of Rat, to shouts of praise from the spectators, followed by the question— *Who was that?* The name *Algaravayir*, not heard in that place for many years, echoed up and down the stone benches.

The rest of the riders streamed in, everyone having to comment.

"A fluke," the seniors said as the riders brought their horses in to be rubbed down.

"She cheated," Pepper Marlovayir declared loyally to his bunkmates, joined by a chorus of agreement, as if loudness could change the facts.

"Nah." Rat flicked his hand out, palm down. "Rode in front of me the entire time. Sheered the edges better'n me. Want to see that horse," he added thoughtfully.

Noren, as winner, was given the choice to go first in the next competition, which was the mounted spear throw. This event was less about speed than about riding ability, as the rider had to bend to the ground, pick up a spear, then lob it at a target fifteen paces to the side, all within the length of the parade ground.

Noren could have been expected to turn it down, but instead she flashed a wide grin and signed that she was ready any time they were. Holly had readied another of their horses as Noren ran to the inside of the gate at the barn end of the parade ground.

The master in charge, already experienced in Hand, asked if she understood: she was to ride out the gate, and bend down to get the spear. Not grab it before she mounted.

She waved that she understood, and remained where she was, watched by puzzled, silent boys and girls. She motioned for Holly to release the horse — and then, to everyone's astonishment, as the animal began an easy canter, she pelted out to intercept, vaulted up over the animal's hindquarters, flipped in the air, and landed on the saddle. Then she locked one foot behind the horse's neck and leaned down to snatch up the spear, whipped it around as she righted, and threw. All in one continuous motion.

It landed in the target without much force, but respectably within the inner circle.

The watchers went wild. Noren looked over at those open mouths and grinned.

Up in the stand, Arrow sighed.

"Why the sour face?" Danet asked. "She's a terrific rider."

"I never thought an Algaravayir would learn useless horse tricks."

Danet's lip curled. "Arrow, why would the Algaravayirs be any different from anyone else? Did you really think they've been hiding generations of Inda-Harskialdnas down there, ready to pop out and lead wars for you when you snapped your fingers?"

Arrow shot her a fulminating look, shuffled his feet, then said, "The competition is in the midden now. You watch. The boys're going to start assing around with trick riding. Useless in battle."

Maybe it was useless in battle, but for entertainment value, there was nothing better. The watchers shouted with excitement, thrilling hearts, nerves, brains. The boys did just as Arrow had predicted, the most flagrant being two Jayad Heseas cousins and Mouse Noth, who rode out side by side on a pair of horses, Mouse behind one cousin. The two bigger boys stood on the animals' shoulders as the horses cantered side by side, and small, skinny Mouse scrambled up to place a foot on each of their shoulders, arms windmilling. Then they tumbled down to their animals' backs amid frantic cheering.

Following that, the Tlennen girls rode out in a pack, leaping from one horse to the other. The next group added headstands and running dismounts. The audience adored it all.

Some insisted on a second go, until Headmaster Andaun himself put an end to that particular event. The morning was strengthening in heat, and they still had the three main horse events ahead.

First was the lance competition.

No girls had signed up for this, but most of them lined up on the wall, watching as intently as the rest of the academy boys.

No one watched more intently than Ran. All sense of competition forgotten, he writhed with jealousy. Those boys with their heels locked down and those lances leveled as their heavy horses charged...what in the entire world could be more fun than that?

But Senelaecs didn't learn lances any more than they rode heavy horses. For the past couple of generations, they had been fighting off the increasingly organized horse thieves from over the eastern mountains, which called for fast riding and straight shooting.

Ran watched, breath held, as all the upper seniors rode out, charging hay-stuffed targets. Those who didn't hit the red in the middle were eliminated, cutting the competition abruptly down to eight: four of the most senior of the lancers, Ghost, Rat, and both princes.

Connar looked impossibly heroic as he rode hard, contrasted with heavy-shouldered Noddy, who slumped in the saddle, but it was Ghost and Noddy who slammed their lances into the hay-stuffed targets time after time, with such strength that the targets sometimes completely burst their ties.

The four younger boys were finally eliminated, Noddy last. Connar retired, oblivious to the cheers of the spectators, and unaware of the female gazes on his striking profile. He struggled to hide his sharp disappointment in himself—all that extra time he'd put into lance work, and he tied with Rat Noth, a year younger. Yeah, he was destined to be a commander, not a rider, except his reading made it clear that everyone naturally followed a commander who could beat them all. Like Inda-Harskialdna.

Behind him the four seniors, red-faced with heat, charged the targets another seven times, until at last the elder Mareca boy won.

Ran, who had watched intently, let his breath trickle out. Even when he gave up his braids, he'd never get to do *that.*

The next event irked him just as much. Out came the wooden swords, and fighting on horseback. Three girls had signed up for this event, two from the far south and one from the Fath-Tyavayir riding. No one else, as women usually didn't train with swords. Many didn't even bother with knife training anymore. Few even learned close combat weaponry for scouting, especially among the Eastern Alliance. Those scouts had for at least a generation been spotting trouble, then riding hot and hard on the kingdom's fleetest horses to report. Their weapon was the bow, and the ride and shoot would be next, with the girls impatient to get started.

But Ran watched closely as the Senelaec girls muttered among themselves, hoping that those swanking Marlovayir boys would go down in defeat fast.

The contestants were released to fight in melee to make up for lost time. Each combatant carried a chalked wooden sword, so anyone with a mark on an arm had to fight with the other hand, and marks across the upper body were considered death blows, as hitting heads was strictly forbidden.

At first the melee was a confusing mob, mostly hidden by dust, but the contestants began to fall away fairly rapidly—mostly the younger ones. As the crowd thinned so did the dust, and the spectators were able to make out the best fighters dueling back and forth, sometimes three or four circling one, who either fought them off and broke the circle, or was eliminated.

Fairly early on, along with all the younger boys, two girls were eliminated. Both were sixteen-year-olds who as yet had more confidence than skill, but the third, a Noth rider who had grown up with brothers, lasted until the mass was down to fourteen. Shortly after, in a tactical rout by Ghost and Stick Tyavayir, five were eliminated one after the other (including one Marlovayir, which brought covert grins to the Senelaecs, and to Connar), before Stick was tapped. That left two seniors, Ghost, and Noddy.

As the two seniors fought each other, Ghost and Noddy dueled, mouths open, sweat flying. Ghost just missed Noddy's neck the same moment Noddy swung from the hip and knocked the exhausted, overreached Ghost clean out of his saddle.

The audience sent up a huge shout. Noddy leaped down and held out his hand to Ghost, his regret plain to see as he helped the boy stand. They caught the reins of their horses and walked off together, Noddy deciding to disqualify himself, though what he'd done was not outside the rules—but he was a lot like the Uncle Jarend he'd never met, remorseful when his enormous strength got him into trouble.

The audience gave the prince a shout. At last there were only two seniors, who by now were too tired to do much more than clack their swords together. One finally got in a strike down the other's back, and the crimson-faced boys retired to gulp down ladles of water as the stable hands took the animals to the water butts.

Then runners-in-training ran out to set up for the ride and shoot—the favorite event.

Anticipation gripped watchers and competitors both as the targets were set up on both sides down the length of the parade ground. Connar, brooding from the sidelines, wished he'd put more time into this instead of those useless lances. At least Noddy was even worse than he was—a thought that made him despise himself so much that he had to move, and walked along the wall to look over the girls stringing their bows. He knew how good everyone was in the upper levels of the academy, but he had no idea how these girls would measure up. He hoped they could beat Rat Noth.

Not ten paces away, Ran Senelaec readied himself. After watching, and yearning, his entire body thrummed with the need to prove himself, to *win*.

The elimination round was for single side, at fifty paces.

They were released to ride down the parade ground, two horse lengths apart, leaving little margin for error. The spectators quieted when Noren began her run. She was competent, but not great; it was clear that she was one of the best riders, male or female, but astonishingly, not a fighter.

When everyone had gone, those who had not hit the center mark every time were eliminated, as by now the sun had nearly reached noon, and they still had all the standing competitions yet to go.

Headmaster Andaun sent one of his twelve-year-old runners to give the command to set up a second set of targets on the other side—a sight that dismayed many of the competitors, most of whom practiced only on one side.

Eliminate, eliminate, eliminate, cheer! That was Rat Noth; one of his left side shots was barely on the edge of the center mark, but anything touching was ruled good. He rode back, shaking his head. Pony Yvanavayir had worked her way up to follow Ghost in hopes of catching his attention. Ghost rode down the parade ground, every shot strong and true.

Pony followed. An excellent shot right-side, which was the customary side for competitions, she rarely shot left-side, and even more rarely both, but she was furiously determined, and her first three shots were straight and true. But then she ran into difficulty: you can't slow, or the following shooter will be on your horse's rump, and if you lag for a heartbeat to align your arrow, each shot puts you shooting backward just that much more.

Her next few shots hit the target, but not the mark, and the last, to the left, flew entirely over the target. She rode back, furious—until she got to the gate, and Ghost, who had just finished drinking, handed Manther's sister a cup, smiled, and said, "Good try."

Pony's fury turned to euphoria, just like that. She walked her horse to the waiting runners, her mind full of anticipation, and she didn't see the rest of her riding's competition.

Just as well. To a girl, all their right-side shots were true, but the left made it clear where the weakness in their drills lay.

Several Marlovayir girls went next, mixed among academy boys. No one from their team was disqualified. The Senelaecs, watching with disgust, moved up in the line, and Ran found himself motioned in behind one of the Marlovayir twins, who looked back and gave him a curled lip.

Ran was incandescent. Ink, knowing him well, sidled her horse up. "Just take the targets. Nothing fancy," she cautioned.

She might as well have saved her breath. Ran had just finished watching two contests that filled him with longing—after a morning in which the Senelaecs had won nothing.

They were all hot and sweaty, their cotton-linen clothes clinging damp to their bodies, grimy with dust. Pepper Marlovayir rode down the ground, his arrows striking true, true, true, true, left and right—and then an arrow slipped in his clammy grip. Just for a heartbeat and he recovered, but he was shooting backward now, as Ran began his ride.

All that pent-up emotion cooled into deliberation. He had been practicing both-side targets since he was small, and this last year, as his strength increased, he'd played with shooting two arrows at the same time.

The crowd went wild as his arrows flew, straight and true, to the center mark, twang, *slam!* Twang, *slam!* Twang, *slam!* Halfway down, the danger mark for everyone, he felt his rhythm slow less than a heartbeat, his breath crowing in his throat. Every muscle in his body tightened as he stood in the stirrups, his sweat-damp shirt and trousers molded to his body, and his robe flapping behind him on the horse's flank as *slam, slam, slam*, the arrows flew fast and hard, smacking into the center mark—

Five rows above the king and queen, a teenage journeyman cobbler, who had been enjoying the contestants' tight young bodies rather than their shooting, pointed as he bellowed, "Heyo! That girl's got a prick!"

Arrow—whose sense of humor had not changed much since he was a teen—let out a guffaw, which spread among those who heard. The king laughed, so did everyone else, as those who heard the laughter but not why nudged their neighbors to find out what the joke was.

Ran heard none of it. His focus was entirely on his form, which was stunning—hand snapping out and down, nipping the arrows from the quiver angled at his side. Aim and strength perfectly matched. *Thunk, thunk*, the final two arrows slammed dead center into the last left, the downfall for so many.

The crowd roared.

Arrow's laughter had died, hilarity replaced with a question. "Who is that?"

"Ranet Senelaec," Danet said dryly.

Arrow slewed around to stare at her. "Connar's wife?" His eyebrows met in an angry line over his brows as his neck flushed.

Before he could begin barking questions, Danet murmured, "Not now."

Arrow remembered the audience around them, and straightened, his hands gripping his knees. Below, Ran rejoined the Senelaec girls in the spot they had adopted as theirs. He became aware of a different quality in the noise then, and a lot of stares.

He turned, bewildered—he was not unfairly expecting a mutual whoop of celebration, as not only had he hit every target with two arrows, but that Marlovayir strut had been eliminated. But the girls seemed more uncertain than celebrative, and they drew closer in unconscious protection.

From habit, Ran turned to find Ink, but right then she was making her run, every shot smacking true into the center.

Young Pan whispered to Ran, "I think they know."

Ran blinked dust-gritty eyes. "Know? What?"

"About you."

"What? No, impossible. Who blabbed?"

Fnor bit her lips against the snicker that wanted to escape, and said in an unsteady voice, "Someone. Yelled out. Said you've got a prick."

"Of course I do," he said with an impatient glance down his length, then the implications began to hit him, piling up in all their disastrous probabilities. He turned his head toward where the king and queen sat, the former looking like thunder even from this distance.

"Oh. Shit," he whispered.

Ink had finished—hitting every target—and came riding back. As she rejoined them, Tdor whispered to her, and her expression turned grim. The last three of the Senelaec riding made their runs, and all three hit the targets, but there was no sense of celebration as one by one they rejoined the group, were surprised at the grim faces, and were filled in.

The nine of them stood together, every wondering, mirthful, or simply amazed glance from those around them as painful as a whiplash. Ink wondered when the king's guards would come to haul them off to the royal dungeon, as the youngest girl—who had just finished a ride as lethal as any of the seniors'—wondered if they'd be shot right there in the parade ground.

By then Headmaster Andaun had caught the rumor, and sent a glance at Commander Noth, stationed at one end of the parade ground, where he was in reach of any runners from the garrison sentries. Noth gave his head a tiny shake. Andaun turned for clues to the king and queen. Arrow stared straight ahead, his mind working furiously, but Danet had been expecting that unspoken question, and her fingers flicked in the *Carry on* sign.

The last four contestants completed their rides, every one of them eliminated, and then, in a dry voice, Commander Andaun read out the names of those who would participate in the second round, with the targets removed now staggered, some closer, some at a far remove, and shifted laterally as well.

When Andaun got to Ran's name, someone in the crowd of academy boys commented loudly, "Shouldn't that be Rana?"

Some laughter rose, drowned by a buzz of conversation as everyone wondered what, why, when, was it some kind of ruse, as the Senelaecs trooped off in a tight pack toward the horses.

This time all the seniors, who worked hardest on lance and sword, were eliminated, and more than half of the academy boys; as future captains they were more likely to be commanding the archers, rather than shooting themselves.

It was the distance shots that did in the younger boys, who didn't quite have their strength yet. More than half the girls found themselves riding back in defeat. Among the Marlovayirs, the oldest three girls were the only ones who survived, one barely, the arrow in the farthest target drooping at an angle. Ink, Ran, Young Pan, and Tdor made it from the Senelaecs, the younger girls all defeated by the distance shots.

The third round had all the targets moved back, the last two at a hundred paces. This time, a Sindan-An, a Tlennen—both cousins to Ran—and Ran were left, Ink disqualified by a heartbreaking finger's width on the last shot, her arrow drooping as if ashamed of having not flown true.

The three final contestants met to get their horses. Tall, dark-haired Marda, born a Sindan and adopted heir to the Tlennens, said to Ran, "I wondered why Cousin Ran moved in with you at Senelaec. How long you been a girl?"

"Since I was born."

Baldy Sindan-An flashed a grin. "What a prime ruse! Cub shoulda let us in on it."

All three turned when one of the headmaster's small runners panted up and squeaked, "Headmaster wants you."

They followed him back to the command post. Headmaster Andaun turned their way. "We're awarding the three of you a tie," he said. "We're running very late, and we still need to get to the standing competitions. Go get something to eat." He pointed to the mess tent.

The two boys saluted. Ran just stood there, not sure what to do with his hands; Senelaecs didn't bother with saluting. As the Headmaster spoke with someone else, Marda squinted against the sun at where the runners were busy hauling all but four of the targets away, and others rolled out carts of wooden weapons. "Well, now's when we get hammered."

Baldy rolled his eyes, shoved wisps of his nearly white hair out of his eyes, and elbowed Ran. "You should run with us some day."

"If I survive today," Ran muttered, the back of his neck prickling; everywhere he turned, people stared.

Baldy snickered, still convinced that his distant Senelaec cousins had pulled a ruse for the fun of it.

They relinquished their now unneeded horses to the stable hands. The two boys turned toward their classmates in the academy, already discussing the results in cryptic academy idiom, and Ran separated off and rejoined the Senelaecs. The prickling worsened with every breath as he tried to imagine how much trouble he was in.

Tdor and her cousin, future runners, had gone off to fetch food while the others stood in a tight pack. During the sword fighting, distance shooting, standing knife and spear throw, and hand to hand events they endlessly speculated, watching sporadically. Ran's desire to compete in the long distance standing archery had withered; all he could think of was how much damage he was going to bring home.

No one noticed Noren's intent assessment of the hand to hand fighting, any more than they noticed the row of royal runners in training behind everyone else, watching closely.

The sun had begun to drop toward the western horizon when the last of the awards were given out. These turned out to be tiny discs of gold with the Olavayir eagle worked into them. Boys could sew theirs down the left arm of their House tunics (right sleeve being reserved for military honors only), and the girls down the front edging of their House robes.

Andaun gave Ran a slightly pained glance as the latter stepped up to win his gold for the ride and shoot, a look that Ran tried to interpret as he walked back to the girls.

He wasn't left to wonder long. When the last award had been given, the academy was dismissed, jarls' offspring to bathe and ready themselves for the banquet to be held in the feasting hall opposite the throne room, and everyone else to rec time or to pack for home.

The Senelaecs were standing in a circle wondering what to do next—poor little Cousin Ranet with tears running silently down her dusty face—when a runner approached. Not one of the headmaster's small boys, but an older royal runner in dark blue. He said to Ran, "Please follow me."

"Why?" Ink said, looking wary. "If you're dropping him in some dungeon, we'll all go together."

"To an interview with the king and queen," the royal runner said, studying those nine worried faces. "Ranet, Ran?"

"I'm more used to Ran," he whispered.

"Ran Senelaec. You are the only one whose presence is required."

The girls exchanged questioning glances, but even Ink didn't quite have the courage to attempt forcing herself into a royal interview. "Hold this," he said, handing her his little gold eagle.

Ink took it and bent a glare on the royal runner as she stated with dire import, "We'll be waiting for you."

SEVENTEEN

Up in the royal chamber, Danet and Arrow faced each other. He crossed his arms. "There are two reasons for a boy to turn into a girl. Unless that boy comes up here and tells us he got born into the wrong body, and I know it happens, then someone made him do it. And there's only one reason why that makes sense. I never expected a stab in the back like this from Wolf Senelaec."

Danet let out a short sigh. "I thought so, too, when I first heard about it."

"Wait. What?" he demanded sharply. "How long have I been kept out of this secret? And who else is in on it?"

"Only me," Danet said, deciding to leave Hliss out, as Arrow was still sore about Andas's disappearance. "It was accidentally found out by a runner. I was angry at first. I thought it was a strike at my betrothal plan. At *me*. But over time, I began to see it differently."

"How is it anything but the back of the hand at us?"

"Think about our history," Danet said. "Not ours, especially. No, even that's not true: Think about how we became king and queen. When that child was born, it was not long after Mathren killed Evred and Kendred. And if you look back farther, around the time we were born, the previous king and queen were killed, the queen being the Jarlan of Senelaec's sister. And so on, back several generations."

Arrow grimaced, and dropped his gaze.

"So, back to us. At the time that boy was born, you declared that second sons were to come to a new academy."

"Which means Wolf thinks I'm incompetent," Arrow muttered. "Both of them."

"At the time," she said, "neither you or I knew if we'd last a day. A month. A year. *We* couldn't see our own future. Everyone knew we weren't brought up to it. Anyway, I waited to see what they would do, and sure enough, they've sent us a perfectly acceptable girl to marry Connar. They call her Ranet. It might even be her name. She looks exactly like Fuss, which is most appropriate, considering that Fuss ought to have been standing here with Evred right now, instead of you and me."

"That's true enough," Arrow said, massaging his jaw. "Yet here I thought Wolf would regard it as an honor, their girl marrying Connar. I was damn wrong."

"Rather than assume motivations, why don't we ask this boy? Alone. Everyone else is talking about it. That can't be helped. I really think, given the fact that there are no actual laws spoken before the jarls about requiring their sons to attend—" When Arrow began a heated comment, she raised her hand. "Let me finish. And half of the spectators heard you laughing when that lout yelled out his discovery. All told, I think handling this situation quietly, whatever you do decide, is the better part of wisdom."

"All right. Have it your way," Arrow said, sighing. The truth was, he wanted that young rider in his army: Given a year or two of practice and strength, boy or girl, Ran would probably be the best shot among the new generation.

Ran sloped along behind the royal runner, covered in sweat-streaked dust, his braids filthy and tangled. He was too inexperienced to perceive that Danet had sent mild-mannered Ivandred as the least threatening person to summon him. Ran might as well have been marching with his hands tied, surrounded by a fierce wing of guards armed to the teeth. Guilt was his worst enemy, as he knew that his parents had not wanted him on this escapade.

And this was the reason why.

When they reached the door to the interview chamber at last, he braced his spine.

The door opened, but no execution squad awaited him. No one was there but the king and queen, the latter seen the once on their arrival, and the former only glimpsed in the royal seat among the spectators at the parade ground.

That was frightening enough.

It was the king whom Ran watched anxiously. On seeing Arrow's irritated frown, his heart sank even further, while Arrow scrutinized the boy. If he'd seen a smirk, much less insolence, nothing Danet could have said would have stopped him from tossing that skinny ass into the lockup for a day or two until his temper cooled. But Ran's expression was nearly green with sick dread and guilt.

In times of stress, Arrow reverted to the truculent youth bullied by Lanrid and his rough Riders. "Was this one of your Senelaec practical jokes?" he demanded abruptly.

"No!" Ran's face drained completely of color, then he flushed from the neck to the ears. "I sneaked away. Da was gone, they're trying to catch those horse thieves out east, and Ma said I should stay home. But...."

"I want to know why this." Arrow indicated his braids. "Are you or are you not a girl?"

"Yes—that is, no. I grew up as one." Ran looked around wildly, tugging at his shirt collar beneath his robe, which unaccountably seemed too tight, though the shirt laces had become loose. As the royal pair regarded him in silence, he groped for words. "I was going to have to give it up anyway. Cub —Mardran, my brother—thinks I'll have to do the Beard Spell in a year at most, and so, they brought out Cousin Ranet to be me, and I'll be Rana, and go with Da when the Tlennens call."

"Do you fight with a sword?" Arrow asked in a much easier voice—it was clear that this masquerade was not Ran's idea. That stupidity lay solely with his parents.

Ran sighed. "No—the girls don't drill with swords. We're, they're, scouts, and if there's trouble, we shoot, and run for reinforcements. Cub started teaching me a year ago, but he doesn't always have time—he rode out during spring with Da. Promised to find me a swordmaster when Cousin Ranet takes my place."

Arrow's eyes narrowed with interest. "Would you go to the academy if you could?"

It's difficult to say how this interview would have gone if Ran had expressed anything else but the honest longing that he'd been feeling all day. "*Would* I?" he exclaimed. "I'd give *anything* to go!"

Arrow's expression cleared. "Run along, then. I'll have a letter for you to carry to your father by the time you leave."

Ran backed up, fist to his chest, a flush of happiness glowing in his filthy face. As he pivoted, poised to decamp, Danet said, "Remind Cousin Ranet that, as my son's future wife, she ought to attend the banquet. She may sit with your Sindan-An or Tlennen connections if she likes. She can sit with us next year."

Ran flattened his palm as he faced her, then he backed hastily to the door, and fled.

The others visibly relaxed when they saw him pelt up, apparently still in one piece. They hirpled toward the barracks as Ran filled them in on the conversation.

Relieved that they were miraculously saved from summary execution, they vented the long hours of intense emotion in high-pitched sniggers and wild talk about what they would have done to rescue him if he'd been slammed into the royal dungeon.

At the barracks door, they fell silent when they saw Pony standing with her feet braced against the frame on either side, fists on hips. Three Marlovayir girls crowded behind her.

"You," she pointed at Ran, "can go bunk with the boys."

"Drop it," Ink said. "Unless you want to take it outside." She shook her sleeve back, revealing a knife sheath on her left forearm.

The Marlovayir girls, mindful of their jarlan's dire warnings, stood silent, poised to mix it up with the Senelaecs if the latter started anything. A fake girl was as good an excuse as any other; one girl bit chapped lips, silently urging Ink to make the first move so they could claim self-defense.

Henad Tlennen stepped up in front of them, turned, and faced the Marlovayirs. "He's not going in the baths with us, so who cares?"

"I don't," Shendan Khanivayir said with false cheer, annoyed with Pony Yvanavayir having summarily chosen herself as speaker for the barracks. "And he could go in the baths with *me* any time."

"I'm there first," called a Fath.

Ran had heard the older girls joking about sex for a year or two, but he still blushed, as another girl he didn't know ranged herself alongside Henad, and said pleasantly, "Isn't it a little late to start squawking about modesty, seeing as he's been with us since we rode in?"

Genis Fath, betrothed to Mardran Tlennen, added, "Do you really think you're so tight he'll look twice at you?"

Ink shoved past Pony, knocking the shorter girl back and ignoring the Marlovayirs, and the rest of the Senelaecs streamed behind her. The girls trooped off to the baths, while Ran slunk around the back of the barracks and made his way to the back barn, where the big tubs of water for the cows were located. No one was there, so he stripped to the waist and plunged his upper half in the magic-protected water, feeling all the grime vanish in that effervescent sensation, a little like bees running all over your skin.

He cleaned up fast, dunked his clothes to be spread out to dry with the others', and rejoined the group, giddy with joy now that a miracle had happened. He was not only saved, but he'd get to go to the academy!

Pony was left complaining to her followers, who paid lip service as they got ready for a night of fun. At least they didn't have to go to the banquet hall with Pony, who had been getting more bossy by the day, not less, though she hadn't won a single event. No one really cared one way or the other about a younger boy living among them as a girl.

Pony discovered that the other jarlate girls had gone in a pack straight from the baths, leaving her to walk alone the long distance to the banquet hall next to the throne room, where she found her older brother Manther sitting with their Tlen cousins. She had to join them, but she looked around for the Faths. Who were busy talking to the Tyavayirs. Ghost did look over twice, smiling. Of course he was smiling at her, she thought, and smiled back.

As soon as the banquet *finally* was over, she raced out after Ghost, ahead of the younger folks streaming toward the city center. It was filled with young people, singing and dancing already in full force in five different places.

With the sun's disappearance and cool baths, everyone's spirits had lifted. Pony caught up to Ghost before he could vanish into the crowd, and in her flirtiest voice cooed, "Show me where I can get the best root brew."

He looked around for his friends, but they all backed off, leaving him with Manther's sister.

"All right," he said.

Behind them, Noren walked with Bunny and Lineas. They had invited Cousin Ranet to join them, suspecting that the younger girl would be lost on her own, until she could be restored to the rest of the Senelaec girls. They worked through a laborious conversation about the horses and their performance, Lineas interpreting, until they found the rest of the party.

Cousin Ranet listened silently, nearly dizzy from the whipsaw emotions of the day. Now that Ran was truly safe, she could secretly revel in the fact that she had been picked to marry the prettiest boy in the entire royal city. She would one day be a princess, which meant all the girls' games would be run by her. She could not imagine a better life, ever, ever, *ever*.

Connar had said very little to her, but that was fine. She was far too shy around strangers to expect anything more. Buoyant with happiness, she skimmed lightly through the crowd when she spotted Young Pan, and she waited to join in the girls' dances.

On the other side of a huge circle, Ran sat cross-legged, robe puddled around him and braid loops flapping on his shoulders as he pounded on a borrowed drum for a group of boys twirling and leaping and stamping, horsetails and coat skirts swinging.

It was clear that nothing was going to come of his masquerade. Keth Eveneth, primed by Salt and Pepper Marlovayir, sauntered up. Ran ignored him and kept playing a galloping counterpoint to the five other girls and boys on various-sized drums.

Keth nudged Ran with his toe. "Why don't you dance?"

"I don't know the boys' dances," Ran said, without missing a beat.

"Are you a girl or a boy?"

"Boy," Ran said.

"Why did you come as a girl?"

"Because I did."

Tdor and Young Pan approached with linked arms. Young Pan thumped Keth hard with her hip, forcing him back a couple of steps. "Ooops," she said over her shoulder as she took his place.

Keth, who found the whole thing hilarious, laughed and retreated to report the exchange to the watching Marlovayirs. They turned away, disappointed that no one seemed ready to make a scene.

Ran drummed in a flourishing finish as the boys finished their dance, sending shrill yips rising to the starry sky.

"Our turn!" Maddar yelled.

"Come on, Ran. This is your last dance," Fnor yelled, pulling Ran to his feet.

Another person readily took the drum, so Ran joined hands with the forming circle and matched steps with the girls. Since the days of remaining unobtrusive were over, he could not resist clowning, dancing with exaggerated swings of his scrawny hips as the watchers whooped and laughed.

While the young people danced and flirted and carried on as if they hadn't exerted themselves in the hot sun all day, inside the banquet room, adults lingered at the long tables, appreciating the cooler air, for those thick stone walls warded the heat effectively.

Arrow and Commander Noth stood against the wall, each sipping dark beer brought up from the deepest cellar. Arrow had already filled Noth in. He ended, "About that Senelaec boy. Maybe I'd better talk to Andaun first. He's going to have to fit him in somewhere—what is it?"

A young stable runner had appeared at his elbow. "The Jarl of Senelaec just rode in," he said. "Stable chief said to come to you direct."

Noth whistled, and Arrow said, "I thought he was riding with Sindan-An." To the stable hand, "Bring him in. No. Not here. Up to the interview room." And as the youngster raced off, he said to the commander, "Want in on this?"

Noth hesitated, then turned his palm down flat. "He's alone, certainly no threat. My guess is, he's ridden for days, hot on his boy's trail. You don't need me there."

Arrow turned his palm up in acceptance and made his way to where Danet was talking to a Fath cousin. His expression caused her to excuse herself.

She and Arrow reached the interview chamber. Arrow said to the two duty guards, "The Jarl of Senelaec is on his way."

One of the guards said, "Is he armed?"

Danet spoke before Arrow, "Probably, but leave him be." At Arrow's scowl, "But stand guard in case."

They walked inside and sat side by side on the mats. Moments later a runner brought in Wolf, exhausted and filthy.

Wolf ranged himself before them, his dark-ringed eyes shifting between the two. He registered their lack of surprise, and said huskily. "I got back from chasing those horse thieves east, and Ran was gone...."

Danet said, "He's in the city with the rest of the youngsters."

"Whooping it up," Arrow added dryly.

Wolf shut his eyes, his shoulders sagging.

"We're waiting to hear why he's been raised as a girl. That clearly wasn't him," Arrow added.

Wolf glanced up, not quite meeting either of their gazes. "Back then. We were afraid."

"I know." Arrow remembered what Danet had said. "Mathren. Evred. Your aunt."

"Not just that. When I was small, my father often talked about the bad stories he grew up with. About the two uncles he lost in the academy when Bloody Tanrid was king."

"Did you think *I* was going to be like that?" Arrow demanded, his temper flashing to fury as he half-started up.

Danet unceremoniously yanked him down again by the coat skirt.

"Here's the thing." Wolf spread his hands. "He said his da insisted Tanrid Olavayir meant well. His idea was to train the boys to toughness, as tough as our army was when we fought the Venn back at the Pass in Inda-Harskialdna's day. Pretty much what you said to us, right, that Midsummer Convocation? We'd be like those days again. What that meant under Bloody Tanrid was brutal endurance tests, floggings every Sixthday for defaulters. Frequent duels, everyone gathered to watch. Many were to the death, until it got out of control, feuds, masters against boys. Jarls turning up with wings ready for war, at the end."

Arrow grimaced. "But that was exactly the opposite of the way Inda-Harskialdna ran the academy. Didn't I talk about the Gand record?"

Danet spoke up here, dry and dispassionate. "You said Inda-Harskialdna a lot, but there weren't any details, just talk about reviving our glorious past. I think what the jarls heard was a lot repeated stuff from the hero ballads and war stories."

Arrow swung around to scowl at her. "You're not saying those are lies?"

"This is what I'm saying." Danet raised a hand. "When I was delving in the records for past oath-promises, I discovered that under the early Olavayir kings, there was an actual edict proclaimed that nobody could talk about the old days under the Montreivayirs. It seems that the first couple of Olavayir kings viewed talking about the good old days not just as criticism, but as treachery. They destroyed a lot of the old academy records—"

"That I know. I didn't know why."

" — and the second and third kings even had patrols watching the border of Choreid Elgaer until they could find an excuse to break it apart, awarding chunks of land to their own people. Which is why those freeholds are there along what used to be the eastern border. And Feravayir grabbed the south as a trade...."

Arrow waved a hand. "I knew about the Algaravayirs' land being broken up, but we're far from Ran, Rana, from this boy and why he's not in the academy."

Wolf ran a grimy hand over his equally grimy face. "I can tell you I grew up distrusting the royal city because all our trouble seemed to come from there. So when you talked about starting the academy, and making us as strong as the days of Inda-Harskialdna, like Dan—the gunvaer said, I was afraid it would be Bloody Tanrid all over again. Or worse, if you couldn't hold the throne." He added, "I know *I* couldn't wake up and find myself king, and expect to hold the kingdom."

Arrow crossed his arms, his tone partly surly and partly defensive. "Your boy wants to come to the academy."

Wolf knuckled his eyes, then dropped his hands. "If he's been around here long enough to see it, and likes what he sees, then I certainly have no objections."

"With that much settled, let's get a meal into you, and you can rest," Danet suggested, looking from one to the other. Understanding seemed to have been reached, but they still reminded her of dogs with their hackles ruffled, tails stiff. "Everything else can wait till morning."

"Sleep, yes," Wolf said, his voice tired. "Bath. But I don't think I could keep anything down. I was on the road before dawn."

"You haven't eaten all day? You most definitely need a bite of something," Danet said as she got to her feet.

Arrow had calmed enough to recognize the anxiety in Wolf's face. It struck him how it must have felt to arrive home after chasing horse thieves for months, to discover that Ran had ridden out with the girls. He recollected how he had felt when Andas was taken away, though he'd known his son would be perfectly safe. Wolf had surely ridden for days imagining the worst.

The last of his resentment faded, and he said in a much milder tone, "Eat a little. Tomorrow I'll take you over to the academy, and you can see it for yourself. Of course they're packing to go home till next spring, but you'll be able to get a sense of things. Much better than seeing it empty at winter Convocation."

Wolf's fear had eased enough for him to become aware of the fact that he stood there alone with an unarmed king and queen while he had two throwing knives at his wrists, two in his boot tops, and a sword strapped across his back. None of which anyone had taken away.

He, like Arrow, was little given to self-reflection, but he sensed the goodwill underlying the superficials just as Arrow recognized the anxiety of a parent.

Wolf struck his fist to his heart belatedly, then said, "I guess you also probably could use a report on what we did out east."

"Tomorrow," Arrow said as Danet opened the door. "I want to hear it all, and you can show me on the map."

Danet took Wolf down the hall in one direction as Bun and Noren approached from the other. They were trailed by Lineas, who on opening the door to Bun's rooms was distracted by the ghostly scent once again, stronger than usual.

EIGHTEEN

Why were ghosts?

Lineas saw the Evred one most often at the entry to the stable, though she had found out that he was killed in a tower. And he hadn't been much of a rider, according to castle gossip. The only thing he'd liked was wine. Maybe he loved the stable when young. It was useless to speculate until she could find someone else who saw them and knew more about them, or until she could actually talk to one.

Noren was excellent company. She got along well with Bunny, but it turned out she didn't see ghosts. Nor did either of her runners. Lineas sighed to herself as Noren signed a good night and passed on down to the guest chamber.

"I miss Noren already," Bun said as Lineas shut the door. "And she's not even gone yet."

"She'll soon be back forever," Lineas reminded her.

"I know, and I mean to be much faster in Hand when she does. Cousin Ranet said she's going to learn it in a year! Cousin Ranet. Isn't that funny that everyone calls her that? They can't *all* be cousins. I wonder if she'll still be called Cousin Ranet when she comes back to marry Connar."

"We can practice Hand now," Lineas signed.

Bun wrinkled her upper lip, for she was tired after the long day, mostly spent cheering for people and horses she liked. But she complied, signing, "I wonder where Connar is, anyway? I saw Noddy with all the big boys, but I didn't see Connar anywhere."

That was because Connar was prowling the perimeter of the celebration, his mood rotten.

He'd been stared at all his life, but now he understood what those long looks meant. During the previous month or so before Victory Day, Connar had begun waking up with saddle wood, and in the baths, learned what the seniors called horseplay. While he enjoyed it while he was doing it, after it was over, his frustration rushed right back. Sex play, brief and intense, was all right, but it wasn't *winning*.

As he walked around in the still, balmy air, he encountered the usual stares, from both boys and girls. If he stared back at the girls, some turned red, others fussed around with their hair, or sidled in ways that drew his eyes downward to shapes he'd hitherto ascribed to his sister and mother.

A girl caught his eye as she danced. He couldn't take his eyes away from the swing of her hips, the shape of her butt when her robe fluttered and swung so enticingly, hiding and revealing. But he didn't know what to do, what to say to a girl. The boys in the baths were blunt. These girls acted in a way that he couldn't interpret, and he hated feeling awkward.

So he walked away from one group busy yakking and boring on about the competitions (who cared if that Senelaec strut with the two arrows turned out to be a boy?), and was looking for a way to distract himself when Fish Pereth, now a garrison runner-in-training, slunk up. Connar's mood, already vile, worsened sharply the moment he spotted Fish's protuberant eyes. At least the sight of him gave focus to his sour mood.

"Get lost," he snarled at Fish, whose habit when they were small of spying and then tattling had endeared him to no one in the academy versus garrison boy wars.

"I was sent," Fish said. He sidled furtive glances to either side in that way that Connar despised, then said, "He wants to talk to you."

"He?"

Fish took a step closer, then said in an undervoice, "Uncle—Master Hauth."

Connar grimaced as he, too, glanced around. The soft summer air carried at least three competing ballads, rising and falling to the persistent beating of drums. Boys and girls ran, walked, strolled, and chased everywhere, in pairs, threes, groups. Connar was alone because he'd wanted to be alone.

Connar sighed. It was clear he wouldn't easily get rid of Fish, and anyway, whatever Hauth had to say might be less boring than all these boneheads bootlicking those who won golds. He rubbed at his bare left sleeve irritably, caught himself at it, and snarled, "Let's get it over with."

Fish ducked smoothly in the narrow space between a saddlery and a glazier. Connar followed him through city alleys until they reached the extreme southwest corner of the castle, where the sheep wintered. They scaled the wall between the sentries, Connar wondering if this was always a blind spot, and would that come in use someday?

They slunk from building to building, drifting outside the outbuildings and the back kitchen garden to the fields between, which the queen had made over to visiting girls. It was empty now. All the girls were in the city adding to the noise.

Back around to garrison winter storage, and finally, they slipped inside a narrow hall, dusty, hot, stuffy, and smelling overwhelmingly of wool. Connar's mood had not improved during the long, hot run. He wished Fish would speak only so he could tell him to shut up, but Fish had seen that scowl and prudently remained silent.

When they reached a door, Fish stepped aside. Connar passed into the lamp-lit room, noticing irritably that Fish was half a hand taller.

Connar stalked inside, and the door shut behind him. Connar crossed his arms, glaring at Hauth, who sat at the other end of the room, cane laid across a table, a pile of papers before him.

Hauth looked up, expertly assessing Connar's scowl despite the throbbing headache from the long, wearying day in the sun. The masters were responsible for the complex logistics of the competitions, as well as monitoring the boys; they'd risen well before dawn and worked ceaselessly until the Games were over, the animals stabled, the equipment stored, and the parade ground swept. But he already knew the heedless young took it all for granted.

Hauth's gaze slipped to the golden eagle stitched across the front of Connar's House tunic, and his mood worsened. He said, "My winter orders will shift me out tomorrow. So we had to meet tonight."

"Why?" Connar demanded sullenly. "There's no more point in those exercises, which by the way were worthless."

Hauth said, "Give it a year. You've barely started to grow."

"I mean everything." Connar snapped his hand away. "I didn't win anything this year. Nothing. And don't tell me to wait a year. Inda-Harskialdna won every damned game from the time he was ten."

Goaded beyond endurance, Hauth retorted, "Inda-Harskialdna wasn't the true king. And he was too stupid to take the throne when he could have."

Hauth shut his teeth, regretting the words as soon as they were out. They should have come out much later, after the boy got through the foolishness he was so clearly verging on: growth spurts, voice changing, beard and body hair, and above all, the unrelenting focus on sex. This was the age when all the adults around you were dolts, when you knew everything, when the future was as hazy as it was limitless, and everything you did was the first and most important event in world history.

Connar's sulky expression—which, on him, still managed to be magnificent, the more because as yet he had no idea of the effect of his splendid looks—altered to confusion. "What?"

Hauth sighed. Maybe it was for the best after all. "The truth. Lanrid was being raised in secret as crown prince—the true heir to the royal dolphin-clan."

"So Mathren was going to murder Evred all along?" Connar backed away, rigid with disgust. "And this is the man you keep telling me was so heroic?"

"Evred never would have held the kingdom. He was a drunken sot. Lazy. No discipline whatsoever. A drunken sot at twenty makes for the weakest sort of king. For a moment, forget what Mathren did, or intended to do.

When there is a weak, lazy, drunken king, it's not a matter of *if*, but *when*, someone stronger comes along, and we can hope their motive is for the good of the kingdom. Everything that Mathren Olavayir did was for the good of the kingdom," Retren Hauth said, his voice husky with conviction. "Lanrid, your father, your real father, should have been king. He was *meant* to be king."

Connar was a few years short of truly understanding the complexity of that emotion, but he knew conviction when he saw it. He stared at Hauth, his wide, unblinking eyes reflecting the lamplight in twin points of gold. He'd gone so still that those flames didn't so much as flicker.

Then he whispered, "Impossible."

Hauth said, "My first loyalty is to dolphin-clan. Which is what you are. The last one."

Connar's unwavering gaze shifted at last, and his hand shook as he passed it over his forehead, then it dropped. "But...what you're saying...." He took a deep breath, and the anger was back. "I'd kill anyone who tried to hurt Noddy. Or Da."

"The king is not your da," Hauth retorted. Why not, since he'd already gone this far.

"Yeah, mine got himself slaughtered, and a lot of people along with him," Connar said bitterly. "Chasing after a traitor. And my so-called mother tossed me into the midden. Ma—the queen, *my mother*. My *real* mother. The birth one is *nothing*. And the king, *my father*, didn't have to take me in. I know they hated Lanrid, and especially hated Mathren the Murderer. I don't care if he's blood-related. He *was* a murderer."

"So," Hauth leaned forward, his teeth showing, "was Inda-Harskialdna. To everyone he defeated. But it was always for a cause. For the kingdom. Mathren would have been the greatest of our kings. You've got his brains, and you're getting his speed and strength. You're still so young. Like every other boy your age, you can't see it, you want everything now."

Connar passed his hand across his eyes again, then muttered, "What I see is, you seem to be telling me without telling me that I should be king."

"Yes."

"Which means killing my *real* family."

"I'm not telling you to kill anyone," Hauth said quickly, seeing Connar poised to run. "I'm oath-sworn to train you, the last of the dolphin-clan. Because anything could happen. Has. And you have to be the first to admit that Nadran-Sierlaef isn't all that..." *fit* "...excited about the prospect of kingship."

Connar looked sightlessly around the small room, without seeing the shelves of dusty account books. Finally he muttered truculently, "If you called me over here to tell me to make that 'anything' happen, I'll...."

Hauth said quickly, "What I wanted to tell you was to keep studying those papers I gave you. Work on self-discipline. Strength. Think about strategy, and tactics. It's true that some seem to take to it naturally, just as some are naturally great singers, or any other skill you can name. Inda-Harskialdna was naturally great at fighting and command. Not everyone is, or we would never talk about him. But that doesn't mean you can't learn from his actions. Teach them to the Sierlaef, if you will, and help him improve. Just...keep learning."

Connar stared, aware that any other time, he would have really been annoyed at being dragged across the entire city by that slinking Fish, just to be jawed at about self-discipline and learning. But now, it was kind of a relief. Because he wasn't being encouraged to be *treacherous*.

"We can meet, or not, in the spring, as you choose," Hauth finished. "I will continue to collect anything that I think might help you in your learning."

Connar banged the door open with the flat of his hand, and was gone in a few quick steps.

Fish, meanwhile, had gone to fetch his father, as ordered. Quartermaster Pereth waited in the tack repair room until Connar stalked by, bootheels rapping on the worn stone floor, then slipped into the records room. "Well?"

Hauth gave a succinct report.

Pereth struck his hand against the lintel. "You lost him."

"Maybe. Maybe not." Hauth dug his thumb into the corner of his eye socket in a vain effort to relieve the pounding headache. "He's at that age where *anything* will send them galloping wild into the wind. He's still angry because he didn't win any of the wargames he commanded this spring. I told Andaun not to put him up against Yvanavayir, but you know Andaun. Thinks it's better for the princes to go against the toughest future captains."

The quartermaster accepted that, and Hauth said reflectively, "Anyway, this I'm sure of, he heard me."

"And stalked off in a temper."

"Which he inherited from that vile Iascan who gave him that black hair. He's easily one of the most jealous, competitive boys in the entire academy."

"You think that's a quality?"

"If it enables him to overcome the mediocrity all around him, yes. It's up to us to discipline him out of it. As for what I said...." Hauth's smile was grim. "I know he'll remember."

NINETEEN

The morning of Noddy's Name Day, Connar was reaching for the last peach tart when Bun snatched it up and ran out. Annoyed, he looked up, but Ma signaled one of her runners to fetch hot ones, then put her hand up to halt Bun's red-haired runner at the door. She signed in Hand, "She's improving?"

Lineas signed back, "We practice every morning and evening." Then she vanished.

Danet got up and went in the other direction, leaving Arrow alone with the boys. Arrow turned to Noddy. "Is it time to assign runners to you? Run your errands?"

Noddy had been staring downward, his shoulders hunched. "No, Da," he mumbled.

Da. Connar kept hearing Hauth's voice whispering *the king* and it was easy to recollect what he'd missed before, that Hauth had never, in all their sessions, said *your father* or *your brother.* He'd always used their titles.

"No, Da," he said, just to be saying *Da.* And he hoped Hauth was somehow spying or listening.

Then he wondered why he didn't get a runner. There was no longer any need for secrecy. He could go work out any time he wanted — with Da's complete approval. But...he glanced at Noddy, who always got that hunched up look whenever that freckle-faced runner Lineas was around. Connar knew why, and he also knew how miserable it made Noddy feel, because Lineas never looked twice at Noddy. She was one of the ones who stared at *him*, though she always looked away again if he caught her at it. But he felt it.

Then he heard an echo of that short conversation with Ma. He'd never even thought about it before, but Lineas was reporting on Bun. Not that Bun would care if she knew, and maybe she did.

That didn't matter. What did was, Hauth had been watching him, Connar, and now he knew why. It had galled him ever since that Victory Day conversation: Hauth watched him and tutored him not because he was smart, or showed the promise of skill, it was all just the accident of his birth.

He fumed as thoughts flitted rapidly through his mind. He now comprehended the significance of those boring lessons they'd sat through ages ago, how you could get babies in two ways. There was the Birth Spell, which had something to do with magic in the long-ago past, but the point was, you had to really want the baby. Or you could get one with sex, but the woman had to chew or drink some herb first to make herself able to get the baby inside her.

Either way, you didn't get a baby by accident. You had to work at it, but out of all the babies in the world, *he'd* been thrown away. Well, maybe that dolt Lanrid might have kept him, if he hadn't got himself killed running after a traitor (and why would he get a baby with one woman while chasing another?) but the woman—he refused to think of her as his mother—had tossed him out.

And Hauth watched him because of *that*.

Revulsion tightened through him. "I like things as they are," he stated.

Da said slowly, his eyes on Noddy, "That says a lot for your self-discipline. But there are some ways having a runner makes life easier." In a very different voice, he said slowly, "Connar, you've grown at least a hand and a half since last year. You two have to be close to your full height."

"Did the Beard Spell before Victory Day," Noddy mumbled.

Connar opened his hand. He'd gone with Noddy, though he only had two cherished hairs on his chin at that point, and scarcely more than that under his clothes. As usual, Noddy had way more hair where men got it.

Arrow flicked his hand in agreement. "You boys been to the pleasure house yet? Or are you fine on your own?"

How could Da not know that Noddy was hot for Lineas? Noddy stared down at the crumbs on his plate as if they were about to get up and attack him. His ears were so red they were almost purple.

Da said, "Noddy?"

Noddy couldn't look up, far too conflicted to explain that girls had been a problem for half a year, now. And it was just girls. At the academy, the boys who liked sex with other boys could easily find each other at rec time or in the baths, but there weren't any girls in the academy, except glimpsed from a distance.

Then came Victory Day, and girls arrived aplenty, but the ones who came up to him called him *Sierlaef*, or *Nadran-Sierlaef*, or acted like...like....

"I wish I wasn't a prince," he burst out.

"What?" Arrow and Connar exclaimed at the same time.

Arrow got it first. "Has someone been—never mind that. Noddy, *have* you gone to the pleasure house?"

Noddy said to his plate, "No."

"Why didn't you speak up?"

"Because Connar doesn't want to yet. I don't want to go alone, and not know what to say, or do, and what if they laugh at me."

Arrow sat back, fists on his knees. "Noddy. I can absolutely guarantee they won't laugh. You could walk in and kick over the tables and pour beer on their heads, and they won't laugh."

"Because I'm a prince," Noddy mumbled.

"Yes and no. They'll just charge you more if you make trouble, whether you're a prince or an assistant stable wander. It's true that princes are going to get special attention...."

Arrow paused, remembering Evred and the Captain's Drum, and the sort of men who'd followed and flattered him. "Look, I can take you to a place where being a prince won't matter. Most of the senior academy boys seem to like it. They have a riding or two's worth of people who deal especially with first timers. Your mother took your sister last year. She obviously survived."

Noddy looked up. "Bun?" Somehow Bun always seemed like an eternal puppy. But she was...nearly seventeen.

Arrow shrugged. "Girls get their full growth sooner than we do, which means they usually take an interest a little sooner. My point is, we can go today if you want. Connar, you, too."

Connar grinned, wondering why he hadn't thought of going months ago. But he knew the answer: because Noddy hadn't been ready.

Arrow said to Noddy, "You don't have to do anything if you don't want to, you can just talk. They're good at making, ah, personal things feel normal, things that might feel awkward with your family or your mates at the academy."

Noddy's entire demeanor brightened. "Yes. Let's do that."

Arrow said, "Wait here. I have to give a couple of messages." He ran out.

Connar eyed Noddy, who looked a little dazed. "Do you really mean that? About not wanting to be a prince?"

Noddy glanced sideways. "It won't happen to *you*. She — they look at you different. They look at me and some of them laugh behind my head. I've seen it. I've heard it. But when they know I'm seeing them, they're full of *oh, Nadran-Sierlaef* and smiles." His voice rose to a squeak on his name.

Connar knew his question was senseless — that Noddy was never going to suddenly come out with a desire to run off and be a stonemason rather than a king. But he couldn't help probing at the questions snarled in his mind, even if obliquely. "Do you ever think about being king?"

Noddy's long, buck-toothed face changed to an expression so rare that Connar couldn't quite define it. He'd only seen it once before, when their favorite dog had died of old age. "No," he said, his voice a deep rumble in his chest. "I don't like to think about Da being dead." He slewed around, earnest now. "But when it happens, you'll help me, right? Like you always do."

"Always," Connar said fervently, then looked away.

Arrow returned then, took his sons off to the Singing Sword, which was everything he promised — and more.

And so, as the sun dropped northward each day, bringing harvest season and cooler weather, Noddy and Connar threw themselves enthusiastically into the new, compelling world of pleasure house sex.

The preparations for Convocation completely escaped them until a cold, sleety day, far too cold for a ride. Connar had spent the morning at the garrison salle with the sword master, and he was prowling restlessly around his room, trying to decide if he'd give in and start reading Hauth's papers again, or ignore them, when Noddy burst in, a blond boy at his shoulder. The newcomer was almost as tall, almost as broad, with the same short upper lip, only in him it managed somehow to look less beaver-like.

This boy gave Connar a mild smile, and said in a soft voice, "Seven days without rain, and it hits us today, when we wanted to ride in looking good. Or at least clean."

Noddy, who never noticed how anyone looked, clapped the newcomer on a shoulder as he said to Connar, "Here's Cousin Tanrid! Our uncle Jarend sent him for his first Convocation."

Connar looked from one to the other, then said, "The one Ma and Pa call Rabbit?"

"They stopped calling me Rabbit when I broke the swords in the sword dance," Tanrid said, in that same mild voice. "Da told me to do it."

Connar stared, trying to decide if this new cousin Rabbit-turned-Tanrid was strutting or...just odd.

"Come with us, Tanrid. We'll show you around," Noddy said.

"I would like that very much. May we look out the highest tower? I want to see how the distance compares with the view from the highest tower at home."

Definitely odd.

The three went out, Tanrid occasionally offering facts from archives. It was clear by the end of the evening, when he was drunk enough to be staring fuzzily, that Tanrid was very bookish.

But he turned out to be an excellent companion, ready to do anything the others suggested, and keeping up effortlessly with that same mild expression. Bun joined them, taking an instant liking to Tanrid.

Everything was smooth on the surface. Underneath, there were currents difficult to navigate.

First, where Bun went, there went Lineas. Noddy couldn't even say what it was about Lineas that gripped him so hard. She was quiet, unfailingly polite, self-effacing. Only someone aware of her every move would notice how her gaze strayed toward Connar, then flitted away quick. He hadn't noticed her until late one day, with golden light slanting down and lighting her hair bright as fire. She stood poised, still as a hummingbird in the air, as she stared at *something*, her lips parted.

Noddy looked, and looked again, unable to see what in a blank stone wall had so arrested her, as his nerves prickled all over his body.

After that he couldn't get her out of his mind.

Second, Connar enjoyed the easy camaraderie until the stormy morning they went down to the salle for practice. Tanrid was nearly as tall as Noddy, and almost as strong, which — in his own mind — left Connar the shortest and weakest of the three.

Connar struggled to hide his anger at being last in everything — most of that aimed at himself. Neither he nor Noddy had drilled every day for at least a couple months. They'd been too busy sleeping in after nights of pillow jigging with their favorites over at the Singing Sword, where most of the academy lancers congregated in season.

The truth was, Noddy didn't really *have* to practice.

As the three walked to the baths to clean up before a meal, Connar vowed to get back to practice every morning instead of once in a while when he felt like it. He was still angry, and unsettled, about Hauth's words.

All right. He was nearly as tall as Da, at least, and even if he wasn't going to get any taller he was *going* to get stronger and faster.

Tanrid (formerly Rabbit) had come with his mother, Tdor Fath, as the Jarlan of Olavayir had chosen to remain in Nevree with Arrow's brother Jarend. Arrow had kept his promise to Jarend, never requiring him to attend Convocation, but that promise did not extend to his son. This was Tanrid's first visit.

While the cousins roamed around entertaining themselves, Danet and Tdor Fath resumed their old habits of talk as if the intervening years had never happened. At first Tdor Fath was slightly disconcerted, finding that gawky Danet had become this eagle-eyed gunvaer, but Danet made it plain much she missed having her to talk to.

"I talk to Arrow, of course. And Noth. And the royal runner chiefs are discreet and sensible. And there are things I only talk about with my sister. But each has things they want to talk about — and then there are the subjects I shouldn't talk about. With you...I feel like I can say anything."

Except she couldn't, really.

Even with Tdor Fath she couldn't bring herself to discuss what still felt like Calamity Senelaec's personal betrayal. Tdor Fath saw the pain in her expression, and misinterpreted it.

"You can," Tdor Fath promised, gratified, but regretting how much that throne had weighed on Danet — she still had nightmares about that last terrible day in the royal city all those years ago. And she could see the effects of that day in the taut lines in Danet's face, which gave her that eagle-eyed look. "You can say anything to me. It won't go farther."

But they only had a day or two before the trumpets began to peal, and their precious free time ended.

The ground was iron-hard, the sky mercilessly clear and cold as the jarls converged on the royal city, for the first time in history riding with their jarlans.

The Jevayir of Jayad Hesea contingent had met the Feravayir party, as was traditional, riding north to stay over at the Cassad castle in Telyer Hesea, then, with the Cassads, set out in a long cavalcade. Carleas Cassad had been looking forward to a pleasant journey until the arrival of tall, bronze-skinned and black-eyed Lavais Nyidri, Jarlan of Feravayir.

The Nyidri family had ruled Perideth before the Marlovans swept in, renamed it Feravayir, and established one of their captains as jarl. The Nyidris had accepted the new rulers outwardly, as had the Cassads, but unlike the Cassads, had nursed for generations a bitter determination to recover what had once been theirs.

Lavais had married the last Feravayir, and after he died during a pirate attack on the harbor when their two sons were small, she ruled in her eldest boy's name. When the news arrived that Mathren Olavayir was dead, she made two strategic moves: She returned to her family name, and married Ivandred Noth, the commander at Parayid Harbor garrison.

The Jevairs and the Cassads both regarded that marriage as a strategic move on Lavais's part. No one was certain of Ivandred Noth's motives, as he'd had a reputation as a straightforward military man who, until that marriage, had lived simply, first to rise with the garrison cooks and last to sleep. Whether he'd been dazzled by those Sartoran airs and graces of hers, or he'd thought to gain a mother for his boys, they'd combined their families, four sons altogether.

She hadn't left her castle since coming back from Sartor as a young woman and began keeping court Sartoran-style, wearing Sartoran fashions and using their manners. Few in the south knew her; they only knew *of* her. And while peace existed between these three main powers of the south, all three were aware that she coveted the Jayad and the Telyer, which her ancestors had once ruled.

So they traveled together amicably enough on the surface.

Though they had to slow in areas slick with ice, the journey seemed far less arduous to the jarls than the last Convocation three years previous, with its howling winds.

The jarlans' experience was different. Left to the company of their gender, by the time the cavalcade reached the royal city (the Jarlan of Feravayir smoothly assuming precedence as her right), Carleas was heartily tired of the long journey, which seemed the longer because each day began and ended with Lavais-Jarlan and her calm, assured command of all topics of conversation.

Carleas murmured to the Jarlan of Jayad Hesea, "She's perfectly willing for us to reveal ourselves, but she's about as communicative as that fan she's always waving about. We'll get nothing she doesn't want to give."

As for Lavais, she was intensely curious to see and evaluate the enemy. Her first jolt of annoyance occurred when they reached the royal city and the single peal for a jarlan rang out, instead of the fanfare for a royal house—proof (as if she'd needed it) that Perideth did not exist in the Marlovan mind.

But she kept her reaction to herself. Though she expected nothing but barbarianism from these Olavayirs, accidental monarchs from an already mediocre family line, she had to admit as she rode into the city that not only was Choreid Dhelerei well kept up, it was a formidable stronghold. Mediocrity, it seemed, knew how to protect itself, she thought as she rode under the alert, watching eyes of sentries.

She needed to assess this queen herself, after that surprising command that jarlans come to Convocation. Hitherto she'd thought it sufficient to send Ivandred Noth. He was excellent as a military commander, and played the part of a jarl well. But for politics he was useless, far too straightforward to comprehend subtleties.

In spite of the fact that this Danet-Gunvaer had had the temerity to force a betrothal treaty on Lavais, she would never let her beautiful, Sartoran-educated son Demeos actually *marry* a Marlovan barbarian unless she had beauty, brains, and wealth to bring—or at least wealth and beauty, and could be swayed to the Perideth cause. He was being groomed for a royal Sartoran marriage.

Her original plan had been to decide which would benefit her most: breaking this betrothal, or taking the princess they called Bunny back with her as a hostage.

The latter plan ceased to be feasible when she observed how many hard-eyed, fully armed warriors guarded this castle alone.

Once inside the second set of massive gates, she despised the unadorned stone. The furniture was sparse and intimidating rather than artistic or fashionable: big wingbacked chairs, raptor-clawed legs on the low tables, and here and there enormous tapestries depicting battle victories.

In the guest room she was assigned to, she scorned the low table with mats on the stone floor, instead of civilized tables and chairs. The dishes were typical clumsy Marlovan ceramic, the wine cups broad and shallow, forcing one to lift them with two hands—it was said to keep knives at bay. She could well believe it. She despised the shallow dishes, utensils only a spoon, and that wood-carved, as if they were all babes in arms. No forks, not even any Colendi eating sticks.

The interview room they were brought to was dominated by an enormous tapestry of a battle. She took in the winged helms and armored

Venn with their elaborate knotwork. Their embroidered figures struggled with men in old-fashioned Marlovan coats, below a cliff on which stood a Marlovan commander in green and silver, standing in a heroic pose accepting the surrender of kneeling Venn.

She indicated the tapestry with her fan. "Is that supposed to be Indevan Algaravayir?"

The other women deferred to a short, graying figure in green and silver. Lavais belatedly realized this had to be Linden-Fareas Algaravayir, descendant of this same hero, as the Iofre said, "It is actually a fairly good representation, we are told, though overlarge, of course. It was sketched from life, and the tapestry given to Indevan's wife Tdor Marthdavan."

Lavais hated having to defer to a princess when she knew herself to be a queen. Especially a princess who had been too stupid to understand her overtures when she had written to suggest that one of the Algaravayir daughters might marry her darling second son, Ryu—the first step in an alliance that could retake the entire southern half of Halia.

Face to face, this woman did not look stupid at all. "Thank you." Lavais forced a diplomatic smile.

Her first glimpse of Danet-Gunvaer, though Danet was ten years younger than she, reinforced her decision to tread lightly and observe. Danet was as plain as a fence slat, her forgettable face dominated by a narrowed, observant gaze. She wore a robe of the purest of blues, hanging in rich folds of unexpectedly exquisite linen. Within the first few moments of greeting, it was clear that this gunvaer knew absolutely nothing of courtly finesse, but she was also dangerous; she not only said what she thought, but appeared to be capable of carrying it out.

As for Danet, one look at Lavais Nyidri, and she knew the woman was trouble. It remained to be seen what kind of trouble.

Calamity Senelaec (though living closer than anyone but the Gannans) was the last to arrive, approaching slowly as she appreciated the massive royal castle and the bustling city surrounding it. When they reached the stable, she helped her runners see to the animals, then begged the closest runner to request an interview with the gunvaer.

Danet had been sitting with Tdor Fath, the Iofre, and the jarlans of Tlennen and Sindan-An. As soon as she heard who had made the request, she excused herself and sent Sage to bring Calamity to her private chamber.

There she waited, aware of her thumping heart, until Calamity dashed impetuously in.

Danet, whose life had not provided much in the way of friends, and Calamity, who had to be loved, searched each other's faces for signs of resentment or anger, and saw only their own expressions mirrored, in faces no longer young, but at nearly forty, far from old.

Calamity yanked off her gloves and knit hat, her braids tumbling out as she said, "I've been thinking about you ever since the Victory Day games, and my son's rash idea to ride here. But it's all right, isn't it?"

Danet understood the real question, which had little to do with that boy's typical Senelaec dash headlong at a ruse, and everything to do with Calamity's typical Senelaec snap decision to lie about his birth.

"It's all right." Danet turned her palm up.

"Truly? I feel stupid," Calamity said.

Danet hesitated, mulling over what to say. Calamity looked and sounded exactly like the girl who'd helped her birth Noddy, and who had made her welcome in the barn attic at Senelaec, yet the first comment to mind was *You feel stupid because you got caught lying.*

Calamity had, in short, broken her trust.

And that was such a hard thing to get back. But here Calamity was, waiting with a slightly hopeful air, and Danet realized that nothing could be the same. They weren't newlyweds married to second sons, there was too much that had changed. But she also remembered something she'd read in Hadand-Gunvaer's letters from a century ago, how trust and liking didn't always match, even if you wished they did.

She still liked Calamity. She would go on as if she still trusted her. So, though she felt the pressure of all the things waiting to be done, she asked after everyone at Senelaec, chatted about children, and finally flicked a glance at Loret, who came forward to open the door. "Go ahead and get settled. We'll have plenty of time for chat later."

Calamity accepted that, her emotions tumbling. It could have gone worse, but it also could have gone better, though she couldn't define how.

She simply had to keep trying.

TWENTY

The army of royal and castle runners had prepared for weeks.

Hliss had worked even longer, making certain that every guest bedroom had new linens, so that when Lavais of Feravayir retired to the bedchamber in her suite, she found herself looking down at fine-hackled, double-bucked bed linens, woven in a complicated honeycomb pattern. Her cotton-silk sheets from Sartor weren't as fine as these. As she slid into the bed and felt the rich whisper of the fabric over her skin, she contemplated the silent message: Danet had, without words, defined the difference between ignorant barbarians and the house of a war king.

It was a sober set of women who gathered back in the interview room on Firstday Morning.

Danet stood before them in her beautiful House robe. "I expect that many of you would rather be in the throne room with the jarls, as this is likely the only time you will ever attend Convocation. But I've sat through every Convocation since Anred-Harvaldar first presided Midsummer of Year Sixty."

She paused, four fingers in the air to indicate the number of Convocations. Numbers, she believed, were solid ground. No one could argue with them. "I can assure you that you will miss nothing," she said abruptly. "They always begin Firstday with unfinished business, which is going to gallop down the endless side trail of arguing about the Nob. Those who like the sounds of their own voices will repeat what they've been arguing about for the past ten years, and certain others will restate what they just heard but in their own words."

Danet paused, and seeing question in some faces, waited, but every woman, from the young to old, remained silent and stiff.

Danet said, "Here's the short version of what will keep them from deciding anything. While Lindeth Harbor pays for itself, the Nob is nothing but a drain; the people of the peninsula don't want us there, but we pay their costs—that is, your taxes pay their costs—according to a century-old treaty. I doubt very much that is going to be resolved now, or even in ten years."

She paused again, assessing the silence. They were still listening. "What I want is to talk to you all face to face, rather than spend five years exchanging letters. My intent is this, to offer your girls the chance to serve in the King's Army."

And that broke the silence.

Danet let them exclaim and ask each other questions they couldn't answer, then said when at last they quieted, "We all know that men are generally bigger and stronger, but we also know that women can be faster — sometimes as riders, definitely in reaction. And in hand to hand, a trained woman isn't necessarily outmatched even if the man is twice her size. You all have grown up hearing how Hadand-Deheldegarthe defended the throne against the Jarl of Yvanavayir, knives against a sword."

A few whispers met this, and a dry laugh from the Jarlan of Tlennen, whose daughters had been riding with the Sindan-Ans against the horse thieves for some time now.

Danet said, "What I really want is to mix girls in with the army in hopes that they might be able to mitigate men's tendency toward fighting for fighting's sake."

The Jarlan of Tyavayir crossed her arms, her dark, thick brows meeting over her thin nose. "As exampled by Hadand Arvandais?"

"I figured her name would come up sooner than later." Danet opened her hand. "To that I'll say the obvious, the fact that it's always her name makes her the exception."

"I realize that." The jarlan tipped her head. "But she was also trained in war. How many Hadand Arvandaises will we create if add girls to the army requirement?"

A short burst of commentary rose. Danet waited until the noise died down and they turned from one another to her again. She said, "First, I'm not proposing your girls be required to join. This is volunteer only, while we see how it goes. Second. Did you really think I hadn't thought of investigating my cousin's training?"

The words "my cousin" caused a short burst of whispers, as quickly silenced.

Danet went on. "This is what I learned from my own brother, and from my father's first runner, who came back down the Pass with the news when my father died defending the jarl. Hadand Arvandais got the same training all your foremothers did, and many of you still get now — odni knife fighting, and horseback archery — but that training was savage. Whoever lost a scrap, or a wargame, got beaten. Punishments were severe. She was raised to further her father's purpose, and she was to be the spearhead. Hadand Arvandais's first move was the assassination of her father."

Rustles and widened eyes met this news.

"I thought he was assassinated by the loyalists," spoke a woman from the back — Danet couldn't make her out.

"So did we. Until a witness reached us, a year later. This was my father's first runner — who died defending the jarl. My father's last act was to send his runner to carry witness, for he'd recognized his daughter's followers, though they wore face masks and dressed like brigands."

Another whisper rose, then subsided as Danet cleared her throat and continued. "Hadand was an exception, not a rule. From everything else I can discover in every written record I can find, most women don't fight because we like to fight, we fight because we must. And when we do, we can be as bloodthirsty as vicious as any man. But when the quarrel is resolved, most of us stop. We don't carry on across borders as far as we can slaughter."

That raised another buzz.

Then Lavais Nyidri said in her smooth, Sartoran-accented voice, "Whom do you fear? Your sons, or the son of the king's brother? The Olavayirs historically do seem to favor fighting one another."

Danet suppressed a sharp spurt of anger. It was a fair question, if rudely worded. "It's true that the Olavayirs have a rough history. I knew that before I married into the family. All I can say is, we've taught our boys that that family history is a warning, and I will also note that my sons are quite loyal to one another."

"They're boys," that same woman called from the back, voice flat with disillusionment. She shifted, and Danet caught sight of her shoulder and arm, recognizing Gannan colors in her robe. "Boys don't usually lead civil wars. Give them five, ten years, then we shall see."

Danet knew it was unfair to judge a woman by an unwelcome stay years ago, so she decided not to respond.

She turned her gaze to those in the front row. "My husband's brother, who by treaty should have been king, begged Ar, ah, Anred to take the throne. I feel confident in predicting that Jarend-Jarl of Olavayir will not change his mind. If you doubt me, you may address his wife, the Jarlan of Olavayir, third from the right, second row."

Tdor Fath rose, unsmiling, and turned in a circle so that everyone could see her face. "Everything she said about Jarend is true." No one missed the air of challenge in her straight shoulders, and the way her gaze snagged unblinking on every pair of eyes raised her way.

More whispers rose, but sudden silence fell when Fareas-Iofre raised her hand up, palm out. "Would you put our daughters in the academy, then?"

"Not right away," Danet said. "I believe the summer games have been a success—you can ask your daughters if I am right. My thought was to restart the queen's training again, for at least a couple of years. Then let them go on the overnight wargames with the boys. See how it goes. If it goes well, try the next step. If it doesn't, then no harm—the girls will have benefitted from sharing training."

"What does the king say?" an old jarlan quavered.

"He says the decision is ours," Danet replied. "It will be your daughters and nieces coming here to train. So talk among yourselves. Talk to me. Let me know what you think before you ride home again. This is an idea, not an edict, at present."

Female voices rose in a high hum.

The Iofre stayed silent, an island in a sea of chatter. Danet noticed, and so was not surprised when the Iofre waited at the door for her when they broke up for the midday meal, after which the jarlans expected to go to the throne room for the jarls' Firstday oaths and Arrow's address.

Danet waved off the hovering runners, and fell in step beside the Iofre, who said, "Ambitious. I can't say I don't follow your thinking."

Danet glanced down at the shorter, older woman, who had gone grayer in the few years since they had seen one another. "But?"

"I did not want to raise this point, because I suspect it might weigh more than it ought, but after your visit I went through Tdor's letters. I wish I'd known about this plan of yours, as I would have reread the pertinent letter, perhaps brought it, but anyway, it seems that Inda did intend at one point to bring girls into the academy. It has to be remembered he was used to serving with women at sea. He said that at ten, boys and girls pay little heed to such distinctions, and if they grow up together in training, by the time they reach the age where the distinction begins to matter, they are so used to one another it is no more a problem than an army with all boys or all girls."

"And?" Danet prompted.

The Iofre looked up, her eyes reflecting the torchlight. "And Hadand wrote back forbidding any such thing. She said, and this much I remember, *Someone has to be trusted to do the real work of the kingdom.*"

They walked together as Danet said, "Interesting. I saw no reference to that exchange in her papers here. Did she elaborate?"

"Not that I recollect—that is, I only have Tdor's end of the correspondence, and since her next letters didn't mention it, I assume the matter was dropped."

They walked a little farther, Danet thinking that though she lived, ate, and slept in the same rooms Hadand had lived in for all those years, though she'd read and reread Hadand's papers, there was still no knowing her mind. Perhaps an ordinary person could never comprehend the mind of brilliance any more than one could define the substance of fire.

A stray thought: did the famous contemplate their own brilliance?

But that sort of pondering was for later. She said, "Hadand was far greater than I could ever hope to be. But her time was different. I wish I knew what happened to her end of that exchange—which makes me wonder how much else we're missing without knowing it."

Danet and Fareas reached the royal guest chamber, where the Iofre turned in the open door, paused, and said, "Hadand's time was different in what sense? You don't just mean the Venn threat."

Danet stood outside the door. "This is another thing I've discovered while delving in the records, that what we consider traditional has never been one thing. Ever."

"True. Very true." The Iofre beckoned Danet in, appreciating how the gunvaer waited on the threshold, though this was her domain. "Before we lived in castles, women guarded the camps while the men rode out raiding. The tradition that Hadand-Deheldegarthe was raised to was women guarding castles instead of camps, though the Iascans never tried to retake the kingdom."

Danet said, "Yes. Other than fighting off coastal piracy, and our taking of the north coast, the worst fighting until the Venn invasion was among us Marlovans. Starting with the first Montreivayir king stabbing the first, and only, Montredavan-An king in the back. And after Hadand-Deheldegarthe used the odni against Mad Gallop Yvanavayir when he tried to take the throne, things began to change again, until we became border scouts, as now."

"Knowing this history, do you believe that bringing women into the army will be an improvement?"

Danet stood just inside the doorway, aware of the press of obligations. People were waiting for her, but this conversation, with this particular woman, at this moment, felt important. "Improvement," she repeated. "This word is...like water, to me. Can't quite be shaped to the circumstances. Do I think warfare will improve? I have no idea how to define improvement within the context of warfare. Do I think that women will be better warriors than men? Not necessarily. Better defenders, maybe."

The Iofre said soberly, "As you said, we can be just as bloody-minded as men when sufficiently roused."

"Yes. But I can't find a single record, and I've looked, that mentioned female captains or chieftains who successfully defended then rode out a-conquering for the sake of glory. They seemed to turn to rebuilding."

"As have men." The Iofre opened her palm. "That's one credit I will grant my ancestor, Inda-Harskialdna. After he brought back the treaty settling the strait, he didn't sweep eastward, creating an even larger Marlovan empire. He went home, and tried his hand at farming until they made him a teacher. We can't resolve the debates about female or male natures, much less establish that there is any such thing. As warriors for millennia have discovered after they break skulls, our brains all look the same. So. To what matters now."

The Iofre dropped cross-legged on the guest-mat that Danet herself had chosen, and glanced at the rapidly cooling meal waiting. "I must discuss your plan with Noren, who might be expected to carry on your designs."

"There's time," Danet said. "If the others agree, I'll call for the queen's training to begin spring a year from now, to once again establish a single standard for female training. There's considerable variation in training, I've seen at the Victory Day competitions. If nothing else, I believe it will be beneficial to regularize it."

Fareas-Iofre said, "Am I to understand that you will teach the old odni, or do you intend to introduce Fox's drills?"

Danet said, "I thought about it. For now, I think we're better off with the odni, which I learned as a girl. If events in the kingdom change, that can change as well. We've only one more thing to talk about: when Noren is to come to us as haranviar."

The Iofre smiled. "I don't know that she's ready to be acknowledged as haranviar with all the duties implied, but she's ready to live in the royal city now. She loves it here. I can send her permanently after she turns eighteen, though I don't know that she'll be ready to marry even then. All her attention has been on acquiring skills."

"The Olavayirs traditionally marry young—boys by twenty-five, girls eighteen to twenty—but that doesn't mean we have to follow this tradition. Noddy isn't even twenty yet, and he's far from ready. She can be haranviar in all but name for a few years, if she and Noddy want. There's no hurry for marriage, but I would like her to be here when I begin the queen's training."

"She'll definitely want to train with the other girls before she can be expected to run it," the Iofre said.

"Of course." Danet laid her hand to her breast in unconscious salute, though she could never have said why she did it. "Thank you for talking to me. Enjoy your meal. The Convocation will resume at the double-bell."

She walked out, to find an unfamiliar runner hovering in the hallway. Belatedly she recognized the wine-colored and yellow edging along the front and sleeves of the woman's sun-faded blue runner's robe: Marthdavan.

The woman said, "My jarlan asked me to petition for a private interview."

Danet made an effort to mentally shift. Marthdavan, another fake daughter—a very troublesome one, about whom there had been minor complaints that reached first the ears of the Fath family to whom this fake daughter was betrothed, and from them to Tdor Fath. She'd sent the letters on to Danet, who'd decided to deal with it later since no one had come to her directly...*aaaaand* apparently "later" was now.

She was going to follow the runner, then remembered that she was the gunvaer, and this jarlan was in the wrong. And the faint throb behind her eyes was no doubt due to the fact that she had not eaten since last evening's hunk of bread stuffed with cheese.

"Bring her to my chamber," Danet said.

When she got there, her third-runner Sage had just brought a meal. Danet eyed the many dishes, and sent an inquiring glance at Sage.

"Loret thought someone might be sticking to your hem when you came back. And she said you haven't eaten since last night."

"Thanks," Danet said with deep appreciation, and tried to get as much into her as she could.

Even so, she'd barely swallowed half a dozen bites before the runner returned with a short, dark-haired woman with wide-set, anxious eyes. She held hands tightly with another woman whose plain clothes offered no clue as to her calling. They stood hip to hip in a way that signaled to Danet that these two were close, maybe even lifemates, though they didn't wear rings.

She waved them both in.

Danet recognized in the set of the jarlan's chin that self-justification equaled guilt, and to cut short a conversation they both would find trying, she said, "I know that your daughter Chelis isn't a daughter—"

"You *know*?"

"Yes. Did you think I was going to send a wing of lancers down to Marthdavan? I know what you feared, and why. What I require from you is a suitable bride for Anderle Fath, so that my entire betrothal plan doesn't unravel. Send me the family name for the records, and we'll be done."

The Jarlan of Marthdavan saluted, a gesture conveying as much relief as respect. "It will be done as soon as I return home."

"Sit. Have you eaten?" Danet asked, and indicated the extra dishes. "As you see, my runner brought extra."

The jarlan dropped crosslegged onto the guest mat, scarcely hearing the dry tone of Danet's voice. The other woman stepped back to stand behind her, but the jarlan whispered something under her breath and tugged on the woman's robe.

With a quick, wary glance at Danet, the woman sat next to her jarlan, again hip to hip, shoulder to shoulder.

Sage uncovered the braised fish, bread, cheese, and darkberry compote. The jarlan and her companion shared the same plate.

"Tell me about your boy," Danet said.

The pair exchanged glances. Then the jarlan sighed as she pulled out her belt knife to cut the fish. "At first we raised him as Chelis, so as not to make a liar of us. He was wild from the time he could speak. We think he would have been wild if we had not braided his hair. One of his uncles fought duels all down the coast until he finally met someone stronger, and his grandfather was…. Well. At ten, when Chelis understood what we had done, he insisted we call him Chana—for Chanrid, the same uncle I mentioned, whom our Chelis, that is, Chana, admired. Then he tried to run away to the royal city, for he thought that the academy meant he could fight all day without discipline or duty."

"There are some who come here with that belief. After they've scrubbed enough stables, it passes," Danet said.

The jarlan pressed her hands to her face as the silent woman's arm slipped around her waist. "We finally sent him to sea. He did not get his first leave for two years, but when he came home, all he talked about was going back. He's with the patrol ships, mostly south, off the Land Bridge. Been in three battles against pirates, so we hear…."

Danet listened patiently to the exploits of this once-troublesome son, who apparently had become an excellent sailor and pirate fighter. At least Danet got to finish her lunch before the two women finally left. She was alone at last, with a chance to reflect on these private conversations. For the most part, it seemed the jarlans were...she wouldn't say with her so much as not against her, Lavais Nyidri of Feravayir excepted.

That one, Danet wouldn't trust as far as she could spit into a wind.

The oaths (as per usual), king's address (short), and commentary (very, very long) dragged on until well past sundown. They were in that frigid room so long it began to seem almost warm, and moisture glistened on the walls from all the exhalations.

Danet and Arrow both noted a different quality to the men's voices with the women present, but each interpreted it differently: Arrow heard swagger, and Danet a tone of self-justification. The rambling repetitions ended only with the ringing of the watch bell announcing the Firstday banquet across the windy passage. Stomachs wringing with hunger forced an ending to the tedium, and the tone of the voices lightened, the usual buzz of men blending with the descant of female voices.

Hot spiced-wine had already been placed on the tables. As it circulated, the waiting line of kitchen staff and runners snaked in and dispersed on a signal, each carrying covered trays of baked spice-fish, cabbage, and cheese. They set these down at the same moment, a fact unnoticed by the hungry guests; even though the latter paid scant attention to anything but their dinner, Kitchen Steward Amreth Tam knew that when the jarls noticed something, it was invariably to complain. There had been bad blood at a Convocation during the first Olavayir's reign because the tables were served one after another, those at the last table seeing insult in the arrival of frigid food when the king's table was half finished eating.

The royal children were present for the first time at this banquet, which gave the jarls a chance to glimpse their future king. Most thought he wasn't much to look at, but approved of those big shoulders. He looked strong enough to sit on that throne there across the hall.

Levais of Feravayir paid no attention to Noddy. Her attention shot straight to that homely daughter, and foundered on disgust. Unless that buck-toothed weed spoke Sartoran and knew something of civilized manners, she would never marry Levais's brilliant Demeos.

Her gaze snagged on the second son. A shame he wasn't a girl. That one would have been suitable for Demeos, at least in looks.

Early Thirdday morning, Sage came in to warn Danet that a jarlan had been standing in the hall before the morning watch bell.

"Who?"

"Wouldn't say," Sage whispered, eyes huge. "She is very old. Wearing Zheirban colors."

"Let her in," Danet sighed.

The white-haired Jarlan of Zheirban stood inside the door, her hands in her sleeves, as if gripping her wrists tight. As the woman drew a shaky breath Danet wondered if she had knives up her forearms, and her body tightened, the old defensive block trembling in her muscles.

But the woman began to sing in a cracked, quavering voice that once had been beautiful:

"When kings die, their quarrels with them

Who will remember

The sons and brothers whose blood they spilled

Whose bones lie scoured by winter's wind?"

She paused for another shuddering breath, and Danet—though irritated and thirsty, prompted by impulse she could not name—sang,

"As the sun returns, it is we their beloveds

Who sing to remember

Spring rains bring new life, but never to us

Our tears shall drown the wind."

"You still remember it," the jarlan whispered.

"Of course." Danet opened her hands. "My mother taught me that it's one of our oldest ballads. The men sing of glory, the women's chorus sings of its cost."

"One of our earliest ballads. From the days before we took the Iascan castles," the old jarlan stated, her unwinking gaze steady from pouched old eyes. "It was one of many grief songs, when woman unbound their hair and rent their robes."

That was *very* long ago, Danet thought. Out loud, she said, "When I was a girl, I sometimes heard men sing it among themselves, but they left off the chorus."

"Did you?"

"No. We sang the entire song." *If we sang it at all.* Danet was not going to get into how impatient Mother had been of any ritual save the Andahi Lament, which was a family duty. In adulthood, it had occurred to Danet that her mother, honest, strong, and hard-working, was oblivious to beauty in any form.

The old jarlan clasped gnarled hands. "You sing it still? And yet we are told it was the royal city that suppressed Andahi Day, and no longer sings the Lament. Was that you?"

Danet sensed that this was not the problem, but she turned her palm up in a gesture of invitation. "Please. Come, sit. It was my husband who laid aside the Andahi Lament, but not for the reason you seem to think."

The jarlan unbent enough to join Danet at her table. She explained the king's feelings about the attack in the Andahi Pass followed by Lorgi Idego's breaking away. The jarlan listened in silence, then out came her true question: "Why do you desire to put our daughters in the fields of blood?"

"I want to prevent fields of blood," Danet retorted, trying not to sound sharp.

Once again, she explained her thinking, repeating the speech she had worked on so carefully since summer. How many people had ignored it that first day of Convocation? Or maybe they didn't ignore it, but some word, some phrase, caused them to fall into their own thoughts, so they missed the following words. It had happened to her often enough.

When Danet came to a close, and fought the impulse to repeat herself into the still-tense silence, the jarlan slowly rose, one hand pressing against a bad knee. She sighed, touched a finger to a loose hair from her thin white braid loop, then said, "I will tell my grand-daughter not to hold our girls back if they wish to come. I believe in your good will."

"I hear misgivings," Danet said. "Share them freely. Please."

The jarlan had started toward the door. Here she paused, looking back. "I've learned that the young are more likely to make our mistakes all over again than listen. So I will say only this: if you train an army, what else has it to do but fight?"

"My husband's answer will be defense," Danet said. "Mine is, I hope they'll spend their lives enjoying their wargames, without ever having to raise a sword in earnest."

The jarlan sighed heavily. "Thank you for talking to me," she said, saluted and went out, wondering how much Danet-Gunvaer had truly heard.

TWENTY-ONE

On New Year's Thirdday night, the first real blizzard of winter struck.

The sun came up next morning, weak and blue, as Lineas shoved her hands into the sleeves of her winter robe.

Bun had insisted on going with Lineas when she went upstairs to the third floor to check in for any new orders. So they ran side by side up to the tower room below the Harskialdna chamber, the command post for the castle watch commander and the runner chief during Convocation.

Bunny knew that Quill had been given the responsibility of overseeing the younger runners during Convocation, which included relaying the constant stream of demands on the kitchens from various servants brought by the guests. She looked around with interest as gray-blue coated and robed people came and went in the room, their voices soft. At Bun's entrance, they stilled, touching two fingers to their hearts.

Bun eyed the slate against one wall, covered with cryptic marks. On a table sticks with colored notches lay lined up, surely conveying some sort of message.

Bun's gaze flicked from these to Quill, tall and slim in his dark blue runner's robe, modestly queued dark brown hair glinting reddish in the lamplight. He'd been standing in the center of the room in low-voiced conversation with two young runners in training.

"You know what to do." He flicked his hand, and the two youngsters took off.

Then he turned to Bun and touched a finger to his chest in salute. "What may I do for you, Hadand-Edli?" His gaze flicked to Lineas, who had been reading the slate and the message wands.

It was no more than a glance, but Bunny saw it, and misread it. "I insisted she bring me," she said, gazing round-eyed at Quill. This had gone very differently in her imagination.

Ever since her last Name Day, Quill had switched from calling her Bunny-Edli to using her given name, and she hated it. Even worse, she hated that polite, formal salute. Nobody saluted a person they wanted to kiss.

The entire room had gone silent, everyone staring at her. "I thought I could offer to help," Bun said in a small voice. "There's a blizzard, so no riding. And I haven't anything else to do."

"That is kind and thoughtful," Quill said in a kind and thoughtful voice, but not the least romantic. "Might I trouble you to pass a message to Sage in the gunvaer's chamber? It's urgent."

Bun brightened as he picked up one of the sticks lying to the left of the pile, and handed it to her. "I'd be glad to!" She took the stick, and turned it over in her hand. "Uh, what do these marks mean?"

"Sage will explain," Quill said, and saluted again. "Thank you very much for your offer."

Smiling. Waiting. Bun gave in to the unconscious pressure to get out the door. But a step from the doorway she resisted, turning. "Lineas?"

"She'll be along in a moment, Hadand-Edli," Quill said in that kindly, polite voice.

As Bun exited reluctantly, Quill whirled and threw one of the sticks directly at where Bun had been standing.

Lineas lunged, her fingertips knocking the stick into the wall with a clatter. There was no getting past the truth: She should have caught it. She'd let her reflexes slow.

She looked up. Quill's timing had been perfect. Bun had vanished with her stick that signified *Delay*, or *Keep the bearer busy*. The only audience was their fellow runners, who turned back to their work, having recognized another one of their frequent tests.

Lineas's timing had been a heartbeat late.

As Lineas placed the stick on the table, Quill said lightly, "Too much Convocation?"

He regretted the words as soon as they were out. Her face had already flamed with shame. He knew how quick, how sensitive she was.

Quill took a step closer, and said softly, so only she could hear, "What did you think of the Jarlan of Feravayir?"

Lineas's first impulse was *I didn't like her*. But she'd been trained out of that error. "Her smile is half-face," Lineas said, meaning that it never reached the woman's eyes. "She gives no information. When she first saw B—the princess, her quick expression was a sneer."

"Yes, Mnar saw it as well," Quill said, and Lineas's breath trickled out slowly as he went on, "Lineas, you know that the princess is betrothed to that jarlan's eldest son. Now that Hadand-Edli is well past sixteen, it's entirely possible that this jarlan will require her to ride back to Feravayir with her. Do you think she will be as safe there as she is here?"

Sick with dread, and disgust at herself for not thinking ahead to the obvious, Lineas put hand to heart.

Quill said, "I know that the princess stays up late, but recently you've been missing drill more often than you've attended. And it shows, as you saw just now."

"I'll be there in the morning," Lineas whispered.

She walked out, shivering from a chill that had little to do with winter's grip. Halfway down the tower stairs she stopped, pressing her forehead against the icy wall.

She, who tried so very hard to be normal, and let her awareness narrow to the immediate, without thinking past that.

No, be truthful.

Her focus narrowed through the day to each evening, when the Olavayir teens gathered. She had offered to serve, which they accepted without thought. It let her, for the first time, be in the same room with Connar for hours. She took care to station herself out of his line of sight so she could watch the edge of his cheekbones, the line of his shoulder down to narrow hips, his beautiful hands as he held his cup, or gestured. So she could listen to the liquid gold of his voice.

That meant her focus had narrowed—to him.

Fierce self-hatred seared through her, but she breathed hard to let it go. One thing she'd learned over the last few years was that anger was another, more dangerous limitation to focus. There was no use in denying herself those evenings. The boys might not notice, but Bun would ask why.

No, Lineas would still go, but she would watch everything else *except* for Connar. It would be good discipline: her job was to guard Bunny, not watch the second prince. And danger, if it happened, would happen suddenly. She could not relax while on duty, no matter how much she loved being around Connar-Laef.

She pushed away from the wall and ran down the stairs, unaware of Quill watching silently from above, fighting against his own guilt and remorse. When he saw her skinny shoulders straighten and her freckled chin lift, relief poured through him. He faded back into the constant stream of activity.

Lineas rejoined Bun in the gunvaer's chamber, where Sage had coopted her to help with setting out the dishes for the breakfast Danet was giving to Calamity and a group of jarlans and first runners connected by family.

When Bun saw Lineas, she carefully set down the good ceramic plates and gave Lineas a tight hug.

Lineas stiffened. Bun knew by now that Lineas had grown up with some mage or other in Darchelde who was sensitive to touch, and so Lineas had only had parental hugs on her home visits. But Bun was by nature tactile; the animals she spent so much time with responded strongly to touch, caress, rub, fondle. Bun had learned not to fondle people the way she handled animals, but she was a hugger. Lineas was startled, as always, then sighed and melted into the hug; she understood right away she had forgotten to school her face, and so she brought out a smile before they let go.

"Are you all right?" Bun asked, wide eyes searching Lineas's face. "What did Quill want to talk about?" She pressed her hands together, her expression hopeful. "Did he want to talk about me?"

"I'm fine," Lineas said, and deflected the truth with a truth. "Quill is like a big brother to me, because we both come from Darchelde. He just wanted to remind me that I've been skipping too many drills."

Bun's eyelids flickered, but before she could speak, Sage clapped her hands. "We're done," she said, examining the table. "Unless you would like to stay for this breakfast, Bunny-Edli?"

Bun wrinkled her nose. "And be the only girl while they bore on about the past, and people I never met? Come on, Lineas, let's go visit Cloud and Silk," naming two mares brought by the jarlans of Tlennen and Sindan-An respectively.

They escaped as the jarlans began arriving.

Carleas Cassad had come with two purposes in mind.

Before riding to Convocation, she'd discussed with the jarl the questions about Colt, the academy, and a possible trip to Sartor for the magic to bring Colt's body and identity to agreement.

He'd said, "I see Colt's situation as a Dei family matter, first. Colt and you are both Deis, with family experience in the question. As for admitting that Barend is not Carleas, this by rights is gunvaer business, but if there is to be trouble, then send for me. I'll talk to the king myself."

So Carleas had decided it was time to address the gunvaer directly. At the end of the New Year's Fourthday breakfast, Carleas kept herself busy finishing her coffee as the others left, the Jarlan of Marthdavan sending back a sympathetic glance.

Danet immediately recognized the intent behind that apparent dawdling and turned an inquiring eye toward the Jarlan of Telyer Hesea, bracing for another attack on her ideas.

Carleas stood in a formal stance and admitted to calling her son a daughter, to which Danet suppressed the urge to roll her eyes so hard they'd hear the clang all over the castle. She raised a hand to stem the obviously-rehearsed flow. "Yes, I know...evil Olavayirs, Bloody Tanrid, all the rest. My only question is this: Do you have a suitable girl to marry the Yvanavayir heir?"

Much chastened by the gunvaer's total lack of surprise, Carleas said humbly, "I do, and she's quite willing. Chelis, daughter to my husband's younger brother, is an excellent manager."

"Good. Then we're done." The gunvaer turned away.

Carleas gripped her hands. "Not quite." She drew a breath, and launched into her second prepared speech.

Danet listened first mildly puzzled, then very confused by the tangle of pronouns. When Carleas came to a close, Danet said, "Let me get this straight. This now concerns an adopted daughter or a son? Which is it?"

"That's part of what makes it so difficult. The castle has been calling Colt she, but out riding, she's he. He's he. Then reverts to she at home, I guess to make life easier, because they've all known her since she came to us as an infant. But Colt is Rider-trained, wants to be a captain, and so — as he — wants to go to the academy, where captains are trained."

"All right, so Colt is a he, and wants into the academy? But doesn't want to go to Sartor for magic transformation?"

"Correct."

Danet clapped her hands together. "Come with me."

Arrow had just returned from the baths, clean but bleary-eyed. He glanced from Danet to Carleas, then sent Danet one of those private fiery looks that she successfully interpreted, so she said, "This concerns the academy. Therefore, you."

And without any prompting, she gave a succinct summary of the dilemma. At the end, she turned to Carleas, saying, "Have I stated it fairly?"

"Fair enough," Carleas said.

Danet waited as Arrow gazed into the middle distance, his brow furrowed. At least, she was thinking, he wouldn't hop out with his usual *Inda didn't have these problems in his academy.* Then it struck her that Inda wouldn't have considered it a problem, not after he'd gone to sea, learning marine defense with all kinds of people.

It had been Hadand Deheldegarthe who —

"Let me get this right," Arrow said. "Your Colt is he out riding, but a she here." He smacked his chest twice, left then right, then pointed at his crotch. "He wants to come to the academy, but doesn't want to travel off to Sartor to get the girl parts cut off, or whatever the healers do by magic, and a prick grown on."

"In essence, that is correct," Carleas said gravely.

"And this Colt refuses to ride with the girls at the summer games — even with the understanding that Danet here wants to start up queen's training again?"

"Correct," Carleas said. "Colt is Rider-trained, good with a bow but better with a sword, and near unbeatable with the double-stick. She — he — needs training to become a captain, which right now is only got at the academy. I thought I would ask, as I'd heard that Ranet Senelaec will be coming to the academy."

"That's easy. No," Arrow said.

"Why not?" Danet asked.

"Different situation. Completely different," Arrow said with a flat-handed sweep. "For one thing, Ranet Senelaec won't be coming as Ranet. He was a boy dressed as a girl. He's coming as a boy."

He paused, thinking that explained everything, just to meet Danet's eyebrow-lift of skepticism, and Carleas's stony expression.

He sighed, hard. "Look. I know people can get born into the wrong sort of body. Anyone growing up with Aunt Hlar, who was born my father's brother Hal, knows *that*. Maybe if Colt came in at ten, and they all grew up together. Boys and girls are puppies at ten. But at seventeen? He can say he's a he all he wants, but we've only got the one bath down there, and there's no hiding the fact that he's got she parts. Unless lightning bolts strike their eyes, those eighteen-year-olds, who only think about three things, sex, fighting, and sex, are going to be looking."

"So?" Carleas retorted. "Everybody looks, then they're done."

"You don't understand," Arrow shot back. "We raise these boys training hard—it's traditional to train them until a year or so after they get their full growth, which means coming into their strength. But with full growth comes sex. And at that age they think about it all the time. All. The. Time. We run them hard partly to build strength, but also to tired them out so much they sleep at night."

"So far you're telling me the obvious."

He wiped a hand through the air. "I'm getting there. So they all bathe together. They grow up knowing there's one end of the baths where the boys who like to play around with boys can get rid of saddle wood. Those who only like girls grow up knowing that's the way it is, and they have to wait for rec time to go into town to the Sword, or wherever. It isn't fair, but it's the way it is. So what happens when I put someone in who looks like a girl the age of their partners at the Sword, but isn't? If I issue special orders about your Colt, then she— *he*—becomes an object of resentment. See? I can tell you who will fight to get Colt's attention anyway, and who will pick fights *with* her. Him. Damn. All I foresee is trouble, making Andaun have to hammer them all, when there's enough going on."

Carleas held up her hand. She thought his reasoning stupid, but she hadn't expected any better from an Olavayir. "As you wish."

"Colt can be a Rider anywhere in the kingdom. But not at the academy. If you wanted to send someone," Arrow stated with some heat, "you should've sent your boy Barend, who you told us was a girl named Chelis."

Carleas reddened. "As it happens, I don't know that that would have borne out. My son never sought to be anything but what he was, which is...that is, he doesn't see himself as a female, but his only interest is in textiles, color, and design. He's certainly no use in a military sense. He was that way before he could speak."

Arrow knew the stories about the crazy Cassads. He said gruffly, "Such boys usually get peeled out early and sent off to the scribes, or back home to be prenticed."

"But all we had were the memories—"

"—of Bloody Tanrid," he cut in to finish with an exasperation that even she admitted was justified.

They parted then, with expressions of somewhat strained mutual goodwill, Carleas to tell her husband that the king had rocks between his ears but at least the question of lying about Barend went better than she'd dared to hope, and Arrow figuring he'd gotten himself through that well enough, though he had a pounding head from too many cups of hot bristic the night before.

Danet left, thinking: That's it, Arrow said it himself. If we put girls in the army, we start them at age ten.

That night, as usual, the young Olavayirs collected in Noddy's suite, attended by Lineas, alert and observant—as far as her experience allowed. So she enjoyed the atmosphere of jokes and rambling anecdotes, careful not to look Connar's way, though every remark, laugh, even the sound of his breathing filled her with the light of summer sunshine.

So she was unaware of the way Connar watched Tanrid, whose popularity made Connar wary, and whose easiest remarks in retrospect seemed...not threatening, but odd.

Like that comment on the tour right after his arrival, when he said that about looking out over the land from up high. Connar had taken that as pedantry at first. Tanrid did like his books, and offered quotations whether anyone wanted them or not. But what if that comment hinted at the possibility of *possession*—the way a king would look over his land?

Connar tried to forget Hauth's words, but he was discovering that consciously trying to forget something made him worry at it in sneaky ways. Like the fact that Tanrid was the *true* heir to the dead Evred, according to the old Olavayir treaty: That is, his father had been designated heir by treaty, and sons follow fathers. That was accepted tradition. Order.

Uncle Jarend had said he didn't want to be king, but what if his son did? Tanrid was older than Noddy, so someone could insist he was the true heir.

Connar watched Tanrid, evaluating his every utterance, as Noddy avoided looking at Lineas—another thing she remained utterly unaware of.

Noddy was very aware of her. He kept his eyes averted, but he listened for her sweet voice, so seldom heard. It reminded him of glass chimes he'd heard at a shop in the city, one that sold fabrics from other lands. And as for her face, people might say that pale, freckled skin was ugly, but he liked those freckles because they were part of *her.*

It never would have occurred to Lineas that anyone would look at her for any purpose but to share a task or hand off an order. After that awful experience at the age of eight, she had preferred to enjoy her crushes quietly, because of course they would always be one way.

At those nightly gatherings she oversaw the snacks of crisped rye biscuits with melted cheese and hot spice wine, enabling Tanrid's first runner and closest friend, Halrid (Floss) Vannath—a cousin whose family was promoted after Lanrid's cousins mostly died at the Pass—to sit with Tanrid, Bun, and the princes, and take part in the chatter.

This particular evening began like the previous ones until Connar, conflicted and restless, heard Noddy's relishing description of lancers' games in a new and sinister light. Eldest sons didn't attend the academy, except for Noddy as the future king.

What if Tanrid, smiling over there as he listened to Noddy going on about the fun he and Ghost Fath had smashing hay targets, decided he wanted to come to the academy? It was possible, even at an advanced age—they'd learned that after hearing that the Senelaec boy was coming straight to lancers.

He cut in, "I'm bored. Who's for Sword?"

Noddy swung around to eye him. "It's blizzarding out there," he protested. "We'd get lost soon's we rode out the gates."

Floss wiggled his nearly white eyebrows. "You've got an entire castle full of good-looking girls. Why cross the city?"

Noddy dropped his head and mumbled something.

Tanrid leaned over. "Cousin, do you mean to say you don't like *any* of them?"

Noddy studied his hands, his ears crimson.

Tanrid elbowed Noddy and cooed, "Your castle girls only like girls? Think we stink?"

"Speak for yourself, jarl of farts," Floss retorted, and eyed Noddy. "They can't all be ring-bound. Or is there some rule that puts you two hounds out of reach?"

"Of course not," said Bun, aware of undercurrents she couldn't define.

Intensely aware of Lineas's breathing a few paces away, Noddy muttered to the cup he was turning around in his hands, "They can't say no, at Singing Sword."

"Of course they can say no," Bun retorted, startled.

Connar shrugged sharply. "The whole reason we go there is that they don't say no."

"There's a river of difference between can't and don't." Bun opened her hands. "They say no, but they aren't *mean* about it. Like Vnat in the bakery." She turned to Noddy and said earnestly, "Say, you go in and you first notice...oh, Liet. But she only goes with girls. She's friendly but not flirty. She introduces you to Nand, who only goes with boys. Nand is friendly *and* flirty and you forget all about Liet."

Noddy's blush had burned right down to his neck. But as this subject had been goading him for months, he let the wine speak. "It's all right, over *there*. But here. If you try to talk to some girl about something that isn't a chore, or something, she turns away, or says she has to work, or she just says no, it all happens in a way that makes you wish you never spoke. And you never even *tried* to kiss her."

Tanrid and Floss exchanged pained glances, Tanrid wishing he hadn't started teasing Noddy. He shifted, wondering how to get out of it gracefully.

Connar didn't trust Tanrid enough to ask what he saw in girls that made their intent clear. It wasn't as if girls leaped into the baths with you and grabbed you, lance at the charge when they wanted a fast tumble, as they did at the north end of the academy baths. There was little or no talk — they knew what they wanted and they got it. The academy slang for that end of the bath was fun-and-run.

But outside of the fun-and-run, where everyone knew the rules...he hated the uncertainty. While roaming the castle grounds, he and Noddy had both overheard Vnat and some of the older kitchen girls' frank scorn in discussing the garrison men while they weeded the garden. Connar loathed the idea of his name coming up, and causing that jeering laughter. It was just as easy to go to the Singing Sword, where everything was a simple trade.

Bun's thoughts arrowed, as usual, straight to Quill. Until the day she noticed him leaning on the gate, watching the lancers practice evolutions, her sexual experiences had been fun. Experimental. None of those had given her that feeling of heat all over, that catch in breath that she got when just *looking* at him.

Yet everything she tried didn't get past his deference, that friendly...*respect.*

She glanced at Noddy doubtfully. He looked exactly as miserable as she felt about Quill. She wondered if Vnat had hurt him, and decided to shift the subject. "At Sword, they get training in how to talk to people. I asked, my first time. Everything was so *interesting.* I asked for a girl first, because I've been kissing girls since I was fourteen, but I never did anything else. Never wanted to. And that was fine."

Noddy still hadn't looked up, but his ears weren't quite as red, so she kept blabbing, "But when I decided to try with a boy, Branid — that's his name — he told me that most of them are family, and grew up into the trade, the children serving the food downstairs, and helping with the drumming and dancing, and when you're a teen, you can go upstairs and learn the skills there, if you want. He said it's fun when you're young, but his da said it's not as fun after ten or twenty years of it, and so a lot of them marry off, or go do something else. Which is why it's mostly young ones."

Tanrid felt terrible about his blunder. He saw Noddy looking less dejected after Bunny's ramble, and jumped in to offer a description of his first time with the Nevree castle baker's lusty daughter, who'd towed him into the cooling room to show him how to bake a cake. "She baked my cake, all right. Three times, until she was sure I had the recipe."

Floss snickered. Bun clapped her hands. Noddy smiled briefly, so Floss told them about his own first time, which at the time he thought a disaster of kingdom-shaking proportion. "I can see why nobody wants to be anybody's first," he said. "My sister told me that at the Rocking Horse in Nevree, they have people who only do firsts."

"I wonder if they laugh themselves sick afterward," Tanrid mused. "At least you never hear about it if they do. Unlike that gabby you-know-who at home."

Noddy smiled, but still wouldn't lift his head, with Lineas standing there; he wondered longingly what her experience was—having no clue that she had no experience at all. Lineas went as Bun's runner to the Sword, but she always stayed downstairs to listen to the music and darn the socks that Bun was forever wearing out at heel and toe.

The subject ended as the jug of spice wine emptied, and everyone parted for the night, Floss muttering privately to Tanrid, "You stepped in it there."

"How was I supposed to know?" Tanrid muttered back. "Poor Noddy."

Bun confided to Lineas as they walked down the hall, "I didn't think Noddy even *noticed* girls. Has to be that Vnat who snubbed him. One of these days she's going to run out of boys to make fun of."

Before the single clang of the pre-dawn bell, Lineas was dressed and ready for knife and contact fighting drill at the royal runners' own salle.

The blizzard, to everyone's relief, blew out overnight, leaving perfect weather for travel, the fresh snow squeaky powder. Those with the longest roads to travel readied in haste.

Feravayir, of course, was one of the longest, so the southern party was first to depart. Twice Danet steeled herself to duty and attempted to get some sense of when Lavais-Jarlan expected Bun to travel to Feravayir to marry Demeos Nyidri. Danet loathed the thought of saying farewell to her daughter, a prospect not made any easier by the jarlan, whose manners were perfect, but whose *manner* was as slick as ice, and about as warm.

Both times Lavais-Jarlan skillfully kept the conversation general, and once Danet was certain that the jarlan was not in any hurry to take in her prospective replacement in order to instruct her in the ways of Feravayir, Danet let the subject lapse with profound relief.

Bun was not given to much reflection, but she was far from stupid, and observant enough in her own way. As she joined her mother in walking to the stable to say farewell to the southern party, Bun muttered to Lineas, "I'm so glad the Jarlan of Feravayir didn't say anything about me having to go south with her. She reminds me of a horse about to bite. Ears like this." Bun cupped her palms slightly, and put them up by her head, signaling a horse a heartbeat away from a kick.

Everything proper was said, and the Jayad Hesea, Feravayir, and Telyer Hesea parties rode out, trumpets blaring in the clear, bracing air—Feravayir of course leading the way.

As she rode out the gates into a fresh world of white under an azure sky, Lavais of Feravayir agreed out loud to the inanities the Cassad and Jayad Hesea jarlans uttered, and silently agreed with none of it.

Danet and Anred Olavayir were war leaders, their castle a fortress. They didn't seem to have heard of the concept of gardens, much less fashion, art, or music. But they were very powerful. She could respect the power they wielded while despising the persons.

Take that bonehead idea of Danet's. Put women in the army to stop men from making war? She suppressed the urge to caw out a laugh of disbelief. As if that could happen! When men got their pricks up for blood, no mere woman was going to stop them. Only when they had shot their bolt into the bloody wreckage of other men would they come home to their women for their rewards.

She could wait. Those young princes were bound to be trouble within the next few years, as Marlovan princes always were unless sent off to get themselves killed first. The bucktoothed one might be too much of a dolt to start it, and it was difficult to say about the northern Olavayir boy, but that black-haired piece of art with those gorgeous, watchful blue eyes was trouble on the hoof. As soon as he got bored with breaking hearts he was going to be breaking heads, anyone with half a brain could see *that* at a glance.

As for that rabbit-faced girl they all called Bunny, if the gunvaer forced Lavais to take her, it would be easy enough to arrange an accident well before Demeos found his Sartoran princess.

She laughed silently to herself as the Cassad woman blathered on about the famous Inda tapestry, and how the fashion for tapestries might come back.

Fashion. These boors had no idea what the word meant.

TWENTY-TWO

Winter sped by, full of activity.

The only time the boys felt the drag of time was when Arrow insisted that they sit in on his meetings with guild chiefs. The round-and-round discussions of where and how to allocate fealty funds was maddeningly tedious, inevitably coming around to the sore topic of the Nob. The boys didn't mind sessions with various garrison staff, but they were heartily sick of hearing about the Nob.

Noddy sat stolidly without catching much meaning, enduring it as he endured extremely hot weather or cold, confident that the discomfort must end. Connar's emotions twisted like the banners in the winds. Kingship would be tedium like this, he told himself. But he knew that kings could and did delegate. Which meant that Noddy, if—no, *when*—he became king, might expect Connar to sit through these boring gab fests....

One day, when the boys thought the state lessons safely over until the next winter, a thaw brought the usual cluster of runners who had been holed up somewhere.

As they did most days, the family gathered for breakfast in the king's rooms, which were the warmest. Bun tore through her food and took off to find out where Quill was, and to figure out if there was a way to get him to stop seeing her as Hadand-Edli. The boys lingered, as neither wanted to go out into the bitter sleet roaring on the rooftops and rattling the windows.

Noddy was reaching for his third biscuit when his father sighed, and tossed a letter over to Danet. "You'd better find a way to manage this."

She took up the letter, the lines between her brows increasing as she read. "The Senelaecs need seed grain *again*?"

"You remember Wolf, his boy, and all their Riders went east all last spring and summer, right?"

"I know that, but we're not getting begging letters from Sindan-An," Danet muttered. "Or Tlennen. I wish Calamity and Wolf would...." She became aware of extra pairs of ears and eyes, and sighed instead. "What is it about the east anyway? Are you certain these constant excursions aren't just playtime for those Riders?"

Arrow got up, and with a flare of coat skirts and his long yellow horsetail, vanished into the far room where he kept his maps and correspondence. Danet sat back on her heels, aware of a pulse of laughter at how Arrow, even with thinning hair and the lined face of a man in his early forties, still walked with the swinging, almost swaggering bounce that had characterized him when they first met.

He returned with a rolled map, glanced at the table full of dishes, then squatted down and snapped the map open on the fresh-swept stone floor. "Look here. I've chalked in every raid. Where, what was lost, and how many. You tell me if that's playtime."

Danet crouched on the other side of the map, her chin on her knees as her gaze roamed the map.

Noddy buttered his roll, got to his feet, and walked out of yet another boring map session. Connar waited, curious; he found himself hoping the Senelaecs, who had sent that annoying boy-girl, would get into trouble, so maybe Da would send him back. No one would want some seventeen-year-old scrub coming into lancers without earning the right to be there, like everyone else had!

Danet glanced up, her eyes narrow. "You're sure about these dates? Is this all rumor from the Eastern Alliance, via half a dozen mouths?"

"These ones with the 'R' are royal runner reports."

"*Those* can be trusted," Danet said. "They only give eyewitness reports. Hmph."

"What do you see?" Arrow asked with a skeptical glance.

Danet said, "I see two patterns. One, early spring dates, the raids are all through here." She swept her hand down south. "My guess is, someone is trying to get in ahead of the jarls' horse studs when they ride out in spring to reclaim their animals sent to winter pasture. When I was young, it was always spring when the horse thieves struck, trying to grab our trained horses. The wild ones being too smart for them."

Arrow turned up his hand. Everyone knew that.

"But the later ones...look. The land below the mountains on this side, according to the maps I had to make as a girl, is barren. These attacks...branching from here and here, well into the dry season...where are they getting their water? Their food? What appears to me is that there's a supply line running through the southern pass." She tapped the straight line bisecting the conical mountains drawn between Sindan-An and Anaeran-Adrani, the map made by someone who had scant knowledge of the geography of mountains.

Arrow squinted down. "I don't see how you're getting that."

Danet sighed. "Because you were trained to defend from Nevree. I've had to learn about supply lines while dealing with the jarls' arguments about the logistics of supporting the Nob, and — oh, never mind. The thing is, you, none of you, think about the *work* in setting up and defending supply lines. The cost. You think about purely military necessity, how many to send, how to place them, for defense or attack."

"The cost is what *you* do," Arrow said. "Better than those scribes of Evred's ever did."

"That's because Mathren kept them blind while he built.... Never mind that." Danet snapped her hand through the air. "Arrow, my point is, if I'm right, these are the kind of supply lines that kings provide."

"Years ago I thought the raiders might be Adranis. You remember, I asked Camerend to send a couple of experienced runners up there to listen for Adrani speech. See if they wore Adrani colors. They came back reporting different languages in the caravan guards. Different fighting styles. There's no law up there in those mountains, so it's natural brigands would roost, but the conditions drive 'em on again, especially when trade caravans are well guarded."

Danet turned a palm up. "The military is your end. What I see...." She smacked the map with the backs of her fingers. "Are numbers too regular to be occasional bands of brigands. Either someone with power and wealth is backing these raids, or else there's a federation of horse thieves the size of an army, because only they could supply raids reaching this far."

Arrow scowled. "If it really is the Adranis coming over the mountains...shit. They must think I'm a bonehead." He glared at the map, mumbling, "This would never have happened in Evred and Inda's day."

They'd merely had to face the Venn, Danet thought. But she decided against saying it. She'd heard enough from Arrow about the bygone days of heroes. *Heroes.* Anytime that word was spoken it threw her back to that stormy day in Tenthen Castle, firelight reflecting in the Iofre's eyes as she described the wreck Inda had been after his heroism.

So she said, "It wouldn't have, because Joret Dei would have put a stop to it."

"True." Arrow's brows lifted. "But. I'm going to send the army up the Pass and clean 'em out clear to the other side."

Danet sat back on her heels. "And have the Adranis declaring war?"

Arrow cursed as he bent over the map. "It's not already war if these are really the Adranis?"

She smacked the map again. "Those plains all along here below the mountains *aren't* our territory. *Or* theirs. They can't claim it any more than we can, right? It's open space, by ancient treaty."

Arrow shrugged. "Right now it seems to be open road for horse thieves. Well, if the Adranis can hire, or pretend to be, horse thieves, then I can send a pack of army-trained horse traders up that way, looking for yearlings. Heh. It's time to try the army — damnation, what now?"

Because Danet scowled at the map, her palm turned down. "First, from the evidence of these dates, it might be too late: so far, my understanding is that every spring they come raiding, then vanish by the end of summer when all the little rivers dry up—"

She paused at a single tap on the door: Arrow's first runner.

"What?" he barked.

"Royal runner chief says, he just received a report you should hear."

"Just what I need, more shit to wand," Arrow muttered. Then, louder, "Send it in." He got to his feet, followed by Danet.

Connar also rose. If it was going to be a lot of reports and talking back and forth, he might as well take off now, and share the juicy news with Noddy. Or what might be juicy news. It would be too stinking unfair if the army thundered east, banners flying, while he and Noddy were stuck playing with wooden sticks on the academy game field another year. By the time they'd *finally* get out of the academy, the fun would be over.

He slipped out and vanished one way as Camerend entered from the other, bringing in a mud-splashed, sodden royal runner from whose gaunt face dark-circled eyes stared out, obviously a man near the end of his strength. Danet and Arrow barely recognized in that frizz-haired, grimy scarecrow Ivandred, one of the best of what they called the long riders, those who traveled great distances—to the Nob, to Parayid Harbor way down south, and even over the Andahi Pass.

Camerend saluted, a gesture belatedly and vaguely echoed by Ivandred. Then Camerend said, "He's just returned from Ku Halir, a hard run."

Arrow and Danet looked at each other, then down at the map. "Ku Halir?" Arrow said. "Something wrong at the new garrison?"

Ivandred said hoarsely, "No. I was sent to Wened Lakeside to run a message...." He bent, coughing.

Danet stepped toward him. "Want some water? Or I can order something hot to drink."

Ivandred fluttered the fingers of his free hand. "Thank you, gunvaer. Got a sip in the stable," he said in a hoarse whisper. "Report right away."

Arrow glanced down at the map. Ku Halir, his new garrison, had been an Iascan trade town on the ancient route from the southern pass. Traders usually stopped first at Wened Lakeside, which was a small trade outpost at the eastern end of the lake, considered the outer boundary of the Sindan-An jarlate.

Ivandred coughed out more dust. "Bad weather, so I stopped at Four Points Inn, to get a night and a meal. I was visiting my brother, so I was riding civ," he added, gesturing down his lanky body, though at this moment he was dressed in the heavy dark blue coat that royal runners wore on the road. "Heard Sartoran. Adrani accent."

"Go on," Arrow said.

"No one up there speaks Sartoran—almost any language but. Adrani, sure, as traders come from there. Shalgan, East Iascan, even Ashka, you'll hear, but not Sartoran," he went on. "I ordered a drink, so I could listen. Two men, one young, one old. The young one said, *But captain, our orders.* The old one said, *I carry the tally.* Right then the innkeeper sent his boy over to serve their food. They broke off, and when the boy scouted off again, the captain just said, *You have your orders. Eat, and ride.*"

Ivandred paused, blinking rapidly, his domed forehead wrinkled. Then, "I didn't know which to follow, so I stuck to the older one. Higher rank, has a tally. He stayed there two days, then it was Restday, with people whooping it up all over. He vanished among them. I rode back to Ku Halir to report. Sent down to carry it to you."

Arrow said slowly, "What's a tally, besides a chalk mark counting things?"

Camerend said, "According to some histories, tallies are tokens, usually gold, silver, or certain kinds of carved and polished stone, used in kingdoms with complex chains of command. Even if one has inherited some sort of military title or rank, no one below royal rank can give orders to a military body without a tally. So, for example, a king might give his tally to a subordinate to move a regiment, say, from here to there. Think of it as the physical manifestation of the King's Voice."

Arrow's brows shot up. "So what you're saying is, there's some army coming over one of the passes?"

Danet glared into space. "Everybody knows the northern pass is blocked up by snow for eight months out of the year, and the rest of the time, it's barely a trail alongside a river. I don't know much about military movement, but it's plain that any army up there would only be able to go as fast as the traders' ox-carts, and two by two at that."

"Not true of the south," Arrow said. "We know there's at least one outpost in the pass."

Camerend said, "There's a walled inn built just below the start of the steep ascent in the southern pass, where traders hire oxen or mountain ponies for going up the pass. We runners sent to the Adrani side always stay there." Camerend tapped a spot on the map.

Arrow turned to Danet. "What if the company was part of your supply lines?"

Danet scowled at the map. "You think the Adranis have taken over that outpost and put warriors there?"

Arrow turned to Camerend, who stood there with his customary mild expression, waiting for orders. Yes, waiting for orders. Arrow considered rapidly. He wanted someone he could trust doing the investigating, someone who knew what to look for. And there was this to say about royal runners— if you gave them specific orders, they carried them out exactly.

The comfort he found in this thought reached too deeply for him to examine it—or even want to examine it. "Camerend, do you have someone you can send east to who would know how to recognize evidence of an army up in either of those passes?"

Camerend gazed out the window as if considering. He'd seen the wariness in Arrow's eyes. He suspected that Arrow, even after a coming up on two decades of rule, still half-expected a knife in the dark.

Camerend had been considering various plans on the walk up the stairs, and how to suggest them. He said slowly, "Lnand could go up the southern pass. If she went as a traveling bard, she might even get into places snowed in all winter. Everyone talks in front of bards. Ivandred here could take the northern pass. Maybe not ride up it. We know what it's like. He might take a position and watch who comes down at our end. He speaks all the dialects up there."

Arrow clapped his hands and rubbed them. "Do it."

Danet tapped the painted mountains with the toe of her boot. "We need this better drawn, showing the folds in the mountains, at least the southern pass, as the northern one follows the river. On this map, these mountains are painted to be pretty, but surely mountains don't all look exactly alike." She remembered those jagged shapes in the distance when she was a girl in Farendavan. "Do they?"

"They do not," Camerend said. "Mapping can be part of Lnand's orders, if you so desire. She's trained."

Danet's expression eased. "If these Adranis, or whoever, are getting supplied from their side at the end of harvest, then sitting tight over winter so they can send raiders in spring.... Arrow, if Lnand finds that outpost suspicious, could you surround it and then capture the raiders directly as they come forth?"

Camerend's lips parted, then he hesitated, watching Arrow rock back and forth, heel to toe, as he, too, scowled at the map. "It's walled, you say? One thing I've learned is that when we took the first castles, it was Iascans who taught us siege warfare. Something we haven't used much of since."

Danet said sourly, "Let me guess. Starving people into surrender hasn't much 'honor' in it compared to spitting someone on a lance."

"Well, the risks are roughly even in a lance charge," Arrow said in a reasoning tone, as if that made all the difference in the world. Maybe it did in his mind, but Danet made no distinction between one miserable death and another. "But one thing I'm sure of: If we laid on a siege over winter, they could sit tight in their warm outpost and laugh at us squatting up to our armpits in snow and ice."

"Right," Danet said. "Well, the military is your end."

Arrow rolled the map, picked it up, and brandished it. "I'm going to show this to Noth. Make sure you find seed grain for the Senelaecs," he added, and to the royal runners, "Good work, Ivandred. Go get some rest, then ride north. Camerend, have Lnand on the road by sundown, while the weather's clear."

Four steps, the door slammed, and he was gone.

Camerend and Quill rode out the city gates during the first real thaw of spring. Quill was about to depart on a tour of Marlovan Iasca, every castle, trade town, and village.

Camerend waited until they were alone under the scudding clouds reflected in drying pools here and there, surrounded by the a stubble of green as far as the eye could see. On the northern horizon a line of black dots moved toward the west, birds returning from the other side of the world.

Camerend halted his horse, and swept his hand around.

"Senrid," he said, "this is your kingdom."

Quill looked around the familiar low hills over which a cold wind softly soughed, knowing that his father did not mean it in any literal sense.

Indeed, Camerend went on as he reached forward to tousle the mane on his favorite mount, "That's what Shendan said to me when I first rode out to make the renewal rounds."

Quill had often wondered what it was like to grow up a hostage, surviving violent changes of king. But he'd learned that his father never talked about his past. *Each new day is a gift, not to be wasted in regret,* he'd said once when asked. Quill was only beginning to comprehend that that word "regret" told him all he needed to know.

Camerend went on, "Your grandson might very well say the same thing to his son, though by then the old exile treaty will be ended, and so our binding to Darchelde. Though we could be kings, we are not, and might never be. We can serve the people of the kingdom with or without a throne."

Quill opened his hand to signify assent. It was as rare for his father to talk generally as it was to refer to his past. He was always present-specific, giving little away of his thoughts.

Maybe that's the way you had to be when you grew up a hostage.

Camerend turned away from contemplating the hazy west under its patchy clouds, and considered how to address his smart, sensitive son without alluding to what he suspected was the quiet heartbreak of a first love. "This is your opportunity to see *everything*. To listen to people and their concerns. If it takes you five years, as it did me, no one will suffer for it. It's early for renewal. I am giving you specific orders to travel, enjoy yourself, and listen to what people want to tell you about themselves."

"All right," Quill said.

Camerend's brief smile faded to a pensive assessment. "Now's the time, when you're young, strong, and heartfree." He glanced at Quill's saddlebag, aware of his son's hand flexing on that last word. Sorrow hurt his heart, but he knew there was no repairing such things with parental sympathy. At least his boy was young, and youth was resilient: by the time Quill returned, no doubt he'd come back with experience under his belt, his current hurt forgotten. "You have your notecase, and the transfer tokens?"

Quill turned up his hand. In an emergency he could perform transfer magic to a Destination at either Darchelde or Camerend's study in the castle, where he had made a Destination. But transfer tokens were faster unless one was very adept at this dangerous, volatile magic. He wasn't all that adept— practice *hurt* so very much.

"Fare well," Camerend said, leaning out to clasp arms with his son.

"And you."

Camerend turned his mount and began riding back.

Quill gazed back, his throat unexpectedly tight. His father had always seemed ageless, but Quill knew no one was ageless. His first stay would be Darchelde, which of course needed no magic renewal, but Shendan was very frail, unable to transfer at all anymore. She might not be there on Quill's return.

As the dappled shadows from a budding tree passed down his father's blue coat and over the flanks of his horse, Quill wondered about that wording, heartfree. Is anyone is ever truly heartfree? He knew his father had not been at his age, and had made a marriage Quill had once overheard called disastrous when the speaker did not know he was on the other side of a stack of scrolls. He knew the "disaster" was not aimed at him, but at the cost to his father.

Quill straightened around and tightened his knees, urging his fresh horse into an easy canter.

It was best to get away from the royal city. He'd seen signs over winter that Bunny's interest was already waning. His absence should free her the faster. As for Lineas...no, it was better to get away until her lingering gaze in Connar's direction wouldn't matter.

TWENTY-THREE

Connar was still brooding over missing a possible attack on the eastern raiders a couple months later, as his Name Day came and went, and spring thawed the world.

So far, nothing had been said about the army riding out, at least. And besides, there was something to be said for being in the top year of the academy at last. The coveted senior barracks, with its own practice court, and closest to the mess hall, was finally theirs.

Connar and Noddy looked around on a rainy, cold morning, buoyant with triumph and anticipation. Both wore new coats, fitted and sashed. Anticipation revealed itself, despite careless attitudes and offhand talk, in the fact that everyone had showed up a day or so early, no matter how far they'd had to ride.

Connar, always listening, overheard someone laughing over the fact that the far south boys had holed up at an inn along the lower river for an entire week, so no one would think they were too eager. Rat and Mouse Noth found them hiding out there, and Mouse was busy telling everyone.

Which was the sort of reckless thing Mouse would do, Connar thought as he chucked the contents of his gear into the empty trunk at the foot of his bunk.

Then he turned around to see who had chosen where, and how much they'd grown. Secretly relieved to find himself the fourth tallest, he bent over to neaten the jumble in his trunk before the bell rang for inspection — some things didn't change — then paused as Lefty Poseid dashed in, eyes wide. "The braids boy is here."

"Where'd they put him?" Gannan asked, grinning.

Lefty jerked his thumb over his shoulder, his lip curling with the extravagant disdain of a senior for the barracks they'd lived in the year before. "With the rats." That was the seniors' pejorative for the class the year behind them, led by Rat Noth.

"Of course they put him in with the rats," Gannan said, irritating Connar with the way he furtively looked around for approval. "He's a rat. Are they duffing him up?"

"Dunno, but I'm going to see." Lefty was gone, his retreating footsteps splashing from puddle to puddle.

Righty, his twin, bolted out the door in pursuit, and the rest streamed after, hoping for entertainment, ancient rivalries temporarily lulled by the presumption of an interloper being thrust among them.

"Out," honked a gangling seventeen-year-old, completely ignored by the seniors, who knew their rights. As this year's leaders, they could go anywhere, a privilege they'd often enough bitterly resented in past years when seniors had seen fit to trample through their barracks.

They ranged themselves along the windows, looking in at a vaguely familiar face: their age, blond hair, a hand shorter than Connar. He was an ordinary enough boy, well put together, square chin, and a wide mouth made for smiling. He'd obviously just arrived, as he stood alone wearing a worn coat that had to have been handed down from a brother, his gear over his shoulder. He faced the rest of the rats, who stood in a semicircle.

Ignoring the new audience, Ran Senelaec said, "Which bunk is mine?"

Six hands pointed to the one by the door.

"Right there, Braids," someone said, and flicked two fingers to an imaginary braid — *braids* in Hand.

Ran tossed his dusty, mud-splattered bag on top of the trunk at its foot and gave them a wry look, having expected both the nickname and the bed. "Worst one in here, right?" And when no one immediately answered, "That's what I figured."

Since his tone had been droll resignation without any heat or resentment, the tallest boy spoke both out loud and with hands, "At least in here, you won't get rained on, as our door faces south. Weather never comes up from the south."

"You might shiver," Baldy Sindan-An put in, turning slightly as he signed, so that David Mareca could see his hands. "But at least you won't smell Basna and Mareca there."

"Says the biggest farter outside the stables," Mareca's hands flashed, his face wrinkled in a grimace of horror. "You'll like the door come summer, Braids. Except yours is the first bunk in inspection."

Ran, who in Senelaec had over winter become Rana, that day underwent another name change that day, one that would stick. He accepted it with a philosophical shrug, more interested in their speed in Hand. He and Cousin Ranet had begun studying the language after the Victory Day games — and as was usual among Senelaecs, what one did, everyone did. Braids had learned a lot, but these boys were so fast he had to concentrate to follow, as some didn't speak at all. It was clear these boys were used to switching between languages without a thought, the same way his Sindan-An cousins switched between Marlovan and their Iascan dialect.

When the pause became a silence, Pepper Marlovayir said in a goading voice, "Do girls fart, Braids?"

"Like a stable after the horses get into the green grass," he said, signing *horses, eating, grass*. He betrayed no reaction to the nickname.

Snickers and guffaws met this sally, then Braids glanced around. "Go ahead. Get 'em out. I know you want to ask."

Thus invited to interrogate him, everyone unaccountably dried up, until Nermand said and signed, "What was it *like?*"

"You mean, what was it like being a girl?" Braids asked, and on seeing an opened palm, "I don't know, what's anything like, when you're used to it every day?"

"Did you really think you were a girl?" someone else asked and signed.

"I didn't think about it at all. Neither did the others. Till we were, I don't know, ten or twelve or so. It was in the baths when they first noticed I was the only one with a prick." Memory: Fnor, who could sometimes be oblivious, asking why he was booted out of the girls' baths. *On account of she's actually a he. Didn't you notice "she's" got a prick?* To which Fnor had said round-eyed, *She does?* "Once they noticed, they thought it was hilarious."

"Your prick?" one of the Marlovayir twins sneered.

"Well, that, and the fact that me being there was the best ruse since since...." He paused, side-eyeing the Marlovayir twins. Both his parents had warned him about starting anything. He could finish if the Marlovayirs went after him, and the Senelaec clan would back him to the hilt, but he wasn't to *start* anything. So he said, "I got sent to the men's bath side, but the rest of my time I spent with the girls."

"Why?" someone else asked.

"Obvious," a scornful voice rose from the Marlovayir side of the room. Braids didn't look. "They didn't want him *here.*"

"Why not?"

That same twin sneered, "Because he was a rabbit—"

Then a boy, hitherto silent, spoke up for the first time, "When he was born?"

The quiet sarcasm was met with a brief, reflective pause, and Braids wondered who this brown boy was: brown hair, eyes, skin, all much the same shade of dull wood. Apparently Brown was something important among them, judging by the lack of retort.

Braids said into the silence, "On account of the stories about Bloody Tanrid," he said. "I guess we lost a lot of people in my family back then."

"Pretty much everyone's family lost someone then," tall, quiet Hana Jevayir commented.

From the open window came the deeper voice of a senior, as lanky, sharp-boned Stick Tyavayir, as popular as Ghost, got right to the question all the oldest were most were curious about. "So if you lived with the girls, and they knew you weren't one, you got laid any time you wanted?"

Braids had loved the camaraderie of his life as a girl, the jokes and stings, the horses and the rides in wind and sun. But those girls had become in some sense like sisters. Cub had offered to take him to the pleasure house at the end of winter, as Braids was almost seventeen, but all he'd really done was talk, trying to figure out who he was and how he was supposed to regard those longtime sisters. He was still growing, and wasn't ready for sex with another person yet, but he could see in the faces around him what they wanted to hear.

So he said, "Sure."

A chorus of howls rose around him.

"I knew it." Stick smacked his hand to his forehead, his expressive face anguished.

"And you're *here*, when you could be with a different girl every night?" someone else moaned.

Braids opened his palm. "The king invited me. I didn't think invitations from kings had a 'no' choice."

The whispers and mutters died suddenly, at the familiar clack-thud of Hauth approaching the door. The seniors faded back, their strut gone, as Hauth rapped out, "Inspection before evening mess."

That sent the seniors in full retreat. Hauth then separated out Braids and the Marlovayir twins with a flick of his cane and a sharp jerk of his chin.

Braids looked sideways to see what he was supposed to do, then followed the twins at a wary distance.

Outside the barracks, Hauth said to the twins, "Everyone has been bored to annihilation hearing about your feud with Senelaec House."

Both twins reddened.

Turning a merciless one-eyed stare from them to Braids, Hauth said, "There are rules for fighting among seniors. Anyone lacking self-control enough to squabble is unable to command. So when your group goes on overnight, you will be supervising the scrubs in stable duty. That's the usual rule. In case you three are wasting time figuring ways around that, there are specific orders for you." He glared at Braids. "*Any* sign of your boneheaded clan feud here, and you go home."

To the twins, whose faces betrayed initial delight, "And *you'll* go home too. Both of you. No questions asked. The night anything happens between the three of you, you'll be riding out of the gates together, under guard."

Pepper began, "But what if he—"

"That's an order from the headmaster. Take it up with him. Do you three understand? Anything overt or covert, and you're gone. We're not going to lose a future battle because your two houses have shit between your ears."

The twins three-fingered their chests, belatedly copied by Braids.

"Then get ready for inspection." Hauth stalked away, aware of his hypocrisy. But the feud between eagle and dolphin clans was different, too much bloodshed to be overlooked. The stakes were not childish ruses and the occasional duel out on the borderland, but the kingdom itself.

And the boy who should be in line for that throne was ignoring him.

The twins dashed back inside, shaking rain off themselves. Braids followed, turning to the nearest boy who wasn't a Marlovayir. "Who was that?"

As there are few pleasures superior to informing the ignorant, the rest of Braids' news barracks-mates spent the remaining time before the bell offering highly opinionated descriptions of the masters.

While they talked, Braids learned how to organize his trunk (something he'd never done in his life) and how to properly sweep the floor, because of course the new boy would get stuck with this job, with many voices offering helpful critique.

After the headmaster came through to inspect and dismissed the boys to the evening meal, Braids followed, exhilarated and worried in a whipsaw of emotions. He was here at last, wearing Cub's old gray coat, his hair in a horsetail, which at first had made his ears feel cold. It had been so strange to train his fingers to pull his hair up high on the back of his head, after years of braids.

On the way into the mess hall—which smelled like rye buns, cabbage, and grilled fish, like home—Braids spied that master with the single eye in a crabby face. Hauth, the others called him, the lance training master. Aware that he was terrible with a lance even after a winter of knocking around with one he and his brother had made, Braids ducked his head as he passed.

Hauth had already dismissed the Senelaec brat from his mind as someone of no importance. His single eye was on Connar, who—unlike every year since their first meeting—sauntered past him without a glance.

Safe in the knowledge that no boy or master could read the women's code (with Senelaec additions), Braids wrote:

Rana Senelaec to His Family:

After a month they let us write letters home. Here is mine. Da, you were right. First thing out of their mouth they called me Braids. Everything is great except they talk so fast in Hand and have a lot of words we did not learn. If you fight you get stable duty at rec time or when the others go overnight. Baldy says it was the first rule on account of Bloody Tanrid. So, Ma, you can stop thinking the Marlovayirs will challenge me to a duel.

The Marlovayirs pretend I do not exist. I do the same to them. I am sure they were planning to get me kicked out the first day. You should have seen their faces when Hauth said if they did they would go home. Me too. They look like weasels to me but I heard Frog Noth (he is only a distant cousin to Rat, kind of like me and Baldy) telling someone the three of us look alike and are we related. I wanted to kick him over the barn roof.

Cub. It was exactly like you warned me. Everybody beat me in sword drill. But the master said at least I had the basics. Thank you for that. It was worth all that time in the icy barn breathing cow breath and goat farts.

The first time we did horseback sword drill Cabbage Gannan the senior captain knocked me right out of the saddle. I was expecting that, only from Marlovayirs. There have been two broken arms so far and a broken leg from bad falls but I know how to roll. So I got back on and after that Rat Noth (he is kind of like a captain though there are no ranks except temporary ones for games) offered to drill extra with me if I did not mind getting up before the dawn watch bell. He is tough but I am learning fast. Nobody can beat me at the ride and shoot. And I win races as often as Rat so no one can call me snail or slow. (The Marlovayirs probably do anyway but they say nothing that I can hear. Also I do not care what they say.)

Lance practice. I was bad at that too. But it turns out what they call light rider boys like me only ride with the lance a few times to know what to do, and then we serve as targets for the boys training for the heavies or else if the big boys are using hay target we go to practice sword on horseback. The big boys really drill hard and there is nothing better to watch. We sometimes act as enemy for the seniors when they drill breaking the line and either fighting on horseback or dismounting and doing double-stick drill. Which means we get to see them break the targets before they drop the lances and come at us with the wooden swords. Both the princes are good but the sierlaef can smash a lance without half trying.

The food is like home. We have to keep our kit neat all the time. I hate that. Everybody thinks it their business to remind me. If your bedding is not perfect you get stuck sweeping. Sometimes I do it on rainy days when Rat and me and Tlennen and Jevayir stop sword drill early. Just to get it out of the way before morning inspection because I know I'll be stuck with it anyway.

When I am tired I wish I was at home where you can stick your shirt and pants on a peg and somebody else comes along and makes sure they are clean. Here we have to dunk our own clothes. And of course sew up the rips. I was surprised at how bad some are at sewing. It was like they never saw the double-satin stitch for extra reinforcing on the armpit insets on coats.

Rat asked me to show him the double-satin because he is always ripping out the right shoulder on his coat and he won't get a personal runner until he gets promotion into the King's Riders. The Marlovayirs ignored me but I noticed later Salt Marlovayir had satin-stitch on the tear he got in his shirt from Basna at contact fighting.

Rat is sort of leader without being called captain, except in games when if we pick he always gets picked. If he is, we win. Not always when others want to be leader or a master picks....

The remainder of the letter was a scrawl of minutiae about what he'd done in the games, and what his bunkmates had done, without once stating the purpose of the games. Nor did he care. Braids' entire ambition was to captain a wing of skirmishers—no life, in his view, could be more exciting.

In contrast, Connar's obsession with winning shadowed him through the day and bled through his nights, frequently giving him nightmares in which the King's Riders galloped through the gate to glory, leaving Connar standing alone.

He didn't tell anyone what he had overheard about the army. If others found out, they found out. But the competition was already so intense, and he knew everyone else would want to win, to stand out, to be chosen to ride with the army when it went east.

Over that first month and a half he avoided Hauth, until after his first command, which ended in a draw due to a sudden thunderstorm. He knew he would have lost. Sick with fury at himself, at Rat Noth, at the academy, and at the world, after a sleepless night he made himself go to the back barn where he'd met Hauth all those previous years.

And there he was, working a young war horse on a longe line. Hauth heard the slow, reluctant footsteps, and relief wrung through him, along with exasperation at Connar's waywardness. Of course that was his mother in him. If he could, he would beat it out of the boy, but short of that, he'd do his best to sweat it out of him.

Connar came up and stood silently, breathing hard. When Hauth brought the animals in for a carrot reward, he glanced aside.

Connar stood there, every line expressive of defiance. "Are you going to assassinate Noddy?"

"What?" Hauth's eye widened. "No!"

Connar's gaze shifted, relief flooding him at Hauth's honest shock.

Hauth's mouth flattened to a grim line. "That, in case you don't know, is called treason."

"But all that you said, last summer." Connar's gaze flicked warily, not hiding from Hauth, who knew the prince well, the ambivalence and guilt and longing that galled Connar.

That was enough moral outrage, Hauth thought. Time to relent. "I told you about your heritage, your dolphin-clan heritage. It's a vow I made, for I was loyal to dolphin-clan, as you know. My goal here is to teach you, for the sake of that loyalty. What you do about it is your concern." And before Connar could speak the *but* shaping his lips, "So let me guess. You're here to rail against Noth because you lost in yesterday's raid."

"No." Connar crossed his arms.

"Good. He'll be one of your best captains someday. You should be glad he's as good as he is. Did you see his strategy?"

Connar's eyes narrowed. "It's the same one he always uses, he leads the middle—"

"Exactly. It's the same one he always uses. It so happens you've got some big, fast, skilled boys in the year behind you. Future leaders for you to put in the field." Time to shift to what he'd overheard in a discussion between Commander Noth and Andaun at the masters' mess the previous evening. "But right now, the problem as I see it is you boys defend against Rat Noth the way you do scrapping in contact fighting, strength for strength. The Noth boy wins because he knows how to field the three flying wedges. And we want that. It's the best way to make you tougher, which will make those you command tougher. You boys tend to stick to what works, which is normal. I guess it's also normal at your age to avoid ventures like tactical retreat. You seem to think that you'll look like rabbits."

Connar scowled. It was true. Connar thought back to the Inda stories about naval battles. He'd initially ignored all those, as ship fighting was useless on land. But this past winter he'd read the ship battles out of desperation, and discovered that Inda's fleet had used all kinds of ruses, including ones that could be called tactical retreats—drawing pirates right into a trap. For the first time, he wondered if that would work on someone besides pirates.

"Second thing," Hauth said. "You lost because you set Holdan to lead your flank attack. That should have been Gannan."

"I hate Gannan."

"So? Noth Ain also won because he put the right man in place for each."

"But Gannan hates me. If I put him in a command of a riding, he'll lose to make me look bad."

Hauth looked incredulous. "You really think Gannan ever wants to lose?" Boys were notoriously short-sighted, but that cynicism had to be another trait inherited from that Iascan woman.

Time and past to train it out of him. "You put the man where he'll do best, and even if yesterday he spat at your feet, if he wins for you, you give him respect. That's what Mathren did, and he built loyalty like no one, *no one*, else."

"That's because he *killed* everyone if they weren't," Connar retorted.

"He did exactly what he said he would," Hauth shot back. "He said he would make the kingdom strong again, and that was what he was doing."

"Building a secret army for himself, using kingdom funds and lying about it? I've heard all about Nighthawk Company." Connar crossed his arms, lip curled, eyes bright with derision.

Hauth suppressed the intense desire to strike that arrogant face hard enough to knock some sense into the brat. But he'd made a vow. "Nighthawk Company would have secured the kingdom, without civil war," he said heavily. "Yes, he was going to take the throne, but Evred would have lost it sooner than later, turning loose all the jarls to fight each other. With Nighthawk Company at strong points, the jarls would have seen strength and order when it was time for Lanrid to take the throne. That's what people really want, the strength that guarantees *order*...."

Connar sighed inwardly and let the order lecture flow over his head. When Hauth saw his inattention, he caught himself, gritted his teeth to rein in his temper, and said, "But that's a debate for when you know more. Right now you're parroting what the king tells you. You'll understand when you get more experience, and one way to get experience is in these games. I'm offering suggestions, not solutions. I'm here to teach what I know, which is heavy cavalry. Not all that useful in tactical retreat."

Connar shrugged sharply, but at least he was listening.

"To get back to my original point, every commander learns sooner or later that you treat your captains well," Hauth said. "Don't give them a reason to turn against you."

"Right," Connar said, his temper easing at the words *your captains*. Annoying as Hauth was, he clearly expected Connar one day to be in command.

They parted, Connar determined to find a new defense besides the usual right, left, and center wedges. *Your captains.* That was the way to address a future commander. No treason in that!

But then came that gnawing worm: "Your captains" could belong to a king as well as to an army commander. *No. No. No.*

Each Restday, as the weeks galloped by, Connar chivvied Noddy into going up to the castle early so that they could get the latest news the moment they could, and Noddy, for his own reasons, complied.

Connar dreaded hearing that the army was about to depart. So far they hadn't. Every Restday, as soon as breakfast was over and he'd heard the news, he holed up in his room and pored feverishly over the Inda papers, the naval battles as well as the old game reminiscences.

Of course he kept coming back to the battle at Andahi Pass. It seemed to Connar that Inda had always liked using surprise flank attacks, first as a scrub running around on a field, and later against the pirates. He used the same plan against the Venn at Andahi Pass—a crazy plan born of desperation, depending on timing in terrible mountain terrain, against far superior numbers.

But it had worked.

Ruses....

His next game gave him Noth on his side, and Stick Tyavayir as opposing commander. Connar put Noth and Ghost at the head of a flying wedge. "I want everybody watching you," Connar said.

Ghost grinned. Rat looked impassive as usual, but Connar knew he'd do exactly as told.

And while the enemy force watched Ghost, Noth, and their spread numbers riding slowly and deliberately as they swung and twirled their wooden swords, two ridings belly-crawled at the perimeter of the designated field, and lay doggo.

Ghost and Noth began the trot, then the canter of a charge, howling and yipping and waving their wooden swords. The enemy flag signaled a line, and they spread, readying to envelope the wedge they knew would hit hard.

But then Ghost's horse bumped into Frog Noth's, which somehow upset the charge—they slowed, then Frog broke and began to retreat.

Ghost, who loved a ruse, began shouting and swearing at him to come back—and rode after Frog, uttering threats. The enemy first line guffawed, and now it was their turn to ride up to a charge as Noth, then the rest, wheeled and retreated in apparent confusion, shouting curses.

And right when the enemy reached a good canter, swords extended, Connar raised his fist, and skinny Basna, hiding behind a boulder with his bow, sent a whirtler whistling into the sky.

All the boys knew that signaled a tactical change—and as the charging enemy looked wildly in the wrong direction, Connar's hidden teams leaped up from where they lay in the mire, and picked them off with efficient speed. The chalk arrows were difficult to control, and ineffective anywhere but close range, especially as the boys hadn't been able to hold them completely above the mud and grass. However, close range was all that was needed: Braids alone accounted for ten before the few survivors were out of arrow-shot.

As one, Ghost and Noth wheeled again, gave chase to the survivors—and it was a complete and total defeat.

Connar thrilled with the hot, wild joy of winning, as all around him his force shrilled the *yip-yip-yip* of victory.

There was nothing better. *Nothing.*

He coasted on the headiness of triumph for the rest of the day, but with dawn of the next, the old anxiety rose: he was still not assured of command on the big game. There were three other serious contenders besides himself for the two command positions: Ghost, Stick, and Rat Noth, even though he wasn't a senior lancer. Connar was fairly certain that his next game would be against Rat, who hadn't had an overnight since the first in the beginning of spring. After all, *he* still had a year of lancers to go.

One warm Restday as spring ripened toward summer, Connar lingered after Noddy and Bun left. He said as casually as he could, "Da. About that report in winter, the Adranis. Is the army going to attack them?"

Arrow grinned. "I like to see you taking an interest." As Connar flushed with pride, Arrow rapped his knuckles on the low table. "Right now, scouts're heading up into the mountains. Once we know what we've got, we'll figure out what to do. Hah, I was so pleased to hear of your win. If we wait until after Victory Day to head east, would you like to ride as an aide?"

Connar did not want to go as an aide. At twelve, he'd served as a runner to the headmaster, and he knew that aides were nothing more than runners attached to some captain or commander. He wanted to be a captain, even if only of a flight, or even a riding. Reading the Inda papers had made it clear what a small force could do if you had the right leader. Inda had taken control of a notorious pirate ship with scarcely a riding.

"Sure," he said, because at least he'd be going. The rest could happen after they got into the field.

He listened to every scrap of talk among the boys, he reread the papers so much he had them memorized. He had multiple questions about what wasn't described. So much was left out, such as exactly what Inda had done before executing these plans. Everything, *everything*, described what happened afterward.

If he was truly going to be a commander, he needed to know *more* than everyone else. It made no *sense* otherwise, but he knew their answer to that: everyone in the academy must be treated the same—given the same information at the same time, whatever your future rank—because there must never be another Sierlaef of infamy, or a Bloody Tanrid, expecting special treatment above the everlasting damned rules.

TWENTY-FOUR

Camerend woke abruptly from a deep sleep. He registered the sound of rain through the weavers' annex open windows, under the distant mutter of thunder. Closer by, the sweet sound of Hliss's breathing.

He rolled up gently onto his elbow to look down at the pure curve of her cheek, the soft line of her jaw above the inward curve of her neck, so beautiful a line it hollowed him to the heart. He had never believed that joy could reach such depth it was near to pain, but an exquisite pain, a knife edge this side of pleasure.

Marriage to Isa Eric had never been joyous, even when Senrid was born. Happiness, yes, but always attended by concern for her wellbeing, and awe, too. Isa's gifts were wondrous, strange, and dangerous, never quite confined to the world of the living. Or rather, a reminder that the world one saw around one was only a part of what existed. If she was right (and she never lied) a very small part.

Now Hliss had come into his life, her gifts a generosity of mind and body that demanded nothing. It had become his delight to give what was never asked.

He smiled and reached, with infinite care, to shift her warm, heavy braid, freeing the loose strands of hair caught in her lashes.

It was then that consciousness woke enough to recollect what had brought him out of sleep: it was the magic alert on his golden notecase.

Awake now, he slipped out of bed, slid on his night robe, then fished the case from the inside pocket and padded noiselessly to the far window, where he thumbed the latch.

The tiny scroll within was written in Old Sartoran, Lnand's handwriting, just three words: Reached Skytalon Peak. The Elsarions have begun building small outposts along the pass. Everyone says to curb the passage of brigands.

Camerend frowned at the paper. Outposts in plural. That sounded admirable on the surface—if it was true. Establishing outposts was something kings did, usually in concurrence with other kings, if said outposts straddled borders.

Camerend lifted his gaze to the view out over the castle walls to the cloud-streaked sky, glowing orange and red between the castellations in the eastern distance.

"Camerend? Something amiss in the chickenyard?"

He had his back to the bed. Sliding note and case back into his pocket, he turned to find Hliss sitting up in the bed, flushed with sleep, but her gaze alert.

He smiled. "Checking the weather," he said. "I forgot it's Restday. Go back to sleep, love."

"Are you coming back to bed?"

"I'm too awake. I may as well get a few chores done while it's cool."

She accepted that with a flick of her upturned palm. Then said, unsmiling, "Is Arrow really going to send the King's Riders east to attack the Adranis?"

As always, there was the question of how much to tell, and the futile wish that the boundaries of trust and obligation would be clear.

Hliss knew nothing of the golden notecases or the royal runners' own communication net. Though she and the king were no longer lovers, Arrow still liked coming by to talk to her and catch up with news of Andas. Camerend's guilt over the fact that he could provide her with daily reports on Andas's doings, but did not, was something he had to live with, and ameliorate as best he could.

As to kingdom affairs, he was practiced in talking around what he knew. "So far, we couldn't find evidence that the raiders are Adranis. Or even their hirelings."

Hliss had been thumbing tired eyes. They had gone to sleep scarcely half a watch ago. She looked up. "Then who is it?"

"We'll find out more when the scouts return, of course," he said, the usual preface. "All we know is that the Adrani king is not behind the attacks—he's too busy with matters on his eastern border. We're not certain about the Elsarions, a very powerful duchas family up there on the Adrani western border. They owe fealty to the Adrani king, but they have a lot of power in their own territory. We may as well call the Elsarions petty kings."

"Elsarion," Hliss repeated on an interrogative note. "Where have I heard that name before?"

"If you studied history beyond our borders, which we runners are required to do, you've probably heard that Sarias Dei—the ancestor the present duchas is named for—lived among us a century ago, until she married into the Elsarions. Her descendants are reputed to be ambitious as well as handsome, charming, and everything you always hear about the Deis."

"I remember now. What I heard was that you can't trust the Deis," Hliss said, smiling. "That was Mother's opinion, of course."

"Currently, according to the last report I received, the new Elsarion duchas is a young woman with a younger brother around the crown prince's age." Perhaps it was time to visit them, making shared family tree an excuse, to discover what he could about them.

"What will it mean, if Arrow sends his army there?" She fought a yawn, her eyes watering.

He said, "I can't predict for certain, of course. Perhaps a show of force might cause the troublemakers, whoever they are, to withdraw and reflect."

Hliss lay back with a sigh. "I hope you're right."

His calm conviction reassured her; so far, everything Camerend said seemed to be so. He *noticed* things. He'd asked royal runners passing anywhere near Farendavan to take the time to stop there, just so they could bring word of Andas, though she had never asked him to. That he would do that meant as much as the letters themselves. Mother didn't write, of course, but Brother did, and when he was riding with the Faths or one of the other clans, either his wife Tialan or his lifemate Hanred wrote.

Of late Andas had added his own scrawls. There was even a picture of a fourlegged animal labeled Dusk, which Hliss guessed was a horse. Hliss treasured the much-folded, chalk-smeared drawing more than diamonds.

Smiling over this memory, she let her eyes drift shut, soothed by the quiet rustle as Camerend dressed.

He dropped a soft kiss on her brow and left, breathing in the clean, heady scent of green things after the rain. Tiny wildflowers were already springing up in cracks between the stones, adding a trace of scent to the air. He splashed rapidly through the courts, reflecting that the castle bees would be out in force before the sun topped the distant hills. Sometimes the creatures of ground and sky made more sense than the humans who disturbed their ancient patterns.

He ducked through the north end archway—and nearly ran into the two princes rushing in from the opposite entrance. "You're up early," he exclaimed, and watched Noddy blush deeply as he looked away, poor soul. He was still sneaking over to watch Lineas drill with the queen and her runners, and thought he wasn't noticed.

Connar's wide gaze, blue as the summer sky emerging from the clouds outside, pinned Camerend. He asked breathlessly, "Is there any news?"

Camerend smothered a laugh as they started up the stairs together. "As it happens, I believe that at this moment the king is meeting with Commander Noth as well as Headmaster Andaun for his weekly report. If that meeting didn't get cancelled, you should hear the very latest at breakfast."

Connar knew that the headmaster met with Da weekly, but that was always at night. Why so early in the morning, and with Commander Noth there, too? Everyone talked about the King's Riders going east—they were only waiting on the scouts.

Maybe Da wanted to take the seniors!

Maybe he wanted to take Noddy and him, Connar thought, heart thundering against his ribs. He and Noddy turned off down the second floor hallway as Camerend kept going up the stairs to the royal runners' floor.

The princes checked with Ma's third runner Sage, on duty at the queen's outer chamber, to discover that indeed, the king was gone, so breakfast would be late.

Connar said he'd go to his room to catch up on his sleep, went inside, then peeked out after the count of ten. As expected, Noddy was loping back down the hall toward the window at the far end, from which Connar knew that Noddy watched Lineas drilling with Ma, Bun, and their runners. Connar had never gone. He had no interest in a pale, freckled little stick like Lineas.

Connar stood poised, breathing hard. Tomorrow was the last combined senior game, and he and Rat Noth were the only ones left for their third commands of the season. Whichever one triumphed would be enemy commander against Ghost Fath in the week long all-academy Great Game out somewhere in the plains.

And here he was, everything in place to make that happen: the family busy, the headmaster as well. A *true* commander noticed the best circumstances in which to act, like Inda Harskialdna when he took over the pirate ship.

And a *true* commander learned everything he could about the enemy, in order to win with the least cost to his own men.

He glanced at the stairway. In practical terms this scouting foray would be the deadliest sneak of his entire life. That was appropriate for the most important game of his entire life, his last chance to win that command over the entire academy.

It has to be me in command.

Conviction propelled him back down the stairs, and along one of the old servant halls to the empty state chambers, and out through the stable entrance to the parade ground, which was constructed to limit distractions to the horses going to and fro. He had to remain unseen by the sentries on the city wall, as the headmaster's annex was located on the other side of the parade ground from the royal residence portion of the castle, where guards were the most alert.

Elation pounded his heart in time with his footsteps as he ran through byways he and Noddy had discovered as boys. There weren't many places one could escape the sentries' eyes, but he and his brother knew them all.

All you had to do was get to the inner north-south wall, then keep low. A pulse of regret when he paused at an intersection; he was so used to having Noddy at his back. But it was better this way. Noddy was terrible with secrets – not blabbing, but he got mopey if something bothered him.

Connar ghosted along walls flanking the upper school barracks, where few boys would be. The lower school were confined to their territory on Restday, where they'd be playing around, but the upper school was nearly empty, boys either on liberty or else working off penalties in the barns or on the far walls as sentries.

Keeping his head bent, Connar slipped along the corrals and, protected from view by the nearer stable, hopped the fence, crossed behind the mess hall, and then entered the headmaster's building from the mess hall side. Again, no one was about.

Heart drumming against his ribs, he ventured inside.

It looked empty, but in fact, Connar was not alone.

Up in the loft storage, one of the headmaster's runners had wedged himself uncomfortably among dusty trunks. This small boy from the Tevaca clan knew that on Restday no one had duty, and the headmaster had been seen setting out into the last of the storm just as the sun was coming up, so—gloating over his own cleverness—he'd retreated to the loft with a stolen feast of honeycakes.

With a twelve-year-old's appetite for any food at any time, the more delicious when illicit, Tevaca was about to get outside of his booty when footsteps caused him to freeze mid-bite.

The headmaster was back already! Terrified, he leaned out, eyes stark...and in cat-walked one of the big lancer boys. Black hair. Was that the prince, Olavayir Tvei? Tevaca's mouth dropped open. He watched in silence as the prince paused to sweep the room. Instinct caused Tevaca to lean back, only a heartbeat before Connar cast a quick glance up at the loft.

Connar, seeing nothing, and remembering from his own days as a headmaster's runner that the loft contained only trunks of old records, turned his attention to what he had come for: the wall behind the headmaster's desk, where the big chalkboard was rested when it wasn't taken out before games.

As Tevaca leaned out with infinite care, not even daring to breathe, below, Connar grinned in triumph. There it was, the complete layout, boundaries and limitations, of the next game! And it was a nasty one—an infiltration assignment, the type Connar hated most. He studied the pins at various points around the city as well as outside the academy walls, which meant no horses. A real blister of a game.

Connar bent closer to the pins, and spotted notes in fake Venn runes at each—obviously code that would have to be broken before they proceeded to the next site.

At least academy codes were always simple. Royal runners were the ones who studied languages and codes; during the long, dull winter days when he and Noddy were small, Ma's runners had given them paper chases over the castle with easy codes to solve, with something good to eat at the end of the trail.

He scanned again, committing the map to memory, as Tevaca watched in trembling silence above. When Connar began his turn to leave, Tevaca jerked backward.

Connar's neck tightened, and he paused halfway to the door to look around more slowly. Had he heard...something? But he stood directly below the loft now, so of course he saw nothing out of place, and his mind was entirely on the headmaster and masters. It never would have occurred to him, with the entire castle as a retreat, that anyone would want to be in that room unless assigned to be there. He listened for a few heartbeats, aware that time was against him, and hearing nothing (again, Tevaca was holding his breath, the honeycake poised in one hand) he shook off the feeling and hastened out.

Only when his footsteps had diminished did Tevaca breathe again. Olavayir Tvei! Was he supposed to be there? Of course he must, or why else would he be? The lancers were intimidating and incomprehensible to the smaller boys, the princes even more so, with their silent hand language.

Tevaca crammed the honeycake into his mouth, chewing furiously. The fun had gone out of his booty, and with it, the taste. Worry, question, excitement boiled inside him. Someone else could turn up!

That thought squelched what was left of his appetite. Sweeping the unfinished cakes into his grubby tunic, he closed one fist around them and with the other scrambled over the side of the loft, landing on the top of a cabinet, then on a table, and to the floor, scorning the ladder resting on the other side of the room.

He stopped, horrified. If he *had* used the ladder, Olavayir Tvei would have noticed it for certain, and discovered him. Horror at the close call made him shiver as he bolted out the door.

He skulked back to scrub territory, dumping the honeycakes in a cache for later—hoping some disgusting greedyguts didn't nab them first. He kept low to north walls so that the castle wall sentries wouldn't spot him. He didn't straighten up until he reached safe ground. Then he sauntered casually in among the boys playing games, with an air of innocence so patently false that if anyone had shown the slightest interest in him, they would have dogpiled on him for summary interrogation.

Pretty soon he was in on a game of racing beetles, but his mind stayed back in the headmaster's annex. He wondered what Olavayir Tvei had been sent to do. Anything the big boys did was interesting.

One thing for certain: secrets were only fun if people knew you had them, and it was so much better to speculate with someone else than hoot questions inside your own head.

He considered the others, and once his beetle wandered off, he elbowed his particular friend, a freckle-faced urchin from the Faldred branch of the Zheirban Riders.

"Where were you?" this friend demanded, well acquainted with Tevaca's appetites. "Pigging extra breakfast buns?"

"Way better. Want to know who I saw? But you can't tell *anybody*...."

As Connar got through the slow hours of Restday, he concentrated on his mental image of the map: destination the winter barn, clues at various sites around the city, fake runes to be deciphered.

It was all useless if he didn't come up with a plan. No, a set of plans, because this wasn't an easy attack or defend problem. He had to defend his searchers, and then guide them to figure out the destination that he already knew, without anyone the wiser. And once they did that, there was still getting there ahead of the enemy.

Was this how you did it, Inda, he wondered as the family settled in the queen's suite, bread and wine at hand for Restday. The silence of Hand, usually so irking, helped him now. Nobody expected him to talk, so he could think about this new idea, that Inda had been no smarter than anyone else, just more sneaky at getting the inside line of communication. Then he'd put together his solutions before anyone knew what he knew. So of course they thought his victorious plans sprang from his head as if put there by magical spell.

By this win Connar would prove that he was ready to move straight into command this very summer. A riding at first, of course. He knew better than to think that he'd be awarded anything larger, though Inda-Harskialdna was commanding entire fleets of pirates when younger than Connar was now. Mere trickery, he reminded himself as Noddy labored away at describing in Hand the overnight earlier that week. Maybe the records lied about that, too.

But these days, nobody made riding captain before twenty, much less higher rank. Asking for it was the same as whining. He had to impress the elders so much that they *gave* it to him.

When Restday Drum and dinner were finally over, Noddy suggested, as he always did, that they all take a ride. Connar knew why Noddy did it, of course: because Bun would always agree, which meant her royal runner would be along as protection. Which, in turn, meant Noddy could sneak peeks at her when he thought nobody was looking, which would keep him occupied, so that Connar could think.

As they finished up the last of the strawberry tarts, Connar snapped an inquiring look at Lineas, who was helping Ma's runners collect the dinner dishes. He wondered what Noddy saw in her. Connar liked both boys and girls, but they had to *look* like boys or girls — the angles on a boy, curves on a girl, both with smooth muscles. Lineas looked like she was made out of string under that dark blue robe she wore.

"Go on," Ma said, as Da went out the other door. "It's a perfect evening, nearly a full moon."

Noddy was of course relishing the agony of being so near and yet so far. Lineas was unfailingly kind, but her tranquil gaze whenever they spoke made it clear she saw him simply as Bun's brother. Though he kept hoping something would change, as usual she was more interested in watching the low shrubs for any passing bands of assassins to leap out than she was in watching him. At least she didn't stare at Connar anymore, which gave him hope.

They circled the city walls, riding over bridges that crossed the slow rivers of summer and dropping the reins to give the horses a night gallop along the northern wall, then curving around to the southwest and past the academy's outer wall.

The moon was well up when they rode back through the city gates. Above, a sentry waved a pennon now that the royal children were back, the bells rang for the night watch, and the gates swung shut behind them. At the stable, lanterns hung around a stall drew their attention. A tall, strongly built young woman strode out, pale braids pearlescent in the ruddy light. Despite the road dust nearly obscuring the dull blue of her runner's robe, evidence of a very long ride, there was a swing to her walk and a lift to her clean jawline that arrested the eye.

The royal siblings walked up, Bun saying, "Do I know you? You look familiar."

"Heyo," she hailed, teeth flashing in a dimpled grin. "You have to be the royal family."

Bun said, "And you?"

The runner smacked her palm to her magnificent chest and said, "Neit, mother-cousin to the Ventdors, Riders to the Jarl of Olavayir. You met my brother Floss. I'm the jarlan's newest long runner. Just arrived. I'm sure your stable people are excellent, but Seafoam here likes my touch." She patted her mare, and they noticed belatedly the eagle-clan blue edging her dusty robe, dark and dull in the ruddly lamplight.

At once Noddy and Bun had to ask how Tanrid was—how Floss was—and in the general exchange while Neit finished currying Seafoam, Noddy found himself distracted by Neit's frank appraisal, a laughing quirk to her eye.

When the mare looked ready for a parade, and munched quietly, she closed the stall door. "Lead on," she said.

Bun did. They moved off in a group, Neit falling in easily beside Noddy, her long legs matching his stride. She moved with an unconscious swing of hip that drew Noddy's eye, but when she smiled at him—she only had to lift her head a little, a new sensation for him—he blushed even redder and looked away. Under the torchlight she gave him a smiling up-and-down. "I must say, Floss was right about you. I do like a man who isn't a weed."

She'd said "man." Noddy's mouth dried. But she didn't wait for him to agonize about fumbling through a response. "Looks like I'll have a night of liberty. Anywhere interesting to go on a Restday evening?"

Even Noddy didn't miss this subtle hint. She wasn't Lineas, but....

He grinned, blushing to the ears. He managed to stutter out an incomprehensible collection of syllables that she took as assent.

Connar backed up a step, then another. He wasn't certain Noddy would hold Neit's attention long (he wasn't certain *he* could) but he wasn't going to stay and find out.

He followed the others through the archway to the stairs. When they reached the first landing, he backed down and darted through the inner door.

He was free. He ran back to the academy through the balmy night air. The lower school was dark, silhouettes briefly blocking the stars low on the western horizon: boy sentries patrolling the far wall. Connar knew from experience they were half asleep. As long as no noise broke the usual night sounds, you could lock your body into a thoughtless shuffle-trudge, your mind slipping into dreams, until the welcome relief let you stumble back to your bunk for what felt like a few heartbeats of sleep.

Light still glowed in the senior barracks windows. Half the boys were still awake. Connar faked a huge yawn as he walked in. By the light of a single candle, Lefty Poseid, Rooster Holdan, and Vandas Noth sat on a bunk playing cards'n'shards, with a focus that meant at least one of them was trying to win his way out of a hated assignment—most likely midnight watch sentry duty.

Across from them, Ghost lay on his stomach, his hair bleached to white in the candlelight. He marked his place in a grubby, limp-looking scroll, then looked down again.

Vandas threw down his cards, then made the sign for Noddy.

"Still castle-side," Connar muttered in the undervoice they all habitually used when others were asleep, though they learned early to fall asleep whatever was going on. He faked another yawn, got ready for bed, and lay with his eyes closed, reviewing the map until images began to slip sideways into dreams.

Jolt. His eyes opened to moonlight streaming in. He *had* slept! Judging by how far the moon had jumped, morning wasn't all that far off, and he still had no sure plans! What was the use of the inside line of communication if he didn't use it?

He slid out of bed, pulled his clothes on, and eased out into the courtyard, where he hunted up tiny pebbles, and laid them on the stone ground in an approximation of the map.

Right. Right. If he had, say, three teams, one to shadow the enemy—no, better for them to lie in wait, depending on which set of rune-clues he was given....

He was still sitting there when footsteps approached. He looked up into the blue light of impending dawn as a big, broad-shouldered silhouette appeared. Connar recognized Noddy, though he sensed a difference in his walk, the swing of his hands.

Connar abruptly remembered his stone map. He suppressed the instinct to strike his stones away: that would be suspicious even to Noddy. No one would know what they meant.

"Connar? What are you doing out here?"

"Couldn't sleep. Headache," Connar said. "So I was reviewing our loss on the Thirdday overnight." Then, belatedly, "All night?"

Noddy's bashful grin and dropped head made it plain what had happened. Connar watched Noddy go on into the barracks to hunt up fresh clothes. Noddy! Neither of them had ever expected he'd be the first to make it with a girl outside of the Singing Sword.

Connar was aware of a vague sense of ill-use. Why did that tall, tight runner pick *him?* He scowled down at his hands, annoyed with himself for that stupid pulse of jealousy. Sex was great, then it was over. He had more important things to think about right now.

By the time they went to breakfast, he had the beginnings of four plans, and when the headmaster summoned the upper school, divided them, and handed off the first coded clues to Noth and Connar, his mind simmered with expectation.

TWENTY-FIVE

Infiltrations were not actually overnights in the sense of camping out, since they were located in the academy, the castle, and perhaps portions of the city, but they were called overnights as shorthand for two-day assignments.

When Connar's infiltration riding reached the winter barn "enemy HQ" just as the evening watch clanged, defended by Gannan, Noddy, and the biggest boys in the upper two classes, they erupted into wild yips and dancing about.

"One day! We did it in *one day!*" The senior class executed a gloat—well deserved, Rat's defeated team had to admit. They were still working on their second scrap of code.

Connar pelted up in time to see Gannan execute two handsprings and a backflip. Cabbage Gannan! Connar hadn't thought that barrel body of Gannan's could manage a somersault.

They started back toward the senior barracks, met by the two deflection teams. Connar gazed at his capering command in the white heat of euphoria.

This is what Inda lived for, he thought as the two teams gathered around him, yipping shrilly and yelling wild words of congratulation. This was how Inda felt after taking the Venn commander's surrender, there on the cliff commemorated forever in that tapestry in the interview chamber. There could not be any joy greater.

They swept off to the mess hall, jubilation ringing off the walls, as the younger boys trailed in more slowly, word of the seniors' win passing back through the ranks.

Tevaca didn't think anything of it until he chanced to be in line four or five down from the famous Rat Noth, who said to tall, auburn-haired Stick Tyavayir (another admired hero), "I don't know how Olavayir Tvei did it. We'd just figured out the second note."

Tevaca felt the words rising, *But he saw the map. Of course he knew.* Then it hit him, what that meant.

For the second time in two days his appetite vanished. No, not possible. The big boys didn't cheat. They just didn't. For one thing, they knew what would happen to them if they did. There hadn't been any public canings for some years, but everybody had heard the history of the last one by the end of their first week at the academy. Anything with that much blood was sure to be passed down exhaustively, to the last sanguinary detail, to equally eagerly horrified listeners.

Tevaca looked around—and met Faldred's wide eyes.

"What do we do?" Tevaca whispered when Faldred caught up to him, his tray piled. No diminished appetite for him, Tevaca noticed sourly. But then he hadn't been up in the headmaster's loft on the sneak.

Faldred's averted gaze and his jerky shrug shot alarm through Tevaca. "You *didn't* snitch," he muttered in a dire undertone.

Faldred looked affronted. "I would never *snitch*, even if they set me on fire and pulled out my eyes." His gaze shifted, and he muttered in a less assured tone, "I only told Eveneth, and he said he wouldn't blab. Come on, Tevaca, you know it was too good to sit on, and besides, I didn't drag your name into it. I just said somebody."

Eveneth—a year older, practically fourteen. *He'd* know how to keep his lips sealed.

Tevaca's appetite returned with the same speed it had vanished...the last comfortable meal he was to have for several days. From cousins to connections, the gossip that Olavayir Tvei had been seen in the headmaster's office the day before the game made its way up the school.

By noon the following day Tevaca was beginning to learn the truth about secrets; at that same meal, as whispers hissed in a wildfire susurrus through the mess hall, Connar intercepted some long looks from much younger boys, difficult to interpret, except that they were materially different from the admiration of the night before.

One of the younger masters, expert in cutting out yapping pups, began following the rumor back and back: "Who told you?" "It was Horseapple Hend!" Horseapple: "My cousin!" "I got it from...." and so on, until he got to Faldred, who, when confronted by a scowling master tapping a yew wand in his hand, after trying "I don't know," gave up Tevaca. He tried to exculpate himself to a circle of stony-faced classmates when he returned from this encounter, assuring them that everybody swore they'd endure fire and flaying rather than blab, but when facing the reality of a cane in a strong master's hand, of course anybody caved.

At mess that evening, Tevaca was absent, which strengthened his barracks-mates in shunning Faldred for being a blabbermouth—to someone in another barracks, no less.

At the other end of the school, Connar was aware of a pool of silence spreading around him and Noddy, the latter blithely unaware, as usual. Connar acted as if nothing was amiss. Because nothing *was*. He'd done what any commander would do—that is, any commander determined to win.

While he was thinking that, the headmaster sent a tearful Tevaca (summarily ejected from the elite squad of headmaster's runners) to execution HQ, the boys' sobriquet for the small, bare room at the other end of the headmaster's building where miscreants awaited investigation and judgment.

The headmaster sat alone, staring in horror at the chalkboard leaning there against his wall, still bearing the map he'd sketched out to show the upper school Firstday morning.

He opened his door to send a runner to Commander Noth, shook his head, and decided it was better to go himself. He shut the door and even turned the old key in the lock, something he'd done maybe twice since his appointment.

Even now he couldn't define why he did it. He thought about what to say all the way up to the garrison captains' wing, where the duty runner, Fish, was dispatched to find Noth.

Fish, expert at winnowing out all the academy gossip, stopped by the quartermaster's to pass the news to his father, then went to locate the commander.

Soon Andaun, a balding, conscientious man who had memorized the Gand manual, faced Commander Noth, each seeing their own emotion in the other's eyes.

Andaun said, "I realize that under the rules, Olavayir Tvei is Olavayir Tvei while on academy-side, but we all know how much that truly means."

"You haven't asked the prince," Noth said—not quite a question, since Andaun had said as much in his summary.

"Just Tevaca. Exhaustively. I'm convinced he didn't make it up. Though he backtracked and rambled and second-guessed himself, two things are consistent: that he saw Connar in my office on Restday, and that Connar spent some time before the game map."

Silence, as a fly buzzed against the window, then Noth hit his knees with his hands. "The king," he said, "is going to be furious."

Andaun sighed. "He has to be told, of course. Before I talk to Connar or after? Or should he be here?"

Noth tapped his fingers gently on a battered side table, the old call to arms drum tattoo. Finally he said, "It's never going to stay in the academy. So trying to keep it within is a fool's game. Why don't you bring Connar here? We'll question him, and whether he confesses or denies, we'll all go to the king."

Andaun got to his feet, then sank down again on the worn wooden bench that had been in that room since Inda-Harskialdna's day. His voice was husky with dread. "What if Connar denies it?"

They couldn't answer that—and in any case, they didn't have to. A runner was sent (not Fish, to his disgust, though he lurked within call as long as he could) to fetch Connar. By then it was quite late, though back in the academy, the senior barracks was lit. As soon as Connar left with the runner, the seniors burst out talking, while Noddy looked from one to the other, totally bewildered.

Connar appeared at Noth's door, blue eyes wide and bright in his beautiful face. He saluted, was summoned within, and Noth said without preamble, "Were you in the Headmaster's office before the Firstday assignment?"

Connar had figured out that he'd been seen somewhere along his path. It was the only explanation for the weird looks and silences. All during the walk from academy to garrison-side, he thought out what to say, and so, with a passionate conviction that silenced both elders, he outlined his reasoning, all the way to Inda-Harskialdna on the cliff.

At the end of that long speech, Andaun said, "Do you understand that you broke several rules?"

Connar knew it to the knots in his stomach, but (so he reasoned) he would feel exactly the same if caught by the enemy. "Does the enemy have rules?"

Noth said wryly, "So Headmaster Andaun is your enemy?"

Connar threw his head back, a magnificent gesture. Unconscious of the effect it had on two men who ordinarily weren't inclined toward their own gender, he said, "I knew I was going to command. I knew I had to win. When you have a war, you get any information you can, however you can, in order to be effective. Inda-Harskialdna said that the purpose of our training is to deliver victory by the fastest way that preserves lives and material."

Straight, Noth and Andaun were both thinking, *out of the Gand manual.*

Noth sent a look at Andaun: It was time to fetch the king. And the queen as well.

Not that you ever fetch a king, of course.

"Wait here," he said to Connar, as Andaun crossed his arms, looking out the window and wishing he was anywhere else.

On the long walk up to the royal residence, he mentally composed his report. Hoping strongly that he was early enough to catch Arrow before he went off to one or another of his favorites, he stopped long enough to send a fast young runner to apprise Connar's parents that he was coming.

When he arrived at the king's suite, the royal parents were waiting, standing side by side.

"What's going on?" Arrow asked.

Noth expertly assessed the king's sobriety. He'd been drinking, but it hadn't reached his eyes yet. Good.

He saluted, to establish the seriousness of the situation, and gave his report.

At the end, Arrow uttered a laugh. "Damn! Connar is a clever little shit—he's not wrong."

Danet was not smiling. "He's very wrong."

Arrow snapped, "What?"

Danet rubbed her eyes. "Is this our fault? Don't you see it, there's no sense of wrong, or right?"

A thought occurred to Arrow, *Just like Lanrid, right was what he pointed at*, but he didn't say it. He knew how much Danet would hate it. "Connar's young, and thinking like a youngster. He wants to win, and he's beginning to think about strategy." He started pacing, as he always did when his gut began to churn.

Danet said, "Is that what you call it?"

Arrow whirled. "Are you saying you want to see him caned a hundred times in front of the entire academy? Because that's what's going to happen if you go on about rules. He's not wrong about what a commander would do in a war situation — and half the school is going to say that. Not just me. We're training future captains there." He jerked his thumb over his shoulder. "*My* captains. Noddy's future captains. Whose purpose is to protect the kingdom."

Danet's arms crossed tightly over her chest. "I do not want to see him caned. I do not want to see anyone caned. Or even hear of it. I told you once how stupid I think such viciousness is, and I listened to all the talk about honor. And I understand that 'honor' is really some sort of invisible boundary that's supposed to rein men in from loosing Norsundrian brutality. That means war has to have rules or it never ends. And you all agreed to this rule."

Her voice trembled. She stopped, pressed her fingers against her lips, and shook her head. "This is something you will have to solve yourselves."

She turned to go, and Arrow, feeling that he'd just been dumped with an impossible choice, rapped out fiercely, "What're you going to say if your girls try something similar?"

She stopped at the door, and looked back, her face ravaged. "If any girl tries something similar," she whispered, "I'll send them all home."

Arrow wanted to follow and yell that she was not only unfair but no help, but he knew that ranting at Danet was not going to solve this mess. He couldn't make her decide, much as he wanted to.

So he nailed Noth with a narrow glare. "What do you think?"

Noth said slowly, as calmly as he could, "My understanding is that all those boys know the rules, and they know the consequences."

Arrow dug his palm heels into his eyes. "Oh, damnation. It wasn't a small cheat, an easy one. The *headmaster's office*. That's like the cheat of all cheats. And if I overlook it because Connar's our boy, we'll never be able to talk about honor again, and have them take us seriously. How I hate that word, honor. Sometimes I don't even know what it means."

Noth said gently, "Then think of it as trust."

When Andaun got back to the academy, it was to discover that a fight had broken out in the senior barracks. By the midnight bell, which reverberated through his aching head, he'd gotten to the bottom of *that* mess, which began with Gannan saying that even if it was true and Olavayir Tvei cheated—and he wouldn't be surprised at all if it was true—nothing would happen because he'd weasel out of it by crying to the king.

And Noddy hit him.

Gannan launched himself at Noddy, several others got in the way of the big boys' powerful fists in trying to stop them, causing a generality of black eyes, cauliflower ears, bruises and contusions.

The senior barracks was put in lockdown (which meant a master had to spend the night with them, something that usually only scrubs got when out of hand), and Noddy, as first offender, found himself at execution HQ with his brother, Tevaca having been sent back to his barracks to await sentence for being out of bounds.

Of course Noddy told Connar everything that had happened. When he got to Gannan's remark, implying that Connar was a weasel—a level of cowardice even lower than a rabbit—Connar's anger at himself for being caught, at Andaun, Noth, and his father for all the blab about rules instead of understanding that winning commanders did whatever necessary, ignited into fury.

By the time the sentence was executed, the day before the entire academy was to take off for the week-long game (Rat Noth now the commander facing Ghost Fath), Connar saw himself as the betrayed warrior among the enemy, going to execution, and determined to die well.

And that's what the entire academy saw. Connar walked out alone, wearing only a shirt, trousers, and boots, and waited, head high, for his hands to be affixed to the crosspiece on the post—which held him up when his feet no longer could.

It was Noddy who broke first, sobbing when the first blood appeared on the white shirt. It was so loud a sound, as shocking as the crack of yew across flesh. By then several small boys were sobbing as well, and two fainted. Others watched with sickened thrill, as did many older boys, but no one moved or spoke: Fear underlay all other emotions. One false step and you could be up there, too.

It seemed to last forever, until it was done. No one seemed to breathe as Connar was freed. No one heard the low mutter, "Don't. *Touch* me."

All they saw was the headmaster's two runners stepping back as Connar swayed rockily away from the post, hands stiff at his sides, head thrown back. He made it maybe five steps on his own before pitching forward onto his face, too quick for them to catch him, utterly unaware of the murmur running through the upper school at his bravery.

Connar was borne off, leaving a trail of dark red drips, and the seniors were dismissed first. When Noddy stepped abreast of the gate, he struck the support post with all his considerable strength. The wood cracked like a lightning bolt hitting a tree. He stood there blinking as his hand dripped blood onto the stone, then he wheeled and walked off to the lazaretto.

Connar was floating on a cloud of green kinthus when Noddy walked into his line of sight, his hand bandaged. Connar drew a slow breath. The pain was at bay, a fierce but distant heat, like a bonfire twenty paces away. That distance would vanish, he knew: green kinthus could be dangerous, and so he'd only have it for a short time.

"Why are you here?" he breathed.

Noddy held up his hand.

"Gannan again?"

"I hit the gate."

"Why?"

Noddy crouched down beside Connar's bed, his red-rimmed eyes on a level with Connar's own, his upper lip long with sorrow. "I didn't want to go. If you couldn't."

Oh, Noddy, Connar wanted to say, fondness and even laughter pulsing through him, then gone again, smothered by the foggy blanket between him and that river of pain. Talking took too much strength. His eyes closed.

"You should've told me." Noddy's voice was husky with regret. "You should've told me. I would've helped you."

But Connar had sunk beneath the waves.

When he resurfaced, his back had ignited into fire again, the rest of him shivering uncontrollably. A face swam into view, sidelit by a single candle. Noddy was gone. Instead —

"Da," he whispered, the word a question.

"Drink this." Arrow held out a cup.

"Don't touch me," Connar managed to utter. If anyone moved him the pain would kill him.

Arrow's eyes gleamed with unshed tears. "I'm sorry, I'm sorry," he whispered, and Connar could see his own agony mirrored in Da's face. Hear it in his voice.

He sucked in tiny sips of air, careful not to breathe too deeply lest his ribs expand and bring another surge of fire down his back. "If it was...?" He stopped there — he didn't even know where that question came from. But it was enough.

Arrow recoiled as if someone had struck him. Then the tears did fall, tracking down his lean cheeks in which the familiar lines had begun to furrow. "It would be just the same, Connar. Just the same. I couldn't stop it. The rules have to be the same for everybody. Here. Your mother thought of this, so you don't have to try to sit, or even raise your head." He held out a sponge, ruddy as all sponges are, dug up from the sea between Halia and Toar. "See, I dipped it in the medicine. You can suck it out of the sponge."

Connar opened his mouth. Warm bitterness spread over his tongue — green kinthus. Arrow dipped the sponge again, and already the fire began to recede, recede, recede, allowing Connar deeper breaths. With the pain sinking, his consciousness faded into sleep.

When Connar woke again, it was daylight, and Ma was there. This time he wasn't shivering, but on fire. Danet laid a cool, damp cloth on the side of his face turned up, and then came the blessed relief of medicine by sponge.

When the pain woke him again, night had fallen, and there was Da. "I begged them for one more day with green kinthus. Then it has to be listerblossom and willow-bark." He held out the sponge.

Connar knew that too much kinthus was dangerous in some way, though not nearly as much as the legendary white stuff. Listerblossom was only good for fevers (and then they added willow bark) and mild aches. But he would take anything he could get.

Unnoticed by either Arrow or Connar, Hauth stood in the doorway, after two days of fierce internal debate. On seeing the king kneeling next to Connar's bed, he backed away, and when he found the healer, asked. "How long has the king been there?"

"Tonight? Since the watch change. Sat there all last night. Queen all day."

Hauth retreated.

Connar did not want to be in the lazaretto when the academy returned, and so he endured being carried up to the castle, where he collapsed in his room, and was given a last half-dose of green kinthus before the pain of the bandage being taken off and fresh keem leaves laid on before another bandaging.

When he woke, Noddy was there. "Ma has to run the girls," Noddy said quickly, a little nervously.

It was those bloodshot eyes, and the tight corners of Connar's mouth. Anger or pain, he couldn't tell, but both grieved him, and he wanted—so very badly—to say, *Why did you do it?* But the answer wouldn't really matter, because the true question was, *Why didn't you tell me?*

It was that bloody trail in the parade court, scrubbed away by nightfall, that had caused a yawning divide between them. Bewildered, deeply hurt, he tried to bridge that chasm with a rush of words, "Lineas will be here at night. She knows how to do bandages and medicine, since me and you don't have runners yet. But if you want Ma, or Da, they said, send for them and they'll come."

Connar tested his breath. He could draw in a bit more before the pain threatened. "Is Da ready. To ride out? King's Army?"

"Day after the competitions, same as before."

Connar braced inwardly. "Who's going with him?"

"No one. I mean, from us. Seniors go on liberty till New Year's, same as always. Then get an assignment at some garrison. Da said, you and me, we'll be sent to different garrisons. Transfer around. We should know them all."

"Great Game?"

"Ghost's army won."

"Good."

Not that Connar really cared, except that it shouldn't be someone from the class beneath them, an insult. Corrosive fury surged: he shouldn't have gotten caught. That was carelessness. He still didn't know who snitched, and if Noddy knew, he wasn't telling.

"Before they left. What did they saying about me?"

Noddy understood that to mean the senior barracks. "Divided. How you'd expect. Gannan, some, go on about cheating. Stick, Ghost, and some think you were smart, and yeah, it was against the rules, but there won't be that kind of rule if we go in the field, and the headmaster should have locked up the board." He looked down. "They'll be back tomorrow," Noddy said. "I told Da I'd sit with him and Ma for the Victory Day competitions. Bun did, too. Neither of us want to be in if you can't be."

Connar said, "You can tell me who wins."

TWENTY-SIX

A larger number of girls arrived to compete in the Victory Day competitions than previously, but Noren Totha of the Algaravayirs was not one of them. When Noren came next, it would be permanently.

Some secretly rejoiced, Pony Yvanavayir among them. Her father, unexpectedly firm, had said that this was Pony's last year playing around with these games. It was time for her to learn some discipline, as her betrothed would be out of the academy the following year, and the Feravayirs might very well expect her to move down south.

Pony was determined to win on this, her last visit to the Victory Day Game. She practiced hard all year. She loved riding the borders. As a child, she had escaped lessons and boring chores in order to ride, causing the entire castle to laugh and look on indulgently—everyone told her she was going to grow up to be a hero like her mother.

But as the years passed, only her father still laughed, and looked at her fondly when she escaped tedious chores or lessons she saw no point in. Being the only female in the Yvanavayir family had given her a taste for leadership —which was fine on patrols, but not so fine during winters, when she continued to ignore, or dump onto others, the chores she found tedious.

The jarl's fondness for his daughter kept the castle staff from saying much —but all that had changed last winter when Eaglebeak brought Chelis Cassad to Yvanavayir. As wife to the heir, Chelis was looked to for castle matters, and as she proved to be an excellent manager, the staff hailed her arrival with growing respect.

All except Pony.

By the time Pony rode out with her carefully chosen riding of fast riders and good shots, the castle breathed a collective sigh of relief. Nobody knew what to do about the strain between Pony and Chelis.

As for Pony, it was a relief to get away from Chelis and Eaglebeak and their tedious moral superiority.

And she had plans.

The first part of her plans paid out—she won second place behind Braids Selelaec in the ride and shoot, and she came in tied for third on the obstacle run, her girls placing close behind her, all to Yvanavayir's credit.

After the awards were handed out, Pony pinned her silver eagles on her robe and set out into the city, determined to celebrate her victory in spite of the weird tension still gripping many of the older academy boys, resulting in a wild atmosphere after the competitions.

Night had fallen as Ghost Fath, sitting in a row in the main square with Rat, Basna, Braids Senelaec, two of Rat's Noth kin, and Stick, was thinking that it had been a weird Great Game. But no one was talking about what had happened to Connar, though that first night in their tent out on the plains, they'd talked about nothing else.

"Three wins, Braids," Basna was saying. "Next year you'll be a swell."

"Swelled head," Frog Noth cracked.

Everybody laughed at this subtle wit, then Braids put his palms out. "I'm humble. I'm humble! Just make sure you remember to salute my shadow every—"

A figure cut in front of Braids, and presented herself before Ghost. His heart sank: it was Manther's sister, persistent as a fly over honey. "Come watch us dance," Pony said, flipping her braids and sticking her chest out. "And then we can get a cold drink. Whatever you like. My treat."

Ghost tried to find a polite excuse, then fell back on postponement. He held up the tankard he'd been sipping from. "How about when I finish this?"

Pony looked down the row, waiting for someone to make space so she could join them. She liked the idea of being the only girl in a row of pretty boys who were all winners, but they just sat there like typically oblivious boy lumps. She hated to think that Ghost was as dull as Rat Noth—but at least he was good-looking. In fact, except for the second prince, he was the best-looking boy in the entire academy.

"All right," she said, forcing a smile. "I'll come back after the next dance!"

Ghost let out a sigh. He didn't want to move. They'd been on strict discipline ever since Connar vanished, and all he longed for was his bed, now that everything was over.

"Does someone else want to go watch her dance?" Ghost asked hopefully.

No one spoke, though Frog sent a sympathetic glance Rat's way, and they all recollected that Rat was supposed to marry her. Rat just sat there looking stolid, as he always did.

While no one would have spared a glance if a younger boy had yelled *Look at this!*, a mighty snort of contempt caused all heads to turn toward whatever might be snort-worthy.

Then Rat launched himself off the bench and darted between knots of teens turning to watch a fight, no, a drunken brawl between a half dozen fifteen and sixteen-year-old boys. Rat hauled his brother out of the midst of the pack with one hand, with the other blocked a wild punch, then he sent three assailants sprawling and bawling imprecations.

A heartbeat later the sentry-alerted city patrol arrived, and the belligerents retained enough wit to hold up their hands in surrender. As the patrol captain issued terse warnings, Ghost became aware of a huge shadow at his side, and here was Noddy.

"Thought I'd come down, say my farewells." A few days apart, and Ghost realized how deep Noddy's voice was. You didn't notice things like that when you heard someone every day.

"How's your hand?" Frog asked.

Noddy blinked at his right hand, still wrapped at knuckles and wrist. "Fine." He shrugged. "Wanted to stay behind with Connar."

"How is he?" Ghost asked.

"Wants me to say he's fine. Sitting up now. Started to eat again," Noddy reported, and the others shifted uncomfortably, murmuring variations on *That's good.*

Noddy stayed a little longer, cheery as always, but his presence was a reminder of events no one wanted to think about. But of course everyone was thinking it—reseeing images much too fresh in memory. Between that and the wildness around them, which probably had the same cause, Ghost was glad when the last bell rang, giving them all an excuse to cross back over to the academy, and rest up before departure the following day.

When morning came, he found himself reluctant to pack his kit and leave the others he'd shared his life with for nearly ten years.

An elbow nudged him. "Will ya miss me?" Vandas Noth cracked.

"I won't miss the reek of your socks."

Rooster collapsed back on his bed, fake-gagging. Then he crossed his arms behind his head.

Silence fell on the somnolent air, all of them more or less aware that their lives were about to change. Boyhood was gone. They'd be effectively scrubs again when they began their rotation among the garrisons, but as men. With the responsibilities of men—command for many. Connar and Noddy at the top, because of who they were. It was the way of things.

Ghost said reflectively, "Ten summers."

Vandas cracked a laugh. "Only ten? Seems like fifty. Was there any class of squeakers more useless than we were?"

"Not a chance," Hana Jevayir said.

"Speak for yourself," Gannan retorted. "Of course, *some* thought they were ready for a crown and throne now."

And Rooster muttered, his gaze on the unvarnished beam overhead, "Why did he cheat?"

Sickness boiled inside Ghost—here they were, back to the same conversation they'd gone over and over that night in the tent, as thunder rumbled in the distance. "We *heard* all that. He thought of it as scouting."

"I can see that," Frog said slowly. "A ruse. I can see it...."

Ghost sensed opinion swinging toward Connar, and then Gannan—of course it was Gannan—said corrosively, "He cheated *us.*"

And there it was, the same tension right back again.

Gannan went on, looking around for approval the way he always did, which irked Ghost to no end, as Gannan went on, "I like a ruse same as anyone. Especially against the beaks. But he let *us* think—"

Frog shot him a sour look. "And let *someone* rat him out?"

Now they were ready for yet another fight. Gannan flushed with anger, and slammed his hand on the wall, a sharp crack. "We've heard it all. Same yap. It's over. Let's get out of here."

"Way ahead of you," Frog said. "I've got just enough for a night at the Sword, and I intend to get my money's worth."

That got them all moving.

Ghost was ambivalent about not saying farewell to Olavayir Tvei. Connar was...like a fast-moving stream, fun for a tumble, but you might hit the rocks suddenly. He'd hated losing, and he was like a sharpened sword with sarcasm, especially with Cabbage over there, yapping at Lefty Poseid to carry both their bags, when anyone could see that one decent word from Connar and Gannan would have fallen all over to please him.

It wasn't what the boys called a heat, Ghost reflected as he hefted his gear bag and walked off to the stable to fetch his horse. Gannan only liked the girls at the Sword. What did you call a heat when you didn't want to kiss and tumble? Cabbage Gannan craved attention and admiration, but so did most. It was just that Cabbage was hungriest for it from Connar, but for some reason Connar hated Gannan more than anyone in the entire academy.

Well, it was over. One thing Ghost wouldn't miss, those early mornings, smash out of bed, drill before breakfast, even when it was raining. He wouldn't miss that at all, though he was probably in for ten more years of it in the King's Riders. At least, after the two years as a garrison scrub, he'd be a captain, and giving the orders instead of getting them.

Lost in reverie, Ghost shuffled behind a pack of lower school boys lined up at the mess hall to get a hunk of nut-and-berry-thickened travel bread and a slab of cheese, which would suffice to get him to a cross-roads inn. Then there was the line at the stable.

Stick, with whom Ghost ordinarily rode, was already gone, along with Braids and the pack of Sindans, Tlens, and Sindan-Ans, all hoping to get in on whatever action the King's Riders would see on their eastward sweep. Stick had been invited to visit by the Sindans, with whom his betrothed was close. The visit was an excuse everyone said out loud might get them assigned as runners or stable hands, but secretly they hoped to get orders as scouts or even skirmishers.

If the Senelaecs were there, that might even happen, Ghost thought as he got in line at the stable. He found Rooster and a couple of the Noth cousins ahead in line, which meant more joking back and forth, until at last they rode out the city gates then parted in their several directions, Ghost heading along the north road.

He sat back in the saddle and let his horse plod through the heat of the day. A canter could come later, when the air chilled.

He'd left the city far behind when he camped alongside a tributary of the river.

The next morning he rose with the sun and continued on, noting occasionally that his horse behaved as if hearing, or sensing, the presence of other horses. He looked back from time to time, but saw nothing beyond the low hills and patches of scrubby trees.

At noon, he reached the next river, and dismounted to lead the horse down to drink. Her ears flicked, and she tossed her head, as if seeing or sensing something. Ghost cast a quick glance around for snakes or animals that might spook the mare, and saw nothing out of the ordinary: The hedgerow to the left was still, and birds sang above a copse of trees off to the right, where a streamlet had carved out a small island in the flow. Nothing. The mare bent her head to the water at last, and he leaned against her side, thinking that a mere week ago, he had commanded half the school in a wargame maybe a day's ride to the west.

The mare's head came up. She shifted, tail lashing.

Ghost turned, one hand scrabbling for his belt knife, to meet a heavy cloth thrown over his head. Instinct forced his hands up, his fingers hooking to claw the thing away from his face. He cursed as he fought, aware that he'd dropped his knife. A force hit the back of his knees, and he buckled, coming down on top of something warm and squirmy. He jabbed viciously with his elbow, causing a yelp of pain, and punched wildly with his other hand as he fought to get the smothering cloth off his head.

His fist connected with another solid form. He rolled, punching and kicking.

"Get him down," someone muttered—a high voice. A girl? A scrub running some kind of prank?

He checked for half a breath, as bodies piled on top of him. His fingers fumbled, reaching, and closed around a skinny arm. He yanked with all his strength, then heard a crack.

"Owww!"

That was definitely a girl's voice. Another body landed on his right arm, pinning it flat. He used all his strength to pull back, dragging the weight with him. Another girl, or a squeaker. Definitely not the size of Gannan or Noddy. He wouldn't have been able to move.

He forced himself to relax, and waited to see what would happen while he assessed the situation.

Harsh breathing, a hissing whisper, then hands closed on his wrists and hauled him upright. Now he let himself go limp, slipped out of their grip, and fell back to the ground. The shrouding cloth stretched tight over his face. It smelled like a winter cloak.

A whisper. "Get him on his horse."

"He's *heavy*."

"Do it."

Ghost grimly enjoyed the struggle as several pairs of hands did their best to tug him to his feet, but he stayed loose, a deadweight.

"He's unconscious," someone finally whispered — as if the stifling cloak prevented him from hearing.

"How? Did anyone brain him?"

"Have we smothered him?"

"He's breathing," someone else said, after laying a hand over his chest. A small hand. And a girl's voice.

So far, it seemed he'd been brought down by a pack of girls. Ghost hovered between irritation and amusement. He decided to keep on being passive since they were obviously not out to gut him.

"You and you and you, get that half. We'll get this half, and put him over his saddle."

Working together, the girls got him into the air, and flipped him over his horse. And then, with efficient speed, a rope wrapped around his wrists, tying them to the stirrup. He checked at that, but found his wrists bound fast.

"I think he's waking," someone said.

"Just make sure he's secure. I want to get well away from this road," came a familiar voice, no longer whispering: brisk, self-assured, but without the sugary smile tone he'd heard from Manther Yvanavayir's tenacious sister.

This is what I get for being polite to her, he thought in disgust.

The horse began to walk, and immediately Ghost regretted his decision. He'd spent years in the saddle — there were some weeks he was more in the saddle than out of it — but never had he spent time thrown over the saddle like a bag. It was the most uncomfortable ride of his life.

The girls rode mostly in silence, except for two whispering in back, too low for him to hear over the noise of the horse's hooves not far below his head. Someone else was talking in front; at one point, he heard Pony Yvanavayir state, "No, it's an *excellent* plan. The worst is over."

"But what about when he wakes up? He's not going to be happy."

"Leave that to me, Fenis, and do as you're told."

It seemed centuries later when they finally halted. Ghost's head ached from hanging over the horse's side, and he was drenched with sweat from the cloak that had been tied about him.

Enough playing around, he decided. Hands unbound his wrists, the shroud loosened, and he slid down and landed on his feet, rubbing at his wrists as the cloak was bundled away by a girl who avoided his gaze.

He stamped his feet, which were painful with pins and needles, and turned to face a half-circle of girls in the fading twilight. Pony stood at the center, looking quite pleased with herself.

"Why did you attack me?" he asked.

"We snatched you," she said briskly.

He felt at his belt. His knife was gone. Not that that mattered. He wasn't going to knife a bunch of girls bent on...what, exactly? "Why?"

"I thought it all out," Pony stated with a toss of her golden braids. "You can claim you had no choice. As for me, if I have to marry, I'd much rather have you than that ugly Rat Noth, the most boring dullard in the world."

Irritation flashed through Ghost at this casual slander of someone he'd lived with, worked with, and striven against, sharing pain and laughter.

"As for you, you can't possibly want to marry that scrawny rat, Leaf Dorthad. Let *her* marry Rat Noth. Two ugly rats. Perfect for each other."

Ghost studied the circle of girls, who studied him in return.

Fenis was not the only uneasy one. This Ghost Fath towered over them all, solid muscle. While all were good with their blades, or Pony would not have brought them, they'd discovered that contact fighting without weapons, especially when you weren't supposed to hurt your opponent, but he could hurt you, wasn't easy. And for what? Pony had promised them that this Ghost Fath had flirted with her, but it was plain to everyone that he wasn't the least bit happy.

As for him, he had to look at the damage he'd done. One girl held an arm close to her side, her face creased in pain; another had a purpling bruise on the side of her head. Those were what he could see; he remembered dishing out some nasty kicks and punches, while no one had kicked, punched, or stabbed him back.

Annoyance mixed with regret as he gave his reddened wrists a last rub, then reached up to reset his hair into its clip.

"I'll do that," Pony cooed, wanting to get her fingers into that pale cornsilk.

He ignored her request. "Let me understand. You're jumping two betrothal treaties, and without asking me?"

"See, you don't have to do anything," Pony said in a reasoning tone. "The gunvaer won't send warriors after *me*, once she finds out you had no choice."

"What if I'd rather go home, and marry Leaf Dorthad?"

"Of course you'll want to marry me, once you get used to the idea," Pony stated with the easy conviction of one who has always gotten what she wanted. "You can adopt in. The Yvanavayirs are an *ancient* family, much older than the Dorthads. Or the Faths. We vayirs all have royal connections going back to the first king, and everyone knows my grandfather died saving the kingdom from the tyrant Jasid-Harvaldar in '33."

"They were traitors a century ago."

Pony flushed, pressed her lips together, tossed her hair, and said airily, "Then stay a Fath. I know they have a fine reputation up north. But if I have my way, you might even end up Captain of Riders, which won't happen up in Tyavayir. I asked." Pony crossed her arms and lifted her chin. "And you'll be married to *me*. Far, *far* better than Leaf Dorthad, with a face like a bullfrog. And sounds like one."

Ghost didn't say anything about Leaf, who had been a friend since childhood. He said slowly, "So my choices are to give in, or tangle with your posse here?"

Pony's eyes shifted, a flush of irritation on her cheeks. "Aren't you listening?"

Ghost dropped his hands, and a tense moment ensued, everyone silent except for some distant birds. Finally he glanced around the circle, his expression smoothed into unreadability. "You say we're going to Yvanavayir?"

"Yes," Pony stated, lips curving upward. "My father will do anything for me. You'll see. Once we're married, we can write to the gunvaer, and suggest she pair Leaf with Rat Noth, so she won't even have to find another betrothal for either of them."

"How about this." Ghost raised his palm. "You have my parole until we reach Yvanavayir."

Pony's smile widened with complacent triumph. "I knew you'd see things my way."

"We'll reach Yvanavayir today," Pony said three weeks later—as if Ghost couldn't guess why the girls paid special attention to their braids and robes, even taking the time to groom their horses.

He returned a polite answer, as he had all through the journey. Pony had done her best to flirt with him, repeatedly inviting him to share her tent. He'd steadfastly insisted he liked sleeping out in the open, even the night a thunderstorm threatened. And when it roared through, he ignored the warm rain and went to stand with his horse on the picket line, soothing and patting it until the lights and noise had faded away to distant rumbles.

Pony, who had flirted her way through the young and attractive Yvanavayir Riders, could not conceive that any man she wanted would turn her down, and assumed he was playing hard to get. Maybe he was even saving their first night for marriage, which she knew some people did. That was all right. She could wait for her reward if she had to.

When the towers of Yvanavayir's magnificent castle jutted above the distant hill, Pony swelled with pride. The girls galloped the rest of the way, dashing down the main street of the town instead of taking the lakeside loop.

Pony loved scattering carts, dogs, cats, chickens, and people in the marketplace, all deferring as they stared (she was certain) in admiration.

She, Ghost, and her posse cantered through the gates, banners snapping in the breeze, and reined up before both her brothers and the steward, who had been busy discussing the planting of winter wheat and peas.

The three looked up. Pony turned her hand in triumph toward Ghost, then froze as Ghost—for the very first time—grinned.

Pony's head turned sharply to discover what he was grinning at. There stood both her brothers, Manther home for his first liberty as a riding captain in the army. His eyes widened, and he yelled, "Ghost?"

Ghost leaped off his horse, tossed the reins to a stable hand just coming up, and then to Pony's astonishment, the two ran into each other's arms—and kissed breathlessly, as Eaglebeak laughed and yelled, "Woo-la!"

"How did you end up here?" Manther demanded when they broke for air.

Ghost said, "Ask your sister."

Manther smiled past Ghost's shoulder at Pony, kissed Ghost again, and said, "Thank you for the surprise!"

Later on that evening, Pony, feeling utterly betrayed, stood before her father after sulking in her room through the midday meal. When she refused to join them for supper, the jarl summoned her.

"Fareas," the jarl said with a pained expression, using the name she loathed.

Fareas was dowdy, an old woman name. She had been called Pony since she was a cute little horse-mad girl with golden ringlets all around her head, everybody's darling. She believed she still was—but not when he said *Fareas* like that. "What."

"Did you really think that capturing and beating up that boy was going to want to make him marry you?"

"We *didn't* beat him up," she retorted.

The jarl put his hand over his eyes. "Half your girls got injured."

"They should have been faster."

"Maybe. But the fact is, all but two of those girls have gone separately to Chelis to ask if they can be assigned to her. The other two, I suspect, we haven't heard from only because they're at home in the village."

"It's not my fault they're stupid. I told them what to do. As for him, he offered parole." She added with an angry flip of a braid, "Now I know why. He could have *told* me he and Manther were two-ing."

"He could," the jarl said seriously, dropping his hand to a fist on his knee, "have made all kinds of trouble. Pony, Eaglebeak is probably right in saying this is my fault for indulging you all these years. But there could be serious consequences from this sort of thing. Have been."

"Before anyone is actually married?" She tossed her braids, mouth sulky, gaze skeptical. "It's not as if anyone made vows. Or even treaties. Except the gunvaer passing down orders. We already know people who've broken those, and nothing happened."

"But it could have. And might, who knows?" He looked through the window, then said, "The fact is, there are some ugly stories about just this sort of thing, not often talked about."

"Like what?" she asked suspiciously.

"Well, there's Dannor Tyavayir, who was married to our own Hawkeye of Yvana Ride Thunder fame. After he died at the Pass, you know she married into the Olavayirs. It was her son who broke off into the dolphin branch, and then took the jarlate. Everyone said she was behind it. Caused a blood feud that might have wiped out two generations, but she'd made enemies of the servants, who lost brothers, cousins, lovers, in the family battles. They got justice their own way. It's said she took a long time to die."

Pony grimaced. "I wish you hadn't told me that," she said with another flip of her braids. "It's not romantic at all. And it's not as if I'd ever *kill* anybody. I thought he liked me, and—"

"Daughter. My point is, she worsened cracks in the family, which brought about generations of bad blood."

"*My* point is, my situation *now* is all the gunvaer's fault. If she wanted the betrothals again, she should have made us go to the new family when we were two."

"Maybe she will," the jarl said. "One thing I know, people will be talking. Probably already are, as half the town saw you galloping up with that tow-haired Fath boy. I'm going to have to send a runner to the royal city, before the gunvaer hears a garbled account."

"Do what you want." Pony hissed a sharp, put-upon sigh. "But two things. One, I refuse to marry Rat Noth. He's stupid, and more to the point, he won't inherit anything. I *won't* be a third daughter by marriage, stuck with all the chores and none of the command. Second, as for picking and getting the person you want to marry, I'm sure I'm not the only one making plans of my own."

TWENTY-SEVEN

During those first, early days, it grieved Lineas whenever she caught herself reveling in watching over Connar. It was despicable to let herself find the smallest iota of pleasure in his pain, so she fought her own emotions through pages and pages of journalized inner turmoil. No detail was ever too irrelevant, such as the quiver of his eyelashes when she strove to remove the bandages without hurting him. Each spasm of pain lacerated her spirits, countered by his unconscious sighs of relief when the herbs took effect.

At first, she and Bun sat together through those summer nights, and Noddy spent as much of each day as he could, around demands by his father to attend guild and governing meetings.

When Danet—satisfied that Connar's recovery was progressing well—pulled Bun aside to aid her in entertaining the girls come for the Victory Day competition, Lineas was left alone with him. She strained every nerve to spare him what pain she could; frequently, especially in those early days, tears ran silently down her face.

During the day, elderly Nath, Arrow's runner of the chamber, took care of Connar. When Connar recovered enough to take notice of his surroundings, he felt awkward waking up to this grandfather-aged, wiry old man during the daylight hours, and Bun's freckled runner by night.

But as the pain began to recede, leaving room for the simplest thoughts outside of it, he found Lineas's touch light, and patient when she untangled the sweaty knots of his hair. She asked no questions, and though he had no interest in whatever went on in her mind, one morning as the shadows began to lift, he caught her heavy-lidded gaze moving slowly across the room.

"A spider?" he asked, his voice husky from disuse.

The sleepiness vanished from her startled gaze, and her face flooded with color. Her lips parted as she hesitated, then she looked away, always resolute in keeping the ghosts to herself, especially now. Evred was so bright and so clear as he walked through the room and vanished into the shadows of the far wall, except for the shadowed pits of his eyes; the hairs rose on the back of her neck. "My apology if I disturbed you," she whispered.

Connar turned away, closing his eyes.

Lineas always bathed twice a day, the second time before she went to Connar's room. She put on fresh clothes that had been laid in sweetgrass. As the days slowly began to wane a little earlier each evening, he found he preferred her ministrations when changing the bandages: Nath was skilled, but her touch was tender (though he did not know the word), and she smelled nice.

Then one evening, as the shadows closed in, Lineas arrived with his supper to discover him sitting upright, wearing only a pair of trousers as he looked out at the twilight sky.

Odd, how seeing him flat on his stomach had only sparked concern, but when he sat facing her, she had to hide the heat of her reaction.

She halted, tray in hand. "If you're feeling much better, I can leave you in peace."

Connar raised a hand. "Tell me what's going on. I'm bored out of my mind. First of all, where's Noddy? I haven't seen him for a couple of days."

Lineas remembered that Noddy had come in one morning to tell Connar where he was going, but the prince clearly didn't remember. With her back to the door, she said only, "He was sent by the gunvaer to aid the King's Riders' supply chief. To teach him about logistics."

"Poor Noddy." He gave a soundless laugh, then winced, one long hand brushing the bandage at his side

As Lineas set out the covered dishes on his table, she struggled to find things to report in a castle that was mostly empty, and waiting on news from the east. Connar ate sitting cross-legged at his table for the first time. Lineas changed his bandage for the night, and by then he was ready for listerblossom and sleep.

A few days passed, Connar gaining strength. Each night Lineas asked if he would like to be left in peace, and each night he kept her there with questions. Reluctant to leave, she always stayed to watch over him even though by now once he slept, it was for the night, but she stayed in case, until dawn's light brought Nath.

Finally an evening came when a dry, hot wind scoured over the stone towers, and she found him as usual sitting by the window, barefoot and shirtless, the bandages much diminished. Most of the weals had pinked over, but his skin was still very tender.

Only one lamp had been lit, to keep the heat down. The light sculpted over his flesh, molding muscle and highlighting the bones of his face, before fading to blue shadow in his hair.

Lineas looked away quickly as she set out his supper. "Which would you like first?" she asked, indicating the pot of listerblossom and the rice dish.

Connar's mood was volatile; he was bored, and restless — this was the longest he'd gone without a tumble since the summer before. But he was not yet ready to go into the city to visit the Sword. Not until he could lie on his back, because he wasn't going to let any lover see that shit back there, and maul him with either pity or scorn. He would hate them both.

He considered Lineas.

She glanced his way, finding his eyes in shadow, his beautiful mouth curved in what almost might be a smile. They watched one another as she busied herself laying out his supper. In the light of that single lamp, her pale skin did not appear as bleachy, and the light softened over shapes and shadows beneath her robe.

By now he recognized desire in others' eyes, but as yet he hadn't had the time or the inclination to do much beyond what was immediately offered in the baths or at the pleasure house.

Time to try. "Leave that. It's too hot for supper. Come sit here with me."

She looked his way, her lips parting. Her cheeks flushed. The wind moaned over the tower, almost overwhelming her soft, "All right."

She perched on the edge of the deep window inset. He already knew that she smelled of soap made of summer herbs, a clean scent. He found it pleasant. Soothing.

He slowly lifted a hand as she sat there still and silent. Nand at the Sword had taught him well. He experimented, lifting his palm to cup Lineas's cheek, then drawing his fingers over her jawline. She turned into his touch and gave him a tentative, tremulous smile.

His fingers drifted down in wordless invitation.

She caught his hand at her breast, her fingers small, the palms rough from knife drill. And then she took him by surprise. "I've...I haven't done this before."

Nand had taught him what to say to that, too: "I am honored you picked me for your first."

He'd thought it a little silly—what was the difference in honor between the first time and the fiftieth?—but he said it, and saw in the widening of her eyes, and the way her pupils changed size, that it meant something to her.

From there it was easy, and exhilarating for once to be the guide with experience.

Later that morning, he returned to the window, from which he could make out the cadenced yells from the garrison drill a couple of courtyards to the north.

When Nath appeared with his breakfast, Connar said, "I want to see to myself today."

The man said, "I'll bring you fresh water." Which he did, then withdrew.

And so, for the first time, Connar was alone, after a good night. A great night. Lineas was all muscle, like a cat—much stronger than she looked—and so *intense*. And yet she had been so careful not to hurt him.

For the first time in memory he felt...tranquil. The hot, corrosive breath of pain, his intimate companion for so long, had receded to a distant cloudbank, and with it anger, questions, regret. Connar sat by the open window as weapons clashed and feet stamped in rhythm in the garrison drill court. He reached tentatively around his left side, wishing he could deal with the bandages himself, for he longed for a real bath, instead of washing from the basin.

His outer door opened — and Hauth walked in.

"Don't you knock?" Connar asked, his good mood gone in an instant.

"If you had a runner, you could choose whom to see and whom to avoid."

"I don't want one," Connar said, as he always had — but with less conviction, after all this time being tended by one of his father's old runners, and a girl. "Why are you here? I thought the Riders were gone."

"They are. The last scout report indicated the raiders were scattering as the streams dry up. There's no need for the heavies to break a line if there is no line. Though we're on alert in case things change. You still don't have a personal runner. You'll be expected to have one, and will probably need a couple by the end of your first year as a garrison riding captain."

"I take it you have one for me?" Connar asked warily.

"Yes. David Pereth."

"Augh," Connar grunted with disgust. "I hate Fish."

"You brats all hated him, and were equally hateful," was Hauth's caustic response, and Connar flushed. "He's excellently trained. Loyal, like his family, to dolphin-clan — his mother is my kin. He's very useful. So use him, especially for those orders you might not give to the royal runners, for example."

Connar's disgust altered to wariness. "So now you're saying I can't trust the royal runners? Or are you going to start with how I, not being Da's *real* son, can't have a royal runner? Because I can tell you you're wrong, they've tried to get me —"

Hauth cut in. "The royal runners' allegiance is to whoever holds the throne."

"What's wrong with that?"

"Nothing. Except...surely, at your age, you don't want every detail of your life blabbed to the king and queen?"

Connar's thoughts went straight to Lineas, who had probably been reporting on his recovery each day. Then he scowled at Hauth. "Fish'll be reporting to *you*."

Hauth said, "I'm loyal to dolphin-clan. As you know. As for young Pereth, if you trouble yourself to win his allegiance, he won't report to anybody but you."

Connar sighed. If he'd had a trusted runner when he went to scout that game slate.... Well. "Send him over. But if he annoys me, out he goes, and I'll get Quill, as soon as he comes back to the royal city." Quill was the first name to mind, not that Connar knew anything about him, other than that he was the royal runner captain's son. Which would make him suitable for a prince.

Hauth heard the challenge in Connar's tone, but kept a prudent silence, having got what he wanted. He left without another word.

Connar stood up carefully, and looked around his tidy rooms. But old Nath and Lineas had only dealt with his bedding and food and his clothes. Fish's fingers would soon be into everything. Not that Connar cared, except for....

He walked into other room, feeling weirdly tall after lying flat for so long. He moved to the trunk beside his desk, grimacing as he knelt and opened the trunk. There, under the books his parents and tutors had given him over the years, were the Inda papers, just as he'd left them. He pulled them out, surprised at how grubby and battered they'd become, until he had them mostly memorized.

He got to his feet, crossed the room, and chucked them into the fireplace, which was cold, of course. But last winter's firesticks lay on the mantel. He tossed them in cross-wise, muttering the spell for fire—and there was enough magic-bound sunlight still left in them to sprout a lick of flame on the edge of a paper. The flame spread and strengthened, the edges of the top papers browning and curling.

He stood there as heat and ruddy light beat over him, watching the words wither and vanish.

Everything according to the rules.

He remembered the conviction in Da's voice when he'd said it. Well, another thing Da believed was that the age of heroes was over, leaving the rest of them to do what they could.

Connar watched the fire as a sort of calm quenched the hot fury inside him. He got it now. He understood. If you didn't like the rules, you became the person who makes new rules.

Before the noon bell, Fish presented himself at Connar's door.

Connar said, "I don't remember your last name—"

"It's Pereth."

"—and I didn't ask you to interrupt me. If you can't stick hearing Fish, then take yourself off." Of course he remembered who David Pereth was, but he'd better get their own rules established.

Fish remained impassive, having expected something of the sort. Being called Fish certainly wasn't new—it was his own brother who'd given him the inescapable nickname. His father had said the evening before, the only thing to do was make the name famous for excellence, so it would become a trophy. Fish also had been warned that the prince was likelier to be nasty-tempered than usual after what he'd endured, but he was still the true king. The future king.

Connar glared at Fish, who—taller than he was by a couple fingers' breadth—had grown into his eyes somewhat, though he was still goggle-eyed. He wore a gray castle runner's robe, his light brown hair neatly queued back. Fish didn't look angry or smirking, or much of anything. And it *had* been a long time since he'd been spying and tattling. Connar hadn't seen him for years, except for the previous summer when he had fetched Connar for the king conversation.

He sighed. "I really want a bath," he said tiredly. "And I can't get these damn bandages off by myself."

Fish turned out to have a deft touch, and for the midday meal he managed to scout out a pot of strawberry compote, though the day before Nath had told Connar that there wasn't any left in the entire castle. Connar remembered that Fish's father was the quartermaster, and decided that maybe this wouldn't be so bad.

When Lineas entered the outer door that evening, carrying Connar's supper as usual, she stopped still, surprised to see Fish straightening Connar's outer chamber.

He gave her a hostile stare. "Put it down and take yourself off. I'm his runner now."

"All right," Lineas responded softly, and as she set the tray down, she said, "What should I call you?"

"Fish," Connar snapped from the bedroom door. Time for another rule. "And *I'll* say who's coming and going."

This new rule would be a whole lot better. He crossed to Lineas and held out his hand.

She took his fingers, brightening into a happy smile. As Connar led her into the bedroom, he said over his shoulder, "Stay out until I call you."

He shut the bedroom door, leaving Fish standing alone, consciously breathing against the gut burn of irritation. He had to remember the goal that Uncle Ret had promised: When Connar was king, David Pereth would be chief of the royal runners, who had rejected him.

While Fish glared down at the tray of cooling food, Noddy backed away from the outer door, which Lineas had left open. He'd returned from a long ride to see how his brother was doing, and to ask if he wanted to share the evening meal.

But he'd seen those linked hands, and Lineas's smile, and he knew what was going to happen—what had happened.

Yes, that hurt a little. At least there was Neit, he reflected as he retreated to his own room. And Connar was definitely better, which made him glad.

WHO'S WHO

Narrator

The same narrator who oversaw the Fox memoir detailing the history of Inda Algaravayir, known as Inda Harskialdna. (Subsequent details in later records.)

Marlovan Jarl Households and Rider Families

(Individuals connected to jarl households listed under that household. For example, Farendavan, under Tyavayir.)

Arvandais (of Lorgi Idego)

Jarl: Hastrid
Jarlan: Starand
Daughter: Hadand "Hard Ride"
Son: Haldren "Hal"
First cousin: Ndiran Arvandais. (Married to **Wolf Senelaec** 3 years, took daughter Marend on dissolving the marriage)
Third-cousins: Farendavan family [see **Tyavayir**]
Anderle Vaskad: sword master and war trainer, first under former king Tanrid Olavayir AKA **Bloody Tanrid**; had early training of **Mathren Olavayir** before moving to north shore.

Algaravayir

Iofre: Linden-Fareas
Daughters (by Aldren Noth): Hadand, Noren (future gunvaer)
RIDER FAMILY: NOTH
Runners:
Pan Totha (runner to Noren)
Holly (runner to Noren)

Cassad [see Telyer Hesea]

Darchelde, (family name Montredavan-An: confined within their own borders for ten generations by old treaty)

Jarlan: Shendan, secret mage chief
Son: Savarend-Camerend, (known as Camerend) chief of royal runners, co-chief of royal runner training, m. Isa Eris
Son: Savarend-Senrid "Quill"

Eveneth

Sons: Camerend, Keth
Daughter: Fnor
RIDER FAMILY: MARECA
Sons: Barend, David
Daughter: Dialen

Feravayir (family name Nyidri)

Acting jarl Commander Ivandred Noth
Sons: Ganred "Rat", Vandas "Mouse"
Jarlan: Lavais
Sons by Lavais and former jarl: Demeos, Evred "Ryu"
RIDER FAMILY: NOTH, PARAYID BRANCH

Gannan

Jarl: Evred
Jarlan: Fareas
Sons: Indevan "Blue", Senrid "Cabbage"
Daughter: Ndand
RIDER FAMILIES: STALGRID & POSEID
Sons: "Lefty" and "Righty Poseid", twins

Halivayir

Jarl: Indevan
Son: Kendred "Bendy"
Daughter: Hadand "Thistle"
RIDER FAMILY: DORTHAD
Leaf Dorthad (betrothed to "Ghost" Fath)
Steward: "Goose" Banth
Nanny

Jayavayir, also known as Jayad Hesea (family name Jevayir)

Jarl: Indevan "Iron Spear"
Grandsons: Hana, Ivandred, Senrid
Holder Khael Artolei: holder of a border territory, maternal second cousin to Nyidris of Feravayir, friend to Nyidri sons

Khanivayir

Jarl: Barend
Jarlan: Mran
Sons: Tanrid "Squeak", Retren "Snake"
Daughter: Shendan
RIDER FAMILY MONADAN

Marlovayir

Jarl: Indevan
Jarlan: Ndara
Sons: Handas "Knuckles", Tlen
Knuckle's sons: twins, Salt and Pepper
Daughter: Tdiran
RIDER FAMILY: STADAS

Marthdavan

Daughter: Lis
Son: Jarend
Chana (once "Chelis")
RIDER FAMILIES: BAUDAN, NDARGA, and **NOTH**
Dannor Ndarga
Lemon Noth, Riding Chief

Olavayir

Eagle-branch
Grand Gunvaer: Hesar
Jarl: Indevan
Jarlan: Ranor
Randael: [deceased]
Randviar: Sdar
Sister: Hlar (born Halrid, third brother), chief potter
Sons: Kethadrend [deceased], Tanrid [deceased], Jarend (married to Tdor Fath)

Offspring: Tanrid "Rabbit", Anred "Arrow" m. Danet Farendavan
Arrow's sons: Nadran "Noddy", Connar [see dolphin branch]
Daughter: Hadand "Bunny"
"Sneeze" Ventdor, second cousin to Jarend and Anred
Runners:
Gdan (runner to jarlan)
Nand (border Rider)
Tesar "Tes" (Danet's runner, niece to Gdan)
Nunkrad "Nunka" (in charge of nursery)
Loret (Danet's First Runner)
Shen (Danet's second runner)
Sage (Danet's third runner)
Halrid "Floss" Vannath (Tanrid's first runner)
Neit Vannath (Jarlan of Olavayir's long runner)
Nath (chamber runner to Arrow)
David "Fish" Pereth (runner to Connar)
Dolphin-branch
Garid [deceased]
Kendred (regent),
Mathren (Commander of King's Riders) m. Fnor Marthdavan
Sons: Lanrid, Sindan "Sinna"
Grandson, by Lanrid and Fini sa Vaka: Connar [see **eagle branch**]
Retren Hauth (maternal second-cousin to Mathren, sent to Nevree as lance master)
Runners:
Thad (Mathren's third runner)
Tlen (general castle runner)
Kend (second Runner to Mathren)

Senelaec

Jarl: Garid
Jarlan: Gdar
Jarl's brother: Tanrid "Tana"
Sons: Camrid "Wolf ", Tanrid "Yipyip"
Daughters: Fareas "Fuss", Carleas "Calamity" (adopted from Noth relations)
Mardran "Cub" (son of Wolf and Ndiran Arvandais)
Marend (daughter of Wolf and Ndiran Arvandais, taken to Arvandais by Ndiran
Ranet/Ran "Braids" (son of Wolf and Calamity, raised as a daughter)
Fareas "Kit" (daughter of Wolf and Calamity)
Ranet (adopted from Keriam family, to replace Ranet in betrothal)
Runners: Pip

Ndara
Young Pan
Ink
Trot
Fnor

Sindan-An

Jarl: Tanrid "Rock"
Jarlan: Ranet
Son: Evred "Baldy"
Daughter: Fnor
RIDER FAMILY: SINDAN (related to the Sindans of Sindan-An and Tlen
Daughter: Pandet Tlen
"Amble" Sindan: Eastern Alliance chief

Telyer Hesea, combined with Faral (family name Cassad)

Jarl: Handas
Jarlan: Carleas Dei
Sons: Aldren, Barend "Chelis" (for a time)
Daughter: Carleas "Colt" (adopted from deceased sister Hlar Dei)
Sister's daughter: Chelis
RIDER FAMILY: NOTH, FARAL BRANCH

Tlen

Jarl: David "Tuft"
Jarlan: Tdan
Son: Garid
Daughters: Hibern, Chelis "Owlet"
Pandet (second cousin)
RIDER FAMILY: SINDAN & HOLDAN
Son: Senrid "Rooster" Holdan
Daughter: Shen Sindan

Tlennen

Jarl: Garid,
Jarlan: Hibern
Son: Mardren "Marda" (adopted sister's boy)
Daughter: Henad

RIDER FAMILY: SINDAN

Toraca

Jarl: Nadran
Jarlan: Faral
Daughters: Fala, Gdir
Sons: Indevan "Horseshoe", Nadran
RIDER FAMILY: TUALAN

Tyavayir

Jarl: Halrid
Jarlan: Hadand "Han"
Sons: Camrid, Tanrid
RIDER FAMILY: FATH
Anderle "Moss": Rider Captain
Sons: Tlennen, Anderle "Ghost"
Daughter: Genis
TRADE FAMILY: FARENDAVAN
Father: Hasta, captain of riders sent by Tyavayir to Olavayir to fulfill treaty
Mother: Fnor (Known to everyone as "Mother") Chief Weaver
Son: Hastrid "Brother"
Daughters: Danet (married to Anred Olavayir), Hlis (Chief Weaver)

Yvanavayir

Jarl: Ganred
Jarlan: Fala [deceased]
Sons: Aldred "Eaglebeak", Manther
Daughter: Fareas "Pony"
Runners: Fenis (Pony's runner)

Zheirban

Jarl: Anderle
Jarlan: Maddar
Sons: David, Camerend
Daughter: Gelis
RIDER FAMILY: LENNACA

Royal Castle and Academy Staff

Jarid Noth: City Guard Captain, promoted to Garrison Commander, interim King's Army Commander
Amreth Tam: Kitchen Steward
Evred Pereth: Quartermaster
Evred Pereth's sons: Halrid (guard-in-training), David "Fish" (runner-in-training)
Evred Andaun: Academy Headmaster
Retren Hauth: Lance master [brother-in-law to quartermaster]
Evred Stadas: archery master
Spindle (castle runner)
Hlis Farendavan, Chief Weaver [see Farendavan]
Mard (runner to Evred)
Tarvan (runner to Evred, then to Jarend Olavayir)

Royal Runners

Shendan and Camerend Montredavan-An, chiefs in charge of the runners, and (first one, then the other) co-chiefs of the royal runner training
Mnar Milnari, co-chief of the royal runner training
Fallon (referred to only) chief trainer of long distance runners
Branid
Ivandred
Hlar Dei [deceased] (sister to Jarlan of Cassad)

Dannor (student)
Cama student)
Fnor (student)
Vanadei (student)
Liet (academy senior)
Ndand (academy senior)

ABOUT THE AUTHOR

Sherwood Smith studied in Europe before earning a Masters degree in history. She worked as a governess, a bartender, an electrical supply verifier, and wore various hats in the film industry before turning to teaching for twenty years. To date she's published over forty books, one of which was an Anne Lindbergh Honor Book; she's twice been a finalist for the Mythopoeic Fantasy Award and once a Nebula finalist. Her YA fantasy novel *Crown Duel* has been in print for over twenty years.

She reviews books at Goodreads and blogs intermittently at Dreamwidth. Find her website at Sherwoodsmith.net.

ABOUT BOOK VIEW CAFÉ

Book View Café Publishing Cooperative is an author-owned cooperative of over fifty professional writers, publishing in a variety of genres including fantasy, romance, mystery, and science fiction.

Book View Café authors include New York Times and USA Today bestsellers as well as winners and nominees of many prestigious awards, including:

Agatha Award
Campbell Award
Gaylatic Spectrum Award
Hugo Award
Lambda Literary Award
Locus Award
Nebula Award
PEN/Malamud Award
Philip K. Dick Award
RITA Award
World Fantasy Award

Book View Café, since its debut in 2008, has gained a reputation for producing high-quality ebooks. BVC's ebooks are DRM-free and are distributed around the world. The cooperative is now bringing that same quality to its print editions.

www.bookviewcafe.com